Here I Am

Here I Am

CONTEMPORARY JEWISH STORIES FROM AROUND
THE WORLD

Compiled & Edited by
Marsha Lee Berkman and Elaine Marcus Starkman

The Jewish Publication Society
Philadelphia and Jerusalem
1998 • 5758

Library of Congress Cataloging-in-Publication Data
Here I am : contemporary Jewish stories from around the world / compiled & edited by
    Marsha Lee Berkman and Elaine Marcus Starkman.
        p.   cm.
    Includes bibliographical references.
    ISBN 0-8276-0654-0 (alk. paper)
    1. Jewish literature. 2. Jews in literature. I. Berkman, Marsha Lee. II. Starkman,
Elaine Marcus.
PN6067.W67   1998
808.8'98924—dc21   98-14407
                                                                              CIP

Typeset by Matrix Publishing Services
Printed by Haddon Craftsmen, Inc.
        An R.R. Donnelley & Sons Company

02 01 00 99 98
10 9 8 7 6 5 4 3 2 1

For Norman, whose encouragement and support have helped to make this book possible, and for our children and grandchildren;

and in loving memory of my mother, Janet Sava Schoenfeldt (1901–1996) who gave me life; my mother-in-law, Sarah Weinstein Berkman (1905–1996) who gave me faith; and in memory of my father, Lee Schoenfeldt, whose own love of knowledge gave my life purpose.

MLB

For Leon, whose love of Jewish culture has brought me to this place; and in honor of my mother, Eva Solk Marcus and our children and grandchildren, Andrew, David, and Isaac;

in memory of my beloved father, David Samuel Marcus, and two loved friends: Talma Zoiberman of Petaḥ Tikvah, Israel, and Sondra Trief of New York and California.

EMS

From east to west, from one end of the world to the other, Jews are scattered and connected.

Edmund Burke, Irish political philosopher, 1781

Contents

ACKNOWLEDGMENTS

Our gratitude to Dr. Ellen Frankel, Editor-in-Chief of The Jewish Publication Society, whose vision and guidance have made this book a reality.

We are indebted to many of the ideas and essays contained in Hana Wirth-Nesher's book *What Is Jewish Literature?*

Thanks to Fred Isaacs, former Head Librarian at the Jewish Community Library in San Francisco, who read our manuscript and made suggestions, and to Jonathan Schwartz, present Head Librarian; to the Jewish Community Library and Judy Baston for giving us a warm and inviting place to meet; to Eleanor Tandowsky of the Reference Services at the Fremont, California Main Library; to the many friends who aided our search, among them, Professor Lois Baer Barr of Lake Forest College who kindly shared her material from Latin America; Jill Kushner of *The Literary Review,* Fairleigh Dickinson University; *Prairie Fire* of Winnepeg, Manitoba; Dr. Shel Krakofsky for his books and articles on Canada; to Florence Miller; Irena Narell; Professor Leonardo Senkman of *Asociación International de Escritores Judíos en Lengua Hispana y Portuguésa* in Jerusalem; Merilyn Weiss and Howard Schwartz for their suggestions; Professor Daniel Weissbort of the University of Iowa; and to the authors themselves, particularly to David Albahari for leading us to other Canadian writers and to Serge Liberman for his Australian bibliography. Many thanks to Marjorie Agosín, Nadine Gordimer, Moacyr Scliar, A. B. Yehoshua, Arlene Kushner, and Anne-Solange Noble of *Éditions Gallimard* for their generosity.

Special appreciation to Albert Chamé who gave us valuable insight into the Egyptian Jewish community; and to Odette Meyers who shared her knowledge and personal recollections of her years in France during the war.

Additional thanks to Ruth Tarnopolsky for reading manuscripts and making suggestions; to Noga Tarnopolsky for directing us to authors and sources; to Ren-na Blevins, our typist, whose good nature sustained us during the preparation of this book. And last, to the many translators who remain behind the scenes, bringing their skills and knowledge of other languages to the English-speaking world.

INTRODUCTION

The need for an international anthology of Jewish writing has never been more timely or more urgent. We live at the end of a century that has witnessed the most cataclysmic event for Jews since the destruction of the Temple in Jerusalem two thousand years ago. Yet despite the tragic loss of European Jewry and the silencing of a whole generation of writers, Jewish literature is flourishing. Through the words of these authors from many of the countries where Jews live today, we experience the richness, the vitality, and the immense variety of Jewish life all over the world—the resurgence of a people still striving to be heard.

Even a few years ago it would not have been possible for us to include many of the writers who appear in these pages. The disintegration of the communist bloc in Central and Eastern Europe and the massive emigration of Russian Jews from the former Soviet Union have enabled a substantial part of our people to reunite with other Jews. Writers until recently almost unknown in the West, such as Norman Manea, who was born in Romania; Ivan Klíma, who lives in Prague; Nina Sadur, from Siberia; and George Konrád of Hungary, are now able to share their lives and experiences with Jews in other parts of the world.

And in Latin America there has been a fertile outpouring of Jewish writing, which parallels the recent popularity of non-Jewish Latin American authors in what is known as "El Boom." By including a number of authors from Central and South America we have presented the distinctive pluralism of this tradition. Emerging voices appear in this collection, such as Marjorie Agosín, from Chile, blending life in her homeland with her Jewish background; Nora Glickman, writing of Jews on the pampas in her native Argentina; and Victor Perera, who remembers his Guatemalan boyhood. They, as well as others from Latin American countries, have emigrated to the United States to escape repression, to find the freedom to write as they please, and to be read by an appreciative audience. Many of them are publishing in both English and Spanish or Portuguese, thus becoming more accessible to Jews all over the world. Yet whether they write in a second exile in the United States or in their own countries, stories by these writers are essential to understanding worldwide Jewish literature.

In addition, the rapid unfolding of events in the Middle East has profoundly influenced contemporary Jewish life not only in Israel, but also in the Diaspora. The conflict between Arab and Jew, as old as the enmity between Isaac and Ishmael, has started to yield to the possibility of a peaceful coexistence not only between Palestinians and Israelis, but also between Israel and other Arab nations. That delicate peace process has been complicated since the assassination of Yitzhak Rabin. The stories of Savyon Liebrecht and David Ehrlich in this volume reveal the specter of Jew against Jew, as well as terrorism by extremist groups on both sides, that has left the future unpredictable and open to change.

In order to understand Jewish life today, we need to consider a larger perspective. A new global society is emerging, fueled by mass media and the ease of travel. The women's movement of the past few decades has impressed a patriarchal religion with the need to adapt to demands for equality. For the first time, the entire world is linked electronically. In the new frontier of cyberspace, Jews in isolated areas of the globe are coming together to share Jewish holidays and knowledge.

Yet the same technology that has made possible so many positive advances has also contributed to the easy extermination of human life. Despite the lessons of the Holocaust, ethnic hatred persists and anti-Semitism has not disappeared. The neo-Nazi movement, terrorism against Jews and Jewish institutions, hate messages on computer-linked systems, harassment on college campuses, and the revival of anti-Semitic literature are sad reminders of our past. These sobering realities underscore the need for an international arena allowing Jewish writers to speak for themselves as they reveal how Jews in many countries are recovering from one of the most tragic catastrophes in human history.

The reunification of Germany, indeed, the fact that Jews are living in Germany at all, further motivated us to expand our vision to probe the relationship between Germans and Jews in our time. We also felt that it was important to focus on the miraculous resurgence of other Jewish communities devastated during the war and later traumatized under Communism.

Finally, we wish to acknowledge and celebrate the unique nature of Jewish life, which as a result of our dispersion, has not been linked to one national territory, shared political history, or national language. The lives of Jews have always crossed boundaries, making a true national literature impossible. In his essay, "On Jewish Storytelling,"[1] Saul Bellow notes that "Jews have been writing in languages other than Hebrew for more than two thousand years."

In the ancient world, Jewish literature was written in Hebrew, Aramaic, and Greek. In the Middle Ages, Arabic, Judeo-Persian, German, French, Spanish, Italian, Ladino, and Yiddish were used. And in our own day, Jews write in many modern languages and Jewish dialects. In their diversity, the contemporary contributors assembled here represent the multilingual and multicultural nature of both Jewish civilization and Jewish literature.

〜 〜

Today Jews are characterized not only by what we have in common, but also by our differences. We are defined by enormous dissimilarities based on our religious affiliation (or lack of it), where we live in the world, the languages we speak, our place in the Jewish community (or outside it), our political views, our age and gender, our sexual orientation. We are observant and irreverent. We are historical Jews, Zionists, Socialists, and not so long ago, Communists. We are secular Jews and Hasidim and mystics, discovering new ways to look at the reality of our lives. We are Jews by choice and Jews of mixed marriages, rich and poor, educated and uneducated. We are Ashkenazim, with roots in Central and Eastern Europe, or Sephardim, tracing descent from ancestors who

---

[1]Saul Bellow, "On Jewish Storytelling." In the introduction to *Great Jewish Stories,* edited by Saul Bellow. (New York: Dell Publishing, 1963). Reprinted in *What Is Jewish Literature?* edited by Hana Wirth-Nesher (Philadelphia: The Jewish Publication Society, 1994).

lived in medieval Spain, or *Edot ha-Mizrakh,* from countries in the Middle East and North Africa.

In all of this diversity, how can we speak of Jewish literature, a literature that resists easy definition? What, in fact, makes these stories Jewish?

✒ ✒

This anthology illustrates the way in which the common threads of Jewish communities all over the world are transmuted into certain universal themes. Although the psychological aftermath of the Holocaust figures prominently in a number of these stories, many other subjects engage contemporary Jewish authors: shared memories of cultural, historical, and religious forces; the experience of the Diaspora and exile; the fear of total assimilation and the search for an authentic identity within secular culture; Jewish ritual and rites; the sense of kinship felt by Jews all over the world; the centrality of Israel in the Jewish imagination; the distinction between Sephardic and Ashkenazi Jews; the bittersweet bite of Jewish humor; and the migrations of the Jewish writer seeking a haven of safety and autonomy.

In "Jewish Dreams and Nightmares,"[2] Robert Alter suggests that Jewish literature "draws upon literary traditions that are recognizably Jewish," while Cynthia Ozick, in her landmark essay, "America: Toward Yavneh,"[3] writes, "The fact is that nothing thought or written in Diaspora has ever been able to last unless it has been centrally Jewish."

And so it is that beneath these contemporary stories lies the ancient source, drawn upon in unexpected ways. Thus, although Nadine Gordimer has disclaimed her identification as a Jewish author, she writes out of the moral disposition of the prophets, like so many other authors who perceive the world through Jewish concerns.

Yet contemporary Jewish literature is affected not only by an enduring tradition, but also by modern literature itself, with a profound debt to its techniques and masters. Latin American writers have been dominated by two modern giants, Jorge Luis Borges and Gabriel García Márquez. Still other authors have borrowed from Kafka or the French

---

[2] Robert Alter, "Jewish Dreams and Nightmares," *Commentary* 45 (January 1968): 48. Reprinted in *What is Jewish Literature?*
[3] Cynthia Ozick, "America: Toward Yavneh," *Judaism* 19 (Summer 1970): 264–282. Reprinted in *What is Jewish Literature?*

literary tradition. Some write out of the precepts of realism; several, such as Angelina Muñiz-Huberman of Mexico, are interested in the spiritual world and metaphysical subjects.

Today there is also a blurring of fiction and nonfiction into a new literary genre. The memoirs of André Aciman and Naim Kattan in this anthology exemplify many of the techniques traditionally utilized in fiction: dialogue, scene, voice, and the unfolding of a narrative.

Contemporary writing is reminiscent of modern media and the clipped, faster pace of film, as opposed to earlier fiction, which was more leisurely and moralistic. In addition, in contemporary fiction there is often a fluid shifting of time and place, a more complex psychological characterization, and an open-ended ambiguity. A number of stories, particularly the American ones, such as Max Apple's "American Bakery," Cynthia Ozick's "Puttermesser," and Steve Stern's "Bruno's Metamorphosis," are self-referential, making the reader aware of the postmodern constructs of the writer composing fiction. Many of these stories also use an original satirical voice and a narrator who is irreverent. Stanislaw Benski's story, "Missing Pieces," begins with the flippant comment, "I'm not typical. I saw no Nazis, SS-men, or Gestapo, I never laid eyes on a German soldier. . . ." Absent is the sentimentality that defined Yiddish literature, a literature of the dispossessed and disenfranchised, or of the immigrant generation seeking to find a place for themselves in the American Dream.

Until recently, Jewish literature has been primarily the province of male writers. In the past twenty years, however, a significant number of women have begun writing, many of whom appear here, their work infused with a forceful sense of independence and marked by strong personal voices that go to the heart of the writers' own lives.

As we began compiling stories, we asked ourselves: What does it mean to be an American Jew at the close of the millennium? Or a Jew living in Argentina, still subject to the bombings that strike at the life of the Jewish community there? Or a Jew living in Israel, whose people come from almost every land and religious leaning, given the task of making peace with the enemy? Or a Jew living in Germany today? Or even Jews such as ourselves, living in northern California, a place open to new ideas, but also having a high degree of assimilation and intermarriage?

After a lengthy process—in some cases as long as a year or two, or more—the stories came forth, often by word of mouth or through recommendations. We decided that this volume would comprise material written and translated after 1975, with an eye toward a new century. Those narratives that look back to the past do so through the vantage point of the present.

From modest compass, the book gradually emerged and began to expand in richness and texture to reveal the tapestry of an entire people. As editors we have been strengthened by its literary rewards and its varied expression of our people's hopes and aspirations, joys and sorrows.

How representative is this anthology of Jewish literature from around the world?

We have tried to choose stories grounded as much as possible in the life of the authors' countries. Yet Jewish writers, with few exceptions, still represent a minority literary voice in their respective regions. France, for example, which has a long tradition of fine writers, including many Jews, yielded few stories that have been translated into English. While we were able to find many women writers in the United States and Latin America, the opposite was true in Western, Central, and Eastern Europe. In fiction from the former Soviet Union, Australia, and Latin America, the theme of exile is particularly strong. Stories from many communities reveal that Jewish life passages are often the last vestigial reminders of a once robust tradition.

Although this collection resonates with the energy of Jewish writing today, we found we were unable to include work from its vast spectrum: fiction of Orthodox life and political stories from the left, the new spiritual counterculture, recent translations from older work in Yiddish. We also had to limit writing from exotic communities that are rapidly disappearing, places where scattered Jews currently live, and the number of fine personal essays we encountered. Instead, we concentrated on the literary expression of fiction and memoir that touch the deepest core of complex human experience and represent vital voices from their respective countries.

We begin with the United States. For writers in this country, the individualism of American life and the freedom of expression we enjoy have produced a prodigious amount of writing. The search for personal happiness and satisfaction, a rebellious sense of self, and an ironically humorous tone—all of which draw on both Jewish tradition and American culture—differentiate our writing from that of other countries.

Dominated a few decades ago by three major male figures (Bellow, Malamud, and Roth), American Jewish writing by the sixties spoke to the contemporary condition of alienation and the Jew as a modern Everyman, an existential prototype of the human condition. Recently, American Jewish fiction has been transformed by an abundance of writers who reflect new ideologies. Although these writers are addressing a number of concerns in a variety of styles, assimilation has become the major subject of our time—the fear that Jews are rapidly disappearing into a bland secular culture.

At the same time, American Jewish writing no longer receives the attention it deserves. As a result of our assimilation—and acceptance—into the fabric of American life, multiculturalism, which has so captivated the public imagination, has ceased to include Jewish writings as a separate genre. Yet American Jewish authors represented here reveal that we are still a distinct ethnic and cultural group within the larger context of America.

In "The American Bakery," Max Apple skillfully captures the tensions that exist for a young Jew growing up enamored by American life. Fascinated with baseball and the English language, he learns about American heroes and the Gettysburg Address, along with stories that recount his grandparents' lives as Jews in Russia and their discomfort with much that the New World has to offer.

Persis Knobbe's "Here I Am," set against the backdrop of the life and death of an American rabbi, describes a young woman brushing up against the confines of religion and family, while Cynthia Ozick's wise and witty story, "Puttermesser: Her Work History, Her Ancestry, Her Afterlife," addresses a serious topic: the intellectual Jewish woman who is attracted to American secular life, but who also longs to return to her roots and the richness of tradition. Ozick's final rhetorical question: "Hey! Puttermesser's biographer! What will you do with her now?" is directed to us: Will we continue to be seduced by assimilation or, like Puttermesser, will we recognize the value of our tradition before it is too late?

The retrieval of this legacy is the subject matter of Steve Stern's "Bruno's Metamorphosis," a story that contains echoes of Kafka. The protagonist, Bruno Katz, a writer who thinks that writing might distract him from his unhappiness, calls up the ghost of Yiddish literature who pursues him in the shape of his own youth and Jewish history. The story, blurred with a surrealistic fictional dimension, is an important lesson: the contemporary Jewish writer needs to return to his or her spiritual origins to draw on the continuity of Jewish life.

Allegra Goodman uses the Passover seder ritual to explore not only Jewish continuity and history, but also the dilemmas—and changes—in the contemporary Jewish family in her acerbically humorous story, "The Four Questions," one of a series of linked narratives from *The Family Markowitz.*

And "Madagascar," by Steven Schwartz, touches a nerve that taps the collective unconscious of the American Jewish community. In this story, the pain between the American-born son who can never truly understand the father's experience, and the father who remains forever at a distance from the son he loves but cannot comprehend, suggests larger implications in our own relationship as American Jews to the Holocaust.

Finally, Elie Wiesel, the conscience of an entire generation, and among the first writers to bridge the silence after the Holocaust, writes in "Kaddish in Cambodia" of the need to connect the ancient ritual of remembering the dead—in this case Wiesel's father who died at Auschwitz—with the massacres in Cambodia and the forgotten dead of the other atrocities of our own day. Wiesel's personal journey around the world from the cloistered, pious life of his boyhood in Transylvania to the years spent at Auschwitz, his sojourn after the war in Paris as a journalist, and then, at last, to a home in America, is representative of the migrations of many Jewish writers today and reminds us of the formative experiences that have made Wiesel an international spokesman for peace.

Canadian Jewish fiction, which in an earlier generation teemed with the density of urban immigrant life, has now broadened to include many contemporary realities that engage Jews everywhere. The search for Jewish identity and selfhood, as well as fears of blending too completely into a North American culture occupy many Jewish writers in Canada today.

In Veronica Ross's "The Ugly Jewess," a woman who has fled anti-Semitism in Germany finds that it still exists in the small Canadian town of Kitchener, forcing her to confront—and to embrace—the Jewish identity that her family has discarded in the New World. And in the hard, male perspective of Matt Cohen's "Racial Memories," the protagonist displays profound ambiguity over his identity as a Jew.

As we observe from the Canadian and American stories, North America has been a comfortable place for Jews to live; nevertheless, these countries do experience unexpected eruptions of anti-Jewish sentiment and undercurrents of tension.

⁊ ⁊

For Jewish writers in Central and Latin America, existing in two cultures is often charged with violence, hate, hostility, and fear. Too frequently, dictatorships and anti-Semitism have created a situation fraught with anxiety for the writer. Aesthetically, many of these authors have been influenced by the magic realism of non-Jewish Latin American writers, which overlays the grim reality of life under totalitarianism with the dreamlike escape of the fantastical. And for many Jews who came to South America to escape persecution, the theme of displacement is particularly strong.

Mexican writer Angelina Muñiz-Huberman is included with writers from Central and South America. Born in Provence after her parents escaped the Spanish Civil War and then brought to Mexico as a child, Muñiz-Huberman's relationship with Judaism is chiefly concerned with exile, both physical and spiritual, which she claims "is my inspiration in life as well as in literature." As a Jew living in the Catholic culture of Mexico, her stories are often removed in time and place from the realities of that country. She asks, "What am I doing here? Where did I come from? What exactly is this place called?" In her work, represented here in the selection, "In the Name of His Name," that is, the mythical search for the Name of God, Muñiz-Huberman draws upon a rich vein of Jewish legend.

In contrast, Victor Perera has written about the violence in his native Guatemala and the difficulty of living there as a Jew. In the selection from *Rites: A Guatemalan Boyhood*, he describes his family's increasing secularization, with religion becoming relegated to life cycle events or yearly observance of the High Holidays, and his own reluctant preparation for his Bar Mitzvah as "a renegade who stole visits inside the cathedral." The story, "Mar Abramowitz," also reveals the wide gulf between the family's Sephardic heritage and the Ashkenazi Jews who came to Guatemala as refugees after World War II.

Marjorie Agosín, poet, critic, and human rights activist, is one of the most prolific of the younger Latin American Jewish writers. Her work is informed by the long tradition of female Chilean writers, as well as by her Jewishness. Using the voice of her mother in *A Cross And A Star*, she writes of three generations of her family in her native Osorno. Chronicling the difficulties she encountered growing up as a Jew in Chile, the narrator observes, "We were always the others. We survived exiles, foreign tongues and jibes from the daily inferno, those foreigners who believed in the Sabbath and prayed to an irate and invisible God." Like Angelina Muñiz-Huberman, Marjorie Agosín bypasses plot and the characteristics of traditional fiction in favor of symbolic language, image, and setting.

Argentina, with the largest population of Jews in Latin America[4] and an active Jewish community, has often been inhospitable to its Jews. Like its neighbor, Chile, it had been plagued by dictators, Nazi war criminals, and anti-Semitism. Yet, despite this hostile climate, Argentinean Jewish literature has been vigorous, mirroring the aspirations of struggling immigrants trying to assert themselves in a repressive environment—or Jewish gauchos fighting the elements, attempting to understand their identity in an alien land. In "The Last Emigrant," Nora Glickman writes of the difficult life—and death—of an Eastern European Jew in the province of La Pampa.

Moacyr Scliar's native Brazil, with its open and ethnically mixed population, has been more tolerant of Jews, who have prospered and rapidly assimilated. In this excerpt from his novel *The Centaur In the Garden,* Scliar relates the story of a creature half human, half animal, born to Jewish parents living on a small farm in the interior of the country, a region once envisioned by Baron Hirsch as a Jewish utopia.[5] Ashamed of their freakish child, the parents try to lose their distinctiveness by moving to the city. Clearly, Scliar has written a fable about personal exile and assimilation in his country. As the major literary voice of the Brazilian Jewish community, and as one of Brazil's most respected authors with an international following, Scliar's concerns are intrinsically Jewish and draw on the Hebrew Bible, the Sephardic poets, the Yiddish masters, and, like Steve Stern, on the modern writer Kafka.

✒ ✒

The European stories, which proved difficult to locate and were often untranslated, are haunted by the Holocaust. Whatever healing is

---

[4]Nearly half of the 430,000 Jews in Latin America live in Argentina, which had an estimated Jewish population at the end of 1994 of 208,000. See U. O. Schmelz and Sergio DellaPergola, "World Jewish Population, 1994" in the *American Jewish Yearbook,* edited by David Singer, vol. 96 (New York: The American Jewish Committee, 1996): 443–463.

[5]Baron Maurice de Hirsch (1831–1896). German philanthropist who founded the Jewish Colonization Association in 1891 to finance large-scale emigration of Jews from Russia to escape poverty and pogroms and to resettle them in agricultural colonies in Argentina and Brazil. For further information see the *Encyclopaedia Judaica,* vol. 8 (Jerusalem: Keter Publishing House Ltd. and New York: The Macmillan Company): 506–507.

necessary, both spiritual and emotional, and whatever institutional rebuilding is possible, will take generations. Worldwide Jewry has not yet recovered from the destruction not only of human beings, but also of outstanding schools of Jewish learning. Three stories from Western Europe describe the psychological aftereffects of the Holocaust.

From Italy, Primo Levi writes in "Southwards" about his return from Auschwitz. Sick and weak after his years in the camp, he encounters two Yiddish-speaking Jews who cannot believe that a Jew who can't speak Yiddish is really a Jew. Although Levi's story is typical of recent Italian Jewish literature in its emphasis on the repercussions of the Holocaust, the Italian Jewish tradition out of which he writes goes back to the second century before the Common Era.

Set in England, Ruth Fainlight's "Another Survivor" recounts the emotional damage experienced years later by a Jew sent to wartime England as a child to escape the Nazis. The story reflects one of the themes of contemporary British fiction—the terrible suffering inflicted by World War II not only on those who were killed, but also on those who survived.

While American Jewish writers have enjoyed the freedom to blend both their Jewish and American backgrounds in their work, reinventing themselves by using American myth and mobility, Bryan Cheyette suggests in his essay "Moroseness and Englishness" that Jewish writers in Great Britain have been more constrained by the homogeneous and fixed nature of English society and literature; they have been unable to express fully their Jewish identity in their writing.[6]

Most contemporary Jewish writing by German Jews addresses the discomfort many Jews still feel in Germany today. Even in the face of emerging neo-Nazism, Jewish authors are openly writing about their pain, and for the first time, many works on Jewish themes are being read by Germans. Older Jewish writers are being republished, and new Jewish writers are coming to the fore. As Jewish life reemerges in their country, Germans are meeting Jews in a dynamic that is constantly in flux.

In "Finkelstein's Fingers," a story noteworthy both for its bold contemporary tone and its setting, the young German Jewish writer Maxim Biller describes a post-Holocaust love triangle: two Jewish men, one, a

---

[6]Bryan Cheyette, "Moroseness and Englishness: The Rise of British-Jewish Literature," *The Jewish Quarterly*, vol. 42, no. 1 (Spring 1995): 22–26. For further background material see Cheyette's *Constructions of the 'Jew' in English Literature and Society* listed in bibliography.

writer from Germany and the other an American professor, share an attraction to a German woman from whom they remain irrevocably separated by their terrible knowledge of the past.

French Jewish literature, once the province of immigrant Jewish intellectuals, is now reemerging, though much of the work is still unread by English-speaking readers. In the excerpts from *The Chant of Being,* French writer Gil Ben Aych, focuses on Sephardic Jews from Algeria, who, along with Jews from Morocco and Tunisia, have migrated to France, creating one of the largest Jewish communities in the world. The conflict between religion and secularism, the desire to hold onto the last vestiges of Jewish ritual life, and the generational tensions evoked by a Bar Mitzvah are familiar themes in Jewish literature all over the world.

Although France has traditionally been known for its liberalism toward writers and artists, French Jewish authors such as the late Edmond Jabès, who was born in Egypt, remind us of its historic intolerance toward foreigners, including Jews, and its betrayal during the war of its Jewish citizens.

✦ ✦

The Central and Eastern European stories included here are dominated not only by the Holocaust, but also by the ghost of Communism and its legacy of literary repression. The rich literary tradition of Russia and Poland is gone. But Prague, with its long and varied prewar Jewish history and its claim to the Golem and Kafka, is experiencing a renaissance. Ivan Klíma, whose works were banned for many years, is writing prolifically in the Czech capital, and is now known worldwide for his short stories and novels. His story, "Miriam," set in the concentration camp Terezín, not far from Prague, depicts how love can exist even in the worst of circumstances.

The fate of Eastern European Jews is perhaps shown most tragically in Poland, one of the largest Jewish communities in the world until the Nazi extermination reduced its Jewish population from three million to a handful of survivors. "Missing Pieces" by Polish writer Stanislaw Benski, recounts the story of two Warsaw Jews, safe in New York during those fateful years, who escaped the horrors that befell their friends and relatives. Afflicted with survivors' guilt, they are driven to fabricate false histories for themselves because they have lost their pasts, like the missing parts of a puzzle. Yet the couple can't help being thankful that they weren't "in a camp, in a ghetto, in the forest, or some other place where they murdered children."

Romanian writer Norman Manea, who presently makes his home in the United States, shows how difficult it was for Judaism to prevail in a godless society after the war. In his story "The Instructor," an adolescent boy living in a Communist state openly resists preparing for his Bar Mitzvah, a ceremony that he feels is now meaningless.

In the former Soviet Union, Jewish literature, written in Yiddish, Hebrew, and Russian, was liquidated during the Soviet period. Yet Nina Sadur, born in Birobidzhan,[7] is representative of younger Jewish writers in Russia still yearning to be heard. In "Irons and Diamonds," she recounts the torture and persecution of a family before they emigrate to Israel. Her story, overlaid with the irony of Jewish humor, reflects the danger, paranoia, and anti-Semitism still present in Russia.

David Albahari, from the former Yugoslavia, concerned with the consequences of totalitarianism in his country, became a central figure behind the "young Serbian prose" affected by postmodernism. One of the many writers in this book influenced by Kafka, Albahari's dreamlike homage in his story, "Jerusalem," the city where "the soul of every Jew dies," mirrors his deep feeling for his Jewish heritage.

Jewish life in Budapest, like Prague, is reawakening, and with it, Jewish literature. Hungarian writer, George Konrád, imprisoned by the Communists for his writings and banned from employment for sixteen years, writes with renewed hope in the future in "Expectations," as he awaits the birth of a child at Hanukkah. This miracle represents not only a new life, but also Jewish continuity as surely as did the ancient battle of the Maccabees for Jewish survival.

⚞ ⚞

---

[7]Birobidzhan is the colloquial name for the area in Russia that was officially called the Jewish Autonomous Region. Although originally a Soviet decision to select Birobidzhan for Jewish resettlement and colonization, many Jews saw it as an ideological alternative to Zionism and as an opportunity for autonomous statehood. Immigration began in April 1928. By the mid 1930s collective farms were established, as well as Jewish village councils and a Jewish theater. However, the Soviet purges of 1936–38 and Soviet policy to restrain Jewish activities throughout the U.S.S.R in 1948, and later purges that year and in 1949, ended aspirations for an independent Jewish life and culture.

See the *Encyclopaedia Judaica,* vol. 4 (Jerusalem: Keter Publishing House and New York: The Macmillan Company, 1971): 1043–1050 and Israel Emiot, *The Birobidzhan Affair,* listed in bibliography.

In the section we have entitled "Other Diasporas," we have gathered stories from countries that defy easy classification into regions—South Africa, Australia, China, Ethiopia, Iraq, and Egypt—although China no longer has a viable Jewish community, nor does Iraq or Egypt, and most Ethiopian Jews have been rescued or have emigrated to Israel.

A pervasive sense of loneliness echoes in South African writer Nadine Gordimer's story, "My Father Leaves Home." Although her work, like that of other South African Jewish writers, has concerned itself with the effects of apartheid, this narrative portrays the inevitable strain on a Jew as he moved not only from one hemisphere to another, but also from one culture to another.

From Australian writer Serge Liberman and a later migration, comes the selection, "Two Years in Exile," in which a young child mournfully observes his mother lost in Melbourne "amongst neighbors, generations, continents, galaxies apart from herself, a foreigner Jew in an Australian marsh." Acknowledging her own alienation, the narrator's mother asks, "Why this wilderness, this curse, this Gehenna?"

Through Isabelle Maynard's "Braverman, DP," we glimpse the historical Jewish community of Tientsin, North China, which, along with Shanghai, was a haven for Jews for a quarter of a century. As Maynard has observed elsewhere, "I have carried China all my life." In this distant place, two Jews, one, a young girl born in China, and the other a survivor of Nazi genocide, find that they are not so different after all.

In contrast to Nadine Gordimer's story of white Jews in South Africa, Shmuel Avraham's account of his difficult journey in the same continent, from Ethiopia to Israel in "Escape Westward," dramatically portrays a black Jew's harrowing life-and-death struggle to maintain his Jewish identity by escaping to the Promised Land. Despite Israel's difficulty in absorbing Ethiopian Jews into its culture, Avraham became a university professor and a leading consultant on Ethiopian Jewish culture.

The selection from Naim Kattan's book, *Farewell, Babylon,* draws a compelling portrait of the once-vibrant Jewish community in Iraq, the site of the biblical Garden of Eden, where "we had pitched our tents . . . from time immemorial." Yet Iraq was also where Jews had "served the hard apprenticeship of injustice," and from here, after many centuries, they were forced into exile. Kattan now lives in French Canada.

"The Last Seder," by André Aciman," from the author's memoir, *Out of Egypt,* reverberates with a similar motif. Aciman describes modern Jews in Egypt celebrating their last seder in that country. After World War II, as both Jewish aspirations for a homeland in Palestine and anti-Jewish sentiment rose in Egypt, Jews again faced persecution, and a decade later, expulsion. Like the ancient wandering Jews who fondly remembered the fleshpots of Egypt, the narrator knows that he will always remember this night, that in years to come "if only for an instant," he will catch himself longing for Alexandria, a city he never knew he loved until he had to leave it.

⤚ ⤚

The establishment of the State of Israel is second only to the Holocaust as the defining event for Jews in the last part of this century. Yet the early romanticism and exhilaration, the sense of pride and new self-esteem, have given way in Jewish writing to a hard look at the political, religious, and social realities of a contemporary land.

The profusion of outstanding Hebrew fiction translated and published in English is a relatively recent phenomenon. Over the past twenty years new writers have appeared and, along with them, gifted translators, who have stimulated an ongoing lively interest in Hebrew as a modern language.

Current literature in Israel reflects the enormous changes that have taken place in the life of the country as it absorbs Jews from many different cultures. The selection from Albert Swissa's *Akud* gives us a finely textured portrait of a Sephardic Jewish family who has emigrated from Morocco. In this story Swissa uses a biblical legend, the story of the *akeda,* the binding of Isaac, to explore a present day father-son relationship, one of the enduring themes of Hebrew and Jewish literature.

Another distinct group is portrayed in the excerpt from A.B. Yehoshua's novel, *Five Seasons,* depicting the adjustment of Indian immigrants in the early eighties to a small town in the Galilee. The story is seen through the eyes of Molkho, the "vatik," or veteran representative of the establishment, who bends the rules of the old socialist bureaucracy with a touch of humor and personal involvement in their lives.

By the time we reach the mid-nineties, the earlier feelings of tolerance in Yehoshua's piece are replaced by far more negative ones in David Ehrlich's "The Store." The story reveals a shocking allegory, both ancient and modern: tribe against tribe, brother against brother. Unrepentant, the narrator blames imagined Arab arsonists for the death of the outsiders who bring their capitalistic way of life to an old settlement founded on Zionist ideals. With profound understated insight, Ehrlich's story teaches us that internal enemies in Israeli-Jewish society can wreak havoc as deep as those threats from the Arab world.

Unlike the protagonist in David Ehrlich's story who uses the Arabs as a scapegoat, Savyon Liebrecht's "A Room On The Roof," indicates a growing trend in Israeli secular literature and life—the struggle to humanize the "enemy" by an Israeli who, despite herself, is attempting to move beyond old stereotypes to understand the other as a human being not so different from herself. Representing a new direction both in Israel and in the Diaspora, Liebrecht's story exemplifies the powerful Hebrew fiction written today by women whose voices have traditionally been restricted to poetry, and reflects Israeli women's active role in initiating change in their society.

Shulamith Hareven is one of the most respected of Israeli writers and the first woman member of the Academy of the Hebrew Language. In her story, "A Matter of Identity," she writes about "Who Is a Jew?" a cardinal question of Jewish law being reassessed by both Americans and Israelis. Like Yehoshua, Hareven uses humor to explore a serious subject affecting many recent immigrants to Israel.

⚘ ⚘

What conclusions can we draw from reading this collection?

As we enter a new millennium, Jewish literature is characterized by unprecedented freedom and a great creative outpouring from an extraordinary number of authors around the world. Writing critically and honestly about contemporary Jewish life, authors are meeting our increased desire to learn about the way Jews live in other cultures and countries.

In contrast to most national literatures, which tend toward homogeneity, Jewish literature draws on two major sources—both the national literature of the writer's country and the Jewish literary canon that traces its origins to the Bible. The tension between these dualities and the rich cross-fertilization that results has produced fresh and original forms. This anthology is a living example of the uniqueness of Jewish literature.

Although dispersed in many lands, we remain a recognizable and significant ethnic group with a collective memory, similar values, religious rituals and customs, even as our lives are redefined for the twenty-first century. As Cynthia Ozick points out in her essay "America: Toward Yavneh," writers who renew the tradition and draw upon Jewish text and allusions, as the authors in this volume have done, endure and create lasting work.

Marsha Lee Berkman and Elaine Marcus Starkman

I

NORTH AMERICA

THE AMERICAN BAKERY

Max Apple

I grew up in the heyday of ventriloquism. The dummy Jerry Mahoney was everyone's sweetheart. You could hardly go a day without hearing a joke about buttoning your lip or having a wooden head.

On the playground of my elementary school I practiced with all my might. I kept my lips close to the chain-link fence so that if they moved I would know it by the cold steel against them. My friends were doing the same. Two decades early, our playground was a herald of transcendental meditation. We were six years old, saying "om" to the fence, each of us hoping for our own dummy, a dummy who would supply all the punch lines, leaving us forever free to roam the playground practicing voice control.

Finally I got my dummy. An elderly cousin, moved by the seriousness of my tight-lipped practice, sent me an expensive one, a three-foot-high Jerry Mahoney in a cowboy outfit and an embossed half-face smile. But by the time my Jerry arrived he was too late; ventriloquism had already faded. The contestants on *The Original Amateur Hour* went back to thigh slapping and whistling through combs. My schoolmates, too, abandoned loneliness against the fence for kickball and pulling girls' hair. My dummy languished then as my wok and my food processor do now.

It took another twenty years for me to cast my voice again, this time into stories rather than dummies. It's a weak analogy, I know, and yet fiction seems sometimes like my dummy, like that part of myself that should get all the best lines. I want to be the straight man so that the very difference between us will be a part of the tension that I crave in each sentence, in every utterance of those wooden lips redeemed from silence because I practiced.

Yet the voice from the silence, the otherness that fiction is, doesn't need any metaphoric explanations. It's true that I tried ventriloquism, but it was my fascination with the English language itself that made me a writer. Its coyness has carried me through many a plot, entertained me when nothing else could. If not for love of words, I couldn't have managed eighth grade sitting next to Wayne Bruining during lunch, listening to the details of his escapades as a hunter. These were not adventure stories of life in the wild; they were the drab minutiae of taxidermy. While I held an oily tuna sandwich, Wayne lectured on how to skin a squirrel. He brought pelts to school and supplied the entire class with rabbits' feet. As Wayne droned on, I wondered in all the words that were new to me if he hunted in fens, glades, moors, vales, and dales. Though his subject was gory, Wayne was a good teacher. I could probably skin a squirrel, based on my memory of his conversations. I imagine that Wayne is still at it somewhere deep in the Michigan woods, showing his own son how to position a dressed buck over the hood of the car and then wipe the knife clean on the outside of his trousers.

My grandmother had a word for Wayne and most of my other friends: *goyim.* It explained everything. The hunting, the hubcap stealing, the smoking, the fighting—all were universal gentile attributes. *Goy* was a flat, almost unemotional word, but it defined everything I was not. There was some difficulty. Grand Rapids, Michigan, in the 1950s was not an East European ghetto, although my grandma did her best to blur the distinctions. World War I and poverty had moved her from her Lithuanian village, but even forty years in the wilderness of America did not make her learn English. She chose, above all, to avoid the language of the goyim. I told her about Wayne and everything else in Yiddish, which was the natural language of talking. I remember being surprised in kindergarten that everything happened in English. To us, English was the official language, useful perhaps for legal documents and high school graduation speeches, but not for everyday life.

My grandmother and I were quite a pair in the supermarket. Proud that I could read, I read all pertinent labels to her in loud Yiddish. The two of us could spend a long time in aisle four at the A&P over the differences between tomato paste and tomato sauce, while all around us gentiles roamed, loading their carts with what we knew were slabs of pork and shotgun shells. We wondered at them, these folks who could eat whatever they wanted and kill their own chickens. My grandma never learned English or strayed very far from her house, but she did glean from the gentiles a lust for technology. Our big nineteenth-century kitchen, which was also my playroom and her salon, was loaded with the latest. Before anyone else, we had an oven with a see-through door, a rotisserie, a Formica-topped dinette, and a frost-free refrigerator. The technology, though clearly "goyish," was never tainted. Sometimes I would come into the kitchen to find my grandmother admiring the simplest object, a cast-aluminum frying pan or a Corning Ware baking dish. Our kitchen needed only a wood-burning stove to become the kitchen in every Russian novel, yet in that old-fashioned place all the wonders of modern America blossomed. My grandmother never trusted the gentiles, but because of the way she savored kitchen gadgets, I know that at some time, probably before I was born, she gave up her fear of pogroms and settled down to take in, through translation and bargains, the available pleasures.

While she daydreamed in Yiddish and Americanized her domain, my grandfather worked in the American Bakery, among ovens that could bake two hundred loaves at once. He wore a white shirt, white trousers, a white apron, and a white cap. His hair was white and fine-textured. Puffs of flour emanated from him as he walked toward me. The high baking tables, the smell of the bread, the flour floating like mist, gave the bakery a kind of angelic feeling. In the front, two clerks sold the bread and customers talked in plain English. In the back, where the dough was rising, my grandpa yelled in Yiddish and Polish, urging his fellow bakers always to hurry. He went to the bakery long before dawn and would sometimes work twenty-four nonstop hours. He was already in his seventies. Twenty-four hours he considered part time. He did not bake what you might think; the American Bakery was true to its name. My grandpa toiled over white bread, sticky air-filled white bread, and cookies shaped like Christmas trees, green at the edges, blood red in the middle. He baked cakes for Polish weddings and doughnuts by the millions. My grandmother preferred store-bought baked goods. Their ghetto curses and old-world superstitions interrupted *I Love Lucy* and *The $64,000 Question*. He wished upon her a great cholera, a boil in her entrails, a solipsism deeper than despair.

My mother spent her energy running the household. My father earned our living as a scrap dealer. His work meant driving long distances in order to buy, and then to load upon his short-wheel-base Dodge, tons of steel shavings, aluminum borings, defective machinery—anything that could eventually be melted back to a more pristine condition. I rode with him when he didn't have to go very far. I had a pair of leather mittens, my work gloves, which I wore as I strutted among the barrels of refuse at the back of the factories. I touched the dirtied metals. I wanted to work as my father did, using his strength to roll the barrels from the loading dock to the truck. When he came home he washed his hands with Boraxo, then drank a double shot of Seagram's Seven from a long-stemmed shot glass. I imitated him with Coke or ginger ale. He alone knew what I wanted and loved. My grandfather wanted me to be a rabbinic scholar, my grandmother thought I should own at least two stores, my sisters and my mother groomed me for a career as a lawyer or "public speaker." My father knew that I wanted to play second base for the Tigers and have a level swing like Al Kaline. I probably love and write about sports so much as a way of remembering him. I carry baseball with me always the way he carried my mittens in the glove compartment of a half-dozen trucks to remind him of his little boy who grew up to study the secrets of literature but still does not forget to check the Tigers' box score every morning of the season.

When I was not listening to the Tigers or playing baseball or basketball myself, I was reading. A tunnel under Bridge Street connected the Catholic school, next to the American Bakery, to the West Side branch of the public library. I don't know what use the Catholic school made of the tunnel, but it was my lifeline. I would have a snack at the bakery, then move through the tunnel to reappear seconds later in that palatial library. In the high-ceilinged reading room I sat at a mahogany table. Across the street, my grandpa in the heat of the ovens was yelling at Joe Post in Polish and at Philip Allen in Yiddish; here the librarians whispered in English and decorated me with ribbons like a war hero, just because I loved to read. The books all in order, the smiling ladies to approve me, the smooth tables, even the maps on the wall seemed perfect to me. The marble floors of that library were the stones of heaven, my Harvard and my Yale, my refuge in the English language. What I learned from those boys' books was indeed American Literature. Wayne Bruining skinning squirrels was too close, too ugly, too goyish. But in the aura of the reading room, *The Kid from Tomkinsville* and *Huckleberry Finn* were my true buddies. I wanted to bedeck them with ribbons the way the librarians decorated me or, better yet, take them through the tunnel for a quick doughnut at the bakery.

When I came home from the library I sometimes told my grandmother in Yiddish about the books. We wondered together about space travel and the speed of light and life on other planets. If there was life on other worlds, she thought it was only the souls of the dead. She urged me to read less and think about someday owning my own store.

I think it was in that library that I finally came to distinguish the separateness of the Yiddish and English languages. I could speak and think in both, but reading and writing were all English. I specialized in reading and writing as if to solidify once and for all the fact that the written language was mine.

My sisters found the language through speaking. They won "I Speak for Democracy" contests; they were the Yankees and Dodgers of debate tournaments. I could barely hit my weight in Little League, but their speech trophies lined the windowsills like mold. They stood in front of our gilded dining room mirror, speaking earnestly and judging their looks at the same time. They used their arms to gesture, they quoted *Time* magazine, their bosoms heaved. My mother stopped her chores to swoon at her lovely daughters. My grandma thought their padded bras were a clever way to keep warm. Patrick Henry himself could not have outdone the rhetoric in our dining room.

My sisters wanted it for me too, that state championship in debate which seemed automatic just because we spoke English. I resisted the temptation as a few years later I resisted law school. I admired my sisters before the mirror and I, too, longed to understand *Time* magazine, but I didn't want to win anything with my words. I just wanted to play with them. I was already in love. Instead of debate, I took printing.

I, too, made words, but words laboriously made, words composed on a "stick," with "leads" and "slugs," words spelled out letter by letter with precise spacing—words that had to be read, not heard.

My hero was Ben Franklin. On his tombstone it said only: BEN FRANKLIN PRINTER.

"Did he make a living?" my grandmother wanted to know.

"He made the country. He and George Washington and Alexander Hamilton, they made the whole country."

"Go on," she said. "You believe everything they tell you in school."

I did believe everything I learned, but I listened to her too. Her stories were sometimes about the very things I studied. She had lived through the Russian Revolution. In a house in Odessa, a shoemaker's daughter, she waited out the war until she could join her baker husband, already sporting two-tone shoes and a gold watch on the shores of Lake Michigan.

She had no political ideology; the Czar and the Communists were equally barbarous in her eyes. Once, though, she did hide a young Jew pursued by the Czar's police. It was my favorite story. To me, that young Russian became Trotsky himself hiding for half an hour among my grandmother's wedding aprons, feather beds, long-sleeved dresses, and thick combs, the very objects I hid among in our Michigan attic.

She didn't care about Trotsky or Ben Franklin, only about her grandson, who she thought was making a mistake by becoming a scribe rather than a merchant. Only once, shortly before she died, did I convince my grandmother that being a scribe was not my intention. "I make things up, I don't just copy them."

"I've been doing that all my life," she told me. "Everyone can do that."

In a way she was right: making things up is not very difficult; the difficulty is getting the sentences to sound exactly right.

I would still prefer to be the ventriloquist—to let the words come from a smiling dummy across the room—but I'm not good enough at buttoning my lip. An awkward hesitant clumsy sentence emerges. I nurse it, love it in all its distress. I see in it the hope of an entire narrative, the suggestion of the fullness of time. I write a second sentence and then I cross out that first one as if it never existed. This infidelity is rhythm, voice, finally style itself. It is a truth more profound to me than meaning, which is always elusive and perhaps belongs more to the reader.

Jacob wrestled with angels and I with sentences. There's a big difference, I know. Still, to me they are angels, this crowd of syllables. My great-uncle who came from the Russian army in 1909 straight to the American West told me he never had to really learn English. "I knew Russian," he said. "English was just like it." He bought horses, cattle, land. He lived ninety years and when he died he left me his floor safe, which sits now, all 980 pounds, alongside me in the room where I write. My eight-year-old daughter knows the combination, but there is nothing inside.

I don't know if that's a trope too—that safe that comforts me almost as if there were a way to be safe. There is no safety—not for my uncle, not for my sentences so quickly guillotined, not for me either. Yet I wish for the security of exact words, the security I knew as a four-year-old reciting the Gettysburg Address at patriotic assemblies in the Turner School auditorium.

I learned the Gettysburg Address from a book of great American documents that my father found in the scrap. It was a true found poem; Lincoln's cadences thrilled me long before I knew what they meant. Abe Lincoln was as anonymous to me as that Russian hiding in my grandmother's boudoir, but I could say his words, say them in English, in American, and as I said them the principal wept and teachers listened in awe to such a little boy reciting those glorious words. My parents coached me in Yiddish as they taught me to say "Four score and seven years ago," but I know that they wanted me to be an American, to recite the Gettysburg Address to prove beyond a doubt that I was an insider to this new lingo, to prove that our whole family understood, through my words, that somehow we had arrived, feather beds and all, to live next door to squirrel skinners.

Perhaps my grandmother was right. A store or two, or even a law office, makes a lot more sense than a love affair with words. At least in a business your goods and services are all there, all out in the open, and most of the time you even see your customers. To confront them and know what you're selling—those are pleasures the writer rarely knows. Believe me, reader, I would like to know you. Most of the time I am just like you, curled up on the sofa hoping not to be distracted, ready to enter someone else's fabric of words just as you are now in mine.

Across the room from me, the safe is stuck half open. My son's tiny socks lie beside it, my daughter's lovely drawing of a horse, the sky, a cloud, and a flower. I wish I could tell you more, and I will perhaps in stories and novels; there I'll tell you more than I know. There I'll conjure lives far richer than mine, which is so pedestrian that it would make you seem heroic were you here beside me. Take comfort, though, in these sentences. They came all the way from Odessa at the very least and have been waiting a long time. To you they're entertainment; to me, breath.

HERE I AM

Persis Knobbe

Aggravation caused my father's heart attack, my mother said, aggravation over me. Rabbi Stern disagreed, saying that all kids rebel and how can you blame anyone for a heart attack. *Mea culpa,* I whispered. *Mea culpa,* whatever that means. The words were musical, forbidden, something to do with guilt.

My father, sitting in a chair for the first time in a week, said no one he knew had been arrested for committing a heart attack. My mother shrugged at a tray of empty teacups. I could see her from the hall where I was eavesdropping. When I leaned into the doorway, she looked up and said calmly, "I'm sure you have better things to do."

She was wrong. When she carried the tray to the kitchen, I resumed my listening post. The rabbi was telling my father not to worry about me.

"The best ones rebel," he said.

"That may be, Rabbi, but this one wants to sing in a church." My father's voice modulated on the last word from major to minor. Then, with pride: "A solo part. From the Messiah."

"Ah, Handel. The Messiah; most of it you will find in Isaiah. Beautiful, I have a recording by the London Symphony. *Halleluyah!* The same word in Hebrew."

"Beautiful? She goes to church every Sunday."

"Morris, read Isaiah, the first lines: 'For the Lord has spoken: Children I have reared, and brought up. And they have rebelled against me.'"

After a long pause, my father said, "A prophet isn't safe in his own house, is that right?" No answer from the rabbi. "And the prophet's wife? That's the worst part," my father said, "what it's doing to her mother."

I suspected my mother said the same about him.

"She's a smart girl," the rabbi said. "She'll figure it out. Try to step back a little. Find the humor in it."

Humor. Did he think this was a joke? Is there humor in driving your parents crazy? My aunt said that was my life's goal. I had no goals, other than surviving the school year and forming a bond with members of the church choir who, at the moment, were my only friends. If, in the process, my parents were knocked off their Jewish thrones, was it my fault?

The rabbi's approach was: Don't take her seriously. He dismissed me completely, walking right past me at the Congregational Church the following Sunday. I was lined up with other members of the choir outside the vestibule. "My God," I said to another alto, "that's my rabbi." Did I say *my* rabbi? I heard myself too late, just as he realized he had passed me.

"Ah, the renegade," he turned back, not surprised to see me. He greeted people on all sides with the easy handshake of a politician, then pulled me aside. "You'll be here for the sermon? Good. I think it will interest you."

Often a guest speaker in churches around town, the rabbi saved his most controversial sermons for those occasions. His first words—"Here we have Jesus as a young Jewish boy"—entered my body through my spinal column, vertebra by vertebra. Did he realize he was in a church? That he was talking to Christian people? I blocked out most of the sermon until the very end when the rabbi, as Jesus, took his prayer shawl, kissed it and chanted in a singsong Hebrew: *"Borchu et Adonoi hamvorakh."*

Then he looked out to the audience, one that had listened in pin-drop silence, unlike his own congregation, and smiled.

⤺ ⤺

"Come in while you're here and talk to me," the rabbi said on the phone. "I want to know how you turned out."

Home for the summer from New York where I was studying music, I had forgotten how cold San Francisco could be in July. I was shivering in cotton pants, T-shirt and my mother's white bumpy sweater, not looking my best, in contrast to the rabbi. In spite of a diagonal scar across his chin, the rabbi was a handsome man. His fencing wound, as he called it, was acquired as a teenager when he fell from a schoolyard fence. The negatives about his looks were also the positives: he was always on the verge of stubble, his complexion was too swarthy, his scar identified him.

Against the dark setting of his skin, his eyes and teeth were sources of light and energy. He was applying the energy to me, convincing me to perform at a Jewish fund-raiser. I surprised him, I thought, by saying yes and prepared to leave when he asked, "Did you read the books I recommended? Your mother sent you copies of Viktor Frankl, Martin Buber?"

"I tried, Rabbi. I'm not sure how much I understood."

"You don't have to understand. Buber is in the moment. Meeting, meeting another person head on. *I and Thou*, eye contact, very important. Relationship, that's the key word. I don't understand it either, I just do it. Sometimes. Not consistently. My wife couldn't take it."

I smiled, knowing how he used his wife to lighten a point. "Try Buber again," he said. "Try another way of looking at people."

His suggestion that I needed improvement provoked a sting of underground tears and an admission that I wasn't reading about Judaism.

"Since when?" he asked

"Since I became an atheist."

k k

"An atheist?" my aunt said. "You give her too much freedom." I was eavesdropping again. They were always talking about me and I had to know what I was up against.

"Buber! He tells her to read Buber? Let him practice some eye to eye, himself." She had visited the rabbi in his study with her written questions about the afterlife. He wasn't interested, she said. "Can you imagine? A rabbi not interested in the afterlife?" She asked him if she would see her love again in heaven. "I was in and out like the doctor's office."

She soothed her neck as she complained to my parents. "He's not a personal rabbi," she said. "He's a *public* rabbi, all that running to marches. There's more to life than what's happening in the world."

I had seen the rabbi march, with a minister on one side, a priest on the other, a trio for a Hollywood poster. Once, in an informal neighborhood protest, I walked beside him and saw him at his exuberant best: talking to strangers on all sides, smiling when one challenged him, fighting the good fight, his rabbinical robe flowing behind him like Prospero's cape.

Before I left for college I decided to surprise my father in *shul* one morning by walking down the aisle and sitting beside my mother. The rabbi was giving his sermon when I made my entrance. My mother, somewhat less thrilled than my father to spend Saturday mornings in *shul,* raised her eyebrows and smiled when she saw me. My father, sitting with members of the Board of Directors on one of the throne chairs, faced the congregation from the pulpit. He leaned forward and lifted his head as I moved down the aisle.

"Continuity," the rabbi was saying, his voice pounding on the podium.

"What's he talking about?" I whispered to my mother.

"Intermarriage," she answered, not looking at me. After Injustice, his favorite sermons were The Perils of Intermarriage and Welcome the Convert. Intermarriage again.

"Boy, they never give up." I shook my head sadly as if I were the only adult in the congregation.

"Sh," my mother said, "I want to hear this."

"What happens to the children?" The rabbi shrugged. "That's what people ask. I ask, what happens to the parents? M.D.'s and Ph.D.'s, high achievers, some of them, and what do they give their children? Jewish surnames. That's the end of it. Do they know that their own minds and emotions were shaped by Jewish thinking? By generations who studied Torah and Talmud in a house where next to God people worshipped education?"

"Ingrates," I whispered.

"Other minorities give their kids an identity, a physical identity; the shape of the eyes or color of the skin and they're stuck with it. We can only give ours the way we live our lives, what we choose to believe, what we choose to remember." That was the summation, I thought, or at least prelude to a pause. A long pause, it developed, during which I interviewed him in my imagination:

Are you saying, Rabbi, that black people can't walk out of their skins and Jews can?
You should know.

What do you mean?
Writing on your college application where it said Religious Choice:
None.
How would he know? Doesn't matter, Rabbi. You said it's what
you choose to believe or choose to remember. I choose to stay
ignorant.
Too late.

He was right. I already knew too much, growing up in a home where they lit the candles every Friday night and said prayers over the first everything, even the first cherry you ate every summer. Being Jewish, the whole heavy business, was right in the center of me. Ignorance was out.

The rabbi sang a few notes from "L'dor v'dor"—from generation to generation—his theme song. "Memory," he said, pacing the edge of the pulpit. "Memory is the color of our skin. The memory of our parents and their parents and the ones who never made it here. The memory of the Six Million. The memory of the holidays, lighting candles to welcome the Sabbath, dancing at weddings, giving a heavy foot to the glass goblet,"—here he stamped his foot and roused the man in front of me— "the bridegroom breaking the glass to remind us of the destruction of the temple."

I saw that my mother was taking it in, smiling her wishful smile when the rabbi spoke of dancing at weddings. I looked at her and asked myself what it would be like to please her, to marry a nice Jewish boy "when the time is right," a phrase she swung over my head as if she alone knew the precise moment. Like the rooster my grandmother once circled around my head to absorb my sins, the concept of the right time had no effect on me. I would make no promises. I knew that no mother, no God, no rabbi would stop me from marrying a man I loved.

The wandering rabbi, my mother called him. He went from Intermarriage to the Resurrection According to Judaism and then, briefly, back to Intermarriage. Next would come Rejection. Yes. Now he was castigating "people who reject their religion without knowing what they're rejecting." Was he looking at me?

"Sad, don't you think: a young person who doesn't like being Jewish; it's hard, it's inconvenient, it doesn't appeal. It's a hassle, I have heard." He was looking at me. "Sometimes it is teenage rebellion, sometimes it matures into self-hatred."

A merciful God had seated my father behind the rabbi so that he didn't see where the rabbi's eyes were focused. He didn't see the prayerbook slide from my lap, as if the flood of embarrassment made my clothing wet and slippery. Fortunately, my mother caught the book in time or it would have made a thud as loud as the rabbi's foot when it simulated the destruction of the temple.

I stood up, ruffling a row of knees as I passed them, including those of my mother's friends. The husband of one of them stood up to let me by. The way he looked through me said he knew everything about me, that I went East to college, that I sang in church on Sundays, that I was a general pain in the neck, in spite of getting very good grades. He wouldn't trade his daughter for me, that was a given.

I walked home wondering how people can say certain things in public. What happened since the day the rabbi advised my father: "Give her a break, find the humor in it." What changed him I'd like to know. I was glad the fog hadn't lifted; it gave me the cover I needed. I walked in short, angry steps, then lengthened my stride as I recovered a sense of myself. "Nobody can tell me who I am," I told myself, beginning to feel hopeful, cleansed, destined for something great. And, even when greatness poured over me, even when I wowed them on Broadway or at least got my teaching credential, I vowed I would never forgive the rabbi. And there would be more to forgive.

❧ ❧

I maintained my boycott of the rabbi for a full year, breaking it to go with my father to *shul* to say a *mi shebeirakh,* a special prayer for my mother's health. I sat beside my father while he stood, praying with the men. His prayerbook in front of him, he looked sideways out of his eyes at me. I had arrived at a place with him where I could do no wrong and yet I could do nothing wonderful. Why was it such a big deal to make your father proud? I was proud of him, standing alone, finishing his prayer, oblivious to the rabbi beginning his sermon. The rabbi stopped in the middle of a sentence and glanced at my father. "It's a distraction," he said to the congregation. Was he talking about my father? "I'm trying to give a sermon; I give the benefit of doubt to the slower readers and still I see stragglers. I cannot wait indefinitely; the congregation cannot wait indefinitely." The rabbi squinted at my father. "Is that you, Morris, is there a problem?" My father did not look up from his book.

"Please. A matter of respect. If not for me, for the office of the rabbi and the hope of the congregation to finish by twelve noon. And still he stands. Will no one speak to him?"

"I'm sorry, Daddy. The rabbi wants you to sit." My father's lips kept moving. He glanced at me, motioned me to be quiet, a short downward push of his arm. Like a child, I tugged at his coat. He gave me a sharper look, an angry one. Why was I annoying him, interrupting his prayer? He had absolutely no idea the rabbi was looking at him. Why would the rabbi speak to him from the pulpit?

Once he sat down he made the connection. The lower part of his face lost shape; his teeth appeared to collapse. "He was talking to me?" my father said. "No respect?"

His head was close to mine. I nodded. He turned forward, facing the altar, shaking his head as if shaking off a dream; *There was the rabbi. Here was the shul.* He took a slow breath and slid his fingers along his prayer shawl.

My father went through the motions for the remainder of the service. He let someone else dress the Torah in its cloth mantel and silver crowns. He stood with me when the cantor, returning the Torah to the ark, circled the congregation, followed by what my mother called the Parade of *Machers,* men who wielded power in the *shul.* "We can leave any time," I told him. He was whispering the words to the *Amidah,* a silent prayer, the signal for men to look at their watches and women to go to the bathroom.

When the cantor sang the closing melody, the rabbi sat up, startled. I wondered if the hand of God had grabbed him by the scruff of his neck. He stood up and took a step forward as the cantor was approaching his high note, an A above middle C. The rabbi waited for the note to end. Then he spoke in a rush, unable to get the words out fast enough. "My old friend. Forgive me. A man so devout, so loving of the word of God. No matter, no matter who it was finishing his prayer, I would apologize. What you were doing Morris, *Moishe,* was more important than what I was saying. Your prayer, in the eyes and ears of God, I am sure held more weight than my sermon."

Too late, Rabbi, I said to myself, that's it. Forget me. Chalk up another loss for your side.

♠ ♠

My parents gave up on enticing me back to Judaism but *nachas,* pleasure from the children, awaited them when I married Leo, a nice half-Jewish boy. My mother was pleased even if it was the wrong half. She told me that according to tradition the *mother* is supposed to be Jewish. "For once," she said, "the woman is more important than the man. When she's pregnant, of course."

Soon after Leo and I were married I dreamed of walking to synagogue with him, arms crossed over my breasts, naked from the waist up,
like the model in the Maidenform Bra ad without the bra. "I know you'll
be mad at me," I said to Leo, "but I forgot my blouse." He assured me
that no one was looking. "Good thing," I said in my dream knowing it
was a dream, "that I'm walking with you and not my father." I was embarrassed but not ashamed.

Part of me was exposed in the dream, the Jewish part. And I was
comfortable with it. Leo helped me with that. The reconciliation was
gradual, the way you begin to accept your parents when you first go
away from home. Leo started me off with Jewish comedians. Then I fell
in love with the hokey music at Jewish weddings. And then it went beyond the ethnic. My reconciliation with the rabbi took longer and was
not complete until my daughter was in her teens, on a day that proved
to be the hottest Yom Kippur on record.

❧ ❧

The heat hit me when I got out of the car. World Series weather,
High Holiday heat. The blowing of the ram's horn for the Jewish New
Year signaled Indian Summer in San Francisco. Leo stayed in the car,
listening to the radio, unable to tear himself from the series game. "I'll
leave at the end of the eighth," he said, "unless it's tied." Annie, our
daughter, was to meet us in temple, where we would spend the day swel-
tering in our velvet seats.

I unbuttoned my linen jacket. At least there was a breeze. I was part
of a small group taking the short cut to temple through a city park. We
walked beside an unused bridle path surrounded by eucalyptus trees. A
horsy smell blended with the eucalyptus in a mixture that always intrigued and repelled me. Pausing at an intersection where my father used
to pause for a second wind or because he got that ache in the back of
his knee, I thought of the Via Dolorosa and smiled. Here I was reliving
my father's aches and pains on the way to temple as if they were Stations of the Cross.

Someone behind me was humming a tune, a Yom Kippur melody,
three descending notes repeating each time one step lower, finally disappearing. Then a woman's voice: "You think the new rabbi will speak
today?" I waited for an answer. Perhaps it was a nod.

A new rabbi? How could they hire a new rabbi? Rabbi Stern was
the temple, the temple was Rabbi Stern. I crossed away from the bridle
path to the residential side of the street, where a Chinese woman waited
with her broom for me to pass. She was used to this small parade on

the High Holidays. I nodded at her, the way Catholic families used to nod at my father when they passed our house on their way to Mass. My father, outside watering our city patch of lawn, enjoyed the civility: this was America.

The descending triplets played in my head like Three Blind Mice in a minor key. See how I ran, I sang in my head. See how I ran from my own religion and then from one to another. And now had I come full circle? God only knew.

❧ ❧

I arrived at the outside steps to the temple, only to be stopped by the hired greeter. He was not the one I knew, with a beard and dark suit and no tie. This one looked more like Security with his khaki jacket and bulging holster. We had a couple of bomb threats not long ago; apparently they had been taken seriously. The guard checked my High Holiday ticket, bowed his head and waved me to move on.

Together with other late-comers, I walked upstairs, up the soft, raspberry carpeting. The voice of the rabbi once could be heard all the way down the stairs to the street: Jeremiah warning the children of Israel. He read to us from the Torah or the *Jerusalem Post* or the *London Times,* setting aside his prepared speech and responding to the moment, this moment in the world, his eyes catching the lights from the stained-glass windows.

There was standing room only when I entered the main floor. The cantor was chanting *Hineni:* Here I am, Lord, in my humility. It was a singular, theatrical part of the Yom Kippur service in which the cantor approached the pulpit from the rear of the temple, singing as he moved slowly up the aisle. I waited, embarrassed to be at the door simultaneously with the cantor, like arriving at the church with the bride. Once he was midway up the aisle I went to my reserved seat as unobtrusively as possible, nodding an apology to the old man at the end of our row, knowing he would not look up from his prayerbook to meet my eye.

"Look," my daughter said, the moment she saw me, "Rabbi Stern."

Sitting up on the pulpit with the assistant rabbi, the choir and all the officers of the temple was a ghost, a wraith. A sunken face rested on a voluminous white gown with the bones of Rabbi Stern in it. On his feet he wore what he always wore on Yom Kippur as a gesture of humility: canvas tennis shoes.

He would not be springing up in those shoes to plead with the congregation for order, not this year, not any year. On High Holidays the main floor of the temple was a meeting place where someone was always moving, kissing, exclaiming. The rabbi would periodically remind us that we were observing the Days of Awe. Today there was more awe than he bargained for.

As latecomers entered, they stopped when they saw the rabbi and plainly gasped. People took assigned seats or stood against the back wall without fuss. No one spoke in an audible voice except for the woman in front of me who was fanning herself with an envelope. She wondered what the rabbi was doing here. "Shouldn't he be home in bed?" she asked. No one answered her. One of the officers on the pulpit took side glances at the rabbi and then looked steadily forward.

The cantor, still singing, paused at the steps to the pulpit. His tone was straight and piercing until he relieved it with a cantorial embellishment. Later in the day, in an act shunned by Jews except on the holiday of Yom Kippur, he would kneel, prostrating himself in a ceremony of cleansing, a reenactment of the High Priest entering the Holy of Holies on Yom Kippur. Most of us openly stared at the rabbi who looked back over our heads, out of his eye sockets, not seeing us.

The couple to my left stood up and Leo slid in past them. He leaned over me to kiss Annie, then took a long time to sit down, not taking his eyes from the rabbi. "What happened to him?" he whispered.

"You can see," I said. "He's dying."

Cancer, I thought. He was going slowly, not like my father, who went like *that*. I snapped my fingers and both Leo and Annie looked at me. The rabbi wasn't going like that. Feeling cold and excluded, as if I had turned to the obituaries and seen the name of a close friend, I wished that someone had called me.

You should have known, my father would have said. *You should have kept in touch.*

Of course. Especially after my father's funeral. "A *shane Yid*," a sweet Jew, the rabbi had called him in his eulogy. There was no thought of asking anyone but Rabbi Stern to preside at the funeral. I remembered how quickly my father forgave the man who made him feel like two cents in front of the entire congregation.

"Not me," my father said when I made an unwise reference to that occasion. "He made *you* feel like two cents. Me, I'm not bought and sold on the open market." My father believed that great men did foolish things. "As long as they don't do them every Monday and Thursday," he qualified.

When the cantor concluded the *Hineni*, Rabbi Stern pulled himself up. His rabbinical gown hung on dust. As he stood, it folded against itself. Never had the congregation been more as one, more riveted than when the rabbi approached the lectern. Would he speak? Did he have the strength for speech?

He waited, his right hand poised as if it were a baton, holding us to the moment. "I have come," he said, "to bid you farewell." We barely breathed as the rabbi raised his hand in a gesture that had once held off applause or stopped a protest. His voice was not the resounding voice of Rabbi Stern but it was audible. "And I would like to ask your pardon."

A member of the choir adjusted the microphone and the rabbi's voice was clearer when he continued. "Every year on Yom Kippur I ask you to go beyond reconciliation with God. That is the beginning. That is the *idea* of atonement. The *act* of atonement is to ask forgiveness of the persons you have wronged."

His eyes were now focused. He was seeing us, recognizing faces. "Over the years I am sure I have offended many of you, if not most of you, if not all of you. I am asking you to forgive me." As his eyes scanned the congregation looking for specific faces, my daughter took my hand and held on hard. Was the congregation expected to make some response? The small clasping movements around me suggested the holding back of a response. Could someone lead us in one?

What about the old man at the end of our row? Whenever I saw him, his shoulders raised in a permanent shrug, I thought: definitely not born in America, definitely been through hell. On Yom Kippur, he gently beat himself, bringing his fist slowly to his breast as he chanted the sins in the *Viddui*, the confession. One beat for each sin: *A-sham-nu*, we bring shame, *ba-gad-nu*, we betray. His voice preceded the congregation as he sang the melody, the descending triplets I heard on my way to temple. I watched the journey of his fist, and I wanted to be held in it, brought to the heart: his and my father's and the rabbi's.

Hineni. Here I am, I wanted to tell them. Was that enough? Here I am? I wanted to say *Forgive me, Father, for I have sinned.* No, that was the other religion. You see, Rabbi? Here I am, always mocking. That was in the *Viddui*: Kiz-*av*-nu, *latz*-nu, mar-*ad*-nu, we deceive, we mock, we rebel. The old man chanted it, beating himself for God knows what, and all I could say for myself was Here I am, Rabbi. Rebbe. Teacher.

Rabbi Stern took a small step back, eyes still burning, with a spreading in the lower part of his face, not quite a smile. It was hard to define a smile where the flesh pressed so close to the bone. The rabbi lifted his head to the crowded balconies, his eyes circling left to right, then the main floor, slowly, right to left, all the way to the back of the synagogue, eye to eye, eyes to eyes. I turned to my daughter but she was looking straight ahead. Beyond her, the old man finally looked up from his prayerbook. He nodded at the rabbi, a quick nod, then slower, his head barely moving.

PUTTERMESSER: HER WORK HISTORY, HER ANCESTRY, HER AFTERLIFE

Cynthia Ozick

Puttermesser was thirty-four, a lawyer. She was also something of a feminist, not crazy, but she resented having "Miss" put in front of her name; she thought it pointedly discriminatory, she wanted to be a lawyer among lawyers. Though she was no virgin she lived alone, but idiosyncratically—in the Bronx, on the Grand Concourse, among other people's decaying old parents. Her own had moved to Miami Beach; in furry slippers left over from high school she roamed the same endlessly mazy apartment she had grown up in, her aging piano sheets still on top of the upright with the teacher's X marks on them showing where she should practice up to. Puttermesser always pushed a little ahead of the actual assignment; in school too. Her teachers told her mother she was "highly motivated," "achievement oriented." Also she had "scholastic drive." Her mother wrote all these things down in a notebook, kept it always, and took it with her to Florida in case she should die there. Puttermesser had a younger sister who was also highly motivated, but she had married an Indian, a Parsee chemist, and gone to live in Calcutta. Already the sister had four children and seven saris of various fabrics.

Puttermesser went on studying. In law school they called her a grind, a competitive-compulsive, an egomaniac out for aggrandizement. But ego was no part of it; she was looking to solve something, she did not

know what. At the back of the linen closet she found a stack of her father's old shirt cardboards (her mother was provident, stingy: in kitchen
drawers Puttermesser still discovered folded squares of used ancient
waxed paper, million-creased into whiteness, cheese-smelling, nesting
small unidentifiable wormlets); so behind the riser pipe in the bathroom
Puttermesser kept weeks' worth of Sunday *Times* crossword puzzles sta-
pled to these laundry boards and worked on them indiscriminately. She
played chess against herself, and was always victor over the color she
had decided to identify with. She organized tort cases on index cards. It
was not that she intended to remember everything: situations—it was
her tendency to call intellectual problems "situations"—slipped into her
mind like butter into a bottle.

A letter came from her mother in Florida:

Dear Ruth,

*I know you won't believe this but I swear it's true the other day
Daddy was walking on the Avenue and who should he run into
but Mrs. Zaretsky, the thin one from Burnside not the stout one
from Davidson, you remember her Joel? Well he's divorced now
no children thank God so he's free as a bird as they say his ex
the poor thing couldn't conceive. He had tests he's O.K. He's
only an accountant not good enough for you because God knows
I never forget the day you made Law Review but you should
come down just to see what a tender type he grew into. Every
tragedy has its good side Mrs. Zaretsky says he comes down now
practically whenever she calls him long distance. Daddy said to
Mrs. Zaretsky well, an accountant, you didn't overeducate your
son anyhow, with daughters it's different. But don't take this to
heart honey Daddy is as proud as I am of your achievements.
Why don't you write we didn't hear from you too long busy is
busy but parents are parents.*

Puttermesser had a Jewish face and a modicum of American distrust
of it. She resembled no poster she had ever seen: with a Negroid passion she hated the Breck shampoo girl, so blond and bland and pale-
mouthed; she boycotted Breck because of the golden-haired posters, all
crudely idealized, an American wet dream, in the subway. Puttermesser's
hair came in bouncing scallops—layered waves from scalp to tip, like
imbricated roofing tile. It was nearly black and had a way of sometimes
sticking straight out. Her nose had thick, well-haired uneven nostrils,

the right one noticeably wider than the other. Her eyes were small, the lashes short, invisible. She had the median Mongol lid—one of those Jewish faces with a vaguely Oriental cast. With all this, it was a fact she was not bad-looking. She had a good skin with, so far, few lines or pits or signs of looseness-to-come. Her jaw was pleasing—a baby jowl appeared only when she put her head deep in a book.

In bed she studied Hebrew grammar. The permutations of the triple-lettered root elated her: how was it possible that a whole language, hence a whole literature, a civilization even, should rest on the pure presence of three letters of the alphabet? The Hebrew verb, a stunning mechanism: three letters, whichever fated three, could command all possibility simply by a change in their pronunciation, or the addition of a wing-letter fore and aft. Every conceivable utterance blossomed from this trinity. It seemed to her not so much a language for expression as a code for the world's design, indissoluble, predetermined, translucent. The idea of the grammar of Hebrew turned Puttermesser's brain into a palace, a sort of Vatican; inside its corridors she walked from one resplendent triptych to another.

She wrote her mother a letter refusing to come to Florida to look over the divorced accountant's tenderness. She explained her life again; she explained it by indirection. She wrote:

I have a cynical apperception of power, due no doubt to my current job. You probably haven't heard of the Office for Visas and Registration, OVIR for short. It's located on Ogaryova Street, in Moscow, U.S.S.R. I could enumerate for you a few of the innumerable bureaucratic atrocities of OVIR, not that anyone knows them all. But I could give you a list of the names of all those criminals, down to the women clerks, Yefimova, Korolova, Akulova, Arkhipova, Izrailova, all of them on Kolpachni Street in an office headed by Zolotukhin, the assistant to Colonel Smyrnov, who's under Ovchinikov, who is second in command to General Viryein, only Viryein and Ovchinikov aren't on Kolpachni Street, they're the ones in the head office—the M.D.V., Internal Affairs Ministry—on Ogaryova Street. Some day all the Soviet Jews will come out of the spider's clutches of these people and be free. Please explain to Daddy that this is one of the highest priorities of my life at this time in my personal history. Do you think a Joel Zaretsky can share such a vision?

Immediately after law school, Puttermesser entered the firm of Midland, Reid & Cockleberry. It was a blueblood Wall Street firm, and Puttermesser, hired for her brains and ingratiating (read: immigrant-like) industry, was put into a back office to hunt up all-fours cases for the men up front. Though a Jew and a woman, she felt little discrimination: the back office was chiefly the repository of unmitigated drudgery and therefore of usable youth. Often enough it kept its lights burning till three in the morning. It was right that the Top Rung of law school should earn you the Bottom of the Ladder in the actual world of all-fours. The wonderful thing was the fact of the Ladder itself. And though she was the only woman, Puttermesser was not the only Jew. Three Jews a year joined the back precincts of Midland, Reid (four the year Puttermesser came, which meant they thought "woman" more than "Jew" at the sight of her). Three Jews a year left—not the same three. Lunchtime was difficult. Most of the young men went to one or two athletic clubs nearby to "work out"; Puttermesser ate from a paper bag at her desk, along with the other Jews, and this was strange: the young male Jews appeared to be as committed to the squash courts as the others. Alas, the athletic clubs would not have them, and this too was preternatural—the young Jews were indistinguishable from the others. They bought the same suits from the same tailors, wore precisely the same shirts and shoes, were careful to avoid tie clips and to be barbered a good deal shorter than the wild men of the streets, though a bit longer than the prigs in the banks.

Puttermesser remembered what Anatole France said of Dreyfus: that he was the same type as the officers who condemned him. "In their shoes he would have condemned himself."

Only their accents fell short of being identical: the "a" a shade too far into the nose, the "i" with its telltale elongation, had long ago spread from Brooklyn to Great Neck, from Puttermesser's Bronx to Scarsdale. These two influential vowels had the uncanny faculty of disqualifying them for promotion. The squash players, meanwhile, moved out of the back offices into the front offices. One or two of them were groomed—curried, fed sugar, led out by the muzzle—for partnership: were called out to lunch with thin and easeful clients, spent an afternoon in the dining room of one of the big sleek banks, and in short, developed the creamy cheeks and bland habits of the always-comfortable.

The Jews, by contrast, grew more anxious, hissed together meanly among the urinals (Puttermesser, in the ladies' room next door, could hear malcontent rumblings in the connecting plumbing), became perfectionist and uncasual, quibbled bitterly, with stabbing forefingers, over principles, and all in all began to look and act less like superannuated college athletes and more like Jews. Then they left. They left of their own choice; no one shut them out.

Puttermesser left too, weary of so much chivalry—the partners in particular were excessively gracious to her, and treated her like a fellow-aristocrat. Puttermesser supposed this was because *she* did not say "a" in her nose or elongate her "i," and above all she did not dentalize her "t," "d," or "l," keeping them all back against the upper palate. Long ago her speech had been "standardized" by the drilling of fanatical teachers, elocutionary missionaries hired out of the Midwest by Puttermesser's prize high school, until almost all the regionalism was drained out; except for the pace of her syllables, which had a New York deliberateness, Puttermesser could have come from anywhere. She was every bit as American as her grandfather in his captain's hat. From Castle Garden to blue New England mists, her father's father, hat-and-neckwear peddler to Yankees! In Puttermesser's veins Providence, Rhode Island, beat richly. It seemed to her the partners felt this.

Then she remembered that Dreyfus spoke perfect French, and was the perfect Frenchman.

For farewell she was taken out to a public restaurant—the clubs the partners belonged to (they explained) did not allow women—and apologized to.

"We're sorry to lose you," one said, and the other said, "No one for you in this outfit for under the canvas, hah?"

"The canvas?" Puttermesser said.

"Wedding canopy," said the partner, with a wink. "Or do they make them out of sheepskin—I forget."

"An interesting custom. I hear you people break the dishes at a wedding too," said the second partner.

An anthropological meal. They explored the rites of her tribe. She had not known she was strange to them. Their beautiful manners were the cautiousness you adopt when you visit the interior: Dr. Livingstone, I presume? They shook hands and wished her luck, and at that moment, so close to their faces with those moist smile-ruts flowing from the sides of their waferlike noses punctured by narrow, even nostrils, Puttermesser was astonished into noticing how strange *they* were—so many luncheon martinis inside their bellies, and such beautiful manners even while drunk, and, important though they were, insignificant though she was, the fine ceremonial fact of their having brought her to this carpeted place. Their eyes were blue. Their necks were clean. How closely they were shaven!—like men who grew no hair at all. Yet hairs curled inside their ears. They let her take away all her memo pads with her name printed on them. She was impressed by their courtesy, their benevolence, through which they always got their way. She had given them three years of meticulous anonymous research, deep deep nights going after precedents, dates, lost issues, faded faint politics; for their sakes she had yielded up those howling morning headaches and half a diopter's worth of sight in both eyes. Brilliant students make good aides. They were pleased though not regretful. She was replaceable: a clever black had been hired only that morning. The palace they led her to at the end of it all was theirs by divine right: in which they believed, on which they acted. They were benevolent because benevolence was theirs to dispense.

She went to work for the Department of Receipts and Disbursements. Her title was Assistant Corporation Counsel—it had no meaning, it was part of the subspeech on which bureaucracy relies. Of the many who held this title most were Italians and Jews, and again Puttermesser was the only woman. In this great City office there were no ceremonies and no manners: gross shouts, ignorant clerks, slovenliness, litter on the floors, grit stuck all over antiquated books. The ladies' room reeked: the women urinated standing up, and hot urine splashed on the toilet seats and onto the muddy tiles.

The successive heads of this department were called Commissioners. They were all political appointees—scavengers after spoils. Puttermesser herself was not quite a civil servant and not quite *not* a civil servant— one of those amphibious creatures hanging between base contempt and bare decency; but she soon felt the ignominy of belonging to that mean swarm of City employees rooted bleakly in cells inside the honeycomb of the Municipal Building. It was a monstrous place, gray everywhere, abundantly tunneled, with multitudes of corridors and stairs and shafts, a kind of swollen doom through which the bickering of small-voiced officials whinnied. At the same time there were always curious farm sounds—in the summer the steady cricket of the air-conditioning, in the winter the gnash and croak of old radiators. Nevertheless the windows were broad and high and stupendously filled with light; they looked out on the whole lower island of Manhattan, revealed *as* an island, down to the Battery, all crusted over with the dried lava of shape and shape: rectangle over square, and square over spire. At noon the dark gongs of St. Andrew's boomed their wild and stately strokes.

To Puttermesser all this meant she had come down in the world. Here she was not even a curiosity. No one noticed a Jew. Unlike the partners at Midland, Reid, the Commissioners did not travel out among their subjects and were rarely seen. Instead they were like shut-up kings in a tower, and suffered from rumors.

But Puttermesser discovered that in City life all rumors are true. Putative turncoats are genuine turncoats. All whispered knifings have happened: officials reputed to be about to topple, topple. So far Puttermesser had lasted through two elections, seeing the powerful become powerless and the formerly powerless inflate themselves overnight, like gigantic winds, to suck out the victory of the short run. When one Administration was razed, for the moment custom seemed leveled with it, everything that smelled of "before," of "the old way"—but only at first. The early fits of innovation subsided, and gradually the old way of doing things crept back, covering everything over, like grass, as if the building and its workers were together some inexorable vegetable organism with its own laws of subsistence. The civil servants were grass. Nothing destroyed them, they were stronger than the pavement, they were stronger than time. The Administration might turn on its hinge, throwing out one lot of patronage eaters and gathering in the new lot: the work went on. They might put in fresh carpeting in the new Deputy's office, or a private toilet in the new Commissioner's, and change the clerks' light bulbs to a lower wattage, and design an extravagant new colophon for a useless old document—they might do anything they liked: the work went on as before. The organism breathed, it comprehended itself.

So there was nothing for the Commissioner to do, and he knew it, and the organism knew it. For a very great salary the Commissioner shut his door and cleaned his nails behind it with one of the shining tools of a fancy Swiss knife, and had a secretary who was rude to everyone and made dozens of telephone calls every day.

The current one was a rich and foolish playboy who had given the Mayor money for his campaign. All the high officials of every department were either men who had given the Mayor money or else courtiers who had humiliated themselves for him in the political clubhouse—mainly by flattering the clubhouse boss, who before any election was already a secret mayor and dictated the patronage lists. But the current Commissioner owed nothing to the boss because he had given the Mayor money and was the Mayor's own appointee; and anyhow he would have little to do with the boss because he had little to do with any Italian. The boss was a gentlemanly Neapolitan named Fiore, the chairman of the board of a bank; but still, he was only an Italian, and the Commissioner cared chiefly for blue-eyed bankers. He used his telephone to make luncheon appointments with them, and sometimes tennis. He himself was a blue-eyed Guggenheim, a German Jew, but not one of the grand philanthropic Guggenheims. The name was a cunning coincidence (cut down from Guggenheimer), and he was rich enough to be taken for one of the real Guggenheims, who thought him an upstart and disowned him. Grandeur demands discreetness; he was so discreetly disowned that no one knew it, not even the Rockefeller he had met at Choate.

This Commissioner was a handsome, timid man, still young, and good at boating; on weekends he wore sneakers and cultivated the friendship of the dynasties—Sulzbergers and Warburgs, who let him eat with them but warned their daughters against him. He had dropped out of two colleges and finally graduated from the third by getting a term-paper factory to plagiarize his reports. He was harmless and simple-minded, still devoted to his brainy late father, and frightened to death of news conferences. He understood nothing: art appreciation had been his best subject (he was attracted to Renaissance nudes), economics his worst. If someone asked, "How much does the City invest every day?" or "Is there any Constitutional bar against revenue from commuters?" or "What is your opinion about taxing exempt properties?" his pulse would catch in his throat, making his nose run, and he had to say he was pressed for time and would let them have the answers from his Deputy in charge of the Treasury. Sometimes he would even call on Puttermesser for an answer.

❧ ❧

Now if this were an optimistic portrait, exactly here is where Puttermesser's emotional life would begin to grind itself into evidence. Her biography would proceed romantically, the rich young Commissioner of the Department of Receipts and Disbursements would fall in love with her. She would convert him to intelligence and to the cause of Soviet Jewry. He would abandon boating and the pursuit of bluebloods. Puttermesser would end her work history abruptly and move on to a bower in a fine suburb.

This is not to be. Puttermesser will always be an employee in the Municipal Building. She will always behold Brooklyn Bridge through its windows; also sunsets of high glory, bringing her religious pangs. She will not marry. Perhaps she will undertake a long-term affair with Vogel, the Deputy in charge of the Treasury: perhaps not.

The difficulty with Puttermesser is that she is loyal to certain environments.

🐦 🐦

Puttermesser, while working in the Municipal Building, had a luxuriant dream, a dream of *gan eydn*—a term and notion handed on from her great-uncle Zindel, a former shammes in a *shul* that had been torn down. In this reconstituted Garden of Eden, which is to say in the World to Come, Puttermesser, who was not afflicted with quotidian uncertainty in the Present World, had even more certainty of her aims. With her weakness for fudge (others of her age, class, and character had advanced to martinis, at least to ginger ale; Puttermesser still drank ice cream with cola, despised mints as too tingly, eschewed salty liver canapés, hunted down chocolate babies, Kraft caramels, Mary Janes, Milky Ways, peanut brittle, and immediately afterward furiously brushed her teeth, scrubbing off guilt)—with all this nasty self-indulgence, she was nevertheless very thin and unironic. Or: to postulate an afterlife was her single irony— a game in the head not unlike a melting fudge cube held against the upper palate.

There, at any rate, Puttermesser would sit, in Eden, under a middle-sized tree, in the solid blaze of an infinite heart-of-summer July, green, green, green everywhere, green above and green below, herself gleaming and made glorious by sweat, every itch annihilated, fecundity dismissed. And there Puttermesser would, as she imagined it, *take in*. Ready to her left hand, the box of fudge (rather like the fudge sold to the lower school by eighth-grade cooking class in P.S. 74, The Bronx, circa 1942); ready to her right hand, a borrowed steeple of library books: for into Eden the Crotona Park Branch has ascended intact, sans librarians and fines, but with its delectable terrestrial binding-glue fragrances unevaporated.

Here Puttermesser sits. Day after celestial day, perfection of desire upon perfection of contemplation, into the exaltations of an uninterrupted forever, she eats fudge in human shape (once known—no use covering this up—as nigger babies), or fudge in square shapes (and in Eden there is no tooth decay); and she reads. Puttermesser reads and reads. Her eyes in Paradise are unfatigued. And if she still does not know what it is she wants to solve, she has only to read on. The Crotona Park Branch is as paradisal here as it was on earth. She reads anthropology, zoology, physical chemistry, philosophy (in the green air of heaven Kant and Nietzsche together fall into crystal splinters). The New Books section is peerless: she will learn about the linkages of genes, about quarks, about primate sign language, theories of the origins of the races, religions of ancient civilizations, what Stonehenge meant. Puttermesser will read Non-Fiction into eternity; and there is still time for Fiction! Eden is equipped above all with timelessness, so Puttermesser will read at last all of Balzac, all of Dickens, all of Turgenev and Dostoevski (her mortal self has already read all of Tolstoy and George Eliot); at last Puttermesser will read *Kristin Lavransdatter* and the stupendous trilogy of Dmitri Merezhkovski, she will read *The Magic Mountain* and the whole *Faerie Queene* and every line of *The Ring and the Book,* she will read a biography of Beatrix Potter and one of Walter Scott in many entrancing volumes and one of Lytton Strachey, at last, at last! In Eden insatiable Puttermesser will be nourished, if not glutted. She will study Roman law, the more arcane varieties of higher mathematics, the nuclear composition of the stars, what happened to the Monophysites, Chinese history, Russian, and Icelandic.

But meanwhile, still alive, not yet translated upward, her days given over to the shadow reign of a playboy Commissioner, Puttermesser was learning only Hebrew.

Twice a week, at night (it seemed), she went to Uncle Zindel for a lesson. Where the bus ran through peeling neighborhoods the trolley tracks sometimes shone up through a broken smother of asphalt, like weeds wanting renewal. From childhood Puttermesser remembered how trolley days were better days: in summer the cars banged along, self-contained little carnivals, with open wire-mesh sides sucking in hot winds, the passengers serenely jogging on the seats. Not so this bus, closed like a capsule against the slum.

The old man, Zindel the Stingy, hung on to life among the cooking smells of Spanish-speaking blacks. Puttermesser walked up three flights of steps and leaned against the crooked door, waiting for the former shammes with his little sack. Each evening Zindel brought up a single egg from the Cuban grocery. He boiled it while Puttermesser sat with her primer.

"You should go downtown," the shammes said, "there they got regular language factories. Berlitz. N.Y.U. They even got an *ulpan,* like in Israel."

"You're good enough," Puttermesser said. "You know everything they know."

"And something more also. Why you don't live downtown, on the East Side, fancy?"

"The rent is too much, I inherited your stinginess."

"And such a name. A nice young fellow meets such a name, he laughs. You should change it to something *different,* lovely, nice. Shapiro, Levine, Cohen, Goldweiss, Blumenthal. I don't say make it different, who needs Adams, who needs McKee, I say make it a name not a joke. Your father gave you a bad present with it. For a young girl, But-terknife!"

"I'll change it to Margarine-messer."

"Never mind the ha-ha. *My* father what was your great-great-grand-father, didn't allow a knife to the table Friday night. When it came to *kiddush*—knifes off! All knifes! On Sabbath an instrument, a blade? On Sabbath a weapon? A point? An edge? What makes bleeding among mankind? What makes war? Knifes! No knifes! Off! A clean table! And something else you'll notice. By us we got only *messer,* you follow? By them they got sword, they got lance, they got halberd. Go to the dic-tionary, I went once. So help me, what don't one of them knights carry? Look up in the book, you'll see halberd, you'll see cutlass, pike, rapier, foil, ten dozen more. By us a pike is a fish. Not to mention what nowa-days they got—bayonet stuck on the gun, who knows what else the poor soldier got to carry in the pocket. Maybe a dagger same as a pirate. But by us—what we got? A *messer! Puttermesser,* you slice off a piece but-ter, you cut to live, not to kill. A name of honor, you follow? Still, for a young girl—"

"Uncle Zindel, I'm past thirty."

Uncle Zindel blinked lids like insect's wings, translucent. He saw her voyaging, voyaging. The wings of his eyes shadowed the Galilee. They moved over the Tomb of the Patriarchs. A tear for the tears of Mother Rachel rode on his nose. "Your mother knows you're going? Alone on an airplane, such a young girl? You wrote her?"

"I wrote her, Uncle Zindel. I'm not flying anywhere."

"By sea is also danger. What Mama figures, in Miami who is there? The dead and dying. In Israel you'll meet someone. You'll marry, you'll settle there. What's the difference, these days, modern times, quick travel—"

Uncle Zindel's egg was ready, hard-boiled. The shammes tapped it and the shell came off raggedly. Puttermesser consulted the alphabet: *alef, bes, gimel;* she was not going to Israel, she had business in the Mu-nicipal Building. Uncle Zindel, chewing, began finally to teach: "First see how a *gimel* and which way a *zayin* Twins, but one kicks a leg left, one right. You got to practice the difference. If legs don't work, think pregnant bellies. Mrs. *Zayin* pregnant in one direction, Mrs. *Gimel* in the other. Together they give birth to *gez,* which means what you cut off. A night for knifes! Listen, going home from here you should be extra careful tonight. Martinez, the upstairs not the next door, her daughter they mugged and they took."

The shammes chewed, and under his jaws Puttermesser's head bent, practicing the bellies of the holy letters.

Stop. Stop, stop! Puttermesser's biographer, stop! Disengage, please. Though it is true that biographies are invented, not recorded, here you invent too much. A symbol is allowed, but not a whole scene: do not accommodate too obsequiously to Puttermesser's romance. Having not much imagination, she is literal with what she has. Uncle Zindel lies under the earth of Staten Island. Puttermesser has never had a conversation with him; he died four years before her birth. He is all legend: Zindel the Stingy, who even in *gan eydn* rather than eat will store apples until they rot. Zindel the Unripe. Why must Puttermesser fall into so poignant a fever over the cracked phrases of a shammes of a torn-down *shul?*

(The *shul* was not torn down, neither was it abandoned. It disintegrated. Crumb by crumb it vanished. Stones took some of the windows. There were no pews, only wooden folding chairs. Little by little these turned into sticks. The prayer books began to flake: the bindings flaked, the glue came unstuck in small brown flakes, the leaves grew brittle and flaked into confetti. The congregation too began to flake off—the women first, wife after wife after wife, each one a pearl and a consolation, until there they stand, the widowers, frail, gazing, palsy-struck. Alone and in terror. Golden Agers, Senior Citizens! And finally they too flake away, the shammes among them. The *shul* becomes a wisp, a straw, a feather, a hair.)

But Puttermesser must claim an ancestor. She demands connection— surely a Jew must own a past. Poor Puttermesser has found herself in the world without a past. Her mother was born into the din of Madison Street and was taken up to the hullabaloo of Harlem at an early age. Her father is nearly a Yankee: his father gave up peddling to captain a dry-goods store in Providence, Rhode Island. In summer he sold captain's hats, and wore one in all his photographs. Of the world that was, there is only this single grain of memory: that once an old man, Puttermesser's mother's uncle, kept his pants up with a rope belt, was called Zindel, lived without a wife, ate frugally, knew the holy letters, died with thorny English a wilderness between his gums. To him Puttermesser clings. America is a blank, and Uncle Zindel is all her ancestry. Unironic, unimaginative, her plain but stringent mind strains beyond the parents—what did they have? Only day-by-day in their lives, coffee in the morning, washing underwear, occasionally a trip to the beach. Blank. What did they know? Everything from the movies; something—scraps—from the newspaper. Blank.

Behind the parents, beyond and before them, things teem. In old photographs of the Jewish East Side, Puttermesser sees the teeming. She sees a long coat. She sees a woman pressing onions from a pushcart. She sees a tiny child with a finger in its mouth who will become a judge.

Past the judge, beyond and behind him, something more is teeming. But this Puttermesser cannot see. The towns, the little towns. Zindel born into a flat-roofed house a modest distance from a stream.

What can Puttermesser do? She began life as the child of an anti-Semite. Her father would not eat kosher meat—it was, he said, too tough. He had no superstitions. He wore the mother down, she went to the regular meat market at last.

The scene with Uncle Zindel did not occur. How Puttermesser loved the voice of Zindel in the scene that did not occur!

(He is under the ground. The cemetery is a teeming city of toy skyscrapers shouldering each other. Born into a wooden house, Zindel now has a flat stone roof. Who buried him? Strangers from the *landsmanshaft* society. Who said a word for him? No one. Who remembers him now?)

Puttermesser does not remember Uncle Zindel; Puttermesser's mother does not remember him. A name in the dead grandmother's mouth. Her parents have no ancestry. Therefore Puttermesser rejoices in the cadences of Uncle Zindel's voice above the Cuban grocery. Uncle Zindel, when alive, distrusted the building of Tel Aviv because he was practical, Messiah was not imminent. But now, in the scene that did not occur, how naturally he supposes Puttermesser will journey to a sliver of earth in the Middle East, surrounded by knives, missiles, bazookas!

The scene with Uncle Zindel did not occur. It could not occur because, though Puttermesser dares to posit her ancestry, we may not. Puttermesser is not to be examined as an artifact but as an essence. Who made her? No one cares. Puttermesser is henceforth to be presented as given. Put her back into Receipts and Disbursements, among office Jews and patronage collectors. While winter dusk blackens the Brooklyn Bridge, let us hear her opinion about the taxation of exempt properties. The bridge is not the harp Hart Crane said it was in his poem. Its staves are prison bars. The women clerks, Yefimova, Korolova, Akulova,

Arkhipova, Izrailova, are on Kolpachni Street, but the vainglorious General Viryein is not. He is on Ogaryova Street. Joel Zaretsky's ex-wife is barren. The Commissioner puts on his tennis sneakers. He telephones. Mr. Fiore, the courtly secret mayor behind the Mayor, also telephones. Hey! Puttermesser's biographer! What will you do with her now?

BRUNO'S METAMORPHOSIS

Steve Stern

Someone was playing a prank on Bruno Katz. A teacher who made no great claims to imagination, he had been trying to write a story. Only just emerged from an abortive love affair, he thought that the writing might distract him from unhappiness.

The affair in question, his first of any endurance, had ended in a literal abortion, when Bruno at thirty-five confessed to his girlfriend Goldie Shapiro his unreadiness to have a child. In terminating her pregnancy, Goldie had terminated her relationship with Bruno as well. Walking, despite some pain, all the way from the clinic where Bruno had preferred not to accompany her, she burst unannounced into his small but tidy West Side apartment.

"You nebbish!" she called him, and blowing her nose, "You spineless worm! You slob!" Then she turned on her heel and slammed out the door, causing a medley of Broadway show tunes on Bruno's phonograph to skip.

This was unfair, Bruno thought, objecting to her latter accusation. Call him what you will, he was not a slob. Though somewhat overweight, he dressed well enough and was neat in his personal habits.

Later on that evening—lonely, downhearted, bored with the routine of his days—he put on his pajamas and bathrobe and sat down to write a story. Though writing had long been a secret ambition of Bruno's, he always found excuses not to begin. Too little experience, he told himself; or was it that he merely lacked inspiration? In any case, there was a drama about the end of Goldie that prompted him to try to write again. And moreover, by depicting himself as a character in a tale, he might find the perspective to help him through this trying time.

Thus, pushing his bifocals over the hump of his nose, he commenced typing. But rather than draw from his present still-sensitive circumstances, he chose for his subject a distant episode. Not untypical of his childhood, the episode nonetheless haunted and frustrated him even now. As what in his life, come to think of it, did not?

The episode recalled an outing to Coney Island with his mother. Game for showing her son a good time, she had taken him on some of the gentler rides, then bought tickets for the funhouse. Little Bruno, frail and scrawny then (the baby fat would come later), had reluctantly taken his mama's hand. He had followed her down a dark corridor at the end of which a neon clown flashed off and on. Past the clown, however, the corridor turned a corner into utter darkness; where Bruno, looking over his shoulder for a light that was no longer there, started to cry. Though his mama assured him there was nothing to fear, he insisted that they turn back. Nor would he stop crying until she had led him safely out into the sunshine, where his terror subsided into shame.

It had been the mature Bruno's intention to finally resolve the incident, to redeem himself by allowing the boy and his mother, if only on paper, to continue on through the funhouse. What they would encounter—for their intrepid exploits would comprise the story—he wasn't quite sure of. He knew only that they would pass from darkness into light, this time without turning around.

Though aware that the word was unpopular, Bruno would have admitted, if pressed, that his method was a kind of therapy. But for the sake of his wounded pride, he was calling it fiction.

The problem, however, had come when, in the course of developing his story, he arrived at the point where the mother and son turned the corner past the clown. Beyond which he could not write. So there he was decades after the fact, educated and grown-up, but still paralyzed in the face of the unknown. A failure of imagination, he'd called it, what was by any other name a failure of nerve. How true to form that on this, his first attempt, he should be stricken with writer's block.

"Give it up," he told himself, shrugging, resting in the assurance that there were other means of diverting oneself. There was, for instance, a whole world beyond his room.

He thought he might try to get back in trim, though who was he kidding? When, in a life led almost exclusively indoors, had he ever been in trim? All right, so he was soft, his flesh pale and tallowy, his frown yielding two or three chins. Still, in rare daydreams he disowned the endomorph, fancied himself angular and spry, leaping from place to place instead of walking. And toward this vision of himself, he tried jogging one evening through Riverside Park.

Winded after a few hundred yards, chafed by ill-fitting sweat clothes, leery of shady characters along the benches, he resorted to a nearby bar. Exercise having failed him, he surrendered to its inverse: debauchery. He would drink himself into a state of indifference. But as drink was never his medium, his over-indulgence left him instead only crapulous and irritable.

Then there was food which—giving himself over to an orgy of eggrolls and blintzes—he flattered himself that he understood. He would eat to forget. Both over-eating and its attendant dyspepsia were, after all, nothing new to Bruno. What he needed was a more radical change of focus, something to get him over his broken heart. If broken heart he had.

So what was next? And of the extremes of behavior left open to him, sex was most certainly the ticket. Albeit a ticket he'd always found hard to get punched. Undeceived by his natty attire and complacent pot belly, women, sensing the driven nature of his needs, had kept their distance. Except of course Goldie, who, with her strabismus and thinning hair, had been as desperate as he.

And thinking of her Bruno had a sudden realization: that there were no regrets. From what then, if not from Goldie, had he been so strenuously trying to divert his thoughts? Why had he departed from his customary routine? The answer came like the handwriting on the wall, or maybe the absence of same. He was still feeling baited by the unfinished page in his typewriter, still hounded and absorbed. All other activities apart from working at his story—so randomly begun—seemed extracurricular, merely the tactics of evasion.

Insomnia, a nuisance of long standing, kept him constantly fatigued. He brooded through the night over his page, wondering how he'd stumbled into such a first-class obsession. He, Bruno Katz, who'd successfully eluded commitments for thirty-five years. How was it that his future seemed suddenly to depend on the advancement of a mother and son through a carnival funhouse?

⤟ ⤞

He'd been lying in bed worrying about what the headmaster had said. This was the headmaster at the prep school where Bruno taught English to rich kids too smart for their own good. He'd told Bruno that afternoon how his preoccupation had been noticed, not to mention his uncharacteristic slovenliness. Though the headmaster, his face grown around his pipe like an old tree around a post, had used a milder word. "Discomposure," that was it.

"If there's anything wrong, feel free to confide in us," he'd said. But Bruno, tempted, usually such a glutton for sympathy, held his tongue. Who would understand?

Then clearing his throat the headmaster had told him he must understand, there were standards to be maintained. This after seven years.

"I'm expendable," Bruno chanted all the way home, trying to get used to the idea.

Complementing his worries was the evidence that he was going to hell. His appearance, in which he'd always taken pride, bore it out: the crest had come unstitched from his blazer, the coarse hair grown over an unwashed collar. His pants sagged from the weight he'd lost in the absence of his appetite. What's more his apartment, kept usually spotless, had fallen into disarray. Nor would Bruno, for all his fretting, lift a finger to halt the deterioration—not if it meant taking time from the primary fretting over his unfinished page.

Then it happened, what had to be someone's idea of a joke. Somewhere during the small hours he'd managed to doze off. He'd dreamed a crazy dream about a skeleton tap-dancing on a tin roof, then was awakened by the cold. Sitting up he saw that his window, always shut, was now open to the mid-winter winds. He remembered the broken lock that he'd meant for some time to repair. Fearful of burglars he switched on a lamp and made an inventory of his effects: his books, his dirty clothes, old phonograph, portable typewriter. What in fact did he have worth stealing? And wrapping himself in a blanket, trembling from more than the cold, he got out of bed to investigate further.

At first he noticed nothing out of the ordinary, neither in bedroom or kitchenette. Though it dawned on him, after he'd inspected the contents of his impoverished refrigerator, that a pint of milk that he'd swear to having purchased yesterday was missing.

"What's going on!" Bruno demanded aloud, hurrying to slam shut the window. Taking up a broom, which he broke over his knee, he wedged the handle above the window frame. And stooping to recover his blanket, he happened to glance again at his desk, at the typewriter about which his world had revolved for some weeks. Then he observed what minutes before had escaped his attention, what astonished him so much he forgot to be afraid.

For the page, which had lain so long in his typewriter three-quarters blank, was now replete with words. Tentatively Bruno edged closer to the desk and examined the page. He saw that, without so much as a paragraph break, his story—stalled forever, he'd thought—had been continued.

"Okay, very funny," he affirmed, not to be caught off guard, unconsciously smoothing back hair that stood on end. "Ha ha," he added without much heart. Then rubbing his eyes against their possibly deceiving him, he read the sentence that took up where his own manuscript left off: at the point where the mother and son turned their corner.

"Then the boichik," it began, "he is cryink in the dark and the mama she is sayink shaineh kin she is strikink a match . . ." In this pidgin manner the typescript rambled on, careless of syntax and punctuation. But despite the homeliness of the language, its lapses into Yiddish, Bruno found himself warming to its tone. He felt that, their primitiveness aside, the words seemed to fairly dance down the page.

The story itself told how the mother led her son through a maze of pitch-black passages, through rooms of tableaux vivants (which may or may not have been wax) that depicted frightening scenes from the little boy's life. In this way, without losing sight of the burning match, the boy followed his mother in wonder past a bully at school, past his own angry father in the act of removing his belt. Then he was led into scenes outside of his own life and times: a Cossack with a whip, a Spanish inquisitor beside an iron maiden. And following the artless narrative to the bottom of the page, Bruno shared in the little boy's wonder, how it mitigated the horrors and rendered them benign.

When the narrative inconclusively ended, Bruno, wanting more, tore the page from the typewriter and turned it over. He looked furiously about the desk as if for clues. But the spell was broken and Bruno was left feeling duped and scared. Trying to catch his runaway breath, he was stuck by two propositions: First, that there were maybe more things in heaven and earth, etc. And second, that he must be losing his mind.

He lay awake until dawn feeling vulnerable, trying to make sense, unable to clear his head for the ringing in his ears. At school during the next few days, stuporously inattentive, he lost what little control he had over his classes. Once the headmaster, alerted by the noise, entered his classroom to find the students amok, some of them smoking marijuana, while Bruno stood gazing perplexedly out the window. After which it was suggested he seek counseling.

Meanwhile Bruno was spending his nights poring over the mysterious manuscript. Unable to explain it, having only ascertained that it was real, he fell back on his original notion that someone was playing a prank. But who? He tried to picture Goldie creeping over the window sill, but stealth was never her strong point. Only after her there was no one he could think of who would have taken such pains for his sake. Nor, by the same token, was there anyone to whom he could unburden himself of such a thing. He had few acquaintances outside of his colleagues at school, whose growing suspicions he didn't want to aggravate further.

Beyond this there was his instinct, new to Bruno, to preserve the secrecy of what had happened. For overriding even his bewilderment was his continuing fascination with the story thus far. Living with it, with its humor and simplicity, he was coming to feel protective of the story and to regard it as a kind of gift. Had it not in fact carried his own narrative further than he'd been able to carry it himself? And for this he felt, leaving aside the question of its origin, that the story was pointing the way for him. Somehow, he felt he was meant to complete it.

Only now he was back where he'd started. He was beating his brains out for the solution to the tale, the telling of which had a drollery that Bruno, at the best of times, could not have mustered. His frustration compounded, he came that close to ripping the text to shreds, to throwing it out the window from where it came.

❧❧

With his situation so was his presence—given the neglect of his former good grooming—degenerating. Passing a mirror, he was interested and appalled at the sight of his alteration: his previously brilliantined hair now matted and elflocked, his face showing cheekbones for the first time in several decades. He would pause for a moment's consideration of how, having pampered himself for so long, he could now forget himself so completely. Then it was back to worrying about the matter at hand.

After a series of warnings he was notified of his dismissal from the preparatory school, an event he'd dreaded as the very worst that could happen. Though when it came it seemed scarcely worthy of his attention, so consumed was he by the story.

"It never rains but it pours," was all he could spare by way of appropriate response. But security was no longer his theme. Money, of which there remained only a couple of week's worth in the bank, was the least of his problems. The story was the thing. And impotent to coax the mother and son a syllable further in their progress, unable to leave them alone, Bruno was at his wits' end.

Then one night at the brink of delirium, no longer responsible for his actions, he yanked the broomstick out of the window. Giddy with anticipation, he lay down with one eye open and waited. Doubts assailed him, apprehension toward his extreme state of mind. Was this what came of keeping too much to one's own company? Then he would have risen to replace the broomstick had not weariness kept him prone, the intensity of the preceding days having worn him out. Amazed that his native insomnia should have failed him on this particular night, he felt himself drifting off to sleep.

He awoke to the cold, leapt from his bed, and rushed to his desk without bothering to close the window. The typewriter was empty, but beside it was a small stack of manuscript pages. These Bruno abruptly pounced upon.

By his goosenecked lamp he read the continued story, marveling again how its ingenious style lured one with impunity through a gallery of horrors.

Having passed through a few more preliminary tableaux, the mother and son came to a scene depicting a medieval attic-like room littered with scrolls. The figures in the room included a rabbi of evil countenance stuffing a parchment into the mouth of a diminutive clay golem. And while the rabbi remained frozen in this posture, the golem, who was the spit and image of the little boy, clamped his teeth over the parchment and began to shuffle slowly forward. Looking on in mortal terror, screaming "Lemme out of here!", the boy clung to his mama's skirts. But his mama only told him "Happy Bar Mitzvah" and shoved him in the direction of the golem. She said,

"Zuninkeh, give him a patsch! Show him what my son is made of."

Then the boy, his heart bursting with fear and pride, begins wrestling with the golem.

"Ridiculous!" exclaimed Bruno, laughing out loud. But if so ridiculous, why the tears streaming down his cheeks, the thrill beyond reason?

Still, he wanted more, wanted to see the fight resolved, the mother and son leaving the funhouse triumphant. But calming down he listened to his better judgment, which told him that the story had ended as it should. Critical faculties engaged, he realized that, for all its ungainliness, it was a modern story. Its unresolved climax was ambiguous enough to satisfy the contemporary reader. There was little left for him to do.

Closing the window, lodging the broomstick in place, he sat down then and there to give the manuscript his finishing touches. Respectful of the tone, interfering as little as possible with the rhythm of the sentences, he discreetly inserted punctuation, dropping the more obscure Yiddish phrases. He was unconcerned now with who might be responsible for the story, feeling that in a sense he was himself responsible, the manuscript being the gift of his muse. Drinking black coffee as the milk in his refrigerator had vanished, he worked through the early morning. By noon the story was completed but for a title. Too impatient to think of anything more fitting, Bruno labeled it simply "A Modern Fable," then stuffed it into an envelope with an ingratiating cover letter and sent it off to an eminent magazine.

❦ ❦

In a couple of weeks he got word from the magazine, saying sorry they were unable to use the story at this time, saying that but for the title which could stand improvement the piece had been much admired; by all means he should try them again. This was all the encouragement that Bruno needed.

"So I'm not crazy," he sighed, rereading the editor's response, as if his sanity had been the issue all along. And having suspended his efforts while awaiting a verdict, having done nothing in fact since submitting his story, Bruno launched immediately into another.

In keeping with the tradition of the funhouse episode, this one also concerned an occasion during which a young boy exhibits faintheartedness. It was drawn of course from Bruno's endless repertoire of such occasions. This particular episode had occurred when, for the purpose of his initiation into a neighborhood gang, Bruno had agreed to crawl through the tunnel of a sewer. This without the benefit of his mama's accompaniment.

He'd been doing all right, had managed maybe fifty yards on his hands and knees through nauseating swill, when the tunnel suddenly turned a corner. At that point the light from the entrance, which he'd kept for reference over his shoulder, disappeared. It was then he reasoned that he didn't like the other boys much anyway. He made a token effort to force himself forward in the dark. But panic overtaking him, he turned around and scrambled wildly toward daylight, toward certain and undying humiliation. Which the older and wiser Bruno prepared himself to erase.

But again he could get no further on his own steam than the story's, that is the sewer's, turning point. There his invention jammed and his newfound confidence slipped away. Nothing left to do but sleep on it, though Bruno was as usual too agitated to sleep.

"I've been here before," he complained to his pillow. In nocturnal vigils he wondered how something undertaken so blithely could change so quickly to headaches and futility.

Meanwhile, his money spent and no more where it came from he contemplated last resorts. Such as pawning his typewriter or looking for a job. How had he let things come to such a pass? His weight loss was now tantamount to atrophy. Seriously gaunt, dark hollows beneath the eyes, hooked nose and Adam's apple prominent, he was swallowed by his once sartorial wardrobe. Furthermore it appeared that his thick and unruly hair had begun to recede. Who was so recently enchanted seemed now to be cursed.

Never far from it, he succumbed to self-pity. Here he was destitute on the threshold of middle-age, living in a pig sty of a room and a half that he was incapable of dreaming himself out of.

"What I've got," he sulked, "is nothing to lose. What I need," a little heartened by the obvious rhyme, "is a visit from my muse."

And again removing the broomstick from the window, he asked himself why he hadn't done it sooner.

As an afterthought he put a pint of milk on the desk and went to bed. Closing his eyes, he fell into a semi-conscious doze, as deep as his slumber ever got these nights. He was listening to what he thought was a rattling radiator, what he came gradually to realize was the sound of typing. Opening his eyes by degrees, he was presented with the sight of a wizened old man at his desk, his feet not quite reaching the floor. Bearded, earlocked, with an embroidered skullcap perched atop his wispy gray hair, he was slouched in a threadbare and shiny black gabardine. His face, creased and glaucous, squinted over his pair of crooked forefingers, which hopped about the keys like a jig on hot coals.

In a film, thought Bruno, this is where I shut my eyes and say it's only a dream. But how could Bruno, who never sleeps, be dreaming? Then shaken by the grotesque and impossible truth of the situation, he sat bolt upright and shouted.

"Go away!"

The little man turned with rust-rimmed eyes and studied Bruno's face, as if looking there for something lost. Instantly Bruno was sorry.

"Come back!" he cried, as his visitor nimble despite his years, leapt from the chair and vaulted through the open window.

With the covers still pulled to his chin, Bruno dared to picture himself giving chase, pursuing the little rabbi through the streets in his pajamas, carrying a butterfly net. In the end, worn out with imagining, he ventured as far as the window. He looked out past the fire escape to the tops of the neighboring roofs, to the moon disentangling itself from a skirmish of aerials. It was, he concluded, an unusually balmy night for early March.

He snapped out of his reverie at the sight of the empty milk bottle. Remarking its drabness in his drab apartment he felt vaguely disappointed. So that was his muse, that shrunken hasidic gargoyle looking more like a scholar than a scribe. Well, what had he expected, an archangel with wings of flame? Beggars, as the saying went, could not be choosers.

In this way he checked his astonishment with ingratitude. He tore the page out of the typewriter, a little thrilled as he examined its contents that he could handle it with such disdain. Which turned to astonishment as soon as he began to read.

Picking up where Bruno'd left off, the story recounted the further adventures of the boichik: how turning a corner, he gets lost in a maze of black tunnels. He gropes along in terror until he stumbles into a cell beneath a manhole cover. In the cell illumined by oil lamps he encounters a hermit, living there in the sewer to escape, so he says, history and a yenteh wife. He has brought with him some holy books, a few zlotys, and a tiny iron stove for cooking his tsimmes on—all mementos of the old country, whose denizens and houses he has crayoned over the concrete walls.

"Don't tell nobody," he entreats the boichik, "and some day all this is yours."

Undiscouraged when the manuscript ended abruptly, Bruno whistled as he worked, playing show tunes on the phonograph as he refurbished the sentences in hand. Later on he went out and borrowed some money from a former colleague who failed to recognize him at first. Then he treated himself to a decent meal.

"I deserve this," he said, but left his cheesecake uneaten. It saddened him that his old relish for food had vanished along with his belly. That night however, though briefly disturbed by the sound of typing, Bruno slept extremely well.

In the morning he cheered the details of the completed story: the touching friendship between the boy and the old man, lasting through the years until the old man passes away. Then the boichik, without a candle, lugs the body wreathed in a kapok life-preserver a mile through subterranean drek. He then drops it in the East River, giving it a shove in the direction of paradise. Afterward, having come into the old man's estate, he says to himself,

"I am blessed!" Which fact becomes small comfort during the course of an otherwise lonely and uneventful life.

As he affectionately edited the manuscript, Bruno, so captivated by the manuscript itself, gave scarcely a thought to its strange originator. Such familiar, if unnameable, chords did it strike in his breast that the story might as well have been his own.

Aware that the title of the previous piece had not been satisfactory, he tried to think of something catchy for the current. Drawing a blank, he told himself it was no sin to be literal, and hastily scrawled "Boichik Inherits" at the top of page one. Then he paused as a maverick thought crossed his mind:

"Maybe I ought to concede the collaboration."

The thought past, Bruno signed his name to the story and sent it off.

In a week he received a five-hundred dollar check from the magazine. Taking his second story they asked to reconsider the first; they praised what they called his knockabout surrealism. By the time the news arrived Bruno was already anticipating a collection of Boichik tales, and had started another.

🔖 🔖

Great days ensued for Bruno Katz. His praises were sung in many quarters, his stories the talk of the town. A mensch, as his muse might have said, was what he'd become. His telephone, silent since his breakup with Goldie Shapiro, was now ringing off the hook. Agents and publishers wooed him; friends he'd not heard from in years called to congratulate. Colleagues from the prep school voiced their approval, hinted at his possible reinstatement—but who needed it? Goldie herself had phoned to say that she too had succumbed to the charms of his stories, and would he maybe care to come to dinner? But no thank you again. Why, with his brilliant future unfolding, should he be content to pick up where he'd left off?

And while he tried to keep his notoriety in some kind of perspective, his head was already turned. On the one hand he told himself don't be greedy, while on the other he was dizzily aware of spoils for the taking. Already he was matching the money he had against what he would make, his loneliness against the women who would inevitably surround him. Of course, he never failed to observe, such fringe benefits were nothing compared to the fulfillment of a finished story.

But for all its promise of glory his new life, as Bruno called it, had come to him a little too fast. Thirty-five years is fast? Yes, when the change came like this: when least expected, when you found yourself a late bloomer who never expected to bloom at all. And so he fell prey to second thoughts. Where he'd initially welcomed so many opening doors, he now feared the threat to his privacy. Solitude was after all the condition in which his stories had been nurtured. Perhaps a more public Bruno might lose touch with his materials. Perhaps he would find his "muse"—the word employed here in its figurative sense—perhaps he would find his muse reluctant to call.

Meanwhile, having signed a contract with the magazine, he was spending money on the strength of a story he'd yet to write. The deadline was drawing near and he'd started nothing. He was strapped for a premise, his new self-importance having eclipsed the old disgraces that had been his themes. The page in his typewriter remained blank, his muse—granted, in a literal sense—apparently not interested in initiating a tale.

So he indulged in expensive distractions, bought extravagant meals, though rich foods no longer agreed with him. To replace the clothes that were now too big, he bought a wardrobe of stylish others, ostensibly to show off his svelte new physique. But in the mirror the clothes mocked him, appeared too young for him, the loss of his baby fat having left him a cadaverous stranger.

His beard had grown unkempt along with his thinning hair, the sight of which prompted a hairdresser to cluck his tongue. Seeking comfort Bruno nearly engaged the services of a call girl, but was discouraged at the last minute by her swivel eye. He was beginning to wonder if good fortune was his cup of tea.

Thinking he might feel better in less shabby surroundings, he shopped around for a new apartment, maybe something overlooking Central Park. But still he lingered in his old cramped quarters, due in part to his exhausted advance, in part to cold feet. As the weather was warm, he slept with the window wide open, his broken broom in the trash, a pint of milk souring on his desk.

But nothing happened. The magazine, after hounding him for a while, left him alone. The phone ceased to ring. His star, which had so swiftly ascended, seemed just as swiftly to be in decline. The desolation that had been his lot was again his lot, only now he was spoiled. Having tasted success, however abortive and brief, how could he return to his squalid obscurity?

"Cinderella," he teased himself, but without humor.

He languished for days, sustaining himself on melba toast and sardines. Now and again an idea might present itself, though Bruno couldn't be bothered to get up and write it down. He preferred to lie across smelly sheets mourning the loss of his prospects, wasting away. But after a week or two even Bruno's misery began to tire of its own company. His resistance down, he concluded this about his ambitions: Easy come, easy go. He was damned in any case, incapable of enjoying the fruits of his labor. And asking himself so why labor, he answered why not.

Thus prompted more by habit than afflatus, Bruno went to his desk and started another story.

It was about (What else?) a writer whose muse had abandoned him; who after a few windfall successes can think of nothing else to write. Who worries that he may have already used up in his stories what notable experiences his limited life has to offer. Then arriving in his composition at the point where the imaginary writer must do or die, must invent or resign himself to having been a flash in the pan, Bruno found himself stuck again.

In its familiarity Bruno's frustration was almost a homecoming. He relaxed amid the fragrances of tar, and exhaust wafted through his open window. Gladly conceding defeat, what was there left to do but pack it in, but to put on his filthy pajamas and go to bed, to take off his pajamas against the unseasonable heat.

Lying in the dark, he picked at the scab of his conscience. Was his inadequacy, he wondered, some kind of vengeance of the muse, wrought for his failing to give credit where credit was due? If so, it was a vengeance he'd been subject to since birth. Perhaps he ought to reconsider the prep school if they'd have him back, reconsider Goldie. But when he compared what he had been with what he'd become—compared the chubby schoolteacher with the specter savaged by obsession—he found to his surprise that he still had no regrets. And besides wasn't it already too late for turning back? On that note, curious to see what if anything the morning might bring, Bruno fell asleep.

He woke up to the heat, unnaturally intense, to the smoke which sent him coughing and choking to the window. Sticking his head out, gulping for air, he saw flames like ragged curtains flapping from the other windows of his building. He heard sirens and tenants hysterically shouting, saw them practically climbing over each other as they raced down the fire escapes. Then prompted by his own sleepless instinct for panic, Bruno wasted no time in following their lead.

He flung a leg over the window sill and bolted down the metal stairs dodging flames. Gingerly he stepped onto the last flight which tipped vertically, spilling him and the others behind him onto the sidewalk. Disengaging himself from his neighbors he scurried to get clear of the building, as the fire trucks arrived.

In the street amid pandemonium—firemen and hoses, disconsolate families, squad cars with flashing lights—Bruno stood alone looking up at the burning building. He was scarcely aware of being jostled in all the activity, so transfixed had he become by the vision of his window burst into flame.

"My life!" he called to the window, dubiously, as if to confirm that no one was there. Fascinated by the disaster, he remained—despite bull-horns and squalling children and the infernal rumbling of the fire itself—surprisingly calm. Despair, he knew, would overtake him in a moment; it would crush him beyond comfort, as who was there to comfort Bruno? But despair didn't come, and in its place he felt (it was almost heretical) a sense of relief. Easy come, easy go.

And since no one stepped up to console him it was just as well, since he'd realized that he was standing mother-naked in the street. Turning he shouldered his way through the throng of onlookers, who ignored him, beating it into the laundromat adjacent his building. Though brightly lit it was empty of customers, everyone having run out to see the fire. In a sweat Bruno lunged for the first machine whose porthole showed tumbling clothes. But opening the dryer he hesitated, diverted by his own gaunt reflection in the window pane. Beyond his reflection he could see the crowd watching the chaos, the men on ladders directing long arcs of water, the flames reaching an awesome height. His heart unexpectedly lifted to the height of the flames, Bruno waved and danced a few steps in his nakedness. Then he pulled out the clothes.

The pants, made out of an itchy black material, were too tight in the crotch, the cuffs reaching to just below his knees. The collarless white shirt, also too small, was stiff and smelled musty, though it had presumably just been washed. There was a vest which, while it constricted his armpits, he slipped on anyway—as his outfit had seemed incomplete. Then heading barefoot for the door he was again impressed with his reflection in the glass, and stood there a moment grinning at his antic transformation.

Once outside, shoving through the crowd that strained at the police barrier, Bruno hadn't a clue as to where to go next. Standing on tiptoe to get his bearings, he saw only confusion, saw the flames dissolving into a red morning sky. And down the street past the burning building, scuttling around the corner at the end of the block, he saw the little rabbi, his fleeing muse.

"Wait for me!" cried Bruno, ducking under a barrier, oblivious to the shouted warnings from the cops. And pumping his legs over aching feet, he gave chase.

ᔫ ᔪ

Turning the corner, he was just in time to see the rabbi disappearing down the steps at a subway entrance. Calling to him in vain Bruno poured it on, taking the steps in a couple of strides, vaulting a turnstile with inspired agility. He reached the platform and leapt on to the waiting train, then about-faced to confirm what he thought he had seen. And there waiting on the platform sans anyone to fill them was a pair of battered black shoes.

"Any port in a storm," thought Bruno, stooping to snatch them up, as the doors closed and the subway jolted forward.

Forcing on the shoes which crimped his toes, he was launched again, sliding the doors between couplings, searching toward the front of the train. He charged down the aisle between the early morning passengers too drowsy to lift more than a brow at his zany attire. Rushing headlong into the foremost car, Bruno spotted his muse. He was seated beside some nurses in his long gabardine, its hem stopping short of his hairy ankles and unshod white feet.

Lunging forward Bruno was abruptly thrown backward, grabbing an overhead strap as the subway squealed to a halt. Risen, the little rabbi looked at him askance, wrinkling his whiskered features quizzically. Then he stepped out into a concourse of Grand Central Station with the former prep school teacher at his heels.

How the figure in front of him, with his scuttling pace, stayed just beyond his reach was a mystery to Bruno. Though it might have had something to do with the fact that, on the point of overtaking him, Bruno was losing heart.

"Wait a minute," he panted, uncertain as to whether he were addressing his muse or himself. And besides, his feet were killing him.

He held onto a pretzel concession to catch his breath, suffering the stares of the passers-by, watching the little rabbi hurry away up a ramp. So what—it seemed the moment to ask himself—what did he hope to gain from such meshugass?

He was bewildered at having come so far afield, at behaving with such mad impetuosity. And here he was looking forward to god-only-knew—to making more of a spectacle of himself than he already was, to springing upon a kosher leprechaun in the middle of Grand Central Station. Demanding what? Fairy gelt? Another story? Which he would transcribe on whose typewriter in what room?

He thought of the fire. He thought that in a film this is where the newsboy shouts: "EXTRA! PROMISING WRITER LOST IN FLAMES!" How buying a paper, he would sigh for the late Bruno Katz—what a waste. Though the prospect, rather than distress him, filled him with a sense of mischief, as if his very existence were a kind of prank. Then it occurred to Bruno, rootless in the world, that he didn't want so much to capture his muse as to follow him home. And as he loped up the ramp from the subway, it seemed that his shoes were giving a bit.

The ramp led to a corridor that opened onto a row of numbered gates. At the farthest of these was a queue of passengers which included the little rabbi, handing their tickets to a uniformed collector to be punched. Beyond the gate a train, breathing steam, stretched along the platform.

Bruno stepped to the rear of the line moving forward until he was asked for his ticket.

"Ticket!" he repeated. "Of course." Then he made a great show of searching his person, while the collector (Had he batted an eye at the rabbi?) frowned suspiciously. Fishing in the pockets of his trousers, which seemed to have grown baggier, he pulled out a slip upon which was printed: NEW YORK ONTARIO & WESTERN RR. Bruno's jaw hung open as the collector, snatching the ticket, punched it and handed it back. Its stamped destination read: LIBERTY.

On board the train, peering over upraised newspapers, Bruno prowled from car to car, but no little rabbi. Instead he found, draped over a vacant seat next to the window, a tasseled prayer shawl. In need of accessories he took up the shawl and wrapped it with a flourish about his throat. Then, undiscouraged, feeling that everything—so to speak—was already written, Bruno occupied the seat himself. He sunk so far into its cushions that his feet barely touched the floor.

In a newspaper that a passenger was holding across the aisle, he could see if he squinted an article about an apartment house fire. Leaning forward he could make out, towards the bottom of the column, something about a writer of promise presumed to have perished. Then the newspaper was fluttering, the train pulling out of the station. And Bruno, exhausted from the chase, lulled by the cadence of clacking wheels, was beginning to nod. He was asleep as the train snaked its way beneath the city, surfacing finally into daylight.

శ్రీ శ్రీ

He woke to blue mountains, the train crossing a river flanked by granite cliffs. As the window—unusually high—began at the level of his chin, Bruno craned his neck to take it all in. He rubbed his eyes and tugged at his scraggly beard while the train hugged the tree-lined slopes. Pitching through tunnels, it burst upon vistas wherein towns appeared. Mountaindale, Woodridge, Fallsburg, Liberty: its name printed across a board shingle hanging from the eaves of a gingerbread station house.

As the voice of a conductor confirmed their arrival, Bruno, trying to shake himself into motion, sighted his barefoot rabbi through the window. He was crossing the wooden platform as if in a hurry to keep an appointment.

"I'm properly out of my skull," Bruno reflected, and shrugged. Getting up he was conscious that, despite having slept in them, he was comfortable in his borrowed clothes; he was conscious that the other passengers seemed larger than himself. This left him hopeful that from now on everything would have extra dimensions. Then in a couple of bounds, sprightly for his years, he was off the train and again on the trail of his muse.

Not bothering to hail him Bruno followed his man down a pleasant avenue lined with ornate shops. The shop windows bore posters announcing the bill of fare at Grossinger's, at the Concord. Then the rabbi, obviously accustomed to this route, turned into a shady residential street. In a block or two the houses ended, petering into a narrow unpaved lane. The lane in turn dead-ended in a garden path with a gate, which the rabbi left open as he quickly passed through.

Following, Bruno had to stifle his laughter, so intoxicating was the fragrant air. Holding his own with the rabbi's brisk pace, he was strolling through bluebells and clover. With his sidelocks, borne on the breezes, occasionally tickling his nose, he was trotting down an incline that grew ever more treacherous and steep.

At the bottom of the defile was a brook with a few stones across it. Over these the little rabbi stepped smartly—a feat that Bruno, shoes no longer pinching, duplicated without effort. Not so effortless was the climb up the slope on the other side. Practically a precipice, up which the rabbi scrambled in defiance of gravity, it was obstacled with jutting rocks. There were grapevines and gnarled spruce trees, whose trunks Bruno clung to in his struggle to keep up. But even in his toiling, he found himself distracted by the flora, sniffing the sassafras and witch hazel whose scents he wondered how he knew. Where in his claustrophobic urban past had he gleaned such woodlore?

Eventually he reached an overhang where he clutched at roots, his feet dangling a dizzy moment in space. Managing at last to haul himself up over the brow of the cliff, he lay panting a while in a bed of moss, then picked himself up and inhaled the view.

The mountains, their tops veiled in mist, were much nearer than they'd appeared from the train. They were distanced now by only a valley in whose hollow was a bluegreen meadow, and in the meadow what appeared to be a village. Though he'd never set eyes on it before, Bruno felt that the scene possessed a certain familiarity. It was the kind you enjoyed when reading the little rabbi's stories, the credit for which he now regretted having taken. Then he realized, looking down through the clustering trees, that his muse was nowhere in sight.

Alarmed, half running, half sliding, Bruno flung himself down the long hill. Stumbling he rolled headfirst over pine needles and leafmold, then got to his feet only to trip and sprawl again amid towering trees. So dense was their foliage that only the few odd coins of sunlight, falling on toadstools, could filter through. Bruno raised himself, dusting off thistles. Left to his own devices in this sinister place, abandoned one might say, he began to have serious misgivings. Though he proceeded, his bravado had left him, and in its place was his old and erstwhile companion fear. To which, having had enough, Bruno shouted,

"Fuck off!"

Koff-foff-off: his voice came back to him in diminishing echoes. And when the echoes had faded away, so had the fear, departing into memory. Then memory itself had grown dim, absorbed by the fear that had fled, taking with it his recollection of why he was here, how he had come, where he had been in all the years (evaporating now) previous to this moment. Then he knew that he'd lost himself, that Bruno—portly, fastidious, fainthearted and friendless, childless—had turned around and gone back where he came from.

"Nu?" he wondered wiping away tears. "So who does that make me now?"

But in any case, as he toddled through shadows, he felt at peace with his emptiness; felt in fact that the grimacing stones, the waist-high ferns, that deserted quarry, that broken chimney, that oak, had at least as much significance as himself.

Picking his way down the remainder of the slope, whistling show tunes, he paused beneath a ruined tree, its barkless limbs as crooked as his fingers. From its bottom-most branch a long gabardine kapote was limply hanging. Taking it down from the tree he put it on and declared it a perfect fit. Then as if prompted by habit, he reached into one of its pockets, looking for maybe a compass? a map? And finding an embroidered skullcap, he placed it over the bald spot in the midst of his wispy gray hair.

He emerged from the trees into a meadow, across which he could clearly see the shingled roofs and smoking chimneys of the village, the cupola of its wooden synagogue. As he scuttled through the tall grass, he made up a story, secure in the knowledge that he had a million more. In this one the village, call it Bobolinka, appears for only a day every hundred years . . .

⤳ ⤶

. . . Bruno Katz, the wandering mayse-teller, returns home for a night. Family and friends pour into the muddy streets bearing gifts—chicken livers, baked knishes, schnapps. These he gratefully declines, protesting that they mustn't spoil him. Later on they gather in the study house where he tells them of his travels. The young are spellbound while the older ones tease him that Broadway has turned his head. In the morning, shalom and he's off again. He goes on foot to the city, the world having broken down in his absence. But as some things never change, he climbs through an open window and, thirsty, looks in an icebox for milk. Then he sits at a desk, his back to the bed where someone is fitfully snoring. In the typewriter he reads an unfinished page about a man whose house catches fire, and making a face, he begins to type.

THE FOUR QUESTIONS

Allegra Goodman

Ed is sitting in his mother-in-law Estelle's gleaming kitchen. "Is it coming in on time?" Estelle asks him. He is calling to check on Yehudit's flight from San Francisco.

"It's still ringing," Ed says. He sits on one of the swivel chairs and twists the telephone cord through his fingers. One wall of the kitchen is papered in a yellow-and-brown daisy pattern, the daisies as big as Ed's hand. The window shade has the same pattern on it. Ed's in-laws live in a 1954 ranch house with all the original period details. Nearly every year since their wedding, he and Sarah have come out to Long Island for Passover, and the house has stayed the same. The front bathroom is papered, even on the ceiling, in brown with white and yellow flowers, and there is a double shower curtain over the tub, the outer curtain held back with brass chains. The front bedroom, Sarah's old room, has a blue carpet, organdy curtains, and white furniture, including a kidney-shaped vanity table. There is a creaky trundle bed to wheel out from under Sarah's bed, and Ed always sleeps there, a step below Sarah.

In the old days, Sarah and Ed would fly up from Washington with the children, but now the kids come in on their own. Miriam and Ben take the shuttle down from Boston, Avi is driving in from Wesleyan, and

Yehudit, the youngest, is flying in from Stanford. She usually can't come at all, but this year the holiday coincides with her spring break. Ed is going to pick her up at Kennedy tonight. "It's coming in on time," Ed tells Estelle.

"Good," she says, and she takes away his empty glass. Automatically, instinctively, Estelle puts things away. She folds up the newspaper before Ed gets to the business section. She'll clear the table while the slower eaters are contemplating seconds. And, when Ed and Sarah come to visit and sleep in the room Sarah and her sister used to share, Ed will come in and find that his things have inexorably been straightened. On the white-and-gold dresser, Ed's tangle of coins, keys, watch, and comb is untangled. The shirt and socks on the bed have been washed and folded. It's the kind of service you might expect in a fine hotel. In West Hempstead it makes Ed uneasy. His mother-in-law is in constant motion—sponging, sweeping, snapping open and shut the refrigerator door. Flicking off lights after him as he leaves the room. Now she is checking the oven. "This is a beautiful bird. Sarah," she calls into the den. "I want you to tell Miriam when she gets here that this turkey is kosher. Is she going to eat it?"

"I don't know," Sarah says. Her daughter the medical student (Harvard Medical School) has been getting more observant every year. In college she started bringing paper plates and plastic utensils to her grandparents' house because Estelle and Sol don't keep kosher. Then she began eating off paper plates even at home in Washington. Although Ed and Sarah have a kosher kitchen, they wash their milk and meat dishes together in the dishwasher.

"I never would have predicted it," Estelle says. "She used to eat everything on her plate. Yehudit was always finicky. I could have predicted she would be a vegetarian. But Miriam used to come and have more of everything. She used to love my turkey."

"It's not that, Mommy," Sarah says.

"I know. It's this orthodoxy of hers. I have no idea where she gets it from. From Jonathan, I guess." Jonathan is Miriam's fiancé.

"No," Ed says, "she started in with it before she even met Jon."

"It wasn't from anyone in this family. Are they still talking about having that Orthodox rabbi marry them?"

"Well—" Sarah begins.

"We met with him." Ed says.

"What was his name, Lowenthal?"

"Lewitsky," Ed says.

"Black coat and hat?"

"No, no, he's a young guy—"

"That doesn't mean anything," Estelle says.

"He was very nice, actually," Sarah says. "The problem is that he won't perform a ceremony at Congregation S.T."

"Why not? It's not Orthodox enough for him?"

"Well, it's a Conservative synagogue. Of course, our rabbi wouldn't let him use S.T. anyway. Rabbi Landis performs all the ceremonies there. They don't want the sanctuary to be treated like a hall to be rented out. Miriam is talking about getting married outside."

"Outside!" Estelle says. "In June! In Washington, D.C? When I think of your poor mother, Ed, in that heat!" Estelle is eleven years younger than Ed's mother, and always solicitous about Rose's health. "What are they thinking of? Where could they possibly get married outside?"

"I don't know," Ed says. "Dumbarton Oaks. The Rose Garden. They're a couple of silly kids."

"This is not a barbecue," Estelle says.

"What can we do?" Sarah asks. "If they insist on this rabbi."

"And it's March already," Estelle says grimly. "Here, Ed"—she takes a pink bakery box from the refrigerator—"you'd better finish these eclairs before she gets here."

"I'd better not." Ed is trying to watch his weight.

"It's a long time till dinner," Estelle warns as she puts the box back.

"That's okay. I'll live off the fat of the land," says Ed, patting his stomach.

"I got her sealed matzahs, sealed macaroons, vacuum-packed gefilte fish." Estelle displays the package on the scalloped wood shelves of her pantry.

"Don't worry. Whatever else happens, the boys are going to be ravenous. They're going to eat," Sarah assures her mother. They bring the tablecloth out to the dining room. "Remember Avi's friend Noam?"

"The gum chewer. He sat at this table and ate four pieces of cake!"

"And now Noam is an actuary," says Sarah.

"And Avi is bringing a girl to dinner."

"She's a lovely girl," Sarah says.

"Beautiful," Estelle agrees with a worried look.

In the kitchen Ed is thinking he might have an eclair after all. Estelle always has superb pastry in the house. Sol had started out as a baker and still had a few friends in the business. "Are these from Leonard's?" Ed asks when Sol comes in.

"Leonard's was bought out," Sol says, easing himself into a chair. "These are from Magic Oven. How is the teaching?"

"Well, I have a heavy load. Two of my colleagues went on sabbatical this year—"

"Left you shorthanded."

"Yeah," Ed says. "I've been teaching seven hours a week."

"That's all?" Sol is surprised.

"I mean, on top of my research."

"It doesn't sound that bad."

Ed starts to answer. Instead, he goes to the refrigerator and gets out the eclairs.

"Leonard's were better," Sol muses. "He used a better custard."

"But these are pretty good. What was that? Was that the kids?" Ed runs out to meet the cab in the driveway, pastry in hand. He pays the driver as his two oldest tumble out of the cab with their luggage—Ben's backpack and duffel, Miriam's canvas tote and the suitcase she has inherited, bright pink, patched with silver metallic tape, dating from Ed and Sarah's honeymoon in Paris.

"Daddy!" Miriam says. "What are you eating?"

Ed looks at his eclair. Technically all this sort of thing should be out of the house by now—all bread, cake, pastry, candy, soda, ice cream—anything even sweetened with corn syrup. And, of course, Miriam takes the technicalities seriously. He knows she must have stayed up late last night in her tiny apartment in Cambridge, vacuuming the crevices in the couch, packing away her toaster oven. He finishes off the eclair under her disapproving eyes. He doesn't need the calories, either, she is thinking. She has become very puritanical, his daughter, and it baffles him. They had raised the children in a liberal, rational, joyous way—raised them to enjoy the Jewish tradition, and Ed can't understand why Miriam would choose austerity and obscure ritualism. She is only twenty-three—even if she *is* getting married in June. How can a young girl be attracted to this kind of legalism? It disturbs him. On the other hand, he knows she is right about his weight and blood pressure. He hadn't really been hungry. He'll take it easy on dinner.

Meanwhile, Ben carries in the bags and dumps them in the den. "Hi, Grandma! Hi, Grandpa! Hi, Mom!" He grabs the TV remote and starts flipping channels. No one is worried about Ben becoming too intense. He is a senior at Brandeis, six feet tall with overgrown ash-brown hair. He has no thoughts about the future. No ideas about life after graduation. No plan. He is studying psychology in a distracted sort of way.

When he flops down on the couch he looks like a big, amiable golden retriever.

"Get me the extra chairs from the basement, dear," Estelle tells him. "We've been waiting for you to get here. Then, Sarah, you can get the wine glasses. You can reach up there." Estelle is in her element. Her charm bracelet jingles as she talks. She directs Ben to go down under the Ping-Pong table without knocking over the boxes stacked there; she points Sarah to the cabinet above the refrigerator. Estelle is smaller than Sarah—five feet two and a quarter—and her features are sharper. She had been a brunette when she was younger, but now her hair is auburn. Her eyes are lighter brown as well, and her skin dotted with sun spots from the winters in Florida. "Oh—" she sighs suddenly as Miriam brings a box of paper plates from the kitchen. "Why do you have to—?"

"Because these dishes aren't Pesah dishes."

Estelle looks at the table, set with her white-and-gold Noritake china. "This is the good china," she says. "These are the Pesah dishes."

"But you use them for the other holidays, too," Miriam tells her. "They've had bread on them and cake and pumpkin pie and all kinds of stuff."

"Ooo, you are sooo stubborn!" Estelle puts her hands on her tall granddaughter's shoulders and gives her a shake. The height difference makes it look as though she is pleading with her as she looks up into Miriam's face. Then the oven timer goes off and she rushes into the kitchen. Sarah is washing lettuce at the sink. "I'll do the salads last," Estelle tells her. "After Ed goes to the airport." Miriam is still on her mind. What kind of seder will Miriam have next year after she is married? Estelle has met Miriam's fiancé, who is just as observant as she is. "Did you see!" she asks Sarah. "I left you my list, for Miriam's wedding."

"What list?"

"On the table. Here." Estelle gives Sarah the typed list. "These are the names and addresses you asked for—the people I need to invite."

Sarah looks at the list. She turns the page and scans the names, doing some calculations in her head. "Mommy!" she says. "There are forty-two people on this list!"

"Not all of them will be able to come, of course," Estelle reassures her.

"We're having one hundred people at this wedding, remember? Including Ed's family, and the kids' friends—"

"Well, this is our family. These are your cousins, Sarah."

Sarah looks again at the list. "When was the last time I saw these people?" she asks. "Miriam wouldn't even recognize some of them. And what's this? The Seligs? The Magids? Robert and Trudy Rothman? These aren't cousins."

"Sarah! Robert and Trudy are my dearest friends. We've known the Seligs and the Magids for thirty years."

"This is a small family wedding," Sarah tells her mother. "I'm sure they'll understand—"

Estelle knows that they wouldn't understand.

"I think we have to cut down this list," Sarah says.

Estelle doesn't get a chance to reply. Avi has arrived, and he's standing in the living room with Ed, Miriam, and Ben. She stands next to him: Amy, his friend from Wesleyan. Estelle still holds back from calling her his girlfriend. Nevertheless, there she is. She has gorgeous strawberry-blond hair, and she has brought Estelle flowers—mauve and rose tulips with fancy curling petals. No one else brought Estelle flowers.

"They're beautiful. Look, Sol, aren't they beautiful?" Estelle says. "Avi, you can take your bag to the den. The boys are sleeping in the den; the girls are sleeping in the sun room."

"I don't want to sleep in the den," Avi says.

"Why not?" asks Estelle.

"Because he snores." Avi points at his brother. "Seriously, he's so loud. I'd rather sleep in the basement."

Everyone looks at him. It's a finished basement and it's got carpeting, but it is cold down there.

"You've shared a room with Ben for years," Sarah says.

"You'll freeze down there," Estelle tells him.

"I have a down sleeping bag."

"You never complained at home," Sarah says.

"Oh, give me a break," Ben mutters under his breath. "You aren't going to have wild sex in a sleeping bag in the basement."

"What?" Ed asks. "Did you say something, Ben?"

"No," Ben says, and ambles back into the den.

"I don't want you in the basement," Estelle tells her grandson.

"Can I help you in the kitchen, Mrs. Kirshenbaum?" asks Amy.

Estelle and Amy make the chopped liver. The boys are watching TV in the den, and Ed and Sarah are lying down in the back. Miriam is on the phone with Jon.

"Did you want me to chop the onions, too?" Amy asks Estelle.

"Oh no. Just put them there and I'll take out the liver, and then we attach the grinder—" She snaps the grinder onto the KitchenAid and starts feeding in the broiled liver. "And then you add the onions and the eggs." Estelle pushes in the hard-boiled eggs. "And the schmaltz." She is explaining to Amy all about chopped liver, but her mind is full of questions. How serious is it with Avi? What do Amy's parents think? They are Methodist, Estelle knows that. And Amy's uncle is a Methodist minister! They can't approve of all this. But, then, of course, how much do they know about it? Avi barely talks about Amy. Estelle and Sol have only met her once before, when they came up for Avi's jazz band concert. And then, suddenly, Avi said he wanted to bring her with him to the seder. But he's never really dated anyone before, and kids shy away from anything serious at this age. Avi's cousin Jeffrey had maybe five different girlfriends in college, and he's still unmarried.

Amy's family goes to church every Sunday. They're quite religious. Amy had explained that to Estelle on the phone when she called up about the book. She wanted Estelle to recommend a book for her to read about Passover. Estelle didn't know what to say. She had never dreamed something like this would happen. If only Amy weren't Methodist. She is everything Estelle could ever want. An absolute doll. The tulips stand in the big barrel-cut crystal vase on the counter. The most beautiful colors.

By the time Ed goes off to the airport, everything is ready except the salad. They dress for dinner while he is gone.

"Do you have a decent shirt?" Sarah asks Ben, who is still watching television. "Or is that as good as it gets?"

"I didn't have a chance to do my laundry before I got here, so I have hardly any clothes," Ben explains.

"Ben!" Estelle looks at him in his red-and-green-plaid hunting shirt. Avi is wearing a nice starched Oxford.

"Maybe he could borrow one of Grandpa's," Miriam suggests.

"He's broader in the shoulders than I am," says Sol. "Come on, Ben, let's see if we can stuff you into something."

✑ ✑

They wait for Ed and Yehudit in the living room, almost as if they were expecting guests. Ben sits stiffly on the couch in his small, stiff shirt. He stares at the silver coffee service carefully wrapped in clear plastic. He cracks his knuckles, and then he twists his neck to crack his neck joints. Everyone screams at him. Then, finally, they hear the car in the driveway.

"You're sick as a dog!" Sarah says when Yehudit gets inside.

Yehudit blows her nose and looks at them with feverish, jet-lagged eyes. "Yeah, I think I have mono," she says.

"Oh, my God," says Estelle. "She has to get into bed. That cot in the sun room isn't very comfortable."

"How about a hot drink?" suggests Sarah.

"I'll get her some soup," Estelle says.

"Does it have a vegetable base?" Yehudit asks.

"What she needs is a decongestant," says Ed.

They bundle her up in the La-Z-Boy chair in the den and tuck her in with an afghan and a mug of hot chocolate.

"That's not kosher for Pesah," says Miriam, worried.

"Cool it," Ed says. Then they sit down at the seder table.

Ed always leads the seder. Sol and Estelle love the way he does it because he is so knowledgeable. Ed's area of expertise is the Middle East, so he ties Passover to the present day. And he is eloquent. They are very proud of their son-in-law.

"This is our festival of freedom," Ed says, "commemorating our liberation from slavery." He picks up a piece of matzah and reads from his New Revised Haggadah: " 'This is the bread which our fathers and mothers ate in Mitzrayim when they were slaves.' " He adds from the translator's note: " 'We use the Hebrew word *Mitzrayim* to denote the ancient land of Egypt—' "

"As opposed to modern-day Mitzrayim," Miriam says dryly.

" 'To differentiate it from modern Egypt,' " Ed reads. Then he puts down the matzah and extemporizes. "We eat this matzah so we will never forget what slavery is, and so that we continue to empathize with afflicted peoples throughout the world: those torn apart by civil wars, those starving or homeless, those crippled by poverty and disease. We think of the people oppressed for their religious or political beliefs. In particular, we meditate on the people in our own country who have not yet achieved full freedom; those discriminated against because of their race, gender, or sexual preference. We think of the subtle forms of slavery as well as the obvious ones—the gray areas that are now coming to light: sexual harassment, verbal abuse—" He can't help noticing Miriam as he says this. It's obvious that she is ignoring him. She is sitting there chanting to herself out of her Orthodox Birnbaum Haggadah, and it offends him. "Finally, we turn to the world's hot spot—the Middle East," Ed says. "We think of war-torn Israel and pray for compromises. We consider the Palestinians, who have no land to call their own, and we call for moderation and perspective. As we sit around the seder table, we look to the past to give us insight into the present."

"Beautiful," murmurs Estelle. But Ed looks down unhappily to where the kids are sitting. Ben has his feet up on Yehudit's empty chair, and Avi is playing with Amy's hair. Miriam is still poring over her Haggadah.

"It's time for the four questions," he says sharply. "The youngest child will chant the four questions," he adds for Amy's benefit.

Sarah checks on Yehudit in the den. "She's asleep. Avi will have to do it."

"Amy is two months younger than I am," Avi says.

"Why don't we all say it together?" Estelle suggests. "She shouldn't have to read it all alone."

"I don't mind," Amy says. She reads: " 'Why is this night different from all other nights? On other nights we eat leavened bread; why on this night do we eat matzah? On other nights we eat all kinds of herbs; why on this night do we eat bitter herbs? On other nights we do not dip even once; why on this night do we dip twice? On other nights we eat either sitting up or reclining; why on this night do we all recline?' "

"Now, Avi, read it in Hebrew," Ed says, determined that Avi should take part—feeling, as well, that the questions sound strange in English. Anthropological.

"What was that part about dipping twice?" Amy asks when Avi is done.

"That's when you dip the parsley into the salt water," Ben tells her.

"It doesn't have to be parsley," Sarah says. "Just greens."

"We're not up to that yet," Ed tells them. "Now I'm going to answer the questions." He reads: " 'We do these things to commemorate our slavery in Mitzrayim. For if God had not brought us out of slavery, we and all future generations would still be enslaved. We eat matzah because our ancestors did not have time to let their bread rise when they left E—Mitzrayim. We eat bitter herbs to remind us of the bitterness of slavery. We dip greens in salt water to remind us of our tears, and we recline at the table because we are free men and women.' Okay." Ed flips a few pages. "The second theme of Passover is about transmitting tradition to future generations. And we have here in the Haggadah examples of four kinds of children—each with his or her own needs and problems. What we have here is instructions on how to tailor the message of Passover to each one. So we read about four hypothetical cases. Traditionally, they were described as four sons: the wise son, the wicked son, the simple son, and the one who does not know how to ask. We refer to these children in modern terms as: committed, uncommitted, unaffiliated, and assimilated. Let's go around the table now. Estelle, would you like to read about the committed child?"

" 'What does the committed child say?' " Estelle reads. " 'What are the practices of Passover which God has commanded us? Tell him or her precisely what the practices are.' "

" 'What does the uncommitted child say?' " Sol continues. " 'What use to you are the practices of Passover? To you, and not to himself. The child excludes him or herself from the community. Answer him/her: This is on account of what God did for me when I went out of Mitzrayim. For *me,* and not for us. This child can only appreciate personal gain.' "

" 'What does the unaffiliated child say?' " asks Sarah. " 'What is all this about? Answer him or her simply: We were slaves and now we are free.' "

" 'But for the assimilated child,' " Ben reads, " 'it is up to us to open the discussion.' "

"We can meditate for a minute," Ed says, "on a fifth child who died in the Holocaust." They sit silently and look at their plates.

"It's interesting," says Miriam, "that so many things come in fours on Passover. There are four questions, four sons; you drink four cups of wine—"

"It's probably just coincidence," Ben says.

"Thanks," Miriam tells him. "I feel much better. So much for discussion at the seder." She glares at her brother. Couldn't he even shave before he came to the table? She pushes his feet off the chair. "Can't you sit normally?" she hisses at him.

"Don't be such a pain in the butt," Ben mutters.

Ed speeds on, plowing through the Haggadah. " 'The ten plagues that befell the Egyptians: Blood, frogs, vermin, wild beasts, murrain, boils, hail, locusts, darkness, death of the firstborn.' " He looks up from his book and says, "We think of the suffering of the Egyptians as they faced these calamities. We are grateful for our deliverance, but we remember that the oppressor was also oppressed." He pauses there, struck by his own phrase. It's very good. "We cannot celebrate at the expense of others, nor can we say that we are truly free until the other oppressed peoples of the world are also free. We make common cause with all peoples and all minorities. Our struggle is their struggle, and their struggle is our struggle. We turn now to the blessing over the wine and the matzah. Then"—he nods to Estelle—"we'll be ready to eat."

"Daddy," Miriam says.

"Yes."

"This is ridiculous. This seder is getting shorter every year."

"We're doing it the same way we always do it," Ed tells her.

"No, you're not. It's getting shorter and shorter. It was short enough to begin with! You always skip the most important parts."

"Miriam!" Sarah hushes her.

"Why do we have to spend the whole time talking about minorities?" she asks. "Why are you always talking about civil rights?"

"Because that's what Passover is about," Sol tells her.

"Oh, okay, fine," Miriam says.

"Time for the gefilte fish," Estelle announces. Amy gets up to help her, and the two of them bring in the salad plates. Each person has a piece of fish on a bed of lettuce with two cherry tomatoes and a dab of magenta horseradish sauce.

Sarah stands up, debating whether to wake Yehudit for dinner. She ends up walking over to Miriam and sitting next to her for a minute. "Miriam," she whispers, "I think you could try a little harder—"

"To do what?" Miriam asks.

"To be pleasant!" Sarah says. "You've been snapping at everyone all evening. There's no reason for that. There's no reason for you to talk that way to Daddy."

Miriam looks down at her book and continues reading to herself in Hebrew.

"Miriam?"

"What? I'm reading all the stuff Daddy skipped."

"Did you hear what I said? You're upsetting your father."

"It doesn't say a single word about minorities in here," Miriam says stubbornly.

"He's talking about the modern context—"

Miriam looks up at Sarah. "What about the original context?" she asks. "As in the Jewish people? As in God?"

Yehudit toddles in from the den with the afghan trailing behind her. "Can I have some plain salad?" she asks.

"This fish is wonderful," Sol says.

"Outstanding," Ed agrees.

"More," says Ben, with his mouth full.

"Ben! Gross! Can't you eat like a human being?" Avi asks him.

"It's Manishevitz Gold Label," Estelle says. "Yehudit, how did you catch this? Did they say it was definitely mono?"

"No—I don't know what it is," Yehudit says. "I started getting sick on the weekend when we went to sing at the Jewish Community Center for the seniors."

"It's nice that you do that," Estelle says. "Very nice. They're always so appreciative."

"Yeah, I guess so. There was this old guy there and he asked me, 'Do you know "Oyfn Pripitchik"?' I said, 'Yes, we do,' and he said, 'Then please, can I ask you, don't sing "Oyfn Pripitchik." They always come here and sing it for us, and it's so depressing.' Then, when we left, this little old lady beckoned to me and she said, 'What's your name?' I told her, and she said, 'You're very plain, dear, but you're very nice.' "

"That's terrible!" Estelle says. "Did she really say that?"

"Yup."

"It's not true!" Estelle says. "You should hear what everyone says about my granddaughters when they see your pictures. Wait till they see you—maid of honor at the wedding! What color did you pick for the wedding?" she asks Miriam.

"What?" Miriam asks, looking up from her Haggadah.

Ed is looking at Miriam and feeling that she is trying to undermine his whole seder. What is she doing accusing him of shortening the service every year? He does it the same way every year. She is the one who has changed—becoming more and more critical. More literal-minded. Who is she to criticize the way he leads the service? What does she think she is doing? He can remember seders when she couldn't stay awake until dinner. He remembers when she couldn't even sit up. When he could hold her head in the palm of his hand.

"I think peach is a hard color," Estelle is saying. "It's a hard color to find. You know, a pink is one thing. A pink looks lovely on just about everyone. Peach is a hard color to wear. When Mommy and Daddy got married, we had a terrible time with the color because the temple was maroon. There was a terrible maroon carpet in the sanctuary, and the social hall was maroon as well. There was maroon-flecked wallpaper. Remember, honey?" she asks Sol. He nods. "Now it's a rust color. Why it's rust, I don't know. But we ended up having the maids in pink because that was about all we could do. And in the pictures it looked beautiful."

"It photographed very well," Sol says.

"I'll have to show you the pictures." Estelle tells Miriam. "The whole family was there and such dear, dear friends. God willing, they'll be at your wedding, too."

"No, I don't think so," says Ed. "We're just having the immediate family. We're only having one hundred people."

Estelle smiles. "I don't think you can keep a wedding to one hundred people."

"Why not?" Ed asks.

Sarah clears the fish plates nervously. She hates it when Ed takes this tone of voice with her parents.

"Well, I mean, not without excluding," Estelle says. "And at a wedding you don't want to exclude—"

"I don't think it's incumbent on us to invite everyone we know to Miriam's wedding," Ed says crisply. Sarah puts her hand on his shoulder. "It's not even necessary to invite everyone *you* know."

Estelle raises her eyebrows, and Sarah hopes silently that her mother will not whip out the invitation list she's written up. This list with forty-two names that, mercifully, Ed has not yet seen.

"I'm not inviting everyone I know," Estelle says.

"Grandma," Miriam says, looking up. "Are you inviting people to my wedding?"

"Of course not," says Estelle. "But I've told my cousins about it and my dear friends. You know, some of them were at your parents' wedding. The Magids. The Rothmans."

"Whoa, whoa, wait a second," says Ed. "We aren't going to revive the guest list from our wedding thirty years ago. I think we need to define our terms here and straighten out what we mean by immediate family."

"I'll define for you," Estelle says, "what I mean by the family. These are the people who knew us when we lived above the bakery. It wasn't just at your wedding. They were at *our* wedding before the war. We grew up with them. We've got them in the home movies, and you can see them all forty-five years ago—fifty years ago! You can go in the den and watch—we've got all the movies on videotape now. You can see them at Sarah's first birthday party. We lived within blocks; and when we moved out to the Island and left the bakery, they moved too. I still talk to Trudy Rothman every day. Who has friends like that? We used to walk over. Years ago in the basement we hired a dancing teacher, and we used to take dancing lessons together. Fox trot, cha-cha, tango. We went to temple with them. We celebrated such times! I think you don't see the bonds, because you kids are scattered. We left Bensonhurst together and we came out to the Island together. We've lived here since fifty-four in this house. We saw this house go up, and their houses were going up, too. We went through it together, coming into the wide-open spaces, having a garden, trees, and parks. We see them all the time. In the winters we meet them down in Florida; we go to their grandchildren's weddings—"

"But I'm paying for this wedding," Ed says.

At that Estelle leaves the table and goes into the kitchen. Sarah glares at Ed.

"Dad," Avi groans. "Now look what you did." He whispers to Amy, "I warned you my family is weird."

"I'm really hungry," Ben says. "Can we have the turkey, Grandma? Seriously, all I've had to eat today was a Snickers bar."

In silence Estelle returns from the kitchen carrying the turkey. In silence she hands it to Sol to carve up. She passes the platter around the table. Only slowly does the conversation sputter to life. Estelle talks along with the rest, but she doesn't speak to Ed. She won't even look at him.

⁂

Ed lies on his back in the trundle bed next to Sarah. She is lying on the other bed staring at the ceiling. Every time either of them moves an inch, the bed creaks. Ed has never heard such loud creaking; the beds seem to moan and cry out in the night.

"The point? The point is this," Sarah tells him, "it was neither the time nor the place to go over the guest list."

"Your mother was the one who brought it up!" Ed exclaims.

"And you were the one who started in on her."

"Sarah, what was I supposed to say—Thank you for completely disregarding what we explicitly told you. Yes, you can invite everyone you know to your granddaughter's wedding. I'm not going to get steamrollered into this—that's what she was trying to do, manipulate this seder into an opportunity to get exactly who she wants, how many she wants, with no discussion whatsoever."

"The discussion does not have to dominate this holiday," Sarah says.

"You let these things go and she'll get out of control. She'll go from giving us a few addresses to inviting twenty, thirty people. Fifty people."

"She's not going to do that."

"She knows hundreds of people. How many people were at our wedding? Two hundred? Three hundred?"

"Oh, stop. We're mailing all the invitations ourselves from D.C."

"Fine."

"So don't be pigheaded about it," Sarah says.

"Pigheaded? Is that what you said?"

"Yes."

"That's not fair. You don't want these people at the wedding any more than I do—"

"Ed, there are ways to explain that, there are tactful ways. You have absolutely no concept—"

"I am tactful. I am a very tactful person. But there are times when I'm provoked."

"What you said about paying for the wedding was completely uncalled for."

"But it was true!" Ed cries out, and his bed moans under him as if it feels the weight of his aggravation.

"Sh," Sarah hisses.

"I don't know what you want from me."

"I want you to apologize to my mother and try to salvage this holiday for the rest of us," she says tersely.

"I'm not going to apologize to that woman," Ed mutters. Sarah doesn't answer him. "What?" he asks into the night. His voice sounds to his ears not just defensive but wronged, deserving of sympathy. "Sarah?"

"I have nothing more to say to you," she says.

"Sarah, she is being completely unreasonable."

"Oh, stop it."

"I'm not going to grovel in front of someone intent on sabotaging this wedding."

Sarah doesn't answer.

⟋ ⟍

The next day Ed wakes up with a sharp pain in his left shoulder. It is five-nineteen in the morning, and everyone else is sleeping—except Estelle. He can hear her moving around in the house adjusting things, flipping light switches, twitching lamp shades, tweaking pillows. He lies in bed and doesn't know which is worse, his shoulder or those fussy little noises. They grate on him like the rattling of cellophane paper. When at last he struggles out of the sagging trundle bed, he runs to the shower and blasts hot water on his head. He takes an inordinately long shower. He is probably using up all the hot water. He imagines Estelle pacing around outside wondering how in the world anyone can stand in the shower an hour, an hour and fifteen minutes. She is worried about wasting water, frustrated that the door is locked, and she cannot get in to straighten the toothbrushes. The fantasy warms him. It soothes his muscles. But minutes after he gets out, it wears off.

By the time the children are up, it has become a muggy, sodden spring day. Yehudit sleeps off her cold medicine, Ben watches television in the den with Sol, and Miriam shuts herself up in her room in disgust because watching TV violates the holiday. Avi goes out with Amy for a walk. They leave right after lunch and are gone for hours. Where could they be for three hours in West Hempstead? Are they stopping at every duck pond? Browsing in every strip mall? It's a long, empty day. The one good thing is that Sarah isn't angry at him anymore. She massages his stiff shoulder. "These beds have to go," she says. "They're thirty years old."

"It would probably be more comfortable to lie on the floor," Ed says. He watches Estelle as she darts in and out of the kitchen setting the table for the second seder. "You notice she still isn't speaking to me."

"Well," Sarah says, "what do you expect?" But she says it sympathetically. "We have to call your mother," she reminds him.

"Yeah, I suppose so." Ed heaves a sigh. "Get the kids. Make them talk to her."

"Hey, Grandma," says Ben when they get him on the phone. "What's up? Oh yeah? It's dull here, too. No, we aren't doing anything. Just sitting around. No, Avi's got his girlfriend here, so they went out. Yeah, Amy. I don't know. Don't ask me. Miriam's here, too. Yup. What? Everybody's like dealing with who's going to come to her wedding. Who, Grandma E? Oh, she's fine. I think she's kind of pissed at Dad, though."

Ed takes the phone out of Ben's hands.

"Kind of what?" Rose is asking.

"Hello, Ma?" Ed carries the cordless phone into the bedroom and sits at the vanity table. As he talks, he can see himself from three angles in the triptych mirror, each one worse than the next. He sees the dome of his forehead with just a few strands of hair, his eyes tired, a little bloodshot even, the pink of his ears soft and fleshy. He looks terrible.

"Ed," his mother says, "Sarah told me you are excluding Estelle's family from the wedding."

"Family? What family? These are Estelle's friends."

"And what about Henny and Pauline? Should I disinvite them, too?"

"Ma! You invited your neighbors?"

"Of course! To my own granddaughter's wedding? Of course I did."

"Ma," Ed snaps. "As far as I'm concerned, the only invitations to this wedding are going to be the ones printed up and issued by me, from my house. This is Miriam's wedding. For her. Not for you, not for Estelle. Not for anyone but the kids."

"You are wrong," Rose says simply. Throughout the day these words ring in Ed's ears. It is he who feels wronged. It's not as if his mother or Sarah's mother were contributing to the wedding in any way. They just make their demands. They aren't doing anything.

Miriam is sitting in the kitchen spreading whipped butter on a piece of matzah. Ed sits down next to her. "Where's Grandma?" he asks.

"She went out to get milk," says Miriam, and then she burst out, "Daddy, I don't want all those people at the wedding."

"I know, sweetie." It's wonderful to hear Miriam appeal to him, to be able to sympathize with her as if she weren't almost a doctor with severe theological opinions.

"I don't even know them," Miriam says.

"We don't have to invite anyone you don't want to invite," Ed says firmly.

"But I don't want Grandma all mad at me at the wedding." Her voice wavers. "I don't know what to do."

"You don't have to do anything," Ed says. "You just relax."

"I think maybe we should just invite them," Miriam says in a small voice.

"Oy," says Ed.

"Or some of them," she says.

Someone rattles the back door, and they both jump. It's just Sarah. "Let me give you some advice," she says. "Invite these people, invite your mother's people, and let that be an end to it. We don't need this kind of tsuris."

"No!" Ed says.

"I think she's right," says Miriam.

He looks at her. "Would that make you feel better?" She nods, and he gets to give her a hug. "I don't get to hug my Miriam anymore," he tells Sarah.

"I know," she says. "That's Grandma's car. I'm going to tell her she can have the Magids."

"But you make it clear to her," Ed starts.

"Ed," she says, "I'm not making anything clear to her."

❧ ❧

At the second seder, Estelle looks at everyone benignly from where she stands between the kitchen and the dining room. Sol makes jokes about weddings, and Avi gets carried away by the good feeling, puts his arm around Methodist Amy, and says, "Mom and Dad, I promise when I get married I'll elope." No one laughs at this.

When it's time for the four questions, Ed reads them himself. " 'Why is this night different from all other nights? On other nights we eat leavened bread. Why on this night do we eat matzah?' Ben, could you put your feet on the floor?" When Ed is done with the four questions, he says, "So, essentially, each generation has an obligation to explain our exodus to the next generation—whether they like it or not."

⤞ ⤝

That night in the moaning trundle bed, Ed thinks about the question Miriam raised at the first seder. Why are there four of everything on Passover? Four children. Four questions. Four cups of wine. Lying there with his eyes closed, Ed sees these foursomes dancing in the air. He sees them as in the naive illustrations of his 1960s Haggadah. Four gold cups, the words of the four questions outlined in teal blue, four children's faces. The faces of his own children, not as they are now but as they were nine, ten years ago. And then, as he falls asleep, a vivid dream flashes before him. Not the children, but Sarah's parents, along with the Rothmans, the Seligs, the Magids, and all their friends, perhaps one thousand of them walking en masse like marathoners over the Verrazano Bridge. They are carrying suitcases and ironing boards, bridge tables, tennis rackets, and lawn chairs. They are driving their poodles before them as they march together. It is a procession both majestic and frightening. At Estelle's feet, at the feet of her one thousand friends, the steel bridge trembles. Its long cables sway above the water. And as Ed watches, he feels the trembling, the pounding footsteps. It's like an earthquake rattling, pounding, vibrating through his whole body. He wants to turn away; he wants to dismiss it, but still he feels it, unmistakable, not to be denied. The thundering of history.

MADAGASCAR

Steven Schwartz

This is a story I know so well.

My father, who is twenty-one, is on his way home from finding food for his family. He has traded a gold brooch for a bottle of milk, some vegetables and a little meat. With his blue eyes and blond hair, my father is the only one in the family who has any chance to pass for gentile on the streets. He makes sure to sit on a public bench, to pick out a paper from the trash and look comfortable, then go on. Among the many edicts against Jews—no traveling in motor cars, no leaning out windows, no using balconies open to the street, no going outside after dark—is one that forbids them to sit on park benches.

On the way home he takes another chance meeting his fiancée in South Amsterdam. Before the deportations started they were to be married; now they must wait until the war ends, each of them hidden in different areas of the city.

After dark when he returns to the apartment cellar where his father, mother, and sister hide, he sees the Gestapo drive up. It is May 26, 1943. Tomorrow he will learn the Great Raid has taken away all the remaining Jews, those in rest homes, in mental institutions, in orphanages, those too sick to walk, those who have cooperated with the Germans thinking it would spare them. Even the entire Jewish Council will be shipped

89

to the labor camps. Now he knows nothing, only that he must avoid the house, that if he is caught out after curfew he will be imprisoned or shot. He steps into a bakery where the baker—a gentile, though trusted friend of the family—offers to hide my father. If someone has informed on the family and the Gestapo do not find all the members, the baker knows they will search the whole block; they have been through here before. They will check the back room, the bins of flour, the attic above. They will tap the floor and walls for any hollow spaces. But, ironically, they will not check the ovens.

The baker tells my father to climb into an oven no longer in use. At first my father resists. He is afraid. Afraid he will die in there. But there is no other way. The Gestapo will not think to look in such an obvious yet unlikely place.

My father crawls in. The sirens stop. His family is taken away to Majdanek, never to return. He lives in the oven until the end of the war, coming out every two hours when business has slowed sufficiently so that he may stretch. Some days the baker stays so busy that my father must be inside for three, four, and once even six hours. Without room to turn over or extend his legs, he remains curled up in a ball. On one occasion, much to his humiliation, he must go to the bathroom in his pants. The baker and his wife kindly provide him with a long apron while his trousers are washed in back. In the oven, he makes up waltzes in his head and has long, complex discussions with himself, marshaling arguments for each side as to which of the two Strausses, father or son, is the true Waltz King, despite the son being known by the title. He re-creates each note of their compositions and discusses the works with a panel of experts, but always delays the final vote another day so he may weigh the evidence more carefully and reconsider the merits of "Joy and Greetings," "Lorelei-Rheinklange," "Shooting Stars," and a hundred others.

⤳ ⤳

After the war my father will listen to music in a high-backed chair. The record player during my childhood, a hi-fi, will be near a whisper in volume, perhaps the loudness at which he originally heard the melodies in his head. When I come into the room, he does not mind being disturbed, but asks me to sit and listen with him. I am ten. "Ah, now," he says raising his hand when the French horns begin to play. "Our favorite part." I do not know if "our" includes me or someone else or if he just speaks of himself in the plural. Soon he closes his eyes, smiles and extends his hand for mine. Although we are sitting down, me at his feet, our arms sway together, my father waltzing with me from this position. Softly he releases my hand, tells me I have good timing and to remember practice practice practice. Mastering the clarinet is no easy task—even for a bright ten year old. He rises from his chair, pulls down the sides of his coat—on Sunday afternoons he wears a jacket and tie at home—returns the record to its sleeve, closes the lid of the hi-fi, and stands with his hands behind his back for a few seconds as though making a silent prayer. Then he says, "Ephram, would you like to accompany me on a walk in the park?" I have my coat on within five seconds.

⤳ ⤳

In ninth grade, I am caught shoplifting. I steal a silver pen from a drugstore. I am taken to the police station in Haverford, the small town where we live outside Philadelphia and where my father teaches European history at Haverford College. My mother is in New York visiting her sisters, so I must call my father. The department secretary informs me that he should return from class within the hour.

"Are you at home, Ephram?"

"I'm at the police station," I say, shocked by my own admission. Perhaps I want to confess right away and get it over with, not hide the shame I feel, or perhaps I want to boast.

Without comment, she makes a note of my situation and promises she will get the message to my father immediately.

While I wait for my father in front of the sergeant's desk, on a plastic chair a faded aqua color, I think how I've wanted to succeed at something, most recently sports. The basketball game I made sure my father attended, positive I would be put in since we were playing a much weaker team, we wound up only narrowly winning, coming from behind. I sat on the bench the whole time. "Very stirring match," my father said afterward, walking me to the car, his arm around me. He knew I felt bad, of course, but there was nothing he could do, nothing I could do.

I lack the speed and agility to be first string; and by this season I have lost interest in sports, don't even try out for the team, and instead have fallen in with a group of kids who hang out at the edge of the parking lot, wear pointed shoes with four-inch Cuban heels, pitch quarters during lunch, comb their hair in duck tails (a style that requires me to sleep with my hair parted the opposite way so that the curls will straighten out by morning), and who generally get in trouble for everything from smoking cigarettes to belching "The Star-Spangled Banner" in back of Spanish class. It is 1964. School has become intolerable.

My father soon comes to the police station. I am released into his custody and we leave the old armory building of massive, buff sandstone, me in a blue corduroy coat that says Haverford Panthers, my father with his walking stick and tweed overcoat, a cream-colored scarf tucked under his chin. He puts his hand lightly behind me and I involuntarily sink back against his open palm, no easy feat going down a flight of steps. I keep expecting him to ask me what happened. Though I know he won't raise his voice, he never does, let alone physically punish me, I anticipate a lecture, as is his custom when I've misbehaved, which to be honest has not happened all that often. An only child, I have learned how to fill my parents' wishes better than my own. They have little reason to find fault with me, so trained am I in the most subtle of ways—a raised eyebrow from my father, a frown from my mother—to find fault with myself first.

"Why don't we walk a little bit, Ephram." We stop at the post office. My father buys a roll of stamps and some airmail envelopes for letters to Holland. We have no relatives over there anymore but he keeps a regular correspondence with friends and some members of the Amsterdam Symphony. Before the war he, too, had studied the clarinet and planned to become a professional musician, a source of conflict with his father who wanted my father to have a career in business like himself. When I was younger I always eagerly awaited the letters from Holland so I could steam off the stamps for my collection.

We sit down on a bench in front of the post office. It is December but the sun is bright enough for us to rest a moment outdoors.

I am prepared to apologize, no longer able to stand my father's silence. At the same time I want to explain that school offers me nothing but hypocrisy, lies, false values and mush-headed teachers who haven't read a book themselves in years, and that I know this frustration has something to do with what I've done. But before I have the chance, he says he wants to tell me something about the war, one subject about which I am intensely interested because I always hope he will speak, as he rarely does, of his own experience.

"You may not know," he says, "that Hitler had several plans for the Jews. The camps came much later, after he had ruled out other possibilities, such as selling Jews to different countries. He also considered sending the Jews to the island of Madagascar. He wanted to permanently exile them there. Not destroy them, just isolate them on a remote island. This was to be his answer to the Jewish question. I have imagined many times what this situation may have been. I see the beaches, I see the shops, I see the clothes my mother and father wear there—light fabrics, colorful, soft cotton, a little lace on holidays. The sea is blue, the houses white. My mother does not like the heat, but my father welcomes it every morning by doing calisthenics on the balcony. They have settled here, done well, as Jews will do most anywhere, even in Nazi Madagascar. But you see how childish this is of me, don't you? That I want there to be a refuge in the midst of such undeniable evil. Perhaps it is why I decided to study history after the war. I have the liberty to make sense of the many possible pasts historians can always imagine—but the duty to choose only one. Sometimes I fail to honor my task because it is too unbearable. I do not think you are in a very happy period of your life now, Ephram. We are perhaps letting you down, your mother and I. I hope, though, that you will see I am far from perfect and struggle to make meaning of things as much as you do. It is my wish only that you will not harm others in the process, nor assault your own dignity. Leave yourself a small measure of respect in reserve. Always. You see, even in my worst memories—and I know nothing that can be worse for a man than to remember his mother and father and sister while he walks free in the world—even here I have left myself an escape to Madagascar. So allow yourself the same opportunity and do not think so poorly of your own promise that you must succumb to the disgrace of crime. You are bright, imaginative, resourceful. Surely there is a way out of whatever hell it is you too experience. I do not doubt that you can do better than this."

Chastened, I sit in silence with my father while we drive home. After his intercession, charges will be dropped by the drugstore. My mother learns nothing of the incident, and I soon separate from the group of misfits I've joined earlier. I also give up the clarinet when I discover—as my teacher agrees—that I feel nothing for the instrument.

✦ ✦

My college roommate freshman year is named Marshall X. Tiernan. I have chosen to go to a small liberal arts college in Ohio that is not too far from Haverford but far enough so I feel I'm leaving home. Every Tuesday afternoon he asks if I can vacate the room for three hours and fifteen minutes (exactly) so he can listen to music.

"I don't mind if you listen while I'm here," I tell him.

He shakes his head. He must have privacy. Marshall X. Tiernan, reedy and tall as elephant grass but not nearly so uncultivated, has an enormous collection of classical records that takes up one quarter of our room. He is studying to be an engineer. Unlike the rest of the men in my dorm, who in the fall of 1968 have grown their hair long and wear patched jeans and army surplus coats, Marshall dresses in Arrow shirts with button-down collars and keeps a well-inked pen protector in his pocket. He has an unfortunate stutter and does not socialize beyond a fellow engineering student he knows from home. We have a respectful relationship, but I can't say that Marshall is a friend.

I agree to leave him alone on Tuesday afternoons, but one time I come back early. I have forgotten some notes that I need to take with me to the library. Expecting to hear music outside the door, I hear nothing and decide to go in. On the bed, with large padded earphones, is Marshall, his thin body rigid as slate. He sees me but does not acknowledge that I am here. His clothes, the sheets, everything is drenched with sweat. His legs tremble, a kind of seizure starts. When the record ends, a composition by Satie, Marshall sits up, quickly strips the bed, throws the sheets in the closet (Tuesday the maids bring new linen), changes his clothes and returns to his desk to study.

We do not discuss the incident.

Shortly afterward he drops out of school and moves home. I have the privacy of my own room, a lucky situation that enables me to spend time alone with Jessica, whom I've met at an antiwar meeting. One night while I am telling her, with some amusement I am sorry to say, about Marshall X. Tiernan, I suddenly stop. Jessica says later the look on my face is as if I've seen a ghost, for that is what happens. I suddenly see— no, *feel*—a twenty-one-year-old man curled painfully in a baker's oven, his body kept alive by music.

**

Thanksgiving vacation my sophomore year I bring Jessica home with me. Several years older than I and a senior in anthropology, she helps my mother with Thanksgiving dinner, talks at length with my father, who retains a lifelong interest in Margaret Mead, and makes such a positive impression on them both that my mother whispers to me as we are about to leave for the airport, *"She's a jewel."*

But at school I sink into a profound depression. My grades plummet and although Jessica tries to stand by me, I manage to chase even her away. She finds her own apartment yet continues to call every day to check up on me. I become more withdrawn, however, and after a while I ask her to stop phoning. I watch television and eat chocolate donuts, drink milk from the carton and stare at the dark smudge marks my lips leave on the spout.

My father appears one afternoon, a surprise visit, he says. I know by the look in his face, though, that he has come because of Jessica. I burst into tears when I see him.

"What has happened, Ephram?" he says.

But I don't know what has happened, only that I can no longer study, I don't care about school and have no chance of passing finals; I don't care if I flunk out.

"Your mother is very worried. She wanted to come with me but I thought it best if I came alone. Is there anything I can do to help you? Is there something wrong in school, you don't like your courses, the pressure perhaps of too many hours ...."

"I haven't been to class in weeks," I say. "I can't go. Even a trip to the store is overwhelming." I start to cry again. "I want to go home. I want to go back with you."

"But what will you do back there?" my father says. "There is nothing at home for you now. You have your studies here, your friends."

I look at my father. As always, he is dressed neatly, and warmly, a blue blazer and gray slacks, a wool vest under his coat. Meanwhile, my apartment remains a mess, dishes in the sink, clothes everywhere, my hair unwashed.

"I'll find a job, I'll work and make money."

"And live at home?"

"Yes, what's wrong with that?"

My father pauses. "I don't know. I would think that you'd enjoy the freedom of living on your own."

"I have freedom and privacy at home. You've never told me what to do or when to come in. I'm not happy here."

"But Ephram, changing the place you live will not solve your problems. You need to get to the bottom of this."

"I don't care, I just want to go home! Can't you understand that?" I am almost screaming. "I have to go back. I can't make it here!"

For the rest of the winter I work in a bubble gum factory near Philadelphia. It is miserable, but the more miserable the better because I feel as if I deserve the punishment of tedious, demeaning work for failing in school. I am paid minimum wage, $1.85 an hour. So much sugar hangs in the air—we throw bags of it into a mixing contraption resembling the gigantic maw of a steam shovel—that the people who have worked for years at the factory have lost many of their teeth. The gum itself comes out on long (and unsanitary) splintered boards that I carry to racks, which are taken to another station where these long tubular strips of bubble gum—more like waxy pink sausages than gum at this stage—are cut into bite-size pieces with a tool akin to a large pizza wheel.

One day at the beginning of spring I receive a letter from the draft board. According to their records my student deferment has expired; I am now eligible to be considered for military service.

My father comes home early from his office hour at school. He himself hates the war, the senseless bombing and killing. He has marched with his college's students and protested the presence on campus of recruiters from a chemical company that makes napalm. He has, in fact, been more active than myself who has withdrawn into the routine and oblivion of factory labor, for which there are no deferments.

"What are your plans?" my father asks.

"I don't know. Canada, I suppose, if all else fails."

"And what is 'all else'?"

"A medical deferment."

"On what basis?"

"My mental condition."

"But you have never been to a psychiatrist. You have no history."

"I don't know then." I shrug. I feel numb, resigned. Why not basic training and then the jungles of Southeast Asia? Could it be much worse than the bubble gum factory?

"You will not go. That is all there is to it. We will make sure of that."

"And how will you do that?"

"We'll hide you, if necessary."

I look at my father and almost laugh. But I can see he is serious, alarmed.

"What are you talking about—hide me? Where?"

He picks up his newspaper and folds it back, once, twice, three times until he has a long strip of news in front of him. It is the idiosyncratic way he likes to read the paper—folding it up like a map until he is down to a small, tight square of information the size of a wallet or obituary. I think that it must make him feel some control over the world's chaotic events to read about them in such miniature, compressed spaces.

My mother brings in a stuck jar for one of us to loosen, and my father puts down his newspaper, which pops open on his lap like an accordion. I am still thinking about his wanting to hide me, aware that the draft has touched off buried fears for him, a flashback to the war, some instinctive response to the personal terror of his family being taken away from him. "I'll get out of it, Dad," I say. "Don't worry. I won't go."

"Don't worry, don't worry, is that what you think is the problem here? You have put yourself in this position, though I begged you not to. What is there to do now but worry!" He stands up. "I am *sick* with worry, if you must know. This is my fault. I should have demanded you stay in school, not let you come here!"

I have never heard him raise his voice like this. His body begins to tremble, and from the kitchen my mother hurries in with her hand over her heart. "What is going on here?" she says. "What are you arguing about?"

"Nothing," my father answers. "The argument is finished," and he goes into his study and closes the door—a sight I am used to from childhood. I hear him weep, but rather than sadness I feel a great relief; finally, something I've done has touched him.

✒ ✒

I do not get drafted but receive a high number in the first lottery. The long and tiresome depression, the deadness I have felt, is replaced with the exhilaration of a survivor, a life reclaimed. I make plans to visit Europe, use the money I've saved from the bubble gum factory to travel for three months. Guidebooks about England, France, Spain, and Italy cover my bed. I pore over them and come up with a tentative itinerary. But when I actually get to Europe, I find I make a detour from England to Holland. I locate the Jewish quarter where my father hid during the war, find his school—the Vossius Gymnasium—and then what I've come for: the bakery. It is still there, although the original owners who saved my father have long ago died. I explain to the current owners who I am; they tell me in broken English that yes, they have heard what happened here during the war, they know about my father and the Koops who saved him; the story is legend. "Does the oven still exist by any chance?" I ask.

They take me to the back, outside to a shed. It is here, covered with a tablecloth. I ask them if I can be by myself for a few moments and they say certainly, no one will disturb me.

A squat and solid object, the oven stands only chest high. I pull open the door and look inside. The opening is deeper than it is wide, the height a little less than two feet. I hoist myself up to sit on the edge. Then I swing my legs around and push my body in feet first. My neck is back against the left edge. I cannot go any farther. My shoulder sticks out too much even when I bend my knees into my chest. I do not understand how he did this, but I am determined to fit inside, so I slide out again and try to enter without my shoes and without my jacket. I tuck my legs under and pull my head inside, my back curved tight as an archer's bow. I hook my finger through the match hole and close the door. The stove smells of mildew and carbon; the scaled roughness of the iron ceiling grates against my cheek. It is pitch black except for the match hole through which I can see. I put my eye up to it and watch. Soon I hear footsteps and I feel frightened, but the footsteps recede into the distance and the bakery becomes silent.

❧ ❧

Many years later my parents come out to celebrate the occasion of our son's fifth birthday. My father helps Philip build the space station they have brought him. I watch them play together, my father with no awareness of the world around him other than this mission to be his grandson's assistant.

While my mother and Judith, my wife, put Philip to bed, my father and I have coffee on the porch. It is a cool summer night and we are in Boulder, Colorado, where the shimmering night sky looks, to my parents, like a planetarium. Judith works in the university's office of communications, while I teach literature. Like my father, I have become a professor.

"What are you going to do now?" I ask him. He is on transitional retirement, half-time teaching, and is scheduled to leave the college next year. "Will you finally go to Europe?"

"Perhaps," he says, "but your mother's back may not permit it."

I nod. The trip out here has cost her a great deal of pain that she has accepted stoically. If she walks for more than half an hour or sits for that long, the result is the same, inflammation.

"Have you thought of going yourself?" I ask.

"I could not leave your mother for that long. She would not be well enough."

My father sits with the hiking boots he has bought for this trip out west laced tight on his feet. They are spanking new and he has already cleaned them of mud from our climb this afternoon. I take pleasure in seeing him so fond of the mountains, so open to the world out here. "You and I could go," I say. "Together. A nurse could help Mother if we went next summer."

"I will give it some thought," my father says, but I can see that the veil has already dropped—the complex configuration of blank terror that can still scare me with its suddenness, the yearning on his face vanished. He has gone to Madagascar.

He empties the coffee he has spilled in the saucer back into his cup. "I have made a mess here," he says, replacing the dry saucer underneath. He stands up. Pulls down the sides of his jacket. Despite the hiking boots, he has dressed for dinner. "Would you like to go for a walk with me Ephram?"

Yes, I say, and get my coat, eager as always.

✑ ✑

Last summer Judith and I took Philip to Europe because I wanted to show him where his grandfather grew up. Though the bakery was no longer there—an insurance office now—I described everything about the original building, and the oven. I held him in my arms while he listened with intelligence and care, and I kissed his long lashes and felt his soft cheek against mine. I wondered what he knew that I would never know about him, what pleased him that could not be spoken. When would he grow past me, leave his fatherland, hack and chop and hew whole forests until he could find one piece of hallowed ground on which to plant the seed of his own self?

One night in our hotel I could not sleep and began to write: "Every son's story about his father is, in a sense, written to save himself from his father. It is told so that he may go free and in the telling the son wants to speak so well that he can give his father the power to save himself from his own father." I wrote this on a note card, put it in an airmail envelope, and planned to send it with its Amsterdam postmark to my father.

The following morning a call from my mother let us know that my father had suffered a stroke. We flew home immediately, and I rushed to see him in the hospital while Judith waited with Philip at the house. My mother was there by his bed. An IV bottle was connected to his wrist. His other arm I saw had purplish bruises from all the injections and from the blood samples taken. The effects of the stroke made him confuse the simplest of objects, or draw on archaic uses—a pen became a plume. A part of his brain had lost the necessary signals for referencing things and faces with words, and now dealt in wild compensatory searches to communicate. When he spoke of Judith he referred to her as my husband, called me "ram" trying to pronounce Ephram, and, saddest of all, could not understand why I had so much trouble understanding him. He had once spoken three languages fluently, and to see him in this state was more of a shock than I could bear. When he fell asleep, I left his room to speak with the doctor, a neurologist who explained to me that a ruptured blood vessel was causing the illogical and distorted speech. Bleeding in the brain. The image for me was vivid, his brain leaking, his skull swelling from the fluid's pressure inside and all one could do was wait.

One day while I sat and read by his bed, he said my name clearly and asked if I could help him get dressed. He had a white shirt and tie in the closet. He spoke with difficulty from the stroke, although his condition had improved and we all believed he would be released soon. I dressed him and because he was cold I put my sweater over his shoulders and tied the arms in front so he looked like a college man again. While he sat up in bed I held onto his hand to steady him, reminded of how we used to waltz together when I was ten. I said something to him that I had carried around with me for a long while, something that had no basis in fact, only in the private burden of a son traversing the globe for a father's loss. "I'm sorry if I've disappointed you," I told him and he answered me in speech slowed by his stroke, "I forget everything, Ephram." I nodded, but then cried later at his funeral because I thought and hoped he had meant to say forgive.

KADDISH IN CAMBODIA

Elie Wiesel

On the eighteenth day (in the Hebrew calendar) of Shevat I found myself in the dusty, noisy village of Aranyaprathet, on the border between Cambodia and Thailand, searching desperately for nine more Jews.

I had Yahrzeit for my father, and I needed a *minyan* so that I could say Kaddish. I would have found a *minyan* easily enough in Bangkok. There are about fifty Jewish families in the community there, plus twenty Israeli Embassy families, so there would have been no problem about finding ten men for *Minḥah*. But in Aranyaprathet?

I had gone there to take part in a March for the Survival of Cambodia organized by the International Rescue Committee and Doctors Without Frontiers. There were philosophers, novelists, parliamentarians, and journalists—myriad journalists. But how was I to find out who might be able to help me with *my* problem?

I would have liked to telephone one of my rabbi friends in New York or Jerusalem and ask his advice on the halakhic aspects of the matter. What did one do in such a case? Should one observe the Yahrzeit the following day, or the following week? But I was afraid of being rebuked and of being asked why I had gone to Thailand precisely on that day, when I should have been in synagogue.

I would have justified myself by saying that I had simply been unable to refuse. How could I refuse when so many men and women were dying of hunger and disease?

I had seen on television what the Cambodian refugees looked like when they arrived in Thailand—walking skeletons with somber eyes, crazy with fear. I had seen a mother carrying her dead child, and I had seen creatures dragging themselves along the ground, resigned to never again being able to stand upright.

How could a Jew like myself, with experiences and memories like mine, stay at home and not go to the aid of an entire people? Some will say to me, Yes, but when you needed help, nobody came forward. True, but it is *because* nobody came forward to help me that I felt it my duty to help these victims.

As a Jew I felt the need to tell these despairing men and women that we understood them; that we shared their pain; that we understood their distress because we remembered a time when we as Jews confronted total indifference. . . .

Of course, there is no comparison. The event that left its mark on my generation defies analogy. Those who talk about "Auschwitz in Asia" and the "Cambodian Holocaust" do not know what they are talking about. Auschwitz can and should serve as a frame of reference, but that is all.

So there I was in Thailand, in Aranyaprathet, with a group of men and women of good will seeking to feed, heal, save Cambodians—while I strove to get a *minyan* together because, of all the days of the year, the eighteenth day of Shevat is the one that is most full of meaning and dark memories for me.

Rabbi Marc Tanenbaum was a member of the American delegation. Now I needed only eight more. Leo Cherne, the president of the International Rescue Committee, was there as well. Only seven more to find.

Then I spotted the well-known Soviet dissident, Alexander Ginsburg, and rushed over to him. Would he agree to help me make up a *minyan?* He looked at me uncomprehendingly. He must have thought I was mad. A *minyan?* What is a *minyan?* I explained: a religious service. Now he surely did not understand. A religious service? Here, by the mined bridge separating Thailand and Cambodia? Right in the middle of a demonstration of international solidarity? I began all over again to explain the significance of a *minyan.* But in vain. Alexander Ginsburg is not a Jew; he is a convert to the Russian Orthodox Church. I still had seven to find.

Suddenly, I caught sight of the young French philosopher

Bernard-Henri Levy, who was making a statement for television. Only six more to find. Farther on, I found the French novelist Guy Suares. Then a doctor from Toulouse joined us, followed by Henry Kamm, of the *New York Times*. Another doctor came over. At last there were ten of us. There, in the midst of all the commotion, a few yards from the Cambodian frontier, we recited the customary prayers, and I intoned Kaddish, my voice trembling.

Then, suddenly, from somewhere behind me, came the voice of a man still young, repeating the words after me, blessing and glorifying the Master of the Universe. He had tears in his eyes, that young Jew. "For whom are you saying Kaddish?" I asked him. "For your father?" "No." "For your mother?" "No."

He grew reflective and looked toward the frontier. "It is for them," he said.

THE UGLY JEWESS

Veronica Ross

A grey November Saturday. Market day in Kitchener, once called Berlin, home of Oktoberfest. From Market Square the white signs of the Jews protesting racism and Holocaust denial look like white angel wings, waving back and forth, back and forth. Or like the handkerchiefs of immigrants on piers and ships: Remember me. Don't forget me. I think of coming to Canada, of the SS Columbia docking in London where I heard English for the first time. And of a mixed-up memory of reading *The Source* pre-literary years ago: a Jewish carpenter? shoemaker? was sailing away from his Italian village. Seeing the Jews gathered on the shore reminded him of candles glowing. Or was it a fire he saw?

I know I have to, I should, walk up along King Street and take up a sign. We were Jews once; now we're not. Is that not incredible?

German Jews had Christmas trees. They served in the Kaiser's army. They hardly knew Yiddish. I think of an aunt who kept kosher when she moved to the States but who said she sometimes yearned for a *Speck Brot*.

As for us, my family, we ate matzahs when we first came to Canada— I remember that—but then it was decided being Jewish was too dangerous: the Nazis might come back. Better hide, better keep the secret.

Through the lobby of Market Square Mall, past Fairweathers (I can use a new sweater, must look later), past the store selling helium balloons with Santa on them I go, and down the escalator to the quilt world of the Farmer's Market.

It's crowded with early Christmas shoppers. Rudolph-the-red-nosed reindeer ornaments made of cinnamon sticks, watercolours of Amish girls feeding ducks, salt dough hearts, gingerbread men, and white feathered birds that will sing on your Christmas tree. There's a dollhouse, handcrafted by a man who also makes wooden puzzles and footstools with roosters etched on them. The dollhouse even has a grandfather clock with hands that turn, and tiny books in a corner shelf.

I really love that dollhouse with its dormer windows and wide front porch, its blue and white exterior, although it's not as wonderful as the dollhouse I had as a child. Mine had two rows of balconies, upstairs and downstairs, with doors that opened to the outside. Glass in the windows, lights operated by battery. A silver wringer washer. The front, painted terra cotta pink, was carved in swirls and flowers. And you could open the slanted roof to reveal the maid's bedroom. What Canadian dollhouse would have a room for the maid? I used the other attic room for the laundry.

What happened to this dollhouse is a mystery. My mother says they gave it to the Y family; my father says no: the Xs got it. Neither family recalls it. Why did they give it away at all? If they did. Maybe it just disappeared in one of the many moves.

Maybe it was, like Heine wrote, a dream. *Es war ein Traum.* Vaterland, Fatherland. All a dream: my grandparents' house in the country, the cherry tree, candles on the Christmas tree, my white wicker doll pram with the pink satin quilted cover and the old china doll, also dressed in pink satin with a pink bouquet of silk flowers pinned to the dress, and a new head with a clear, rosy complexion, unlike the body, with its cracked glaze. That doll, and others—Angelika with the long braids and blue dress—disappeared too.

Cobblestones, streetcars, red railway stations, carpets beaten on a clothesline, marzipan, and apple cake. Snowy trees, stars shining in the night sky while I am riding on my father's shoulders.

And the temple my two grandmothers took me to. Only a room, I think. Upstairs, somewhere in the city. All that remained, after the war. Folding wooden chairs. A man with a beard bending over me. He gave me—cookies? Chocolates? The opening cupboard in front. I remember that. It was winter, late fall. I was warm in my coat, as I am now.

The Jewish cemetery, visited when I was an adult. I paid a donation for the upkeep of the grave of Oma R., not my Oma, my granny, but the grandmother of cousins who had been in Riga. The cousins' mother died in Riga, after liberation, because she was fed too much, too soon; the father in Theresienstadt. My great-grandfather was buried in the same cemetery. I have Oma R's *Siddur,* given to one of my grandmothers, and inscribed: "In memory of my beloved husband Isaak/Julius who died 29 Kislev, 5704, 26 December, 1942, in Theresienstadt."

Downstairs, where the food is sold, Mrs. Martin greets me with her unassuming smile. Her Mennonite white prayer covering is in place over her greying hair. I often buy from her: apple butter, sticky buns, Dutch apple pie, shoofly pie, leaf lettuce in the spring. "So good with sour cream." I am ashamed of my nicotined fingers in front of her, although if she notices she does not let on. If I slapped her face she would forgive me. She makes me think: I want to be good. Turn the other cheek, forgive my enemies, avoid conflict, help others. In the 1500s they drowned and killed her ancestors for their Anabaptist beliefs, but here she is today, up since four A.M., selling her baking.

Her goodness and faith are so appealing. Could I be like her? I'm not sure who I am. Maybe I could. My husband is descended from the Mennonite Hostettlers, who died during an Indian raid because the father would not let his sons take the guns they used for shooting wildlife to defend the family. All died, except the old mother—"fleshy of hip"— and a son who was out with the buggy, courting.

It's an honourable heritage, I tell my husband, who is descended from the courting son.

Rick says, "To hell with that." He would have shot, he said. And yet, I know Kraft dinner would have to turn to diamonds before he would raise a hand in anger, especially against me.

I buy buns, stick them into my purse. Move past the stalls selling meat. I need something for dinner. I could buy steak, maybe find a cauliflower in the garage where the vegetables are sold. But do I want to have to carry things today?

Upstairs again. I drift into Coles, buy the *New Yorker,* which I cram into my purse. Spin the racks at Fairweathers. Cotton sweaters for $14.99, in the earth tones I like, and I could use a scarf too, even if they're only polyester. But my bag feels so heavy, and I'd have to dig through the whole mess to find my wallet.

I need to sit down. Upstairs, in the food court, I drink coffee and have a smoke while I read the *New Yorker.* It's starting to snow out, I see, a grey snow that turns to rain before it hits the pavement. I'm not wearing boots. My feet would get soaked through if I walked up King Street. I can catch the bus downstairs and be home in ten minutes. If I decide to take the bus, I could even return to Fairweathers and buy the sweater. Two sweaters, why not? Go back to Coles, buy a book to read on the bus and while I wait for it. There isn't much in the *New Yorker* this week. And if I'm going right home, I can pick up steak too.

Go home, make a pot of tea, do the cryptic puzzles in the *Globe and Mail,* bake some bread. . . .

Outside, I have to wait for the light to change. It's really wet and my feet are definitely going to get soaked. And there's a hole in my leotards, right on top.

The light changes. Turn right, go to the bus stop, or cross the street?

Across the street I stand in front of the Valhalla Inn and look in the windows of Erika's Bavarian Fashions at dirndls and German picture books, at wooden puzzles and beer steins. Once, there was Christkindle—a Christmas bazaar—at the Valhalla. I went, looking for presents and ornaments, and found Ernst Zundel positioned by the pool. "Buy a painting by a famous name—a Zundel painting." A fashion parade of dirndls and loden coats, youngsters in Bavarian dress, and an elderly couple accompanied by their German Shepherd dog, proceeded under Zundel's gaze.

Rick called the newsroom of the local paper when I got home, but by the time the reporter arrived at the Valhalla, Zundel was gone.

I wrote a poem:

Outside, snow.
Christians pamphleting.
Inside Valhalla:
From the pool,
Odin and Edda
Siegfried too
Watch the dirndl parade.
Across the room,
The stout man rises.
"Invest in a Painting by a Famous Name—
A Zundel painting."
Orange sunset, oily trees.

I think of yellow light
Of lovely light
Of "Wedding of the Butterflies"
Of Ilona Weikhova
Bloc Four
Colouring in the lines.

Close up, the signs are not angel wings or fluttering handkerchiefs. They are just—signs. White Bristol board affixed to the slats of wood. Remember the Six Million. Down with Racism. Never Forget the Six Million.

Round and round the protestors march in a long circle in front of the store where David Irving has been invited to speak. Across the street, on the other side of King, two or three cops watch. Non-protestors— Irving supporters, I guess, look on from the front of the store and the doorway leading to the apartment upstairs. Young punks, black leather and shaved heads, young women with dyed blonde hair and high-heeled boots. One woman has a cute boy with her. She's chewing gum. "Yeah, sure, tell me six million really died," she laughs.

But an older man in a respectable overcoat stands with the punks. And a middle-aged woman with a neat hairdo and a leather jacket stands beside him.

I need a sign.

"Heading West," someone tells me.

I swivel my head. Are they joking with me?

"Heading West," the woman repeats and laughs, recognizing my confusion. She nods in the direction of a store called "Headin' West" and I go in and pick up a sign.

I walk and walk. Round and round. I don't know these people. A policeman comes over and says not to crowd the sidewalk. Please. A tray of take-out coffee is delivered to the punks. They've been joined by two older men, one with a video camera.

I get into conversation with one of the protestors. The weather. It's cold, yes. He's been here since eleven.

"I thank you from the bottom of my heart for supporting us," he tells me.

I don't know what to say to that. I keep walking.

"Look at the monkeys," the man with the camera says in German to his companion. *Affen.* I understand perfectly.

"They're not human," his buddy replies.

"Not white, that's for sure."

They laugh. The man with the video camera turns it on. He balances it on his round sweatshirt-covered stomach and leans back to get a better angle.

Round and round I go. Will the film be shown at neo-Nazi gatherings, beery get-togethers celebrating Hitler? *Affen,* I hear again. Does anyone else here understand what they are saying? I wonder. If they know Yiddish, maybe.

"They should all be dead," I hear.

I catch the cameraman's eye. He swivels the lens right at me. I stare at it as I walk by.

"Look at the ugly Jewess," he chuckles, keeping the lens in my direction.

Yes, well. I imagine my face is flushed from the cold and whatever make-up I applied that morning has worn off. My wet hair is straggling around my shoulders. I'm wearing an orangey-beige nylon coat that used to be my sister's. Her pregnancy coat, against the cold of Montreal, "down-filled," but it's really polyester-lined. And there's the hole in my leotards.

"Yeah, the ugly Jewess," his buddy agrees.

Kuk mal die hässliche Jüdin an.

Look at the ugly Jewess.

It is absurd and crazy, nutty and screwy, but the words that jump into my mind, the words that I whisper without moving my lips are: Thank you.

RACIAL MEMORIES

Matt Cohen

The beard of my grandfather was trimmed in the shape of a spade. Black at first, later laced liberally with white, it was also a flag announcing to the world that here walked an Orthodox Jew. Further uses: an instrument of torture and delight when pressed against the soft ticklish skin of young children, a never empty display window for the entire range of my grandmother's uncompromising cuisine. To complement his beard my grandfather—indoors and out—kept his head covered. His indoor hats were *yarmulkes* that floated on his bare and powerful skull; the hats he wore outside had brims that kept the sun away and left the skin of his face a soft and strangely attractive waxy white. White, too, were his square-fingered hands, the moons of his nails, his squarish slightly-gapped teeth, the carefully washed and ironed shirts my grandmother supplied for his thrice-daily trips to the synagogue. A typical sartorial moment: on the day before his seventieth birthday I found him outside on a kitchen stepladder wearing slippers but no socks, his suitpants held up by suspenders, his white shirt complete with what we used to call bicep-pinchers, his outdoors hat—decked out in style, in other words, even though he was sweating rivers while he trimmed the branches of his backyard cherry trees.

Soon after I met him, I began remembering my grandfather.

Especially when I lay in bed, the darkness of my room broken by the thin yellow strip of light that filtered through the bottom of my door. Staring at the unwavering strip I would try to make it dance. "Be lightning," I would say. "Strike me dead; prove that God exists." And then I would cower under my sheets, waiting for the inevitable. That was when I would remember my grandfather. Standing alone with him in the big synagogue in Winnipeg, the same synagogue where he must have sought God's guidance in dealing with Joseph Lucky, looking up at the vaulted ceilings, holding his hand as he led me up the carpeted aisle to the curtained ark where the Torah was kept.

And then he showed me the words themselves. God's words. Indecipherable squiggles inked onto dried skin not so different from the tough dry calluses on my grandfather's palms.

Also full of words was the high bulging forehead of my grandfather. Everything he said to me in English, which he spoke in a gently accented cadence I had difficulty understanding, he would repeat in Hebrew, which I couldn't understand at all. Cave-man talk, I would think, listening to the guttural sounds. He showed me, too, the separate section where the women sat. I was amazed at this concept of the women being put to one side, just as later I was to be amazed to discover that when women had "the curse" they spent their nights in their own dark beds, left alone to bleed out their shame.

My great-great-uncle Joseph, the one after whom I was named, served in the cavalry of the Russian czar. This is true, and I still have a photograph of a bearded man in full uniform sitting on a horse in the midst of a snowy woods. After two years, during which he was promoted once and demoted twice, my ancestor deserted and made his way across Europe to a boat that took him to Montreal. From there he caught a train on which, the story goes, he endeared himself to a wealthy Jewish woman who owned a large ranch in Alberta. We could pause briefly to imagine the scene: minor-key *War And Peace* played out against a background of railway red velvet, cigar smoke and a trunk filled with souvenirs. Unfortunately the lady was married, so my uncle ended up not in the castle but out on the range, riding wild mustangs. (Also, it has been claimed, singing Yiddish folk songs to the animals as they bedded down beneath their starry blankets.)

And then my uncle Joseph struck it rich. Sitting around the campfire one night, he reinvented the still with the help of an old horse trough and a few lengths of hose. All this is according to my father; he was the historian-in-exile, but that is another story. The rest of the family claims he was only trying to make barley soup. Maybe that explains how my uncle became known as Joseph Lucky.

Having made his fortune and his name, Joseph Lucky began sending money to the relatives. We've all heard about those Russian Jews: semi-Cro-Magnon types covered in beards, furs, dense body hair, living without flush toilets or electricity in a post-feudal swamp of bone-breaking peasants, child-snatching witches and wicked landowners. Having helped his blood relations through the evolutionary gate of the twentieth century—to say nothing of destroying the racial purity of his adopted homeland—my uncle asked only one thing in return: that the newcomers settle in Winnipeg, well away from his field of operations. When they got established, he came to pay a visit. By this time the wealthy Jewess had died and, because of a jealous husband, my uncle Joseph had moved on from his life on the range to "business interests." Another photograph I possess: Joseph Lucky standing on the Winnipeg train platform, winter again, wearing matching fur coat and hat and framed by two enormous suitcases, which my father tells me were made from "soft brown leather you could eat."

This was before the First World War, before my father was born. Also before the war was my uncle's demise. What had happened was that for causes unknown he was put in jail. After a few months he wrote to his nephew, my grandfather. The letter was written in Yiddish, using Hebrew characters—the same formula that my grandmother employed to torture my mother decades later. I've seen the letter; my grandfather showed it to me when I was a child. He opened the envelope and out blew the smell that made a permanent cloud in my grandparents' house, a permanent storm-cloud to be exact, always threatening to rain down the pale greenish soup that my grandmother claimed was all her frail stomach could support.

My grandfather was a strong man. Once, when a neighbour's shed was burning down, he carried out two smoke-damaged pigs. The image of my grandfather, wearing his inevitable satin waistcoat and box *yarmulke* walking down the street with a sow over each shoulder, has never seemed improbable to me. I can image him, too, poring over the letter from his benefactor. Caught between his duty to help a relative, his distaste for my uncle's way of life, and his own poverty. According to my father, my grandfather never answered the letter. Instead, after waiting two weeks he gathered what cash he could and took a train for Edmonton. When he arrived he discovered Joseph Lucky had died of food poisoning and that his body had been claimed by someone whose name had not been recorded. My grandfather always feared that his delay had killed Joseph Lucky. That is why my father felt obliged to give me his name. Also because, he always insisted, Joseph Lucky had likely died not of food poisoning at all, but had been bribed away from the jail (body claimed by an "unrecorded stranger"!—who could believe that?) by a rich client and spent the rest of his days happily riding some faraway range.

"If you could credit a Jewish cowboy . . ." my mother would protest and shake her head. But that was where Joseph Lucky was lucky, I didn't have to be told. Somehow he had escaped being Jewish, wiggled out from under his fate and galloped off into that carefree other world where you were not under a life sentence or, to be more exact, perhaps you were under a life sentence of mortality (even an assimilated Jew finds it hard to believe in Heaven) but you had been promoted to a different part of the sentence: instead of being the object, you were the subject.

❦ ❦

"Did you hear the one about the rabbi's wife?"

"No," I say. We are lying on the centre of the school football field, six of us in a circle, face to face with our bodies extended like the spokes of a wagon-wheel. It is late September, a cool heart-breaking twilight. At the word "rabbi" my stomach has suddenly tensed up and my hipbones start to press against the hard ground.

"This sausage salesman comes to the door . . . Are you sure you haven't heard it?" The five of us are the offensive backfield of our high-school football team: the wheel of which I am the only Jewish spoke.

"I'm sure," I say. I look up over at the boy who is talking. The fullback. A power runner known as Willy "Wild Bill" Higgins. He's the one we need when it's late afternoon, November, and gusts of cold rain are sweeping down the river valley and turning us into sodden little boys who want to go home. That's when Wild Bill—it's me who gave him the name—drives forward with his cleats spitting out gobs of mud, knees pumping up into the face of anyone crazy enough to tackle him.

"All right," he says, "forget it. Don't get your cock in a knot."

All evening, over my homework, I'm left wondering. Something to do with a circumcision no doubt. Animal sex? Two weeks ago a girl I asked to a dance told me her father wouldn't let her go out with a Jew. I'm at my sixth school in ten years but I still can't get used to breaking the ice. Can't get used to the fact that it never breaks.

At eleven o'clock the phone rings. It's another spoke of the wheel—
a small spoke, like me. "Don't let dickface get you down," he says. The
first thing I think is how glad I am that this is happening over the telephone, so my friend can't see my eyes swelling up with unwanted tears.

Idiot, I say to myself. *Thin-skinned Jew.* "Doesn't matter," I say
aloud. "Except that maybe I missed a good joke."

Peter Riley laughs. He's a skinny Irish kid whose father has lung cancer. Sometimes, after school, I go home with him and we sit in the
living-room with his father, feeding him tea and watching him die. "She
says she only eats kosher," Peter Riley says.

I start a fake laugh, then stop.

"Not funny?"

"Not funny to me."

"Join the club," Peter Riley says.

"What club?"

"You name it."

"The Wild Bill Fan Club," I say, a little chunk of the past—another
school, another group of boys—jumping unbidden out of my mouth.

✑ ✑

Leonard lived above the garage attached to the house my grandfather bought after he moved to Toronto to be nearer the brothers, sisters, aunts, uncles, cousins, etc. The spider's web of relatives in Toronto
didn't include my own parents: they had already learned their lesson and
were hiding out in Ottawa, on their way to greener fields. As a gesture
to family solidarity, however, they had sent me to the University of
Toronto. There I was not only to carry my parents' proud banner in the
world of higher learning, but to act as unofficial delegate and sacrifice.
Leonard, not a relative but a paying boarder, was also at the university;
ten years older than I, he had the exalted status of a graduate student
in religious philosophy. "He doesn't eat kosher," my grandmother confided to me in the kitchen, "You can tell by his smell, but he goes to
shul every morning and he doesn't make noise."

In a room with my grandparents, Leonard was so well-behaved and
courteous that he hardly seemed to exist. Once out of sight, however,
he became the main subject of my grandmother's conversation. "Did
you see how he wiped his mouth?" she always began, as though she had
spent the whole time doing nothing but watching Leonard compulsively
snatch at the napkin. And then Laura, a cousin slightly older than I who
had sealed her reputation by going to a drive-in at age fourteen with a

married man (self-made, rich from vending machine concessions), would point out that once again the insides of Leonard's nostrils were flaming red because—she had seen him at it through his window—every night he spent an hour yanking out his nasal hairs in order to combat his other urges.

"Wanna see my place?" Leonard invited, while we were drinking tea after a Sabbath lunch.

I followed him out the back door, along a path worn through the grass, and we arrived at the metal stairway leading up the outside of the garage to Leonard's room. Immediately I found myself thinking this arrangement was ideal because it allowed Leonard to come and go as he pleased, even bringing company with him if he wanted. Or could. An unlikely possibility I thought, following the shiny seat of Leonard's grey-and-black checked trousers up the final steps.

The first thing I noticed was the mirror where Leonard was reported to carry on with his nose. It hung above a dresser from which the drawers jutted out, each one overflowing. The cartoon chaos of the room continued. Piled over every available surface were dirty clothes, newspapers and magazines, empty pop bottles, wrappings from candy store food. Even the desk of the graduate philosopher was a tower of babble—unsteady stacks of library books interspersed with sheaves of folded paper. Ostentatiously draped over the back of the chair was a strangely mottled towel. Stepping closer I saw that the towel was, in fact, heavily stained with blood.

"War wounds," Leonard said.

At lunch I had already noticed Leonard's soft white fingers, his unmuscled arms blotched with freckles and covered with a sparse layer of white-orange fur.

"They're crazy for it then. Ever notice?"

I shook my head.

"Read Freud. The power of taboo. Close your eyes. Imagine it. You're in the dark with the woman of your dreams. The smell of sweat and blood. Smells so strong you can taste it. Get up from the bed and your dick is dripping with it."

My eyes weren't closed. I was looking at Leonard. His eyes were boring straight into my face. "You some kind of a pervert?"

Leonard looked puzzled. Encouraged, I continued with a further inspiration: "If you didn't pick your nose, it wouldn't bleed."

Leonard shook his head. "You're going to study philosophy, kid, you need to have an open mind. I told you the truth."

"Don't make me laugh. No woman in her right mind would come into this rat's nest for more than five minutes."

At which point Laura opened the door, came and stood by Leonard's chair, practically sticking her chest in his face while he patted her bum. "Isn't this great? Look, we're going to drive you downtown and then we'll pick you up later for dinner. Isn't this place unbelievable?"

*   *

Laura and Leonard are halfway up the greys, exactly at centre ice. From where I line up on defence I can see the steam billowing from their Styrofoam cups of coffee. They grin at me. "Go get 'em," Leonard shouts and his voice echoes in the empty arena. This is intramural hockey, a house-league game taking place close to midnight. The only other spectators are a few couples who have discovered that the shadowed corners of the varsity rink are good for more than watching hockey.

My legs are tired. There are lines of pain where the blades of the skates, which don't quite fit me, press into the bones of my feet. One of my shoulders has already begun to ache as the result of a collision against the boards. Peter Riley looks back at me. He is our centre. A quick skater with dozens of moves and a hard wrist-shot, he is the only one who really knows how to play. The rest of us make up a supporting cast, trying to feed him the puck and to protect our goalie, a non-skating conscript whose main virtue is that he has the courage to buckle on his armour, slide across the ice in his galoshes and risk his life.

Most games we just give the puck to Peter and he scores with tricky unstoppable shots. Now we're in the finals and they've got the strategy to beat us. Two, sometimes three, players shadow Peter, sandwiching him every time he tries to dart forward. The rest of us are often left in the open but compared to these other bigger, stronger players, we are ineffectual midgets. Somehow, however, our goalie has risen to the occasion. With a couple of minutes to go in the game we are only one goal behind.

The referee looks back at us. I bend over my stick. My rear end is sore from numerous forced landings. Riley winks at me and then nods his head for good measure. I know what this signal—our only signal—is supposed to mean: when the puck is dropped he will gain control—then I am to skate by at full speed so that he can feed it to me and send me in.

As the puck bounces on the ice I'm already driving forward, and by the time I've crossed centre ice the puck—via Riley—has arrived at my stick. I'm alone, the crowd of two is screaming. I'm going as fast as I can but I can hear the ice being chewed up behind me, long powerful strides gaining on my short choppy ones. The hollow ominous sound of steel carving ice, Laura's amazingly loud voice—I lift my stick back preparing to blast the puck before I'm overtaken—and then something has hooked my ankles and I'm sliding belly-down.

No whistle so I'm up again. Peter has somehow recovered the puck from the corner and is waiting for me to get in front of the net. This time I'm going to shoot on contact, no waiting; again my stick goes back. Then I'm swinging it forward, toward the puck, already feeling the sweet perfect impact of the hard rubber on the centre of my blade, already seeing the net billow with the tying goal. Suddenly the curtain comes down. A blast to my forehead so intense that I lose consciousness falling to the ice. Get up, dazed, glove held to my head. Start skating again, vision foggy, towards the puck, until I see that everyone else has stopped, that my glove and hockey stick are covered with red, that the clouding of my vision isn't dizziness but a veil of blood over my eye. Leonard and Laura are rushing towards me.

There are words, too. "Jew. Eat it, Jew," I thought I heard someone say. The words are rattling in my head like pebbles in a gourd but I'm too confused to know who put them there. Laura's got a handkerchief out of her purse, it's soaked in perfume, soft white cloth with a pink stitched border. The pebbles are still rattling in my skull and I can't stand them, have to do something about them, twist away from Laura and skate towards the big boy with blood on his hockey stick.

But Peter Riley is already there. When the boy hears me coming, turns towards me, Riley twists—twists and straightens his legs as he sends an uppercut deep into the unpadded belly. Mine enemy collapses to the ice retching. His team prepares to rush ours. By now I have felt my cut with my bare finger; a small gash above the left eyebrow that opens and closes every time I move the muscles in my face.

Before anything can happen there is a sharp blast of the whistle. The referee, who is also the Dean of Men and who hands out suspensions for fighting—from the university, not just from hockey—is holding the puck and standing bent over the spot where he wants play to begin again.

"Sir," Riley says, "one of our players is bleeding."

"Have his friends take him to the hospital."

As I'm clumping along the wooden gangway, Laura's scented hanky pressed to my wound, Leonard is calling my dean a "Jew-baiting bastard, an anti-Semitic son-of-a-bitch who would have spent his afternoons cracking open teeth to get at their gold fillings."

By three o'clock in the morning, when I am sharing a mickey of rye with Peter Riley, my wound has been reduced to a small throbbing slice covered by a neat white patch. And Riley is telling me that the dean shook his hand as he left the dressing room.

As I fall asleep, the words are still with me. I am lying in the dark. The first time I heard such words, such words said by other than my own, I was ten years old. I was in a new school that year, but friends had come quickly and life seemed suddenly to have grown wide and easy. Then one day, late in the fall, my friends turned on me. There were three of them. "Jew," one of the said. "Jew," said the other two. We had been standing in a vacant lot on the way home from school. Talking about nothing. One of them pushed me. A nothing push, not really a punch, something I wasn't sure whether or not to ignore.

"Jews are Christ-killers," one of them said.

"Christ-killers," the others repeated. The words unfamiliar to all of us.

Now I can see they didn't know what to do. Something their parents had said would have put them up to this, probably without intending anything specific.

There were more shoves. I shoved back. "Christ-killer," they were saying, still trying to convince themselves. "Run," one of them said.

"No."

"Run," said the biggest one. He slapped me across the face, knocking my glasses to the grass. When I bent to pick them up, he covered them with his foot. I reached anyway. As I pulled them out from his shoe he stamped on my hand.

"Run."

I held my glasses tightly. The other two boys, the ones I had thought were my friends, had backed away. Without my glasses their faces were foggy and distorted. I put my glasses on. My friends had pebbles in their hands.

"Run."

I ran, hating myself from the first step. As I did a shower of rocks fell gently on my back. One boy, the biggest, chased me. I was smaller but faster. I vaulted over the fence—clearing it the way I'd had to in order to become a member of the club they had invented—the Wild Bill Fan Club—then ran to the back door as the one boy still chased after me. As I opened the door, he reached in. To grab? To punch? A reflex action? I slammed the door on his hand.

For a week I walked back and forth from school alone. Stomach broiling. At night I couldn't wait to be in bed, alone, lights out. Then finally the world of fear I'd been containing all day in my belly could expand, spread out, swallow the make-believe theatre of pretend-niceness that surrounded me during the day. In the dark, instead of daring God to show himself as I used to, I listened for the sound of convoy trucks on the road, knocks at the door, policemen's boots on the stairs. And if they weren't going to come? I eventually had to ask myself. Did that mean that in this new world there was safety after all? That my great-great uncle Joseph Lucky truly had led us out of the wilderness and into the promised land?

One afternoon recess, during the compulsory all-school no-rules soccer game, mine enemy was delivered. Head down, dribbling the ball forward at full speed, running straight at me while being chased by fifty screaming boys. An hour later we were standing on either side of the door of the principal's office. Him with scratched cheeks from the gravel he fell into when I tripped him, plus a swollen lip from the only punch I had managed to land; me with bloody nose and ribs, rearranged from the fight-ending bearhug.

I still remember the principal's suit. A blue-grey plaid too long for his short legs, worn cuffs, lapels sporting a maple leaf pin. In his hands, very small, was a thick leather strap. Without comment he reddened our palms. Then we were out in the hall again, the door closed behind us. No handshakes, no words of mutual consolation, no smiles. But by the time the school day had finished, the underground telegraph had turned us into folk heroes, victims and survivors of the principal's best, warmly united members of the Wild Bill Fan Club once more.

≽ ≼

I am in Laura's bedroom. Laura is in her dressing gown, then takes it off to try on her dress. Laura encased in sterile white brassiere and panties surrounded by tanned skin. The body is untouched, an uninhabited countryside, a national park waiting for its first visitor; but her face is the city. A long curved jaw stubbornly set. Lips painted what Peter Riley called "North Toronto Red." Brown eyes, Jewish eyes, eyes that I knew my friend found sympathetic and embracing, but that to me looked hardened with all the calculations they had made.

I am in Laura's bedroom because I have been delegated the task no one wants. Why me? Instead of, for example, my father? The explanation for this lies in other stories, stories too long and intertwined to tell, stories not about Joseph Lucky and Laura and Leonard, but stories about my parents. Most of all my father who had decided by now to complete his escape and was residing (with my mother, of course—herself a sub-ject not to be broached without lengthy explanations) in Sydney, Aus-tralia, where he was attempting to unknot the city's bus schedules.

"This is crazy. I'm supposed to talk you out of marrying my best friend."

"So talk me out."

"He's a shit. His father's dead and his mother drinks too much. So does he. His brother is a lawyer and makes deals with politicians. His sister goes to church on Sundays. Five years from now he'll be screwing his secretary. How's that?"

"You can do better."

"He's a Catholic. Secretly he hates Jews but he hasn't got the guts to say it. He's marrying you in order to destroy you. When you have children he'll drag them down the basement to a priest he has hidden in the furnace and baptize them."

"At least we'll have a house."

"Tell me," I suddenly say. As if I'm thinking about it for the first time, and maybe I am. "Why *are* you marrying outside? Really why?"

Laura looks at me. For a second it seems that my question has truly surprised her, cracked the shell. Then I realize that she's only waiting for me to back down. "I love him," she says. Her voice is so wooden as she pronounces this formula that I can't help believing her.

"But answer my question."

"Crazy boy."

She crosses the room to where I am sitting on her bed. Bends over me and kisses the scar above my eyebrow. Then my lips. A slow kiss that leaves me bathed in her taste and scent. "I couldn't marry a Jew. It would be like incest, if you know what I mean. Did I ever show you this? Grandpa gave it to me."

Dear Nephew,
You will remember me. I am your wicked uncle, Joseph Lucky.
A few years ago I came to visit you and the rest of those whom you call your family. As always, I brought gifts. As always, they were greedily snatched and then scorned. His money is dirty, they would like to say, since they have none. You alone wrote to thank me. I kept your letter, nephew, because I, a childless old man, wanted to dream about what might be possible. I imagined such things, nephew, as bringing you to live with me and making you a partner in my various enterprises. That is the letter I should

have written you because you might have been the one to change my fate. Too late now. Now I am in jail, starving because despite everything you might have heard about me I refuse to eat anything but kosher food. To tell the truth, even the smell of pork chops is enough to turn this old stomach. Nephew, I beg you to come and see that I am released, or at least fed. When you arrive I will give you the name of a lawyer who can arrange things.

Love from your fond Uncle—

"What about the other letter? The one my father has?"

"There were lots of letters. Each one written as though the others had somehow failed to arrive. Not all of them were sent to Grandpa either."

"And when he went to Edmonton?"

"He never went. No one did. They let him die because they were ashamed of him." Laura puts on her dressing gown and lights a cigarette. "You think Peter's cousins are on their knees right now? Begging Peter not to marry me?"

"They should be."

❦ ❦

An hour later I am at Leonard's. Stiffening the spine so that I can report the failure of my mission to my grandparents. "You are the outsider," Leonard is explaining to me, "the perennial third man. You think it's because of your shiny metal mind. Forget it. You're outside because you're a Jew. And that's why Laura is marrying your friend. She grew up being outside and now she wants to be sure she'll be outside forever. Except that she won't because ten years from now the whole world will be people like you and Laura, people trying to get away from themselves. And you know what will happen then? Laura will decide she's unhappy. She'll start to drink or have an affair or run away to a kibbutz in Israel. The next time you see her, middle-aged, she'll say that she wasted ten years of her life. She'll ask you why you let her get married."

"Why did I?"

"Because you want to do the same thing."

Leonard was dressed in his *shul*-going suit. Black without stripes or flecks. Shiny seat bottom. Pockets padded with yarmulkes and hankies just in case someone needed an extra. Soon we would be going to the bride's house, which was where the wedding would take place—under the supervision of a Unitarian minister who didn't seem to believe anything overly offensive.

"And you? I thought you were the one who was so hot for her."

After my grandfather's first heart attack Leonard had evolved from paying boarder to man of the house. Now he even had a job—as a history teacher at the Orthodox Synagogue Hebrew Day School. Leonard the responsible citizen was heavier, jowled and his hair was turning a dull grey at the temples. And then he smiled. With the memory of whatever had transpired between him and Laura, I thought at first, though what could have linked this prematurely middle-aged perpetual bachelor to the ripe and bursting Laura was hard to imagine. "Never," Leonard said. "I promised myself years ago to a young woman of strong character who takes care of her mother in Vancouver."

"And when did you meet her?"

"The summer I went to study in New York. She was on the Holocaust committee."

"How romantic."

Leonard gave me a look I hadn't seen since the day he explained his bloody towel. "You're a fool. Helen is the perfect woman for me in every way." He turned to his desk. In his student days it had been heaped with scholarly texts. But since the summer in New York, the philosophical treatises had been pushed aside, first to make room for bulky volumes on the Holocaust and then, more recently, for the history primers he needed for his job. From a drawer stuffed with letters he pulled a picture of a squarish-looking woman with a young smile and a surprising splash of freckles across her nose. "When her mother dies—"

My grandparents are waiting for me in their parlour. Like Leonard, like my grandfather, like Laura's own father waiting resignedly at home, I am dressed in a suit. An almost new suit, in fact, the one I bought a few months ago when I graduated from law school. Eventually I will wear the same suit, the same white shirt, the same gold cuff-links to my grandfather's funeral. The cuff-links were his gift to me on my Bar Mitzvah. On that occasion, a few weeks after my thirteenth birthday, I had needed new thick-heeled shoes to push me over the five-foot mark. One sideburn had started to grow, but not the other, and this unequal hormonal outburst had been accompanied by the very unmasculine swelling of one of my nipples. For some reason this swollen nipple ached when I sang, especially when my voice cracked in public, which it did dozens of times during the painful delivery of my *moftar*. Afterward my grandfather, his breath thick with rye, had delivered me a bristly kiss and pinched my arm so lovingly that I carried the bruise for a month.

Now they are sitting stiffly and waiting, elderly patients bracing themselves for the bad news. Stubborn but helpless. I beg them to at least come to the reception, for Laura's sake. This is the compromise everyone had been hoping for—avoiding the wedding but joining the celebration.

My grandfather is looking placidly about the room. His most recent attack seems to have taken away his electricity. He is perpetually serene, almost vacant. Even his shining and muscular skull seems to have lost its power; now the skin is greyer, listless. I try to imagine what might be going on inside. Weather?

My grandmother is twisting her hands. Everything considered, she has big diamonds. "We'll go," she announces. "The mother of those bastard children was born a Jew and so the children can still be rescued, God willing, after the father has left."

⤐ ⤐

"Assimilated," Leonard says. He pronounces the word slowly, savouring, then repeats it. First he stares at me—a Leonard who has emerged in the ten years since his own marriage, a Daddy Leonard with a rounded bulldog face, muscular cheeks, blue eyes that have spent so many long nights poring over his Holocaust documents that they have turned the skin surrounding them into dark crater holes—then he swings his head to Laura for confirmation. She nods, Laura whom I've known forever. Laura who is prettier than ever, but whose face seems more angular because she decided to replace her contact lenses with glasses when she started taking Hebrew lessons again.

I am sitting by the window. It's still open, a souvenir from the golden warmth of the October afternoon. Now it's evening and a cold breeze sucks at the back of my neck, but no one is thinking about the heartbreak of Indian summer.

Laura is kneeling on the floor. Her floor, the floor of the living-room of her and Peter Riley's North Toronto house. While she kneels she staples posters to sticks. NAZI JEW KILLER the posters all read.

"I can't believe how *assimilated* you are," Leonard says, pleased with himself now that he has found the word for me. "How *typical*. I won't say you're a coward. When it comes to being punched in the face, you're ready. When they call for volunteers to get baked, you'll probably run to the train. *Bravo*. But ask you to stick your neck out and stand up for yourself—all of a sudden you turn into a lawyer for some Jew-baiting creep."

"Listen to yourself," I say. "You're filled with hate. Do you think

Jews are the only people in the world who have ever been killed? Even during the Second World War there were three million Poles who died. Gypsies were sent to concentration camps too. Do you think the Holocaust gave the Jews some sort of moral credit card? Do we get to trade our dead for Palestinians? Is it one for one or do Chosen People get a special rate of exchange?"

"I have never killed anyone. But I am proud of my people when they defend themselves."

"Violence poisons," I say.

"God is violent," Leonard comes back.

Bang-clack, bang-clack, goes Laura's stapler. Now she's finished her signs, a dozen of them. In a few minutes it will be time to carry them out to the family-size station-wagon. While the "family"—twin four-year-old daughters—sleeps, Peter is to baby-sit. And while Peter baby-sits, Laura and Leonard are to drive the signs out to the airport, where Leonard has been tipped off that an East German cabinet minister someone claims was once a concentration camp guard is to arrive for inter-governmental trade discussions.

Laura and Leonard stand up.

"I'll go with you," I say.

Leonard's face breaks open. "I knew you would." He moves forward, hugs me. All those years living above my grandparents and now he smells like they used to—the same food, the same soap, the same sickly sweet lemon furniture polish. I can't help smiling, thinking about Leonard's youth as I knew it; tortured nasal passages, a white towel soaked with what he claimed was menstrual blood.

We stand around for a moment while Leonard phones home. At the other end, apparently saying little, is his woman of perfect character, the devoted Helen who had borne him four children and seems to make a virtue of obeying Leonard. They live in the main house now—my grandparents left it to them—and the room above the garage is consecrated to books and pamphlets detailing the attempted destruction of the Jews. Lately they've added slides, films, one of those roll-up white screens with little sprinkles on the surface. You know what I mean.

We all drag the posters out the front door to the waiting station-wagon. A few leaves crackle and drift in the cool breeze. Lights are on in all the houses around us. It's the moment when children have gone to bed, tables have been cleared, televisions have been turned on or attaché cases opened. We're on the lawn waiting for Peter to open the back hatch when a neighbour walking his dog stops to talk. The subject of conversation is, of course, the weather, the growing possibility of snow, the desire to spend one last weekend at the cottage. Only while the neighbour is agonizing over his big decision—whether or not to dig trenches so that he can keep the cottage water turned on until Christmas—does he notice the NAZI JEW KILLER signs. He says he is going to dig the trenches after all, if the weather is good, you have to think of the future, and besides he has always wanted his children to share his own dream, a white Christmas in the country.

✦ ✦

At the airport a small band of the faithful were waiting on the fifth floor of the parking garage. We got out of the car, distributed the signs. According to Leonard's information, the former concentration camp guard was due on an Air Canada flight from London. The plan was to meet him at the Passenger Arrivals gate.

There were ten of us. Too many, with our NAZI JEW KILLER signs, to fit into a single elevator. Laura went with the first group—Leonard too—so I was left with four strangers to descend in the second shift. One of those strangers became you, but only later. Sharing our elevator were two passengers with their suitcases. At first they paid us no attention—then, reading our signs, they shrank back.

By the time we had left the elevator and were walking towards the Arrivals gate, Leonard's group was surrounded by airport security officials and police. We raised our own signs and began to approach them. But before we could be noticed Leonard had gotten into a shouting match with one of the officials. "Never lose your temper needlessly," Leonard had lectured us in the Riley living-room. But, as Laura told me later, Leonard had already called his friends at the television station and promised a confrontation. When photographers with television cameras on their shoulders and assistants carrying portable lights began to run towards the struggling group, Leonard turned towards them. Soon, the official forgotten, he had positioned himself in front of one of the cameras to make a speech about a country that denied its own citizens free expression while protecting foreign "criminals against humanity." Then there was one of those incidents that is not supposed to happen, a relic from other countries, other eras: just as Leonard was working himself to a climax, a policeman smashed his truncheon into the back of his head, sending him falling face forward onto the floor.

Later that night I could watch myself on the television news as I entered the circle of light, knelt above Leonard and turned him over so I could see on his face, running with blood, a half-smile of triumph. You weren't in the picture. "Communist," shouted a voice from off-camera, but no one laughed.

➢ ➢

Driving to the liquor store Peter Riley and I are already drunk. Actually, we have been drinking all afternoon. It's the kind of day that deserves drinking, a Toronto December special that is cold but snowless, a gritty colourless day that merges pavement and sky. Peter's shirt is open. The tuft of red hair at the base of his neck has gone to flat silver; silver too is the colour of the red mop that used to peek out the holes and edges of his football helmet. To heighten the effect he's wearing a leather jacket left over from our university days; "U of T 66" is blazoned across the back in white. Looking at him, at myself slumped uncomfortably beneath the seat belt, I am reminded of the men Peter Riley and I used to go and watch during the summer in Ottawa, fat and powerful men with big paunches and thick arms who played evening softball at the high school diamond. Strong but graceless, able to swat the ball a mile, but stumbling around the bases in slow motion, the evening athletes had always seemed an awesome joke to us. "Battles of the dinosaurs," we called their games, delighting in their strength, the kaleidoscope of grunts and sweat and beer-fed curses.

At the liquor store parking lot we climb out of the car and stand, side by side, looking up at the clouds. We aren't two baseball players, I am thinking, among other things; we are two middle-aged lawyers, partners in a small firm. We are tense, overtired, mind-fatigued businessmen taking a day off to drink ourselves into oblivion because it's the only cure we know for the fact that while eating lunch we reminded each other that Leonard had died exactly six weeks before. Not that either of us had ever considered ourselves admirers of Leonard. Still.

"Among other things" includes the sound of the dirt falling onto Leonard's coffin, his family's uncontrolled grief, the talk at the funeral about another martyr to anti-Semitism. You were present, silent, beautiful, though your face was pinched with cold. We started walking towards each other at the same time and before we had ever told each other our names, I was asking you for your telephone number. Also at the funeral were the wide circle I see once every few years at such events. Aunts, uncles, cousins at various removes who have come not because they think of Leonard as a martyr or support his politics but because they remember Leonard as the faithful boarder who helped my grandparents through their old age, the daily *shul*-goer who, even when my grandfather was eighty years old, patiently shepherded him back and forth to the synagogue.

Some of the aunts, the uncles, the cousins at various removes are themselves getting old now. Short stocky men and women in their seventies, eighties, even the odd shrunken survivor who was born in the last century. Many of them, not all, were born in Russia and came out of the mythic peasant crucible to Canada where they gradually adorned themselves in suits, jewellery, houses, coats, stock-market investments until finally, at this group funeral portrait, they could be seen literally staggering under the weight of their success.

I find myself looking at Peter Riley's open shirt again. "For Christ's sake, do up the buttons, you'll get arrested."

"Undo yours," Peter Riley says. "In the name of the Wild Bill Fan Club, I formally dare you to undo your buttons."

"For Christ's sake," I say again, this time wondering why on this occasion it is Christ I invoke—Leonard must have been right. An occasion, to be precise, on which Peter Riley and I have already emptied one bottle of scotch, to say nothing of a few beer chasers, and now find ourselves at 4:33 P.M. in front of the Yonge Street liquor store in search of a refill. Near the liquor store is a shop where we can buy newspapers, mix, cigarettes, ice, candies. Even twenty years ago, when we were underage, we went there to buy Coke for our rum.

"I'll go to the liquor store," I say, "you get the other."

The scotch hits me while I am alone in the heated display room. "The last of the big drinkers I am not" is the sentence that comes into my mind—spoken by my father. But my father is dead, possibly along with whatever part of me is his son. "Never shit on our own doorstep," my father also told me. Translation: you can go to bed with non-Jewish girls but don't bring them home. I move down the counter and settle on a bottle of *Famous Grouse* scotch whisky. When I present my order the cashier makes a point of staring at my unbuttoned shirt. He has straight oiled hair into which each plastic tine of the comb has dug its permanent trench. My age or older. Skin boiled red by repeated infusions of the product he is selling. Looks a bit like Wild Bill near the end, I finally decide, but not enough for me to tell him about the fan club. I look into his eyes. Tough guy. He doesn't flinch. Meanwhile the store is empty, we could go on staring like this forever. "I'm having an identity crisis," I imagine saying to him, "I mean I was born Jewish but I don't feel comfortable carrying NAZI JEW KILLER signs."

≫ ≪

That night I dream about the hearse, a sleek powerful limousine. You aren't in the dream but the rest of us are. We're sitting behind the driver: Laura in the centre, Peter Riley and I surrounding. Behind us is the coffin and its presence somehow makes us even smaller than we are, reminding us that Death is the queen bee and we humans are just worker bees keeping Death supplied. It is nighttime, the time of night when time does not exist.

The hearse is carrying us down University Avenue. Wide, empty, stately, the street conducts us to the American Embassy where there is one other car, an ambulance with its rotating light winking "He's nuts" into the sky. The attendants, bored, are leaning against the ambulance and talking to the lone policeman.

Crouched on all fours, his weight on his knees and hands, Leonard is howling like a dog at the closed door of the American Embassy.

When he sees us he interrupts to wink, then turns back to his howling. After listening for a while I realize that his howl is in fact controlled, a merely moderate howl you can howl until dawn or at least until newspaper reporters arrive. I turn to relay this news to Laura and Peter Riley, but as I turn I see they have been transformed into the ambulance attendants, while I have somehow ended up on my knees, baying at the door. When Leonard tries to arrest me I leap at his throat, bringing him to the ground and tearing at him until I wake myself up with my screams.

≫ ≪

At the funeral the men took turns throwing shovelfuls of earth on the coffin. Into the silence small stones and earth rattled against the dull wood. I couldn't help listening, I couldn't help watching, I couldn't help crying at the thought of Leonard dead. At some point I discovered you were still standing beside me. Anonymous in your black coat, bare fingers gripping each other in the frozen air, thin black shoes with the toes pressed together. When the service was over we walked toward the parking lot, climbed into my car, drove to a hotel.

Now this hotel is my train. You are my benefactress, wealthy in the dark cream skin that you inhabit, the mysterious odours of your mysterious places, your eyes that becalm everything they see. Under your protection we ride our wild animals into the twilight. Until beneath our starry blankets we find a way to sleep—out on the range, in this room that hovers in an otherwise unmarked universe, that exists for no other purpose than the mutual exploration of mutual desire. *Assimilated,* as Leonard used to say; against our nonexistent will we have been assimilated into this compromised situation—two unrecorded strangers claiming each other with words sight touch smell until we raise spark enough to join our foreign bodies.

II

CENTRAL AND SOUTH AMERICA

IN THE NAME OF HIS NAME

Angelina Muñiz-Huberman

Abraham of Talamanca pondered long upon the word of God before making his decision. He had studied the signs and portents of the world. He had read and reread the Great Book and sought its revelation. Somewhere he would find the divine word. He felt a profound anxiety, though he did not know why; he knew only that the answer was there somewhere and he could not find it. Not that the world was mute, but that he could not understand its language. Not that God was silent, but that he could not hear Him. He continued to search and time continued to pass. To be possessed by a certainty that cannot be explained, a truth that cannot be proven. A sound that has no time. A color that cannot be painted. A word that cannot be deciphered. A thought that cannot be expressed. What then does he possess? How can one live by doubt, divination, foreshadowing?

⤞ ⤝

Abraham of Talamanca senses his ideas spinning round and round in the confined and infinite chaos of his mind. Arrows fly in his head and at times he supports his head in his hands, so heavy it seems to him. And then comes the pain. It begins with his eyes, which, as a source of enlightenment, embrace much and suffer much. He who does not see, does not weep. He who does not weep does not ache. A sword stroke at the center of his skull. Pain that makes a fiefdom of his arteries, a whip of his nerves and a torment of his muscles. Abraham, who loves light, flees into darkness; he searches for the word and flees into silence. Pain imprisons half of his head, while the other half struggles for lucidity. But the battle is never won; pain triumphs, and with his hands Abraham covers his eyes: no light, no word. Thus he loses days, which turn to nights, nights of the soul, which become darker and darker.

⇜ ⇝

But the answer does not appear. After thirty days of constant pain in which the unafflicted side of his head rested no more than the afflicted, he made his decision. He would go in search of the Sambatio, the distant river of the Promised Land, the river that flows six days a week and ceases on the Sabbath, or perhaps instead flows on the day of the Sabbath and ceases on the other six. The frightful roar of the rushing river, which carries rocks, not water, and sand, and which on the seventh day, shrouded in the clouds, keeps total silence. The river protects, for him who crosses it, the paradise inhabited by the Ten Lost Tribes. If he should manage to reach it, Abraham the Talamantine, and if he should manage to cross it.

⇜ ⇝

He would leave behind his books, his studies, his prayers, his meditation. He would try the paths and byways of pilgrims and wanderers, soldiers and vagabonds, merchants and adventurers. Tranquility and wisdom would be lost along the way. He would go unrecognized, and lose himself among the rest. To be lost and alone, and so to find himself more deeply. And with the cool of the dawns and the dust of distant places, he would forget that search for the unknowable. He would breathe deeply the air of mountain and sea. He would belong to nothing, to no one. The absolute freedom of one who has only himself. He would try for once to be God. Impossible to be integral; always dual; always the divine presence. I speak to myself and He answers me, spark of eternity. Can't one be alone? Absolute solitude? No, no, no. He always appears, God, the One without a name, the One sought after, desired, never found, He who requires perfection. So we wander, with Abraham of Talamanca, in search of the unsearchable.

Abraham prepares his departure, taking few possessions, fulfilled in himself. The pain has disappeared. Now he knows what he seeks; he seeks the name of God and he knows that it will appear when he crosses the final river at the end of the long journey. He seeks the meaning of the word, that which is beyond asking. He cannot accept the imperfection of the sign. The difficult connection between things and their name. The attempt to enclose in the space of a word the idea of perfection, of unity, of infinity, of creation, of plenitude, of supreme good. God is a conventional sign. How can one find its true essence? *Baruj ha-shem.* Blessed be His Name.

To approach immensity little by little. Slowly twining the links of the chain. More slowly still ascending the steps toward illumination. Losing ourselves in the partial and fragmented reflection of a thousand facing mirrors. And still aspiring to rise higher and higher. That longing to fly that is only achieved in dreams. To climb the mountain. To arrive at the summit of pure air and blue sky. Below, seas and rivers and lakes.

⟡ ⟡

Through open fields and enclosed gardens, along paths and byways, up and down, the road unwinds before Abraham the wanderer. And when the land runs out and sand borders the water, he furrows the water and creates light foam and soft waves, which, uncreating, erase his vain steps. The sun is ensconced in an immense blue cradle, and the four phases of the moon as well. When at length the sea loses its freedom and the high rocks force it to recede and close upon itself, the foot of the wanderer again falls upon the worn sand, so often tread, so often shifted and displaced.

⟡ ⟡

The Holy Land he touched not only with his feet but also with his hands, raising the fine dust to his lips, kissing it. Only then did he begin the pilgrimage. Eyes, feet, hands, lips, eager. Whether the ancient tomb, the golden rock, the stones of the desert. And then, northward, in search of the Sambatio. In search of the revealed word. But the river is a mirage. It appears and disappears. It recedes and overflows. It sings and is silent. It approaches and withdraws forever. For years, hope detains Abraham. Then certitude detains him. Meanwhile, the word has sounded, he knows that it is there, that it circulates within him: like the blood that flows through his body, it fills him to overflowing. It encourages him, nourishes him, gives him life. It has no form but that given to it by the vessel that contains it. It moves freely, flawlessly, smoothly. It has no equal.

⟡ ⟡

Abraham no longer speaks. He no longer writes. The Word has eliminated words. The Name is. The Revelation cannot be communicated. Silence fills everything, finding its proper form.

Abraham has stopped searching for the Sambatio. The name of His Name flows in his veins.

Translated from the Spanish by Lois Parkinson Zamora.

MAR ABRAMOWITZ

Victor Perera

Soon after my tenth birthday Rabbi Toledano warned Father that he had neglected my religious education, and said I was in danger of growing up a godless heathen. Alarmed, Father looked up from his ledgers and registers and saw that Rabbi Toledano was right. His firstborn and only son, three short years from Bar Mitzvah, could not read a word of Scripture. This was hardly my fault. Our lingual tender at home was a secular hash of native slang and Ladino Spanish: "*Manga tu okra, ishto; 'scapa ya tus desmodres*" (Eat your okra, animal; enough of your foolishness). Hebrew was for off-color jokes and adult secrets.

Father's alarm grew when he learned that his only male heir was a renegade who stole visits inside the cathedral, whose best friend was a mestizo goy of scant scholastic attainments—a male heir, furthermore, who gaped imbecilically when you quoted Talmud at him or asked him to recite the Commandments.

Father's first step was to teach me a Hebrew prayer that I was to repeat every night before retiring. The second was more drastic. After years of getting by as three-holiday Jews we began observing the Sabbath. At dusk on Friday evenings Father took me to the synagogue, where he tried to teach me my Alef-Bet. But his patience was short and his mind would drift continually to business matters. If I did not pronounce the strange syllables perfectly on my second or third attempt he would snap his prayer shawl in my face, or slam the book shut, which instantly slammed my mind shut and turned my tongue to lead. After a half-dozen lessons I succeeded in memorizing the blessing to the Torah, which ends *"Barakh atah Adonai, noten hatorah"* (Blessed art Thou, oh Lord, who giveth the Torah). On the following Sabbath Rabbi Toledano called me to the altar and I recited the blessing before and after, pretending to read a passage from the scroll, moving my lips to Rabbi Toledano's words like a ventriloquist's dummy.

Father's lessons lasted only through Yom Kippur, after which the Christmas rush set in and he had to be in the store late on Friday evenings and all day on Saturdays. He gave up trying to teach me himself and engaged for my religious instruction a Polish war refugee, Mar Israel Abramowitz.

Mar Abramowitz did not attend services in our temple. With a dozen or so other Ashkenazi refugees from Eastern Europe he worshipped in a tiny downtown loft that was said, by those who had never been inside it, to smell of rancid butter and pickled herring. Only on the High Holidays were the Poles and Litvaks allowed to defile our synagogue, and they had to sit toward the rear, next to the women.

Although I did not learn Hebrew for another two years, I was very early inculcated with the gospel of Sephardic caste. If all other Jews were Chosen, we were the Elect. We Sephardim were sole heirs to a remote but glorious Golden Age whose legacy we could batten on, without any effort on our part, until the Day of Judgment. At the end of the Golden Age we had nobly suffered the Inquisition, which resulted in our Expulsion from Spain and resettlement in a place called Diaspora. One day we would all reunite in the Promised Land, Eretz Israel, and begin an even more glorious second Golden Age, with God's blessing.

My earliest remembered "proof" of our legacy came at Yom Kippur. Toward the middle of the liturgy, before the blowing of the ram's horn that signaled God's presence among us, two men were summoned before the Ark: chinless, rail-thin Eliezer Cohen, a failure at business, and fat, famously henpecked Shlomo Kahan. Cohen and Kahan, whose names identified them as members of the priestly elite, first prayed in unison before the Ark. At a signal from Rabbi Toledano they draped their shawls over their homburgs and turned to the congregation, faceless. They were instantly transformed into hieratic mummers, impersonators of God's mystery, as they swayed from side to side with both arms raised, chanting His words in antiphonal responses.

Of course, it never occurred to me that Ashkenazim might have their own Cohens and Kahans to communicate God's blessing.

Mar Israel Abramowitz had been a successful lawyer in Warsaw before the Nazis came. Father said he had spent years in a concentration camp, but Mar Abramowitz did not talk of this and I never thought to ask him. I was not at all certain what a concentration camp was and had no special curiosity to find out. I know only that it was a place where Jews suffered.

Suffering appeared to be Mar Abramowitz's chief occupation. He was a thick-set man in his middle fifties, with tufts of gray hair at either side of a squarish bald head. His bifocal glasses magnified a hollow look of grief in his eyes. His breath stank most of the time; nearly all his remaining teeth were black stumps. He had an ingrown right thumbnail, which he continually stroked. It was several sessions before I understood that the sighs and moans punctuating our lessons had no connection with me.

Mar Abramowitz managed to teach me enough Alef-Bet so I could read a little Hebrew, but his suffering got the better of him before we could start on comprehension. I soon learned to take advantage of his infirmity. If his breath smelled especially rank and he stroked his nail more than usual, I knew I could get out of doing the drills and coax him into telling Bible stories instead. I liked these exotic tales, which Mar Abramowitz delivered with a heavy Slavic accent and his usual grieved expression. As he got into them, however, his eyes would soften and he would grow almost eloquent, despite his poor Spanish. The Old Testament stories seemed to ease his suffering as much as they enhanced my tonic sense of truancy from serious study.

In my youthful wisdom I knew they were mostly fables. I lent no more real credence to a talking snake, the burning bush, the parting of the Red Sea than I gave the prince who turned into a frog, or to Billy Batson's instant metamorphosis into Captain Marvel with the magical word Shazam. The fighting and killing, on the other hand, I understood perfectly: David and Goliath, Holofernes and Judith, the Canaanites and the Babylonians, these made eminent sense. The battle between the forces of good and the forces of evil, as I realized, as Tarzan and Kit Carson and Buck Rogers and President Roosevelt realized, was unending—and part of man's natural estate.

There was a custom in our temple of auctioning off ritual honors on the High Holidays. Rabbi Toledano or his sexton would pace up and down the aisles, chanting the bids aloud in Hebrew (while keeping the score on the fringes of his shawl) so they sounded to my ears indistinguishable from the liturgy: "I have thirty-five to open the Ark from Isaac Sultan in praise of the Lord. . . . Forty . . . forty-five from Lázaro Sabbaj in praise of the Lord. Shmuel Benchoam bids fifty quetzalim to open the Ark in praise of the Lord, blessed be His Name. . . ."

On Simḥat Torah, in reward for the scant Hebrew phrases Mar Abramowitz had dinned into my head, Father bought me the bearing of the Scroll from the Ark to the Bimah. I crept along the aisle with the red velvet Torah—junior size—hugged to my chest as worshipers crowded around to kiss it. The Scroll was weighted down with a chased shield, chains, silver horns, and other ornaments, each separately bid for by the congregation. My fear of dropping the Torah and profaning Holy Scripture caused my feet to throb inside the corrective boots I wore for fallen arches.

My performance of this ceremonial honor evidently assuaged Father's conscience, for he never bought me another.

One week Mar Abramowitz did not show up for our lesson because, Mother said, he wasn't feeling well. (She used the Ladino *hazino* to dignify his unwellness.) But I guessed he was only suffering. I pictured him crouched in a corner of his room, breathing his foul breath, stroking his ingrown thumbnail, the grief-stricken eyes sunk deeper than ever in their sockets. He failed to come the following week and the week after that. When he finally appeared, I hardly recognized him. He had shrunk from a corpulent middle-aged man to a wizened gnome. The sag of his shoulders inside the loose-fitting jacket gave him the derelict look of a tramp. Only his sunken black eyes had life. The bifocals exaggerated what I recognized even then as the haunted, pinpoint gleam of madness.

Mar Abramowitz had come to excuse himself that he could no longer keep up my lessons because of his illness. His apology was rambling and disconnected and went on long after Mother assured him that she quite understood, and he was forgiven. Then, to my intense shame, Mar Abramowitz began to moan and cry aloud, right in our hallway, so that the sounds reverberated throughout the house. Mother fetched her handbag and placed in Mar Abramowitz's bony hand a folded bill. Brushing his eyes, he executed a courtly bow, pocketed the bill, and kissed Mother's hand before he shuffled out the door.

Three years later, on returning from the States, we learned that Mar Abramowitz had hanged himself.

FROM "OSORNO"

Marjorie Agosín

THE SOUTH

Night and its presence of rain like a watchman of sounds, like a care-taker of the rhythm of the trees. It is through the rain and the thickness of the fog that I return to the south as if to a distant time of sweet love. I return to Osorno as if finally rediscovering that space where I learned about processions between the mist and about the sound of the rocks and mud between our hands.

I approach the moss and stumble upon small rivulets drenched by the frost, and there is the door with its enormous copper and bronze padlocks that brought us to discover a place beyond the light and there is the window that made us feel the perverse innocence of children who know how to look and be seen.

The house alone, uninhabited with that smell of time and moistened history. The furniture like deflowered fans and between the cracks, be-hind the thresholds I see the faces of my mother and my dead brother.

1993

Southern Chile stretches out before my gaze like an intermittent and sacred landscape. The long expanses of earth sometimes acquire ingenuous and dreamy forms for the navigator. My country is a blue strip of land resembling the fish of the earth. I tremble going through it conserving that subtle poverty of the humble folk who still remain within their brightly painted homes that emit gray vapors of coal and dignified misery.

I travel through southern Chile at daybreak looking at the reddish and golden dawn like a sunflower where women with birdlike voices forever appear in order to sell fresh bread, beef jerky, and whole milk, a milk that is fertile and foreign to the pain of barefooted children who perpetually plod along trying to learn to read.

In the late afternoon, I go to Plaza Yungay where I used to swing with my winged dresses. The yard of my house is now a corner grocery store but I still see it resplendent with chickens and herbs. How much I have won and lost in my voyages! However, above all else I maintain my language and the capacity to be astounded before horror. The garden of my house is like the heart of a savage girl.

I walk toward the center of the city and there before me is the German Club where they would let my father, the Jew, enter only after lunch hour. The ritual repeats itself. I appear suspicious to them even though I am blonde. My eyes are too defiant, I smell like the poverty along the public roads and they don't permit me to enter.

This time I walk as if nothing could astonish me and the feeling of being violated from everywhere is so immensely familiar to me. I walk through Osorno and see the same men of the war years, this time more robust and doleful, darkened by their bureaucratic suits. They savor their German language and treat the Indians of the south with the same insolent arrogance of before. Osorno continues to be invaded by generations of Germans and Nazis who have not yet learned to appreciate the tolerance of the Chilean people. Besides their sausages and exquisitely well maintained homes, the legacy of the Germans in Chile is almost null and void.

I walk along the sidewalks of this provincial city. It is summer in the southern hemisphere and the smell of peaches, fruit, and wild flowers stretches out like an inexhaustible tablecloth of human life. The people in the street: the vendor of herbs, the knife sharpener, and the organ grinder with the little parrot who supposedly assures us of good fortune, still remain witnesses of a life whose past is an extended and tranquil time.

It is Sunday and the sky seems to fill up with balloons. I am in love with the light, the air and life. This time no one persecutes us and the war years are like a disfigured silence. In the distance, in a strategic place in the city, I pass by the German school building where thirteen-year-old children like me would file by a huge and perfidious swastika. Today the firefighters of the German Club repeat the same ritual.

When night falls and it seems as if southern Chile were filling up with the shadows of birds, I walk through the streets of my childhood again and think that I still have a country to which I can return and call my own.

It was here that I learned to look at the strips of crimson sky and here where my father would go to the train station looking for those made destitute by the war, bringing them white shirts and bright bouquets of copihue blossoms, the national flower of Chile that is found amid the mountains and snowcapped peaks.

Dazzled and lost as if blindfolded, I find the roads that will take me to my house, my garden and orchard. I stop before the beautiful antique shop because I am reminded of the porcelain dolls that my Grandmother Helena hid within her trunks. I enter the store as if treading through a narrow pass and I am confronted with immense portraits of Adolf Hitler. The man says that they are very popular, that the Germans in Osorno still are accustomed to hanging them on their walls. He suggests that I look at them up close, that they are authentic. He talks to me about Adolf Hitler with an enthusiasm and spectacular passion that frighten me. My blue eyes look at him anxiously with that millenary fear of the Jews. I imagine that my head is a blazing forest. I imagine myself bald and boneless without eyes. I imagine thousands of pitch-black jail cells and a universe of deep walls without an exit.

Osorno of 1993, how little you have changed. Antique dealers continue carrying their most prized possessions in their shops: portraits of Adolf Hitler, and I, terrified, go out to look at the birds of Chile, the storks and the thrushes, and I see my father waiting for the last train. . . .

February 1993

Raquel's indistinguishable house is located a short distance from the municipal square. I come to visit her by surprise, even though she intuitively waits for me with our favorite welcoming food: empanadas and a dark thick red wine. Raquel embraces me and leaves her crutches leaning against the family piano. Then I remember when they shouted at us: "There go the cripple and the Jew." I remember the voices of the children in the German school who wanted to hit her for being lame and for having a Jewish girlfriend. I also evoke the memory of my Aunt Luisa who was her best friend and chose her as her lady-in-waiting for the impoverished beauty contest of the province. The unusual spectacle of a cripple carrying a Jewish girl's scepter of orchids was as memorable as that clamor of broken glass in the funeral parlor the following day.

And here we are as if time had stopped on the peripheral beauty of a coffin. Her living room is spacious and silent. She, herself, reminds me that it was here where we would play inside the coffins arranged according to their social class. The coffin lined in red satin occupied a tier of extreme importance in the living room of the funeral parlor and the one adorned in poplin, a lesser spot. The ones without a lining were for the peasants and political prisoners. . . . Who said that death makes us equal?

Raquel, with her slow-gaited movements, tells me that this Osorno is just like the one that existed in 1938, that there are still large Nazi enclaves, that in many sectors of the city only German is spoken, and that Germans still don't allow marriages of impure blood with Chileans. There are still shrines for Hitler and I tell her about that young German fellow in the antique shop across from the square who offered me a picture of the Führer at a good price.

Osorno appears before my gaze like a great nocturnal mirror. I advance along its paths and tremble before the familiarity of that which no longer is. I step into the mist and from afar I perceive volcanoes, fog, and clouds of smoke. I dream about Osorno as if it were changeless. I dream about the thresholds and my mother's hands celebrating the harvest with clusters of golden wheat.

I have dreamt about absences and about trains void of fear. Only a whistle in the terrifying night makes me relinquish my skin and memory. The pain increases as in births, tearing and mute. In the distance a bandurria bird sends me a signal with its multicolored music.

Last night the stars formed an enormous branch of blue lights and behind the windows, the first view of my town appeared looking at me as on that day in which I went to the school of the Indian children and they kissed my hair.

I think about my country and it hurts me. It is a borrowed region of vast plateaus, knolls, and snowcapped peaks. Nevertheless, I sleep and tremble within it, unable to avoid it. I love it and shiver in its kiwi and peach fragrances. I am a knoll of rubble before its majesty, round like a womb foretelling good luck. From so much pain and happiness, I immerse myself in my country and become again that little girl lost on the southern frontier. My return journey is also like a train advancing in the darkness.

Sitting opposite aged memory, I approach and care for it; it is a passing and intermittent music, a circle of red flames like the tousled hair of women in love. One day I began to listen to my mother and she told me about her years in southern Chile before and after the Second World War. Bewildered, she told me to tell her sacred and dark, painful and stirring story.

For a long time I approached her words, like warm blankets and dangerous roads. Sometimes their silence made me stop before the proximity of horror.

A Cross and a Star relates the personal experiences of my mother. I gathered them together, made them speak, arranged the episodes, and transformed myself into a thirteen-year-old girl from a province in southern Chile surrounded by Nazis, Christians, and native inhabitants from the region. This is the story of foreigners and exiles and it doesn't matter if I forgot your name because you are also in the dark dwellings of memory, crossing the dangerous thresholds of all bygone times.

Translated from the Spanish by Celeste Kostopulos-Cooperman.

THE LAST EMIGRANT

Nora Glickman

Old Leiserman is dead, the emigrant, Baruch Leiserman. The news shook loose memories of my hometown in the province of La Pampa. I remembered how much closer he was than my grandfather, or any uncle for that matter.

As the days grew longer, Mama would take me along on visits to see him and his wife, Sara. Around five, Dad might be engaging a customer in some interminable discussion about renewing an insurance policy and Mama would take advantage of the opportunity to escape from the office and would go to look for me at home.

It was just a few blocks away; we walked. Lanuse's bar exhaled its beery and smoky breath that followed us as far as the corner. The Viners and the Shames would set up their wicker chairs next to the entrances of their respective stores to be able to kibitz with each other. The women seemed older than the men; they rocked slowly and chatted in Yiddish mixed with Spanish. Then we would pass Litner's bakery where a furry, dirty dog stretched out and blocked the sidewalk, undoubtedly paralyzed by the languid, penetrating aroma of freshly baked loaves. Or perhaps by age. Anyway, Mama would buy a few pastries there and Mrs. Litner would keep her posted on the rheumatism that was swelling her knees as well as on her mother who lay dying in the room in back. Mama always listened quietly: things seemed to worsen at a comfortable rate, and there would be months and months to enjoy the same pastries and the same conversation.

Sara Leiserman would treat us to a tureen full of toasted sunflower seeds, with *leykach,* honey cake, and we took our tea *prekuske* style, Russian tea, biting lumps of sugar as we drank. I liked to dip the sugar a little bit at a time and watch it turn brown in the hot tea. Then Sara would take a nap. She was always tired, and Mama stayed to chat with Baruch. I went to the storehouse in back, cradling corn in my dress and feeding it to the chickens around the patio. Sometimes I threw a handful as hard as I could just to see them run and cackle a little. Other times I chased them and plucked their feathers. Baruch's old roan always stood by the water trough; he scratched his neck against its rusty edge, though he never cut himself. I would fill a bag full of grass for him and hang it on his neck to see him through the night.

Mama would still be talking when I went back in the house. I listened to them while going through Sara's shoe-box full of yellowing photographs. Baruch talked about the Russian Revolution, the ear infection he inflicted on himself to avoid the draft—it still acted up now and then—and the labor unrest in Buenos Aires. Mama commented on the articles from the Yiddish newspaper. She was big on Israel, Zionism, and the kibbutzim, although Baruch didn't see any advantage in a Jewish homeland. "It's better for them to hate us separately; a Jewish state surrounded by Arab enemies won't last very long as a democracy." Just to needle him, Mama would make me sing *"Wir furn kayn Eretz"** and then sing along even louder than me. Then it was *"Zog mir shvester Leybn, vos ich vel dir freign"*† where Leybn declares her intentions to grow oranges in Israel and forget about the Diaspora. Mama put everything into those songs; she seemed to feel herself nearer to Israel, free of the burden of the *goles,* the Diaspora.

Baruch made fun of her, grimacing with an impatient *Achhh,* waving away the songs with his thick and hairy hand. Then all of a sudden, he would grab me around the waist and say, *"Danushka mayns, zing mir 'unter'n vigele,' "‡* which was his favorite song. I complied willingly and sang that and other songs while they hummed along in time. Baruch had a certain way of closing his eyes and arching his thick, bushy

---

Wir furn kayn Eretz: We are traveling to the land of Israel.
†*Zog mir shvester Leybn, vos ich vel dir freign:* Tell me, Sister Life, what I want to ask you.
‡*Danushka mayns, zing mir 'unter'n vigele':* My Danushka, sing 'Under the Cradle' to me.

eyebrows, creating a magic, irresistibly appealing space in front of his forehead. When he opened his eyes again, it was as if he had woken up with a shudder. I don't know if it was pleasant or not, because he usually preempted discussion with some mundane observation.

It was during these visits that Mom did Baruch's bookkeeping, and there was always an argument. She would marshal two or three figures—and show how he could replace the carriage with a used pickup, how if the outer hall were blocked off—the one leading to the grapevines—the house wouldn't get so cold during the winter, how it was better to have one laborer year-round rather than employ three just for the harvest. . . . Baruch would raise his hands to his cheeks, pressing them hard, telling Mama how the plague of grasshoppers had ruined everything two years before, and how when the Perels' fields went up in smoke just before the harvest, his was saved only because the wind changed direction; how another fire like that, or perhaps hail, like in '51, could leave him penniless, and then what would become of him? You always needed to keep something in reserve.

Mama would get exasperated. Her eyes flashed. "You're just an old tightwad and you'll never invest in anything, you old hardhead, you'll never get anywhere that way." Then, a few minutes of truce during which nothing could be heard except the crackling of the fire. Sunflower-seed husks piled up on the checkered tablecloth, or fell to the floor.

❧ ❧

Back in the office, Dad would be grouchy, doing sums, tearing up sheets of paper and tossing them into the wastebasket—somehow he never missed, although he never seemed to try very hard. "You left Blanca alone at the cash register and she made some mistakes again . . . you left without posting the balance." "It's not as if I'm your employee," Mama replied. "Blanca gets paid to be a cashier, not me." Dad kept on crumpling paper into little balls and looking over his notes. There was no more discussion, though she stayed and worked until the evening. How could she just drop everything to go and see that *shlimazl*, that poor, lazy Baruch? What did she see in him? But she stood up for him—"He's got *seykl*. He thinks. He reads more than all of you put together, he should never have stayed in this crummy little town, this Bernasconi, Bernashmoni." And then, *shoyn*, that's enough! and the matter was closed.

But Dad did feel sorry for Sara. She was stuck with Baruch. She survived the pogrom in Russia, she lived through it all in Vilna by a miracle, though now, in Argentina, her luck had run out. She used to tell how she was the only one to hide in time when the Cossacks broke into her uncle's house; she saw everything and forgot nothing. The hooligans broke up the furniture with their sabers, tore up the comforters and the pillows and filled the room with feathers. They gutted Sara's uncle, a large man, and filled him with the feathers. Her aunt wailed and they tore her eyes out before killing her. I can't remember exactly what they did with the girls. Sara was an orphan and lived with them. After the pogrom my *zeyde* brought her to Argentina, passing her off as his daughter. Sara was quiet and withdrawn. She seemed to rub her complaints off her veined hands by rubbing them into her apron. According to Dad, Baruch never even looked at her before taking her to wife—and probably never looked at her after, either. His first wife had died while giving birth to her fourth child and the others were still small. It was clear that he couldn't handle them by himself, and there was Sara, available, submissive. Mama says that people are just the way they are, and if Sara wanted to be a martyr, she got what she wanted.

We had moved several years before to Bahía. Every summer we passed through Bernasconi, but just because it was on the way to the farm. Sometimes we dropped in to say hello to the Leisermans, but it just wasn't the same anymore. Dad came along with us, and the visits were always cut short so we could see as many friends and relatives—and offend as few—as possible.

☆ ☆

Baruch's accident happened at his farm, a short distance from the town. He apparently saw the tornado coming; nobody better than he could read the pinkish streaks in the clouds—like an old-time gaucho he understood the menace implicit in the motionless air, suspended like in a photograph. So Baruch must have anticipated the inexorable advance of the dark column that swallowed everything in its path and he, Baruch, the headstrong emigrant, had to thwart it, defeat it, just long enough to get his four panic-stricken cows into the barn; he went out alone to close the gates and protect his cattle.

The farmhand just happened to be in town that day. When he returned the following morning, he found Baruch among the wreckage, a hundred yards from the barn, in the middle of a huge puddle left by the storm. Baruch rolled into the mud, dragging with him all the plants he ever seeded during his life there. What would he have been thinking? About the cows that wouldn't make it? Whether he had enough supplies in reserve? The unfinished business? No: he probably just closed his eyes, just like when he liked a song, and then knitted his brow and let himself go, carried away in his magic poncho.

Translated from the Spanish by John Benson.

A SMALL FARM IN THE INTERIOR, QUATRO IRMÁOS DISTRICT, RIO GRANDE DO SUL SEPTEMBER 24, 1935– SEPTEMBER 23, 1947

Moacyr Scliar

One's first memories, naturally, cannot be described in conventional words. They are visceral, archaic. Larvae in the heart of the fruit, worms wriggling in the mud. Remote sensations, vague pains. Confused visions: a stormy sky above a tempestuous sea; from between dark clouds, a winged horse majestically descending. It advances quickly over ocean and continent, leaving behind beaches and cities, forests and mountains. Little by little its speed diminishes, and now it glides, describing large circles, its mane rippling in the wind.

Below, bathed in the moonlight, is a rustic wooden house, isolated and still. From its windows a weak yellow light shines out into the mist. A short distance away is the stable. Farther on lies a small patch of woods, and beyond them the wide fields. Among the thickets of trees, small animals fly, run, leap, and crawl, hiding themselves, chasing and devouring each other. Chirps, squeaks, trills.

A woman's sharp scream echoes through the valley. Everything grows hushed, motion arrested. The winged horse glides through the air, its wings outstretched. Another scream, and another. A series of screams— and then silence again. The winged horse circles the house again and disappears without a sound into the clouds.

❧ ❧

It's my mother who is screaming; she is having a baby. Her two daughters and an old midwife from the vicinity attend her. She has been in labor for hours, but the baby shows no signs of coming. Her strength is drained; she is almost fainting. I can't stand it anymore, she murmurs. The midwife and the girls exchange anxious glances. Should they call the doctor? But the doctor lives forty kilometers away—is there time?

In the neighboring room are my father and brother. My father paces back and forth as my brother, sitting on the bed, stares at the wall before him. The screams come more and more frequently, one after another, and between them are curses in Yiddish that make my father shudder: "That criminal! He took us from our home and brought us to this hell, to this place at the ends of the earth! I'm dying, and it's his fault, the murderer! Oh, my God, I'm lost, help me!" The midwife tries to calm her; everything's all right, Dona Rosa, don't panic. But her voice betrays her anxiety: by the light of the lantern the midwife looks in alarm at the tensed, enormous belly. What was inside it?

My father sits down, burying his head in his hands. His wife is right, he is to blame for what is happening. All the Jewish colonizers of the region, who had come from Russia along with him, had already gone to the cities—Santa Maria, Passo Fundo, Erechim, or Pôrto Alegre. The revolution of 1923 had expelled the last remnants of the colonization.

My father insisted on staying. Why, Leon? my mother asks, Why this stubbornness? Because Baron Hirsch placed his trust in us, he answers. The baron didn't bring us here from Europe for nothing. He wants us to stay here, working the land, planting and harvesting, showing the goyim that Jews are just like everybody else.

⪻ ⪻

A good man, the baron. In 1906 Russia had been defeated in the war against Japan, and the poor Jews—tailors, carpenters, small businessmen—lived in miserable hovels in the small villages, terrorized by the threat of the pogroms.

(A pogrom: drunken Cossacks would invade the village, charging on their crazed horses against children and old people, flailing their sabers in all directions. They would kill the citizenry, loot and burn the village, and then disappear, leaving the echoes of screams and neighing behind them in the tormented night.)

In his mansion in Paris, Baron Hirsch would awaken in the middle of the night in great alarm, hearing the sound of hoofbeats. His sleepy wife would say, it's nothing, Hirsch, go back to sleep, it was just a nightmare. But sleep would not come for the baron. The vision of black horses trampling lifeless bodies would not leave him. Two million pounds, he murmured to himself. With two million pounds I could solve the problem.

He saw the Russian Jews living happily in faraway regions in South America; he saw cultivated fields, modest but comfortable homes, agricultural schools. He saw children playing among the trees. He saw the iron tracks of the railroad company (in which he owned a great deal of stock) advancing into the virgin forest.

≫ ≪

The baron was very good to us, my father repeats constantly. A rich man like him wouldn't have needed to worry himself about poor people. But no, he didn't forget his fellow Jews. Now we have to work very hard so as not to disappoint such a charitable, saintly man.

My parents do work very hard. It is a thankless existence: clearing the land, planting crops, treating the livestock for parasites, carrying water from the well, cooking. They live in fear of everything: drought, flood, frost, hail, insect plagues. Everything is difficult, they have no money, and they live isolated from other people. Their nearest neighbors live five kilometers away.

But my children will have a better life, my father consoles himself. They'll study, become well educated. And one day they'll thank me for the sacrifices I made. For them and for Baron Hirsch.

The screams cease. There is a moment of silence—my father raises his head—and then the crying of a newborn baby. His face lights up. "It's a boy! I'm sure it's a boy! From the way it cries, it has to be!"

Another scream, this time a savage cry of horror. My father jumps up, standing immobile for a second in confusion. Then he runs to the next room.

≫ ≪

The midwife meets him in the doorway, her face splattered with blood, her eyes popping out: "Oh, Mr. Leon, I don't know what happened, I've never seen anything like it, it isn't my fault! I guarantee you that I did everything just as it should be done!"

My father looks around, not understanding. The daughters are huddled together in a corner, sobbing in fear. My mother lies on the bed in a stupor. What's happening here? yells my father, and then he sees me.

I am lying on the table. A robust, pink baby, crying and moving its little hands—a normal child from the waist up. From the waist down: the hair of a horse. The feet of a horse—hooves. A horse's tail, still soaked with amniotic fluid. From the waist down, I am a horse. I am—and my father doesn't even know the word exists—a *centaur*. A centaur.

My father approaches the table.

My father, the colonist Leon Tartakovsky. A rough, hard man who has seen many things in his lifetime, horrible things. Once a peasant man got stabbed in an argument and my father stuffed his entrails back inside him. Another time he found a scorpion in his boot and killed it with his great fist. Yet another time he put his hand into a cow's uterus to deliver a calf that was wedged crosswise. But what he sees now is by far the worst. He shrinks back, leaning against the wall for support. He bites his fist; no, he must not scream. His scream would break all the windows of the house, would carry across the fields, would reach the slopes of the Serra do Mar, the ocean, the very gates of heaven.

He can't scream, but he can sob. Sobs wrack his large body. Poor man. Poor family.

🐎 🐎

Once the initial shock is past, the midwife assumes control of the situation. She cuts the umbilical cord and wraps me in a towel—the biggest one in the house—and puts me in the cradle. Here she encounters the first difficulty: I am very large. My feet—that is, my hooves—hang out. The midwife finds a crate, lines it with blankets (Did you think of straw, midwife? Confess, did straw cross your mind?) and settles me there. In the days that follow the brave woman takes care of the house and the family: she cleans, washes, and cooks, taking food to each person in turn. She insists that they eat and keep their strength up. They have suffered a severe shock, these poor Jews, and they need to recuperate from it.

Most important, she takes care of me, the centaur. She gives me my bottle, because my mother only cries and can't stand to look at me, much less nurse me. She gives me baths and keeps me clean—not an easy job, for my feces are those of an herbaceous creature and give off a fetid odor. Then the midwife understands that I need green stuff, and mixes finely chopped lettuce leaves in with the milk.

(Many a time, she is to confess in later years, she ponders suffocating me to death with a pillow. It would end the family's torment. Nor would it be the first time. She had once strangled a one-eyed child born without arms or legs, squeezing the delicate neck until the single eye became glazed in death.)

He really isn't bad looking, she sighs, as she places me in the crate to sleep. His features are agreeable, and he has pretty brown hair and eyes. But from the waist down . . . awful! She has heard of monsters, creatures half chicken, half rat; or half pig, half cow; or half bird, half snake; lambs with five legs; werewolves; she knows all these creatures exist, but never dreamed she would someday be taking care of one. Go to sleep, little one, she murmurs. In spite of everything, she likes me, this woman embittered by the deaths of her own four children.

My sisters cry all the time. My brother, who always was quiet and strange, becomes quieter and stranger. As for my father, he has work to do, so he works. He clears land, mows hay. Chopping down trees with his ax, attacking the ground with his hoe, he gradually rediscovers his self-control. Already he is able to think without falling into the depths of despair. Painfully, he seeks explanations, formulates hypotheses.

He is a man of few insights. Though descended from a family of rabbis and learned men, he himself is very limited. Even back in the Russian village, he had gone to work in the fields because of his lamentable mistakes in interpreting the Talmud. God didn't give me a very good head, he always says. Still, he trusts his instinctual good sense; he knows how to interpret his own reactions, like the hair on his arms standing up, the pounding of his heart, or the heat of his face. All these things are communications. Sometimes he has the impression that God speaks to him from inside, from a point situated between his navel and the top of his stomach. He is searching for a certainty of this kind. He wants the truth, no matter how sad it may be.

Why has this happened to him? Why?

Why was he chosen for this, and not a Russian Cossack? Why he and not a peasant, or another farmer of the region? What crime had he committed? What had he done wrong that God must punish him in this way? No matter how he cross-examines himself, he cannot manage to pinpoint any sins. Not serious ones, at any rate. Smaller faults, perhaps. He once milked a cow on the Sabbath, the sacred day of rest, but the cow's udder was full; he couldn't leave her lowing in pain. And he didn't even use the milk, he threw it away. Sins? No.

As he convinces himself of his innocence, a doubt emerges: Is the centaur really his child?

(Centaur. I am to teach him this word someday. At this point he is not much versed in mythology.)

But immediately he is stung with remorse. How can he think such a thing? Rosa is absolutely faithful to him. And even if she weren't, what sort of father could sire such an exotic creature? There are strange people in the region; grim, surly half-breeds, bandits, even Indians. However, he has never seen anyone with horses' hooves.

There are lots of horses in the area, even wild horses, skittish beasts whose whinnying he sometimes hears in the distance. But—a horse! There are perverted women, capable of making love with all sorts of creatures, he knows. Even with a horse—but his Rosa isn't one of these. She is a good, simple woman, who lives only for her husband and children. A tireless worker, an excellent housekeeper. And faithful, very faithful. A little irritable, a bit sharp at times, but kindhearted, wise. And true to him.

Poor woman. Now she lies motionless on the bed, wide eyed and apathetic. The midwife and her daughters offer her soup, rich broths; she shows no reaction, says nothing, and does not accept the food. They try to force her mouth open with a spoon, but she refuses to open it, keeping her teeth stubbornly clenched shut. Nevertheless, a few drops of liquid, a few particles of egg, a few chicken fibers enter her mouth, and she involuntarily swallows them. No doubt this is what keeps her alive.

Alive, but quiet. Mute. Her silence is an accusation to her husband: It's your fault, Leon. You brought me to this place at the ends of the earth, this place where there are no people, only animals. My son was born this way because I looked at so many horses. (She could supply other examples: women who laughed at monkeys and whose children were born hairy; women who looked at cats—their babies mewed for months.) Or perhaps she would cast doubts on his family history: you have lots of disease and deformity among your relatives: your uncle who was born with a harelip, your cousin who has six fingers on each hand, your diabetic sister. In short, it's your fault! she might scream. But she doesn't. She hasn't the strength.

Besides, he is her husband. She has never been attracted to any other man, nor indeed even thought of another. Her father said to her: You will marry Tartakovsky's son, he's a good boy. And thus her destiny had been decided. Who was she to argue? As of matter of fact, the choice of young Leon didn't displease her. He was one of the handsomest boys in the village, strong and cheerful. She was lucky.

They were married. At first it wasn't so good . . . sex, that is. He was rough and clumsy; he hurt her. But soon she grew accustomed to him, and actually enjoyed lovemaking. Everything went well—until they were awakened one night by the trampling of horses' hooves and the savage yells of the Cossacks. They ran and hid in the forest near the river and remained there, trembling with fear and cold, watching the light cast by the burning village. The next morning they went back to find the main street full of mutilated bodies, and the houses in smoking ruin. Let's get out of here, said Leon gravely. I want nothing more to do with this accursed place.

Rosa didn't want to leave Russia. Pogroms or no pogroms, she liked the village. It was where she belonged. But Leon's mind was made up. When the emissaries sent by Baron Hirsch arrived, he was the first to volunteer for the Jewish colony in South America. South America! The terrified Rosa imagined naked savages, tigers, gigantic snakes. She would take the Cossacks anytime! But her husband would not discuss it. Pack the bags, he ordered. Pregnant and panting for breath from her exertions, she obeyed. They embarked from Odessa on a cargo ship.

(Many years later she would still remember that voyage with horror: the cold, and afterward the suffocating heat, the nausea and the odor of vomit and sweat, the decks crowded with hundreds of Jews, the men in berets, the women with scarves tied over their hair, the children who never stopped crying.)

My mother arrived in Pôrto Alegre sick and feverish. But her odyssey was not yet finished. They had to travel to the interior, first by train, then in horse-drawn wagons over a trail cut through dense forests, to get to the colony. A representative of the baron was awaiting them. Each family received a section of land—my father's was the most distant—a house, tools, and livestock.

My father awoke singing every day. He was very happy. My mother wasn't. She found life in the colony worse—a thousand times worse— than in the Russian village. Days of backbreaking work, nights inhabited by mysterious sounds: chirps, squeaks, rustlings. Above all, the invisible presence of the Indians watching the house. My father made fun of her. What Indians, woman! There aren't any Indians anywhere near here! She would grow quiet. But at night, when they sat beside the stove drinking tea, she would see the Indians' eyes in the burning coals. In her nightmares the Indians would break into the house, mounted on black horses like those of the Cossacks. She would wake up screaming, and my father would have to calm her.

Still, little by little she became more accustomed to the place. The birth of her children, in spite of the difficult deliveries, was a consolation. And the thought that her children were being brought up in a new country, with a real future, actually was a source of enthusiasm to her. She began to feel quite happy. But Leon was never satisfied—three children weren't enough for him. He had to insist on a fourth. He wanted another son. She resisted the idea strongly, but in the end gave in. It was a difficult pregnancy; she vomited constantly and could hardly move about with her enormous belly. I think I'm going to have four or five, she would groan. Moreover, she was bothered by hallucinations: she would hear the sound of gigantic wings rustling above the house. Finally, the long painful labor—and the monster.

✎ ✎

Maybe it's something temporary, thinks my father hopefully. Like his wife, he too has heard of children who were born hairy like monkeys—but after a few days they lost their hair. Who could tell, maybe this was the same sort of thing. What they must do was wait a bit. Perhaps the hooves would fall off and the hide come loose in large pieces, letting the belly and normal legs appear, a little atrophied from having stayed inside the dark cavity so long. As soon as they were freed, however, they would begin to move, the quick little legs. He would give his son a good bath and burn the repulsive leftover parts in the stove. As the flames consumed them, everything would be forgotten like a bad dream, and they would be happy again.

✎ ✎

The days pass, my hooves don't fall off, my hide shows no cracks whatsoever. Another idea occurs to my father: it's a disease. And perhaps curable. What do you think? he asks the midwife. Could it be a disease, this thing my son has?

The midwife can't say with any certainty. She has seen some strange cases: a child that was born with fish scales, another that had a tail— only ten centimeters long, if that, but indisputably a tail. Is there a treatment? Ah, that she doesn't know. Only a doctor could say.

A doctor. My father knows that Dr. Oliveira is competent. Perhaps he will have an answer, perhaps he can solve the problem of the horse-baby by means of an operation, or even some injections that, when given in the hindquarters, might cause the hooves to dry up and fall off like broken branches, and make the hide peel away to reveal the beginnings of normal legs. Or with drops, pills, tonics—Dr. Oliveira is acquainted with a wide variety of medicines, one of them would surely work.

But one thing torments my father: Would Dr. Oliveira keep the baby's existence a secret? The anti-Semites could very well use what had happened as proof of the Jews' connection with the Evil One. My father knows that for much less than this, his ancestors were roasted in ovens during the Middle Ages.

But he can hesitate no longer. A son's life is more important than any risk involved. My father hitches the mare to the wagon and goes to town to speak to the doctor.

🌺 🌺

Two days later Dr. Oliveira appears, mounted on his beautiful roan. A tall, elegant man with a carefully trimmed beard, he wears a long cape to protect his English tweed suit from the dust of the road.

"Good day, what a pleasure to see you!"

He is a jovial, talkative fellow. He pats my sisters' heads affectionately as he comes in, greets my mother, who doesn't answer him—she still hasn't recovered from the shock. Here is the child, says my father, pointing to my crate.

Dr. Oliveira's smile disappears, and he actually draws back a step. The truth is that he didn't believe my father's story; he made no hurry to respond to his summons. Now, however, he is seeing the thing with his own eyes, and what he sees leaves him stunned. Stunned and horrified. A seasoned professional, he has seen many upsetting things, many ugly diseases. But he had never seen a centaur. A centaur takes him beyond the limits of his imagination. Centaurs are not listed in medical texts. Which of his colleagues has ever seen a centaur? None of them. Neither have his professors, nor the luminaries of Brazilian medical science. This case was without doubt unique.

He sits down on the chair that my father offers him, removes his gloves and regards the little centaur in silence. My father anxiously tries to read his face. But the doctor says nothing. From his suit pocket he takes a fountain pen and a leather-bound notebook and begins to write:

A strange creature. Probably a congenital malformation. Impressive resemblance of the inferior-posterior members with equine parts. As far down as the umbilical scar, a normal, well-built child. Below this point, body is mulelike. Face, neck, and trunk show smooth pink skin; there follows a small transitional zone of thick, wrinkled tegument heralding what is to come farther down. The blond hairs that cover the skin in this zone become darker and darker, and there appears, cruelly, horsehide of a bay color. Also haunches, shanks, pasterns, hooves, tail, everything resembling a horse. Penis particularly notable, being monstrously large for a newborn baby. A complex case. Radical surgery? Impossible.

My father cannot contain himself. "Well, Doctor?"

The startled doctor looks at him with hostility.

"Well, what, Tartakovsky?"

"What is it? This sickness my son has."

It isn't a sickness, says the doctor, putting away his notebook. So what is it? asks my father insistently. It's not a disease, the doctor repeats. And what is to be done? My father strains to control his voice.

"Unfortunately, nothing," replies Dr. Oliveira, getting up. "There is no treatment possible for a case of this type."

"No treatment possible?" My father cannot take it in. "Aren't there medicines for this?"

"No. There are no medicines."

"Or any type of operation?" My poor father is ever more anguished.

"No. No operation."

My father is silent a moment, then makes another attempt. "Maybe if we were to take him to Argentina . . ."

Dr. Oliveira puts his hand on my father's shoulder.

"No, Tartakovsky. I don't think they would have any treatment in Argentina for a case of this type. In fact, I doubt that any doctor has ever seen a thing like this, a creature so . . . unusual." He looks at the little centaur moving inside the crate and says in a low voice:

"I'll be frank, Tartakovsky. There are only two things to do: let him die, or accept him as he is. You must choose."

"I've already chosen, Doctor," murmurs my father. "You know the choice is already made."

"I admire your courage, Tartakovsky. And I am at your disposal. There isn't much I can do, but you can count on me."

He takes up his medical kit. "How much is it, Doctor?" asks my father. The doctor smiles. "Oh, please, there's no charge."

He starts toward the door. But then an idea occurs to him, an idea that makes him turn around sharply.

"Tartakovsky . . . Would you mind if I photographed your son?"

"What for?" My father is surprised and suspicious. "For the papers?"

"Of course not," the doctor assures him, smiling. "It's for a medical journal. I want to publish an article about this case."

"Article?"

"Yes. When a doctor comes across a case as rare as this one, he should publish the things he observes."

My father looks at him, then looks at the little centaur. I don't think it's a good idea, he mutters. The doctor insists: I'll cover his face, nobody will know he's your son. I don't think it's a good idea, repeats my father. Dr. Oliveira won't be dissuaded: it's a journal that is widely read by doctors, Tartakovsky. It could even be that one of them would have a suggestion for treating the problem.

"But you yourself just said that there is no treatment!" shouts my father.

Dr. Oliveira realizes he has committed an error. He clarifies himself: What I said was that there is no treatment available yet for cases of this type. But in the near future a medical colleague might discover some new drug, some operation. And then he'll remember what he read in the journal, get in touch with me—and who knows but that something can be done for your son?

✑ ✑

My father ends up agreeing. How can he do otherwise? But he imposes conditions: Dr. Oliveira has to bring his own photographic equipment—a large camera on a tripod—because my father will not hear of photographers. Strangers here, no.

The preparations for the photos are complicated. They shackle my hands and feet, but even so I switch my tail nervously and they have to tie it down too. When they put a black cloth over my head I begin to cry. Stop this, for the love of God! screams one of my sisters. Shut up, growls the doctor, struggling with the old camera. Now that I've started this, I'm going to finish it. The magnesium flare explodes, causing my sisters to scream in fright. Get them out of here, Tartakovsky, orders Dr. Oliveira. My father orders them out of the room, and the midwife as well. The doctor continues taking pictures, frame after frame.

"Enough!" yells my father, beside himself. "That's enough!"

The doctor perceives that the man has reached the limit of tolerance. Without a word, he bundles up his camera and other paraphernalia and takes himself off.

(He sends the photographs to Pôrto Alegre to be developed. A total failure, they are dark and blurry, and worst of all, do not show the lower part of my body clearly. One can discern that below the waist there is something different, but one cannot distinguish exactly what it is. To his great disappointment the doctor realizes that he cannot use the photographs. They are inconclusive and don't really prove anything. If he published an article with illustrations of that kind he would be accused of lying. He ends up throwing the photographs away, but he keeps the negatives.)

⤝⤝

Little by little the household returns to normal. The family begins to accept the presence of the centaur.

The two girls—sensitive, sweet-tempered Deborah, twelve, and spirited, intelligent Mina, ten—take care of me. They like to play with my fingers and make me laugh; they even forget the grotesque body—not for long, of course, because the nervous movements of my hooves bring them back to reality. Poor little thing, they sigh, it isn't his fault.

Bernardo also recognizes me as a brother, but for different reasons. He is jealous; he feels that I monopolize everyone's attention in spite of being a monster. He actually envies me: he would like to have four hooves too, if that's what it takes to win our sisters' affection.

The midwife continues to help the family, and my father does his work in the fields, but my mother remains supine, immobile, her gaze fixed on the ceiling. My father, worried, fears she may have gone mad. But he doesn't do anything; he doesn't call Dr. Oliveira. He avoids upsetting her. He wants to give her time; he waits for the fearful scar to heal. At night, he leaves a lamp lighted in the room, for he knows that terrors multiply in the dark. In the dark, the plant of madness puts down roots, stretches out runners, grows luxuriant. In the dark hideous visions proliferate like worms in rotting meat. It is by lantern light that my father removes his clothes (not his underwear; one shouldn't be seen naked.) He lies down softly. He doesn't touch her, because he can feel her pain as if in his own living flesh.

His wise, patient conduct begins to yield results. My mother shows small signs of recuperation: at times a moan, at times a sigh.

One night, as though sleepwalking, she gets up and goes to the crate where I lie. My father anxiously watches her from behind the door—what might she be doing?

For a few seconds she stares at me. Then, with a cry—"My son!"—she throws herself upon me. Startled out of my slumber, I begin to cry. But my father smiles, murmuring, "Thank God! Thank God!" as he wipes his eyes.

᠉ ᠉

Now that the family is reunited once again around the table, now that everything is all right, my father decides that it's time to circumcise the child. A religious man, he has to fulfill his obligations. It is necessary to introduce the boy to Judaism.

Cautiously, fearing her reaction, he presents the matter to my mother. She limits herself to a sigh (from that time on she is to sigh a lot) and says, "Very well, Leon. Call the *mohel*, do what has to be done."

᠉ ᠉

My father hitches the mare to the wagon, which is used only on special occasions such as these, and goes to town in search of the *mohel*. He tells him he had a son and without going into details (without saying the boy is a centaur) asks him to come and perform the circumcision that very day: the time prescribed by the Law has already run out. And the ceremony would have to take place on the farm, because the child's mother was ill and couldn't travel.

The *mohel*, a small hunchbacked man who blinks his eyes constantly, hears the story with growing distrust. The whole thing smells fishy to him. My father insists: let's go right away, Mohel, it's a long trip. And the witnesses? the *mohel* asks. Unfortunately I couldn't find any witnesses, says my father, we'll have to perform the circumcision without them. No witnesses? The *mohel* likes this less and less all the time. But he has been acquainted with my father for some time and knows he is a man to be trusted. Besides, he is used to the oddities of country people. He gets his bag of instruments, his prayer book and prayer shawl, and climbs into the wagon.

On the way my father begins to prepare him. The boy was born with a defect, he says, trying to affect nonchalance. The *mohel* grows alarmed: is it serious? I don't want to have the child dying of the circumcision! No, no, not at all, my father calms him, the child is deformed but very strong, you'll see.

They arrive at sunset, the *mohel* complaining about the difficulties of working by lamplight. He gets out of the wagon muttering and cursing. The family is gathered in the dining room. The *mohel* greets my mother, pays my sisters compliments, recalls that he performed Bernardo's circumcision: that one there gave me a lot of work! He puts on his prayer shawl, asking where the baby is.

My father takes me out of the crate and places me on the table.

"Good God!" cries the *mohel,* dropping his bag and cringing backward. He turns and runs for the door. My father runs after him, grabs him. Don't run away, Mohel! Do what has to be done! But he's a horse! screams the *mohel,* trying to get loose from my father's strong hands, I have no obligation to circumcise horses! He's not a horse, yells my father, he is a defective child, a Jewish son!

My mother and sisters weep softly. Seeing that the *mohel* has stopped fighting, my father lets go of him, locks the door. Staggering, the little man leans against the wall with his eyes shut and body trembling. My father brings him his bag of instruments: come on, Mohel. I can't, the man groans, I'm too nervous. My father goes out to the kitchen and comes back with a glass of cognac.

"Drink this. It'll help you feel better."

"But it's not my custom—"

"Drink!"

The *mohel* empties the glass in one swallow. He chokes, coughs. "Better?" asks my father. Better, moans the *mohel.* He instructs my father to hold me on his lap, and takes his ritual knife from the bag. But again he hesitates. Have you got a good hold on him? he asks, looking over his spectacle rims. Yes, says my father, go ahead, you don't need to be afraid. Won't he kick me? asks the *mohel.* There's no danger, my father assures him, come on.

The *mohel* draws near, and my father separates my hind feet. And there they are, face to face, the penis and the *mohel,* the huge penis and the little *mohel,* the small fascinated *mohel.* Mohel Rachmiel has never seen such a penis, he who has performed so many circumcisions. He senses that this will be a transcendent experience, the greatest circumcision of his life, the memory of which will go with him to his grave. Horse or not, it matters little. There is a foreskin, and he will do what the Law prescribes for Jewish foreskins. He takes up the knife, drawing a deep breath . . .

The *mohel* is an expert. In a very few minutes the deed is accomplished, and he drops back into the chair exhausted as my father tries to soothe my howling, wrapping me up and walking back and forth with me. Finally, I grow quiet, and he places me in my crate. My mother feels ill; Deborah and Mina have to help her to bed.

More cognac, says the *mohel* in an almost inaudible voice. My father serves him a glass and pours another for himself. In spite of everything, he is pleased; the Law has been fulfilled. He invites the *mohel* to stay overnight with the family: we have a bed for you, sir. The *mohel* jumps up. No! I don't want to! Take me back! As you like, my father answers, surprised and confused—why all this shouting, now that the worst is over? He puts on his coat: I am at your disposal. The *mohel* gathers up his instruments, stuffs them back in the bag, and without taking leave of anyone, opens the door and gets into the wagon.

The return trip is made in silence. They arrive at the *mohel's* house in the wee hours of the morning, the roosters already beginning to crow. How much do I owe you? asks my father, helping the old man out of the wagon. Nothing, the *mohel* mutters, you don't owe me anything. I don't want anything. Very well, says my father, holding him, but there is one thing. This matter will stay between us, do you hear? The *mohel* looks at him with loathing, jerks himself loose, goes inside his house and slams the door. My father settles himself again on the wagon seat, clucks to the mare. The tired animal begins to move. He is returning to the farm, to his family, to little Guedali.

⤳ ⤶

A few weeks later I take my first steps. The equine portion of my body develops faster than the human portion. (And will it grow old sooner? Will it die earlier? The following years are to prove that it won't.) My hands still move without definite purpose, uncoordinated; my eyes don't identify images, nor do my ears distinguish between sounds. Yet already my hooves trot about, carrying a body that can't hold itself erect but oscillates grotesquely like that of a doll. They can't help laughing, my parents and sisters (but not my brother) at the baby's obvious surprise: now he's in his crate, now out in the yard—from which they hastily remove him. One thing my father determines immediately: Guedali is not to go outside the limits of the farm. He can run about in the fields nearby, pick wild blackberries, bathe in the stream. But no one must see him. A man of experience, Leon Tartakovsky knows the cruelty of the world. It is necessary to protect his son, who is, after all, a fragile creature. When strangers come to the farm, I am hidden in the cellar or in the barn. Wedged between worn-out tools and old toys (headless dolls, broken cars) or among the cows that silently chew their cuds, I become painfully aware of my shanks, my hooves. I am obliged to think of something called horseshoes. I become conscious of my thick, beautiful tail, of my enormous penis with its circumcision mark. I become aware of my belly (huge, how could my poor little hands scratch such a big belly?) and my long intestines that digest and assimilate my food, often inadequate for a horse's organism, although for humans—and especially for Jews, tasty: beet soup, fried fish, the unleavened bread of Passover.

(Of course, before this, I had already formed a vague notion of my monstrous body. Imagine this example. Lying in my crate when I was a few months old, I must have brought a hoof up to my mouth, as babies always do with their feet; the hoof would have cut my lip, and from the sharp pain, from that hurt, there must have remained the notion of conflict between hardness and softness, between the brutal and the delicate, between the equine and the human. Doubtless I vomited that night.)

Little by little, a sense of my own oddity germinates within me, incorporating itself to my very being, even before I ask the inevitable question dreaded by my parents: Why am I like this? What happened for me to be born this way?

To this inquiry my parents respond evasively. Their answers only increase the anguish that is to permeate my whole being—an anguish going back to my most remote beginnings; back, I believe, to the image of the winged horse. This anguish is to crystallize, deposited permanently as it were in the marrow, of my bones, in the buds of my teeth, in the tissue of my liver. But my family's love acts as a balm; the wounds heal, the disparate parts unify, the suffering acquires a meaning. I am a centaur, a mythological creature, but I am also Guedali Tartakovsky, the son of Leon and Rosa, the brother of Bernardo, Deborah, and Mina. I am a little Jewish boy. Thanks to these realities, I don't lose my mind. I face the fearful whirlwind, journeying through the blackness of many nights, and emerge dizzy and weak on the other side. It is a pallid smile that Mina sees on my face in the morning, but this smile is enough to make her clap her hands with joy.

"Come on, Guedali! Come on and play!"

Mina loves plants and animals. She knows the name of every tree, identifies the songs of the regional birds, and can predict the weather by their flight. She fishes better than anyone, takes up serpents and spiders in her hands, runs through the fields barefoot without cutting herself on the thorns, and climbs trees with amazing agility. Touch him here, she says to Deborah, see how soft his coat is. The timid Deborah comes closer. Her fingers caress me, play with my tail. (The memory of this sensation is to stay with me for many years; whenever it is evoked my coat stands up, waves of voluptuousness rippling over my hide.) If I lie on the ground, they lie down too, leaning their heads against my haunches. How nice it is to be here, says Deborah, looking at the sky. (A cloudless sky, without winged figures.) Mina jumps up: let's play tag! I trot slowly on purpose, letting them catch me. They double up with laughter.

Bernardo watches us from a distance. As time passes, he becomes more and more withdrawn. My father loves him; he is an industrious boy, a great help in the fields. He also has extraordinary mechanical ability. He improvises farm tools, makes kitchen utensils that my mother exhibits proudly, and builds traps for mice and rabbits. But he hardly speaks to me, in spite of Deborah and Mina's insistence. He prefers to ignore me. I might have shared a room with him, but my father, sensing his hostility, decides to build another room for me, an addition to the house. These living quarters are ample, with an independent door through which I can come and go as I like. And really, it's better that I don't walk around inside the house too much. My footsteps make the walls shake, and the crystal wineglasses my mother brought from Europe, her only treasure, tinkle dangerously inside the china cabinet. But meals must be taken together as a family. I stand near the table, holding my plate; my father tells stories from the Bible and my mother watches vigilantly to make sure I eat enough. Little by little they discover the peculiarities of my diet: it must be abundant (I weigh as much as several children my age) and above all, it must contain lots of green, leafy material, as the midwife realized early on. In consequence, my father plants a big garden from which I daily consume heads of lettuce, cabbage, and celery. I grow strong and well developed.

There are other problems: that of clothing, for instance. My mother knits pullover sweaters adapted to my body. They terminate in a sort of blanket to cover my back and hindquarters, for southern Brazil is cold in the wintertime. These jobs are a comfort to her, although she never manages to recover completely from the original shock she had at my birth. Many times she looks at me with an air of hurt surprise, as if asking herself, What is this thing? How did this creature ever come forth from my womb? But she says nothing; she hugs me tightly, although she avoids touching my coat, being allergic to horsehair.

During the Revolution of 1893 tales were told of a mysterious creature, half man and half horse, who would invade the Legalist camps at night, grab a poor young recruit, take him to the riverbank and cut off his head. It wasn't me. I wasn't born until much later.

❦ ❦

From a book on the legends of southern Brazil, Deborah teaches me to read. I learn with great facility. Negrinho do Pastoreio and Salamanca do Jarau are already my friends, part of my everyday life.

I enjoy Deborah's reading to me. I like to watch her writing or drawing. And above all I like to hear her play the violin.

❦ ❦

The violin had been in my family for generations. My grandfather, Abraham Tartakovsky, had given it to my father, hoping to transform him into a great virtuoso like the many others who sprang up in Russia during that period: Mischa Elman, Gabrilovitch, Zimbalist—all young Jewish prodigies. But my father didn't like music. He learned to play the instrument unwillingly, and as soon as he got to Brazil he put it away in its case and forgot about it. Deborah discovered the violin and asked my father to teach her how to play it. She had an excellent musical ear, and learned at once. From then on she practiced every day.

❦ ❦

A beautiful scene:

Standing in her sunlit bedroom one morning, Deborah plays the violin. Ecstatic with joy, her eyes half shut, she executes pieces that she knows by heart: "Dream of Love No. 5" and others. I watch her through the window. She open her eyes and notices me, giving a little start. Then she smiles. An idea comes to her: Do you want to learn to play too, Guedali?

Do I want to! More than anything else. We go down into the cellar—which from then on becomes our studio—and there she shows me the finger positions, the movements of the bow. I learn quickly.

❦ ❦

I wander through the fields playing the violin. The melody mingles with the sighing of the wind, with the birdsongs and the trilling of the locusts; it is all so beautiful that my eyes fill with tears. I forget everything, forget that I have hooves and a tail. I am a violinist, an artist.

"Guedali!" cries my mother from a distance. "Come and eat!"

Eat? I don't want to eat. I want to play the violin. I play it upon the hillsides, in the marshes with my hooves submerged in the icy water, in the thickets where the leaves of the trees drop onto my haunches and cling to my wet coat.

а а

A rainy afternoon in September. High on a bank, I play a melody I composed myself. Suddenly there is a loud pop: a string has broken. I stop playing and stare at the violin. Then, without thinking, without hesitation, I automatically throw it down into the stream below. The muddy waters carry it slowly away. Trotting along the bank, I accompany its movement. I see it catch on a submerged tree trunk, I see it sink. And then I go back home.

On the way I realize what I have done. Now what? I ask myself, upset. What will I tell them? I gallop back and forth, lacking courage to go in.

Finally I open the door. Deborah is sitting in the dining room, reading by lantern light. I lost the violin, I tell her from the doorway. She looks at me, incredulous: "You lost the violin, Guedali? But how?"

I lost it, I repeat, my voice trembling and insecure. My father comes in: What's all this about, Guedali? You lost the violin? I lost it, I insist, I left it somewhere, I can't remember where.

They all go out to look for it, carrying lanterns. For hours they walk through the fields. Finally they are convinced: the violin is truly lost. And it will be ruined with the rain that is now falling in torrents. They go back to the house. Deborah locks herself in the bedroom, crying, and Mina reprimands me for being so careless.

а а

Late that night, I try to kill myself.

All alone in the basement, I work a large nail out of an old rotten board. I plunge it again and again into my back, my belly, my hooves, biting my lips so as not to cry out. The blood runs; I don't stop, but keep on wounding myself. At that moment Bernardo appears, having come in search of a tool. He sees me: What on earth are you doing? he asks in alarm. As soon as he realizes the truth he advances towards me, trying to disarm me. I resist him. We fight, and he ends up getting the nail away from me. He runs to call Deborah and Mina.

They come, they bandage me up. And for the rest of the night they stay with me, telling me stories to entertain me. Stories of dragons and princes, pixies and giants, witches and sorcerers. It's no good, sisters, I say, I wish I could be people, people like Papa, like Bernardo. Confused, they don't know what to say; they recommend that I pray a lot. And so I do, thinking about God until I fall asleep. But the figure that appears to me in my dreams isn't that of Jehovah; it's the sinister winged horse.

> ⤝ ⤝

In the weeks that follow, I avoid my family. I don't want to talk to anyone. I gallop through the fields, going ever farther away. This is how I meet the Indian boy.

He is coming out of the woods as I walk down the trail. The sudden encounter makes both of us stop short. Surprised and suspicious, we stare at each other. I see a naked bronze boy holding a bow and arrow—a huntsman. I know about the Indians' existence from the stories my sisters tell. But what does he think of me? Do I seem strange to him? Impossible to know. He gazes impassively at me.

I hesitate. I should run away, I should go back home, as my father recommended, but I don't feel any desire to flee. I move closer to the Indian, my right hand raised in a signal of peace, repeating, "Friend, friend," like the white men in my sisters' stories. He remains motionless, looking at me. I should offer him a present, but what? I don't have anything. An idea occurs to me. I take off my pullover sweater and hold it out to him, "Present, friend!" He doesn't say anything, but he smiles. I insist: "Take it, friend! Good pullover! Mother made!" Now we are very close to each other. He takes the pullover, examines it curiously, smells it. Then he ties it around his waist. He gives me one of his arrows and draws slowly backward about twenty steps. Then, turning his back, he disappears into the forest.

I go back home and lock myself in my room. My father comes to call me to dinner; I tell him I won't be there, I'm not hungry. I don't want to talk to anyone. I lie down, but I can't get to sleep, I'm too excited. My life is already changed, for I found a friend. The arrow clutched to my chest, I make plans. I will teach the little Indian boy (I've even guessed his name already: Peri) my language, he will teach me his. We will be great companions, Peri and I. Together we will explore the forest. We will have secret hiding places, pacts, rituals. And we will never leave each other.

I can hardly wait for morning to come. I run to the place where I met him, taking a few precious offerings: toys I got for my birthday, the fruits that were in season, and a necklace of my mother's that I pilfered through the window. She likes this necklace a lot, I know. But one should do anything for a friend, even steal for him.

The little Indian is not there. Why should he be? I don't know. I only know that I was certain I would meet him there, and I can't believe he didn't come. I go for a short walk around the area; I climb a hill and look off into the distance. Nobody. I enter the forest:

"Peri! It's me!"

He doesn't appear. I wait hours for him. Nothing. Disappointed, I go home, lock myself in my room, refuse once again to eat. (My belly, my horse's belly, rumbles, but my dry mouth wants nothing to do with food.)

The next day I go again to the meeting place. And the next day Peri again fails to come. Finally, I am obliged to conclude that the boy has abandoned me. Not even the Indians want anything to do with me, I think bitterly.

Once again it is my sisters' affection that sustains me. They play with me and take my mind off my troubles. Thanks to them, I begin to smile again.

But I don't forget Peri. Maybe something happened to him, I think, maybe he got sick; he might still try to find me. I know Indians are very good at following a trail. Sometimes I wake up in the middle of the night imagining that someone is knocking on the door of my room.

"Peri?"

It isn't Peri. It's only the wind, or our dog Pharaoh. I sigh, feel for the arrow that I keep under my mattress, and go back to sleep.

≈ ≈

Throwing violins in the river or no, trying to kill myself or not, finding a friend and losing him, I go on living.

Life is very calm on the farm. Weekdays are full of hard work, with which I begin to help. Indignantly, my father opposes my pulling the plow, but now I cultivate my own garden, and plant corn too; the ripening ears with their golden grains peeping through the husks give me a deep pleasure.

On Friday nights, everyone dresses up in their best clothes. We gather around the table, where the crystal goblets brought from Europe sparkle upon the white tablecloth. My mother lights the candles, my father blesses the wine, and thus we celebrate the arrival of the Sabbath. We also celebrate Passover and the Jewish New Year. We fast on Yom Kippur—when the rest of the family goes to the synagogue in town. On these occasions my father and the *mohel* exchange pointed glances without saying a word.

The wheat is planted in season; chickens hatch, lay eggs, are sacrificed. The cows calve. Once (a terrible time) a cloud of locusts passes over the farm, fortunately without causing much damage. The seasons follow one another. According to my father these are good years, bringing neither too much dry weather nor excessive rain. From him I learn about the phases of the moon, and he also teaches me songs in Yiddish. We all sing together around the great wood-burning stove where a pleasant fire flickers. We drink tea with cookies, many times there is popcorn, hot piñon nuts, baked sweet potatoes. The picture of the united family is a charming one, from which it is almost possible to conjure away the vision of the half-horse (lying on the floor and partially covered with a blanket) that is the other half of the half-boy. It is almost possible to look at my face—at eleven, I am a good-looking lad, with brown hair, lively eyes, a strong mouth—and at my upper body, and forget the rest. I can almost relax in the warmth of the fire and let the time go by without thinking of anything.

🐎 🐎

But my parents don't forget, nor relax, nor stop thinking, especially my father. Many times he gets up at night to watch me as I sleep. He looks at me fearfully, full of foreboding: my sleep is agitated, I mumble things, move my hooves. He stares hard at my large penis: a circumcised penis, but still a horse's penis. What woman (Woman: my father doesn't even ponder any other type of female creature. A mare, for example, never crosses his mind. For my father, I am a growing boy, a boy with abnormal appendages, perhaps, but nevertheless a boy.) would accept him, he asks himself, what woman would ever go to bed with him? A prostitute, maybe, a crazy or drunken woman, a degenerate. But a girl from a good Jewish family, like Erechim's daughters, for example? Never! they would faint if they ever saw him.

Still, my father knows, someday his son Guedali will feel desire for a woman. Irresistible desire. And what will happen then? My father doesn't even like to think about what might happen on a spring night in September.

🐎 🐎

The eve of Guedali's twelfth birthday.

A very hot night, even for September. Insupportably hot.

On that night, the boy can't get to sleep. Restless, his face burning, he will roll from one side of the straw mattress to the other. (It's a hard-on; his great penis is erect, throbbing. What to do? Masturbate? Impossible: his fingers refuse to touch the parts of a horse.) Unable to endure any more, Guedali will go out the door and into the open fields. He will rub against trees, dive into the river, but nothing will calm him. He will gallop aimlessly, startling the nocturnal birds.

On a neighboring farm, near a rough fence made of tree trunks, he is to meet the herd of horses. Mares and stallions, motionless beneath the moonlight, staring at him.

The centaur will creep up softly. The centaur will see a mare, a beautiful white mare with a long mane. The centaur will caress her silky neck with trembling hands, the centaur will murmur sweet nothings in her ears. The centaur: mouth dry, eyes wide, the centaur will suddenly mount her. And the whole place goes wild, the animals running up and down, throwing themselves against the fence, as the centaur yells, "I'm gonna do it! Shit, I don't care, I'm gonna do it!"

Past caring, he will satisfy himself quickly, like someone who wants to die. Then he will run to the river and take a purifying bath.

(His hoof will step on something buried in the muddy bottom. The violin?) He will go back home and sneak into his room as silently as a thief.

⚘ ⚘

But the story is not to end there. Up to that point my father can go, at least in hallucinated imaginings. But there is more.

⚘ ⚘

The mare begins to follow Guedali about.

At night the centaur wakes up, restless, and hears the supplicating whinny: the mare is there outside the window of his room.

Guedali hides his head under the pillow. Useless. He can still hear her. He gets up, tries to chase her away: "Get out of here! Beat it!" he snarls under his breath, terrified of waking his parents. But the mare doesn't go away. Guedali throws rocks at her, hits her with a broom handle. Useless.

She follows him about in the daytime, too. Her owner is forced to come and get her. Intrigued, he remarks to Leon, "I don't know what's gotten into Magnolia, she's forever getting loose and coming over here." He saddles her; she rears, balks, refuses to leave the place. The man whips her, digs his spurs into her sides and finally they go off at a gallop, disappearing in a cloud of dust. From his hiding place in the cellar, Guedali breathes a sigh of relief. But when night falls—whinnying. In the wee hours of the morning, a thought occurs to him: could the mare be pregnant? The possibility terrifies him. The image of another centaur, of a horse, or worse—of a monster with a horse's body and a man's head, or a horse with human lips, or human ears, or a filly with a woman's breasts, or a horse with human legs—these images will not let Guedali find peace.

Nor will Pasha. Pasha, the great bay stallion, the mare's erstwhile mate, whom she now despises. Pasha will come after him, wanting revenge. And Guedali will not be able to avoid the final battle.

One night Pasha might bang on Guedali's door with his hooves. Guedali would yell, "Enough is enough!" and go out to meet his adversary beneath the excited gaze of the white mare.

It would be hooves against hooves, and the fists of the boy against the stallion's teeth, a terrible fight. Physically, the stallion would have the advantage; if Guedali bit him, he would barely scratch his bay hide. The centaur's blows would be strong, but Pasha's jaw is stronger yet. And Guedali's intelligence? Would it be superior to instinct, to the fury of the animal fighting for his life and his mate? Would Guedali have the presence of mind to arm himself with a butcher knife, and use it at an opportune moment?

☙ ❧

My father confides his fears to my mother. She doesn't miss her chance: then let's leave here, Leon. I've always told you we should go somewhere where there aren't so many animals, so many horses. Let's move to the city, Leon. There are good doctors there, hospitals—maybe they'll know of some treatment available for our son. We have our savings, you can open a business. And we'll live someplace out-of-the-way, where nobody will discover Guedali.

Leave the farm? my father asks himself, walking through the fields. The idea disturbs him, for he is very attached to the place. He likes to plow, to plant wheat, to feel the ripe heads of grain between his fingers. Besides, wouldn't leaving the land be a betrayal of Baron Hirsch's sainted memory? My father hesitates.

But sudden events force him to make up his mind.

☙ ❧

I am discovered.

And by none other than Pedro Bento, the son of the neighboring rancher, a boy of dreadful character. Mounted on the speedy Pasha to pursue a runaway calf, he strays onto our land.

My father and I are far from the house, planting wheat in a distant field. He is irritated: I came along against his will. And precisely as he is telling me that he doesn't like me to expose myself so much, Pedro Bento appears. Run, Guedali! screams my father, but it's too late; before I can move, Pedro Bento is beside us. He jumps off his horse and comes near, examining me in wonder. He tries to touch me, and I draw back in fear, while my father, anguish stamped on his face, watches helplessly, not knowing what to do.

"What animal is this, Mr. Leon?" asks Pedro Bento. "Tell me, what is this thing? Where did you find such a funny creature?"

My father stutters a confused explanation, and ends up asking Pedro Bento to keep what he has seen a secret. He offers him money. The boy takes it, promising that he won't tell anyone, but he imposes a condition: he wants to come back every day to look at me. My father had no choice but to agree.

So Pedro comes back every day. He starts conversations with me, and I respond in monosyllables. But I begin to like him. He is friendly, he tells interesting stories. Will he be my first friend? Will he be to me what Peri wasn't?

One day he invites me to go for a walk in the fields with him.

As usual, he rides Pasha, and we set off at a trot. He seems different to me; excited, eyes shining, he doesn't answer my questions. From time to time he gives a long whistle. And suddenly, as we pass through some woods, he jumps off his horse and onto my back.

"What do you think you're doing?" I cry, surprised and irritated.

He laughs and lets out cries of triumph, and at once I see why: three big boys, Pedro's brothers, come out of the woods.

"See?" he yells. "See there? Was I lying?"

Crying, terrified, I rear and whirl around, trying to get free of him. I can't. Accustomed to breaking untamed horses, Pedro Bento clamps his arms around my neck, almost strangling me. Finally, I take off for home at a gallop. Then he gets scared.

"Stop, Guedali! Stop! Let me down! I was just kidding!"

I don't care. I don't listen. I don't stop running until I reach home. Startled by the noise, my father comes out of the barn. "Ah, son of a bitch!" he cries, beside himself. He tears Pedro Bento from my back, knocks him over with a blow, and pounds him until he is out cold on the ground, his face bleeding.

❧ ❧

That night there is a storm. It rains without stopping for two weeks. The wheat crop is ruined. The flooding waters erode great chasms in the red earth. Things start to appear: strangely shaped pebbles, arrowheads, clay pots. And the skeleton of a horse, a complete skeleton, resting on its side with head stretched forward and jaws open, its eye sockets full of clay.

Let's go away from here, says my father. Let's go to the city.

❧ ❧

It is painful for me to leave the farm. My hooves have always known the pastures, the earth; would they accept the concrete of the city? I trot through the fields for the last time, saying goodbye to the trees, birds, the stream. I murmur farewell to the cows and calves. In the place where I met Peri I leave a present, a shirt wrapped up in a newspaper.

I go back to my room, look around me, and sigh. In spite of everything, it was good living here.

❧ ❧

Not having a truck nor knowing how to drive, my father has rented two enormous horse-drawn wagons for the move. In one of them, driven by my brother, go a few household things: furniture, clothes, the crystal goblets brought from Europe, the photograph of Baron Hirsch. In the other, which my father drives, go I, well hidden by a canvas cover. My mother and sisters go by bus.

The midwife comes to say goodbye. Crying, she embraces me, dampening my coat with her tears. May God protect you, my son! She gives me a package sent by Dr. Oliveira. It contains the negatives of the photographs he took of me. Together with a note saying that I should destroy the negatives myself or else keep them as a remembrance if someday, by means of some treatment, I become a normal person.

Shortly before we set off, the *mohel* appears. He says nothing, only hands me a prayer book in Hebrew and a richly embroidered prayer shawl, and goes away.

And so we begin our journey.

Of this trip I retain only confused memories: my father's figure sitting on the driver's seat, wrapped in a country farmer's cape, rain running off his hat brim. The wet backs of the draft horses shining in the pallid light of early dawn. The narrow, muddy road. The trees with broken branches. The whitish skull of a steer impaled on a fence post. Blackbirds perched on the barbed wire.

We advance slowly, stopping often. We cook our own meals and sleep beside the road. At night I stretch my legs, numbed from the prolonged immobility. I trot through the nearby fields, mount a little hill, rear up on my hind legs, pound my closed fists against my chest, let out a savage yell. Bernardo looks reprovingly at me, and my father cries, come back, fool! Do you want them to discover us? I come back at a gallop, stop in front of him and hug him. He is a tall man, but I am even taller due to my long legs, and I have to bend over to whisper into his ear: "I'm happy, Father." (It's true, I am happy.)

We go back to the campfire. My brother quietly prepares rice, his hard face illuminated by the firelight.

✒ ✒

Finally we arrive in Pôrto Alegre. My father sighs in relief: here you'll be at peace, my son. Nobody will stare at you. City people don't care about anything.

Translated from the Portuguese by Margaret A. Neves.

III

WESTERN EUROPE

SOUTHWARDS

Primo Levi

I had been walking for hours in the marvellous morning air, draw-ing it deeply into my battered lungs like medicine. I was not very steady on my feet, but I felt an imperious need to take possession of my body again, to reestablish a contact, by now broken for almost two years, with trees and grass, with the heavy brown soil in which one could feel the seeds chafing, with the ocean of air wafting the pollen from the fir trees, wave upon wave, from the Carpathians to the black streets of the mining city.

I had been wandering around like this for a week now, exploring the environs of Katowice. The pleasant weakness of convalescence ran through my veins. At the same time, powerful doses of insulin also ran through my veins, prescribed, found, bought and injected in agreement by Leonardo and Gottlieb. While I walked, the insulin carried out its prodigious work in silence; it ran through my blood searching for sugar, took care of its diligent combustion and conversion into energy, and dis-tracted it from other less proper destinies. But there was not much sugar available; suddenly, dramatically, almost always at the same time, the supplies ran out; then my legs folded under me, everything grew black and I was forced to sit on the ground wherever I was, frozen and over-whelmed by an attack of ferocious hunger. At this point, the labours and gifts of my third protector, Marya Fyodorovna Prima, came to my aid; I took a packet of glucose from my pocket and swallowed it greedily. After a few minutes, light returned, the sun grew warm once more and I could begin my walk again.

When I returned to the camp that morning, I came on an unusual scene. In the middle of the square stood Captain Egorov, surrounded by a dense crowd of Italians. He was holding a large revolver, which, however, he only used to emphasize the salient parts of the discourse he was making with broad gestures. Very little of his speech could be understood. Basically only two words, because he repeated them frequently; but these two words were heavenly messengers: *"Ripatriatsiya"* and *"Odyessa."*

So, we were to be repatriated via Odessa; we were to return home. The whole camp instantly ran wild. Captain Egorov was lifted from the ground, revolver and all, and carried precariously in triumph. People bellowed in the corridors: "Home! home!" others turned to their luggage, making as much noise as possible, and throwing rags, waste paper, broken shoes and all sorts of rubbish out of the window. In a few hours the whole camp emptied, under the Olympian eyes of the Russians; some were going to the city to take leave of their girls, others quite simply to paint the town red, others still to spend their last zloty on provisions for the journey or in other more futile ways.

Cesare and I also went to Katowice, with this last programme in mind, carrying our savings and those of five or six comrades in our pockets. For what could we hope to find at the frontier? We did not know, but we had seen enough of the Russians and their ways so far, as to make it seem unlikely that we should find a money exchange at the frontier. So common sense, as well as our euphoric state, counselled us to spend the not excessively large sum we possessed to the very last zloty; to use it all up, for example, in organizing a large Italian-style dinner, based on spaghetti *al burro,* which we had not eaten for so long a time.

We walked into a grocery store, placed all our money on the counter, and explained our intentions to the shopkeeper as best we could. I told her, as usual, that I spoke German but was not German; that we were Italians about to leave, and that we wanted to buy spaghetti, butter, salt, eggs, strawberries and sugar in the most opportune proportions for a total of exactly sixty-three zloty, not one more nor one less.

The shopkeeper was a wrinkled old woman with a shrewish and diffident air. She looked at us closely through her tortoiseshell glasses, then stated flatly, in excellent German, that according to her we were not

Italians at all. First of all, we spoke German, albeit somewhat badly; then, and above all, Italians had black hair and passionate eyes, while we possessed neither. At the most, she would concede that we were Croats; in fact, now that she thought about it, she had met some Croats who resembled us. We were, quite indisputably, Croats.

I was quite annoyed, and told her abruptly that we were Italians, whether she liked it or not; Italian Jews, one from Rome, and one from Turin, who came from Auschwitz and were going home, and we wanted to buy and spend, and not waste time in futile discussion.

Jews from Auschwitz? The old woman's look mellowed, even her lines seemed to soften. That was another matter. She took us into the back room, made us sit down, offered us two glasses of real beer, and at once poured forth her legendary story with pride, her epopee, near in time but already amply transformed into a *chanson de geste*, refined and polished by innumerable repetitions.

She was aware of Auschwitz, and everything relating to Auschwitz interested her, because she had run the risk of going there. She was not Polish, but German; formerly, she had owned a shop in Berlin, with her husband. They had never liked Hitler, and perhaps they had been too incautious in allowing these singular opinions of theirs to leak out in the neighbourhood; in 1935 her husband had been taken away by the Gestapo, and she had never heard of him again. It had been a terrible blow, but one has to live, and she had continued her business till 1938, when Hitler, *"der Lump,"* had made his famous speech on the radio in which he declared he wanted to start a war.

Then she had grown angry and had written to him. She had written to him personally, "To Mr. Adolf Hitler, Chancellor of the Reich, Berlin," sending him a long letter in which she advised him strongly not to wage war because too many people would be killed, and pointed out to him that if he did he would lose, because Germany could not win against the whole world; even a child could understand that. She had signed the letter with her name, surname and address; then she had settled down to wait.

Five days later the brown-shirts arrived and, on the pretext of carrying out a search, had sacked and turned her house and shop upside down. What did they find? Nothing. She had never meddled in politics; there was only the draft of the letter. Two weeks later they called her to the Gestapo. She thought they would beat her up and send her to the Lager; instead they treated her with loutish contempt, told her they should hang her, but they were convinced she was only *"eine alte blöde*

Ziege," a stupid old goat, and that the rope would be wasted on her. However, they had withdrawn her trading licence and had expelled her from Berlin.

She had lived from hand to mouth in Silesia on the black market and other expedients, until, as she had foreseen, the Germans had lost the war. Then, since the whole neighbourhood knew what she had done, the Polish authorities had created no difficulties about granting her a licence for a grocery store. So now she lived in peace, fortified by the thought of how much better the world would be if the rulers of this earth had followed her advice.

🖎 🖎

At the moment of the departure, Leonardo and I gave back the keys of the surgery and said goodbye to Marya Fyodorovna and Dr. Danchenko. Marya appeared silent and sad; I asked her why she did not come to Italy with us, at which she blushed as if I had made a dishonourable proposal. Danchenko intervened; he was carrying a bottle of alcohol and two sheets of paper. At first we thought the alcohol was his personal contribution to the stock of medicaments for the journey, but no, it was for a farewell toast, which was dutifully drunk.

And the sheets of paper? We were amazed to learn that the Command expected from us two declarations of thanks for the humanity and correctness with which we had been treated at Katowice; Danchenko also begged us to mention his name and work explicitly, and to sign the papers, adding the title "Doctor of Medicine" to our names. This Leonardo was able to do and did; but in my case it was false. I was perplexed, and sought to make Danchenko understand this; but he had no time for formalism such as mine, and rapping his finger on the paper told me angrily not to create difficulties. I signed as he wanted; who was I to deprive him of a little help in his career?

But the ceremony was not yet over. Danchenko in turn took out two testimonials written in a beautiful hand on two sheets of lined paper, evidently torn from an exercise book. My testimonial declared with unconstrained generosity that "Primo Levi, doctor of medicine, of Turin, has given able and assiduous help to the Surgery of this Command for four months, and in this manner has merited the gratitude of all the workers of the world."

🖎 🖎

The following day our perpetual dream became reality. A train was waiting for us at Katowice station; a long train of freight cars, which we Italians (about eight hundred) took possession of with cries of delight. First, Odessa; then a fantastic journey by sea through the gates of the Orient; and then Italy.

The prospect of traveling some hundreds of miles in those dilapidated boxcars, sleeping on the bare floor, did not worry us at all; nor were we worried by the derisory food supplies provided by the Russians: a little bread, and a packet of soybean margarine for each car. It was a margarine of American origin, heavily salted and as hard as Parmesan cheese; evidently destined for tropical climates, it had finally come into our hands by a series of unimaginable accidents. The rest of our supplies, the Russians assured us with their habitual nonchalance, would be distributed during the journey.

The train, with its cargo of hope, left in the middle of June 1945. There was no escort, no Russian on board; Dr. Gottlieb was responsible for the convoy, for he had attached himself spontaneously to us, and had taken on himself the cumulative duties of interpreter, doctor, and consul for the itinerant community. We felt in good hands, remote from all doubt or uncertainty; at Odessa the ship was waiting for us.

The journey lasted six days, and if in the course of it we were not forced by hunger to turn beggars or bandits, and in fact reached the end in a reasonably healthy condition, the credit was exclusively Dr. Gottlieb's. It became clear immediately after our departure that the Russians of Katowice had sent us on our journey blindly, without making any arrangements with their colleagues at Odessa or at the intermediate stages. When our train stopped at a station (it stopped frequently and for long periods because regular trains and military transports had precedence), no one know what to do with us. The stationmasters and the military commanders watched us arrive with doleful surprise, only anxious to rid themselves in turn of our inconvenient presence.

But Gottlieb was there, as sharp as a knife; there was no bureaucratic complication, no barrier of negligence, no official obstinacy that he was unable to remove in a few minutes, each time in a different way. Every difficulty dissolved into mist in the face of his effrontery, his soaring fantasy, his rapier-like quickness. He came back from each encounter with the monster of a thousand faces, which lives wherever official forms and circulars gather, radiant with victory like Saint George after his duel with the dragon, and recounted the rapid exchange, too conscious of his superiority to glory in it.

The local stationmaster, for example, had demanded our travel warrant, which notoriously did not exist; Gottlieb told him that he was going to pick it up, and entered the telegraph office nearby, where he fabricated one in a few moments, written in the most convincing of official jargon, on some scrap of paper that he so plastered with stamps, seals and illegible signatures as to make it as holy and venerable as an authentic emanation from the Top. Another time he had gone to the Quartermaster's office of a Kommandantur and had respectfully informed him that eight hundred Italians had arrived in the station with nothing to eat. The Quartermaster replied *"nichevò,"* his stores were empty, he needed an authorization, he would see to it tomorrow; and he clumsily tried to throw him out, like some importunate mendicant; but Gottlieb smiled, and said to him: "Comrade, you haven't understood me. These Italians *must* be fed, and today, because this is what Stalin wants"; provisions arrived in a flash.

But for me the journey became a boundless torment. I must have recovered from my pleurisy, but my body was in open rebellion, and seemed to scoff at the doctors and their medicines. Every night, during my sleep, fever swept treacherously through me; an intense fever of unknown nature, which reached its peak near dawn. I used to wake up prostrate, only semi-conscious and with a wrist, an elbow or a knee numbed by stabbing pains. Then I was only capable of lying on the floor of the boxcar or on the platform, a prey to delirium and pain until about midday; after which, within a few hours, everything returned to normal, and toward evening I felt almost well. Leonardo and Gottlieb looked at me perplexed and helpless.

The train ran through endless fields, sombre towns and villages, dense wild forests that I thought had disappeared thousands of years before from the heart of Europe; the conifers and birches were so thick that they were forced desperately upwards, competing for the light of the sun in an oppressive verticality. The train forced its way as if in a tunnel, in green-black gloom, amid bare smooth trunks, under the high continuous roof of thickly intertwined branches. Rzeszów, Przemyśl with its grim fortifications, Lemberg.

At Lemberg, a skeleton city, destroyed by bombardment and the war, the train stopped for an entire night in a deluge of rain. The roof of our car was not watertight; we had to get down and look for shelter. We and a few others could find nothing better than the service subway: dark, two inches of mud, with ferocious draughts. But as punctual as ever, my fever arrived in the middle of the night, like a merciful blow on the head, bringing me the ambiguous benefit of unconsciousness.

Ternopol, Proskurov. The train reached Proskurov at dusk, the engine was uncoupled, and Gottlieb assured us that we should not leave until the morning. So we prepared to sleep overnight in the station. The waiting room was very large; Cesare, Leonardo, Daniele, and I took possession of one corner, Cesare left for the village in his capacity as purveyor, and returned soon afterwards with eggs, lettuce and a packet of tea.

We lit a fire on the floor (we were not the only ones, nor the first; the room was covered with the remains of the innumerable bivouacs of people who had preceded us, and the ceiling and walls were black with smoke, as in an old kitchen). Cesare cooked the eggs, and prepared plenty of well-sugared tea.

Now, either that tea was far more robust than the sort we were used to, or Cesare had mistaken the quantity; because in a short time we lost every trace of sleep and tiredness, and felt ourselves kindled into an unusual mood—tense and alert, hilarious, lucid, and sensitive. As a result, every act and every word of that night has remained impressed on my memory, and I can recall it as if it were yesterday.

Daylight disappeared with extreme slowness, at first pink, then violet, then grey, followed by the silvery splendour of a warm moonlit night. While we were smoking and talking gaily, two young girls, dressed in black, were sitting next to us on a wooden box. They were speaking together; not in Russian, but in Yiddish.

"Do you understand what they're saying?" asked Cesare.

"A few words."

"Up and at 'em, then. See if they'll play."

That night everything seemed easy to me, even understanding Yiddish. With unaccustomed boldness, I turned to the girls, greeted them and, trying to imitate their pronunciation, asked them in German if they were Jewish, and declared that we four were also Jewish. The girls (they were perhaps sixteen or eighteen years old) burst out laughing. *Ihr sprecht keyn Jiddisch; ihr seyd ja keyne Jiden!*" "You do not speak Yiddish; so you cannot be Jews!" In their language, the phrase amounted to rigorous logic.

Yet we really were Jews, I explained. Italian Jews: Jews in Italy, and in all Western Europe, do not speak Yiddish.

This was a great novelty for them, a comic oddity, as if someone had affirmed that there are Frenchmen who do not speak French. I tried to recite to them the beginning of the *Shema*, the basic Hebrew prayer; their incredulity grew weaker, but their merriment increased. Who had ever heard Hebrew pronounced in so ridiculous a way?

The elder one's name was Sore; she had a small, sharp, mischievous face, rotund and full of asymmetrical dimples; our difficult, halting conversation seemed to cause her piquant amusement, and stimulated her like tickling.

But if we were Jews, then so were all those others, she said to me, pointing with a circular gesture to the eight hundred Italians who filled the room. What difference was there between us and them? The same language, the same faces, the same clothing. No, I explained to her; they were Christians, they came from Genoa, Naples, Sicily; perhaps some of them had Arab blood in their veins. Sore looked around perplexed; this was extremely confusing. In her country things were much clearer; a Jew was a Jew, and a Russian was a Russian, there were no two ways about it.

They were two refugees, she explained to me. They came from Minsk, in White Russia; when the Germans had drawn near, their family had asked to be transferred to the interior of the Soviet Union, to escape the slaughter of the Einsatzkommandos of Eichmann. Their request had been carried out to the letter; they had all been sent three thousand miles from their town, to Samarkand in Uzbekistan, near the Roof of the World, in sight of mountains twenty thousand feet high. She and her sister were still children at the time; then their mother had died, and their father had been mobilized for service on a frontier. The two of them had learnt Uzbek, and many other fundamental things: how to live from day to day, how to travel across continents with a small suitcase between the two of them, in fact how to live like the fowls of the air, who labour not, neither do they spin, and who take no thought for the morrow.

Such were Sore and her silent sister. Like us, they were returning home. They had left Samarkand in March, and had set out on the journey like feathers abandoning themselves to the wind. They had traveled, partly in boxcars and partly on foot, across the Kara-kum, the Desert of the Black Sand; they had arrived at Krasnovodsk on the Caspian Sea by train, and there they had waited until a fishing boat took them to Baku. From Baku they had continued by any means they happened to find, for they had no money, only an unlimited faith in the future and in their neighbour, and a natural virgin love of life.

Everybody around was sleeping; Cesare listened to the conversation restlessly, occasionally asking me if the preliminaries were over and if we were getting down to brass tacks; then, disappointed, he went outside in search of more concrete adventures.

At about midnight the quiet of the waiting room and the girls' story were abruptly interrupted. A door, connecting the large room by a small corridor to another smaller one, reserved for soldiers in transit, flew open violently, as if blown by a gust of wind. On the threshold appeared a Russian soldier, almost a boy, drunk; he looked around with absent eyes, then started forward, head lowered, lurching fearfully, as if the floor had suddenly tilted under him. Three Soviet officers were standing in the corridor, engaged in conversation. The boy soldier braked as he reached them, drew himself stiffly to attention, and gave a military salute, which the three returned with dignity. Then off he started again, moving in semicircles like a skater, cleared the outside door miraculously, and could be heard vomiting and gulping noisily on the platform. He came back with a slightly less uncertain step, once more saluted the impassive officers and disappeared. After a quarter of an hour, the identical scene was repeated, as if in a nightmare: dramatic entrance, pause, salute, hasty crooked journey across the sleepers' legs toward the open air, evacuation, return, salute; and so on for an infinite number of times, at regular intervals, without the three ever giving him more than a distrait glance and a correct salute.

So that memorable night passed until my fever conquered me once more; then I lay on the ground, shivering silently. Gottlieb came, and brought with him an unusual medicine: half a litre of raw vodka, illicitly distilled, which he had bought from some peasants; it tasted of must, vinegar and fire. "Drink it," he told me, "drink it all. It will do you good, and in any case we have nothing else here for your illness."

I drank the infernal philtre not without an effort, burning my mouth and throat, and in a short time fell into a state of nothingness. When I woke up the following morning, I felt oppressed by a heavy weight; but it was not the fever, nor a bad dream. I lay buried under a layer of other sleepers, in a sort of human incubator of people who had arrived during the night and who could find room only on top of those already lying on the floor.

I was thirsty; thanks to the combined action of the vodka and animal warmth, I must have lost pints of sweat. The singular cure was wholly successful; the fever and pains had definitely disappeared and returned no more.

The train left, and in a few hours we reached Zhmerinka, a railway junction two hundred miles from Odessa. Here a great surprise and fierce disappointment awaited us. Gottlieb, who had conferred there with the military Command, went along the train, car by car, and informed us that we should all have to get off: the train was going no farther.

Why was it going no farther? And how and when would we reach

Odessa; "I don't know," replied Gottlieb, embarrassed: "nobody knows. I only know that we have to get off the train, settle ourselves somehow on the platform, and await orders." He was very pale and visibly disturbed.

We got down, and spent the night in the station; Gottlieb's defeat, the first one, seemed to us a bad omen. The next morning our guide, together with his inseparable brother and brother-in-law, had disappeared. They had vanished into emptiness, with all their conspicuous luggage; somebody said he had seen them talking to Russian railwaymen, and in the night climbing on to a military train going back from Odessa to the Polish border.

We stayed at Zhmerinka for three days, oppressed by a sense of uneasiness, frustration, or terror, according to our temperaments and the scraps of information we managed to extort from the Russians there. They manifested no surprise at our fate and our enforced stop, and replied to our questions in the most disconcerting of ways. One Russian told us that it was true, that various ships had left Odessa with English or American soldiers who were being repatriated, and that we also would embark sooner or later; we had food to eat, Hitler was no more, so why were we complaining? Another one told us that the previous week a trainload of Frenchmen, traveling to Odessa, had been stopped at Zhmerinka and directed toward the north "because the railway lines were cut." A third one informed us that he had personally seen a trainload of German prisoners traveling toward the Far East; the matter was clear, according to him, for were we not also allies of the Germans? All right then, they were sending us as well to dig trenches on the Japanese front.

To complicate matters another trainload of Italians coming from Rumania arrived at Zhmerinka on the third day. They looked totally different from us; there were about six hundred men and women, well dressed, with suitcases and trunks, some with cameras slung around their necks—almost tourists. They looked down on us, like poor relations; so far they had traveled in a regular train of passenger coaches, paying for their tickets, and were in order as regards their passports, money, travel documents and collective permit for Italy via Odessa. If only we could gain permission from the Russians to join up with them, then we too should reach Odessa.

With much condescension, they gave us to understand that they were persons of consequence; they were civilian and military officials from the Italian Legation at Bucharest, as well as certain other persons who, after the ARMIR* had been dissolved, had stayed in Romania with various duties, or to fish in troubled waters. There were whole family groups among them, husbands with lawfully wedded Rumanian wives and numerous children.

But the Russians, in contrast to the Germans, possess little talent for subtle distinctions and classifications. A few days later we were all traveling together toward the north, toward an unknown goal, at all events toward a new exile. Italian-Rumanians and Italian-Italians, all in the same cattle cars, all sick at heart, all in the hands of the inscrutable Soviet bureaucracy, an obscure and gigantic power, not ill-intentioned toward us, but suspicious, negligent, stupid, contradictory, and in effect as blind as the forces of nature.

Translated from the Italian by Stuart Woolf.

---

*ARMIR: Italian Army in Russia

ANOTHER SURVIVOR

Ruth Fainlight

He's fifty now, but the day his mother and father took him to the
railway station with the one permitted suitcase, clutching a satchel
crammed with entomological collecting equipment he refused to leave
behind, that chilly, too-harshly-bright day of a windy, reluctant spring,
was in 1938, and he was twelve years old. With the other children lucky
enough to be included in this refugee group going to England and their
agitated and mournful parents, they moved to the far end of the platform in an attempt to make themselves less conspicuous. Rudi recognized two of the boys from last year at school. Since the holidays he had
been kept at home: Jewish students were no longer acceptable; nor were
they safe. A few children had begun to cry, unable not to respond to the
tears their parents tried so hard to repress. The entire group emanated
a terrible collective desolation, unaffected by an individual attempt to
put a good face on matters, or hopeful talk of a future reunion. For all
of them, it was their last sight of each other, their last goodbye. Sharing a stridently upholstered couch with three men as withdrawn into
their separate worlds as he is, staring unseeingly at other patients moving restlessly around the crowded day ward, Rudi's face is still marked
by the same appalled expression that had settled on it that morning so
many years ago.

His parents belonged to families who had lived in the city for generations. Though Rudi was an only child, there had been many houses and apartments where he was welcome and at home, many celebrations to attend and cousins to play with. The family ramified through the professions: doctors, lawyers, academics, architects: one of those cultivated, free-thinking manifestations of Jewish emancipation whose crucial importance to the European spirit only became apparent after its destruction. His father had been a biologist, his mother a talented amateur pianist. At night, in the dormitory of the school he was put into by the same kindly people who had organized his rescue, he tried to make himself sleep by seeing how many themes he could bring back to mind from the music she had played. He remembered their apartment full of the sound of her piano, and himself creeping up behind her, steps deadened by the soft Persian rugs whose silk nap glinted like water in the mote-laden beams of afternoon sunlight coming through creamy net curtains, hoping to reach the piano stool and put his hands over her eyes before she even realized he was home from school.

That was the picture he had kept on the iconostasis of his mind during the years when there was no news of them at all. That, and another one—walking in the country one Sunday with his father. Even now, through the distraction of hospital life, he distinctly remembers the surge of pride and intellectual excitement when he suddenly understood what his father was explaining about the particular structure and composition of the hills around them—a lesson in geography and geology; and he remembers, also, how he called upon that memory to sustain him through every boyhood crisis.

Though he mastered English quickly and did his schoolwork well, the only thing that really interested him was the prospect of taking part in the war and adding his energy to the battle against Nazism. But he never managed to see any fighting or even get onto the continent of Europe before it ended. And then, after seven years of suspense, of great swoops between optimism and an absolute conviction that he would never see his parents alive again, the camps were opened up and the first reports and pictures began to appear. The effort he makes, even now, is to shut off parts of his mind, to push all that information away. Nightmares, day-mares—black, white, bleeding, disemboweled, flayed: Goyaesque mares with staring, maddened eyes had been galloping across the wincing terrain of his brain ever since. But he was not able to stop collecting facts, nor stop imagining how every atrocity he heard or read about might have been suffered by his parents.

Then he calmed down, came through it—another survivor. So much time passed that he could even acknowledge how privileged and fortunate he was, weighed in the balance of the global misery. Every morning over breakfast he could read in the newspapers stories of war, famine, torture, and injustice, and be no more affected by them than the newspaper readers of that time were by the catastrophe that engulfed him and his family. He was healthy, prosperous, successful. His wife had not left him. His children were growing up. His work presented no real problems. It was just that now, after more than thirty years, he was overcome with a most intense yearning for his mother. He felt as though he were still a boy of twelve, gone away from home for the first time: the adoring son of a proud, doting mother (that identity which in truth had been his, which had been waiting all this time for him to admit to and assume) who cannot be diverted by promises of even the most fabulous pleasures if they will keep him away from her one moment longer. And the strength of this feeling made him aware of how much he had repressed when it had really happened.

For the first time he was able to remember what his mother had been like before the war. During the intervening years, memory had been blotted out by imagination, which is always stronger. He had only been able to imagine her as a victim, not as a woman at the height of her vigour and self-confidence. This release of memory from the prison of fear had brought about her resurrection.

❧ ❧

Twenty years ago when Rudi and Barbara found their house, the streets between Camden Town and Primrose Hill were neither fashionable nor expensive. They had lived there ever since, while houses around them changed hands for ten and twenty times what they paid. It had been fixed up and periodically redecorated but basically retained the style of the era when they moved in: austere and utilitarian, student-like; with white-walled, charcoal-grey and neutral coloured rooms intended as the background for rational living. He had been attracted to Barbara because she seemed so rational. Nothing about their house reminded him of where he had lived until the age of twelve. The two interiors were entirely different.

Barbara had never been interested in how the house looked. Since the last of the three children started school she had trained and qualified as a social worker, and was out for most of the day and quite a few evenings. Rudi, who had become an accountant after the war, found he was bringing more work home, and often spent whole days at his desk in the big open all-purpose room on the ground floor. There was nothing wrong with his corner—it had been especially planned so that everything necessary was within reach; but sitting there one early winter afternoon he looked around and wondered how he had lived for so long in this bleak, characterless environment. At home, he thought—and became aware that home was not this house at all—everything had been so much prettier and more comfortable, more comforting, too; gratifying to the eye and the spirit in a way the room he now sat in gave no indication of understanding or allowing for. He had a strong, momentary hallucination of his mother as she must have been in 1933 or 1934, perfumed and elegantly dressed to go out for the evening, walking a few steps through the door and glancing around. He had become inured to and then unaware of the frayed, stained upholstery they'd never bothered to replace after the children had outgrown their destructive phase. Through her slightly slanting pale blue eyes, he saw the muddy, formless paintings friends had given them years ago which remained the only decorations, and watched them narrow with distaste and incomprehension before she disappeared without having noticed him.

Walking home from the tube station next day, Rudi was surprised by how many antique shops had opened in the district. A lamp on display reminded him of one in the dining room of his childhood home. It had stood on the right-hand side of a large, ornately carved sideboard, and he had loved the winter evenings when its opalescent glass shade glowed like a magic flower. Antique shops had always made him feel ignorant and gullible, but he forced himself to go inside. The lamp was more expensive than any comparable object he had ever bought, and as he wrote a cheque he was sweating as though engaged in the commission of a fearful, dangerous crime. Standing and lit on his desk, the lamp made everything in the room seem even more nondescript. He could not stop looking at it.

"Oh, that's new, isn't it?" Barbara remarked as she hurried through the house between work and a meeting, tying a headscarf over her short blonde hair. "I forgot some papers," she explained, "or I wouldn't have come back. I've left something for supper for you and the children."

"That's really beautiful. I'd like to do a drawing of it," Faith said. She was the elder of the two girls, and had just become an art student. Though circumstances had made him an accountant, Rudi often wondered if he had betrayed his potential. He thought of himself as an artist manqué. Faith was the only one of the children who took after him. It would be hard to tell that Mavis and Tony had a Jewish father. They were much more like Barbara's side of the family.

Most fathers he knew would be more likely to spend time on the weekend with sons rather than daughters. But Tony had never given him an opportunity to develop that sort of special relationship. When not at school the boy was always out somewhere with friends—an eminently social being. Mavis, the baby of the family, had been her mother's girl from the start, and so Rudi and Faith had been left to make their own Saturday excursions. Visiting museums and galleries with her combined pleasure and anguish. He was grateful for the opportunity to view paintings or statues that had excited and drawn him back to them over and over again as a young man, but that he had not seen for years. It was wonderful to watch Faith's knowledge and appreciation increase, to witness the development of this lovely, perceptive creature. The anguish came when he remembered visiting museums with his mother; when he recognized the inherent sensitivity of Faith's responses, so similar to what his mother's had been; when his pleasure at her responses made him aware of what his mother must have felt about him.

Often they would set out with no particular destination, call in at bookshops or wander around street markets. Now Rudi had an aim, and they would search for pictures, rugs, china, bits of furniture—anything that reminded him of the comfortable bourgeois home he had grown up in. Faith thought it perfectly natural to buy so much—while he found it much easier to spend money in the company of his pretty, auburn-haired seventeen-year-old daughter than when he was alone. He had loved her from the first sight of her hour-old face. What had touched his heart so profoundly, though he had not known it at the time, was an unmistakable and strongly marked resemblance to his mother. The echoes and parallels and actual duplications between his daughter and mother incremented like compound interest once he began to look for them. Because of this, he felt he had to do whatever he could to help her, as though the years torn from his mother's life could be made good somehow if Faith were happy and fulfilled.

ᘒ ᘐ

The difference between his recent acquisitions and the rest of the furnishings gave the house a hybrid quality and disturbed them all. Rudi began to be irritable and dissatisfied, suspecting that he would never manage to achieve a convincing reproduction of his parental home. It was becoming harder to summon up his mother's image with the same marvellous tangibility. The lamps and rugs and little tables were useless magic. And yet even the memory of her first, vivid return as the person she really had been, instead of only the dehumanized victim that was all he had been able to imagine since the war, was enough to change his relationship to everything.

He found it difficult to believe that he and Barbara were actually husband and wife. She was so calm, so settled and busy and mature; like a kindly, abstracted nurse. He'd had a nursemaid rather like Barbara when he was about six years old. Apart from commenting on the amount of money he must be spending, she seemed benignly indifferent to the transformation of the house. In bed, though, when the light was out and he took her warm, silent, acquiescent body into his arms, he could not stop himself from imagining that she was his mother. Frequently, he felt about to burst into tears. The sight of his glaring eyes and pale, tense, puffy face in need of a shave, repelled him when he caught sight of it in the bathroom mirror.

Rudi had avoided talking to the children about the war, the camps, and how his parents died. He had never even managed to give them any explanation about their connection to Judaism. Now he felt it was too late to begin, and was bitterly ashamed of his cowardice. Of course his mother would have wanted her grandchildren to know everything. Perhaps that was why she had come back, and, because he was not fulfilling his duty, the reason for her withdrawal. This thought put him into a deep depression for several days. But that Saturday afternoon on the Portobello Road with Faith, he saw a dress very like one his mother used to wear, dangling from the rail of an old-clothes stall. It gave him an idea. If his mother would not appear of her own free will, dressing Faith in similar clothes might force her back.

Faith was delighted with the dress and hurried him home so she could try it on. The others were out and the house was empty. When Faith came down the stairs Rudi was astounded by the uncanny resemblance. This was not a fantasy or hallucination, but a solid, breathing figure of flesh—a revenant: his mother even before he had known her, before his birth, when she had been a young girl. He was awestruck and terrified. Unaware that she was being used for conjuration, his daughter had innocently assumed the identity of a dead woman.

He had succeeded beyond his imaginings. His mother was in the room—but how many of her? There was the young girl incarnated in his once more recognizable daughter (recreated in any case by the natural laws of genetic inheritance): the two of them fused into this touching being for whom he had been trying to make the appropriate setting with every object purchased, and another—the one he had not wanted to meet again ever.

It was the victim who had haunted him for years. Perhaps those lamps and rugs had not been bought to lure back the girl and untroubled woman, after all—but to ward off this one. Gaunt, dirty, cowed, huddled defensively near the foot of the staircase and wearing the threadbare clothes of a camp inmate, she glared with sick, unrecognizing eyes toward him. The sight made him want to die. He could see them both at the same time, they were only a few feet apart, though inhabiting separate universe.

"Take off that dress!" he commanded. "Go upstairs and take it off right now!"

Faith stared with amazement. "I don't want to take it off." The concentration camp woman vanished at the sound of her voice. "I like it. I want to wear it all the time. It's lovely. The girls at school will all want to have dresses like this."

"You look stupid in it," he said desperately. "You look ridiculous."

"I don't think I do." Her expression was defiant and challenging.

The only way to control his fear of breaking down was to stiffen his spirit with anger. Faith could not understand what was happening. "Take that dress off immediately or I'll tear it off." She knew he would, yet refused to obey and stood her ground.

He had crossed the empty space between them in less than a moment. The cloth was soft and old and gave easily. She screamed with shock and fear. The turmoil of his emotions was sickening. He thought he would lose consciousness. She was in his power and he was tormenting her like a camp guard who could not resist exercising that power, as though she were his specially chosen victim. There must have been someone who singled out his mother in the same way.

She pulled away from him, clutching the torn dress together, and ran up the stairs. "Fascist!" she shouted, her voice thick with tears. He opened the front door and walked out of the house.

It's dark and cold, but he walks rapidly ahead, with no plan or choice of direction, completely indifferent to where he is going, his mind quite empty. After a time, the emptiness on all sides makes him realize that he must have crossed the road and climbed Primrose Hill. He tries sitting down on a bench, but the moment he stops moving, he is swamped by such self-contempt that he cannot bear it, so he starts walking again. He knows that if he goes back he will break into Faith's room and probably beat her to death. His stride lengthens. He is walking down Park Road now, down Baker Street, crossing Piccadilly, crossing the river, a tall, thick-bodied man unable to stop walking. He is going to keep walking until a car knocks him down or someone fells him with a blow, until he reaches the end of his endurance and drops in his tracks.

from *THE CHANT OF BEING*

Gil Ben Aych

They entered the active phase of preparation. There was intense busyness, a little like the days when the seamstress came to the house in Tlemcen, Algeria. Jeannette, Simon's mother, was running all about. She had to see to the reception at home. Joseph, Simon's father, was overcome. He was in charge of coordination with the synagogue and the rabbi, and had to invite the guests.

Gilberte, a cousin from Versailles, came to help out. Aunt Rosette, too. She lived in Créteil and often aided her younger sister following the birth of a child or at other exceptional moments. She would stay on rue Truffaut, in Paris, at Jeannette's and Joseph's place, as she did now. The trip seemed very long to her, and she would repeat that "back in Tlemcen, the distances weren't the same, here we're really far apart, do you realize how long it took me to get from Créteil to the 17th arrondissement, here . . . !"

Jeannette and Rosette had prepared a considerable number of main dishes and cakes, little omelettes and *méguinas:* patties made of egg and potato, stuffed with fresh vegetables, topped with lamb brains cooked in parsley.

Gilberte asked Simon if he believed. If he had faith. He answered no. Just like that. He added that it was to please his grandparents and receive gifts that he had agreed to the Bar Mitzvah. Or the communion, as they called it at Simon's house. But he had learned otherwise from the Hebrew school he attended last term with his brother Abram, and from a neighbor, a European Jewish woman; and from certain family acquaintances who were studying Hebrew. They taught him that a Jew did not take "communion," he had a "Bar Mitzvah" to mark his accession to religious adulthood. The nuance seemed decisive and distinctive. Nonetheless, the words "Bar Mitzvah" had a biblical or theological connotation that his parents did not attach to "communion." "Communion" was a more fitting word for a specific act in time, a good excuse for a festive family gathering.

In the afternoons, they sent out the last invitations, to people whose addresses they had only just gotten. They sat around the table, putting stamps on envelopes. The sun's rays flooded the old wooden floor, and their faces shone. The women ate dates to pass the time.

⟨⟨

They got up early. Joseph went quickly downstairs to warm up the car. He waited, honking the horn from time to time, to hurry them up. Jeannette reacted by asking: "What's wrong with Joseph? Why is he getting so worked up, today of all days?" The day of his Bar Mitzvah. The day. This day. Today is the Bar Mitzvah.

They washed up. They had installed a little shower in the kitchen. They did not have one before. Simon and Abram put on their "nice suits," with white socks and new black loafers. Jeannette kept saying: "Don't press down the back of your shoes," worried as she was about things staying in good shape. She watched over everything. She shut off the gas jets and closed the blinds (it seemed to Simon as though they were leaving for several months). The neighbors were astonished at all the activity, but were simply told of the good news, the Bar Mitzvah, without further comment. It would have been necessary to go into detail about differences in religion and ritual, and no one really felt like it. Except for the baker's wife, who offered them some candy before they set off.

The conventional, general silence that the Christian neighbors kept in the face of an act so meaningful, so revelatory of religious identity, was nothing new to Simon, who had had a clear, sharp perception of it on his arrival in France in 1956. It seemed as though the silence of the others, in the face of something so different (not to mention anomalous or even monstrous), were a kind of respect, a self-contained, mute, unspeakable deference, the mark of a relevant, significant distance. "People" knew! "People" knew that Simon's family (*not* "was" Jewish but . . .) "was-not-Christian!" They were known to be different. And Simon realized this was known.

Nonetheless, Simon suspected that speaking of these differences would allow the real differences, the true ones, to be understood; but he then felt, at one and the same time, shame and the need to keep a distance. Shame because it was not right for a boy of his age, thirteen years old, to teach adults, who perhaps knew the score after all. Perhaps. Distance, a need to keep a distance, because he realized that to speak of the difference would only attract attention. Attention to the difference, not to Simon. And since Simon did not want to attract attention, he preferred to remain silent. Like everyone else. No. Like Simon. Simon, already, did not like to "attract attention."

They jumped into the grey Peugeot 403, crossed the outer boulevards, and arrived at the synagogue of the 18th arrondissement where the Bar Mitzvah was to take place.

It was near the rue Custine, and Rabbi Judas, his father Joseph's cousin, who lived on rue Stephenson, would be there. It had become more and more difficult for him to get around, because of his age, but Joseph insisted on his being there. He, and none other, would officiate at the ceremony.

They entered a bright, bare, vast room. In the center, towards the front, stood the men; and in back, towards the side, the women took their seats. There was a sort of wooden rostrum, covered with an immaculate embroidered cloth, white and pomegranate-colored velvet. At the forefront were the *sepharim.* *

In comparison to the grandiose synagogue Simon had known in Tlemcen, the one here seemed laughable and almost shabby. It made you feel as though Jews had no place in France and hid in order not to call attention to their activities. Were their activities reprehensible? Not as far as I know, said Simon to himself. Why was it so small? The tiny synagogue. The narrow Jew. Shrunken Judaism. European cleanliness and skimpy Judaism. Back there, in Tlemcen, in Algeria, the synagogue took up almost an entire block; here, you went in through the door of a house like all others. This detail mattered. Simon asked his father why and was told that it was a question of "lack of funds." Simon only half-believed him but decided to make do with half a belief. He said to himself, baldly,

---

Sepharim (Hebrew): scrolls.

it may be hard to believe but so it is. Not believing his own eyes, Simon closed them, and believed. Simon would believe. He finally opened his eyes. It was time. It was high time he opened his eyes. That was the very purpose of a communion. Today's the communion. Today?

They began with the short morning prayer, during which a strip of leather is wrapped around the arm. Likewise, a kind of cube, made of the same material and containing biblical verses, is held on the forehead by a band of leather we strap around our heads. The tefillin. The faithful Jew, literally tied to the texts, his forehead marked with the sacred seal, devotes himself to the ritual morning prayer—an act of allegiance to God that Simon found hard to accept but took delight in, because of its incongruous, unexpected, almost obscene character. He was on the rostrum. (Strange to think that addressing God was something strictly personal! For a long time, he was obsessed by a problem present in all religions, but more pronounced in Judaism because of its minority status. If God is supposed to be there for all of us, he must "really" be there for each of us. He's "our" solo player. Mine. The great universal dialogue and private monologues. Generalized, pervasive cacophony. Universal harmony. Because we are there and because we speak. It's us.)

Simon wore a new *tallit* given to him by his godfather, the other Simon. He liked the silky material of the prayer shawl and especially the soft white fringes hanging at the ends. You put it on your shoulders and you were covered before God. He also wore a small red velvet skullcap that his aunt Esther, a seamstress, had made him from leftover material. But the skullcap annoyed him. It was too small and kept falling off. It wasn't a real silk skullcap, embroidered with Hebrew writing, like the ones adults wore. They helped him. They helped him several times to put it back on.

Simon liked embracing the *sepharim*. It seemed as though he were embracing the entire world and its eternal spirit. He felt like crying when he held the sacred scrolls in his arms. He recited his portion without really understanding it, because he had learned it by heart, over a three-month period, during Bar Mitzvah lessons at the synagogue. He did recognize some words. Whence his ability to associate or connect words from other languages—Arabic, French, English, even German or Spanish—with their Semitic "roots," when the occasion presented itself. (Thus *zit* in Hebrew, becomes *zeit* in Arabic, keeps the *i* to become *huile* in French, loses the *u* and gains an *o* to make *oil* in English. Languages can transform or keep consonants at their leisure. Z stays *z* as one moves from Hebrew to Arabic, it switches from *z* to *h* going from Arabic to

French, there's no more *h* in English, *öl* in German turns the *i* into an umlaut on the *o,* ending up with *zeitoun* meaning "olive" in Arabic and Zeitoun as the last name of one of his friends in fifth grade. Zeitoun. *Z* and *t* from the ancient Hebrew disappear, the *i* remains. A straight stick standing up and on the top a point or head. Man walks vertically through history, on the ground. And the history of words goes on, unremittingly, underneath. Languages referring to each other. Words calling words. Our words calling out to each other and beyond.) Whence also the knowing, unspeakable, joy of posting oneself, of being posted at the source of a phenomenon that concerns everyone. Speaking. Writing. Communicating. And using words whose far-removed origins and semantic aura he, Simon, sometimes knew. Semantic. Semitic. Fast-found mimicry among languages. A primitive effect. Writing.

He was rather unhappy when he had to put the *sepharim* back in the lovely ark that looked like a little house. He would have wished to keep them longer or even take them home, so beautiful were they. He liked the little silver towers perched on their very tops and at the ends of which hung little bells of sorts.

What impressed him particularly was the finger you hold to follow the text. He preferred by far to read from right to left. This was quite a change from his school books that all looked alike with their ugly pictures. Here things were strange and uncanny. Simon felt he was part of an elite. Yes, an elite. Or more exactly a group that resembled no other and that was truly distinctive. Here, he was far from all his friends and even tended to scorn them. Not having had the same experience as he, they would never understand things the way Jews could. They. The others. Simon thus displayed a sureness that quickly turned into superiority. Simon read. In Hebrew, Simon read. He read. Simply enough.

The rabbi helped him follow the text. Simon took special care in reading his portion because what pleased him above all, as though it were his duty, was that no classmate should do so well as he or get so good a grade. Not even the Polish or Russian Jews, whom he learned then to call Ashkenazim, a word he easily remembered because his father's boss in Algeria was named Ashkenazi. Services were different at their synagogues.

Moreover, Simon hardly understood how Jews could be designated by a word with the syllable *az.* The thing seemed impossible to him, even comical, in short: contemptible. Laughable. This contempt Simon transferred onto the Ashkenazim themselves. In his eyes, they were hardly Jews.

He had had, however, more than once, the opportunity of learning that impossible things were indeed possible. So he was not unduly surprised. When Simon thought this way, he opened his eyes wide, to absorb what he saw. Stunned, Simon would absorb and forget. He would forget. Simon would forget. Simon was jubilant, detesting the Catholics. He also detested that notorious Ashkenazi, with whom his father had fallen out because he tried to cheat him of his due.

At the time, paradoxically, the relationship between German and the word "Ashkenazi," despite historical events, was not obvious. The association, hidden in the recesses of the unconscious, was taboo. Only much later did he find out that Ashkenazi meant "German" and Sephardi "Spanish." In this way, certain words conceal in their depths connotations or meanings that emerge later. Certain words, and their chrysalises.

Moreover, Simon liked Hebrew pronunciation, the *shin* and the *bet,* the lack of vowels and the greatly condensed vocabulary. It was indeed a communion, a means of communion among members of a minority who assigned to it a unique quality. When the rabbi addressed him—Simon—by name, reciting in Hebrew the names of his father and mother, of his grandfathers and grandmothers, of his great-grandfathers and great-grandmothers, Simon, he, Simon, wiped away tears with a brand-new handkerchief. Brand-new. He heard the women say amen and pray in Arabic as they extolled him. (That the women prayed in Arabic, while the men read Hebrew, added to the confusion, kept Simon from separating Jews and Arabs clearly and distinctly, at least as far as his family in Algeria was concerned. Those women praying, were they Jewish, were they Arab? The question reflected the fact that in Algeria only men were considered fit to learn Hebrew. If a woman knew Hebrew—unless she were a notable scholarly exception—she simply repeated prayers recited a hundred thousand times over. By men!) He turned to the left where there stood a table covered with pomegranate-colored velvet embroidered with gold thread. He continued reading from another book. He thought of all the weddings he had attended, and felt as though he himself were getting married to everyone and no one. Getting married. To everyone and no one.

This idea enraptured Simon, even as it embarrassed him. Only long afterwards did he grasp its exact significance, when he realized that everyone was close to him and no one was close to him, really close to him, to himself, to self. He had married himself having become a man. Communion.

When he arrived at the last lines of his reading, a girl cousin threw sugar-coated almonds at him. He embraced Rabbi Judas, who had a full white beard; his father, Joseph, who stood at his side; his mother, Jeannette, as he came down from the rostrum; his grandmothers, Etoile and Hanna. A member of the synagogue came forward to ask the women to return to their places. Jeannette retorted that she was allowed to kiss her son at his communion, on the day of his communion. God would not mind.

Simon received several gifts. Uncle Jacques handed him a completely white envelope, inscribed with his first name, which intrigued him. He saw the joy, the true happiness, on his family's lips. He remained on the rostrum. Simon. On the rostrum.

It was his brother's turn, his brother Abram, his junior by two years, who liked Hebrew less and whom they had managed to convince even though he did not understand why he had to go through the same thing again. The same thing as Simon. After Simon had done it. His *tallit* was on crooked and kept sliding around, the black leather cube made him appear one-eyed, his skullcap rode down his neck. When he pulled up his sleeve in order to wrap the leather strip around his forearm, he seemed half-undressed, as though he were waiting to be examined by a doctor or getting on his pajamas. His shirttails emerged from his trousers.

He was rather embarrassed and annoyed, he was unsure of his portion and the rabbi kept correcting him because he either read the wrong line or mispronounced words. The worshipers, egged on by Uncle Jacques, began to laugh and make comments. Although absorbed in his reading, Abram raised his head from time to time to cast a curious glance at Judas or to gauge the onlookers' response. His gestures triggered a comic reaction, which then redoubled. So that at the end of a slight half-hour of torture, the rabbi cut things short. Cut Abram's portion short.

Uncle Jacques called out: "We should have said, 'Encore!!! Encore.'" A legend came to be, which attributed the remark to Abram.

Simon's chagrin, the unspeakable dream, the obvious glance, the future presence, the narrow Jew, the semantic aura, Abram's remark.

❧ ❧

A few female cousins were in charge of the record player and switched among Arabic songs, rock music, and slow dances.

Debates started between partisans of one or another kind of music. Upon hearing "modern" music, Hanna turned to Grandmother Etoile and said, "*Cassement de tête.*"* Etoile answered, "*Rass tertek,*" which meant exactly the same thing, but in Arabic.

By listening to his grandmothers, or others, repeat in Arabic what they had just said in French, Simon began to appreciate the differences between the two languages and sense the originality of each. If the phrase meant exactly the same thing in French and Arabic, then there was no reason to say it in both languages. Nonetheless, they said it, repeated it, in both languages. Etoile and Hanna would repeat it. That proved that one language (in this case, Arabic) brought in a nuance that was absent from the other. Here, *rass tertek* added to *cassement de tête* the idea of incessant repetition and irreparable damage. Rock was thus perceived by the two Arab grandmothers as a kind of monotony as well as a sort of smashing, a violent cracking, a total break.

When Simon thought about such things, he liked to go from one language to the other and enjoyed, really enjoyed, the art of nuances. An art of nuances that moved between the local idiolect (the Judeo-Algerian Arabic of Tlemcen) and a mixture of a colonized people's approximate French (which he heard around him) and standard French (which he learned at school). Simon thus had the best reasons to perceive nuances. He appreciated distinctions. He was distinguished. Languages distinguished him. Thus Simon began to forge a language: a language that was not Arabic, or Hebrew, or French. A language. His language. Simon's language.

Others thought that it was not right to play such music on a communion day. This was no ordinary celebration, like a birthday party. The religion had to be respected. So they put Samy el Magrebi back on, along with other Jewish singers who performed liturgical chants in a singsong. The debates stopped. Calm returned.

Translated from the French by Alan Astro.

Cassement de tête (French): splitting headache, deafening noise.

FINKELSTEIN'S FINGERS

Maxim Biller

1.

We sat with our backs to the street, on broad, comfortable leather stools, and over the bar hung a mirror. In the mirror one could see Broadway, which down here, near the World Trade Center, at the southern tip of the city, with its empty warehouses and discount outlets, seemed cold and mean. It was getting dark, and as the streetlights came on, one after the other, I was stirred, as someone else might have been at the sight of a particularly well-turned sunrise.

The woman with whom I was talking had approached me a few minutes earlier. Suddenly she was standing there, her lips quivering in a foolish and uncertain way, and then she said, out of the blue in German, that I looked just like the Hungarian poet Miklós Radnóti. But of course, she continued, she knew who I really was, and she said it in the tone of those people who think they have an undeniable claim on anyone whose photo they've seen in the newspaper.

She was old, and although older women don't interest me much, I took a good look at her. I liked the roundness of her eyes and the fluttering of her false eyelashes. I liked the way her pouting lips quivered whenever she fell silent or was pensive. And her white, nearly skinless face with two long furrows around the mouth reminded me, in the halogen lighting of the coffee shop, of a beautiful Etruscan death mask.

I had offered the woman a seat, but she didn't want to talk about me at all. She merely inquired politely how large a printing had been done of my last book, and remarked contemptuously on the controversy that had erupted over it. Then she said, just as out of the blue as before, that I did not deserve Radnóti's face and eyes; I, the child of prosperity, had no idea what Life and Literature were really about. Finally she began to talk—about herself, about Miklós Radnóti and Professor Finkelstein.

Who was she? The wife of a Hamburg attorney who had one day simply gone off the deep end.

She had three children, a dog, and a master's degree in American literature, and one evening a month she had an open house in her large apartment on Klosterstern, with food and live music. She was friends with young artists, whose paintings she bought. Her familiarity with the cultural sections of the German papers was matched only by that of the people who wrote for them. Apparently she had read every line ever written by Updike and Nabokov, Faulkner and Henry James. When she became pregnant the first time, she had given up everything for marriage and family, and now she was finally fulfilling her old dream: taking a course in creative writing at Columbia University.

And who was Professor Finkelstein? To her, a monster, a sadist, a tormenting spirit, who had decided from the outset to show his student from Germany what the score was.

"A person can speak frankly with you," she said to me. "You don't give a damn about taboos and sensitive subjects."

"You bet your life."

"Then listen: Finkelstein is small potatoes in America. I know that for a fact—the other students told me. He got his teaching position only because of his race."

"You mean—"

"Of course. They all stick together, most of all here in New York. I've heard there are actually people who pass themselves off as Jewish in order to have a chance at making it professionally."

"That's pretty funny, isn't it."

She looked at me amiably and smiled. "Well, if you want to call it that . . ."

I looked into her white face, then raised my eyes. In the mirror over the bar I saw a man get out of a taxi and lean in the window on the taxi's passenger side. His body jerked nervously, and he was waving his arms. Suddenly the driver jumped out of the car, tore open the trunk, and began throwing newspapers, books, and clothing onto the sidewalk. They wrangled with each other a little longer, then the driver drove off in a rage, while the man gathered up his things. He leaned against the plate-glass window of the coffee shop. He was breathing heavily, and his glasses were bent. As I observed his face, I was startled—he looked so much like me. The same small face, tangled red hair, broad, heavy jaw with an over-bite and a scar on the lower left. He even wore a jacket similar to mine, and he seemed to have the same small, somewhat squat build . . .

2.

"You aren't listening to me at all," said the woman next to me, offended.

I looked at her hard, and made an effort to appear focused and polite, but suddenly I couldn't remember who she was or why I was talking with her.

"May I go on?" she asked sharply.

"Yes," I answered slowly, "of course . . ."

"All right . . . The second time the class met, Finkelstein stood up in front and read one of his own short stories," she said.

Again I looked in the mirror. It had gotten dark in the meantime, people were rushing back and forth, cars glided along Broadway, red and yellow lights turned into sparks, threads, and exploding points, and for a moment the nighttime image in the mirror froze into a photograph. There was nothing more to be seen of my double.

"Excuse me," I said, "I'm really listening to you now."

"Do you know what the story was about?" she said.

"Haven't the faintest."

"Guess!"

"Sex?"

She shook her head.

"Love?"

"No."

"Betrayal?"

"No."

"The city?"

"No, not that either."

"Then what?"

"Come on, you'll get it."

"The Holocaust?"

"Exactly!" she exclaimed cheerfully and loudly. "The Holocaust!" Then a shadow passed over her Etruscan face, and she said, "Finkelstein's story was about a former Polish partisan who trades her New York apartment for a country home in Connecticut and from then on is pursued in her dreams by SS-men."

"Not bad."

"In the end she wakes up in the middle of the night, shouts, 'They're coming, they're coming,' dashes to the kitchen, and smashes all her dishes to smithereens."

"I've heard worse."

"You may be right, you're the writer," she said, and then she leaned her shoulder against me. The pressure grew as we talked on, so much so that I began to wonder about her.

"After Finkelstein finished reading it," she said, "he melodramatically laid the manuscript of his story, which has of course never been published, on the lectern. He paced back and forth across the seminar room like a trial lawyer in a Hollywood film as if we were the jury, and then planted himself smack in front of me and said smugly, 'So, Anita, how do you like the story?'"

She looked at me expectantly.

"You should change professors," I said, "if Finkelstein doesn't appeal to you."

"Of course, no problem. In the end, one can change everything: professors, history, your father, your mother, even the country you come from."

"What do you want from me?" I snapped at her, and her old white cheeks immediately filled with blood. They turned red and firm and hard; and suddenly her face looked green, then yellow, no longer like a beautiful death mask. It was like one of those hollowed-out pumpkins Americans spook each other with at Halloween.

She pulled her shoulder away, stood up, laid a five-dollar bill on the counter, and left without a word of farewell. In the mirror over the bar I saw her linger in front of the subway station, loiter around a newspaper stand for a while, take a few steps in the direction of Midtown, toward Chambers Street, then turn back and go down the steps to the subway.

3.

I kept looking outside; I gazed into the mirror above my head. I was glad to be rid of the German woman, but I found it even more reassuring that my double had not appeared again. Finally I pulled my book out of the inside pocket of my jacket and opened it. I had brought it to New York because I had been hoping to find an American publisher, but I had soon given up; two telephone conversations with agents who'd been recommended to me had drained me of my courage. I was reading my stories again now, for the first time since they had appeared in Germany six months earlier, but I didn't understand them. I skimmed over words and sentences as though they were just pretty geometric patterns and lines. Then the door to the coffee shop opened, I heard soft, dragging footsteps, I heard a gentle sigh, and Anita from Hamburg was sitting next to me again and pressing her shoulder against mine.

"You have to help me," she said.

I quickly put the book away. "What's happened?" I asked.

"I have to hand in my term paper by tomorrow . . ."

"What is it?"

"A short story."

"And what am I supposed to do?"

"Write it."

"My English is atrocious."

"I could translate it."

"In one night?"

"In one night."

"How much have you written already?"

"Not a line."

"A nice little victory for Professor Finkelstein, right?"

She took the five-dollar bill from the counter and rolled it up.

"The topic?" I said.

She slid the bill back and forth between the palm of her hands. "Guess!"

"Sex, love, betrayal?"

She smiled, and now she was as beautiful and striking as at the beginning, and then I smiled too, and we said in unison, "The Ho-lo-caust!"

"Here." She laid a black-and-white photo on the counter. The photo showed a young man with eyes half closed and a cigarette in his mouth. He had a small face, a broad jaw with a scar on the lower left, freckles, and light hair, probably red. "Here," she said, "this is Finkelstein's topic. We're supposed to write about Miklós Radnóti. Three thousand words."

4.

I glanced in the mirror. Nothing, not a trace of my double. Broadway was emptying out, and the façades of the buildings, with dark, barred windows above the stores, were gradually acquiring that nocturnal shade of sepia.

"I don't know," I said.

"Please!"

"Tell me about him first. Maybe something will come to you."

"Nothing will come to me. I can't do it, I simply . . . You're the writer."

"Come on now! Get started!"

"All right, I'll try," she said, and then pressed onward, rapidly, breathlessly, without hesitation: "Miklós Radnóti was born in 1909 in Budapest. He translated Apollinaire and Hölderlin into Hungarian. He was a poet himself. A good poet. He had a chance to escape from the National Socialists, but in the summer of 1939 he returned to Hungary, after a trip to France. He thought Admiral Horthy would never allow anything worse to happen."

"And what's the story?"

"The story is his death. What else would it be?" said Anita. She hissed at me, "I'm sure Finkelstein, that Holocaust worshiper, thought this up just for my benefit."

"You're paranoid." I replied with a quiet, sadistic smile. "So, how did this Radnóti die?" I asked her.

"They found him a year after the war."

"Where?"

"He was halfway between Budapest and Vienna. In a large pit. He had had to shovel it out himself, along with some other prisoners."

"I see. So how many corpses were there?"

"Twenty-two," she said.

I beckoned to the waiter. He leaned over the narrow stainless countertop and filled our coffee cups. I liked the sweet, weak New York coffee. I drank it constantly, five or six times a day, and with every sip I thought about having to go back soon. I had only a week left.

I offered Anita a cigarette, and she stuck it behind her ear, to be precise, between her ear and the thick, quilted edge of her wildly patterned cap, which she'd probably bought in a second-hand shop on St. Mark's Place. Then she ordered a doughnut for each of us.

"What did they do to them?" I asked.

"During the last autumn of the war, the SS marched them for months through Wallachia. From Heidenau, near Bor, by the way of Belgrade and Novi Sad all the way across Hungary to Győr. Anyone who couldn't keep going was done for."

"And Miklós Radnóti couldn't keep going?"

"No, apparently not."

I felt the pressure of her shoulder, and then I noticed that she was inching her foot along the footrest. She brought her foot up and finally pressed it against the inside of my shin. She turned her face toward mine, and she came so close that I could see little red and blue veins in her temples. Her negroid lips had a smoky flavor, she was sweating very slightly on the back of her neck, and I think she had on that rare, old-fashioned Chanel scent that always gives a suggestion of grass and gasoline.

It was just a short kiss, very short and very hard.

"And what's the twist on the whole thing?" I asked afterward.

"When the mass grave was opened after the war," she said in a friendly tone and then brushed the back of her hand over her wet lips, "they found a sheaf of poems in the pocket of Radnóti's windbreaker. He'd written them in the camp at Heidenau and also on the death march to Győr. So Finkelstein says. I have no way of checking. It wouldn't surprise me if this was just one of his hoaxes."

"A nice little Anne Frank story . . . Are the poems any good?"

"Finkelstein says Celan couldn't hold a candle to Radnóti. But no one ever undertook to disseminate his work."

"I don't know if I can do anything with this," I said softly.

"Of course you can," Anita replied. She took Radnóti's picture from the counter and stuck it in my jacket pocket, next to my book.

"I really don't know . . ."

I was still wavering, but she paid no attention. She took my fingers in hers, squeezed them until they hurt, and then said, "Tell me where you live."

"Right around the corner."

"Right around the corner," she repeated. Then she put another five-dollar bill on the counter, pulled the cigarette I had given her out from behind her ear, and lit up . . .

Once outside, before we turned onto Chambers Street, I glanced into the coffee shop. There he sat in the window, at a small table—my double. He was drinking tea and sorting his newspapers and books. He had laid his clothing, in a bundle, next to him on the floor. He seemed agitated, distraught, but not at all crazy, and I suddenly had the impression that he and Anita had secretly smiled at each other through the plate-glass window . . .

"OK, Anita," I said to her, "we'll show your Finkelstein."

5.

I've been to New York often, but every time I leave it's as though I've never been there. And that's why every time I go I hardly remember it, only the light, which is entirely different from ours in Europe; all I know is that if you take the highway to Long Island, past the huge white cemeteries of Queens, you can see even more distinctly that the light in America has something subdued and tender about it, as if a huge red filter were suspended over the country . . .

This time I was staying with a friend on Chambers Street, between Broadway and Church, and, except for the first couple of days, I was there alone, because soon after I arrived he flew to Munich to visit his parents. I fed his two cats, brought in the mail, and checked the answering machine. Now and then he would phone from Munich to see if anything was new. Otherwise I had nothing to do, and I decided right at the beginning not to bother anymore about placing the American rights for the book. And then I fell into that mixture of restless curiosity and constant fatigue that takes hold of me in almost every foreign city. I covered TriBeCa in all directions, went down to Wall Street, and from there to Battery Park, where I stared at the Statue of Liberty for a few minutes. I walked to SoHo every day, went to the galleries and boutiques, ate lunch at the vegetarian restaurant on Greene Street, and then took the subway home, to sleep or watch television. In late afternoon I would often go out again. I would sit for a while in the coffee shop on the corner and then take the subway wherever I felt like; I would decide on the platform or on the train . . .

I still recall vividly how two days before leaving, I stood on the riverside promenade in Brooklyn Heights and looked across the East River toward Manhattan. I saw the island with its densely crowded skyscrapers, and then I turned around, and there were these little Brooklyn townhouses behind me. I still recall wandering through the Lower East Side

afterward, eating blintzes with sour cream in a Jewish cafeteria and over-
hearing the owner firing his Vietnamese cook. And most of all, I recall
how I stopped in front of a bookstore to look in the window, and the
owner came out and had *payes* under his black hat and was wearing
Hasidic garb. He closed the shop, pulling down the metal shutter, and
as he hurried away it occurred to me that it was Friday noon and Shabbat would be beginning soon, and then I noticed that all the streets
around me had suddenly emptied out, and that was certainly the most
beautiful moment I have ever experienced in this city . . .

6.

Two months after my return from New York, I came across an article by Anita in *Die Zeit*. It was called "In the Labyrinth of the Past,"
and it was about Professor Finkelstein, his Jewish origins, and Anita's
experiences in Finkelstein's creative writing class. I was thrilled, and I
read the article straight through—as I always do when a topic discussed
in a newspaper or magazine is something I know a lot about. Anita first
described the torments and self-doubt she had had to endure as a German in Professor Finkelstein's class, and at this point she twice referred
to him as the "great, wise, and understanding American of Polish-
Jewish extraction." She wrote that it had been a brilliant piece of strategy the way he had sharpened her historical consciousness through cir-
cumspect inquiries into her biography. But of course she had had to
work through the entire grieving process alone; she would never forget
the day when Professor Finkelstein had sent her to a seminar on Holocaust literature. There, when she was in the middle of reading the gripping poems of the unknown Hungarian-Jewish poet Miklós Radnóti, a
dam had suddenly burst inside her, whereupon she had dashed all the
way across the campus to Finkelstein's office to make her confession at
last. Weeping, she told of her mother, who at every parade had elbowed
her way to the front to be kissed or hugged by the Führer. Raging, she
talked about her father, who had first worked at IG Farben in Lud-
wigshafen, later at the plant in Auschwitz. Yes, and then she described
to the professor her own personal postwar drama, the silence at home,
her father's drinking, her mother's depression, and her own craziness
during the student revolt of the sixties. Finally she kissed Finkelstein's
hand to beg his forgiveness for everything her people had inflicted on
his. "And thus," Anita concluded, "began my friendship with Professor

Finkelstein. We exchange letters, we telephone each other sometimes, and he has promised he will spend Christmas at our house on the Lüneburg Heath."

I smiled. Once again I smiled my conceited Jewish sadist's smile, and then I noticed the photo next to the article. According to the caption, it was Professor Finkelstein, and it was the very photo that Anita had laid on the counter that time in the coffee shop.

I stopped smiling. I folded up the newspaper and looked around me. I was sitting in an Italian restaurant on Isestrasse. It was Saturday afternoon, the last weekend before Christmas, and there was no one in the place except me and the waiters. I had got up late and was only now having lunch. Just as I was about to order coffee, I felt a cold draft hit my legs. The door opened, and in came Anita, accompanied by two very handsome young men. Both had short black hair and lean, bright faces, and surely they were terribly in love with the older woman at their side.

Anita didn't see me. She sat down at the bar with her back to me, and not until twenty or thirty minutes later, when she had already paid and was getting ready to leave the place with her two friends, did she turn around. She recognized me at once. She took a cigarette, stuck it behind her ear with a smile, and all at once everything was as before, in our coffee shop on Broadway . . .

Of course Anita was no longer wearing her New York cap. Her hair was pulled back tightly and smoothly, she wore a string of pearls around her throat, a cashmere sweater, and gold earrings. She looked spirited and youthful, not crazy and lonely as I remembered her.

So we meet again for the first time, I thought, and now, seeing her so rich and vital and contented, I didn't regret a bit what had happened on that fall evening in New York . . . First we had talked a bit about literature, and then, after I had written her paper, had spend half the night fucking . . .

I got up and went over to Anita. "So," I said, "how did Professor Finkelstein like our story?"

7.

Aha, he thought, aha . . . This crazy German has actually fallen in love with me . . . Finkelstein got up from his desk, took off his reading glasses, and laid them on the manuscript of Anita's story. All through the course he had been waiting in suspense for her final paper. He didn't care if she had talent; he just wanted to know if she would write about him, whether she might even declare her love, and now it had happened exactly as he had pictured it.

Finkelstein had always hated his German student, because of her enraptured gaze, because of the pushy way in which she leaned on the lectern during breaks. He found her unattractive and too old, and even though he had thought a few times about tying her hand and foot to a dirty, wobbly hotel bed, he always pushed the thought aside as one of his more aberrant fantasies about the Nazis. Finkelstein hated the Germans; he would never travel to their gloomy, idiotic country. He understood their problems, but he simply wasn't interested in them, and several times he had had to restrain himself when Anita posed her stupid, woeful, German questions in class, in that weak, whiny, woeful voice of hers.

Now Finkelstein was standing in the bathroom. He looked in the mirror at his little Yeshiva student's face with the broad, heavy jaw and the scar on the lower left where the neck began. He ran his hand through his crisp red hair; it feels like wire, he thought, and then it occurred to him that he had actually seen Anita at his coffee shop that evening when Ruthie had kicked him out once and for all. She had been talking to an odd-looking foreigner at the bar. Suddenly he found himself thinking only one thought: One must be fair!

He rushed into his study, turned on the computer, and went to work. "Your text, Anita," Finkelstein began his comment, "is fluent, readable, and at times cleverly constructed. You have apparently attempted, through the use of a split character, to convey the real and simultaneously paranoid element in the Holocaust experience of the descendants on both sides, the side of the victims as well as of the perpetrators. In the process you lose your narrator in the labyrinth of your character-duplicating machine . . ."

Finkelstein jumped up, making, as he always did when he was writing and a word or phrase didn't come to him, furious chewing movements with his mouth. He started to whistle something, he thrust his hands into his pockets, pulled out a few coins and began counting them absentmindedly, but the next moment he was sitting on the chair again, pounding the keys of his computer.

"Even if one can surmise," Finkelstein wrote, "who the narrator, his double, and the (fictional?) poet Miklós Radnóti are, and how these emanations are related to each other, in the last section only confusion and misunderstanding result when you make 'Professor Finkelstein' (I'm a

good sport!) the double of all the previously introduced figures. What are you trying to say? And what, by the way, was your point with the little obscenity in the last paragraph? I know it is fun to write such things—but despite Miller, Bukowski, and Roth (all of whom I consider imposters, by the way), the world is not yet ready for this . . ."

Was that too harsh? Finkelstein wondered. It didn't matter one way or the other to him. But then he hunched over the keyboard again. "You have talent, Anita," he wrote. "You have a good control of language and a knack for creating atmosphere, and if you keep working at it, you can become a real writer some day. There are many writers who have started out at a more advanced age than you. So, good luck for the future, and if you come to New York again, stop by and see me; we could have dinner together.—Sam Finkelstein, Ph.D., Department of English, Columbia University."

The professor crossed his arms behind his neck, scratched himself vigorously behind both ears, and read through what he had written. But when he was about to turn off the computer, his fingers jerked back to the keyboard, as if of their own volition. "Wait, dear Anita," Finkelstein's fingers wrote, "how about tomorrow night? There's a little Japanese place on my block, clean and cheap. We could go there and talk about literature a bit, and later . . . A little joke between writers, Anita. Which of us knows if what we write is really true? So I will call you tomorrow morning, you wonderful German weeping willow!"

Finkelstein smiled. That was really a good idea he'd come up with. And so simple! He'd been masturbating every night for months, conjuring up images of Ruthie, and he had finally earned himself a little real sex.

He stood up and looked out the window. He saw the two blinking towers of the World Trade Center. To the left, in a long, deep, straight line, Broadway's dim tail of lights stretched through the dusk. Damn it all, the little weeping willow was right again, Finkelstein thought. In this part of town Broadway really did look pretty cold and mean.

Translated from the German by Krishna Winston.

IV

CENTRAL AND EASTERN EUROPE

MIRIAM

Ivan Klíma

My father's cousin was celebrating her engagement. Aunt Sylvia was short, had a large nose, and was suntanned and loquacious. Before the war she'd been a clerk in a bank; now she'd become a gardener, while her intended—originally a lawyer—was employed in the food supply office. Quite what his job there was I didn't know, but Father had promised us that there'd be a surprise at the party and he'd smacked his lips meaningfully, which aroused enthusiastic interest in my brother and me.

My aunt lived in the same barracks as us, in a tiny little room with a small window giving onto the corridor. The room was so small that I couldn't imagine what it had ever been intended for. Probably as a storeroom for small items such as horseshoes, whips (the place used to be a cavalry barracks) or spurs. In that little room my aunt had a bed and a small table made from two suitcases. Over the top suitcase she had now spread a tablecloth and laid out some open sandwiches on a few plates cut out of cardboard. They were genuine open sandwiches covered with pieces of salami, sardines, liver pâté, raw turnips, cucumbers, and real cheese. Auntie had even prepared some small cakes with beet jam. I noticed my brother swallowing noisily as his mouth began to water. He hadn't learned to control himself yet. He'd never been to school. I had, and I was already reading about wily Ulysses and forgetful Paganel, so I knew something about gods and the virtues of men.

This was the first time I saw the fiancé. He was a young man with curly hair and round cheeks that bore no trace whatever of wartime hardships.

So we met in that little room with its blacked-out window. Nine of us crowded into it and the air soon got stale and warm and laden with sweat, but we ate, we devoured the unimaginable goodies that the fiancé had clearly supplied from the food supply store, we washed down the morsels with ersatz coffee that smelled of milk and was beautifully sweet. At one point my father clinked his knife against his mug and declared that no time was so bad that something good mightn't occur in it; its many significant events—he would only list the defeat of the Germans at Sebastopol and the British offensive in Italy—now included this celebration. Father wished the happy couple to be able to set out on a honeymoon in freedom by the next month, he wished them an early peace and much happiness and love together. Better to be sad but loved, Father surprised everybody by quoting Goethe, than to be cheerful without love.

Then we sang a few songs and because supper was beginning to be doled out we had to bring the party to an end.

When I returned with my billycan full of beet bilge I saw the white-haired painter Speero—Maestro Speero, as everyone called him—sitting by one of the arched but unglazed window openings. He too had his billycan standing by his side—except that his was already empty—while on his lap he held a board to which he had fixed a piece of drawing paper. He was sketching. There were several artists living on our corridor but Maestro Speero was the oldest and most famous of them. In Holland, where he came from, he had designed medallions, banknotes and postage stamps, and even the Queen had allegedly sat for him. Here, although this was strictly forbidden, he sketched scenes from our ghetto on very small pieces of paper. The pictures were so tiny that it seemed impossible to me that these delicate lines were created by that elderly hand.

On one occasion I had plucked up my courage, put together all my knowledge of German and asked Herr Speero why he was drawing such very small pictures.

"*Um sie besser zu verschlucken*"—all the better to swallow them—he'd replied. But maybe I'd misunderstood him and he'd said "*verschicken*"—to send—or even "*verschenken*"—to give.

Now full of admiration I watched as his paper filled up with old men and women standing in line, all pressed together. They were no bigger than a grain of rice, but every one of them had eyes, a nose and a mouth, and on their chest the Jewish star. As I stared intently at his paper it seemed to me that the tiny figures began to run around, swarming over the picture like ants, till my head swam and I had to close my eyes.

"Well, what do you think?" the white-haired artist asked without turning his head.

"Beautiful," I breathed. Not for anything in the world would I have admitted to him that I too had tried to people pieces of paper with tiny figures, that in my sunnier moments, when I allowed myself a future outside the area bounded by the ramparts, I pictured myself in some witness-bearing occupation—as a poet, an actor, or a painter. Suddenly a thought struck me. "May I offer you some soup?"

Only then did the old man turn to me. "What's that?" he asked in surprise. "Have they dished out seconds already? Or are you sick?"

"My aunt's got married," I explained.

Herr Speero picked up his billycan from the ground, there wasn't a drop left in it, and I poured into it more than half my helping of the beet bilge. He bowed a little and said: "Thank you, thank you very much for this token of favour. God will reward you."

Except, where is God, I reflected in the evening as I lay on my paillasse, which was infested with bedbugs and visited by fleas, and how does he reward good deeds? I could not imagine him, I could not imagine hope beyond this world.

And this world?

Every evening I would anxiously strain my ears for sounds in the dark. For the sound of boots down the corridor, for a desperate scream shattering the silence, for the sudden opening of a door and the appearance of a messenger with a slip of paper with my name typed on it. I was afraid of falling asleep, of being caught totally helpless. Because then I wouldn't be able to hide from him.

I had thought up a hiding place for myself in the potato store in the basement. I would wriggle through my narrow window, after locking-up time, and bury myself so deep among the potatoes that no SS-man would see me and no dog get scent of me. The potatoes would keep me alive.

How long could a person live on raw potatoes? I didn't know, but then how much longer could the war last? Yes, that was what everything depended on.

I knew that fear would now creep out from the corner by the stove. All day long it was hiding out there, cowering in the flue or under the empty coal bucket, but once everybody was asleep it would come to life, pad over to me and breathe coldly on my forehead. And its pale lips would whisper: woe ... betide ... you.

Quietly I got off my paillasse and tiptoed to the window. I knew the view well: the dark crowns of the ancient lime trees outside the window, the brick gateway with its yawning black emptiness. And the sharp outlines of the ramparts. Cautiously I lifted a corner of the blackout paper and froze: the top of one of the lime trees was aglow with a blue light. A spectral light, cold and blinding. I stared at it for a moment. I could make out every single leaf, every little glowing twig, and I became aware at the same time that the branches and the leaves were coming together in the shape of a huge, grinning face that gazed at me with flaming eyes.

I felt I was choking and couldn't have cried out even had I dared to do so. I let go of the black paper and the window was once more covered in darkness. For a while I stood there motionless and wrestled with the temptation to lift the paper again and get another glimpse of that face. But I lacked the courage. Besides, what was the point? I could see that face before me, shining through the blackout, flickering over the dark ceiling, dancing in front of my eyes even when I firmly closed my eyelids.

What did it mean? Who did it belong to? Did it hold a message for me? But how would I know whether it was good news or bad?

By morning nothing was left of the joys or the fears of the night before. I went to get my ration of bitter coffee, I gulped down two slices of bread and margarine. I registered with relief that the war had moved on by one night and that the unimaginable peace had therefore drawn another night nearer.

I went behind the metal shop to play volleyball, and an hour before lunchtime I was already queuing up with my billycan for my own and my brother's eighth-of-a-liter of milk. The line stretched toward a low vaulted room, not unlike the one inhabited by Aunt Sylvia. Inside, behind an iron pail, stood a girl in a white apron. She took the vouchers from the submissive queuers, fished around in the pail with one of the small measures and poured a little of the skimmed liquid into the vessels held out to her.

As I stood before her she looked at me, her gaze rested on my face for a moment, and then she smiled. I knew her, of course, but I hadn't really taken proper notice of her. She had dark hair and a freckled face.

She bent over her metal pail again, took my mug, picked up the largest of the measures, dipped it into the huge bucket and emptied its contents into my mug. Hurriedly she added two more helpings, then she returned my mug and smiled at me again. As if by her smile she were trying to tell me something significant, as if she were touching me with it. She returned my mug full to the brim and I mumbled my thanks. I didn't understand anything. I was not used to receiving strangers' smiles or any kind of tokens of favour. Out in the corridor I leaned against the wall and, as though I were afraid she might run after me and deprive me of that irregular helping, I began to drink. I drank at least two thirds of the milk, knowing full well that even so my brother would not be cheated.

In the evening, even before fear crept out from its corner, I tried to forestall it or somehow to delay it. I thought of that strange incident. I should have liked to explain it to myself, perhaps to connect it with the old artist's ceremonial thanks and hence with the working of a superior power, but I decided not to attach such importance to my own deed. But what did last night's fiery sign mean? Abruptly it emerged before my eyes, its glow filling me with a chill. Could that light represent something good?

I made myself get up from my paillasse and breathlessly lifted the corner of the blackout.

Outside the darkness was undisturbed, the black top of the lime tree was swaying in the gusts of wind, clouds were scurrying across the sky, their edges briefly lit by summer lightning.

Next day I was filled with impatience as I stood in the queue, gripping my clean mug. It took me a considerable effort to dare to look at her face. She had large eyes, long and almond-shaped and almost as dark as ersatz coffee. She smiled at me, perhaps she even winked at me conspiratorially—I wasn't sure. Into my mug she poured three full measures and handed it back to me as if nothing were amiss. Outside the door I drank up three quarters of my special ration, watching other people come out with mugs whose bottoms were barely covered by the white liquid. I still didn't understand anything. I drifted down the long corridor, covering my mug with my other hand. Even after I'd finished drinking there was an embarrassing amount left in it. And she'd smiled at me twice.

I was beginning to be filled with a tingling, happy excitement.

In the evening, as soon as I'd closed my eyes, I saw my flaming sign again, that glowing face, but this time it had lost its menace and rapidly took on a familiar appearance. I could make out the minute freckles above the upper lip; I recognized the mouth half-parted in a smile, the almond eyes looked at me with such a strange gaze that I caught my breath. Her eyes gazed on me with love.

Suddenly I understood the meaning of the fiery sign and the meaning of what was happening.

I was loved.

A mouse rustled in the corner, somewhere below a door banged, but the world receded and I was looking at a sweet face and felt my own face relax and my lips smile.

What can I do to see you, in the flesh, to see you here and now, and not just across a wooden table with a huge pail towering between us?

But what would I do if we really did meet?

By the next day, when I'd received my multiplied milk ration and when a gentle and expressive smile had assured me I wasn't mistaken, I could no longer bear the isolation of my feelings. I had at least to mention her to everybody I spoke to, and every mention further fanned my feelings. Moreover, I learned from friends that her name was Miriam Deutsch and that she lived on my floor, only at the other end. I even established the number of her room: two hundred and three. We also considered her age—some thought she was sixteen and others that she was already eighteen, and someone said he'd seen her twice with some Fred but it needn't mean anything.

Of course it didn't mean anything. I was sure no Fred came away with a full mug of milk every day. Besides where would my beloved Miriam get so much from?

By now I knew almost everything about her, I could even visit her any time during the day and say ... Well, what was I to say to her? What reason could I give for my intrusion? Some pretext! I might take along my grubby copy of the Story of the Trojan War.

I brought you this book for the milk!

Except that I must not say anything of the kind in front of others. I might ask her to step out into the corridor with me. But suppose she said she had no time? Suppose I offended her by mentioning the milk? It seemed to me that it was improper to speak about tokens of love.

But suppose I was altogether wrong? Why should such a girl be in love with me, a scrawny, tousle-haired ragamuffin? I hadn't even started to grow a beard!

Right at the bottom of my case I had a shirt that I only wore on special occasions. It was canary yellow and, unlike the rest of my shirts, it was as yet unfrayed about the collar and the cuffs. I put it on. All right, so it throttled me a little but I was prepared to suffer that. I also had a suit in my case but unfortunately I'd grown out of it. My mother had tried to lengthen the trouser legs but even so they only just reached my ankles and there was no material left to lengthen the arms. I hesitated for a moment but I had no choice. I took my shirt off again, poured some water into the washbowl and washed thoroughly. I even scrubbed my neck. When I'd put on my festive garb I wetted my hair and painstakingly made an exemplary parting. I half opened the window, held the blackout behind it, and for a while observed my image on the glass. In a sudden flush of self-love it seemed to me that I looked good the way I was dressed.

Then I set out along the long corridor to the opposite side of the barracks. I passed dozens of doors, the numbers above the hinges slowly going down. Two hundred and eighteen, two hundred and seventeen, two hundred and fifteen . . . I was becoming aware of the pounding of my heart.

Miriam. It seemed to me that I had never heard a sweeter name. It suited her. Two hundred and seven. I still didn't know what I was actually going to do. If she loved me—two hundred and six, good Lord, that's her door already over there, I can see it now—if she loves me the way I love her she'll come out and we'll meet—two hundred and five, I've slowed down to give her more time. The door will open and she will stand in it, and she'll smile at me: Where have you sprung from?

Oh, I just happened to be walking past. Meeting the chaps on the ramparts, usually walk across the yard.

I stopped. A stupid sentence, that. Why couldn't I have thought of something cleverer?

Hi, Miriam!

You know my name?

I just had to find out. So I could think of you better.

You think of me?

Morning till night, Miriam! And at night too. I think of you nearly all through the night!

I think of you too. But where have you sprung from?

I don't really know. Suddenly occurred to me to go this way rather than across the yard.

That seemed a little better. Two hundred and four.

You see I live on the same floor.

So we're really almost neighbours. You could always walk along this way.

I will. I will.

Two hundred and three. I drew a deep breath. I stared at the door so intently that it must surely sigh deep down in its wooden soul. And she, if she loved me, must get up, walk to her door and come out.

Evidently she wasn't there. Why should she be sitting at home on a fine afternoon? Maybe she'll be coming back from somewhere, I just have to give her enough time. Two hundred and two. I was approaching one of the transversal corridors that linked the two longitudinal wings of the barracks. I heard some clicking footsteps coming along it.

Great God Almighty! I stopped and waited with bated breath.

Round the corner appeared an old woman in clogs. In her hands she was carrying a small dish with a few dirty potatoes in it. Supper was obviously being doled out already.

The next day I saw Miriam again behind the low table with the iron pail full of milk. She took my mug and smiled at me, one helping, a second, a third, she smiled again and handed me my mug. How I love you, Miriam, nobody can have ever felt anything like it. I leaned against the wall, drank two thirds of the message of love and returned to my realm of dreams.

I didn't emerge from it till towards the evening, when the women were coming back from work. I washed, straightened my parting, put on my special suit, but I felt that this was not enough. I lacked a pretext for my festive attire, for our meeting, and even more so for telling her something about myself.

Just then I remembered an object of pride, a proof of my skill. It was lying hidden and carefully packed away in the smaller case under my bunk: my puppet theatre. I had made it out of an old box, painted the stage sets on precious cartridge paper saved from school, made most of the various props from bits of wood, stones and small branches collected under the ramparts, while I'd made the puppets from chestnuts, cotton-reels and rags I'd scrounged from my mother and others living around us.

I took the box out of my case. It was tied up with twisted paper ribbon. The proscenium arch, the wings and the rest of the scenery, the props and the puppets—they were all inside.

Hi, Miriam!

Hi, where have you sprung from?

Going to see a chap. We're going to perform a play.

You perform plays?

Only with puppets. For the time being.

How do you mean: for the time being?

One day I'll be an actor. Or a writer. I also think up plays.

You can do that?

Sure. I pick up some puppets and just start playing. I don't know myself how it's going to end.

And you play to an audience?

As large a one as you like. I'm not nervous.

And where did you get that theatre from?

Made it myself.

The scenery too?

Sure. I paint. If I have enough cartridge paper. I've done our barracks and the metal shop and the gateway when a transport's just passing through . . .

I tied the ribbon around the box again. It looked perfectly ordinary, it might contain anything—like dirty washing. I undid the ribbon once more, pushed two puppets out so their little feet in their clogs were peeping out under the lid, as well as the king's head with its crown on, and then I tied the box up again. Then I set out along the familiar corridor.

I've also written a number of poems, I confided.

You write poetry? What about?

On, various things. About love. About suicide.

You tried to kill yourself?

No, not me. Two hundred and ten. My breath was coming quickly. A man mustn't kill himself.

Why mustn't he?

It's a sin!

You believe in that sort of thing?

What sort of thing?

God!

Two hundred and seven. Dear Lord, if you exist make her come out. Make her show herself. She doesn't even have to say any of these things, just let her smile.

You believe in him?

I don't know. They're all saying that if he existed he wouldn't allow any of this.

But you don't think so?

Maybe it's some punishment, Miriam.

Punishment for what?

Only he knows that. Two hundred and four. I stopped and transferred the box from my left arm to my right. Suppose I just dropped it and spilled everything? It would make a noise and I could pretend that

I was picking up the strewn pieces. I could kneel there for half an hour, picking things up.

Miriam, come out and smile at me. Nothing more. I swear that's all I want.

The following day she took my mug but I wasn't sure whether she'd smiled as warmly as the day before. I was alarmed. Suppose she didn't love me any longer? Why should she still love me when I couldn't summon up enough courage to do anything? Here she was giving me repeated proof of her favour and what was I doing.?

One measure, a second, a third, a smile after all, the mug handed back to me—how I love you, Miriam. My divine Aphrodite, it's only that I'm too shy to tell you but nobody can ever love you as much as I do. Because I love you unto death, my Miriam!

In the evening they began to come round with deportation slips. And after that every day. Never before had such doom descended upon our ghetto. Thousands of people were shuffling toward the railway station with little slips on their chests.

And meanwhile every afternoon three helpings of promise, three helpings as a token of love, three helpings of hope. I returned to my room and prayed. Devoutly, for all my dear ones and for all distant ones, but especially for her, for Miriam, asking God to be merciful toward her and not to demand her life; and they called up all my friends and most of the people I knew by sight, the cook from the cookhouse and the man who handed out the bread. Corridors and yards fell silent, the streets were empty, the town was dead. On the last transport went my father's cousin, short Aunt Sylvia, along with her husband who'd worked in the food supply office. They'd barely been together three weeks and this was to have been their honeymoon trip in freedom. But perhaps, I tried to remember my father's words, it was better to suffer and be loved than to be joyous without love: I was only just beginning to understand the meaning of the words he'd quoted from the poet. A few more days of anxiety in case the messengers appeared again, but they didn't, and the two of us remained behind! Now I won't hesitate anymore, now at last I'll summon up my courage. While the terror lasted I couldn't speak of love, it wouldn't have been right, but now I can and must. I'll no longer walk past her door but I'll address her here and now, on the spot, as she returns my mug to me.

This evening at six, under the arch of the rear gateway—do please come, Miriam.

No!

You will come, Miriam, won't you?

No!

Could I see you some time, Miriam? How about this evening at six by the rear gateway? You will come, won't you?

The queue was shortening, there was hardly anyone left now with a claim to a mouthful of milk.

My knees were almost giving way, I hoped I wouldn't be scared at the last moment by my own boldness. She had my mug in her hand, I opened my mouth, one scoop, not the big one, the smallest one. As for her, she was looking at me without smiling. Could it be she didn't recognize me? I swallowed hard, at last she smiled, a little sadly, almost apologetically, and returned my mug to me, its bottom spattered with a revolting blueish, watery liquid. But this is me, Miriam, me who . . .

I took the mug from her hand and walked back down the long corridor at whose end, in front of the arched window, the famous Dutchman was again sitting with his squared paper.

What was I to do now?

I was still walking but I noticed that I wasn't really moving, I wasn't getting any nearer to the famous painter—on the contrary—and everything around me was beginning to move. I saw the old man rocking on his little chair as if being tossed about by waves, I saw him changing into his own picture and saw the picture floating on the surface of the churned-up water.

I didn't know what was happening to me. All I knew was that she no longer loved me. A sickeningly sweet taste spread in my mouth, my cheeks were withering rapidly, and so were my hands. I was only just aware that I couldn't hold the light, almost empty, mug and I heard the metal ring against the stone floor of the corridor.

When I came round I saw above me the elderly face of Maestro Speero. With one hand he was supporting my back, while the other was moving a cold, wet cloth across my forehead. "What's up boy?" he asked.

It took me a moment to return fully to merciless reality. But how could I reveal the real cause of my grief?

"They've taken my aunt away," I whispered. "Had to join the deportation transport. The one who got married."

Mr. Speero shook his white head. "God be with her," he said softly, "and with all of us."

Translated from the Czech by Ewald Osers.

THE INSTRUCTOR

Norman Manea

He spoke little, his voice more tired than severe. Now and then he frowned; when he did, his gestures took on some animation.

He was on edge. He shifted the blunt pencil stub from one hand to the other, twisting it nervously between his fingers. It was no longer possible to ignore him. Then the bizarre, staccato soundtrack started up: he blew his thick, veined nose repeatedly. His voice came through muffled against a white and foggy background.

His sentences were sometimes spoken with a strange vibrato that meant they shouldn't be taken seriously. At other times he pretended to joke, as if he were avoiding something painful and secret.

"Why is it that the children of the learned are rarely learned? So that it can't be said that learning is hereditary!"

It wasn't the lesson itself so much as the pauses following such diatribes that lengthened the silences between them so horribly. Embarrassment at waiting for something you were in no mood for. In the presence of this odd and shabby teacher, the afternoon's colors slowly faded.

Every day was a whirlwind for the boy. Barely four years had passed since the end of the war. He had been parachuted into a sunny valley; sweet smelling houses, fat aunts, pathetic old men. His eyes, always alert, had barely been able to withstand the bewilderment. The silky sweet caresses had begun. The tinkling voices of small cousins; the delirium of trays full of pastries; the frolicking with ribbons and beads; cups of milk; soft shiny shoes; ink-stained school benches.

April dust in his nostrils; starched linen, morning, voices, flames, the rainbow, the clatter of promises, the sun blinding you on the swing. He had opened himself entirely and was ready to get started. He had made up the lost classes; devoured textbooks, even those others found dull; he swallowed everything; always hungry, concentrated, impelled by his own thirst.

Later, the first conflicts: the calm and the compromise became oppressive. The looks his family gave him were irritating. His parents transmitted a kind of silent alarm to each other that made them appear shy and ridiculous.

By the second lesson, that fool had clarified his position:

"I don't want to waste your time or mine. I can leave, but someone else will come. I knew your grandfather, I know your mother. That's why I've agreed to be here."

The teacher wasn't what he expected. Humbly dressed: a petty functionary, a shopkeeper—the kind that never touches the merchandise—a bored provincial accountant. White hands with burst blood vessels. He was plump, small. His voice was slightly hoarse, his black hat wide-brimmed. Upon his arrival, contrary to the boy's expectations, he had hung it on the coat rack. You had to look very carefully to see the silk skullcap—the color of his bald spot—on his head.

He looked like a neighbor who had dropped by for some unimportant business, let's say to cheer up some invalid. To engage in conversation, give advice, simply to share one of those problems that life delivers unexpectedly. An unknown relative called upon in a difficult moment. But he wasn't a neighbor, he lived who knows where, and he wasn't a relative at all. No, no.

Often inattentive, lost in thought, he would wipe a big white handkerchief over his hot red forehead and its protruding veins. Then he would fold the handkerchief carefully and return it, one corner sticking out, to the pocket below his lapel. The other handkerchief, the one reserved for his nose, the trombone—white too, but gathered in a ball—swelled in the breast pocket of his vest.

The schoolboy he came to see so reluctantly was a sullen partner. His black eyes searched the teacher's for long moments without blinking, but the boy wasn't as rebellious or as insolent as he had expected.

The boy's mother had begged the teacher to try; he was her last hope.

The old man had kept his head lowered and did not look at her; as she spoke, he perhaps remembered a dark, slender young woman whose beauty only ten years earlier had made heads turn. This pale woman, bent and always in a panic, seemed much older—she already looked like her mother, who had perished in those cold and disastrous regions from where few had returned. "You know, he's not like the others; for about a year now, it's as if he hated us all. He leaves and doesn't come back until late in the evening, with all kinds of books; he doesn't talk—only a word or two—as if we were a constant imposition. He avoids us, he'd be happier if we didn't exist." Only for her suffering did the teacher reluctantly accept the role.

The first time the man showed up was on a Monday afternoon. It was raining. He did not have an umbrella; wet and shrunken, he had crept along under the eaves. He knocked at the window, as arranged. The boy was home alone. The teacher took off his dripping hat and wet black coat. He was wearing a vest; under the vest, undershirts and sweaters. A small white beard. His pale silk skullcap was barely noticeable. Sharp eyes, pink cheeks freshly shaven. A wide, knotted forehead. He had already buried his thick nose in the handkerchief and was blowing hard, playing for time. "You shouldn't speak to him as to a child, don't attack his new ideas, avoid them; forgive him, he is blind," the mother had most likely advised him. As he sneezed into the handkerchief, the stranger was probably recapitulating everything he knew about the silent young man sitting to his right.

"You're about to turn thirteen, to become a man. That's why I've been called. The ceremony is not complicated. The language is old, beautiful. The greatest book of all was written in it. That is why the language has survived to this day. Precise, like geometry ... I know you like mathematics. You'll find it interesting."

This old rubbish did not interest the rebellious boy at all. He was sure that he could defend himself against all this, that he could meet head-on whatever clever trap they might lay for him.

"I'll teach you to read it. The pronunciation, the rhythm of the phrases, the tenses. They're complicated. And that will be all, don't worry," continued the guest, folding the handkerchief and stuffing it in the breast pocket of his vest.

He had gotten up and turned toward the coat rack. He picked up a fat brown briefcase that was peeling in places. Where had he kept the briefcase and when had he put it down there?

The teacher picked the case up and rested it against the leg of the table. Bending over, he took out a thick old black tome and a thinner volume that looked like a primer. Then a kind of envelope made out of a black cloth that he laid on the table, on top of the books.

"Our men bear witness to their affiliation through two tests. One is permanent and private, and this is done at birth, as you probably know. The second is public, visible. . . ."

From a little black cloth sack he took out two strange bundles. Two small black leather cubes mounted on a somewhat larger square, also made of leather, to which long, thin leather thongs were attached.

"These are placed, one on the left arm, the other on the forehead. The leather comes from an unblemished animal, as the law requires. The arm is bound first. Preference is given to the deed, to action. When we made the covenant, we promised that we would carry out the commandments, and only later would we try to understand them. In observing them we have also learned to grasp their meaning. I hear you know a little philosophy. We are servants of the One whom we have acknowledged and who has chosen us."

Was this a dialogue? He rattled on as long as he pleased. This was no more than static interference on a soundtrack.

"I know this doesn't interest you. Well, let's gloss over the explanations. I thought I'd mention them, as a curiosity. Then the other is put on the forehead. There should be no break between these operations. Nothing to separate the idea from the gesture, the sentiment from the act that inspires and expresses it."

Before leaving, the teacher made sure to show the schoolboy the first pages of the new primer, the strange letters with which he had to become familiar for the next time.

It was getting late; his parents had not returned yet. The stranger gathered his things, wrapped himself up in his still-damp coat, and mumbled something unintelligible as a farewell. Darkness clouded the window. Silence, solitude, absent parents; there was no one to whom he could express his contempt for this hour of nonsense.

"They are placed on the left arm, next to the heart, and on the head. A covenant! Of all peoples on earth You chose only me. The people had said: He is ours and He is the only One! I, in turn, grant you uniqueness!"

Now it was night, he was alone. The cold and damp room resounded with the pompous words.

He couldn't forget his parents' pleas, their reproaches over his estrangement and brutality, as if the earth were once again falling into that dark, greenish mire from which they had just emerged. Nor could he forget the nights when the threat of the past came alive with the shiny steel eyes of guns aimed to fire. Nor could he forgive himself that he had finally given in. He was furious that he had been swayed by their insistence and their tears.

A man, he was entering the ranks of men! But he wouldn't let himself be dazzled by incense and old rubbish, nor by stories about his great-grandfather, who at the age of thirteen had married his great-grandmother, aged eleven, nor by sacred leather cords, the skin of unblemished animals, long-winded prayers. And at the end of the ceremony there would be a short speech. Then he would be offered—as between men!—a small glass of brandy, a small piece of cake, stale jokes.

It was only while recollecting their past that he found himself part of his family. For the rest, no bridge remained. After all they had lived through, suddenly he was seeing them from a great distance. They seemed childish, ridiculous. They did not even believe in the ceremony for which they were preparing him. It was just the need for yet another sign that all was normal. Nothing else but the rush to accumulate proof, to have relatives and neighbors and former friends confirm that, yes, everything was in order, that life had reaccepted them, that it was just like *before,* that they were the same as before. All customs had to be properly observed: the spectacle for which they had invited such a learned and benign quack was but one instance of the staged scenes to which they were prepared to submit themselves, hour by hour, day in and day out.

He was a man, the only one among them! His eyes were dilated with fury. A true fighter would have recognized in him, he had no doubt of it, a worthy companion. What a man thinks at thirteen is as important as what he will think at thirty.

Adults, sure of themselves, meted out verdicts, made senseless speeches, told banal anecdotes, repeated endless stories whose thread they had lost. No, flashed the hostile eyes of the implacable and self-important boy, he would not be like them. One weakness, then another, then another: a real man would have avoided such confrontations, he would have demonstrated that he was in control of his powers and of his isolation. In vain he tried to avoid painful compromises. He thought he was going to die of shame from the botched rebellion, from the crying that did not surface but twisted him inside. He was overcome by dizziness; he wanted air, light, water, a refuge where no one could find him.

He had been holding his jacket in his hand for several minutes. Soon his parents would be back, and there would be an overly cheerful reunion.

Outside it was no longer raining; if he hurried he might still catch the film, or he could wander the streets. He would come back late, when they could no longer ask him anything.

He returned late. In the kitchen he found the tray with bread, butter, a glass of milk. He drank the milk, then carefully pulled out the book hidden under the cupboard.

They were sleeping, or pretending to; it did not matter. They had become used to his extravagances and no longer nagged at him about rules.

He pulled the lamp closer and opened the book. The inflammatory first phrase had repeated its clear black cadence to him many times: "A specter is haunting Europe . . . A specter is haunting Europe." The sound became deafening. "All the Powers of old Europe have entered into a holy alliance to exorcise this specter." The thundering voice filled the entire screen, you could no longer see anything but those burning syllables: "The history of all hitherto existing society is the history of class struggle. . . . The bourgeoisie, wherever it has got the upper hand, has put an end to all feudal, patriarchal, idyllic relations. . . . It has left no other nexus between man and man than naked self-interest. . . . It has drowned the most heavenly ecstasies of religious fervor, of chivalrous enthusiasm, of philistine sentimentalism, in the icy water of egotistical calculation. In a word, for exploitation, veiled by religious and political illusions, it has substituted naked, shameless, direct, brutal exploitation."

On Wednesday the teacher appeared again, punctually, along with the rain. This time he had a huge patched umbrella and a shiny black raincoat closed up to the neck. Quickly, without introduction, he turned to the alphabet and the first words.

They started with grammar: nouns, pronouns, verbs. Ordinary teaching, like geography or history or algebra. The old man did not find it hard to admit that the young man was a good student. The instructor was not stingy with praise; the best, he finally mumbled.

Encouragement before the approaching holidays. A cold, rainy fall, clear days, the end of September, the household strictures. They did not beg him again, as they had a year earlier, to join them under the vast, cold cupolas. They were keeping their word, they did not ask the impossible of him: they did not expect there to be any connection between the lessons of Monday, Wednesday, Thursday, and reality. So they were not serious, they were not consistent.

Thursday's lesson, conjugating irregular verbs—and the verbs of this rigorous language were proving to be mostly irregular.

The lesson ended a little early. The great expert closed his book more quickly than usual. It was over, but it was not. In his chair, his head lowered between his shoulders, he was no longer looking at his student.

"For us, forgiveness is not simply a hypothesis. It has been proved, it has taken place. After forty days of prayer, in place of the destroyed tablets we were given new ones."

His speech was slow, hoarse. He took out the wrinkled white handkerchief from the breast pocket of his black vest but did not use it, as usual, to blow his trumpet of a nose. He held the handkerchief in his fist, on his right knee, next to the leg of the table.

"For us, penance follows rather than precedes judgment. The judgment must remain fair, unswayed. For us, conscience—you understand the word, you probably use it every day—for us, moral judgment is not irreversible."

Concentrating, he did not look up, as if he were whispering only to himself. But, the joker, he still found time for ironies; he had not forgotten his tricks. But the shrewd, respectful distancing of "us" and "you" no longer had the effect it had earlier. The old man knew the weight of words; otherwise he would not have used them with so much difficulty, panting, hoarse, leaving long pauses between them.

"The believer, that is, the learned man, we could call him that, that would suit you better, he must realize that sin does not lead inexorably to divine punishment. Our conscience allows for recuperation; forgiveness is possible."

Evening had descended; it was quiet, and hard to interrupt him. The words emerged slowly. At long intervals they erupted—uncertain and fragile, they seemed to be asking for a prudently warm reception to be able to rise, to make themselves heard.

"At the New Year the righteous are judged according to the strict letter of the law. Only the righteous deserve severity. On the day of forgiveness, during the great fast that follows the New Year, those in the middle, those who are neither like this nor like that—the ordinary ones, the owners of good deeds and bad—are judged with clemency. And the sinners can repent. They too can be forgiven if they change their ways. Misdeed against God, of course! Misdeeds against people must be forgiven by people."

He had grabbed his impeccable handkerchief out of the pocket under the lapel of his jacket and buried his trumpet deep in the white silk square. The other handkerchief was on the corner of the table. At some point he must have opened his fist; the linen ball, the one he used for his large troubled nose, was forgotten. He didn't drag out the process; he simply stuffed the handkerchief back under his lapel.

"Created free, that is, subject to mistakes, we are offered forgiveness by the law itself. Repentance follows, it does not precede, judgment. Judgment must remain above influence, fair. Can true repentance alter the past? Therefore, alter destiny? The future would no longer be a rigorous consequence of past events! Moral judgment is not irreversible. The law permits forgiveness."

Meanwhile he had gotten up slowly, with difficulty. You would have thought he needed a long time to readjust to walking, to the room, to normal movement. But he had quickly put on his hat, his coat, had picked up his briefcase; he had nodded his head and mumbled something, nothing; he opened the door, went into the hall, and was gone.

The house was empty on holidays. Something austerely festive would hover around the freshly dusted walls. The clean room was deserted, cold, mysterious. His parents were away, in that world to which the rebel no longer went. Beneath the high chandeliers of the golden cupola, between the narrow old benches, among other outcasts, hidden by the long white shawls of silk, they were murmuring, swaying to the refrain of the prayers, bending, with abandon, to the ground—the fury of their humiliation transformed into vanity and defiance.

Solitude, quiet—but it was impossible to think. He felt uneasy in that suddenly huge and empty room, where the old man's words still hovered.

"These are the most important days for us. Forgiveness is not simply a hope—it has been granted. Only the righteous deserve a severe judgment. Sin does not lead implacably to punishment. Forgiveness is possible, but only for misdeeds against God. Those committed against men must be forgiven by men. Forgiveness is not quite an absolution. The new tablets were given to the sons of those who had worshipped the golden calf. That is, for their descendants, penitent and forgiven. The second edition was not as great, however. Moral time can be recuperated. Forgiveness is possible, it has been proved. But forgiveness does not absolve! In the Ark, next to the new law, we preserve the shards of the first tablets."

He would have preferred his parents to be there to share that silence. He would have shamed them with his muteness and disapproval as punishment for their timid guilt!

The table covered with velvet, the closed cupboards wiped clean of dust. Sparkling windows, fresh curtains. It could have been pleasant, cozy, yet it was only ambiguous, tortuous.

He rushed to the vacant lot, among the noisy and tough neighborhood boys. He returned late, sweaty, worn out by the running. At the door Lică greeted him with a tasteless joke. The house was still lighted: candlesticks were burning, the white tablecloth shone. His parents, elegant, stiff, avoided looking into each other's eyes. It was as if they did not even see the dirty, cynical wanderer in the doorway.

Just what year had begun *for them,* only folklorists of Near Eastern antiquity or those who read coffee grounds could have known. But honored parishioners, it *is* October 1! You know that very well because yesterday you got paid. The year did not follow nebulous and sanctified legends; the year was coming to an end . . . winter was coming, but not according to *your* lunar calendar, in which the oxen still pulled a wooden plow.

Instruction continued, however, in the exercise of divine linguistics. The verbs, adverbs, nouns multiplied. Outside, it was snowing thick and fast on the newer, dissident religions.

⤐ ⤐

The lessons continued rigorously. Gone were the pathetic theological digressions, but now came the rules: grammar, vocabulary, translation, composition. An agreement of limited participation. Again Monday, Wednesday, Thursday, conjugations, declensions, adjectives, numerals, attributives, complements, predicates, vocabulary, translation, composition. The black coat on a hook, the black hat on a hook, the briefcase next to the coat rack, the crumpled handkerchief to blow in, the white formal handkerchief. The short, stocky middle-aged gentleman—who could have been from the tax office or the forestry services or from nowhere at all, a court clerk, a tailor, a doctor's assistant, a violinist, a cashier, a detective: a conscientious, laconic scholar, within the limits of the contract.

The schoolboy discovered late and by accident that after the end of the lesson a film, a popular short catering to the tastes of the masses, was screened in the kitchen. The boy was just going there to get a drink of water when he caught the hoarse voice of the speaker. He retreated into the sepia shadows. "Saturday morning on his way to prayers, the rabbi from Berdichev met the town rebel. To confront the rabbi publicly, the rebel took out his pipe and lighted it. The rabbi stopped before the sinner. You must have forgotten that today is Saturday. No, I haven't forgotten at all, the rebel replies insolently. Then you probably don't know that we are not allowed to smoke on Saturday. Not at all!

I know all your laws, replies the rebel. The rabbi from Berdichev does not allow himself to be provoked. Then he raises his eyes and speaks to the sky: Did you hear? He's challenging your commandments. But you have to admit: no one can make him lie! That was the rabbi from Berdichev, kindness incarnate. He saw only good. . . . But after taking a few steps, he turned again toward the boor, who remained standing in the street in confusion. Why are you doing this? Because I'm an atheist! said the rebel, puffing himself up. So you're an atheist, mumbles the rabbi from Berdichev thoughtfully. Aha, hmm. And at which yeshiva and with whom did you study? What do you mean, yeshiva, what kind of yeshiva? stammered the rebel. Well, after all, you can't be an atheist unless you study the holy books. That was the rabbi from Berdichev, wisdom incarnate."

An allusion? Is he in fact speaking about the sinner he's now teaching? Is he kindness incarnate? So, the uninvited guest also poked fun at his student after souring three of his afternoons a week with moldy fruit.

The film droned on lazily. The merchant of anecdotes and soporifics continued with the same generous narratives:

"One day a young man comes to see the rabbi: I've been married for several years, I don't have any issue, I'm desperate, my wife and I want to have children. All right, says the rabbi from Berdichev, go home, you'll have a child. Nine months later, the young man returns, joyous: a son is born. Soon afterward, another solicitant comes to see him: I want a child, I've been married for five years, help me. He receives the same answer: go home, you'll have a child. A month passes, another two go by, another two, the promise is not fulfilled."

As the boy listens, the floor squeaks; it is a narrow space filled with baskets, bags, pots, only a step to the tiny, pantry-sized kitchen with its open door. You need the skills of a tightrope walker to stand there and not make the floor creak beneath your feet.

"The young man returns furious and embittered: You promised and it has not come true, I'm in despair. The old man shrugs his shoulders: What can I do? For you it was impossible. The wretched man insists, shouting: Why not for me? Why was it possible for the other? Because the other, after he left me, went straight to the store and bought a baby carriage! What did you do? the old man asked him. I don't know, I don't remember, stammered the blockhead. Well, that's why . . . that was why it wasn't possible, the rabbi sighed sadly. That was the rabbi from Berdichev, faith incarnate."

The weeks went by. Monday, Wednesday, Thursday: declensions, conjugations, translation, composition. "The rabbi from Berdichev said: Once I saw a thief the moment they caught him. I heard him murmuring: Tomorrow I'll have another go at it, I'll be better next time. The thief taught me that you have to start again every day." Again Monday, Wednesday, Thursday, the hat on the hook, the handkerchief, a-choo, grammar, vocabulary, translation. "The rabbi from Kotsk used to say: Prayers in hell are more sincere than those in heaven. That was the gloomy rabbi from Kotsk. He would shout: I prefer a dyed-in-the-wool idol worshiper to a half-believer! His last words: At last I'll see Him! Face to face!"

Another week: verbs, adverbs, prepositions, conjugations.

"Every nation can be understood by its language and grammar. Look at the English, dignified and democratic: both the king and the garbage man write 'I' with a capital letter. And we ... for us there is no formal 'you.' We call everyone by his first name, and we all have a direct connection with God, without intermediaries."

Again, the coat, hat, briefcase, handkerchief, notebooks full of rules and signs, the stop in the kitchen; the lady of the house offers him a cup of coffee: "The rabbi from Berdichev, the kindest of men, once broke off in the middle of his Yom Kippur prayers. He looked up and shouted, 'Today we are all prostrated before You, waiting for Your judgment. But I say, *You* shall be judged by all who suffer and die to sanctify Your name, Your laws, and Your contracts!' On another occasion, he murmured, 'I am not asking You why we are persecuted and massacred everywhere and under any pretext, but I would like to know at least if we are suffering for You.'

"And the rabbi from Kotsk struck his fist against the table and roared, 'I require that justice be carried out! That the Supreme Legislator subject himself to his own laws!'"

❧ ❧

The ice on the eaves was melting; the girls had reappeared, and with them their heady spring scent. The vacant lots roared with big soccer matches; in the morning and at dusk spring vertigo intoxicated the youth, who whirled around and around, poisoned by exotic breezes. Drunken roosters, conceited dogs, and music-crazed cats danced around the fences to the syncopated rhythm of madness.

A documentary of the times recording its events, burdens, and problems would register that on Monday, Wednesday, Thursday there was nothing but old parchments and scrolls: spring was not discussed, nor the international labor day, which was going to be celebrated the following Thursday, nor what had happened during the war or at school, nor the passionate films about the days of doubt and triumph. All this was dust for future archives.

The stranger seemed beaten, tired; he no longer jumped out of his chair, blurting words. The phrases rolled out evenly, in a steady tone, as if from an automaton. He didn't feel the urge to attack, to wait for a reply. He satisfied himself with a modest indifference. Sunken cheeks, watery eyes. He sweated a lot, panted. His large irritated nose with its wide purplish nostrils troubled him constantly. He blew with gusto into the handkerchief the size of a napkin, then crumpled it up and slipped it hurriedly into the breast pocket of his heavy gray winter jacket, which was buttoned over his vest and woolen sweater, which covered his shirt, which was held tightly closed at the neck by the big knot of his tie.

He had lost the fight. He should have understood long ago that his tricks served no purpose. Perhaps he was sick.

⤞ ⤝

At the end of May, the selection of candidates for the summer camp would be announced at school. Everybody was excited by this prospect.

Whether by coincidence or not, just then, when no one would have expected it anymore, the psalmist recovered his taste for chatter, the courage of familiarity. Again he was playing the part of an old relative passing through town and happy to exchange a word or two, to allow a joke or a piece of advice to slip out, just like that, by accident. Thoughts, anecdotes, questions, pleasantries, it soon became clear that, in fact, they were perfidious attacks! That's what was decided by the boy and Lică during their dialectical discussions. Cunning and perfidiousness: there was no other way to explain why the great actor had returned to tricks that had proved useless.

"Let's call it learning, not faith. You who are thirsty, seek water! That is one of our sayings."

The appeal was no more than a hidden trap from which thin, curved, poison-tipped arrows whizzed out.

"Faith exists where it is allowed to gain admittance. You too have allowed faith to enter. Even if it is not the right one."

And further, after a resumption of conjugations, declensions, translations:

"Do you know what we say? Even if it goes in one ear and out the other, still a trace is left along the way. Too young? A temporary defect! You're losing this disability with every passing day."

Finally, before putting the black bowl over his bald spot, he would push the pedal *"you—us,"* which he had taken up again with fervor.

"When all is said and done, beliefs aren't all that different. I see that you have saints. But we don't have them! Saints, no, we don't have that. No man is so righteous that he can be good without sinning. There are wise men, naturally. So we had better call it learning, that will suit you too."

Look where it gets you: you make one concession, then another, until bang, the stranger slaps you in the face. You did not hit back in time; he knows that now you can't! You can't anymore.

Now he knew that something had changed: for the moment the rebel's hands were tied; anything could be done to him. His parents had found out about the camp. A fine bargaining chip had been offered them. They were suddenly in control and could use it without scruples: in the event you are chosen, if you want to have our consent, you'll have to be kind to Mr. Teacher Accordionist Carpenter Detective, whatever he might be, for all the nonsense he has had the goodness to share with you in between sneezes every Monday, Wednesday, Thursday, his eminence, our very hoarse benefactor.

The instructor had been informed about the blackmail; there was no other explanation for the oblique, increasingly cutting familiarities.

"Every beginning is dizzying. And happiness? As if that were anything. . . . Suffering, only suffering gives weight to time! Write this down, you can write down anything you want, I know who you are, the company you keep. I know you feel guilty that you're here listening to this old-fashioned idiot. Guilt can be vengeful, I am used to it. I hear you appear on the podium for celebrations. You hold conferences, you recite, maybe you also write poems, the red kind. Write it down, write it down, I'm not afraid."

The sequence accelerates in rhythm with the chatter. "The verses written on parchment speak of love, reward, punishment. The truth, in other words. And about freedom. Do you know of anything more important than these delusions? You consider man guilty. You always suspect him. But do you think *we* don't? We say: You have been born, therefore you are guilty."

Shooting was becoming difficult; the camera turned toward the window, then the sky and the trees in the yard.

"Unanimity? Every man is unique, not only God! In the old days our highest court very rarely condemned anyone to death. Only for truly extraordinary crimes! Even then, however, the people did not praise their judges for that. But there existed a provision that automatically annulled the death sentence: if the sentence was passed unanimously. It's suspicious, comrade, what can I say. Are you taking notes? Look at that, maybe you're interested. Do you want to turn me over to the Inquisition? There have been many cases, it wouldn't be the first time. Write it down, son, write this down too: 'The wise man in fur.' A man shielded from the cold feels free to think he's smart. For you people, it's not even a matter of wise men. You have saints. In fur."

What is one supposed to make of that? Sunday morning, in the laziness of the colorless hours, the candidate tries to inject surprise by officially announcing the summer event to the conspirators. Extraordinary scene! Wide eyes, happiness, kisses, as if they hadn't known anything about it. They seem sincere: the head of the family rushes out to buy a bottle of wine; the lady of the house runs over to the neighbors' with the news. Such perfect acting, spontaneous, without the faintest sign of hostility or deviousness. One is almost ready to believe them. No question of opposing the trip, they were proud, happy. Try to understand what is going on now! Such cunning seemed to be too much for their warm hearts. And yet no, no, one had to keep one's eyes open; no detail should be ignored.

There was no longer any doubt—the small, apparently inoffensive, perspiring, hoarse man was hiding behind his innocent game and inexpressive mask; he was an expert schemer! The parents' pained tenderness and his otherworldly geniality were no more than modulations in falsetto. The playful or aggressive words, the high didactic professionalism, hid more than they disclosed. The pedagogue was their powerful secret weapon.

When it was lesson time the house suddenly became quiet. This was unusual. Nothing ever interrupted the continuous circulation from the kitchen into the room, from the room into the hall. Slammed doors, chatter, relatives, neighbors, friends, white-collar workers, Martians, Neanderthals, there was constant turbulence. The appearance of old what's-his-name, however, instantly stopped the merest sound, the slightest movement.

In the room, the grammarian goes hoarse with his anachronistic phonetics. Not a word is to be heard, there isn't even a breeze from the yard. Even if eyes and ears are spying, the doors seem securely locked, the rooms empty; the walls, suddenly thick and porous, absorb all noise. The soundtrack starts suddenly; the movements take on speed.

"You say to deceive your fellow man is a sin. Our elders say to deceive God is childish. Of course. But to deceive yourself, in whom both man and God reside? Be careful, be careful of this."

He kept it up that way, excited, aggressive. When he wanted to focus on a special point that he did not have the courage to express outright, he would modulate his voice dramatically or gesticulate rapidly as though ready to grab his adversary by the shoulders and shake him. "Pay attention, pay attention to this." One did not know what to expect from his commotion. The old man allowed himself to be transported to the point of frenzy by the onrush of his delirium.

Bizarre ideas, not at all innocent. "You can take notes, go ahead, write it down." He knows that it is easier to keep calm when taking notes, like an automaton, than to have to listen.

The parents had pinned all their hopes on the instructor. A few seconds before his arrival they would disappear, vanish, as if they didn't dare disturb his mission. Or perhaps they felt some guilt toward him; it couldn't be ruled out. Was guilt the mysterious element in their relationship? Was their guilt—the boy's guilt—the explanation behind their obvious subordination? One week he didn't show up. Because of illness, that's what they said. They became helpless, stumped, as if life had lost its focus.

Like a miracle, a bizarre compensation, rumors of a polio epidemic suddenly seized their attention. The disease was spreading quickly in this district or that, in this boarding school or that.

Disarmed, barely hiding their panic, each day his parents brought fresh disturbing news. So-and-so from this village, that village. So many in this city or that. Special care should be taken by those who had been through the difficult years, those weakened by fear, by hunger. The undernourished, fussy, sensitive, weak children. Particularly vulnerable were those who had suffered in the war! They say that a tailor's daughter who had been in the same concentration camp with us . . . Crowded places, poor sanitation, should be avoided. Movie theaters, swimming pools, summer camps were particularly disastrous, because all kinds of people from all over the place come together. The trains too, of course—especially when you've got a long trip ahead of you, a very long trip. They emphasized this information with obvious conviction.

They would unfold the map and pore over the train schedule, looking for Radna. From there a bus would take the Pioneer leaders, the school political guardians, to the castle. At camp the danger would be increased; the risk was catastrophic. As if their wailing and exaggeration could have upset anyone! They laid their traps, made insinuations, threats, gave advice, and then waited for the effect.

The old man reappeared, his thoughts elsewhere. Who could guess why. The rehearsals accelerated, but he did not exert himself; he only repeated summary instructions about the text and acted out stage movements.

"They are placed on the left arm, next to the heart, and on the head. Every day for morning prayer, except for Saturdays and holidays." When he left, the big black hat covered him completely, like a sort of umbrella.

On his last day, during the dress rehearsal, the instructor remained silent, apathetic for half an hour, as if he were hiding in his own shell. One might give in to pity if one wasn't careful! One could have believed that the man was someone else entirely! We do not know whom to admire, Maestro: the famous folklorist, well known in academic forums, as the myopic mathematician who sits in the second row insists; the former advocate for the poor, the scandal of the community, as Lică the know-it-all cousin believes; or the secret philanthropist peddling wisdom and sneezes. He was a kind of legend, or so he seemed with his one and only heavy black suit, in full summer, as if nothing could touch or move him.

But the cold, cough, and sneezing would not stop, no matter how untouchable he believed himself to be. He continued to sit in silence and frown in the direction of the star of the performance.

But surprise! He began to speak, quietly and with difficulty, almost in a whisper, looking straight at his listener. They were nonsense words without the least connection to the immediate and glorious duties of the actor whom he had trained with so much patience, nor to the glorious past that some said he embodied.

"Our magnificent contribution, and ours alone, is this sacred and venerable day, its royal majesty, the Sabbath! We were the first to introduce rest, a symbol of freedom and rebirth!"

Gradually he had raised his voice; he would have shouted had his hoarseness allowed it.

"And of dignity, sir! The symbol of creation! After six days the Lord rested, as we do too. We gave the idea to the world, mind you! And the Holy Book is divided into fifty-four chapters, that's how many joys there are in a year, comrade!"

Then why did you talk to the peasants about cooperatives and phalansteries, why did you defend the atheists and rebels, why did you argue with my grandfather in the temple only to save him later from that horrible trap laid for him . . . and why do you continue to respect an outdated tradition, all these ridiculous customs inherited like a weight, from our ancestors . . .

There hadn't been time for these questions: the hat, coat, and handkerchief had disappeared. He had left. Brusquely, without a word.

The next day, beneath the tall chandeliers, the film became festively colored. A hushed cool hall, the strange smell of old, unfamiliar plants. No one but the boy's father, standing a step behind him, saw his momentary hesitation before he touched the scrolls. The left arm covered, the forehead held tightly in the circle of leather, the black cube in the center. A tense and pale candidate under the sacred white silk shawl in which they had wrapped him. The speech had been perfect, the diction clear. The actor's father, a true gentleman, impeccably dressed, had emerged suddenly, or so it seemed, from his secondary role. And his mother was crying, naturally, as was the rest of the vulnerable and emotional audience.

The instructor had not come to the ceremony. His oddness justified any assumption. Lică had come up with a new invention: he claimed the old man had recently insulted a Party boss, a man he had once defended in court when the Communist Party had been illegal. Moreover he was said to have done so in public. In the process he had alienated everyone and managed to have himself disbarred. He was now thrust into poverty, rejected, ridiculed. If this was true, all the more reason why ceremonies might annoy him, Lică explained from under his extraordinary new mustache. His mission had in fact ended, continued Lică, and there would be no reason for the man to expect final thanks from this spoiled Pioneer.

The epilogue—with brandy, congratulations, and sweet pastry—did not last long. On the street the young man again confronted the lazy, torrid indifference of summer. The burning pavement sank under his steps; the heat melted the solemnity of the day.

A week later the early-morning train started for Radna, at the other end of the country. A long journey with many stops to pick up other Pioneer leaders along the way.

A day and a night on dusty wooden benches. In every district another hero climbed aboard; each a fighter who had proved that he had excelled at his brave and important mission. This was the first international summer camp, with special guests. The boy arrived exhausted: he had thrown up constantly.

They were transported, crowded on top of their suitcases, in a truck from the station to the edge of the forest. A blue sky, white puffs of dandelions, a round sun, fields and hills, a marvel. Although they were tired, they sang; they were happy, proud to represent their country.

At the edge of the wood, twenty Bulgarian Pioneers were lined up waiting for them. They were in uniform; their ties were skinnier, shinier. On their heads they wore white cloth hats that looked like pith helmets.

The scene is colored in summer hues, a panoramic image: the road, the trees, the camp housed in the castle of a former ruling monkey. Flags, trumpets, files of men, gatherings, games, meetings. In the morning, exercises, in the evening, campfires, speeches.

They are preparing for elections; there is a lot of commotion around a stalwart, handsome, brown-haired boy; the children whisper that he is from the capital.

Only a few days after the elections are over do copies of the Pioneer magazine arrive. The boy picks one up, overwhelmed, bashful, proud. The title on the second page sparkles, emphatic and red. Two whole columns! He hides the copy so that no one may catch him looking at it; he does and does not want to be discovered. He becomes friends with a Bulgarian Pioneer leader; they exchange stamps. The boy reveals his secret, and soon word is out; his torment ends.

Naturally his prestige grows. Everyone wants to know everything about him; envious, they barrage him with questions. The instructors introduce him all around. They look at him with interest, ask him questions on everything, nod approval, smile. The next day at roll call they raise their hands to greet him. He does make friends with one of them, a student at the film institute. He looks like a movie star. Slim, cold blue eyes, a Greek profile, the shoulders of an athlete, windblown hair. He is very cultivated, carries on long discussions about Engels's *Anti-Dühring* and Rolland's *The Soul Enchanted*. But also about books unfamiliar to the boy. In deep thought, the young man talks about his life to his friend, the instructor, under a shady tree. How, freed from the camps, they still stayed over there for almost a year, how he had then started school, had even had time to become a Soviet Pioneer Scout. The student is amazed and repeats the story to the others. In the next few days the director and the head instructor ask him for details; even the cook develops a soft spot for him. The director expresses his regret that he hadn't known all these things before the elections. A popular hero, a cultural authority! At the first campfire meeting he recites his sonorous verses to peace.

Always busy, happy, he has no time to unpack his suitcase. Only later does he discover, hidden at the bottom among the towels, a red silk pouch. He closes the case quickly so that he won't be seen; he turns the key in fury. He is not going to touch those objects, it is all over—he isn't going to continue with the masquerade! He should have thrown it out immediately, the pouch containing those bewitched leather thongs—or, better, have burned it, if he had had the courage. He would do it in the next few days. But he puts it off; he does not find the right moment. He is never alone. He also postpones writing the letter that would inform them of the definitive break. In the dormitory and at roll call and at mealtimes he cannot manage to be by himself; there is always someone who is looking for him. But he had made sure to hide the silk pouch at the bottom of his suitcase, covered with handkerchiefs and socks, stuffed beneath his underwear. He keeps feeling for the key in his pocket.

The following week, the reel is changed; the pace quickens, an uproar, an episode with parents and doctors. On the evening before an official inspection prompted by rumors of polio, fresh sheets and blankets are brought in. A great bustle: beds are moved so there will be fewer per dormitory. Windows are washed, floors scrubbed with turpentine. Lights-out is sounded late. The night sequence: moon and pine trees—the panorama facing the dormitory, where the little men cannot sleep because of their agitation and the smell of turpentine. The night swallows movement, but you can still hear voices; trucks unload cases of bottles and boxes of vegetables. The noise ends only toward morning.

At dawn everyone is dizzy; morning exercises do not take place. The yard is filled with stacks of cases, mineral water, all kinds of boxes and packages. At roll call it is announced that the camp will receive an important visit. The truth was that they all felt wonderful, even though they had drunk water from the tap. Too many in the dormitory? No one minded—there were happy, friendly scuffles. It was not quite clear what the guests wanted to hear; after all, everything had been terrific; they were all happy.

The delegation appears at noon: a fantastic meal. But the mineral water has a funny taste—it stings your tongue. The young man is placed next to a doctor, on the other side of whom sits a woman who is enraged and silent. The boy is being interviewed and gives all the appropriate answers: the sheets are changed regularly, we wash our hands six times a day, we are eight to a dormitory room, we drink bottled water, the food is like this, exercise is like that, everything is as it should be. The delegates seem satisfied; they consult among themselves, go for a walk in the woods once more, and in the evening they leave. After dinner, his friend the instructor slaps him on the shoulder merrily: "Bravo, you're a man I can trust. You can help me with a job."

The next day the young writer becomes his assistant. They lock themselves in a room in the afternoon and work until late.

At the end of the week, two long-haired fellows with heavy filming equipment on their shoulders come from Bucharest. His instructor friend had probably suggested that he be used in the film. He does not complain; carefully he makes a selection of verses for the Saturday-night campfire, an homage to the beloved Iosif Vissarionovich.

The lens focuses on the field, the moon, the straight black pines, the silent audience of centuries. The night smells of pine needles. The instructor puts his arm around his protégé: a closeup of their faces, then the two continue on their walk through the woods.

"There's no point in going back to yesterday's discussion. You're an intelligent, fair-minded boy; of course, the memories have become deeply ingrained for some of the war's children, it is only natural. But this has no connection with . . ."

"That's exactly what I was saying, too: this cannot have any connection. Then why is it necessary to . . . After all, we're happy here, it's wonderful. Why should we control . . ."

"Oh, here we go again. Congratulations on your verses. You have a way with words, Maestro! Where did you ever pick up words like 'kabbalistic' or 'heresies,' what were you saying there, terrestrial, a terrestrial calendar, for everyone. We don't have saints, either naked or covered in furs. Good, comrade, that's right. Her Majesty the Light . . . nice! . . . severity is only for the righteous . . . we believe in you, just as you believe in us . . . Son, you're a man of culture! All right, I'll stop, I understand. Look, you've got a letter."

He hands him the envelope. His father's beautiful, elegant writing. The boy looks at it for a long time and hesitates. The instructor can no longer restrain himself—he begins to laugh.

"I haven't opened it, for God's sake."

He kept laughing—he could not stop. He had gone on ahead, laughing with unpleasant heartiness. The boy stops, pale. He does not open the envelope; with a frown he watches the departing figure of his companion. The unopened letter, was it an exception? If so, yet another reason for starting the discussion again! Surely, each would repeat his argument and fail to convince the other, nor even make him understand. It would end with the same patronizing pat on the shoulder. A man shouldn't get upset. Between friends there should be no room for condescension. But when seriousness is taken for childishness ... The instructor used any pretext to avoid real talk; he put up a sort of soft wall between them.

In fact it would have been very annoying had the instructor read the letter.

I hope you did not get angry about what you found in the suitcase. I know you are not going to use them. But Mother insisted. We hear all kinds of rumors about polio. She thinks that these things might protect you.

The concerned tone and careful words did not alter the boy's decision to send a letter announcing his separation from the family. He had a lot to do—he was almost never alone, that was true. But now everything became more difficult. Had the instructor really not opened the letter? Does this mean he wouldn't open the reply? What about the answer: to write it, not to write it?

He had objected to the reading of letters from the very beginning. The panic and the rumors of an epidemic had worried some parents so much that they had not only registered official complaints but had also alarmed the children about it; some had even come all the way to the camp to convince themselves that all was well. This was not, the boy maintained, a sufficient motive for the snooping. In fact, what difference would it make if the letters ...

He had objected, but he had consented. He too would have to subject himself to the general rule. "I should have written the letter. And in the most categorical of terms. And put it in with all the envelopes ready to be checked."

He couldn't write about the strange objects hidden in his suitcase. He would have had to explain, at least to the instructor, what it was all about.

He was angry to be connected once more to the shadows from which he was now estranged. Yes, he was sure he was estranged. He had taken another road, it was clearly another road. And yet he felt guilt and shame.

He avoided looking at the others, became taciturn. Sometimes he felt nauseated; perhaps he also had a fever. His friend the instructor was kind and concerned, and asked him repeatedly whether he was sick. He was giving him a chance to open up.

The boy hesitated before speaking: "I can't look my roommates in the eye—I know what is in their letters. Not even at the other campers sometimes. For example, the handsome boy from Bucharest who was elected commander. Now I know how much he despises the rest of us, what he wrote about the showers, about the food." The soundtrack came to a stop suddenly, like a sob. The mentor was smiling. He stretched a powerful, tanned hand across the table and squeezed the boy's small and shaking one.

"Forget these things, there's no point. Don't torture yourself anymore. It's my mistake. I shouldn't have involved you in this. After all, you told me about those fears and sufferings. I should have realized. All right, starting tomorrow, you don't have to come anymore."

But the young dreamer returned on the next day, and on the following days, after lunch, at the usual hour, in the narrow office with the naked walls, a table, and two chairs. The instructor did not send him away. It was a friendly gesture, gentle and indulgent, toward a dreamy, fragile artist. They worked in silence and left together for their dormitories. The boy can't fall asleep. Outside the window in the night he sees the fiery eyes of a nameless bird.

Only a few days before leaving, he managed to draft a letter. He was in the infirmary, where he had been put for observation: he complained of headaches, nausea, that his legs weren't steady, that he couldn't sleep. They gave him all kinds of pills. Finally he slept. Still he was pale, taciturn, his eyes shone, as though blinded by a strange flame.

> I understand you are worried about polio. There are no cases here, but there is cause for concern. The sheets were changed only when they came for inspection. Then they gave us good things to eat; we drank bottled water. Now they even forget to boil it. We don't wash much. We are fine in the dormitory, though there are many of us. It's crowded in the showers. The doctor hasn't been here in a week. The nurse has no patience; she just got engaged. But I hope to get out of here in one piece.

He knew these lines would punish his parents, the censor, and the rebellious writer himself. He asked the nurse to put the letter in the mailbox by the director's office. From the window he carefully followed the blond as she went to lunch. He saw her drop the envelope into the mailbox.

That same evening they allowed him to leave the infirmary. In the dormitory, he pulled out the suitcase from under his bed. It was untouched, dusty, the way he had left it. He unlocked it. Raising the lid only a fraction, he put in his hand and felt around. Everything was in place.

There was only one day of camp left. That afternoon he did not go to meet his companion. In the evening, a pleasant surprise. Those strong guys, the cameramen, had returned with the film.

At the canteen the film was screened. Morning exercise, roll call, model airplanes, craft classes, dance classes, the campfire, the entertainment programs, meals, excursions, the dormitories, the showers, the volleyball field. Our boy/actor shared the leading role with the commander from Bucharest. He was on the screen for almost two minutes: with the trumpet, at the shower, at the reading, with the flag, next to the Bulgarian boy.

When the lights were turned on, they all clapped. The instructor waved but did not come near him.

The next day, the camp closed in a festive atmosphere. At noon the groups were taken to the station.

The trip back seemed even longer. Heat, crowding. He kept throwing up. There seemed to be endless stops; he did not have the strength to squeeze the hands of those getting off. He would doze for a while, wake up suddenly in a sweat, struggle to reach the toilet and vomit. He had not been able to take out the red silk pouch; he was never alone.

Finally, just before arriving home, he fell asleep. At times, the long silver snout of a phosphorescent shark shone in the black window.

He woke up at the station. Through the window he saw them waiting nervously and impatiently. He was the only one left in the compartment. He still had time to open the suitcase and pull out the pouch. He felt the cube, the leather thongs, and the rustle of the shawl. His hand shook holding that hidden explosive. A frightening, dangerous contact. Furious, he threw the bundle under the seat.

He got off the train, relieved and suddenly cheerful. He told them that everything had been as wonderful as in a fairy tale. They made no comment. Had they received the letter? No one brought it up. He told them about his Bulgarian friend, with whom he planned to exchange letters and stamps. At home he unpacked in front of them. Not a word about the missing object.

They were pleased that the holiday had been such fun. But they seemed tentative. He told them about the upcoming cinematographic event of which he was the star. They seemed truly moved.

But the anticipated film arrived only months later: fall had settled in over the little town, hunched under sleet and nocturnal winds. A time of rapid growth, of sleeplessness among his books in his cell.

In the belly of the clouds, unseen birds shrieked in the twilight. The little provincial town swayed languidly. In the evening the hills, intoxicated by resin, rolled recklessly toward the mouth of the devil; on the burning roofs, cats and billy goats danced on pyres. The young man takes rigorous walks under the town hall clock, his eyes toward the stars. Aloof, contemptuous, without illusions, proprietor of solitude, keeping step to the rhythm of a number of grand phrases. To deceive the Lord is childish. . . . To deceive your fellow man is a sin. . . . Error above, error below.

Proud, distant, like any beginner; each step marked yet another start. Poor: without error above, without error below. He avoided crowds, skirted market squares, stadiums. He kept away from assembly halls, churches, movie theaters. He stoically bore his poverty, wounds, grandeur, old age, which had come—who would have believed it—so quickly. Look, in only two months. Everything changed, his gait, his voice, smile, vision. He listened to music until late in the night: records, records, until he lost himself in a faint. In the melodic waters of dawn resounded the flap of long metallic wings.

Yet even in the depths of melancholy he would have to watch that childish documentary about the country's first summer camp. He went to the movie theater; it was a Wednesday, around ten in the morning. He realized how judicious his choice had been: at that hour people were at work or at school. The few spectators, wanderers of no importance, did not deserve his attention; their curiosity could be ignored. He picked a spot as far away as possible from anyone.

The program merited no more than condescension. What could a short, ten-minute film show? A castle, a forest, a troop of pleasant-looking little schoolboys! The tall entrance gate, the flags, the volleyball games, the field trip, the campfire, the roll call, the swimming pool. Everything staged, stylized; they would omit the nurse, the showers, the narrow censor's office, and the beautiful secret hiding places in the field. The hero would appear, probably, in two illustrious, banal sequences, to touch soft-hearted souls with his idiotic, childish smile.

The clock showed one minute past the hour. A few more seconds. . . . He closed his eyes; on his inner screen images of the sky and of the town. A different film: a broken-up street, an old building, a tapering roof; an ordinary room, a table, a chair, another chair, at which sits a schoolboy hunched over books and notebooks. He writes, draws rapidly, or he sits there, perplexed, with an absent look. Another scene: the face of an old man, a bird, a tiger's snout, the barbed-wire fence. He takes notes feverishly: the instructor, tousled hair, handkerchief, Mother, rolls of parchment, a gaunt vulture, the scaly tail, the black hat; the castle, the tiger, the flags, the spiral horn, the bird. He mumbles constantly as he writes. Now all that is left is the pallor of a frowning boy with big eyes. Again, he mumbles as he looks at his drawing: you're here on the page, where are you always flying to . . . stuck for good, he writes down another word, draws, takes notes. It is not quite clear what he is doing and what he is saying; he seems caught up in the mission that has been entrusted to him. Suddenly he looks at his watch and rushes to the coat closet. He takes out his beret, his coat. He slams the front door behind him. Outside, a damp fall, the streets are dirty, slippery. He walks to the front of a narrow building, stops at the box office window, goes into a hall, and sits in the back, on the right, near the exit.

Now the real film starts. Green hills, summer, a castle. Truckloads of schoolboys, flags. Roll call, the volleyball field, the campfire. Roll call, the forest, the infirmary, the games. Next to the flag, under the flag . . . reciting in front of the fire, in the field. A shy, photogenic smile.

The bored spectator gets up. He stops at the snack bar, buys himself a chocolate bar and some juice, and leaves hurriedly.

Out in the street he buries his face in his collar. He heads for the high school, absorbed in his thoughts. In the air, unseen, a gaunt bird, a flame. He touches his temples, his brow. Suddenly he hears the hoarse words of a stranger.

"What are you doing here, young man?"

With a frown he looks up. He can't stand such familiarity. The man is standing before him, a gentleman of medium height in a black coat and hat. A plump, sagging face, deep circles around the eyes, a white, neglected beard.

"Don't you recognize me anymore?"

They are standing under the eaves of a repair shop, protected from the damp wind that is lifting whirlwinds of bronze-colored leaves around them. The young man allows himself a moment's hesitation.

"It's possible that we know each other. This very summer I had, I believe, interesting discussions with you, dear instructor, about Mr. Dühring and about a novel by Romain Rolland. If I'm not mistaken, we even debated certain problems we had come across during our censors' work. You know, without telling you I took the liberty of taking some unsuitable letters. In the evening, before falling asleep, I would reread the delicious childish confessions, full of candor and cunning."

The old man stares for a few moments, as if he had suddenly been struck by paralysis. But then he smiles patiently.

"No, you're mistaken. We met in the home of some nice people, your parents. I took the liberty then of telling you about the Sabbath, our most important holiday, exclusively divine, when the Creator granted Himself a day of rest."

The old man hasn't lost the knack. I've got to give it to him, he is an educated man, in spite of the familiarity with which he stops passersby. But if he hopes for dialogue, he is fooling himself.

"I hoped you would understand that I am to blame if my daughter does not do homework on Saturday. I put it into her head. Learning becomes faith after a while—what could she do? I wonder, my son, if you've participated in the decision to expel her because of that. You would have had to. You had an important political role in your school. You were a group leader. They counted you among the believers, the soldiers, the killers. They gave you great power, dangerous power. Yes, yes. They taught you to enjoy this poison."

Really, he is fooling himself if he hopes for dialogue. No, he could not be stopped at all. Look, he is back at it again. "Yes, my pupil, were you silent when they took the decision? Perhaps you even spoke in favor of it? Unanimity, I know that all your resolutions are unanimous. Is it possible that you didn't catch her name, that you'd forgotten mine? Wischnitzer, that's my daughter's name, too! You aren't capable of such ugliness, am I right? Maybe you didn't even know her, my good boy. She's only thirteen, a mere child. Among our people, only the boys are men at this age!"

From the repair shop under whose eaves they had stopped, the loud sounds of a lathe invaded the street.

"Your parents asked me to instruct you. I refused for as long as I could. They knew about my daughter, what you had done. But they insisted. I couldn't forget your grandfather. No, I couldn't refuse him, my boy. Should I have brought this up at the very start?"

If this hoarse gentleman expects dialogue, he is wrong.

"You mustn't think that I'm judging you. I don't have that right. But I thought I'd take my leave of all of you, we're emigrating . . ."

The young man could bear no more. He suddenly awakened from his shock, hurt and angry, but the old man had disappeared.

"Didn't you teach me, comrade, that our daily history is a history of class struggle, that we have to fight the enemy at every moment, without illusions, without philistine sentimentalism? Without religious fervor, without childish feelings? No, I really didn't know your daughter,

Comrade Berdichev. It is possible that I was there when the decision was taken. The little monster followed his mission, my dear instructor. He kicked out many. Didn't you teach me that judgment must remain above influence, unswayed? It must. One came from a bourgeois family, another refused to write on Saturday, and yet another joked about our saints. Yes, you are right, I tasted power. Yes, I swallowed the poison, my instructors hoped that I deserved this honor, this horror. . . ."

The stranger had left without offering his hand. Better alone! Without parents, instructors.

Grandparents, cousins, neighbors, aunts, instructors, parents; one after another, they leave the country. He smiled guiltily. Orphaned. He was alone on the street.

An extraordinary odyssey, yes, one that demands an inkwell. So he thought, the conceited little prig.

The cloud had descended over him; he was lost in it. But with that hellish buzzing in his ears, he couldn't concentrate at all on important thoughts.

He started off quickly toward the school, bent over, burrowing like a lathe through the morning fog. Now he began to run feverishly, besieged. His narrow shadow had come closer; it was filling the screen.

Translated from the Romanian by Anselm Hollo.

MISSING PIECES

Stanislaw Benski

I'm not typical. I saw no Nazis, SS-men, or Gestapo, I never laid eyes on a German soldier, and never heard a bomb or a mine explode. I learned of all this after my return. Yes . . . I spent the entire war at my brother Isaac's in New York City. Nobody in my family perished, nobody was gassed, nobody was shot in the forest or starved to death in the Ghetto. As a Warsaw Jew, I'm an exception, and to tell you the truth, it's embarrassing. I wrote a long letter to my brother, telling him about all the horrors I heard. I waited six months for a reply. Finally he sent me a postcard from some scenic place in Florida, with this message: "Don't dig up the War, you'll make yourself sick. You suffer from indigestion as it is. Remember how you caught pneumonia when you were with us? So take care of yourself. Greetings from my Hannah and from Aunt Luba. Your brother."

After a long search I found myself a wife who also had not been in the Ghetto, who had spent no time in a camp, and had not lived through the Occupation in the forest. She was in Uzbekistan the whole time—in Samarkand and later Tashkent. She returned from the east and I from the west, but we're compatible.

My wife, Rose, speaks a little Russian and Uzbek, while I know a little English. She cooks rice dishes, even the desserts have rice in them, while I remember the hamburgers and the pizza I had in a bar on Twelfth Street.

Anyway, I said to my Rose: "Listen, dear, I can't stand being an exception, I want to be like everyone else. People look at me as if I were abnormal, or they think I'm lying."

"You're an honest man," said Rose, "but a little absentminded. You don't even remember your shoe size."

"That's not what I mean, dear," I explained. "I, Gabriel Lewin, need a new curriculum vitae."

"You have a fine curriculum vitae," she protested. "Any Jew would be proud to have such a curriculum vitae. Who else spent the War in Manhattan, U.S.A.? Who else, in nineteen forty-three, strolled peacefully down Fifth Avenue or Broadway, and ate in kosher restaurants, and had matzah on Pesaḥ? Who else in Warsaw managed that? Nobody else!"

"People don't believe me," I said. "And I can't blame them."

"Maybe they're jealous."

"Maybe, maybe not. In any case, it's hard to live with."

So Rose took some blank sheets of paper out of a sideboard drawer, and we got to work. It was a complicated job. She decided to redo her curriculum vitae, too. Every evening we sat at the table and put together our life histories during the Occupation.

We began with September, 1939. Although Rose was not in Warsaw then, she recalled several radio bulletins from that period, and conversations about the War, in the village of Nowojelnia where she lived with her parents. We constructed two pages of my curriculum vitae out of this. I learned how long the Nazi air raids lasted, what was bombed and where, and that on September 7, Major Umiastowski over the radio asked all male inhabitants to leave the city. In my new curriculum vitae, I stayed in the capital, and from September 7 to September 20 (Rose didn't remember the exact date—toward the end of the month, in any case) bombs fell on my street: high-explosive, incendiary, delayed action, and some that, because of sabotage back in German factories, did not go off but lay peacefully in the middle of the street.

Before I went to America, I lived at Przebieg Street No. 2 on the fifth floor, and from our window you could see into a room on the fourth floor of the house across the street. My grandmother told me that Mr. and Mrs. Jung lived there, and that their daughter had emigrated to America and was not called Jung anymore, but Young with a Y and an O. Miss Young made a great career for herself there, she got a part in a film, then a Hollywood contract, and became a star. I wasn't sure if this was true or not, but I added a passage to my curriculum vitae about going down to the air-raid shelter with the Jungs and their telling me about their daughter, the great actress Loretta Young with a Y and an O. Such details add realism. Rose approved of the idea.

A description of the Germans' entry into Warsaw I found in some library books. The trouble started in 1940. Reading, we filled ourselves with so many atrocities that we couldn't eat, drink, sleep, or think like normal people anymore. This went on for days.

One sleepless night, Rose sat up in bed and said: "Gabriel, according to my new curriculum vitae, I couldn't have survived. I must have died of a heart attack. Because I can't stand the sight of blood. I used to run away when the *shochet* came to kill the chickens and ducks, I cried when I cut my finger. I could never have lived through those horrors of nineteen forty, and we have three more years to go, nineteen forty-one, nineteen forty-two, and nineteen forty-three."

"If all Jews were like you, dear wife," I said, "the whole Ghetto would have dropped dead, and the Nazis wouldn't have had anything to do. I, on the other hand, have enlisted in the Jewish partisan army and am now in the forest fighting the Germans as becomes a young man of courage."

"Nobody enlisted to join the partisans," Rose explained to me, her brother having been with the underground in the Polesie region. "You had to get yourself detailed to it by order, and that wasn't so easy."

I deleted the part of my curriculum vitae that described me as an underground soldier, and put myself in occupied Warsaw again, but outside the Ghetto, on the Aryan side, where I lived with the Wieczorek brothers on Marimoncka Street, under the identity of a relative of theirs who had been expelled from Nazi-annexed Poznán. The old Wieczorek couple were well-known to my parents and grandparents. We used to play hide-and-seek with Wacek and Adam near the Citadel, and when we were bigger, it was Indians, and when we were bigger still, we went on long walks along the Vistula toward Młociny.

My curriculum vitae was coming along nicely. Rose also added to hers a few "gallant adventures," as she called them, and so after a few weeks we got to the year 1943.

"No, there is no way we could have lived through that," said Rose, and burst into tears. "Don't ask me to survive the destruction of the Białystok ghetto. And I won't have you suffer in the one in Warsaw."

"Why Białystok?" I asked her.

"Because I wrote that I escaped to Białystok, to my uncle Oscar Weisberg," she said.

We were sitting at breakfast. I pushed my plate away, set the glass of milk aside, and looked at Rose. She was crying: her eyes were closed tight, but tears were running, one after the other, down her wrinkled cheeks.

"Don't cry, silly!" I said loudly, perhaps a little too loudly, to cover my pity for her.

"I am crying out of grief, but also with a tiny gladness," she sobbed. "Grief for my family and the loss of so many innocent people, yet I can't help being happy that I wasn't in a camp, in a ghetto, in the forest, or some other place where they murdered children, since I was a child then."

"Nineteen years old is not a child," I said. "There were babies, toddlers there. Like our neighbor's Marylka. She was only three, and you can imagine . . ." I got up and went to the window. In the sandbox down in the yard, children were playing—squealing, laughing, skipping, rolling in the sand. A boy in red pants and white shirt was crying, while another boy, a little taller, patted his little ginger-haired head. A girl in a green dress was reading a book, bent over so that one couldn't see her face. Beside her stood a boy holding a transistor radio to his ear. I asked my wife to come to the window and said:

"Imagine that suddenly, from behind the house on the corner, and from behind the garage and the shed, step German soldiers, field police, SS-men, and they surround the sandbox. The children go on playing, not seeing them or sensing the danger. At last the boy with the radio notices the Germans and screams. He throws the radio to the ground and tries to flee. The girl runs after him, clutching her book, and a few other children run. But it is too late. . . . The SS-men form the children into a double column and march them to the street, where trucks have pulled up. The children are off to the ovens. And there among them is Marylka, who has knocked at our door every day and said, 'Good morning, Auntie. Good morning, Uncle.' Now she won't knock at our door anymore."

Silently we stood together at the window. Then we went back to the table.

"I know a woman who has only the second half of her curriculum vitae," mused Rose. "The first half got away from her, and she can't find it."

"You mean Janeczka?" I asked

"Yes," she said. "I was thinking of Janeczka."

We had met Janeczka in a dairy bar. We used to drop in there for blintzes. She worked in the kitchen, but later became the cashier. She always greeted us with a smile. She had big black eyes, long eyelashes, and tawny skin. The other girls called her Gypsy. One summer day we saw her near the Old Watchtower, sitting against a wall. She beckoned to us. When we went up to her, she said, "I sprained my foot and can't walk. Could you help me?"

I flagged a taxi, and we took her to a first-aid station and then to her place. We became friends. She visited us; we visited her. Then, during one of our evening conversations, she told us:

"I don't know who I am. I don't know who my mother was or my father. Mrs. Eliza, who took me from a children's shelter in nineteen thirty-eight or nineteen thirty-nine, died on Freta Street during the Warsaw Uprising. I was wounded in the foot by shrapnel—the same foot I sprained at the Watchtower that time. A gentleman and a beautiful lady took me under their wing. Her name was Teresa Anna. I wasn't with them very long. I ended up in the orphanage."

"I'm searching for my parents, for the house in which I was born. If the house is gone, the street must surely be there, the lot, or something. I walk all over Warsaw, checking, one after another, the prewar streets, in Praga, in Wola, in Ochota, in Mokotów. I know I'll find that street."

"When I close my eyes, I see a dark room and two beds. I see the face of a young woman in a gray beret, and there is a necklace of little red corals around her throat. I've seen this for years. I remember three gaslights in the street, but nothing more. Sometimes I have doubts, I wonder if maybe I made up those pictures from my childhood. My childhood is like the missing piece of a puzzle—a small piece, but so important."

Rose went back to the window. She opened it wide, and you could hear the mingled sound of laughter, talk, and the shouts of children playing.

"How good it is that it's day, that it's warm, and that children are playing in the sandbox," said my wise wife.

And just then it occurred to me that Janeczka's eyes were exactly like those of my little cousin Esther in Scarsdale, New York.

Translated from the Polish by Walter Arndt.

IRONS AND DIAMONDS

Nina Sadur

The Rosenfelds—six or eight of them—were Jews who lived in Magadan. They liked it, in a grudging sort of way. Until, that is, Israel came bobbing up out of nowhere in the distance, sad-sweet as Turkish Delight. From across the other side of the world it caught them in its glance from under heavy eyebrows, and called its children to itself. Their hearts were wrung. The Rosenfelds said to each other: let us go, so that our children may have a homeland, so that our children's children may never even realize there is such a thing as "foreign exile" in the world.

The older Jews cried, they didn't understand why Magadan should be a foreign land to them; harsh and hungry as the Magadan region may be, it was where these eight Jews were born, and their parents were born there too, none of them were born in Israel, and they felt frightened. But they had to go, so their children could be born in Israel—one, two, three—and so afterward they could say: there, see that curly-headed child running along on gold-skinned legs, and his little heart is light, and the gentle breeze of childhood delight blows through his heart; this child knows no other country, this child belongs here. Rejoice! They wanted to taste this exceptional joy.

All the Rosenfelds sold their flats and moved into their nephew Alik Rosenfeld's solitary single room while they waited to be let out. They were cramped now, but this rather disjointed group of kin (the great cold expanses had scattered them a little) were surprised to realize that this intolerable overcrowding was not irritating; quite the opposite, it pressed them closer together. Even though they all had spacious apartments before, not like the Russian working class—there's no denying the Jews know how to live well!

And here they are pressing close up against each other in Alik's little one-room shell, and not understanding why they aren't irritated, and suddenly they realize that in Old Testament times people lived like this— that was the whining chord of the old patriarchal days sounding on the strings of their hearts before their wanderings began.

In the evenings the old folk gathered at the window and discussed in low voices how much grief there was—it seemed there was no more than there was cunning; and there was about as much happiness as there was peace. But glancing around in search of happier fates was pointless; all around in harsh Magadan, in the silence of its winter evening, the lives glowed all the same. The same but not the same—they had to tolerate this unloving land to the end, not knowing that their lives were simply one long act of endurance.

The old folks looked out the window at the bluish snow and sighed, recalling the squeaky deerskin boots of their childhood. They wondered to each other whether they would be able to learn the heavy chocolate-block Hebrew, and if they could, then what would become of this language they were speaking now, each whispering to himself, so the others wouldn't hear: "My native tongue." They began to feel awkward speaking in this foreign language, their only one, and so the old folk often said nothing, just gazed out the window at the brilliant bluish snow. Where were the tracks of those little deerskin boots? The snow shone with a stern regal radiance.

Meanwhile the young folk dreamed in the kitchen. Alik Rosenfeld, a skinny green youth with a knack for painting colorful pictures, listened to the turgid beat of his own little heart. He knew there were great pictures ahead of him—the ones he would paint in Israel. The other young folk were dreaming too: the girls dreamed of timbrels and flowing finery, the youths dreamed of fat bags of money and decorous early evening discussions as the sun flooded the sky of Israel with fire. And the little ones frolicked there at their feet. They were dreaming of flying in an airplane.

The sale of the flats brought the Rosenfelds twenty thousand rubles. It was decided to use the money to buy diamonds in the jeweler's shop and carry the hard, spiteful little stones to Israel. Probably so that southern land would realize at last how unbearably bright the snow shines in Magadan in the evening. Of course, the Jews were being cunning: the USSR does not allow diamonds to be carried out to other countries. The USSR couldn't give a damn where, even if it's to France. It doesn't allow it, and that's all! There was something not quite clear in all this. You save up, and then you go to the shop and buy a diamond that takes your fancy with your own money, not its money—not the USSR's. While you're buying it, the USSR says nothing, it plays dumb, and then as soon as you want to take the stone away to another country, it starts yelling that the stone's its property. Then why didn't it buy it itself? It's not clear. Not at all. Too much for any sensible man to grasp, this. He takes one look at the dangerous gleam of the stones, says to hell with it, and moves on. No point even thinking about it, you could go crazy. For instance, if it's the USSR's property, then why does the USSR put its very own property up for sale? Just to let you wear it for a while? The USSR's kind of odd. To hell with it.

Our Jews decided to outwit everyone. Of course, it wasn't exactly clear just how you could outwit the USSR; after all, it's not a person, it doesn't really seem to exist. Not until it squeezes you tight between its four letters. Until your ribs crack. But Jews can't help being cunning. Once they're on fire with passion for these diamonds, they're bound to go thinking up moves and consulting in whispers, with their long noses touching each other. But you have to understand them—after all, these little pieces of glittering stone are so incredibly hard because masses and masses of money are packed inside them. It's very convenient—instead of dragging around a plump sack of greasy pieces of paper, you can just carry two or three of these hard little stones and know your money's right there! Especially if you're flying away like they were. They couldn't go barging onto the plane carrying sacks, could they? Of course they all agreed to take the convenient diamonds. And in order to stop the USSR from shouting itself hoarse, they decided to hide them in secluded parts of their bodies. Since the USSR had no body (who was it, anyway?), it wouldn't guess about these secret human recesses. They asked the girls. They blushed and consented.

They went to the jeweler's shop. At first they'd sensibly intended to send two or three of the most cunning Rosenfelds to choose the best, the most sparkling, the hardest stones. In any event, after a shouting match, the entire gang trooped along, including the little ones who were dreaming about flying on an airplane.

They flocked in. The Jewish girls immediately wandered off around the shop in various directions, bending their flower-faces in fascination over the flower-brooches, which trembled at the sight of the beautiful girls beyond the glass, and reached up toward them. But they weren't allowed to flirt for long. They were all herded together into the diamond department, and there they lay, glittering like bullets from the black velvet—diamonds. The diamonds lay there quite without hope, quite withdrawn into themselves, not dreaming of an owner, hostages of the USSR (which had nowhere to wear them). The diamonds were spiteful and solitary. And now here were these excitable, clamorous Jews goggling at them with their brown eyes. The diamonds' lives were virginally brief—only just out of the factory, and now here were their owners already! How much light, how much light there was hidden in them—it blinded their warm eyes through the glass—we are yours!

The Rosenfelds bought two rings and two earrings. Four diamonds in all, not counting the diamond crumb around each of the stones. The entire staff of the shop helped the Rosenfelds. A painstaking, bright-eyed salesgirl demonstrated on her own fingers and then on her ears just how much brilliance there could be in these stones. The vague manager politely served his rich customers. Our Jews had never known such attention. They knew that *over there* all shop-assistants were like this. They tested the situation by putting on airs and being capricious, they insisted on having the box changed. The painstaking salesgirl smiled with her calm eyes, the manager fussed elegantly.

At home they all touched the diamonds with their own hands. The girls were allowed to try them on, and when one of them put on all this finery, she underwent an elusive change, becoming subtly prettier, and all the others waved their arms and cried out in delight. This was how pale green skinny Alik inadvertently fell in love with lazy Masha, when for one terrible moment she was illuminated for him by the gleam of the stones. Afraid even to raise his eyes and look at Masha, Alik said that in Jerusalem he could buy more stones just like them. Masha shrugged. For fairness' sake they also gave the diamonds to the little ones, who said they were a plane's headlights. They were put to shame by shouts that a plane doesn't have headlights, but searchlights, and the diamonds were taken away. After that they decided to hide them for the time being. To keep them safe until they flew off on the plane.

There were a lot of Rosenfelds. About half of them were extremely nervous types, in conversation they raised their voices and gesticulated violently. The words came pouring out of them quicker than their thoughts. And a turgid stream of feelings sometimes totally swamped the meaning of the words. People like that could quite easily blab about the precious stones. They decided it would be good if only old Isaiah knew. Let him hide them on his own. Everyone would go out of the flat for a while, and he would take his time to look around and hide them. The Rosenfelds went outside and raised their heads to look up at the window. But cunning old Isaiah switched off the light. There was a gentle sigh from the Rosenfelds. But they understood that was how it had to be. In the meantime, old Isaiah went into the bathroom, pried up one of the tiles on the floor and put the diamonds under it, then stuck the tile back and washed the floor. After that Isaiah switched on the light in the window and the Rosenfelds realized that everything was already hidden.

That evening was unusually quiet. In this small flat that was now home, four powerful new strangers had made a glittering appearance. Who were they? What would they bring to the Rosenfeld family? Happiness. They would bring quiet happiness. And they would bring tempestuous happiness. They would bring the happiness that each one wanted. It was happiness because it was different for everyone. Each had his or her own. And they would bring it.

The young folk felt somehow shy. The old folk sat modestly by the window. The little ones hardly frolicked at all.

The Rosenfelds smiled furtively at each other. They went to get washed in the kitchen. They went to bed early.

Weep, O ye children of Israel! Weep, O ye Jews! At the dawn hour, the traitor clicked! That metal catch betrayed them at dawn with a click—it was always a traitor, it knew it would betray them, it was just waiting for its chance: with a click like a pistol when you raise the hammer, the executioner-lock flung wide the gates.

. . . At dawn, the time when sleep does you most good, the lock on the door gave a light, dry click: the door hovered, it moved out from the wall and a draft entered, with four others. At that very moment (when the traitor clicked), as though at a command (the click was the command) the Rosenfelds one and all opened their eyes together and held their breath in the faint hope that they were not here (the Rosenfelds). That they, the Rosenfelds, were not only not in this flat, but not anywhere. And never had been. Never would be. Not in any corner of the earth. Let it spin there among the constellations of the worlds, in the abyss of cosmic space, the Rosenfelds were nowhere! Have you seen the Rosenfelds? No, we haven't. They're not anywhere. How do I find them then?—What's the problem? Warmest regards to Doba from Odessa—you know who from. Such joy! May God grant Doba happiness! So where can we find Doba?—There is nowhere she can be found. There's no such thing as Rosenfelds. How does the world carry on spinning in the infinite abyss of cosmic space without them?—It just goes on spinning the way it always does. They've gone!

But there was the clear sound of some of the little ones involuntarily wetting their beds. The Rosenfelds and the four others heard it quite distinctly. The four waited until they finished gurgling (little ones must not be rebuked too sharply or they might develop weak bladders), and turned on the light.

"There they are!"—the four saw them.

The four were dressed in plain clothes, neat as four letters of the alphabet.

Whichever way they stepped, black eyes gleamed at their feet, alive, waiting. The Rosenfelds lying there.

The four said: "Rosenfelds, where are the diamonds?" The Rosenfelds involuntarily turned away from Isaiah, so that the four would not guess which of them knew about the diamonds. "All right then," said the four, "we'll find them ourselves." They began rummaging around. Like a hungry man eating a chicken. When they'd rummaged everywhere, the four said to the Rosenfelds: "Well?" They could see that one of them, with the skinny neck and the big eyes, was under unbearable strain—he must be a new boy. He could burst out sobbing and kill someone. "We didn't find them," said the four. "We're going to torture you and worm it out of you, you hear, Rosenfelds? We're going to smooth out every one of you here with a hot iron." Large beads of sweat stood out on the new boy's upper lip.

Since the gags stopped the Rosenfelds from yelling while the ironing was being done, the little ones decided it was compulsory, like an inoculation at the kindergarten, and they lined up in a queue, whimpering a bit, it's true, but with their little shirts held up. Now and then the new boy stole over to someone and cuffed them lightly round the ear. He crept up with extreme caution, and the gaze he directed into the eyes of his chosen victim was white. Madness glimmered in the new boy's face. There was a smell of roast meat from the Jews. One of the four puked. In among the crowd of Rosenfelds someone began a high-pitched whining. It was like a song in the distance. Or a heavy branch in sultry heat. Or the word "Jerusalem." The new boy suddenly stopped with his head lowered tensely, stood there for a moment, gave a sigh and dropped. But the Rosenfelds really hadn't the slightest idea of singing. They were deadly afraid. They'd been glancing timidly at Isaiah, so he would tell where the diamonds were, but Isaiah was bluffing it out, looking straight ahead of himself, right through the irons and the Rosenfelds, looking right through the wall out into the cosmic abyss into which the Rosenfelds should withdraw instead of wandering over the green lawns of the earth.

"Jew, come here," they called Isaiah.

Isaiah went.

The man calmly placed the hot iron on Isaiah's sunken belly and glanced anxiously into his eyes. Isaiah realized that the man was afraid Isaiah might die. But Isaiah knew he wouldn't die. This wasn't the first time. And he hadn't died. He hadn't died in the German concentration camp. He hadn't died in the Soviet concentration camp. He wouldn't die now. When would he die? Isaiah decided to look inside himself to see if he could die. He looked—no, he couldn't. In Isaiah's belly, somewhere up towards the chest, above the guts, lived something that trembled and ached. That was were the whining came from, that the new boy had taken for a song and fainted. It wasn't a song. It was just Isaiah's internal arrangement, the same as all the Rosenfelds. The Rosenfelds lacked the fine sense of their own dignity that the four had. And of course, none of them could carry that gleam of truth in their eyes. All they had was the thread of life, whining in the eternal presence of danger. Isaiah wanted very much to squeal and weep, but he was too old, he didn't have the strength. He squealed and wept in the German concentration camp. And in the Soviet concentration camp. He would rest with the iron on his belly and only start squealing and weeping from weakness, from grief that he was not able to prove that he, Isaiah, wanted very much to live.

". . . diamonds!"

Isaiah said they were under a tile in the bathroom.

"Why did you keep quiet, Jew?"

Isaiah hadn't been keeping quiet. Isaiah had simply forgotten about them as soon as the traitor-lock gave out its click. If they had said to him straightaway: "Isaiah, give us those worthless stones," he would have handed them over straightaway, but he wasn't able to, because something incomparably more important was going on, something that had been going on for hundreds of centuries—*recollection*. The only thing with which Isaiah secretly reproached God was this—"Why, Lord, did you give the Jews the same love of life as the other innocent peoples?" But God did not hear Isaiah, because the reproach was secret.

. . . In the plane the Rosenfelds glanced around curiously. They liked it. The little ones pressed the buttons, and every time smart young men and women came. They smiled at the little ones with clean teeth and prattled gentle baby talk. There was laughter dancing in their eyes. The little ones' mouths gaped wide in fascination. The old folk, of course, were sitting by the windows. Their legs swathed in blankets. Little pillows under their heads. They liked these comforts. They liked flying engulfed first in blue, then in white. They were afraid of the airplane, but they wouldn't admit it amongst the little pillows and the blankets. The young folk drank soft drinks and pretended they'd been flying like this all their lives. All the scarlet triangles on their bellies had turned eternally brown and they didn't hurt anymore.

Old Isaiah didn't have even a single drink of lemonade. He was sitting in the very back of the plane and he could see the curls on the backs of the Rosenfelds' heads. The iron had cauterized his parting with Magadan somewhat. But when the pain passed, Magadan was still lying there on the bottom of the old Jew's memory after all. In snow, or some smell, or fragmentary sounds. . . . But right now Isaiah was thinking of something else. He was trying to understand why once again the Jews' impetuous cunning had led them to pretend they were the same as everyone else. Why had they built themselves the State of Israel? Why were they rushing to it from all over the world? So they could pronounce that awkward and alien word "homeland?" Then Isaiah wondered how many jackets the Rosenfelds had brought with them. And were there enough sweaters for the little ones? First there seemed to be enough, then there weren't. Old Isaiah was getting old and his thoughts were a little confused. There was just one thing he didn't want to think about—when and how would they start to torture Jews in Israel? He knew it wouldn't be straightaway. And he tried not to think about it in advance, because he loved being alive.

The airplane was bearing the Jews further and further away. The Jews were flying in a blue sky, with the USSR looking up into the blue sky—see, there's the white trail . . .

. . . The tear-washed diamonds went back to the black velvet in the shop.

Translated from the Russian by Andrew Bromfield.

JERUSALEM

David Albahari

I first said "Jerusalem" when I was eleven years old. We were sitting
around the large dining room table and closely following my father's index finger as it traveled over a map of the Balkans. "Belgrade, Niś,
Skopje, Gevgelia," said Father, following his finger, and then he lifted
it from the map as if the border were real. "Salonika, Athens, Piraeus,"
he added. "Here," he tapped Piraeus with his fingertip, "we will board
a ship, and then"—he flipped several pages until he arrived at a map of
the Mediterranean—"Rhodes, Cyprus, Haifa." He looked at us carefully, one by one, Mother, my sister, then me. "And, God willing, we
shall see Jerusalem." The last word fell upon me, draped me like a cloak
(which I was to recognize, many years later, in the sky above Zion), and
I felt called upon to repeat it. I said "Jerusalem." Meanwhile, Father's
face twisted, crumpled, and leaning on his hands—which whitened from
the weight of his body—he began to cry.

Memories are, of course, tricky, even though they are all we have to
feel that we truly exist. Jerusalem, the word, had undoubtedly traversed
our apartment before that day. Father certainly must have mentioned it
in conversations, in commenting on the daily news or while he was dic-
tating to Mother a letter for our relatives. Perhaps he said it while he

was reading a prayer for the holidays, blessing the bread and the wine. I recently leafed through his old prayer books and tried in vain to make out the Hebrew letters that make the word *"Yerushalayim."* Letters that lay mute like my father, like my ignorance, which has made of me a certain stranger.

I did learn a few things. One of them was that Jerusalem may be the only city to which every visit is like dying. Every time I have left it I feel as if a part of me has died. Sometimes a body part, sometimes an elusive feeling that circles around the heart, sometimes one of the many layers of the soul. I talked about this with Father. He halted in the middle of the room and spread his arms. "Regarding Jerusalem," he said, "I am a living corpse." Even then I was taller than he was, and I mused how I could easily put my arms around his waist or his rear and lift him high into the air. I carried him, but only when he was dying: twice helping ambulance drivers, once up the stairs, a second time down, and then many times all by myself, all those days while he lay helpless in bed. Nothing of his earlier lightness was left then. He had wasted away, indeed, but his body seemed to grow denser—it changed its specific weight, it dragged everything downward with it. I carried him from the armchair in the living room to the bed in the bedroom, and when I set him down my arms would still be under his body. I would lay my head on his chest and listen to its deep silence.

It couldn't go on for long. Judging from the documents, my father died within two or three months. Judging from memory, his death arrived from afar, like a traveler riding on a slow horse, like a huge wave whose tousled crest rears over us like a cobra. I have never seen a cobra. I am relating all of this only because I believe that simple things (death) can be invalidated using complex structures (storytelling), though I should have figured out a long time ago that simplicity is more convoluted than any complexity. There is no labyrinth more twisted than a straight road connecting two small towns along the shore of the same river.

Whatever the case, my father died and I kept on going to Jerusalem. One clear night, for instance, I stood on the flat roof of the Catholic orphanage and looked out into the square courtyard of the adjacent Arab house. The door was open, a curtain of colorful beads was hanging in the doorway, and light in the form of an elongated trapezoid lit the stone doorstep and a pair of worn slippers. Another time, when I was walking up a steep street, I watched the powerful thighs of a woman who was carrying a basket filled with fruit. Everything changed on the down-hill slope. The sun was setting and its rays poked in under the eyelids. I remembered how I went to a church with white walls, only above the altar was Jesus' figure, framed by a circle of a darker color. And in the twilight above the noisy street I sat on the terrace of an Arab restaurant and ate hummus and pita bread.

All this turns to crumbs with the ineffable yet familiar taste of death. That night when my father suffered a stroke, I woke up in the moist Tel Aviv night and tried, in the dark, to remember what had jerked me awake. I heard how my father moaned, I rushed to get up, and then the space between our beds seemed to stretch. I felt as if I were slogging endlessly through darkness, but I may have only been bouncing in place. Father's sheet was hovering in the air like a flying carpet, and what had looked from afar like an oar was, in fact, his arm. It hung by the bed, white and unreal, and the tips of his fingers brushed the floor. He must have heard me come over, because he turned his already twisted face to-ward me and lifted his other arm, grabbed me by my undershirt, yanked me to him, the seams began to rip, you could clearly hear in the dark-ness how the fabric was tearing. I had to kneel, and his head nestled onto my shoulder. I took his head in my arms and my fingers felt the tiny curls of his hair. I thought how it would be best if we could fly out the open window on that sheet, straight into the night, straight to Jerusalem. I've always wanted to see Jerusalem from great heights.

Then on my stomach and thighs I felt the pressure of his limp arm, and I realized that death had already moved in on him. Perhaps there, in Tel Aviv, on the shore of the Mediterranean, I should have been think-ing of crabs living in snail shells: this would be a fitting image for the life that remained in the unliving shell of his body. Instead of this, in my mind's eye I saw the whiteness of Jerusalem stone, then that unreal moment of early evening when the entire city turns to flaming gold.

It is odd: sometimes when something vanishes it is enough to close my eyes; but sometimes you have to open them. This world is two-faced and imperfect.

There can be no comfort—I am certain—in this. A month later I brought my father back to Belgrade on Swissair. Jews used to come to the Land of Israel to end their lives there; now they go to end them some-where else. Oh, that is just one more of my fabrications. Actually, the soul of every Jew dies in Jerusalem, regardless of where the body hap-pens to be. My father's body finally gave up the ghost at a Belgrade clinic. It was late summer, the beginning of early autumn, and people were still going around in shirtsleeves. I remember that I suddenly felt weightless, horribly weightless; I even wondered whether I might fly. And then someone phoned and said he had died, and words suddenly became pointless.

Translated from the Serbian by Ellen Elias-Bursać.

EXPECTATIONS

George Konrád

HANUKKAH 1995

We are waiting for the child to arrive and take its place among us.

There is much preparation for the arrival. Guests are assembling in a way that reminds me of the ancient wise men of the East, though they are hardly all from the East, there are many more than three of them, and they are not coming on camels. We greet each of them, and they, in turn, clink their glasses, have a bite, and draw their breaths in peace. Then they raise their glasses to the child, the bringer of light whom we await.

Next to its small cradle we sit, dispensing with words, while the one day's supply of oil burns for eight. The child is still to come, still barely the image of us who are already formed, still capable of becoming anything at all. It could come any day now: in the form, as it happens, of a little girl, whose name might be Zsuzsa, Vilma, Franciska, Magda, or something else. The little coat, hat, and soft blanket stand in expectation, as do the siblings and the grandmothers, friends, and neighbors— and I, the father, a grandfather in age. More than anyone else, the one who carries her is waiting, because this little one is long and heavy, and has not turned her noggin downward, so her mother feels it pressing against her heart.

Now is the beginning of winter, when we step onto the crackle of dry, brown leaves as we walk out of the house-gate, when the shivering mama cat on the porch curls up with her five black and white kittens, when the streets grow dark in the afternoon, when grim prophesies sound at home and abroad. At this season the self-conscious person tortures himself (if not others), thinking he has neglected something that can no longer be set right, because what happened, after all, *cannot* be set right; it is frozen into time's vault, filed away in the storehouse of the cosmos. Today, or tomorrow, you can do good—but not yesterday.

At times like this it is common, too, to await the arrival of the one who might know what we still do not, the one who will set us on a new road, mark a new beginning for the grand experiment. At times like this we await the next breath, the next bite of food, the next touch, the sun's next zenith and nadir, the next moment of self-abandon, the message, the walking papers, the verdict, the gate's opening, the darkness behind and the light ahead, the dousing of lamps, the moment of repose. Our hope is that someone else will do it—that the next generation will do it for our own.

Perhaps they will be more humane than we, more clear-sighted, more courageous, kinder—in a word, more perfect (though we would also not deprive them of the gift of frailty). They are, after all, born of us, but handsomer, more winning, with an advantage provided by their new-formed bodies and their simplicity. *This* person, still zero years of age, will surely set us right, no matter how much she may fling about in protest; she will acquit us of enormous charges, even as she sews unforeseen stitches into the great family carpet.

We wait, then, and make preparations, focusing our attention on the hour of arrival, though we still have the strength to rejoice on these dark, lengthening mornings at those who are already here, those who still live among us as well as those carried far off by the winds. I have the strength to be glad that I have lived to see this day, this eternal today, on which, at my advanced age, the past assumes greater importance than the future, and planning is obscured by reminiscence.

Even should such imaginings of the future be pure illusion—because my race may now be truly run, because this coffee and this toast may be my last breakfast—I nevertheless retain the right to gaze over the barrier-gate, out over the romantic juncture of the century's and the millennium's end. It takes self-control to peer optimistically into the third millennium. All that we have lived through will be, for this new arrival, the history of the former century. All that happens to her will be, for me, the next century's novel, now coming into being thanks to my children.

I see before me the faces of our dead, the expression with which *they* would look upon the newborn, if only they could stand here around her bed. My father would be ninety-eight. He would not say now what he said on the night of his death: "Now, my son, you see that a man's life amounts to nothing." I understand the differences between us, and know how I perpetuate him, both in the way my mind works and in the way I clasp my hands behind my back when I walk—just like one of my sons.

For now, the mother still carries the child within her, but later, the little one will carry us, knowingly or not, and will pass us along to as yet nonexistent strangers, who will bear a ridiculous resemblance to us.

I owe to this living creature about twenty years of my attention and cultivation, and she—let me be honest—could receive no greater gift. We will have a little more to do: one more place setting at the table, one more free will with its irritating and enchanting aspects. The eyes of my mother, eighty-nine, are sparkling now. She was a bit weaker over the summer, but is now, to all appearances, growing stronger. People need to have someone to give to, and the stork is happy to oblige them by depositing a package somewhere in the vicinity. Now, bundled with our expectation of the little one in swaddling clothes, we anticipate many other events—the breast's unbuttoning, the cleaning and wiping up and caressing—and by this time next year we will be holding her hand, which will try to free itself from our grip, and then, seeking safety, creep back.

If all goes well she will be returning our smiles by spring, and by summer will be scampering after her brothers on all fours; by fall, she will be shaking the bars of her walker or crib—Out! Out!—and a year from now, during the holiday of light and expectation, she will be making her own way, performing ever more complex operations, with goals of her own: Over there! In! Up! Down!, wanting to go in every direction, to spin, drop, swim, fly, grab, kick, spread out. This little lady will have needs: she will want nothing less than the entire world. It will not be hers, probably, but why throw in the towel at the outset?

ᴥ ᴥ

"So many messiahs!" I say to myself as I peer through the fence of the kindergarten, so many exceptional, anointed persons, designed by fate to be undying candle flames for those around them. We will listen to the affairs of her life—there will be many things to tell of—and laugh, if she wants to make us laugh, and wonder at the clever maze she spins, and at her sense of humor in telling a story. And she will sit on our knees and laugh at the same silly things her siblings did, and probably we ourselves did, once.

We are awaiting a playful person, who will take joy in things that others find tortuous. For she will know the way to the bottomless well, the unwinking light, the undying fire. We await a little woman whose soul will dominate over fatigue, which means that even if she has nothing, she will be rich.

Translated from the Hungarian by James Andrew Tucker.

V

OTHER
DIASPORAS

MY FATHER LEAVES HOME

Nadine Gordimer

The houses turn aside, lengthwise from the village street, to be private. But they're painted with flowery and fruity scrolls and garlands. Blossoming vines are strung like washing along the narrow porches' diminishing perspective. Tomatoes and daisies climb together behind picket fences. Crowded in a slot of garden are pens and cages for chickens and ducks, and there's a pig. But not in the house he came from; there wouldn't have been a pig.

The post office is made of slatted wood with a carved valance under the roof—a post-office sign is recognizable anywhere, in any language, although it's one from a time before airmail: not a stylized bird but a curved post-horn with cord and tassels. It's from here that the letters would have gone, arranging the passage. There's a bench outside and an old woman sits there shelling peas. She's wearing a black scarf tied over her head and an apron, she has the lipless closed mouth of someone who has lost teeth. How old? The age of a woman without oestrogen pills, hair tint charts, sunscreen and antiwrinkle creams. She packed for him. The clothes of a cold country, he had no other. She sewed up rents and darned socks; and what else? A cap, a coat; a boy of thirteen might not have owned a hand-me-down suit, yet. Or one might have been obtained specially for him, for the voyage, for the future.

Horse-drawn carts clomp and rattle along the streets. Wagons sway to the gait of fringe-hooved teams on the roads between towns, delaying cars and buses back into another century. He was hoisted to one of these carts with his bag, wearing the suit; certainly the cap. Boots newly mended by the member of the family whose trade this was. There must have been a shoemaker among them; that was the other choice open to him: he could have learnt shoemaking but had decided for watchmaking. They must have equipped him with the loupe for his eye and the miniature screwdrivers and screws, the hairsprings, the fish-scale watch glasses; these would be in his bag as well. And some religious necessities. The shawl, the things to wind round his arm and brow. She wouldn't have forgotten those; he was thirteen, they had kept him home and fed him, at least until their religion said he was a man.

At the station the gypsies are singing in the bar. It's night. The train sweats a fog of steam in the autumn cold and he could be standing there somewhere, beside his bag, waiting to board. She might have come with him as far as this, but more likely not. When he clambered up to the cart, that was the end, for her. She never saw him again. The man with the beard, the family head, was there. He was the one who had saved for the train ticket and ship's passage. There are no farewells; there's no room for sorrow in the drunken joy of the gypsies filling the bar, the shack glows with their heat, a hearth in the dark of the night. The bearded man is going with his son to the sea, where the old life ends. He will find him a place in the lower levels of the ship, he will hand over the tickets and bits of paper that will tell the future who the boy was.

➹ ➹

We had bought smoked paprika sausage and slivovitz for the trip—the party was too big to fit into one car, so it was more fun to take a train. Among the padded shotgun sleeves and embossed leather gun cases we sang and passed the bottle round, finding one another's remarks uproarious. The Frenchman had a nest of thimble-sized silver cups and he sliced the sausage toward his thumb, using a horn-handled knife from the hotel gift shop in the capital. The Englishman tried to read a copy of Cobbett's *Rural Rides* but it lay on his lap while the white liquor opened up in him unhappiness in his marriage, confided to a woman he had not met before. Restless with pleasure, people went in and out of the compartment, letting in a turned-up volume of motion and buffets of fresh air; outside, seen with a forehead resting against the corridor window, nothing but trees, trees, the twist of a river with a rotting boat, the fading Eastern European summer, distant from the sun.

Back inside to catch up with the party: someone was being applauded for producing a bottle of wine, someone else was taking teasing instruction on how to photograph with a newfangled camera. At the stations of towns nobody looked at—the same industrial intestines of factory yards and junk tips passed through by railway lines anywhere in the world we came from—local people boarded and sat on suitcases in the corridors. One man peered in persistently and the mood was to make room for him somehow in the compartment. Nobody could speak the language and he couldn't speak ours, but the wine and sausage brought instant surprised communication, we talked to him whether he could follow the words or not, and he shrugged and smiled with the delighted and anguished responses of one struck dumb by strangers. He asserted his position only by waving away the slivovitz—that was what foreigners naturally would feel obliged to drink. And when we forgot about him while arguing over a curious map the State hunting organization had given us, not ethno- or geographic but showing the distribution of water- and wildfowl in the area we were approaching, I caught him looking over us, one by one, trying to read the lives we came from, uncertain, from unfamiliar signs, whether to envy, to regard with cynicism, or to be amused. He fell asleep. And I studied him.

There was no one from the hunting lodge come to meet us at the village station ringed on the map. It was night. Autumn cold. We stood about and stamped our feet in the adventure of it. There was no stationmaster. A telephone booth, but whom could we call upon? All inclusive; you will be escorted by a guide and interpreter everywhere—so we had not thought to take the telephone number of the lodge. There was a wooden shack in the darkness, blurry with thick yellow light and noise. A bar! The men of the party went over to join the one male club that has reciprocal membership everywhere; the women were uncertain whether they would be acceptable—the customs of each country have to be observed, in some you can bare your breasts, in others you are indecent if wearing trousers. The Englishman came back and forth to report. Men were having a wild time in the shack, they must be celebrating something, they were some kind of brotherhood, black-haired and unshaven, drunk. We sat on our baggage in the mist of steam left by the train, a dim caul of visibility lit by the glow of the bar, and our world fell away sheer from the edge of the platform. Nothing. At an unknown stage of a journey to an unknown place, suddenly unimaginable.

An old car splashed into the station yard. The lodge manager fell out on his feet like a racing driver. He wore a green felt hat with badges and feathers fastened round the band. He spoke our language, yes. It's not good there, he said when the men of the party came out of the bar. You watch your pocket. Gypsies. They don't work, only steal, and make children so the government gives them money every time.

∾ ∿

The moon on its back.

One of the first things he will have noticed when he arrived was that the moon in the Southern Hemisphere lies the wrong way round. The sun still rises in the east and sets in the west but the one other certainty to be counted on, that the same sky that covers the village covers the whole earth, is gone. What greater confirmation of how far away, as you look up on the first night.

He might have learnt a few words on the ship. Perhaps someone who had preceded him by a year or so met him. He was put on a train that travelled for two days through vineyards and mountains and then the desert; but long before the ship landed, already he must have been too hot in the suit, coming south. On the high plateau he arrived at the gold mines to be entrusted to a relative. The relative had been too proud to have explained by post that he was too poor to take him in but the wife made this clear. He took the watchmaking tools he had been provided with and went to the mines. And then? He waylaid white miners and replaced balance wheels and broken watch faces while-you-wait, he went to the compounds where black miners had proudly acquired watches as the manacles of their new slavery: to shift work. In this, their own country, they were migrants from their homes, like him. They had only a few words of the language, like him. While he picked up English he also picked up the terse jargon of English and languages the miners were taught so that work orders could be understood. *Fanagalo:* "Do this, do it like this." A vocabulary of command. So straightaway he knew that if he was poor and alien at least he was white, he spoke his broken phrases from the rank of the commanders to the commanded: the first indication of who he was, now. And the black miners' watches were mostly cheap ones not worth mending. They could buy a new one for the price he would have to ask for repairs; he bought a small supply of Zobo pocket watches and hawked them at the compounds. So it was because of the blacks he became a businessman; another indication.

And then?

Zobos were fat metal circles with a stout ring at the top and a loud tick tramping out time. He had a corrugated tin–roofed shop with his watchmaker's bench in a corner and watches, clocks, and engagement and wedding rings for sale. The white miners were the ones whose custom it was to mark betrothals with adornments bought on the installment plan. They promised to pay so-much-a-month; on the last Friday, when they had their wages, they came in from the hotel bar smelling of brandy. He taught himself to keep books and carried bad debts into the Depression of the Thirties.

He was married, with children, by then. Perhaps they had offered to send a girl out for him, a home girl with whom he could make love in his own language, who would cook according to the dietary rules. It was the custom for those from the villages; he surely could have afforded the fare. But if they knew he had left the tin shack behind the shop where he had slept when first he became a businessman, surely they couldn't imagine him living in the local hotel where the white miners drank and he ate meat cooked by blacks. He took singing lessons and was inducted at the Masonic Lodge. Above the roll-top desk in the office behind his new shop, with its sign WATCHMAKER JEWELLER & SILVER-SMITH, was an oval gilt-framed studio photograph of him in the apron of his Masonic rank. He made another move; he successfully courted a young woman whose mother tongue was English. From the village above which the moon turned the other way there came as a wedding gift only a strip of grey linen covered with silk embroidery in flowers and scrolls. The old woman who sat on the bench must have done the needlework long before, kept it for the anticipated occasion, because by the time of the distant marriage she was blind (so someone wrote). Injured in a pogrom—was that a supposition, an exaggeration of woes back there, that those who had left all behind used to dramatize an escape? More likely cataracts, in that village, and no surgeon available. The granddaughters discovered the piece of embroidery stuck away behind lavender-scented towels and pillowcases in their mother's linen cupboard and used it as a carpet for their dolls' house.

The English wife played the piano and the children sang round her but he didn't sing. Apparently the lessons were given up; sometimes she laughed with friends over how he had been told he was a light baritone and at Masonic concerts sang ballads with words by Tennyson. As if he knew who Tennyson was! By the time the younger daughter became curious about the photograph looking down behind its bulge of convex glass in the office, he had stopped going to Masonic meetings. Once he had driven into the garage wall when coming home from such an occasion; the damage was referred to in moments of tension, again and again. But perhaps he gave up that rank because when he got into bed beside his wife in the dark after those Masonic gatherings she turned away, with her potent disgust, from the smell of whisky on him. If the phylacteries and skullcap were kept somewhere the children never saw them. He went fasting to the synagogue on the Day of Atonement and each year, on the anniversaries of the deaths of the old people in that village whom the wife and children had never seen, went again to light a candle. Feeble flame: who were they? In the quarrels between husband and wife, she saw them as ignorant and dirty; she must have read something somewhere that served as a taunt: you slept like animals round a stove, stinking of garlic, you bathed once a week. The children knew how low it was to be unwashed. And whipped into anger, he knew the lowest category of all in her country, this country.

You speak to me as if I was a kaffir.

➶ ➶

The silence of cold countries at the approach of winter. On an island of mud, still standing where a village track parts like two locks of wet hair, a war memorial is crowned with the emblem of a lost occupying empire that has been succeeded by others, and still others. Under one or the other they lived, mending shoes and watches. Eating garlic and sleeping round the stove. In the graveyard stones lean against one another and sink at levels from one occupation and revolution to the next, the Zobos tick them off, the old woman shelling peas on the bench and the bearded man at the dockside are in mounds that are all cenotaphs because the script that records their names is a language he forgot and his daughters never knew. A burst of children out of school alights like pigeons round the monument. How is it possible that they cannot be understood as they stare, giggle and—the bold ones—question. As with the man in the train: from the tone, the expression on the faces, the curiosity, meaning is clear.

Who are you?

Where do you come from?

A map of Africa drawn with a stick in the mud.

Africa! The children punch each other and jig in recognition. They close in. One of them tugs at the gilt ring glinting in the ear of a little girl dark and hairy-curly as a poodle. They point: gold.

Those others knew about gold, long ago; for the poor and despised there is always the idea of gold somewhere else. That's why they packed him off when he was thirteen and according to their beliefs, a man.

⚜ ⚜

At four in the afternoon the old moon bleeds radiance into the grey sky. In the wood a thick plumage of fallen oak leaves is laid reverentially as the feathers of the dead pheasants swinging from the beaters' belts. The beaters are coming across the great fields of maize in the first light of the moon. The guns probe its halo. Where I wait, apart, out of the way, hidden, I hear the rustle of fear among creatures. Their feathers swish against stalks and leaves. The clucking to gather in the young; the spurting squawks of terror as the men with their thrashing sticks drive the prey racing on, rushing this way and that, no way where there are not men and sticks, men and guns. They have wings but dare not fly and reveal themselves, there was nowhere to run to from the village to the fields as they come on and on, the kick of a Cossack's mount ready to strike creeping heads, the thrust of a bayonet lifting a man by the heart like a piece of meat on a fork. Death advancing and nowhere to go. Blindness coming by fire or shot and no way out to see, shelling peas by feel. Cracks of detonation and wild agony of flutter all around me, I crouch away from the sound and sight, only a spectator, only a spectator, please, but the Cossacks' hooves rode those pleading wretches down. A bird thuds dead, striking my shoulder before it hits the soft bed of leaves beside me.

⚜ ⚜

Six leaves from my father's country.

When I began to know him, in his shop, as someone distinct from a lap I sat on, he shouted at the black man on the other side of the counter who swept the floor and ran errands, and he threw the man's weekly pay grudgingly at him. I saw there was someone my father had made afraid of him. A child understands fear, and the hurt and hate it brings.

I gathered the leaves for their pretty autumn stains, not out of any sentiment. This village where we've rented the State hunting lodge is not my father's village. I don't know where, in his country, it was, only the name of the port at which he left it behind. I didn't ask him about his village. He never told me; or I didn't listen. I have the leaves in my hand. I did not know that I would find, here in the wood, the beaters advancing, advancing across the world.

TWO YEARS IN EXILE

Serge Liberman

1.

I wear out my first pair of pants on the fringe of swelling suburbia, where everything is mine. The sandy quarry belongs to me; and the scrub, the rocks, the potholes filled with mud, and the mounds of loam, crumbling and sinking beneath my feet as I watch the builders pushing back the borders. Home is where the feet run most freely, and I make my home anywhere, wherever there is dirt, wherever there is dust.

"What will your mother say?"

Mrs. Walters, spraying her delphiniums next door, shakes a pitying head.

Oh, to tug at the mole that sits on her chin. What bliss.

She stabs a forefinger upwards, probing for gaps in transparent void, and accuses me with her question, compelling, squeezing from me a display of shame and contrition and of whatever other humiliation she would have me feel. For she is a mother—though Colin's and not mine— and I am a son, and for each of us there are roles that we must play. So while Mother, my mother, is sequestered in Flinders Lane pumping stitches into the seams of blouses, this other mother shakes her head and probes at the void, cowing me into a shame I don't feel, my own

290

fingers all the while itching, twitching to pluck at that prickly monster on her chin.

Colin, when he comes home from school, is a good boy. He takes off his pants, folds them like royal linen, and replaces the holy gear with ragged blue jeans smeared and bespattered with paint and charcoal and grime. School is school; home is not its extension. Not in the Walters' rule-book anyway, where between school and home there is a demarcation, expressed most eloquently in a change of pants.

"What *will* your mother say?" This time more emphatic, crushing her words between teeth of steel, the harsher impact tempered by the swishing and lapping of spray on her delphiniums and gardenias.

"Mother's not home," I manage, quite irrelevantly.

"Humph." A puff of wind escapes from flaring nostrils in an upturned nose. Haughtily, mightily, with the airs that exalt her own virtue for being such a real, good, caring, stay-at-home, look-after-baby mother. Not like Mother, my mother . . .

But go betray Mother and tell this paragon of motherhood that I have only two pairs of pants. And that the other pair is in the cupboard, waiting for Sundays and visiting. Go tell this woman that, for folk who one year before came to this country with less, two pairs of pants are gifts of Providence. Go tell her . . . go tell her anything when she is a mother and I a son, and Mother, my mother, sits in a dingy dusty crowded workshop pumping away at a Singer, squeezing from its clatter and hum a pound of steak, a down payment, a doctor's fee, a bus fare, a shirt. So I mime remorse as well as I can, hang my head, shrug a shoulder, bite a lip and toe into a clump of weeds on the nature strip.

Oh, to pinch that porcupine on the chin.

It is her own good lad, going against his will, I'm sure, who delivers me from the leaven of her scorn with a reminder clamoured from the window, "Mum, the roast is burning!"

And Mum, with an "Oh, my dear" and a "Wouldn't you believe?" drops the hose as if it had teeth, and clatters up the stairs on hollow heels to rescue that wretched charred roast whose vapours drift out now, thick and sickly, to suffocate the bowed acquiescent flowers that the abandoned hose is still watering.

Colin's face behind the window is a smirk. There is little else to it, unless vegetable ears and freckles amount to anything. He is a good lad. He changes his pants on coming home, earns a few pennies selling Saturday's *Globe* outside the Plaza, and shows his flair for music, of a sort, as he blasts his trumpet in a fanfare of violence.

His mother's prodding fingers on his hands, he points to the hose, still swishing and hissing into the roots of his mother's flowers.

"Will ya' be a sport, mate, and turn off the tap?"

"Do it yourself," I would prefer to say, but I have tasted, felt, Colin's strength before. So I make for the tap and watch, not him, but the rubber tubing shorten and convulse in a final protest and fall limp, like lead now, upon the grass.

"Ta, mate," he says and ups his thumb. Transfixing a wad of void around his nail before disappearing into the deeper crypts of his red-roofed box that to him is home. Leaving me to wear out my pants on the fringes of swelling suburbia. Alone. Where Northcote ends. Waiting, in quarries, in potholes, on rafters and gums, for Mother's bus, or Father's, to bring them back from Flinders Lane where they pound out a life in this newer distant home.

2.

Mother cannot forgive Melbourne, upon which, she says she has merely stumbled. Nor Europe, now left behind. And even while her feet tread the dry dusty earth of this firmer quieter shore, the ship of her existence floats, homelessly, on an ocean of regret and dejection, of reproach and tears.

We tread on our shadows, coming home. Behind us sinks the mutely drowning November sun, as we walk between two rows of red-brick cubes, set behind ordered squares of green, each fringed by delphinium and rosebush in a flush of conformity.

In which Mother is lost.

"Nice day," says Mrs. Walters, smiling ever so nicely and resting on her broom to watch her husband and son thrash the shuttlecock through the air. The grass squelches under her husband's heavy bulk, while Colin, thin, lanky and nearly all bone skims over the surface as if to tread harder would mean to cause eggs to break.

"Good weather we're havin'," Mrs. Walters tries at conversation once more. Her mole invites. Only to betray. Like her smile.

"Yes," says Mother, only now really noticing the weather at all. For factory interiors know no seasons.

" 'Ope it lasts," hopes Mrs. Walters, resuming her sweeping in a last ritual before sunset.

"Good shot, Dad." Colin leaps high to arrest the flight of the shuttle, but fails. Dad trills with the mirth of his success.

"Now serve it to me, son."

The boy is dutiful. His left hand tosses up the feathered object, his right hand draws back, pauses, quivers and swipes at the white plumage. His straight orange hair, parted in the middle, rises and falls with each stroke, like flaps.

"Hit it up, Dad." And Dad hits up, wildly, deliberately, giving to the shuttle the velocity of his own laughter.

The plumed cone wings and spins in reeling convulsions, hangs tremulously in midair, loses life, falls and thuds upon Mother's shadow at her feet. She recoils as though she herself has been struck. Her lips allow a murmur to escape, but Polish I don't understand and her curse remains her secret.

In one bound, two, three, Dad is over the fence, bending to pick up the battered shuttle and looking up at Mother through flushed amused eyes, his breath strong and rancid, a brew of stale tobacco from the lungs and beer from deeper wells.

"Sorry, dear lady," he wheezes, his sorrow as true and deep as vacuum.

"You're a bit wide of the mark, Dad," his son calls from behind him. "Eh, Mum, did'ja see that shot?"

Dad stands up now, erect, as big and red as an ox. His right forefinger aims at an imaginary mark of Cain on my brow. "Good boy you got there. Like to see a lad helpin' his mum."

Mrs. Walters stands beside him. "Yeh, 'e's a good lad." She tosses her head upwards, though really she is looking down.

"Yes," says Mother again, more nervously, pushing me forward as though the Walters were evil eyes falling upon me.

Behind her own door, within her own walls, her breath, smothered by apprehension, or disgust, escapes with relief.

Of all misfortunes available to the children of this earth, she bemoans, Melbourne was the one she had to choose. Melbourne, a tail torn from the rump of the world, where she is lost, amongst neighbours, generations, continents, galaxies apart from herself, a foreigner Jew in an Australian marsh. Like satin in tweed, perfume in tar, crystal in clay.

"A wilderness we have come to. What a wilderness this is."

In the evening, our neighbor sings a song, or strangles it rather in his throat. Sings about a doggie in the window; sings a song he has caught like some contagion he would get rid of by passing it on. Sings, hoots, whoops, croups, then pauses, mercifully, for a semiquaver rest, to raise the bottle to his trumpet, and then sings again, sucking in air sibilant

with froth, throwing a toad's belch into his turbulent sonata for coun-
terpoint. Daytime would swallow up his song, would digest it, absorb
it, lose it without real loss in the symphony of clatter and roar of cars
and motor-mowers and machines. But the evening is sated and regurgi-
tates the serenade, and lets its breezes take it wherever they will to splash
the sky and darkness with a cacophony of echoes. While in our own dim
kitchen, Father reads the *Jewish News,* about Ben Gurion and Peretz,
about Jerusalem and Warsaw, singing, if he is moved to sing, in a muted
hum, something private, something mellow, not giving his neighbours
cause for even the slightest moment to remind themselves of him. While
Mother would throttle every sound between iron and collar as she presses
tomorrow's shirt, the moisture under the metal hissing, like herself:

"Why this wilderness, this curse, this Gehenna?"

And then the silence. Of midnight. And of Sundays. Of midnight and
the wind rattling the window frames and treetops brushing against the
tiles or the muffled hum of a distant car bringing to Mother wisps of
memory, memories of crowded courtyards and homely faces, of a Yiddish word and a rebbe's touch, in a cosier world now swept away. And
then the silence of Sundays when not even grass stirs, lest its whispers
be too loud in the unreality of cool, shimmering morning crystal. Sleeping city. Dumb city lying drunk, until the brittle crystal is broken by a
milk horse still limping from sleep and by the wheels grinding and the
bottles rattling behind it. Then silence again, briefer and less durable,
breached now by Father as he goes out with bucket and spade to scratch,
scour and scrape up from the bitumen the horse's straw-coloured gift to
feed his drooping tomatoes and struggling lemon tree.

Mother hates both the noise and the silence, a silence that is yet not
a true silence.

"A wilderness, a wasteland," she mutters, fingering the curtains as
she watches Father at his work of adjustment, and, daring to aim higher,
casts her sight upon the empty lots beyond the crossing.

And the street, the cubes of red, the square gardens, the confines of
her wasteland do not protest.

3.

A wilderness. Five miles from the city's heart, Mother feels as if she
were in a country town, a Siberian sovchoz or a displaced persons' camp
again. Far away is High Street with its sprawl of shops, offices, arcades
and picture-theatres. Further still, a light year away, there is—she

knows—a Jewish face, a Jewish word, a Jewish melody. But at our end, her very existence is enshrouded in a pall of silence and of loneliness, while beyond, past the next crossing, along the dry, cracked, and dusty unmade road stretches an empty nakedness that, for Mother, is worse even than the silence and the loneliness. And more threatening.

But the nakedness is being covered. This, Mother does not, cannot, will not see. Men in blue singlets and high gumboots blast the subterranean rocks, uproot wild shrubs, maul the earth and pound it into submission, cowing it to receive the edifices they are determined to erect upon it. The dry hard earth does not yield itself too readily. A thing of pristine virtue, it is too frigid, too severe to penetrate with tact. But muscle, machinery, dynamite, and cursing overcome its resistance, and from the barren surface rise up wooden skeletons upon which brick and cement become flesh. Then are doors fitted, windows inserted, tiles slotted into place. Then, in a day, or two, or three, paths become cemented, bare surfaces covered with topsoil, seeds sprinkled, bulbs planted, and the house becomes a home as weak slender shoots become grass and reluctant buds blossom into full flamboyant colour.

So is a house built. So do the little coloured boxes of suburbia grow. House upon house coaxed to completion by the hum and roar of machines, by the vigour of men's curses, and by the laughter of a ten-year-old boy. My laughter. For as I swing by my arms from the horizontal beams and climb upon the rafters of each rising skeleton, in my imagination, which soars, I build it too, reaping as payment splintered knees, calloused palms, and grit in the eyes. With my help, the perimeter where we live is pushed back and the city swells, enveloping us more rigidly within the carbon solidity of conformity.

Mother detests the perimeter. Father, with his tomatoes and lemon tree, tries to adapt. But I, a bird on the rafters soaring high, thrive and flourish and grow within that wilderness. For the wilderness, the vacant lots, the wooden scaffolds, the quarry, the mounds of loam, even the ringwormed patches where puddles form belong to me. Its melody I have adopted, I know its silences, which are not truly silences, and treasure the emptiness. More than Mother could know. It has its own taste, a taste of that deeper, more remote Australia that Mr. Cook teaches about. The Australia of open spaces, red deserts, towering gums, shearers, swagmen, jumbucks and wheat. Inspired by his mission to make me one of his Aussie kids, Mr. Cook brings me books, pictures, stories by Lawson, odes to Clancy and to the man from Snowy River. My appetite he cannot satisfy. He tantalises my nostrils with the scent of eucalyptus and

I swallow in mouthfuls whatever he feeds me. And—Mother should never know—I grow to love this country with the fervour of a proselyte, for the wilderness is mine. I become Mr. Cook's best pupil, his model child, his favourite. The questions he poses, he asks me to answer. The answers I give no one else knows. Mr. Cook, who should know better, beams as he makes his way between the desks towards me, and laughs as he places his thin tendinous hand upon my shoulder, saying, too loudly, "Well, son, you're a regular Aussie now." Brian Simpson on my left sniggers. Russell McLean laughs, while Jim Reilly, Fisticuffs Jimmy to the boys, sharpens his knuckles, which he will pound into me after school.

"Sissy! Teacher's pet! Sucker-upper!" he hisses behind raised fists. His blows hit whatever target he chooses. His mates urge him on. My left eye swells and darkens, I taste my own blood and tears.

"You're a regular Aussie now, eh?" he mimics from behind his fists. "So show us boy, show us."

Mr. Cook, who has stayed behind, now appears. The cheer squad flees and Fisticuffs Jimmy with it. This reed of a man again puts his mischievous hand upon my shoulder. It is dry, unfeeling leather, hairless and cool. It hints at barrenness and reminds me of the eucalyptus and gum, of open spaces and of the legend called Australia. I would like to love it still, but it has become remote, something not of my world at all but something that merely winked and taunted me with scented promises. Even the closer wilderness upon which I have helped to build with calluses and laughter mocks at having fooled me. And under Mr. Cook's withered solicitous hand now wiping my face of its blood and its tears, I weep, I weep, weep for the bruise that throbs around my eye and for the loss of a treasure that might have remained mine.

4.

School ends. It is December. Month of warmth, excitement, festivity. Of respite from school and playground bullies. Of crystal skies and reluctant clouds; of crickets, sparrows, dandelions. Of Christmas, of Hanukkah.

Colin stands upon the fence. I pray that it may tumble. His Highness stands upon his throne, casts a haughty eye, or a net, over Father's horticultural cripples, and asks, directing his inquiry to someone not at his feet but perched, monkey-like upon his shoulder.

"What are *you* gettin' for Christmas, mate?" himself itching, bursting to tell of promises made to him.

Christmas? What is Christmas? I ask myself, as I engrave a nail track into that too-sturdy fence. My ten years have not yet taught me. There *was* some fantasy performed at school, on the day before term's end. A Mary, a Joseph, three wise men with long black beards, bearing gifts, following a star, then craning their necks over a cradle that cradled a doll of plastic and straw. Ella Plotkin, the grocer's broad-nosed, fat and ugly daughter, played Mary—for acting at least she had a gift—and Peter Hughes, a blade of straw himself, so thin and so fragile, trembled through the rites of Joseph. While I, small, compact, chosen because unnoticeable, was made an angel in the company of twelve on a platform mercifully at the back.

"Well, mate, whatcha gettin'?"

What is Christmas? I ask myself. But him I answer, because I must, "Don't know yet."

"Well, I'm gettin' a cricket set," he says, finally bursting, so smug, almost drooling. The palings of the fence creak under the tremulous rolling of his mirth. The fence sways. Now for vengeance, I dare to hope, now for justice. But the fence stands firm. And if Colin has disappeared from his throne, it is because he has jumped off, not fallen nor crashed nor succumbed to my prayer.

"Colin is getting a cricket set for Christmas," I tell mother. "What are you buying for me?"

"My precious child," Mother softens the blow to come. Her fingers, thin, a little crooked, the pulps flattened from pressing all day on seams, ruffle my hair.

"For us, there is no Christmas. Only Hanukkah."

Hanukkah? What is Hanukkah? I ask myself, wanting but not venturing to escape from beneath her consoling palm. There is an illustration, I remember, in one of my books. A Temple of marble and cedar, soldiers prostrated before its altar, curtains, candles, lights marking miraculous days. That is Hanukkah. And also a time—blessed season— a time for receiving gifts. So, Christmas, Hanukkah, what's the difference? Gifts are gifts and know no distinctions.

And I get my gift. A table tennis set—bats,* a net, a ball.

"For Hanukkah," Mother says, with love, as the gift becomes mine.

"For Christmas," I say to Colin, he at my feet now and *I* upon the throne.

I wait for green envy to consume his face—teeth, freckles, pumpkin ears and all—I wait for those mocking lips of his to set and his nostrils

---

Bats: Paddles.

to bristle with the sap of unrewarded yearning. Oh, imminent moment of exultation.

But instead his eyes narrow into foxes' slits and his nose sharpens and his lips tighten, tighten taut into the tensed string of a bow, until drawn to the limit of their endurance, they yield and collapse, releasing shaft after shaft of hissing laughter that lashes and stings, that cuts and pierces. Our two yards combined cannot hold his scorn as it rolls, and tumbles, and trips, and sprawls on all sides, over wooden palings and creeping passion fruit into the Mertons' and the Sullivans', and the Mackenzies' and the Holts'.

"They're for babies!" he hisses, convulsing into giggles. The servant before the throne dares to be master.

I study my bats, see nothing to mock. Their borders are smooth, the edges well-filed; the handle is layered with ply, the palm cups it with professional ease; the sandpaper on their surfaces is clean, glistens as light plays upon the grains.

"Rubber!" he shrills, "rubber, rubber!"

And between shafts of his taunting, mocking, riveting laughter, in moments of sense between convulsions, his body, his hands, his teeth, his very screech describe the rubber bats that true champions use.

And against the real life-size cricket bat he now brings out from his own house and the red leather-cased ball that mirrors the sun's more muted laughter, my own precious treasure pales, pales from a gift of parental love to a heartless, cruel act of treachery.

5.

The wound heals, while others fester.

December is the year's unwinding. Padlocks silence the schools. The hum and roar of bulldozer and drill die away. Dry dust settles upon the building lots, the wooden skeletons stand stunted and stark, and timber and brick lie in mounds in the midst of rubble and loam.

We kick the dust, Colin and I. And swing from the beams, nails barbing our sleeves, rafters scraping skin. We play. Not out of friendship. But merely because we have met in passing and the earth has not opened to swallow either of us. His shirt is a pepper-pot of holes, his jeans are split and grimy and torn at the cuffs. And his heels are worn down to wedges and the uppers frayed. He is a good lad, this Colin, wearing his out-of-school outfit to be torn, mangled, soiled. Out there, on civilisation's perimeter.

And in our dress, he would make of me his twin, as he kicks dust over me and throws wet sand down my neck, and probes and pokes and pulls and jostles, shoulder against shoulder, hip against hip, in a jest and ecstasy that is private.

Then, sated, or bored, he remembers something and has enough of play.

"Ta-ta, mate. See ya' at carols tomorrow night. Ya' must come. At twelve. Outside the Morgans'. Under the mistletoe."

And he turns to go home. Leaving dust and sand to settle for other opportunities.

Mother, at dinner, says her piece about my shirt. And wonders, aloud, who I think will buy my next pair of shoes. We have just finished eating the herrings and tomatoes. Mother is clearing the plates.

"I'll take him to the factory with me," jokes Father. Whether to buy cheap shoes there or to work for them, I can't tell. But I laugh, to please him, and because I have something to say and need allies.

"I must go to carols tomorrow night."

Mother is serving the soup. Chicken soup again, with noodles, for the third day in a row. While from next door, a roast tickles the nostrils. A myriad globules struggle afloat, a myriad bare lamps flicker and shimmer and glint upon the surface, reflecting themselves in these agitating oily orbs.

"Yes," Mother says, "I will wake you." The ladle clatters confirmation against the pot.

Father looks at her. But her back is already turned as she steadies the pot upon the stove. And if Father has on his tongue a remark to loosen, he chooses instead to suck it down with the noodles. While I gulp mine with a helping of delight. For, surprise too great to countenance, I am going to carols tomorrow night. Outside the Morgans'. Under the mistletoe. At midnight.

And in the labyrinths of private fancies, I rejoice.

Until Mother, sated without having eaten, her hands knotted at the knuckles, starts to rock and heave in her seat, and sets sail upon an oft-sailed sea.

"We must move," she says.

Father, having just licked and smacked his lips, winces under what may swell into an accusation.

"Out of this wilderness," she adds.

The wind, this time, blows more gently. The sails flag. And Mother stops rocking, loosening the rudder she clasps between her palms. And, lapping me with eyes that could quieten storms, she draws breath, her bosom rises and lists, and she folds herself around me.

"My precious one, my little one." Meaning, what is to become of you?

Thursday night, to be awake at the time of carols, I draw the blind early and sink into bed, even though the colour and smells and sounds of day still nudge at my window. Mrs. Walters waters her delphiniums and gardenias, her husband bays at a reluctant moon, while Colin, their good lad, violates and torments "Come All Ye Faithful" on his trumpet. Mother darns my socks in the kitchen, Father reads about Warsaw and Tel Aviv and hums to himself. Fragile breezes break upon my window, crickets chirrup, a sparrow chatters on the sill, then flies away, flies away with my thoughts, my imagination, my dreams, holding them firmly, resolutely, until—until my eyes open, suddenly, to the glare of a blue and brilliant Christmas Day. Wheels, hooves, and bottles clatter along the street outside. Then there is silence, fragile, transient silence, followed by the scrape-scrape-scraping of metal against asphalt as Father shovels up the horse's straw gift for his lemon tree and tomatoes.

I could weep, and would, if tears and sunshine were meet companions under the same canopy of blue. But I don't, not until that evening when Colin, sensing blood, or amusement, creeps up from behind and seizes me with devils' claws.

"Don't ya' like our Christmas songs, mate?"

He is over me. As always. I lie spread-eagled on my back, the grass beneath cold and moist and unyielding, his knees pressing down, a vice on my outstretched arms, my own legs achieving nothing towards liberation. His face, freckles and all, scowls. His nostrils, black pits, flare. His mouth is a menacing crypt of fillings and carious teeth.

"We kill Jews, do ya' know?" Words are his sole weapon, but the roots of my hair burn, as though he has set me on fire. The throb in my arms is as nothing against this fire.

"I am not a Jew."

This, I thrust into every cavity in his teeth. And into the hollow of his throat.

Which makes him laugh.

I hate his laughter. If I could, I would seize it, throttle it, encase it, bind it to anchors of lead. If I could. But free, as malice is free, his laughter reaches all horizons.

"Colin, darling," Mrs. Walters calls from her porch, intruding upon his mirth. "It's time to come inside."

He leaps up, pressing his knees for a last time into my arms and knuckling me in the ribs.

"Well, must go now. I won, mate."

Leaving me crucified on grass still moist, my back cold and green, my arms aching, my ears throbbing with the laughter of his scorn. . . .

The wound festers, where others have healed.

I tell Mother everything. A weak shallow vessel, I can't contain it all.

Mother is a rock. Standing firm; absorbing my pain. Face set hard, chiselled marble, with cheeks suddenly high and cold. Touch, and freeze. I tell her everything, tell her more than everything. Adding things that might have happened, probabilities that Colin might have been capable of, had not his Mum, unknowingly, delivered me from his malevolence. I tell her everything. Hoping, praying to heat stone, to force a glow that might make her avenge all hurt and devour that freckled killer of Jews.

Father, too, has heard, but it is Mother who speaks.

"Did you hear your son?"

His silence torments like pain. He puts down his paper and rubs the bridge of his nose with forefinger and thumb.

"Your son is no longer a Jew."

Ancestry and progeny have parted. The son has abandoned his past.

"What a country this is. There is no God here. See, now, what a *shegetz* is growing up under our roof."

My arms ache. My ears throb. With Colin's cavernous laughter. And Mother's submission, and Father's cowed silence.

Just one word against that devil. Mother! Father! Don't beat him, don't even tell his father. But lay blame where blame is due, and curse him, him, and not me.

Mother salts and peppers tomorrow's soup with her accusations. Father—the hairs in his nostrils are too long and grow also from his ears—enshrouds me with the broad *tallit* of his hands and searches for contact deep within my eyes. Which burn. Which burst.

"Mother!" I plead. "Father!"

Mother empties out the cup of her existence.

"We must move from here. See what this wilderness, this wasteland is doing to your son. Little brothers, blessed sisters. How have we sinned? Who is right in this world? And who is wise? And who is safe? Chaim to Siberia, Reuven to the gas chambers, Sonia to America, Shimon to Israel. Leaves, feathers, scattered and dispersed, while we, silly, blind, pitiful *yiddelekh* sink to the bottom of a barren trough, in exile, without a Yiddish book, a Yiddish word, a Yiddish geist."

"Mother!" I try again, still seeking justice. Even though the plea sticks in the throat, trapped in a gurgle of incoherent meaningless sound.

And I discover a remarkable thing then. I discover that parents, too, can feel. Mother is weeping. A wind has blown against the rock. And it has crumbled. And disintegrated. With rivulets winding down the crevices and wrinkles beside her nose.

"My lost child, my precious one," she says, burying my head in her breast, under a new *tallit*, a *tallit* woven of love and belonging, which I sense, or know, I shall wear forever. As Mother wears the number on her arm.

Evening comes and passes. With sleep, for me, a century away, a universe away. Evening merges into night. Darkness overtakes the shapes of chimneys and trees, which now disappear, dissolving into the void outside my window. Colin blasts upon his trumpet while his father takes to crowing "Silent Night" in the loudest of baritones, then "Good King Wenceslas" amid the clinking of glasses and bottles and cutlery. Father sits in the kitchen, and Mother too, silently grieving over their *shegetz*. From behind a quilt of cloud, stars emerge. Solitary and nameless, meekly unassertive, as if to apologise for their very existence amidst the blare of Colin's trumpet and the scorn of his laughter and his father's raucous song. I watch them, am entranced by them, become as one with them. Until above the stars, Mother's face appears. Pale and drawn, wrinkled and in pain, quivering, throbbing, as each star becomes a tear. Shed for me.

6.

Soon after, we move.

Goodbye, I shout to the neighbours. Goodbye Colin. And to you, Mrs. Walters, whose horny growth I shall now never pluck, goodbye. Sprinkle your gardenias with your devotion and shower your good lad with your love. And thrive on the dust of your wilderness!

Colin, swinging on the gate, smiles wryly, or squints, and raises a phlegmatic hand.

"Come and see us some time."

"Yes," I reply, "I will." The promise is genuine, from the heart, from the heart of a child with plenty to learn.

And before I can say goodbye again, he has turned his back, then takes one step, two, three up the stairs, and disappears. I see his smirk behind the glass of his window and his rash of freckles and that hollow mouth whose laughter has mocked so often. But it is only a memory that lingers there. Not Colin himself, not him. For he has already returned to his trumpet or his crystal set or to devising other mischief.

Goodbye, I shout again. This time to no one in particular. But rather into the transparent air, idling mutely over green unruffled suburbia as Father places a box of kitchen utensils into my hands to take to the car.

We are on the way. Haii, I want to call out, we are moving! And to move is better than standing still!

Through the rear window, I see the wilderness recede with each crossing, moving further out of reach. Enough of sand and tadpoles, of quarries and mud. Enough of building boxes and pushing back borders. I have earned my share of calluses and grit in the eye. Goodbye, my wasteland. I loved you once. Before your people, with their special venom, ruined my love.

Father watches only the road ahead. Mother holds my hands. Her expression is solid. Impenetrable, the firm chiselled marble she must have worn when leaving Warsaw, Russia, Germany, France. Her chest barely moves with her breathing. Only the eyelids, blinking out of necessity alone, yield any hint of awareness.

So we move; come out from exile. Into a fruitshop set in the hub of chaos, in the greyer, rowdier, cruder centre of St. Kilda where Father rises early and Mother breaks her nails over potato and swede* and succours the needs of her thirsty soul as she picks out from their boxes the mouldy lemon, the bruised apple, the withered grape. Grey is the color of St. Kilda and fetid its every corner where I parcel out bits more of my childhood. Not grass, nor tree, nor flower dominate, but glass and brick and spouting and stone, all smudged, peeling, leaking, rusted, cracked. The street stifles under a pall of beer and rotting meat, it reeks of humus and dander, but here, here where the cats breed amongst potato sacks and the Herald boy shouts in adenoidal tones, and the drunkard staggers and reels, begging for a shillin' or a zak outside the Coat-of-Arms, here I thrive, I grow and thrive like some wild and reckless resilient shoot.

Mother complains still, but her cup is drained of its former bitterness. Three doors away is Glicksman's kosher butchery, opposite is Krampel's winestore, and within walking distance stand Rothberg's bakery, Kantor's bookstore and Glazer's delicatessen. Mrs. Tuchinski, fat and breathless, wails about her rheumatism, but recited in Yiddish, which is Mother's bread, the plaint is a melody plated with gold. The Kaplin-

---

Swede: Rutabaga.

skis buy from her and the Fleischmans and the Orbachs, each giving wings to memory reaching back into homelier times. And when I tell her of Harry Lewin who is in my class or of Benny Danziger or of Sophie Grundman who is the rabbi's daughter, an inner light pierces through the shroud of her weariness, to glow, to burn in a private fervour. And she touches my hair. Touches, smoothes, soothes, with hands coated with potato dust and love. Mother is gathering together again the splinters of her shattered self.

One evening, in the midst of reeking onions and wilted lettuces, Mother encourages.

"There is a boy in your class. Joseph Leibholz. His mother came in today. He sounds a fine boy."

I seek him out, but cannot reach him, reach *into* him.

I try. "Your mother knows my mother," I say. And then ask, "What games do you play?"

He stutters from shyness and looks away.

"None especially . . . Oh, . . . chess sometimes . . . And draughts. . . ." Each phrase is a minor explosion of sound, each burst a revelation.

"Not cricket or ping pong or tennis?"

I see from his clean neat pants that he is an indoor boy, not one to roll in dust or chase after tadpoles or climb on the rafters of rising houses. When he shakes his head, it is not with regret, but with the contentment in knowing that what he does and what he is suffices.

"I . . . I also play the violin," he says.

Slowly over the following weeks, I learn that he traverses regions that I have never yet encountered.

He is tall and slender and pale, and hugs the shadows, both around him and within. A fringe of strawlike hair sits over his forehead, his fingers are long and tapering candles of wax. And his eyes are drifting and dreamy, their colour that of distant oceans and as unfathomably deep. He doodles, he draws. He reads music as others read books and in the shadows that are his alone, composes poems that Miss Quantrell praises in front of the class. I try to penetrate but he will not be penetrated.

"Will you play cricket with me?"

He shakes his head. "I'm not good at it."

"What about footy after school?"

"I don't want to."

"But why not?"

"I don't like it."

"It's easy."

"No."

His distance, his difference, inflames. He excludes everyone, but I can't bear to be excluded.

"All right, then," I say, "have it your way." And in the days that follow, I set about him in different ways.

I kick dust into his face and splash ink over his sketches; I bruise him with my knuckles and poke hard fingers into his ribs. I call him "Fiddler," "Sissy," "Sucker-upper," and mock at him with barbs honed with venom.

He does not whimper, this saint, nor resist, nor retaliate, though he is taller and could swallow me alive. His is the manner of martyrdom, denying the ultimate satisfaction to the victor of seeing pain.

Until one day, after I have tripped and spread-eagled him on the ground, he fixes his eyes, so blue and ocean-deep, upon me and stammers, as though rocks sat on his tongue,

"Why . . . do you try . . . so hard . . . to hurt?"

I have forgotten the original reason; the victim has always been so vulnerable and the opportunity ever-present. I have no ready response so I laugh. I laugh, with the laughter of the victor, and fill the schoolyard with my mirth, which spreads and tumbles and rolls into the street, its spiralling coils to be met there by another's laughter, by raucous hateful echoes that suddenly singe the memory and brand my own mockery with disgrace. For Colin has appeared. Colin. Not the real Colin, but his image, come to taunt the taunter and persecute the persecutor.

Later, Mother, wiping moist and grimy hands, takes me aside.

"Is it true that you've been hitting Joseph and fighting with him?"

I make sounds to deny, but the lie falters, strangles, still in the throat.

"His mother came in today. Is it true?"

I kick at the lettuce leaf trodden into the floor and squeeze a tomato until it splits. Silence is confession.

"What will become of you? Tell me. We have left the wilderness but the *shegetz* is still under our roof."

The juice of the tomato drains into my hand. Its seeds slip through my fingers to spill on to the floor. They are your bones that I am crushing, Colin, and your blood that is being spilled.

"What *will* become of you?" Mother asks again, the rock of her fortitude beginning to crumble.

I cannot bear to look. I dread the appearance of those tortuous rivulets in the crevices of her cheeks. But she raises my chin with a hand become grubby and coarse, and sucks at my eyes with her own. Her brow is drawn, and smudged with dirt.

"We have left the wilderness," she says. "But have we really brought it with us?"

Jagged teeth of shame gnaw at the marrow of my being as, under Mother's gaze, I suddenly feel for Joseph and sense his pain. His sketches, his violin playing, his poems—suddenly these return and, through the loom of memory, weave themselves into the warp of my earlier indifference, in turn, to dominate.

When, next day, I sit beside Joseph, I worship where, before, I had mocked. He sketches and I admire. He doodles and I imitate. He reads his music and I, cleaving, search among the dancing notes a pattern, a design, meaning. And when Miss Quantrell recites again a poem of his, I listen, and find it in myself to praise. To praise that which the wilderness, through default, had taught me to despise. The pallor of Joseph's face yields to a softer bashful glow. And gradually, the barriers fall as, caution his mentor, he admits me into the vast ocean of his dreamy drifting eyes where, chastened and converted, I find depths I have never known.

In that moment, I drown Colin. I seize that pagan laughter of his, throttle it, encase it, bind it to anchors of lead. With delirious fervour, I stifle his father's beer-sodden song and, with bliss too fabulous to contain, I pluck at his mother's bristled mole and trample upon those delphiniums and gardenias that she sprinkles with her very soul. Somewhere lies the perimeter I have helped to extend, the suburbia I have helped to cover. The quarries are filled, the puddles cemented. Little red boxes have taken their place. Somebody else scrapes up the milk horse's precious gift. While here, far away, even in this grey drabness of my newer home, my joy swells, and rises, and soars. And transcends as, through Mother's and through Joseph's depths, I purge myself of the wilderness, of that wasteland, where a splinter of my childhood has, in our wandering, been lost.

BRAVERMAN, DP

Isabelle Maynard

Braverman was a DP. Displaced person. He came into my life cautiously and departed several months later, almost without a perceptible trace. What he left was a smudge on my membranes, one that I could never rub out and that became as familiar as the smallpox stamp on my left thigh. I was ten when he slipped into my life and he, I thought, was ancient. For three months a thin wall and a quilt separated my room from his.

At the time, we lived at my grandmother's house on Davenport Road across the street from the thickly walled British Embassy and several blocks from the sluggishly yellow Hi Ho Canal. My grandmother lived in the front room downstairs, the one closest to the door so she could be the first to answer a ringing doorbell. Her room was filled with lavishly framed photographs of relatives around the world. Cousin Ethel, who looked like Loretta Young, from San Francisco, Aunt Haya from Australia, and Aunt Dina from New York. I had never been outside North China. Often I stood before them trying to penetrate the world beyond the stiff photographic poses but all I saw were the studio backdrops.

My parents and I had two rooms upstairs. Across the hall from us lived my aunt and uncle. The fourth upstairs room was occupied by Mrs. Leff, an elderly widow. Downstairs was the Brachtman family—mother, father, and son. Mrs. Kipness and daughter Vera shared the room next to Grandmother. The room closest to the kitchen was settled by the Lerman family—mother, father, son Ben, and a grand piano. In a wing off the kitchen, in two dingy and windowless rooms, lived our two Chinese servants. Although they had been with my grandmother for years, they were known simply as Cook and Boy.

A total of seventeen souls ate, slept, conversed, made love, quarreled and made up, cried and laughed under my grandmother's roof. All activity was muted and hushed, performed discreetly and with an exquisite awareness of the close proximity of others.

One bathroom served the entire household and everyone got their turn without a push or a shove. Bodily functions were bravely accommodated and an unwritten schedule was strictly adhered to. Folks downstairs had first turn, folks upstairs went second. Mrs. Leff was given special preference because of her age and was pushed forward to first place whenever she arrived. "Thank you, thank you" she whispered shyly. Mrs. Kipness, although not elderly, also got preferential treatment because of her "delicate stomach." With eyes demurely cast down, she too would slide to the front of the line. Children went last.

Standing in line one day, with my mother holding the towel and bar of soap for both of us, she said, "You are going to have to give up your playroom."

"Why? It's not really a room, anyway. It's just a closet." I was referring to the unused large closet with a window, but doorless, that separated my room from my parents'. Too small to be used as a living space, it had been given to me to store dolls and toys. I had grown to love it. My mother had hung a lace curtain on the empty door frame, tacking it down with thumbtacks. Often I lay on the floor watching the sun catch the lacy patterns and then bounce them on the walls. Every day at four in the afternoon I could hear the muted sounds of Ben Lerman's piano practice seep through the floor cracks.

"We're expecting a Mr. Braverman. Rudolf Braverman. A DP. From Germany. He is to have that room."

"When?"

"Tomorrow. You'd better take your things out. Later today."

German refugees were trickling into my part of the world. There was a new girl, Eva, in my class from Berlin. A dentist from Bremen had set up shop on Victoria Road. I had visited a new ear, nose, and throat specialist from Hamburg who had opened up a practice on Mercy Road.

"It's only a closet. Not big enough for a person. And it's right next to my room, just inches away from my bed," I wailed, panicking at the invasion of a strange man, "Will a door be put up?" I pleaded. "Maybe, if we have time," my mother replied. I imagined the man, no doubt with a hideous guttural accent, probably speaking only German, a stranger, an alien, plunked down in our midst. New people coming into the community was one thing, but a total stranger right next door to me was totally unacceptable.

"Well, the place is big enough for a single man. It will have to do. He can't pay much rent." My mother disappeared into the bathroom for her turn.

"What's a DP?" I asked Ben standing behind me in line. Ben, who had a head that looked far too big for his body, wore oversized horn-rimmed glasses and was often described by people as a "genius, he'll go far some day." He bared his teeth as if he were about to spit and said, "A displaced person, you dummy. Don't you know? Braverman is escaping from the Nazis. Probably has been tortured, probably is very sick, probably has lost oodles of family. I hear his daughter was murdered. They never tell us anything but I hear. I listen."

I didn't like Ben but I respected him. He seemed to understand the adult world, living on the periphery of their talk and gossip, often allowed to stay behind during conversations when I was told to "go and play." His story about the coming of Braverman did not reassure me. Now I would have not only a stranger in my room, but possibly a sick stranger with a murdered child. Maybe she had been my age. What was her name? I wondered. A taut sliver of excitement coursed through me and I leaned on the wall for support.

Later that day I transported my belongings from the closet back to my room. My mother took down the lace curtain and in its place hung a thick faded quilt. Cook and Boy brought up a camp bed and a small night table. Nails were pounded into the walls. A tall spindly lamp with a faded fringed lamp shade that didn't fit and had to be tied with a string completed the decor. "Well, it's ready for Mr. Braverman," my mother told me. "He's been through a lot, he'll be tired."

All day I peered out of my window, stood at the front door, even went outside in the garden to watch for Braverman. I wanted to see him before he saw me. I wanted to know the size, shape, and smell of the intruder. It would be like seeing the operating room before I had my tonsils out. Seeing him first would give me an advantage, an upper hand. I lay in wait for Braverman but he never showed up.

I went to bed in a room overflowing with toys from the playroom.

In the middle of the night I woke up, as I often did, listening to the night sounds. I heard Mrs. Leff's furtive coughs, the rattling of the spoon against glass as she mixed cough medication with hot water from the kettle on the burner she kept in her room. The steps creaked as someone from downstairs crept upstairs into the bathroom. A few minutes later the muffled flush of the toilet. The tapping of the broken shutter against the outside wall. Familiar sounds. Now a new sound was added, one that I could not describe. A tiny crackling sound, soft and rustling. It was coming from the closet! Crack. Whir. What was it? I tried, but could not define it. Sleep overcame me as the surrounding quiet of the house embraced me. I dreamt of giant mice munching on strange red pellets while in the background Ben played the Moonlight Sonata with relentless vigor, over and over again.

Next morning, toothbrush and towel in hand, I met a stranger in the hall. He too carried a toothbrush and towel, both of us obviously heading for the bathroom. I was surprised to find him so small and thin-boned. Wispy white hair hung around his ears, a scraggly mustache hid his lips. He walked airily on the balls of his feet as if contact with the ground was painful. Seeing me, he hesitated, looked around furtively and lowered his hooded eyes. He whispered something in a foreign language—it sounded like an apology—clicked his heels and retreated, crab-like, into the closet. He reminded me of the sea anemones I used to disturb at the beach who would close up and back away from my invasive toe. The thought that I could be the invader was an intriguing one. And he a frightened grownup?

Washing my teeth at top speed, I combed my hair and rushed back to my room. Leaning into the quilt as close as I could without disturbing its folds, I tried to hear what was going on inside the closet. I knew Braverman must be in there, I had seen him go in, but there were no sounds, no movement coming from the other side of the quilt. I curbed the urge to move the quilt, to peek in, feeling that would constitute a raid. Somewhere in me burgeoned the idea of fairness, privacy, of delicacy. I was learning patience.

For the next few days I did not see Braverman at all. He was obviously avoiding me and had established a bathroom routine that did not coincide with mine. I imagined him creeping out of his room when most of the household had gone to work, or maybe waiting till midnight when we were asleep. The fact that Braverman was making all these plans to dodge me filled me with a sense of wonderment. I ached to boast about it to Ben but decided against it. Ben, no doubt, would put me down or offer a totally different explanation filled with words I could not understand.

Several nights later I was again awakened by the crackling sounds. This time I forced myself to stay awake and listen intently. They were definitely coming from the closet. There was no light there. Whatever Braverman was doing, he was doing in total darkness. I heard the creak of his camp bed, the scraping of something heavy against the floor. I heard the popping sound of a paper bag being opened followed by evenly spaced crackling sounds. I ran down the list of possible things that could make such a noise. He was sorting things in his suitcase. Brushing his teeth. Scratching the wall. Burying small bodies—this gave me goosebumps. Finally I decided that Braverman was shelling peanuts in the middle of the night. This went on for at least half an hour at which point I heard the sound of a paper bag being shut. I had made my first discovery feeling a surge of triumph; Braverman was a night eater and he ate peanuts.

Just as I was about to doze off I saw a shadow in my doorway. A small bundle of fear settled in my ribs as I watched this ghostly apparition. It did not move, just kept looking in my direction. Then he started crooning a song, the words of which I could not understand, but they were strangely soothing and vaguely familiar. I fell asleep.

Early next morning, on my way to the bathroom, I met Braverman in the hall. It was earlier than my usual time and I expected that he had not anticipated seeing me. He was fully dressed in a shabby suit, shiny at the elbows and wrists. A crumpled fedora with grease spots and well-worn shoes with patches on the sides completed the outfit. He was carrying a battered briefcase with a broken clasp. I must have startled him for he stood frozen in his tracks, gasping short bursts of air as if to make himself even smaller than he actually was. I had the feeling that he wanted to disappear, to evaporate in front of me. He held the briefcase close to his body as if burying himself in it.

I smiled at Braverman and in my mind a bevy of questions erupted. Why do you eat peanuts in the middle of the night? Why do you eat in the dark? Do you need a better lamp? A flashlight? Was that you standing in my doorway? What was the song you sang? But all I said was "Good morning." He stared at me, then in a raspy voice that sounded like it came from a deep well, whispered, *"Guten morgen"* and scurried away. There was a strange look in his eyes, a look of terror and yearning. It was a look I had never seen before but I was strangely unfrightened by it.

On my way out I met Ben—both of us going to school. We never walked together but occasionally exchanged a few words on the front steps. I had absolutely no desire to be seen with Ben. "The weird one," my friends called him.

"What's it like sleeping right next to Braverman?" he said.

"I'm not sleeping next to Braverman," I indignantly replied. "Braverman has his room and I have mine."

"He's a strange duck," whispered Ben.

"What do you mean—strange?"

"Never talks to anyone. I started a conversation with him, asked him about Hitler. He just looked past me and fled."

"Maybe he doesn't want to talk about some things," I said, proud of my observations.

Ben glared at me. "It's his history. Makes him strange. Wanna hear something? Well, yesterday I heard Mrs. Kipness tell Mrs. Leff that Braverman spent several years in hiding. In a dark cellar. With rats. All over him. Mrs. Kipness said it was totally dark in the cellar and they had to lower his food to him through a hole in the floor."

"You're making it up."

"I am not," said Ben and started walking away.

"All right, come back. Tell me more."

"Well," said Ben coming back to me with a smirk on his face. "Well, Mrs. Leff then said she had heard that the rest of his entire family— wife, daughter, and mother were taken away one night when he was gone. He came back to the apartment and there was no one there and he went off."

"What do you mean—off?" I said with irritation. Ben had a way with implications, looks, insinuations, that drove me crazy.

"Off. Cuckoo. Crazy. Mrs. Leff says he went on a rampage and killed someone. That very night."

"You're making it all up," I gasped. "You're just making up stories."

Ben was unshaken. "And you know what else I think? I think Braverman may have killed other people with poison."

"Why poison?" I demanded.

"Because I heard Mrs. Kipness say that Braverman used to be a pharmacist and you know . . ." Ben's voice trailed.

"You know . . . what?" I shouted.

"Well, they have access to all sorts of drugs and poisons." Ben looked at his Mickey Mouse watch. "Time to go." I watched him hoist his book satchel over his shoulder and lope off.

Part of me was convinced that Ben was making up stories about Braverman, that he was showing off, making up for his lack of friends by weaving tales to impress me. But he did hang around grownups and was able to pick up bits and pieces of forbidden information. I shivered feverishly thinking of Braverman as a murderer but I couldn't quite make myself believe it. There was gentleness, there was sadness, mystery, but there was absolutely nothing abrasive or violent about Braverman. Ben must be wrong. But there was something to the story that rang true—the fact that Braverman used to eat at night in the cellar without light. He was used to eating in darkness.

For weeks I tried to time my bathroom routine with the comings and going of Braverman but he continued to evade me. At times I still woke up to the shelling of peanuts. Once I dreamt that he was standing beside my bed and softly crying. He carried an object in his arms that I suspected was a gun or an ax and I woke up in a sweat to see him standing in the doorway staring into space. Silhouetted against the moon his cheeks glistened as if with tears.

"It's a nice night," I whispered into the dark, feeling a great urge to comfort him.

Braverman shuddered, reeled as if struck and scuttled back into the closet without a word. I felt a strange protectiveness for him, the feelings I used to have for wounded animals. Once I had tamed a frightened quivering little squirrel by sitting very quietly at a distance. It had been weeks before the timid creature would take something from my hand. I would wait for Braverman.

I went about the business of growing up as summer drew near and the mimosas bloomed blood red. I went to the piano lessons with Mrs. Hochlachkina and dance class at Mme. Voitenko's School of Dance. I waited for summer to begin and education to stop. Braverman and I had reached a comfortable plateau. We never spoke but I let him stand in my doorway and look at me. He never came inside the room, as if there was a magical line that separated his world from mine, a line not to be crossed. From my bed I listened to his night eating.

❧ ❧

Early one morning I lay in bed, feeling the burgeoning of a cold and with it the delicious thought of not going to school, and through slitted, crumb-caked eyes watched the door being pushed forward slowly. A hand appeared and gently deposited a bag precisely in the doorway. I listened for disappearing footsteps, but there were none. My cold-fogged brain dreamt it was Braverman and that he had flown away, like a bird, into the morning sun. Groggily I got up to pick up the bag, which was tied with a red string. Inside were two dozen peanuts. They were all shiny and plump, not a wizened one amongst them. Obviously care had been taken with this gift and a certain cockiness brewed gently in me thinking of the attention bestowed on me.

Later that afternoon we met in the hallway. I, in my rumpled house-coat, was on my way to get some hot tea to soothe a gravelly throat. He doffed his hat at me, and with his head still at a rakish angle, looked at me seriously from beneath his bushy eyebrows. A dappled sun surrounded us as if in a magic circle, making me feel quite elegant despite my tousled attire. I felt almost grown up. Braverman was probably not ancient at all, I thought. Maybe middle-aged.

Coming home from school one day I saw Braverman sitting by himself at a table in Victoria Cafe. He was wolfing down a bowl of soup, his hat still on, his small body perched on the edge of the chair as if prepared for flight. I noticed the bobbing of his Adam's apple with every swallow and his twitching left leg. It was the first time I had ever seen him outside our house and the first time I had ever seen him eat. He looked smaller, furtive, secretive. Suddenly he looked up and caught me staring. He began to tremble, got up shakily, leaving a pile of uneaten food on his plate and looked around as if he had been caught in an obscene act. "Mr. Braverman," I said. "I didn't mean to disturb you. Go on eating." But the glass that separated us was too thick and he did not hear me. He disappeared into the bowels of the restaurant, moving towards the kitchen, avoiding the front door. I toyed with the idea of running to the back door and confronting Braverman but decided against it. Confronting wounded animals was not the best way to gain their trust.

The next day I ran into Braverman outside Vassili's Deli on Dickenson Road. What stunned me was that this time he was actually talking to someone. A woman with lots of lipstick, a tight red skirt, very tall heels and a high pompadour hairstyle. He didn't see me until I got quite close to him. When I greeted him, he looked around wildly, a frozen grin on his face. Perspiration ran down his cheeks and he wiped that with a huge flowered handkerchief. Hurriedly he left his companion, careened down the street bumping into people, loping along in a zigzag manner, coattail flying. I watched until he disappeared around the corner, wondering what I had done to cause this crazed flight. His companion seemed quite nonchalant about the whole episode, lit a cigarette and vanished into the deli. Perhaps she was a Nazi sent to kill him. Or question him. Maybe she had brought bad news. Or maybe she had brought good news from Germany and he was so excited he just danced away.

I decided to approach Ben, even though I knew he might laugh at me.

"You ninny," said Ben, predictably sarcastic. "You're a total ninny. Braverman was making contact with a prostitute. He saw you, got embarrassed and fled. That's all there is to it. A Nazi agent indeed. You're crazy."

"What's a prostitute?" I questioned humbly.

"Grow up! Don't you know? All right. A prostitute is a woman who engages in promiscuous sexual intercourse for money."

"How do you know that?" I squeaked, overwhelmed by the series of unfamiliar words all in one sentence, torn between making a fool of myself and enticing Ben's wrath.

"Because I read the dictionary. Don't you ever read the dictionary?" Ben said staring at me with his watery eyes hidden behind his glasses.

"No. But why was he embarrassed? Why did he run away?"

Ben threw up his hands. "Because you are a child. Because I guess he likes you—heaven knows why. Because he doesn't want you to know he does those things. Maybe because he doesn't want you to tell your grandmother. I don't know. Think for yourself." Ben turned on his heels and left.

I decided to take matters into my own hands. Perhaps Braverman did really like me. Maybe I reminded him of his murdered daughter. Maybe that's why he stood watching me at night. As soon as I could I would go inside his room and look around. Find clues there and unveil the mystery.

The next day I watched Braverman leave the house with his battered briefcase. With a beating heart I stood by the quilt, inching towards the part in the middle which would lead me into the privacy of Braverman's nest. What would I find there? Bones? Skeletons of his family? I pulled the quilt and quickly stepped inside. It was tinier than I had remembered, a small sliver of a room, not more than seven by four feet. The camp bed was meticulously covered with grandmother's blanket. A faded sweater and a raincoat hung primly, side by side, on two of the nails that had been hammered in. The other two nails stuck out garmentless. There was something pathetic about that. Braverman obviously had only two pieces of clothing. No pictures on the wall, no books, no slippers, no rug, not even a pillow. Instead of a pillow he had neatly rolled up a shirt. There was monumental desolation in the room. I could hear it and smell it.

It felt like the time my favorite dog had died, the time my best friend told me she was moving away, the time when trees are dead in winter and you cannot imagine them ever becoming green again. There were no clues. Only sadness.

"You really shouldn't be here." My mother stood in the doorway.

"It's so . . . sad . . ."

"Mr. Braverman is a sad man. A very sad man."

"Why doesn't he have things? They might make him happier."

"Things probably remind him of the past, the sad past. Things bring back memories and pain. Maybe Mr. Braverman thought if he didn't have things he wouldn't have the pain."

This was an incomprehensible thought. Things had always comforted me. I slept surrounded by my stuffed animals, my two cats at my feet. How could Braverman exist without things? No point in approaching Ben. He had become increasingly irritable lately and his piano sessions were now three hours long. The rumor in the house was that Ben was studying to go to a conservatory and become a great pianist. Since no one had left town for years, ever since the war had started, it was difficult to imagine what conservatory Ben would go to. I realized then that grownups were dreamers and made up things to while away the hours.

I began to dream of giving things to Braverman, to make up for all the things he did not have. Giant red velvet pillows, thick piled rugs, a lace tablecloth. But mainly I dreamt of feeding him nectar-sweet pineapples, juicy oranges, and chocolate covered cherries. With money collected through the years from birthdays, I bought chocolate covered almonds and cherries and my favorite marzipan chocolate wafers. I left them precisely in the middle of his doorway under the quilt. Then I slipped discreetly back where I could hear, but not see, his hand pick up the package. There was something delicious in having this arrangement where things appeared and disappeared silently from doorways.

He continued to leave me bags of peanuts. On the occasions when we met in the hall Braverman now smiled shyly at me, the smile starting tentatively on his upper lip and then growing to the sides of his mouth and even entering his eyes. It was the best Braverman could do and I loved it.

On June 4th Braverman was slinking down the hallway with his brief-case and another small package. He walked downstairs and I heard him talking to my grandmother. I bent over the bannister to listen.

"I'll never forget your kindness. Never," I heard Braverman's raspy voice speaking in Yiddish and some Russian.

"You will be well," I heard my grandmother reply but could not fig-ure out from her intonation whether it was a question or an order.

"I will be well. The job in the cloakroom of Club Kunst will be good. There is a small room—behind the cloakroom—for me."

"If you need help, you know where to come."

"Thank you," replied Braverman doffing his hat and for some rea-son lifting his head in my direction. Then he smiled and slightly bowed his head. I heard the door softly closing as he let himself out.

I rushed back to the closet. Maybe he left something for me. The quilt was gone. When had it been taken down? The place was empty—no cot, no lamp, no night table. Even the nails had been pried from the wall and lay in a small neat pile on the windowsill. I was about to walk out when I noticed a small bag of peanuts neatly tied with a red string made into a little bow. I opened the package and started eating them.

I sat on the floor, watching the sun rays, listening to Ben's piano playing, feeling unfathomably happy at having known a sad man, at having seen him smile, at having been watched by him, at having not unfolded the whole mystery, at having the foreign invader turn into an unerasable bump in my heart. We had become accomplices in close liv-ing, Braverman and I.

from "ESCAPE WESTWARD"

*Shmuel Avraham**

Once Yakov and I decided to leave Ethiopia and drove into the rural area, I was able to relax and to concentrate on the details of our escape. The first village we reached was shabby, but it was a place where Yakov knew a few people, none of them Jewish. We felt that by going there we would be far away from the city of Gondar and thus would have no trouble finding shelter.

That first night, we slept in a very run-down house, although I wasn't really able to sleep. Not only was my mind in a turmoil, but the bed was infested with bugs.

The next day was Shabbat, but it was not easily observed there. Yakov slipped out of the village and found a young man—related to both of us—who was willing to guide us into the jungle. We felt it was important to use a relative in this situation, where trust was so essential.

I worried about involving a Jew, however; if he were caught with us things would go very hard for him. Still, we didn't seem to have any

---

*Shmuel Avraham's name—but none of his story—has been changed to protect his family.

choice. The only way we could have relied on someone non-Jewish was if we were able to pay generously, but we had very little cash.

Our guide agreed to come back before dawn the next morning to take us out of the village and help us on our way to the jungle. He knew the route up to a certain point; we planned to meet with other relatives along the way who could guide us from one area to the next. I gave him thirty *birr* as encouragement. I had no fear he would betray us, but somehow it made it easier for me; I did not want to feel that I was using him unfairly.

There were a number of paths out of the village that would take us to the main road. The next morning, a Sunday, at about four thirty, we went to the meeting place we thought we had agreed on. But there must have been a misunderstanding: we waited and waited, but no one came.

I thought I remembered the way out from a time in my childhood when I had gone with my mother to visit an uncle and aunt. I also had some familiarity with the area as an adult—I had stopped at every Jewish village in Gondar, at one time or another, during my work in the field. We forged ahead on our own. I told Yakov I had an idea of what we could do if we were caught: "The village of your birth is in this direction. If anyone asks us, we can say that we are going there because it is the mourning week of your mother."

"And after we pass that village, then what?" he wanted to know.

"Then," I said, "we will be headed toward a village where there is a school. We will say we started out to spend the seventh mourning day at your birth village. First, we are heading toward the school because I have business there, and by nightfall we will go back to your village."

I don't think anyone would have cared what our excuse was. We were kidding ourselves, but it made us feel better to think we had a plan.

As we started our walk, our greatest fear was the arm associations. They were armed by the government and maintained checkpoints along the road we were planning to take. It was their job to guard against so-called antirevolutionaries;* if they suspected anything, they were allowed to search you. We were worried we might get sent back to Gondar City if we got caught.

Luckily, that day happened to be Kibella, a Christian holiday. Early

---

*At the time of this story, Ethiopia was under the rule of a Marxist regime. Although anti-Marxist, Avraham was not connected with any of the antigovernment movements, among them, the EPRP, Ethiopian People's Revolutionary Party or the EDU, a group that wanted to restore the line of Haile Selassie.

in the morning, everyone went to church and then returned home to celebrate with feasting and festivities; it was the day before the beginning of Lent, when there would be fasting. So no one paid attention to us on the road. We certainly hadn't calculated on this advantage and we thanked God that it happened.

About midday, we arrived at a Jewish village. Although I had relatives there, we headed directly for the village school. I did not want anyone to see us—it would have been dangerous for all of us.

We opened one of the classrooms and entered; a small child came in and saw us. He ran to tell others and someone, assuming we had come to the village for a school inspection, came to meet us. I told Yakov in English that we must pretend to be working in order to protect the people. Others from the village joined us. There were inquiries made, which I still remember, concerning the water supply, a clinic, and a wonderful synagogue that had been built there by JOS.*

My relatives in that village had recently celebrated two weddings. The first one was held shortly after I had started work and I had been too busy to come. The second one had taken place just the previous week. I had been invited, but forgot all about it. Now, arriving in the village, I suddenly remembered, and it seemed the right thing to do to go and visit the family, chat, and celebrate. They had *tella,* a beer, which normally I never drank, but I sat and ate with them.

Everyone in the village wound up seeing us, which did not make us happy. Our fear was that if we only ate and visited with certain families, later they would be in danger for having associated with us. We realized that we had to visit with every family in the village so that none would be tarred by our presence and one family could not accuse another.

We spent a whole day visiting, moving from one household to the next. We drank quite a bit of the *tella* over the course of the day. I didn't feel intoxicated because I was so tense; my body was working to its maximum, trying to be diplomatic and alert at the same time.

The last place we visited was the synagogue. There we made a donation of ten *birr* each, for our protection. I prayed, deep in my heart, and I wept.

"God," I said, "make the whole thing successful, up until Jerusalem.

*JOS: Jewish Organization of Service, a philanthropic organization in Ethiopia that took over the whole educational structure for Ethiopian Jews at the time of the 1974 revolution.

After I am in Jerusalem for a day, I will not care if I die." My prayers were very deep and long; I had never prayed that way before. Everyone who was in the synagogue became very quiet. As I prayed I was able to see my whole journey, as if it came in the name of God. I saw all of the problems, all of the difficulties I would suffer on the way, and I saw how I could cut through all of it and reach Jerusalem. . . .

✦ ✦

. . . We had a full night's walk ahead of us, and Yakov was already extremely tired. It had been a terrible time for him. He was just ending the mourning period for his mother. During the past week, he had spent many hours visiting with people and weeping and he had not slept. Then the beer he drank had made him drowsy. When we went outside for the early part of the night, I stayed awake, but he was so exhausted he fell asleep as he was still talking to me.

When the guides came, I woke him. His eyes opened, but he moved as if he were still asleep. Along the way, we saw someone off in the distance with a flashlight and our young guides became nervous and began to run. I ran after them. Yakov, suddenly alert, tried to follow. From behind me, I heard a horrible sound. Yakov's boot had slipped on a rock. I looked around and saw that his leg was dislocated and twisted at a terrible angle. I ran back to him and twisted his leg in the other direction—there was another horrible sound, but it was back in the right place. However, Yakov was in pain and for days he was unable to walk.

That night, the guides and I took turns carrying him, one of us holding him under each arm. It was a dark night with no moon. We went up hills and down hills. Even when we came to a gorge and had to go on hands and knees, we managed to carry him. It was a terrible night, but we managed to pass the dangerous checkpoint.

Early Monday morning we reached the next village, where Yakov's sister lived; no one had seen us. His sister was still in her mother's village, for the seventh day of mourning, but her husband was there and greeted us.

Yakov washed his leg, massaged it, and then rested. I wanted to leave again that night for another village on the far side of Gondar, where it would have been difficult for the Public Security men to reach us. The village was Tivari and it had a special significance for me: it is the place the Kfar Batya teacher had mentioned when he'd asked me to return to the JOS program. I hadn't forgotten.

Because of the holiday, I knew it would take awhile before they discovered we were missing and came looking for us. I calculated that we had until Tuesday, and thought we should be well on our way to Tivari by then. However, it was very difficult for Yakov to walk.

Later that morning, a man came after us from the village we had just left. The father of the boy who had joined us wanted his son back. The boy understood his parents' danger and went willingly enough; actually, we were relieved that he was gone.

Yakov's sister Devorah, his brother-in-law, Simcha, and their children, had only lived in the village for a month. Although it was Simcha's birthplace, family quarrels had driven them to Ambober. A feud had broken out between Simcha's father and brothers and his uncle and cousins so serious it had caused a rift in the village, with one group living in the upper village and one in the lower. Only very recently, because of a wedding that was planned, had mediators brought the two sides of the family together; and there was still a great deal of tension.

A difficult political situation in Ambober had made Simcha and Devorah decide to come back to their home village. Because they had just returned, the *tukul** they were using was a poorly built one full of holes. Anyone could see in from the outside, which made it rather dangerous for us.

However, Simcha didn't want us to leave; he asked us to wait until Devorah returned. Not only would she prepare food for our long journey, he told us, but we would still be in the village for the wedding the following day. But he understood it was best if we were not seen, so we left the village during the day and hid in the jungle, returning at night to eat and sleep.

We were outside of the village on Tuesday when the wedding took place and guns were shot off in celebration. Because of the way the village was constructed, with a rise on one side, we were able to hear everything clearly from our jungle hiding place. I listened to the dancing and laughing and paid attention to the sound of the guns exploding.

On Wednesday, Devorah and her son returned from her mother's village. She told us that on Tuesday, Kabeda had come to Gondar to pay salaries and had realized Yakov and I were missing. He thought that we might have gone to Yakov's birth village for the seventh day of mourning and sent people there looking for us. When he found out we were not there, he alerted Public Security. A report had gone to the police and they were now out looking for us.

---

*Tukul: Forty or fifty square meters of round straw huts.

I realized that they couldn't be far behind. Their network of communications was good and, in fact, they did come close to catching us. We were now in a dangerous area without transportation, moreover we had been seen in the village on Sunday. Although we could be reached only on foot, it wouldn't be terribly hard to trace us. I was afraid that vulnerable fellow Jews would be used against us to reveal our whereabouts. I was determined not to be caught and tortured by Major Melaku; I preferred to keep running—it would be better to take the chance of being killed along the way.

The police sent a Jew into the village where we were hiding, who pretended he had come to join in the wedding festivities. He carried a message, which he said was from a Jew in the Teda area to a Jew in that village. The message was: "Now is the time that we will have a belt." To have a belt is to have pants; to have pants is to be a real man. The implication was that Yakov and I, having the upper hand, had reduced the authorities to less than real men. Now was the time for the people in this village to show themselves to be real men by catching us.

Repeating a story calculated to destroy us, the man also said we had stolen six million *birr* from a government bank. Once the word went out to the professional bandits—the *shiftas*—that we were carrying a large sum of money, it would be the end for us. "If you have them killed along the way, the government will excuse you and will reward you."

The villager who received the message was the groom's father, who had not been on good terms with Simcha. It suited him to make trouble for Simcha at the same time that he attempted to destroy Yakov and me. The man had contacts with *shiftas*, and he got in touch with them. There was no way for them to be sure we were in the village, but it was a good guess we were somewhere in the area near Yakov's sister.

I had told Simcha beforehand that staying in the village would be playing with fire. "It's not like anything you've ever been involved in before. I don't want anyone to be hurt on my account. Please, let us run, try to avoid us, there's no point in keeping us here." But Simcha did not want to let us go.

He intended to serve as our guide for the next leg of our journey. He knew he had to be seen at the wedding first or his absence would be noticed immediately, and there would be a strong suspicion as to where he had gone. So he asked us to remain for a few more days. Of course, this also pleased Devorah—it was important to her to spend more time with her brother.

On Thursday, we were hiding outside the village, when Simcha's son came to tell us that an old woman from a nearby village had come into their house as a visitor. Simcha wanted to know if we minded. Of course, we did. The possibility of a leak of information was too great, even though it might be done innocently. It would be dangerous for the people who were helping us.

Simcha arranged for us to go to his brother's house that night. Four of us went: Yakov, myself, and our two guides. We ate there and Simcha's brother asked us to sleep in his house. I was worried and refused; I needed to be certain we would have a way out and I knew that the longer we stayed the more problems there would be.

"Find a place outside for us to sleep," I said. "We can't sleep inside anymore." I was feeling very closed in.

There was a wonderful place to sleep outside. Because the village was troubled by bandits who came at night and stole property, Simcha's brother had built a bed up in a large tree, so as to be able to scout the area from above. You could look out and see everything, without being seen. The only problem was that if you were discovered, you were caught with no way out.

The four of us spent the night in that tree. It was the middle of the night; there was bright moonlight. The others were fast asleep and I was dozing—I did not feel safe enough to sleep soundly. Suddenly, a small dog began to bark furiously and I jumped awake.

In the moonlight, I saw a man circling Simcha's *tukul*, peering in where he could. He had long hair and a scarf tied around his head: the mark of a *shifta*. In his hands he held a kalatchnikov, a sophisticated Soviet-made automatic rifle.

While I watched, I remembered something that had happened during the day. We had been hiding outside of the village while the wedding was still being celebrated. The sounds coming from the celebration were wonderful; there was dancing and I remember that I had listened carefully to the kinds of weapons that were being shot. Most of the weapons were very primitive, so that I heard a simple "boom-boom, boom-boom."

Then, suddenly, I became conscious of a new sound: "tat-tat-tat-tat." It was a kalatchnikov, which meant someone new was on the scene. He could have been either a soldier or a so-called antirevolutionary; they both used this automatic weapon. As I had listened during the day, there had been no way for me to guess which. Now, lying in the tree, I knew that the people who were after us had reached us. We had lingered in one place for too many unnecessary days.

It seemed to me that even though we were far away from Gondar, in an area of the highlands controlled by antirevolutionaries, there was a direct link from this *shifta* back to Major Melaku in Gondar.

I began to pray; however, this time it was not for myself. I prayed for the villagers who were now in danger. Perhaps we would get away— but after we left, they could be taken to prison.

We decided that on Friday morning we would move to a village that was not Jewish. Everyone was up very early. Devorah made coffee and prepared food for us to take along; she also gave us a small donkey for carrying it.

Before we could go, however, they had to perform a *woof,* a ritual that would give us a sign of our future. Before embarking on a trip, these people go outside, listen for the call of a particular kind of bird, and then wait for the bird to fly by. If the bird comes from the right, it means that you will succeed in your venture; if it flies from the left, you won't; if it flies from behind, you will die.

The bird call they heard was from the right direction; we would succeed. Although I had no faith in such a thing, I later wondered if one reason we did succeed was that these people believed we would. What I believed is that if we succeeded it would be because we had prayed.

Leaving was difficult. The people wanted to say a leisurely farewell and they couldn't be blamed. Who knew if we would ever see each other again? Devorah cried because her mother had died only a week before, and now her brother, adored by the family, was going far away.

In another situation I would have appreciated this slow goodbye, but I remembered what I had seen during the night. I didn't want to terrorize these good people, yet all I really wanted to do was run from there as quickly as I could. I felt the need to make up for the days we had lost by staying too long in that village.

Simcha and his brother came with simple firearms, to accompany us and be our guides. Simcha's son also came along, as well as one of the original young guides who was going to go all the way with us. The other young guide turned back at this point. I walked alongside Simcha, rushing as much as I could. No one else in our group was as driven as I was to get out quickly.

Our two guides, Simcha and his brother, each carrying one of the guns, spread out for our protection—Simcha in front leading the way, and his brother at the rear. I bumped against his leg as I walked along because of my constant impulse to bolt and run. There was only one main road we could take out of the village. It went up and down hillsides and there was one high spot, shortly beyond a crossroad, which gave control of the entire area. As we approached that strategic high point, a bird flew out from our left, made a series of strange noises, and flew on to the right.

Simcha was shocked. He stopped to make sure his gun was properly loaded. "Ah," he said, *"ha-Kadosh, Barukh Hu."* He saw the bird as a sign from God. "Get down!" he told us.

And I knew that the *shifta* with the kalatchnikov I had seen during the night had to be up ahead on the top of the hill. It would have been the logical place for him to wait for us, but I did not see him. While off to our right, that crazy bird did not stop his cry.

Then Simcha changed his mind about the direction we should take. He broke off a branch from a tree and left it as a marker for the other members of our party, who followed behind. They would understand that they shouldn't continue on the road as we had planned, but should turn to the right along the crossroad.

Eventually we reached a Christian village where Simcha had an acquaintance. No one else thought so, but I worried that the *shifta* with the kalatchnikov was tailing us. I was the only one who had seen him clearly at night and I understood from his eyes that he was a crazy, determined man. As we moved away, I thought about this man, and considered what his next move might be. I knew who he was. Back in Gondar I had heard about him and his six *shifta* brothers.

We were taken to a house in the village and graciously received. As the rest of our group came in, they kept looking backward as they walked. I saw that and knew immediately that they had been followed. They came into the compound of the house we were in, and then I saw the man I had seen the night before: his features, the scarf on his head, the way he held the gun. The image was all clear in my mind—it was him. Two other men were with him—sure enough, two of his brothers, all with similar complexion and features.

"Please," I said to the man of the house, "don't let them in here. Find someplace else for them." I knew that according to our culture he would give them a place to stay if they needed one. The owner of the house gave them a small *tukul* some distance away.

We were given some food and drink and talked for a while, but things became very uncomfortable. Some years ago Simcha had known the father of these *shiftas*. In those days, he had been a wealthy man; his seven sons only became *shiftas* after the revolution, when their land had been confiscated. As a boy, Simcha used to visit the father, who was so fond of him that he thought of him as family.

Now, while we were eating, Simcha went to see the three *shiftas* in their *tukul*. He greeted them and told them he was escorting us to some nearby mineral waters for therapeutic treatment.

"You are lying," they said to him. "We know they have stolen six million *birr*. But we are not greedy. All of us here ought to share it." Simcha came back very upset; he knew the story wasn't true. I wasn't even able to pay him for his assistance to me.

Then I discovered that unknowingly we had entered right into the territory of the *shiftas*. They had second families in the village; in fact, the daughters of our host were their second wives.

I still hadn't figured out how that story of the six million *birr* had been carried exactly to the village where we were. But however it had happened, it seemed to me that now we were trapped. I decided that at least we could make it obvious that we weren't carrying the money.

Yakov carried a bag. He had put some antimalaria capsules and some underwear in it before we had left his house. I hadn't come from my own house, and so I was not carrying anything. I had put a carton of Winston cigarettes in Yakov's bag, and nothing more. Women from the village were sent in to the house to serve us and to act as spies. I opened the bag in front of them and spoke to Simcha. "Six million *birr*? Where do they think we carry it? There is nothing in here. We are anti–Major Melaku. We know that the people in this area are anti–Major Melaku. We are brothers."

The women looked at me with widened eyes; I had clearly succeeded in agitating them. They served us coffee, and then ran off to report what I had said, returning later to watch us again.

We had to get out of there and I was prepared to run at any cost. But now the *shiftas* were ready to negotiate using Simcha as an intermediary. They came down from their ransom of six million *birr* to three thousand. A thousand *birr* was the going price for a life in that area— what was paid as compensation when someone was killed, so that there would be no blood revenge. They wanted a thousand *birr* for each of us trying to escape: for me, Yakov, and our young guide.

We did not have anything near three thousand *birr*. I had about four hundred. We were as good as dead. We had no choice but to try and cheat the *shiftas*.

We put together all our cash. Yakov had about 500 *birr*; from my pocket there was 420 *birr;* our guide had 60 *birr.* We couldn't cheat with this—what was there, was there. But we had merchandise. There were two watches. I said one was worth 350 *birr* and the other 250 *birr.* And we set a value of 500 *birr* on one of our firearms.

We gave all of this as an advance on what we owed. In addition, Simcha stood as our guarantor, giving up his gun as a pledge that we would deliver the rest of what we owed. The owner of the house then served as guarantor for Simcha, which made it possible for him to have his gun back for as long as he was our guide. Our host pledged that Simcha would return to surrender it.

I was feeling very angry about having been trapped in this way. If it were still Tuesday instead of Friday, this would never have happened, and I began to wonder on whom we could rely. But the *shiftas* told us we could go and I thanked God for that.

They accompanied us for a while and as we walked, I noticed that my physical appearance had intimidated them. They said that I looked like a trained soldier and they kept their distance from me. But after I had removed my jacket in the warm sun, they moved closer to me; they had suspected I was carrying a pistol inside it.

Carefully, I began to ask them questions, trying to find out how they had come to trap us. I assured them that I was not angry. They told me that two weeks earlier the government had burned their property and taken their cattle away; they had then received a message saying they would be forgiven by the authorities and would get their cattle back if they "acted like men" and came after us. The message had come from a JOS man; it was someone I knew.

I had done favors for the man who had sent the message. I was greatly agitated and kept thinking that this was not yet the end of what Major Melaku would try.

We were approaching a large river called the Guang. The *shiftas* said goodbye and turned back, watching us from a high point as we continued on our way. Once they were gone, Simcha told us that he had no intention of surrendering his gun to them after he returned. He felt it would be dangerous and he was furious with the way they had acted. After all, they had grown up with him.

It was a hot day. We approached the bank of the river and suddenly a large snake began moving toward us. How it moved past Yakov and the donkey, I do not know, but it came directly at me. I was wearing bright orange boots of heavy leather, which had been brought from

Geneva for the JOS field workers. In an instant, the snake had wound itself around my leg and sunk its fangs into my boot. Luckily, the leather was thick enough to prevent the fang from penetrating to my foot, but when I looked down I saw that the leather had turned black where the poison had spread.

Then the snake slithered on to the ground and turned over. I took my walking stick and hit it so hard it divided in two. I was in such shock that at first I didn't realize what I had done. The tail end of the snake twitched; the head seemed still alive—its black tongue flicked in and out, and it looked at me with its terrible eyes. I stepped on its head with my full weight and it exploded, insides splattering out.

One of the *shiftas* up on the hill saw it and called out to me that it was good luck.

We ate some of the food Devorah had given us and drank from the river. Then we crossed it and moved on. By nightfall we had arrived at a non-Jewish village. Simcha was friendly with people who lived there.

It was Shabbat; we rested for the day and prayed. Our prayer was that we would reach Jerusalem peacefully.

There was a farm association nearby, whose chairman was a member of the family Simcha knew. He understood very well what we were doing, but would not expose friends. He politely asked us not to go out of the house—he did not want to be caught helping us.

We ate. They tried their best for us, but the food was not kosher. However, we had no choice—it was better to eat than to starve.

We had planned to leave the next morning, but our host told us we couldn't go until we received a sign from the birds, and the birds weren't ready. "Oh," I said, "unless the birds are finished in Armachiho, Shmuel cannot go out?" Everyone laughed, but this was what they really believed and I wasn't a bit happy about waiting for the birds.

I was worried about our guides—Simcha and his brother. I said to them, "The *shiftas* are going to make trouble for you if you don't pay the guarantee or surrender your gun. Besides, your feelings have changed so that you cannot live near these people comfortably anymore. Please, go back now and get your families and go out of the country. Or, at the very least, leave the area, go to lower Armachiho, to a liberated antirevolutionary area."

They said they were willing to go on and then, along the way, decide whether to go all the way out with us. But I decided that they had to go back. They were far from their original area and far from their families. Only one of them was familiar with the territory we were headed toward. I wanted to see them return home quickly and get their families and save themselves.

They did go back but, not alert to the dangers, they moved slowly without protecting themselves. It turned out exactly as I had feared. The security forces had traced our route through the villages and figured out who was also absent from a village when we left it. Our guides were caught, put in prison, and tortured. For six months they suffered. When I heard about this after I was out, it sickened me, but there was nothing I could do.

There is a saying of Mao Tse-tung's that goes, "A friend of my friend is my friend, an enemy of my friend is my enemy, and the enemy of my enemy is my friend!" But it certainly did not work that way in Armachiho. We were running from Melaku, and the *shiftas* had been destroyed by Melaku—we were all equally opposed to Melaku. Yet, the *shiftas* were not willing to protect us on that account. In fact, they participated in exposing Simcha and his brother to the government, and once Simcha was in jail, they came at night and took all his property, in retaliation for the fact that he had not surrendered his gun to them when he returned to the area.

Once Simcha and his brother had headed back, we were left in the village without guides and without money. However, I told the people we were staying with that if they would provide guides, we would pay. Of course, I didn't tell them it was safer for non-Jews, which was why I wanted them.

Two people came and told us they would lead us out. "How much do you want?" I asked.

"Four hundred *birr*," they said.

"Okay," I told them.

On Sunday the birds didn't cooperate; we couldn't go. On Monday, finally, the birds were ready to give the sign—it was all right. Our new guides brought two donkeys with them. There was a shortage of salt in the area, and they were going to use the four hundred *birr* to buy large quantities of salt in Sudan and then return to sell it.

Shortly after starting out, we came again to the river we had crossed on Friday. As we had done before, we took the time to wash ourselves, but now, for the first time, we also washed our clothes, which was most pleasurable.

Another good thing happened because I washed my clothes—in a pocket of my jacket I discovered money I hadn't noticed previously. On that very last workday in Gondar, I had stopped for coffee in a hotel before setting out for Ambober and had bought a pack of cigarettes, paying with a one hundred *birr* note. The change from the one hundred *birr* had been in my jacket pocket all of this time. I was glad I hadn't found it sooner or I would have given it to the *shiftas*.

We put our clothes back on, still wet, and remained by the side of the river for a while. Then we continued on our way, crossing for the second time.

We didn't travel far; in about two hours we came to a village where we met a wonderful non-Jewish family. I had heard of them before, because of important things they had done in helping others. The son of the family had been killed as he fought with antigovernment forces near the border, so they were fiercely anti-Melaku. The man was a priest, but he did weaving. Almost always this is something the Jews of Ethiopia did; most non-Jews would not: "Weave? Like a Falasha?" To me, it showed that he respected our culture, and I loved him for it.

At night, we didn't sleep in the house; we were taken outside beyond the field to sleep. There was a man with a gun who stood guard over us. It was wonderful, because we were protected. I was fearful of snakes, however, and I thought that one might come up from the earth, even while the man watched.

The next morning, Tuesday, one of the sons of this family asked me if I would like him to buy me cigarettes. I had already tried the local tobacco. It grows wild, and some had been brought to me. I rolled it myself in old newspaper, but it almost killed me when I smoked it. "You can get cigarettes?" I asked him.

"Yes," he said. "Mohammed goes in to Gondar to buy them and sell them to the antirevolutionaries." The place was full of antigovernment people who had come from all over the country to "liberate" the area.

I gave him ten *birr*. "Bring me what you can," I told him. "Nasty ones, cheap ones, I don't care."

He came running back in a few hours, without cigarettes but with new information. He was a member of EDU, the underground party that was at that time trying to reestablish the rule of Haile Selassie's line, and he had connections. His face was completely changed. He was angry—and fearful. He said that fifty soldiers and a military district governor, from a distant area, were coming to search for two men. The two men, of course, were myself and Yakov. It was clear that high government officials were involved.

Major Melaku had wired a message about us to three border areas,

Hummara, Abderafi, and Metema, which were all controlled by the army, and people had been waiting for us along all the main roads of those border territories. We weren't so stupid that we would have walked the roads openly; we would have gone at night as we approached the border. But it actually turned out to have been fortunate that we were delayed along the way. Had we gone directly, we would have been caught. When we hadn't shown up, they had decided to fan out back into the areas controlled by antigovernment people, until they either spotted us or convinced someone to tell them where we were. They were coming from the direction that we were headed toward.

The army also hoped to accomplish something else while sweeping through the antigovernment area. Such things as large oxen were smuggled across the border regularly and sold in Sudan by the antirevolutionaries. Officials wanted to control this at the same time as they looked for us.

My mind started to work furiously again, and the old priest and his wife began praying. Then the young man—who was very small in size, but was very much a true man—went to his *gotah*,* and put the simple gun he had been using down into it and pulled out a very sophisticated machine. It was all iron, Chinese-made.

He ran outside with this gun and hid behind a shelter of branches known as a *gudib,* which had been prepared beforehand as camouflage, in case he ever needed it. A man wanted by the government, he was always alert. He waited there, where he could not be seen, ready to shoot anyone who approached. He didn't know how much damage he could inflict before he was hit himself, but he knew at least he would die while trying to protect his family.

One of the guides became very agitated: "My children, what will happen?" This was not the usual behavior for a guide who was responsible for protecting us. He was supposed to hide his fear, remaining brave even in the face of danger. I judged him to be a weak person, from whom we could expect very little. But we kept him because he knew the way out and we needed him. Besides, we were not likely to find a better guide—people in that region tended to get particularly nervous in the presence of police or government officials.

I waited until the old man had finished his prayer and then simply asked, "Which is our way out?"

He showed us. "This way and in that direction!"

Gotah: Large circular mud and grass containers used to store grain.

"But aren't the soldiers coming this way?" I asked him. "What would happen if we went round about and out the other way?"

"Ah!" he said, because he suddenly was reminded of something. He called one of the guides, "Ato Hailu, do you remember the time we went by this road and across the back to here?" They knew each other, the guide was a relative of the old man's wife.

The guide thought for just a second. "Ah! Yes!" he said. He turned to me and Yakov. "Let's run out of here. Now is the time."

Quickly the guides loaded the donkeys and we left. Up on a hillside to the right of the house, a large wild goat was grazing. A man in a nearby house, not aware of our presence, shot the goat, and it came tumbling down the hillside to our right. The old priest was watching us leave and saw what happened. "You are saved," he said. "There will be no more obstacles, not ever again!" The *woof* was in our favor.

Now we walked the long way around, in order to avoid the army. We went northward, down a hill and far from the main road, and came to a river that snaked its way back and forth across our path. In the course of one and a half days, we had to cross it eighteen times. Then we found our way back to the main route, past the area where the army was moving, and continued going for several days more.

On the road, we met oxen merchants from lower Armachiho who were going toward the Sudanese black market. It was their practice to buy oxen cheaply in their area and sell the animals at a high price across the border. Then they would buy salt inexpensively at the border and return to sell it at inflated prices.

They spoke the original peasant Amharic—which differs from the peasant Amharic of Gondar—with a little Arabic from the Sudanese merchants thrown in. Because they moved back and forth between different areas, their dress was a mix of styles. They wore some Sudanese clothes and some Ethiopian peasant clothes, with a touch of modern style.

We traveled with a small group of these oxen merchants. Their presence gave us protection and made us less visible. Because our guides were local people, these merchants knew them. This made it safer for us: even though the merchants suspected we were not peasants, they wouldn't touch us.

At one point we came across *shiftas* who were tying up some merchants. That's when I changed into peasant's clothes brought from the village. I had left on my boots, which were not like peasant shoes, and one of the guides advised me to take them off and load them on a donkey. The black plastic peasant shoes I had to wear were lightweight and had ventilation, but were very hot. The clothes were not only dirty and smelly, they were infested with lice.

I tried my best to pass as a peasant, but it was almost impossible for me. Even though my skin was darkened black from the sun, it was soft and smooth, not rough and worn like a true peasant's. Unlike the peasants, I wore underwear. Once I was checked for that—someone pulled away my pants and looked to see what was underneath. And my speech, no matter how hard I tried, was never really peasant's speech, the accent was wrong, so that even though I was with others who were rural people, I was repeatedly singled out as someone from the city.

Or I would be asked if I was from EPRP—Ethiopian People's Revolutionary Party. Depending on the area we happened to be in, sometimes I would say "yes" and sometimes "no." I always said no when I was sure I had been identified as someone from the city.

We had traveled so far and long that we had now come into a semi-desert area—for hours on end no water was available. We carried water with us, first from the river we had crossed on our first days out, and later from waterholes we found along the way. Sometimes our water was gone long before we came to another source; at other times we suspected the water was polluted and then we had to take our chances. We heard stories about people who had died from polluted water.

To avoid checkpoints, we often walked at night. The people who manned them were savage and would have killed us quickly. When we approached the main road, we worried about being picked up by government people, but we couldn't go too far from the road. Although we were using a compass, we were afraid we might totally lose our way.

One very hot day something happened that I will never forget. A merchant had pointed out a bird that knows how to locate honey. I was curious enough about this to stop and watch what was going to happen. The bird flew straight to a large tree and just sat there, squawking. The merchant split the tree open and found a beehive inside—in that terrible heat, the bees were in a stupor and unable to sting. He pulled the honeycomb out onto a rock, cut off a large piece, and handed it to me. I loved honey and took it gladly. But in the heat it made me incredibly thirsty. I felt crazy, it was more than I could bear.

Because of how I suffered, we changed our direction to look for water. On the way, we met a man who pointed out a place. We didn't know it then, but he was a Jew on a mission, and I have since met him in Israel.

We went where he directed us, and as we approached, the odor was unbearable We didn't see any water, there was just a terrible smell. The land was flat and soft. In that area, a riverbed sometimes flooded over, and the water was beneath the surface. You had to dig down with your hands and walking stick to find it, which was not difficult. Lions in the area were able to dig with their paws to get to the water. They would drink, and then urinate nearby so that their urine seeped down through the porous soil back to the water, which is why the area smelled the way it did.

We had no choice; we had to have water. I got down on the ground and dug through the urine-soaked soil until I found dirty water, using my dirty clothing to filter out the impurities that were floating in it. I placed my clothing over the water surface and sucked the water through, holding my nose so that I couldn't smell it. I drank and I drank that way. Then the others did the same. Incredibly, we did not get sick.

We rested for a short while and came back to drink again, before going on our way. Within an hour, I was horribly thirsty all over again. I took a leaf off a branch and chewed it, hoping to, at least, have some saliva. My mouth was completely dry and I was becoming dehydrated.

Five hours later we arrived at a place where there was flowing water. Bugs flitted here and there on the surface and fish darted below. This life told us it was clean water. I immersed my body in it all the way up to the top of my head. Then I raised my nose above the water level, opened my mouth, and just let the water flow into me, swallowing mouthful after mouthful.

When I left the water and stood in the heat, I lost it all. It was too much for me and I became violently sick. I drank a second time and was sick a second time.

I went back a third time. This time I held what I drank. Then I took off my stinking peasant's clothes and washed them in the water. There was no soap, of course, but I did manage to make those clothes smell like the water, which was a blessing.

All of us were exhausted, and so we slept for half an hour and then our guides brought us food. In spite of my first anxieties about them, they had turned out to be good people who cared for us well. Many evenings when we stopped to rest, they washed our legs, and massaged our muscles deeply, so that we could sleep in a relaxed state and be refreshed by morning.

Along the way, we had trouble passing urine, perhaps because there was no water in our bodies. It was a terribly painful business. The guides helped us with this too, with a substance called *chilka,* which had been prepared for us in the second village we had been in. Special black seeds were roasted and then ground into a powder. When we had difficulty, the guides mixed this powder into water and once we drank that, we were fine.

For many days we continued at night, in order to avoid the checkpoints. Then on the last day we reached the area between Metema and Abderafi, near the Guang, the big river we had crossed twice before. When we crossed it again we would be in Sudan. It was 1:00 A.M. when we approached this final border. There was the sound of a truck in the distance, and sometimes we could see lights from afar. Our guides told us where we were and that the activity was coming from Sudan.

Usually Yakov tired quickly, but on this night he was the most energetic of us all, as if he had finally accepted where we were going. He reached the river first, while we lagged behind. When I got there, I just fell down and slept. I remember that the guides went down to the river and got water and made *chilka* for us to drink, and that when they washed my legs the water was cold. Then they massaged me, and I slept without knowing where I was. That night, while Yakov was so energetic, I was exhausted. And it is here, while I slept, that I dreamt my last dream about my father.

Early the next morning, I awoke feeling confused. Merchants who had come from different areas were sitting around near me: it was a marketplace and from the other side Sudanese came to buy things. I had seen Sudanese people before, but now I was still half asleep and the atmosphere felt very alien to me. The Sudanese from the south and west are very big people, very dark-skinned. They wear strange-looking, long white robes with wide sleeves, called *jelebiya*. I stood up suddenly, remembering that I had just escaped and that I was at the Ethiopian border.

Written in collaboration with Arlene Kushner.

from *FAREWELL, BABYLON*

Naim Kattan

Before we moved to the new Battawiyeen suburb, we had lived in
the old neighbourhood near the Meir Synagogue. Our house was across
from the *Alawi*, the wheat, corn, and rice storehouses. In summer we
moved our beds to the roof and a white iron enclosure provided privacy
from glances of passersby. Small holes at the top let us look out on the
street without being seen. Often at sunset, before I got into bed, I would
spy through these openings on the muffled throbbing of the outside
world. Once a week the Bedouins would come with their camels. They
would sit them down just across from our house and feed the animals
as they unburdened them of sacks of grain. Where did they come from,
these vigorous men with their chiselled faces, who conversed with their
camels with the familiarity reserved for humans? Very ugly animals, with
their small heads, jaws in constant motion, their humps and their bodies covered with enormous callouses.

I would beg my mother to lift me above the enclosure. Speaking to
the closest Bedouin, I would shout with the secret satisfaction of crossing boundaries that adults would not have the audacity to transgress:
"*Ammi, Ammi*. Uncle, Uncle."

The respect I owed to every older man required me to use this fa-
milial term. In these circumstances, it tasted of the forbidden. In the

Muslim dialect, I would address the stranger. The tall Bedouin would spin around his *Akal* and turn his head. Trembling with fear and courage, I would toss off, in my best Muslim dialect, "May God help you." And the man, still talking to his camel, would answer, "May God keep you, my son." And so he became my uncle and I his son. In the world of childhood, I was neither Jew nor Muslim, and without running any risk I could speak directly to a Bedouin.

☙ ❧

Living on the fringe of the Muslim world, we could sense its strangeness, which was often transmuted into exoticism. For us it was also a world of hostility and compromise. We were close to the Muslims and consequently it was imperative that we avoid their blows, appeal to their goodwill. As long as they left us alone.

When a Jewish mother reprimanded her son, she would call him a Muslim. The Muslim mother returned the insult by calling her offending son a Jew.

My paternal grandmother was skilled at manipulating her power. She lived with my unmarried uncle in the suburb of Aadhamiyah, a predominantly Muslim district. Here and there a stray Jewish family was crowded into the end of a street in this cluster of Shiites and Sunnites. Often the bus that took us there made a detour to Kadhimayn, a sacred place for the Shiites. In the distance we could see the gilded mosque, which was considered the most beautiful in the country and, it was said, in all the countries of Islam. We would get off the bus in front of another mosque, more modern but no less impressive.

I often went with my father to visit his mother. We would go along the street where the mosque stood and cross the covered market, a cool and salutary pause in the summer months. We came to the path edged with gardens before passing the palaces where our most distinguished citizens lived. Through the grille came the scent of roses and jasmine that perfumed the garden of Rashid Ali, who had declared war on Great Britain in 1941. Moved by a childish veneration, I would slow down, forcing my father to linger with me before the great house of the poet Al Zahawi. We finally came to the few Jewish houses stuck between the river, the palaces, and the gardens.

My grandmother enjoyed great prestige among the wives of the more eminent citizens and their servants. In everyone's eyes, she was "the doctor's mother." She relentlessly lavished advice and remedies and she had drugs to take care of irritated eyes, upset stomachs, and stiff backs. No one was concerned about her medical competence, even less that of my uncle. He dreamed of one day becoming a doctor but meanwhile he worked as a laboratory technician. A trifling distinction. Did he not work in a hospital and wear a white smock, even at home? Was he not a great English doctor's right-hand man? My grandmother never missed the chance to take advantage of all these titles. Besides, it would have been the height of ingratitude to question the goodness and knowledge of a woman who offered her remedies and advice and never asked for anything in return. People received care without having to move or see a doctor, without spending the day in hospital corridors. My uncle did not interfere with his mother's growing prestige; on the contrary, he often came home from the hospital laden with potions and pills, which she would judiciously distribute.

It was only partly true that my grandmother received nothing in return for her generosity. I was in a good position to know. The gardeners used to open the grilles of their masters' gardens for us. I was set loose among the oranges, blackberries and apples. I could pick as much as I wanted. My grandmother, though, warned me about the demon of greed. When the prohibition was removed, stripping the trees soon became a tiring game that lost its attraction in favor of walks along paths that give off the perfume of orange blossoms. The overpowering sun on the street seemed like the memory of a distant world. And every time our teacher of Tanakh reminded us that the Garden of Eden described in Genesis was situated in Iraq, my mind drifted through my grandmother's gardens.

I must have been ten when she made me promise to be good for a whole week. As a reward, she would take me to a great celebration at the home of some Muslim friends.

The ceremony took place on the other shore of the river Tigris. My grandmother could bring just two grandchildren and my brother and I were the privileged ones. We got into my uncle's boat to cross the river. He rowed, not suffering anyone else to touch what he called, with a smile, his ship. The other shore, inhabited entirely by Muslims, had always seemed unreal to me and I had never thought I would set foot on it. I held my grandmother's hand tight for reassurance. My admiration for her was boundless. She was powerful with all the esteem of the Muslims; and the marks of respect, of deference even, with which they received her made her grow in my eyes.

We followed the dozens of families who were rushing toward the house of one of the leading citizens. Two of his sons, aged seven and nine, were being circumcised. He had invited the whole neighbourhood to the feast. His neighbours, servants and relatives could take advantage of the great event to have their sons circumcised free.

Drums were throbbing. Orchestras strolled through the streets announcing the news to the world. Finally the fateful hour arrived. The children came out of the tent that had been put up specially, surrounded by their parents, holding in their hands their wounded, painful manhood. The rhythm of the drums grew and the children's cries were drowned in the uproar. It was a time for happiness and joy. When the passage of a child into adulthood was announced, all cries of pain were buried in an outburst of gaiety. From the depths of their kitchens, the women, busy all day preparing the meal for the guests, let out their strident cries.

At nightfall, rugs were spread all along the street and tablecloths laid over them. Two rows of men took their places around the tablecloths, separated by steaming meats and enormous platters of rice and fruits.

Our hosts had not pushed their hospitality to the point of inviting us to appreciate a huge variety of dishes. Besides, my grandmother, terrified as she was by the sly and frightening behavior of the germs my uncle was always talking about, would never have allowed me to put my hand into the plates from which the dozens of guests took their portions of stuffed mutton and rice with oil.

These customs were quite unlike our own. Circumcised eight days after our birth, we had no memory of our bleeding manhood. However, we participated without hesitation in the joy, because any such outburst, no matter how strange its reasons, invited the spectator to share.

I remember another spectacle, the *Sbaya,* with terror. There is a reason for Jews to describe the *Sbaya* as a scene of horror and savagery.

Some distant cousins of my father lived in the Shiite section, a rare thing for Jews. The *Sbaya,* the Muslim "passion," took place before their windows. Every year they shared their privileged vantage point with about thirty friends and cousins. My mother was prepared to miss the show so as not to expose me to needless fear, but my grandmother reassured her: I would be fast asleep before the procession had even started.

All the shutters were closed except for a small crack that did not let in any light. No one outside would suspect the presence of the curious. We pressed our heads against the edge of the shutters so that we could view the spectacle. We did not say a word, afraid of our own whispers. The excited crowd could attack any sacrilegious spectators. I was afraid of the demoniacal perturbation of this human wave and I dreaded my own shadow. I resisted the nightmare and struggled to prevent it from taking hold of me. Tomorrow I would be walking on this earth that was being transformed before my eyes into a Gehenna bursting from the depths of time. This unleashing would be indelibly imprinted on my mind unless I did not eventually repulse its images and phantoms. I can still see the bare-chested men, panting in the chains that bound their arms and legs, waiting open-mouthed for a drop of water to quench their thirst, unbearable but sought and accepted. They flagellated themselves and inflicted as many blows on themselves as on their companions. They were reliving the slow death of Hassan and Hussein, martyrs for the faith. There were even more men armed with swords and daggers. The unfurling of the apparatus of war and of a panoply of green-and-black banners attested to the passage of death—so that the faith might triumph and live. I crouched down in bewilderment. I was convinced that the slightest gesture would signal my presence to that multitude of demons. I closed my eyes in an attempt to banish the spectacle, to exile it into an unreal domain. My mother, wanting to assure herself that my curiosity had finally been overcome by sleep, murmured my name. I did not reply. Could not the utterance of my name reach the ears of the armed men, bearers of black banners? The dramatic game, the ritual of total release—was it not the precursor of the *Farhoud?**

Translated from the French by Sheila Fischman.

Farhoud: Pogrom.

from "THE LAST SEDER"

André Aciman

Two days later the third blow fell.

My father telephoned in the morning. "They don't want us any-more," he said in English. I didn't understand him. "They don't want us in Egypt." But we had always known that, I thought. Then he blurted it out: we had been officially expelled and had a week to get our things together. *"Abattoir?"* I asked. *"Abattoir,"* he replied.

The first thing one did when *abattoir* came was to get vaccinated. No country would allow us across its border without papers certifying we had been properly immunized against a slew of Third World diseases.

My father had asked me to take my grandmother to the government vaccine office. The office was near the harbor. She hated the thought of being vaccinated by an Egyptian orderly—"Not even a doctor," she said. I told her we would stop and have tea and pastries afterwards at Athinéos. "Don't hurt me," she told the balding woman who held her arm. "But I'm not hurting you," protested the woman in Arabic. "You're not hurting me? You *are* hurting me!" The woman ordered her to keep still. Then came my turn. She reminded me of Miss Badawi when she scraped my scalp with her fingernails looking for lice. Would they really ask us to undress at the customs desk when the time came and search us to our shame?

After the ordeal, my grandmother was still grumbling as we came down the stairs of the government building, her voice echoing loudly as I tried to hush her. She said she wanted to buy me ties.

Outside the building, I immediately hailed a hansom, helped my grandmother up, and then heard her give an obscure address on Place Mohammed Ali. As soon as we were seated, she removed a small vial of alcohol and, like her *Marrano* ancestors who wiped off all traces of baptismal water as soon as they had left the church, she sprinkled the alcohol on the site of the injection—to *kill* the vaccine, she said, and all the germs that came with it!

It was a glorious day, and as we rode along my grandmother suddenly tapped me on the leg as she had done years earlier on our way to Rouchdy and said, "Definitely a beach day." I took off my sweater and began to feel that uncomfortable, palling touch of wool flannel against my thighs. Time for shorts. The mere thought of light cotton made the wool unbearable. We cut through a dark street, then a square, got on the Corniche, and, in less than ten minutes, came face-to-face with the statue of Mohammed Ali, the Albanian founder of Egypt's last ruling dynasty.

We proceeded past a series of old, decrepit stores that looked like improvised warehouses and workshops until we reached one tiny, extremely cluttered shop. "Sidi Daoud," shouted my grandmother. No answer. She took out a coin and used it to knock on the glass door several times. "Sidi Daoud is here," a tired figure finally uttered, emerging from the dark. He recognized her immediately, calling her his "favorite *mazmazelle.*"

Sidi Daoud was a one-eyed, portly Egyptian who dressed in traditional garb—a white *galabiya* and on top of it a grossly oversized, gray, double-breasted jacket. My grandmother, speaking to him in Arabic, said she wanted to buy me some good ties. "Ties? I have ties," he said, pointing to a huge old closet whose doors had been completely removed; it was stuffed with paper bags and dirty cardboard boxes. "What sort of ties?" "Show me," she said. "Show me, she says," he muttered as he paced about, "so I'll show her."

He brought a stool, climbed up with a series of groans and cringes, reached up to the top of the closet, and brought down a cardboard box whose corners were reinforced with rusted metal. "These are the best," he said as he took out tie after tie. "You'll never find these for sale any-where in the city, or in Cairo, or anywhere else in Egypt." He removed a tie from a long sheath. It was dark blue with intricate light blue and pale orange patterns. He took it in his hands and brought it close to the entrance of the store so that I might see it better in the sunlight, hold-ing it out to me with both hands the way a cook might display a poached fish on a salver before serving it. "Let me see," said my grandmother as though she were about to lift and examine its gills. I recognized the tie immediately: it had the sheen of Signor Ugo's ties.

This was a stupendous piece of work. My grandmother looked at the loop and the brand name on the rear apron and remarked that it was not a bad make. "I'll show you another," he said, not even wait-ing for me to pass judgment on the first. The second was a light bur-gundy, bearing an identical pattern to the first. "Take it to the door," he told me, "I'm too old to come and go all day." This one was love-lier than the first, I thought, as I studied both together. A moment later, my grandmother joined me at the door and held the burgundy one in her hands and examined it, tilting her head left and right, as though looking for concealed blemishes, which she was almost sure to catch if she looked hard enough. Then, placing the fabric between thumb and forefinger, she rubbed them together to test the quality of the silk, peev-ing the salesman. "Show me better." "Better than this?" he replied. "*Mafish*, there isn't!" He showed us other ties, but none compared to the first. I said I was happy with the dark blue one; it would go with my new blazer. "Don't match your clothes like a pauper," said my grand-mother. The Egyptian unsheathed two more ties from a different box. One with a green background, the other light blue. "Do you like them?" she asked. I liked them all, I said. "He likes them all," she repeated with indulgent irony in her voice.

"This is the black market," she said to me as soon as we left the store, the precious package clutched in my hand, as I squinted in the sunlight, scanning the crowded Place Mohammed Ali for another horse-drawn carriage. We had spent half an hour in Sidi Daoud's store and had probably looked at a hundred ties before choosing these four. No shop I ever saw, before or since—not even the shop in the Faubourg Saint Honoré where my grandmother took me years later—had as many ties as Sidi Daoud's little hovel. I spotted an empty hansom and shouted to the driver from across the square. The *arbaghi*, who heard me and immediately stood up in the driver's box, signaled he would have to turn around the square, motioning us to wait for him.

Fifteen minutes later, we arrived at Athinéos. The old Spaniard was gone. Instead, a surly Greek doing a weak impersonation of a well-mannered waiter took our order. We were seated in a very quiet corner, next to a window with thick white linen drapes, and spoke about the French plays due to open in a few days. "Such a pity," she said. "Things are beginning to improve just when we are leaving." The Comédie Française had finally returned to Egypt after an absence of at least ten years. La Scala was also due to come again and open in Cairo's old opera house with a production of *Otello*. Madame Darwish, our seamstress, had told my grandmother of a young actor from the Comédie who had knocked at her door saying this was where he had lived as a boy; she let him in, offered him coffee, and the young man burst out crying, then said goodbye. "Could all this talk of expulsion be mere bluffing?" my grandmother mused aloud, only to respond, "I don't think so."

After a second round of mango ice cream, she said, "And now we'll buy you a good book and then we might stop awhile at the museum." By "good book" she meant either difficult to come by or one she approved of. It was to be my fourteenth-birthday present. We left the restaurant and were about to hail another carriage when my grandmother told me to make a quick left turn. "We'll pretend we're going to eat a pastry at Flückiger's." I didn't realize why we were *pretending* until much later in the day when I heard my father yell at my grandmother. "We could all go to jail for what you did, thinking you're so clever!" Indeed, she had succeeded in losing the man who had been tailing us after—and probably before—we entered Athinéos. I knew nothing about it when we were inside the secondhand bookstore. On one of the stacks I had found exactly what I wanted. "Are you sure you're going to read all this?" she asked.

She paid for the books absentmindedly and did not return the salesman's greeting. She had suddenly realized that a second agent might have been following us all along. "Let's leave now," she said, trying to be polite. "Why?" "Because." We hopped in a taxi and told the driver to take us to Ramleh station. On our way we passed a series of familiar shops and restaurants, a stretch of saplings leaning against a sunny wall, and, beyond the buildings, an angular view of the afternoon sea.

As soon as we arrived at Sporting, I told my grandmother I was going straight to the Corniche. "No, you're coming home with me." I was about to argue. "Do as I tell you, please. There could be trouble." Standing on the platform was our familiar tail. As soon as I heard the word *trouble,* I must have frozen on the spot, because she immediately added, "Now don't go about looking so frightened!"

My grandmother, it turned out, had been smuggling money out of the country for years and had done so on that very day. I will never know whether her contact was Sidi Daoud, or the owner of the secondhand bookstore, or maybe one of the many coachmen we hired that day. When I asked her in Paris many years later, all she volunteered was, "One needed nerves of steel."

✍ ✍

Despite the frantic packing and last-minute sale of all the furniture, my mother, my grandmother, and Aunt Elsa had decided we should hold a Passover seder on the eve of our departure. For this occasion, two giant candelabra would be brought in from the living room, and it was decided that the old sculptured candles should be used as well. No point in giving them away. Aunt Elsa wanted to clean house, to remove all traces of bread, as Jews traditionally do in preparation for Passover. But with the suitcases all over the place and everything upside down, nobody was eager to undertake such a task, and the idea was abandoned. "Then why have a seder?" she asked with embittered sarcasm. "Be glad we're having one at all," replied my father. I watched her fume. "If that's going to be your attitude, let's *not* have one, see if I care." "Now don't get all worked up over a silly seder, Elsa. Please!"

My mother and my grandmother began pleading with him, and for a good portion of the afternoon, busy embassies shuttled back and forth between Aunt Elsa's room and my father's study. Finally, he said he had to go out but would be back for dinner. That was his way of conceding. Abdou, who knew exactly what to prepare for the seder, needed no further inducement and immediately began boiling the eggs and preparing the cheese-and-potato *buñuelos.*

Meanwhile, Aunt Elsa began imploring me to help read the Haggadah that evening. Each time I refused, she would remind me that it was the last time this dining room would ever see a seder and that I should read in memory of Uncle Nessim. "His seat will stay empty unless somebody reads." Again I refused. "Are you ashamed of being Jewish? Is that it? What kind of Jews are we, then?" she kept asking. "The kind who don't celebrate leaving Egypt when it's the last thing they want to do," I said. "But that's so childish. We've never not had a seder. Your mother will be crushed. Is that what you want?" "What I want is to have no part of it. I don't want to cross the Red Sea. And I don't want to be in Jerusalem next year. As far as I'm concerned, all of this is just worship of repetition and nothing more." And I stormed out of the room, extremely pleased with my *bon mot*. "But it's our last evening in Egypt," she said, as though that would change my mind.

For all my resistance, however, I decided to wear one of my new ties, a blazer, and a newly made pair of pointed black shoes. My mother, who joined me in the living room around half past seven, was wearing a dark blue dress and her favorite jewelry. In the next room, I could hear the two sisters putting the final touches to the table, stowing away the unused silverware, which Abdou had just polished. Then my grandmother came in, making a face that meant Aunt Elsa was truly impossible. "It's always what she wants, never what others want." She sat down, inspected her skirt absentmindedly, spreading its pleats, then began searching through the bowl of peanuts until she found a roasted almond. We looked outside and in the window caught our own reflections. Three more characters, I thought, and we'll be ready for Pirandello.

Aunt Elsa walked in, dressed in purple lace that dated back at least three generations. She seemed to notice that I had decided to wear a tie. "Much better than those trousers with the snaps on them," she said, throwing her sister a significant glance. We decided to have vermouth, and Aunt Elsa said she would smoke. My mother also smoked. Then, gradually, as always happened during such gatherings, the sisters began to reminisce. Aunt Elsa told us about the little icon shop she had kept in Lourdes before the Second World War. She had sold such large quantities of religious objects to Christian Pilgrims that no one would have guessed she was Jewish. But then, at Passover, not knowing where to buy unleavened bread, she had gone to a local baker and inquired about the various qualities of flour he used in his shop, claming her husband had a terrible ulcer and needed special bread. The man said he did not understand what she wanted, and Elsa, distraught, continued to ask about a very light type of bread, maybe even unleavened bread, if such a thing existed. The man replied that surely there was an epidemic spreading around Lourdes, for many were suffering from similar gastric disorders and had been coming to his shop for the past few days asking the same question. "Many?" she asked, "Many, many," he replied, smiling, then whispered, "*Bonne pâque*, happy Passover," and sold her the unleavened bread.

"*Se non è vero, è ben trovato*, if it isn't true, you've made it up well," said my father, who had just walked in. "So, are we all ready?" "Yes, we were waiting for you," said my mother, "did you want some scotch?" "No, already had some."

Then, as we made toward the dining room, I saw that my father's right cheek was covered with pink, livid streaks, like nail scratches. My grandmother immediately pinched her cheek when she saw his face but said nothing. My mother too cast stealthy glances in his direction but was silent.

"So what exactly is it you want us to do now?" he asked Aunt Elsa, mildly scoffing at the ceremonial air she adopted on these occasions.

"I want you to read," she said, indicating Uncle Nessim's seat. My mother stood up and showed him where to start, pained and shaking her head silently the more she looked at his face. He began to recite in French, without irony, without flourishes, even meekly. But as soon as he began to feel comfortable with the text, he started to fumble, reading the instructions out loud, then correcting himself, or skipping lines unintentionally only to find himself reading the same line twice. At one point, wishing to facilitate his task, my grandmother said, "Skip that portion." He read some more and she interrupted again. "Skip that too."

"No," said Elsa, "either we read everything or nothing at all." An argument was about to erupt. "Where is Nessim now that we need him," said Elsa with that doleful tone in her voice that explained her success at Lourdes. "As far away from you as he can be," muttered my father under his breath, which immediately made me giggle. My mother, catching my attempt to stifle a laugh, began to smile; she knew exactly what my father had said though she had not heard it. My father, too, was infected by the giggling, which he smothered as best as he could, until my grandmother caught sight of him, which sent her laughing uncontrollably. No one had any idea what to do, what to read, or when to stop. "Some Jews we are," said Aunt Elsa, who had also started to laugh and whose eyes were tearing. "Shall we eat, then?" asked my father. "Good idea," I said. "But we've only just begun," protested Aunt Elsa, recovering her composure. "It's the very last time. How could you? We'll never be together again, I can just feel it." She was on the verge of tears, but my grandmother warned her that she, too, would start crying if we kept on like this. "This is the last year," said Elsa, reaching out and touching my hand. "It's just that I can remember so many seders held in this very room, for fifty years, year after year after year. And I'll tell you something," she said, turning to my father. "Had I known fifty years ago that it would end like this, had I known I'd be among the last in this room, with everyone buried or gone away, it would have been better to die, better to have died back then than to be left alone like this." "Calm yourself, Elsica," said my father, "otherwise we'll all be in mourning here."

At that point, Abdou walked in and, approaching my father, said there was someone on the telephone asking for him. "Tell them we are praying," said my father. "But sir—" He seemed troubled and began to speak softly. "So?" "She said she wanted to apologize." No one said anything. "Tell her not now." "Very well."

We heard the hurried patter of Abdou's steps up the corridor, heard him pick up the receiver and mumble something. Then, with relief, we heard him hang up and go back into the kitchen. It meant she had not insisted or argued. It meant he would be with us tonight. "Shall we eat, then?" said my mother. "Good idea," I repeated. "Yes, I'm starving," said Aunt Elsa. "An angel you married," murmured my grandmother to my father.

After dinner, everyone moved into the smaller living room, and, as was her habit on special gatherings, Aunt Elsa asked my father to play the record she loved so much. It was a very old recording by the Busch Quartet, and Aunt Elsa always kept it in her room, fearing someone might ruin it. I had noticed it earlier in the day lying next to the radio. It meant she had been planning the music all along. "Here," she said, gingerly removing the warped record from its blanched dust jacket with her arthritic fingers. It was Beethoven's "Song of Thanksgiving." Everyone sat down, and the adagio started.

The old 78 hissed, the static louder than the music, though no one seemed to notice, for my grandmother began humming, softly, with a plangent, faraway whine in her voice, and my father shut his eyes, and Aunt Elsa began shaking her head in rapt wonder, as she did sometimes when tasting Swiss chocolate purchased on the black market, as if to say, "How could anyone have created such beauty?"

And there, I thought, was my entire world: the two old ones writhing in a silent stupor, my father probably wishing he was elsewhere, and my mother, whose thoughts, as she leafed through a French fashion magazine, were everywhere and nowhere, but mostly on her husband, who knew that she would say nothing that evening and would probably let the matter pass quietly and never speak of it again.

I motioned to my mother that I was going out for a walk. She nodded. Without saying anything, my father put his hand in his pocket and slipped me a few bills.

Outside, Rue Delta was brimming with people. It was the first night of Ramadan and the guns marking the end of the fast had gone off three hours earlier. There was unusual bustle and clamor, with people gathering in groups, standing in the way of traffic, making things noisier and livelier still, the scent of holiday pastries and fried treats filling the air. I looked up at our building: on our floor, all the lights were out except for Abdou's and those in the living room. Such weak lights, and so scant in comparison to the gaudy, colored bulbs that hung from all the lampposts and trees—as if the electricity in our home were being sapped and might die out at any moment. It was an Old World, old-people's light.

As I neared the seafront, the night air grew cooler, saltier, freed from the din of lights and the milling crowd. Traffic became sparse, and whenever cars stopped for the traffic signal, everything grew still: then, only the waves could be heard, thudding in the dark, spraying the air along the darkened Corniche with a thin mist that hung upon the night, dousing the streetlights and the signposts and the distant floodlights by the guns of Petrou, spreading a light clammy film upon the pebbled stone wall overlooking the city's coastline. Quietly, an empty bus splashed along the road, trailing murky stains of light on the gleaming pavement. From somewhere, in scattered snatches, came the faint lilt of music, perhaps from one of those dance halls where students used to flock at night. Or maybe just a muted radio somewhere on the beach nearby, where abandoned nets gave off a pungent smell of seaweed and fish.

At the corner of the street, from a sidewalk stall, came the smell of fresh dough and of angel-hair being fried on top of a large copper stand—a common sight throughout the city every Ramadan. People would fold the pancakes and stuff them with almonds, syrup, and raisins. The vendor caught me eyeing the cakes that were neatly spread on a black tray. He smiled and said, "*Etfaddal,* help yourself."

I thought of Aunt Elsa's chiding eyes. "But it's Pesah," I imagined her saying. My grandmother would disapprove too—eating food fried by Arabs on the street, unconscionable. The Egyptian didn't want any money. "It's for you," he said, handing me the delicacy on a torn sheet of newspaper.

I wished him a good evening and took the soggy pancake out onto the seafront. There, heaving myself up on the stone wall, I sat with my back to the city, facing the sea, holding the delicacy I was about to devour. Abdou would have called this a real *mazag,* accompanying the word, as all Egyptians do, with a gesture of the hand—a flattened palm brought to the side of the head—signifying blissful plenitude and the prolonged, cultivated consumption of everyday pleasures.

Facing the night, I looked out at the stars and thought to myself, over there is Spain, then France, to the right Italy, and, straight ahead, the land of Solon and Pericles. The world is timeless and boundless, and

I thought of all the shipwrecked, homeless mariners who had strayed to this very land and for years had tinkered away at their damaged boats, praying for a wind, only to grow soft and reluctant when their time came.

I stared at the flicker of little fishing boats far out in the offing, always there at night, and watched a group of children scampering about on the beach below, waving little Ramadan lanterns, the girls wearing loud pink-and-fuchsia dresses, locking hands as they wove themselves into the dark again, followed by another group of child revelers who were flocking about the jetty past the sand dunes, some even waving up to me from below. I waved back with a familiar gesture of street fellowship and wiped the light spray that had moistened my face.

And suddenly I knew, as I touched the damp, grainy surface of the seawall, that I would always remember this night, that in years to come I would remember sitting here, swept with confused longing as I listened to the water lapping the giant boulders beneath the promenade and watched the children head toward the shore in a winding, lambent procession. I wanted to come back tomorrow night, and the night after, and the one after that as well, sensing that what made leaving so fiercely painful was the knowledge that there would never be another night like this, that I would never eat soggy cakes along the coast road in the evening, not this year or any other year, nor feel the baffling, sudden beauty of that moment when, if only for an instant, I had caught myself longing for a city I never knew I loved.

Exactly a year from now, I vowed, I would sit outside at night wherever I was, somewhere in Europe, or in America, and turn my face to Egypt, as Muslims do when they pray and face Mecca, and remember this very night, and how I had thought these things and made this vow. You're beginning to sound like Elsa and her silly seders, I said to myself, mimicking my father's humor.

On my way home I thought of what the others were doing. I wanted to walk in, find the smaller living room still lit, the Beethoven still playing, with Abdou still clearing the dining room, and, on closing the front door, suddenly hear someone say, "We were just waiting for you, we're thinking of going to the Royal." "But we've already seen that film," I would say. "What difference does it make. We'll see it again."

And before we had time to argue, we would all rush downstairs, where my father would be waiting in a car that was no longer really ours, and, feeling the slight chill of a late April night, would huddle together with the windows shut, bicker as usual about who got to sit where, rub our hands, turn the radio to a French broadcast, and then speed to the Corniche, thinking that all this was as it always was, that nothing ever really changed, that the people enjoying their first stroll on the Corniche after fasting, or the woman selling tickets at the Royal, or the man who would watch our car in the side alley outside the theater, or our neighbors across the hall, or the drizzle that was sure to greet us after the movie at midnight would never, ever know, nor ever guess, that this was our last night in Alexandria.

VI

ISRAEL

from *AKUD**

Albert Swissa

At dawn the boy awoke with a jerk as if he'd been bitten by a snake, even though his father, Mr. Pazuelo, had touched his shoulder gently, as one who takes pity on a child called to a man's task. The room was cold and dark, and he imagined he could feel on his face warm puffs of air, the heavy breath of his five brothers, who lay in a heap all around him. The excitement that had gripped his small body since last night, when his mother and father had spoken to each other in French, roused him to look carefully at his surroundings, and to listen.

A murmur was the first sound he heard, when his father woke him with a kind of reticent mumble. He couldn't speak because he hadn't yet cleansed his hands, and impurity filled his body. Besides the darkness and the steamy sweet smell of his brothers' breath, a sharp, sour stench of socks hung in the air.

That was the living room; his sisters slept in the other room, which served as both foyer and dining room. Outside, rain railed against the porch and the trees and the earth. He could hear the hollow metallic howling of the drainpipes fixed to the shafts inside the tenement. Someone closed and locked a door, then descended the stairs heavily; then came the sound of coughing and spitting, and brisk steps vanishing down the length of a corridor. His father was earnestly whispering *birkat*

---

*Akud (Hebrew): Bound.

*ha-nekabim** and from the hall the syllables sounded like the slurping of a sweet being sucked in a boy's mouth. He pronounced the word *nekabim* with stress on the k and the b. Every so often one of his brothers would scratch his head as if seized by a frenzy.

Yochai plunged his head under the blankets and curled up into his belly with importunate petulance, the edges of his heels touching his buttocks. He breathed in the stench of rank rag that rose from the blanket, which also served as a cover for the *hamin†* on the Sabbath. His feet were still cold, even though he had rubbed them hard that night before going to sleep. His only consolation was in the warmth of his hands, pressed deep between his thighs.

What had Isaac thought on the morning of his binding? Yochai recalled last Rosh Hashana, when he had stood with his father at the lectern used by the cantor and the *tomech*.‡ There was silence in the sanctuary; the ark was opened, revealing Torah scrolls that stood expressionless, gallant popes in splendid vestments, as if still unaware of the judgment. His father began to sing sweetly, beseeching *Et Sha'arei Ratzon,*§ his voice splitting the silence that had made the congregants tremble. The boy enfolded himself in his father's prayer shawl, clasping his knee.

Suddenly his father's voice had broken. For a moment, the silence had lingered. Then words rent the air sharply, nasally. The congregants hid their faces in their prayer shawls, some of them bowing into their prayer books. Quiet, restrained weeping could be heard amid the mumbled words of prayer, then wordless cries burst forth. His father, for years the principal cantor, could not go on. Someone in the congregation hinted that the *tomech* should continue the prayer, but the *tomech*, who respected his father with a kind of awe, instructed the congregation to join together in the song of the binding of Isaac.

**Birkat ha-nekabim*: Blessing of the apertures. Said after voiding, following the ritual washing of the hands. The blessing expresses man's wonder and gratitude for the perfection with which God has endowed the human body.

†*Hamin*: A traditional dish of meat, potatoes, and beans set to cook on a low flame early Friday morning, and consumed at the main Sabbath meal on Saturday.

‡*Tomech*: Because High Holiday services are long and fatiguing, a "supporter" or *tomech* is chosen to assist the cantor if he cannot continue. In small, orthodox congregations, it is customary for both the cantor and the *tomech* to be laymen.

§*Et Sha'arei Ratzon*: Hymn sung in Sephardic congregations on Rosh Hashana immediately before the blowing of the shofar. The hymn is a poetic, somewhat embellished, account of the story of the binding of Isaac.

Fear overcame the boy. Feeling he was about to fall, he tightened his grasp on his father's thigh as if he feared he would lose him. Father's going to be slaughtered—they'll slaughter me too—Mother will cry! Father's a criminal—he's bad! Father's afraid—Father, he's the slaughterer, a certified slaughterer. He slaughters chickens too—he confesses, an awful crime, so very awful, like in Sodom—what do they want from him, what has he done, why does he cry so—for God's sake, make him stop!

At school they didn't know what Isaac had thought. Abraham was the whole story. Isaac hadn't known, he'd asked his father Abraham where they were going, and Abraham had said that only God knows where man is going when he goes. But when they bound him he must have known, because they don't just go binding someone like that. But later on in the legends it said that Isaac knew, and that in his righteousness he was glad to be God's sacrifice.

Yochai heard his father laying *tefillin*, and so got up and hurried to get dressed. A chill passed through him as he dipped first one hand and then the other into the cold water. He tried to touch the water with just the tips of his fingers, and didn't dare get any water near his face. His father was already waiting for him by the door, wound in prayer shawl and tefillin, his right hand resting on the *mezuzzah* as he prayed for the welfare of his household. They stopped before the puddles at the edge of the portico while his father gathered up the tips of the fringes of his prayer shawl, to keep them from getting wet. The boy skipped over the puddles, a few paces behind his father, who was completely hidden within his prayer shawl. In the raging wind and sprays of rain, Yochai's father looked to him like an abominable snowman. They were going to the first service of morning prayers.

Mr. Pazuelo stopped at the entrance to the shelter of tenement number eleven, and listened to the prayers that began with the story of the binding and the sacrifice. He took care not to enter the synagogue before the congregation had reached the *Baruch She'amar*.* At that point all would rise in honor of He who had said "and the world was formed," and not in honor of flesh and blood. Congregants who rose in his honor caused Mr. Pazuelo anguish, for he feared they were depriving him of his reward in the world to come.

Yochai continued walking mechanically through the dim hall, then suddenly froze in his tracks. Eliahu the moron pushed his smiling,

Baruch She'amar: "Blessed is He who has said." The prayer marks the second part of the morning service, comprising songs of praise to God. It is customary to rise for the singing of this prayer.

deathlike face toward Yochai from under the electric memorial lamps. Reb Eliahu, as the elders of the neighborhood called him, was a distant relative of his father's, who in his youth had been his father's playmate. One day, Eliahu's father had taken his son to see how chickens were slaughtered; as a result, Eliahu had lost his mind, and his body had taken the shape of a slaughtered chicken. His head and neck were outstretched, his right arm extended as if to strike. Sometimes he would flail at the air, his elbow contorted, until the arm again went limp. His clothes were fetid, and his body stank of kerosene and chewing tobacco. Yochai detested him because sometimes, without any warning, he would pull from his jacket pockets bloodied, severed chicken heads that he'd gotten from the housewives of tenement eleven. Yochai couldn't fathom that it was possible to eat the heads of animals.

Recovered, he went to sit in his distant corner, under the fluorescent lamp lit in memory of his eldest brother, who had died under mysterious circumstances. Beside him sat two hoary old men, covered from head to toe in black *jalabiyas,** like two monks who had taken the vow of silence. Now and again they would poke their heads out toward their hands and pluck up wads of tobacco, snorting in a way that frightened Yochai.

About thirty fluorescent lamps lit the narrow shelter, all of them dedicated to the memories of congregants who had died of old age or of various diseases, or who had lost their lives as soldiers, or who had been run over in the streets. Yochai would shift his gaze from one lamp to another trying to decipher beneath them the initials and names of those sanctified. His eyes slowly closed, and he felt himself on an endless descent down a narrow passageway lit by a bright light that came from nowhere. He hadn't grown old, hadn't served in the army, nor had he been crushed to death; yet his classmates were weeping bitterly, led by Mrs. Oren, the music teacher. "We have hung violins in the darkness" she shrieked, until the swelling under her left earlobe expanded and burst, and she lost her voice. The friends he had left behind now wailed in disarray, and Rabbi Sokolowski, the homeroom teacher, began to rave.

Yochai started out of his sleep, his whole body shaken. On his neck he could feel the grip of fingers poised to poke into his throat, and his whole body bristled. With an effort he raised his head, and his gaze met the lizardlike eyes of Eliahu the moron, who suddenly stuck out his hand

---

Jalabiyas: Ankle-length, hooded robes which are the traditional dress of men in the Middle East.

like a long tongue and hit him with a prayerbook. "Sleepin' at prayer, huh?"

The old men around him snickered with hollow mouths, their faces black holes. The boy sailed a pleading glance toward his father; but the latter stood like a statue before the cantor's lectern, every fiber of him sunk in prayer. Tears sprang to Yochai's eyes; now he felt the full weight of sin. Again he turned his gaze toward his father. There wasn't a soul in the world who could pardon him as his father sometimes did with his merciful, quiet, attentive gaze that said: "Watch and guard your soul: It is all you have in the world, and that is not much." Now the father was chanting the mourner's prayer, with his son answering "amen" after every line, as if to say: "Yes, Father."

Translated from the Hebrew by Marsha Weinstein.

from *FIVE SEASONS*

A. B. Yehoshua

The next day he informed the office that he was making one more trip to the Galilee and received permission and authorization for expenses. On Thursday morning, which proved to be muggy and overcast, he went to do some shopping, returning home to find the cleaning woman, whom he had not encountered in weeks. At first, he tried keeping out of her way by shutting himself in his room, but she seemed in a particularly gay mood, singing while she beat the rugs and coming in to talk to him, pleased to find him at home. "You're looking better, Mr. Molkho," she said in the end. "Much better." When she finally departed, leaving a silent, sparkling house, it was already twelve o'clock. The promised car had not arrived. At one, he went to the kitchen to make himself something to eat. If I want to claim lunch expenses, he thought gloomily, I'll have to write myself out my own receipt. As soon as he finished eating, he decided, he would summarize the file and get rid of it.

At two the doorbell rang. It was the driver, a burly Arab of about Molkho's age who came from a village near Zeru'a. "How come you're so late?" Molkho scolded him. Despite the man's explanation that he had lost his way for two hours and couldn't find the address, he debated whether to go; but in the end, the thought of the girl and the car expenses prevailed. "You'll have to bring me back, though," he warned the driver, who, however, disclaimed all knowledge of any such responsibility. His job was to drive Molkho to Zeru'a; perhaps someone else would return him. Again Molkho hesitated; then he went to get the file, put it in his briefcase, added a pair of pajamas and some slippers wrapped in a newspaper just in case, and put on some old, heavy shoes. "Let's go," he grumpily said to the Arab, locking the door of the house.

The car turned out to be an old pickup with a load in the back and the Arab's wife, a large peasant woman dressed in black, in the front. Before Molkho could protest, he was made to sit between them, and they started out, driving slowly and with a great clatter of the engine in the heat of the day. Every now and then, they turned off the main road to make a delivery to some remote Arab village that Molkho had never even heard of. Sweatily squeezed between the driver and his wife and dismally cursing his fate, he watched the road go by while throwing hostile glances at the man shifting gears, an operation that was conducted each time with great caution but little sign of expertise. After asking where the man knew Ben-Ya'ish from and being told that the council manager had close ties with the nearby Arab villages and even helped them with their books, there was nothing left to talk about and they drove on in silence, the Arab's wife dozing with her head resting lightly on Molkho's shoulder. By the time they began the climb into the mountains, his eyes, too, began to close; periodically he nodded off, found himself tilting against the peasant woman's heavy breasts, and sat up again with a start. The trip took three hours and included a stop in the driver's village—which looked like something from the wilds of Anatolia—where the woman got out, took off her shoes, and slipped into her house while her husband unloaded the remaining crates and invited Molkho, still rubbing the sleep from his eyes, to come in for a cup of coffee. He went to the bathroom, which surprised him by its cleanliness, and returned to the sitting room to find the coffee waiting there. "I understand you lost your wife," said the Arab. Molkho was nonplussed. Was it written all over his face? But no, the man had heard of it in Zeru'a. What else had he heard there? Molkho asked. Nothing. They just told him to bring Molkho in his truck.

It was 5 P.M. when he reached the school building. Though he saw at once in the mild afternoon light that it was locked and deserted, he did not feel at all surprised; on the contrary, something had told him all along that Ben-Ya'ish would not be there. The fields had yellowed a bit in the ten days that had passed, but here and there he saw summer flowers he hadn't noticed the last time, and on the whole, the place seemed more livable. He walked between the houses, feeling watched by dark silhouettes of Indians. "It's that man from the ministry again," he heard someone say. Slowly he crossed the shopping center, where this time, as though out of compassion, people avoided his eyes.

He walked on to the little house on the hillside, passing under the tall, humming pylon and once again experiencing the sense of déjá vu, though this time it was possible that his previous visit was the cause of it. Ben-Ya'ish's house was locked and silent, the lowered blinds preventing a glimpse inside, but when he knocked on the door, he thought he heard a sound there. "Mr. Ben-Ya'ish?" he called out. "Mr. Ben-Ya'ish?" But the sound stopped, and Molkho, all but trembling with anticipation, walked back down the hill to the house of the treasurer, whose daughter opened the door. "Where's your father?" he asked, feeling himself turn as red as her polka-dot dress. She seemed to have grown smaller since last he had seen her, but her gaze was as pure and earnest as ever. Her father, she said, was in the hospital. "In the hospital? How long has he been there?" he asked, his heart sinking. But he had gone only that morning and would soon be back, she informed him, her thin, finely wrought hand on the door, uncertain whether Molkho wished to enter, perhaps even concerned that he might sleep in her bed again. Nor was he at all sure himself how proper it was to be alone with her in the house. He felt unsteady, as if squatting inside him were a sexless little gnome who had fallen in love with a nymph. Behind her he could see her bedroom with one end of her antique bed, its blanket thrown off, and the heavy furniture. She followed his gaze earnestly, a joyless, humorless, somber little Indian, just like her father. "Do you want to wait here for him?" she asked. "No," Molkho said, "I've come to see Ya-ir Ben-Ya'ish. Do you have any idea where he is?" "He was waiting for you all morning at the school," said the girl, raising an arm as if to fend Molkho off. "You should look for him there." "But the school is locked," he said patiently, "I just came from there," and when she said nothing he continued, "Why don't you show me where the secretary lives, that music teacher." She glided outdoors in her bare feet, explaining to him how to get there; yet touching her so lightly that he barely felt her, as though she were made out of air, he said, "Take me there yourself, please. Just put on some shoes first." And so again he followed her between the houses, looking at her matchstick legs in their sneakers while trying to carry on a conversation, first asking her about her mother and when the new baby was expected, then about the cow, and finally about the wild ravine, the name of which he had forgotten. But she did not know it either and was not even certain that it had one. All she could tell him was that if you walked a ways down it, you came to a waterfall. "What waterfall is that?" Molkho asked. "Oh, just a waterfall."

The music teacher turned pale when Molkho arrived with the girl. "It's you? You came after all? But when? We'd already given up on you." "*You'd* given up?" he snickered. "Yes, we waited for you all morning. Ya'ir was beside himself. An hour ago he took the bus to Fasuta to look for the driver." While Molkho related what had happened, she hurried to give him a chair and a drink, and told the girl she could go. Molkho, though, did not want to stay in her house either, for it was noisy with children and too full of cheap bric-a-brac and glassware. He had a deep urge to stroll in the honeyed spring light, vigilant though forbearing in the knowledge, which both pleased and touched him, that the council manger was afraid of him, but determined to meet the young man and do what he could to console him. "Never mind. I'll take a walk around and wait for him at their house," he said to the music teacher with a nod toward the girl, who stood frozen for some reason in a corner. "Is your father back?" the music teacher asked her. "He will be soon," said the girl. "Then find Mr. Molkho a place to rest," said the teacher, happy to get rid of him.

And so once more Molkho walked behind the girl along the path between the houses, aware of the surreptitious stares cast his way. "Where's the trail leading to that waterfall?" he asked her. She guided him to it, leading him across a field to a broad dirt track. "Well, then," he said, "I'll go down and have a look and come right back." She was reluctant to leave him there, though. "You'd better let me show you the way." "There's really no need to," answered Molkho, not trusting himself alone with her in the ravine. "I'll find it by myself. Just please take my briefcase back to your house." And indeed, the request reassured her, so that she stood there watching him set out, squinting through her comic glasses with a sudden, sweet flutter of her eyes. The broad trail soon narrowed and grew rocky, bushes and boulders blocked the way, and moisture from an unseen source softened the earth beneath his feet, which glistened a turfy green. And yet the more tangled and difficult the path became, the more lustrously vibrant grew the light. The far side of the ravine was hidden by the thick bushes, and from time to time he had to slide down a steep rock on his bottom. Should he stop and turn back? But the winding trail lured him on, the damp earth giving off new smells, joined now by a metal pipe, no doubt for sewage or irrigation, which snaked downward through the lush undergrowth, in which it seemed strangely out of place. Molkho followed it, treading on it now and then to make sure he could find his way back through the thickening brush. He skirted little puddles of water and crossed other paths joining this one, trodden grassless by hikers. It grew darker, there was a pungent smell of dust and rushing water, the walls of a little canyon rose on either side of him, and then all at once he was standing in a clearing of golden light and there was the waterfall.

It was not nearly as small as he had thought it would be. Falling gilded by the sunlight into a gray-green pool that trickled off in an unseen direction, the water burst forth from mosses that concealed a lipped groove in a boulder. He sat on a rock facing it, enjoying the coolness of the air and gazing at some unfamiliar purple flowers and at a weeping willow whose little leaves were like delicate ferns, the sharp scent of artemisia riveting his senses. Here was a place of eternal wakefulness, and though he failed to remember it, he felt sure he had been here as a boy, for the Scouts would never have missed it. How his wife would have liked it too! Places like this made her fall profoundly silent, her judgmental nagging briefly stilled. How sad to think of the lost peace this cascade would have given her! And yet it was years since they last had taken a pleasure trip, and then, too, they never went on foot. Even before she fell ill, she had always been too tired to go anywhere on Saturdays and had passed the time irritably glancing at the weekend papers and uttering her jeremiads. "Stop reading all that junk," he would say to her. "It's all a lot of lies and exaggerations. Why let it get to you." But she simply saw in this one more sign of the dangerously Levantine, apolitical naïveté that was leading the country to catastrophe. Now she was rotting slowly, decomposing in the earth, and he was by himself, squatting comfortably on his heels in Levantine fashion across from the marvelous waterfall, overcome by sorrow and longing. He picked up a pebble and chucked it into the pool.

Just then he heard a rustle of branches and the sound of children, and a minute later the children themselves appeared, staring down at him from further up the ravine, having followed him apparently from the village. He beckoned to them. At first, they hesitated; then, the bigger ones first and the smaller ones after them, they descended like a herd of dark goats and stood with an unwashed smell in a circle around him while he chatted with them easily and patted their heads and backs, until suddenly, green with envy, the girl appeared and drove them away, her father having returned and sent her to look for him, afraid he might be lost. Molkho laughed. "Has Ben-Ya'ish come back too?" he asked. But the girl hadn't seen him.

And so, yet another time, he found himself walking behind her, his eyes on her thin, skimming legs as he climbed arduously up the steep path with the children scrambling in his wake like a pack of nimble monkeys. At the entrance to the ravine, he found her father waiting in the company of two or three other anxious men, all apparently afraid he had taken leave of his senses. "What were you looking for down there?" they asked. "Nothing," said Molkho, brushing off his clothes, "just the waterfall. Your daughter told me about it, so I went down to have a look." "You walked all the way to the waterfall?" they marveled, making him wonder how old a man they took him for. "Yes, is that so unusual?" he replied before asking them about Ben-Ya'ish. But Ben-Ya'ish, it appeared, was still being looked for. "Never has a bureaucrat been given such a runaround by a citizen," sighed Molkho pensively with something like inner satisfaction, basking in the mild, clear light that made the whole world look transparent. "Well, I suppose there's nothing to do but wait for him," he added, turning to go to the Indian's house.

Though the Indian seemed unprepared, he had little choice but to join Molkho, who was already striding purposefully toward the house, in front of which he found his briefcase. Perhaps they'll offer me the girl's bed again, he thought, but instead he was ushered into the familiar living room and asked if he wanted some coffee. He accepted and sat drinking it, trying once more to elicit the details of the man's illness, at least the names of the drugs that he took. But the Indian was no more forthcoming than before, and perhaps he really knew nothing about it, as if his illness were someone else's that he had merely borrowed for a while. Remembering with longing his sleep of ten days ago, Molkho stole a tender glance at the girl's room. "He's playing a game with me, this Ben-Ya'ish of yours," he sighed, tired from the trip and his hike in the ravine but doubtful whether he could fall asleep so late in the afternoon, especially since the soporific wind was no longer blowing. "Maybe he's just afraid of me, but he's playing with fire," he continued, trying to make the Indian feel a measure of guilt or, at least, responsibility. But the Indian too, so it seemed, had despaired of understanding the council manager; sitting straight-backed on the edge of his chair beside his daughter, who appeared, with the light glinting off her glasses, to imitate his movements with unconscious precision, he said sulkily, "I told him he had nothing to be afraid of, that you were a reasonable man and would give folks like us a fair hearing. But I guess he's afraid you won't understand his method of bookkeeping and there'll be trouble."

There was a long silence in the room. The cow mooed longingly in her shed, and Molkho sat back in the little armchair, surprised at his inner serenity, which the Indian, perhaps because he feared another session of sleep, appeared to regard with apprehension. "So you really think he won't show up?" asked Molkho. "I honestly don't know," said the Indian. "But were is he now?" asked Molkho. The council manager, replied the Indian, was last seen departing for the Arab driver's village; since then, he hadn't been heard from and the music teacher had gone to look for him. "He promised me a ride back to Haifa too," Molkho said. The Indian, however, had no idea how such a promise might be kept. "When is the last bus out of here?" Molkho asked. In fifteen minutes, was the answer. Yet he made no move to rise from his chair, too entranced by the silent aura of the girl to tear himself away. I must be going crazy, he thought, gazing at her bare arms and legs, on which, near the ankle, there was a fresh, thin scratch. "Your daughter cut herself," he told the Indian. "Perhaps you should put on a Band-Aid." "It's from the ravine," explained the girl, rubbing the dried blood off with some saliva. "Well, then," said Molkho, reaching for his briefcase, "I guess I'll be on my way." He stepped out into the charmed evening, cut behind the house, paused to regard the big cow in her shed, and continued along the path that skirted the village, which he now seemed to see for the first time in all its pathetic decay: the unwatered fields, the untended hothouses, the abandoned chicken coops, the half-empty cowsheds, the tractors rusting beneath their tattered tarpaulins, the forlorn wildflowers in a sea of yellowing thistles. The whole place, he thought, was like a dying patient who lets the doctor do what he wants with him. The villagers he passed looked at him unseeingly, sometimes keeping in step with him awhile before falling behind or forging ahead. The dead keep giving us orders, he thought, not without satisfaction, recalling, while continuing his tour of the village, how his wife would send him out for such walks to perk him up from the long hours of sitting by her bed, mechanically making small talk—but just then he froze, for there, in the little shopping center, a bus had just pulled in and was disgorging weary-looking passengers returning from work, among them the Indian's pregnant wife, who started out for home on her short, knobby legs. Why, it's the last bus, he realized with a panicky yet oddly happy sensation, watching it pull out past the perimeter fence while feeling how, bright but invisible in the lingering light, someone was shadowing him, perhaps Ya-ir Ben-Ya'ish himself, who, in the most childish case of corruption Molkho had ever encountered, had used government money as a slush fund for the local inhabitants.

He continued to describe a large circle, following the perimeter fence from point to point, leaving nowhere unexplored, not even the distant spot on the hillside where another huge pylon shunted its lines into town. Though the sun had already set, it was still bright out, as if, by fiat of the Ministry of the Interior, for which he worked, daylight saving time had stopped the earth in its tracks and kept the long, glimmering twilight afloat. How his wife would have loved this slow, light-drenched evening, she who was always so afraid of the oncoming night! He had now reached the northern limits of the settlement, where the fence began doubling back, still without finding the last trace of a park or paved road that might allow him to file a less incriminating report, and so he turned and headed southeast, watching his shadow grow longer and thinner in the dimming reddish light until it became a faint specter. A large, heavy woman, none other than a very red-faced and out-of-breath music teacher, was running after him, shouting and waving her hands. He stopped and regarded her sternly while listening to her news, uncertain whether the catch in her voice was from heartbreak or hilarity. Ben-Ya'ish, it seemed, had just called. "Where is he?" Molkho asked. "You won't believe this," said the music teacher, "but he's in Haifa. He never went to Fasuta at all. He went straight to Haifa, because he was sure that the Arab had never picked you up. He just called from somewhere on the Carmel. Isn't that were you live? Then he must be right near your house! But he's already started back, so you may as well wait for him here."

"Wait for him?" whispered Molkho, almost amused by the infinite impudence of the man. "You want *me* to wait some more?" he asked, staring at her half-menacingly and half-comically while the light behind her went on dying, flattening the children in the playground near the shopping center into black paper cutouts. The music teacher, however, did not seem to see the irony of it. "Yes," she said, matching him stare for stare, "that's what he told me to tell you. He'll feel terrible if you leave now." Once again Ben-Ya'ish's feelings were being flaunted as though they were those of an innocent child who must be prevented from suffering at all costs! "First of all," said Molkho sharply, with the smile of a man who has seen everything, "first of all, I want a telephone. A real one on which I can talk. After that, I'll tell you my decision." Apparently the music teacher had had just such a contingency in mind, because jingling in her hands were the keys not only to the office but to Ben-Ya'ish's house, which was now offered to him as a sanctuary. And so together they walked back to the school, where children were still playing soccer; there she unlocked the front gate and the office, switched on the light, and hurried off with the excuse that she had left something cooking at home, flinging the keys on the desk of the disorderly room like a title deed.

His first call was to his younger son, whom he informed that he might not be coming home that night, grateful that his children were already grown up and no longer dependent on him. Then he phoned his mother in Jerusalem to say hello, and was asked where he was calling from and why he sounded so distant. "I'm in the Galilee," he said. "The Galilee? What are you doing there?" "I'm here on business," he told her. "But it's already night," she remonstrated. "So what?" he asked. "So be careful." "All right, I'll be careful," promised Molkho, wondering whom to call next. Perhaps his cousin in Paris, to whom he had not spoken or even written a thank-you note since he got back? It was a tempting thought, but fearful the call might be traced to him, he refrained. He glanced again at his files, which seemed suddenly quite pointless, locked the office door behind him, and wandered down the dark corridor, wondering whether compositions were still hung on the walls as they were when he was a boy and even entering several classrooms, turning on the light in each; but there were no compositions, just pictures of flowers and animals. Which class was the girl in? Unless she had skipped a grade, he guessed, she must be a fifth-grader, and finding her classroom, he spent a long while there and even sat in one of the seats. In general, the school surprised him by being so clean and orderly that he considered praising it in his report as the single bright spot in the village. Even the bathrooms were well kept, and he was especially impressed by the little child-size toilets. Now there's creative thinking, he mused, sitting on one of them and trying to imagine how a child would feel on it.

At last he locked the front gate of the school and put the keys in his pocket. Many eyes, he felt, were on him in the darkness, wondering about the long-suffering but persistent ministry whose loyal representative he was. He walked back to the shopping center, which was now crowded with people and brightly lit by neon lights. In the café, which was doing a brisk business, small children ran back and forth between the tables. People looked at him warmly now, their former reserve gone, as if by virtue of the keys he was no longer the outside inspector but a local, if still temporary, resident, and he sat down at a table, nodding to people he knew, while the dark-skinned café owner, as unshaven and unkempt as ever (did he ever wash his hands? Molkho wondered), hovered silently behind him like a shade. If he wants to serve me more cannibal stew, thought Molkho, I'm afraid I don't have an appetite. In fact, his hike to the waterfall and his evening walk had so satisfied him that he didn't feel like eating anything, not for all the receipts in the world, and all he asked for was a cup of tea, unsweetened, please. Meanwhile, a small crowd had gathered approvingly around him, praising his patience in waiting for Ben-Ya'ish, who was sure to arrive and set everything to rights, since he had only their good in mind. Why, if Molkho hadn't stayed, Ben-Ya'ish would have been disappointed—they all would have been!

From that, they passed to other things. What did Molkho think about the situation in Lebanon? And what did he believe would happen now that the army was withdrawing? He should know that just because they lived near the border and had suffered from PLO attacks was no reason to blame them for the frightful war. They felt for the soldiers who were killed in it, yet there was no denying it had given them three years of peace, without a single shot or shell fired at them. What would happen now? Would they have to go back to living in shelters? They talked on and on, about the present prime minister and the former prime minister and the prime ministers before him and who was better and what was good and bad about each and life in general, and even asked Molkho about himself. Why, these people are folks just like me! he thought. When the television news came on, they all fell silent, watching the pullout from Lebanon with its loaded trucks and tank carriers. Just then a flame-faced boy came running up to him: Ben-Ya'ish had phoned! He was already in Acre and hoped that Molkho would wait.

The report was received with satisfaction, and when the news was over the café dimmed its lights and the customers rose and drifted out. "There's a movie now. Why don't you come?" they said to Molkho, who decided to join them, wondering whether he could put in for overtime. He was led to a part of the village he hadn't been in before and shown into the local cinema, apparently a renovated chicken run, which was soon packed with more people than he would have guessed lived in the place, many of them young couples. The natives are stirring, he thought, looking up at the high corrugated-tin ceiling on its wooden rafters and down at the seats, which seemed to be ordinary house chairs spread in a semicircle on the dirt floor, which still smelled of chicken manure. A large sheet hung at one end of the hall and a projector occupied a table in the middle, while in a far corner mint tea and sun-flower seeds were being served to the audience, which stood around jok-ing and laughing at the children who were caught sneaking in. The In-dian girl's mother was there too, seated with a peaceful look on her face, wet wisps of freshly washed hair sticking out from under a black ker-chief, her large belly protruding and her eyes already glued to the makeshift screen. Molkho sat near her and waved a friendly hello, which she returned with a smile after a brief hesitation. All in all, he now felt welcomed by the villagers, who seemed content with him as well as cu-rious.

The lights had gone out and the reel was being wound when he felt a hand on his arm. It was the music teacher. "I've got good news," she said. "Ben-Ya'ish just called from Karmiel. He's halfway here!" By now, Molkho had the feeling that Ben-Ya'ish was less an actual person than a collective identity passed from one villager to another, but making no comment, he stretched out in his chair, sipping slowly from his mint tea. The movie, which was in Turkish or Greek, was amateurishly made and promised from the outset to be a rather erotic, if not out-and-out porno-graphic, film about high-society sex in a luxury hotel on some Mediter-ranean coast. The female lead was a dark-haired, buxom woman, not pretty but vivacious and bold, even oddly maternal, to whom the audi-ence responded with a buzz of whispers and a cracking of sunflower seeds while Molkho scooped up some dirt from the floor and let it trickle through his fingers until only a few crumbs were left, raising them to his nose and inhaling the aroma of chicken dung flavored with poultry feed. Meanwhile, the actors on the screen having dramatically stripped and begun making love, the audience fell quiet, its every breath audible, its eyes narrowed as though with somnolence—Molkho's, too, though he was also beginning to feel hungry. Idly he sat watching the passion-ate embraces, wondering whether they were real or shammed, his head lolling heavily; but suddenly, as if a rusty old motor inside him had sud-denly turned over, he felt his member grow stiff, and he frowned deeply, sickened and titillated at once.

The lights were kept dimmed when it was time for the reel to be changed, leaving people to whisper unseen in the dark. Someone knelt in front of Molkho. It was a young woman who said, "Ben-Ya'ish called again! He caught a ride to Kiryat Shmonah." "Kiryat Shmonah?" echoed Molkho mirthfully, for the council manager, it seemed, had overshot his mark and now had to travel back the other way. "Yes, but he'll try to get back here tonight. You may as well stay." As if by now he had any-where to go!

The movie ended at eleven. Heavily the audience rose and stretched itself, yawning disappointedly. Molkho exited behind the Indian's pregnant wife, who waddled on her short, crooked legs like a big duck; she was, he noticed when she smiled at him, slightly cross-eyed, like her daughter. The moon was just rising in the starry sky, and it was very cold. Briefcase in hand he walked silently by her side, adjusting himself to her slow pace. The audience began to disperse, and she, too, chose a path and struck out on it, quickening her tiny steps as if pursuing the stomach that preceded her. It takes guts to go to the movies when you're so close to giving birth, Molkho thought. Not that there was any reason for concern, for even if she were to deliver right here and now, in the middle of the path, there were still lights in many houses and the village showed no signs of going to bed. On the contrary, the later the hour, the livelier things seemed: shadowy figures could be seen carrying work tools, a tractor chugged somewhere nearby, and there was an overall sense of definite, if rather vague, activity.

The lights were on in the Indian's house too. He was waiting up and did not seem surprised to see Molkho appear with his wife, as if it had been clear to him all along that the visitor was fated to sleep there. Did he want to eat anything? asked the man, who was wearing pants and pajama tops, in a low but wakeful tone of voice. Molkho, though, did not want to bother his host—who, surrounded by his piles of books, appeared at this midnight hour to be full of intellectual vigor—and agreed only to drink a glass of wine with him. "Ben-Ya'ish is on his way. Everyone says so," Molkho whispered, and the Indian nodded, though the whereabouts of the council manager did not seem to concern him unduly. While his wife took out fresh sheets and cleared the living room couch, he went to his daughter's room, lifted her in her sleep, and carried her out like a folded ebony bird. Molkho tried to help, catching hold of the girl's leg and feeling a wave of warmth when her large, sleepy eyes, without their glasses now, opened for a moment to regard him. The woman spread the child's sheets on the couch, and the Indian laid her down and covered her. Then her bed was remade with fresh sheets for Molkho, who was given a towel too. "I'm sorry to be such a nuisance," he said happily, "but what could I do? This Ben-Ya'ish of yours is playing games with us all."

The door shut behind him. Shut, too, were the windows and blinds of the room, which still was warm from the girl's sleep. He put his briefcase on the desk and paused to look at the schoolbooks scattered there, careful not to touch the glasses that lay opened on top of them and stirred his pity in some unclear way. He debated whether to put on the pajamas he had brought or to lie down in his underwear and decided in the end that he needed the pajamas to sleep. Why, he thought, full of wonder at himself, he hated sleeping in other people's houses and this is the second time this week I'm doing it!

There was a knock on the door. It was the woman, who had come to bring him an extra pillow, her eyes on the floor as if embarrassed to see him in pajamas. "I know I'm inconveniencing you," whispered Molkho again, "but it's not my fault. He pulled a fast one on all of us. He's playing games with me." Slowly he stretched out on the child's bed, not feeling at all tired, convinced he would never be able to sleep. In his mind he replayed the scenes of the movie and once more smelled the manure, and then thought of the pregnant woman hurrying on crooked legs down the moonlight-spangled path, of the cow in its shed, and of his sexual desperation, picturing the girl being carried like an ebony bird, the kernel of pure desire hidden in her folded wings. Why here? he began to argue bitterly with his wife. What do you want from me? How can you say that I killed you? But he knew she wouldn't answer and the silence surrounding him would never be broken, for the days were gone when there was someone to know whatever was on his mind, even at a distance: as soon as he phoned her from the office, she knew just what he was feeling and thinking. Now he was free to do as he pleased, and so he rose barefoot in the dark, carefully lifted the glasses from the desk, held them up, kissed them, fogging the lenses with his lips, wet them slightly, dried them, folded them, and put them back in their place. I've never been so exhausted in my life, he thought, lying down again in preparation for a sleepless night while listening to the crickets and the sound of a tractor.

And yet, despite himself, he fell asleep, waking up five hours later with a feeling of amazement at having gotten through the night. As in his distant days of army service, he rose at once and dressed, made the bed, and put on his shoes in a jiffy. Then, returning his things to the briefcase, he opened the window and leapt straight out into the grainy light of the thick mist swaddling the mountain. Soon the sun would be up. Shivering with cold, he stopped to relieve himself by the cowshed before stepping inside to look at the cow, who stood there alertly as if expecting company. Wondering if cows had feelings, he took a friendly step toward her, tapping her bony forehead with his fist and folding her ears in two like cardboard. No, they didn't, he concluded, stepping back outside with his briefcase. The rim of the sun appeared over the hill, directly above Ben-Ya'ish's house, the windows of which, he noticed, were

open. And indeed, hurrying up to it, he found its bed occupied and woke
the sleeper at once.

It was Ben-Ya'ish himself, a young man in heavy flannel pajamas
who resembled a student more than a politician and lay beneath a pile
of quilts surrounded by electrical appliances. "I'm so terribly sorry," he
said, smiling at Molkho guiltily, already apologizing before he was
awake. "Please, please forgive me. We kept getting our signals crossed.
Why, I went all the way to Haifa just to see you, and getting back from
there wasn't easy. Why didn't you sleep here? I told my secretary to give
you the keys, and all the account books too. You've got me wrong and
I'll prove it. I know, I know, you looked for the road and the park and
couldn't find them, but I'll show you all the plans. There were just so
many out-of-work men who had used up their unemployment checks
that I had to dip into the budget to help them, but we'll balance the
books yet; everything will add up in the end. Maybe you can show me
the best way to do it, because I'm really not very experienced. I mean,
I know the money was budgeted for development, but how can you develop a village that's starving to death?"

Molkho sat there listening quietly, incapable of anger, resigned to
defeat by this sleepy, stubble-cheeked, bright-eyed young man, toward
whom he was feeling increasingly sympathetic. In the end, he knew, he
would not even be able to scold him, especially not now, when he had
just seen the sun rise in its glory on men in need of mercy. And so he
waited for him to dress and drink his coffee, and followed him outside
into the still chilly but now clear morning, feeling slightly feverish as he
was led to a field with some saplings and bushes that had apparently
been planted the night before in lieu of a park and, thence, greeted by
cheerful good-mornings, to the other end of the village, where some fresh
piles of sand and gravel dumped on a path beside an oil drum full of
bubbling tar were meant to signify a road. There was even a steamroller,
painted green like a picture from an old children's book. Ben-Ya'ish
talked on and on, waving documents and plans. "Just show me the best
way to state the facts," he begged Molkho, "the best way to keep us
out of trouble, because more trouble is the last thing we need." And in
the end, that was just what Molkho did.

Translated from the Hebrew by Hillel Halkin.

A ROOM ON THE ROOF

Savyon Liebrecht

That summer she sat on the patio under the rounded awning of the Italian swing, as the straw fringes intertwined with the edges of the cloth dome rustled softly, sounding like forest noises, her eyes on the red glow flowing from the western horizon at sunset, her baby already standing on his own two widespread legs, his fat fingers grasping the bars of the square playpen made of interlocked wooden bars. The lily-like hibiscus waved its circlet of toothed leaves bound in an envelope of buds, only their heads looking out of the long, laden calyxes, pouting like the lips of a coquettish girl, the abundant tranquillity all about deluding merely the part of her that was asleep in any case, not the part that was driven, tensed toward something beyond the apparent silence, knowing the restlessness of someone under eyes constantly prying but always unseen.

That early winter—the mud, the puddles of cement, and the rusty fragments of iron—already seemed distant and impossible, with the three Arab men giving off the stench of wood smoke and unwashed flesh. The men with their bad teeth and mouths, with high-heeled shoes that were once fashionable, now looking oversized, with the leather crushed under the heels.

In her dreams they still visited her sometimes, coming too close to her, which, perhaps, where they live too, could be interpreted as what they might have meant to hint, though perhaps it was done inadvertently. For a long time she wondered about it: did Ahmad draw close to her unheedingly, touching her legs with his rear as he dragged a sack of cement, with his back to her? And later, was it by chance that his elbow touched her breast when he passed by her, balancing a bag of lime on his shoulder, while she raised her arms to the lintel of the door to check the concrete rim as it dried? And did Hassan really believe that she would invite him inside the apartment on that black night when he came back for his coat?

That summer, for a long time after they went off without ever reappearing, she avoided the roof when it was dark, fearing that they might pop up from behind the high potted plants. Sometimes, when she happened to wind up in the back corner, which was imprisoned within three walls and used, for the moment, as a storage area, and she saw the tools they left behind and never came back to collect, a chill would climb her back like a crawling creature with many legs, stirring a column of water in the depths of her belly like the pitching that afflicts you when you're seasick.

But there was no one to accuse. She had brought the thing down on her own head. And if her baby wasn't slaughtered, and her jewels weren't stolen, and nothing bad had happened to her—she should bless her good fortune and erase those two winter months from her memory as if they had never been.

Yoel, her husband, had been opposed to the idea from the moment she had brought it up, still just an idle word in her mouth and still lacking that fervor, that stubbornness, and that unyielding feeling of necessity that were later to possess her.

"A room on the roof?" He twisted his face and took off his glasses as he did when he was angry. "Do you know how filthy construction is? Do you have a notion how many tons of soil and rocks will fall on your head when they break through the ceiling for the stairs? And I don't see why we need another room. There are already two unused rooms in the house. And if you want sunlight—you have half a dunam of private lawn." Against her rebelliously pursed lips, which for a long time, until his patience first broke down, were to emit a defiant silence, he added: "How is it you suddenly got the notion of building? What do you need that for, with a four-month-old baby?"

"So why did we take the trouble of running to the engineer and the municipality to get a building license?" she countered his argument. "And didn't we pay all the fees and the property improvement tax and all that?"

"So we'd have it in hand," he replied, "so that if we want to sell the house one day—it will be more valuable, with the license already in hand."

But the idea had already struck root, twisting up inside her with its own force, like an ovum that had embraced the sperm and was now germinating, and the fetus was already stretching the skin of the belly, and there was no way of putting that growth to sleep.

All that time she was wrapped up in her firstborn son Udi, who summoned her from her dreams at night. She would come to him with her eyes almost closed, as though moonstruck, and her hands turned over the tiny baby clothes of their own volition. On her walks, pushing the baby carriage across broken paving stones, past piles of sand, she found herself lingering around houses under construction, raising her head to see the men walking with assurance on the rim of high walls, amazed, learning how stories grow, windows square themselves in dark frames, shutters fan out panel by panel from an enormous yellow device looking like arm bones with the flesh scraped off them.

From one of the yawning holes that would be a window, someone shouted at her with an oriental accent: "You looking for someone to service you, lady?" She blushed as though doing something wrong and pushed her baby away in a panic. Near a building which she often passed, as he looked into the carriage, a contractor told her, "Excuse me for saying this, but this is no place to wander around with a baby. Dirt and cinderblocks or pieces of iron sometimes fall around here, and it's very dangerous."

After she started leaving Udi with a babysitter in the mornings, a woman who took a few infants in her home, she would go to those places in her old trousers, worn at the knees, climb up the diagonal concrete slabs, supporting herself on the rough rafters, grope in the darkness of stairwells still floored with sand. Here, she would later say to herself, she saw them face to face for the first time, in the chill damp peculiar to houses under construction. They came toward her from corners that stank of urine, all of them with the same face: dark, boiling eyes, sunk in caves of black shadows, hair cut in the old-fashioned way, shoes spotted with lime and cement, and dusty clothes. Here too their peculiar odor came to her nostrils: sweat mingled with cigarette smoke and soot. While she exchanged words with the Jewish foreman, the Arab workers would cast oblique glances at her; down on all fours laying floor tiles; panting as they transported sacks of cement or stacks of tiles; running to ease the effort; ripping out hunks of food with their teeth; half a loaf of bread in one hand, an unpeeled cucumber in the other.

Some foremen were irritable, refusing to answer her questions, dismissing her with a contemptuous gesture and continuing to give directions to their workers, ignoring her as she stood behind them, abashed, feeling how the Arabs were laughing at her inwardly, in collusion with their Jewish foreman. But sometimes the foremen answered her willingly, watching as she took down what they said in her notebook, like a diligent pupil. As she turned to leave they would say with amusement, "So we have to watch out for you, huh, you're the competition!"

In her notebook the pages were already densely packed with details about reinforced concrete, the thickness of inner and outer walls, various gauges of iron rods, a sketch of the way the rods had to be fastened for casting concrete pillars, the ceiling, plaster, flooring, conduits for electricity and water, tar, addresses of building materials manufacturers. She hid her notebook from Yoel in a carton with her university notebooks. Once, when he said, "What's going on? Zvika said he twice saw you coming out of the building they're putting up on Herzl Street," she looked straight at him and said in her usual tone of voice, "Probably someone who looks like me." And he responded, "It's about time you changed your hairdo. Last week I saw someone from behind, and I was sure it was you. She even had the same walk and the same handbag."

Afterwards, when everything was ripe, like a girl come of age, Yoel came back from work one day, and his eyes were troubled. He said: "They want me to go to a training course in Texas for two months. We're getting a new computer. I said I couldn't leave you alone with the baby. Let them find someone else." She answered firmly, alarmed at the swift feeling that leapt up in her like the shock wave of an explosion: "I'll be quite all right—you should go." And when the tempest had died down within her she thought: a sign had been sent from heaven.

The day after she saw him to his plane, David, the Jewish foreman, came accompanied by three Arab workers, members of the same family, looking amazingly like each other. They all wore old woolen hats. They sat on the edges of the chairs, careful not to dirty the upholstery, with their eyes cast down most of the time. Only occasionally would they raise their eyelids and cast a quick glance at her and the apartment, squinting at the baby on her lap. David wrote down some kind of agreement on a piece of paper, explaining some sentences in Arabic, and they nodded their heads in consent. David copied their names from a form he'd brought with them and their identity numbers from the creased documents they took out of their pockets, a description of the dimensions of the room they were to build, detailing the thickness of the walls, the number of electric sockets and their place in the room, the break through the opening for the stairs, the type and color of the plaster, and beside these, the amounts to be paid as the work progressed. Before signing, she insisted that a final date be clearly written, obligating them to finish the work within two months, before Yoel's return.

Then the three of them stood up at the same time and headed for the door. There, on the threshold, after she thanked him for his good offices, David answered: "Think nothing of it, dear lady. It's because I can see you're a fine girl, with a sporting character. Not many women would do something like this. So here's to you! And if you need something, ask for David in the Hershkovitz building any time. Good luck! They're good workers, up on scaffolds from the age of fifteen," and in her ear softly, "Better than ours, believe me."

Sitting on the open roof that summer opposite the sky spread above her with rows of painted white clouds, hearing her baby babble, his voice rising and falling as he tried out his vocal cords, she thought: how did things go so far that those men, whose gaze avoided her eyes, who shrank in her presence with shoulders bowed, as though narrowing their bodies, answering her questions with a soft voice, as though forever guilty, how did it happen that in November they sat on the edge of the chairs that first evening, and by December they were already marching through her house like lords, turning on Yoel's radio transmitter, opening the refrigerator to look for fresh vegetables, rummaging through the cabinet after fragrant shaving cream, and patting her baby on the head?

⤳ ⤶

At first they still seemed to her like a single person, before she learned that Hassan had elongated eyes, whose bright color was like the band of wet sand at the water's edge. Ahmad had a broad nose, sitting in the middle of his flattened face, between his narrow eyes, his lips thick like those of a Negro. Salah's ears pricked up and his cheeks were sunken. Only the pimples on his face gave it some thickness, making it look like the thick skin of an orange.

On the first day, they arrived in an old pickup truck that had once been orange, but now on its dented face there were only islands of peeling paint, and its windows were missing. They got out and unloaded gray cinderblocks near the parking lot. Then the truck pulled away with a grinding noise, returning in a short while with a long wooden beam on top. After a short consultation among themselves, the truck was parked in the parking lot and the beam laid on an angle, the lower part leaning on the back of the truck and the top rising above the edge of the roof. Until the baby started crying inside the house, she stood at a little distance, her hands in the pockets of her slacks, and watched how one of them drew out a tangle of ropes with a saddle-shaped yoke at the end. He stood on the roof and harnessed himself with knots, looking like a coolie in a historical film. One of his mates loaded block after block in the basket on the rope, and the worker on the roof pulled them up along the flat beam, while the third worker, standing on the edge of the roof leaned over and gathered the bricks one by one. Examining them from below, she saw how their faces grew sweaty with the effort, and their hands got dusty and were scratched by the rough blocks. By the time she had put the baby to bed and come out again, she saw they had unloaded the rest of the blocks on the lawn and disappeared with the truck, though she hadn't heard the sound of the motor. The next day, after turning the matter over during sleepless hours, she decided she must demonstrate her authority over them, and she was ready and waiting for them in her window, cradling the baby in her rounded arms, anger breathing force into her movements. From the window she shouted at them as they approached: "Why did you leave work in the middle yesterday? And today. . . ." She looked at her watch with a clumsy movement, stretching her neck over the baby lying at her breast. "Today you come at nine! You said you'd start working at six! This way you won't finish in ten months!"

"Lady," said the one with the gilded eyes, insulted, "Today was police roadblocked. Not possible we leave early before four morning, lady."

Something in her recoiled at the sight of the beaten dog's eyes he raised up toward her in her window, at his broken voice. But she, tensing her strength to suppress the tremor that awoke within her, threatening to soften her anger, shouted: "And yesterday what happened? Was also roadblocked?" Maliciously she imitated his grammatical error. "You went away and left half the blocks down there on the grass."

For the first time she saw the movement that was later to become routine: the jaws clamping down on each other as though chewing something very hard, digging a channel along the line of his teeth. Later she was to learn: that's how they suppress anger, hatred. They clench their teeth to overcome the wild rage that surges up, that only rarely breaks out and flashes in their pupils.

"Yesterday my friend Ahmad, he hurted his, the nail his finger."

Behind him his companion raised a bandaged hand, and she looked out of her pretty window, framed with Catalan-style curtains, feeling how the three men in their tattered work clothes were defeating her, looking up at her from their places.

And two hours afterwards, when she had fed and changed the baby and put him to sleep in his cot, her mind was constantly on the uncomfortable feeling that had dwelt in her ever since her conversation with them, when she had spoken to them with cruel irony. Now, knowing full well she was doing something she shouldn't, but still letting the spirit of the moment overcome the voice of reason, she went out of the front door carrying a large tray, with a china coffee pot decorated with rosebuds, surrounded by cups with matching saucers and spoons with an engraved pattern, and a plate of round honey cakes. She stood there holding the heavy tray, her head raised, debating whether to put the tray down on the marble landing of the stairs and climb up the wooden ladder that leaned against the building, reaching the edge of the roof, and to invite them down for coffee, or perhaps it would be better to call them from where she was. Constantly aware of her ridiculous position, she suddenly discovered she didn't remember any of their names. Then a head peeked over the edge of the roof, and she found herself calling to him quickly, before he disappeared: "Hello, hello, I have some coffee for you." Ashamed of the shout that had escaped her, she put down the tray and got away before one of them came down and brought her offering up to his companions.

That afternoon, placing her wide-awake baby in his cot, she put on old jeans and Yoel's army jacket and climbed up to the roof to see how they were getting along with the work. The tray with the rosebud pattern coffee pot and the pretty cups stood in a corner of the roof, cigarette butts crushed in the remainder of the murky liquid in the saucers. She stood and looked for a long while at the sight, which she would recall afterwards as a kind of symbol: the fine Rosenthal china from the rich collection her grandmother had brought from Germany heaped up carelessly, lying next to sacks of cement and heavy hammers.

"We finished the concrete rim," said Hassan. who seemed to have taken upon himself the task of spokesman. "Now we have to put water and it dry."

"Is it twenty centimeter?" she spoke like them.

"It twenty to the meter," he took a metal measuring tape out of his pocket.

"Is it two centimeters over the edge of the floor?"

It seemed to her they exchanged hurried glances, as if they had conspired together before she came, and she grew tense and suspicious.

"Did you bring it up two centimeters above the floor?" she repeated her question, her voice sharp and higher than at first.

"It twenty to the meter," he told her again.

"But does it come out above the floor or not?"

"Level with the floor," he spread out his hand to emphasize his words, with a satisfied expression, like a merchant praising his wares.

"That means it's no good," she said.

"Why no good, lady?"

"Because the rain will leak in," she said impatiently, her anger rising at the game he was playing with her while the concrete band was drying steadily. "It has to be two centimeters higher. That's what David said to you, and that's what's written in the contract."

"We say David twenty centimeter."

"At least twenty centimeters," she corrected him, her voice rising and turning to a shout. "And of that, two centimeters above the floor."

"There is twenty centimeter, lady," he said again, his voice like a patient merchant standing up to a customer making a nuisance.

She pursed her lips as if to demonstrate the conversation was useless. She threw her legs over the low wall around the roof and placed her feet on the rungs of the ladder.

"I'm going to get David," she said to the three men standing and looking at her, anxious to see how things would turn out. "If that's the way you're starting—then it's no good," she added. She went down the ladder with a rush to show them the bellicose spirit that animated her steps, inwardly calculating how long it would take her to get to the building on Herzl Street and locate David, and whether it would be better to take Udi with her, or leave him in his cot and hope he was asleep. Planting her feet on the ground, she strode vigorously toward her car, determined to call David in before the concrete band dried. Then she heard a thick voice calling to her from the roof: "Lady, you don't need David. We add two centimeters."

She turned her face upward, suppressing the feeling of relief and victory that surged up through her anger, seeking the three dark heads bunched together. "Quickly then, before it dries," she said in a loud, hard voice.

That evening, her sister Noa told her, her voice coming from Jerusalem mingled with those of other people: "You made a mistake about the coffee. Let them make it themselves, and don't serve them anything anymore. If they get into the house—you'll never get rid of them."

"Don't worry. No one gets into my house without an invitation," she shouted, over the strangers' voices.

But the next day, in the doorway, smiling to her with his eyes as yellow as the winter sun, Hassan, whose name she had learned, said to her, with gentle bashfulness in his voice: "Yesterday lady make coffee. Today I make coffee like in my house." From a plastic bag he withdrew a container of coffee that gave off a fragrance like that in cramped spice shops where coffee grinders crush the dark beans into aromatic grains.

Taken aback by the friendly gesture, as though they hadn't sparred with each other the day before, as though she hadn't been racked all night long with worrying how she would mobilize the police and the courts if they tried again to violate the agreement they had signed, she took a step backward, and before she grasped what was happening, he slipped through the space between her body and the door jamb, stepped over to the range, and put the plastic bag on the marble counter. With precise, expert movement, he took out a long-handled blue coffeepot and a spoon, took a spoonful of coffee, added sugar that he poured out of another bag, and filled the pot with water. Then after fiddling lightly with the lighter and the knobs on the stove he lit and placed the coffeepot on the glowing ring. She observed his motions with astonishment, stunned at the liberty he took in her kitchen, her eyes drawn to his graceful, pleasing movements, knowing danger was latent in what was happening in front of her.

He stood on one foot, his other foot to the side, like a dancer at rest, peeking into the coffeepot now and then. A hissing rose from it, heralding the onset of boiling, and the spoon in his hand stirred without cease, with a fixed circular movement. He said: "We put two more centimeter of cement from yesterday." And she answered: "Fine. I hope there won't be any more problems. David told me you were good workers—so do things right."

Then she combed her hair and washed her face, and before she could change out of her soft mohair shirt that had once been burned in the front by a cigarette so she only wore it around the house, she found herself sitting at the table with his two fellow workers, for whom Hassan had opened the door with a hospitable gesture while she was spreading a cloth on the table in the breakfast nook.

"That's coffee like in our house," he said, looking at her, the smile on his lips not reaching his eyes She sipped the thick, bitter beverage, and smiled involuntarily: "You mean the coffee I made yesterday wasn't good?"

"It was good," he answered quickly, drawing the words out, alarmed at her insult. "Thank you very much. But we like it this way, strong coffee." He clenched his fist and waved it toward her with a vigorous motion, to emphasize his last word.

She heard Udi crying in the next room. This was when he usually had his first bottle of cereal. She excused herself and got up, feeling their eyes on her. She took Udi out of his cot, wrapped in a blanket decorated with ducklings, and carried him into the breakfast nook. Then she placed the bottle of cereal that had been standing on the windowsill in his hands, and it was already lukewarm. Ahmad looked as though hypnotized at the sapphire ring Yoel's parents had given her for their engagement, and the others looked at the baby curled up at her breast in his bright blanket, drinking the cereal with his eyes shut. Hassan suddenly smiled, and his eyes brightened. He enjoyed the sight of the tranquil baby, and he brought his face close to him and said fondly, "You eat everything—you be strong like Hassan."

Months afterwards she would remember that morning with dismay, when she had sat with them for the first time, as though they were at home there, drinking from cups like welcome guests, eating off the violet lace tablecloth her mother-in-law had brought from Spain, looking at her baby over their cups. She sipped the bitter liquid and only part of her, the part that didn't laugh with them, thought: could these hands, serving coffee, be the ones that planted the booby-trapped doll at the gate of the religious school at the end of the street? Her heart, which had been on guard all the time, began to foresee something, but it still didn't know: this was just the beginning, appearing like a figure leaping out of the fog. From now on everything would grow clear and roll down like boulders falling into an abyss. The future would clearly be a fall—and no one could stop it.

⇗ ⇖

In the afternoon, as she gathered up the toys Udi had scattered on the carpet, there was a knock on the door. Hassan appeared with a sooty aluminum pot in one hand and a plastic bag imprinted with the name of the supermarket on the main street in the other, a friendly smile of familiarity on his lips, and he said: "Excuse. Can put soup on fire, lady?"

She stood in the doorway, guarding the border, with her hand extended overhead on the doorframe as if halting all entry. But the warm smile on his face and the way he had asked the question didn't leave room for refusal. The blocking arm slipped down, and with cordial hospitality, as though to mask her first hesitation, she moved her hand in an arc and said, "Please, please." Anger at herself welled up inside her for treating him, despite herself, as a welcome guest.

She went back to gathering up the toys, stealing a look at the way he put the pot under the tap with steady movements, like an expert, boiling water in the blue coffeepot that he pulled out of the bag, finding the barrel-shaped salt cellar in the right-hand drawer, knowingly manipulating the knobs of the range. While she arranged the toys in Udi's room, as he slept between the duckling blanket and the Winnie the Pooh sheet, there stole into her—still faint, still resembling discomfort—the fear born of having people trespass, pushing her boundary back and pretending they were unaware.

When she returned, the other two were already with him in the kitchen. One was cutting vegetables into her new china bowl. The other was standing at the open refrigerator, his hand in the lower vegetable drawer. By the look on his face she could tell he'd been caught in the act. His hand, rummaging among the vegetables, stopped where it was.

"Need cucumber, lady," he said, stepping back.

She went to the refrigerator, slammed the drawer home and took a cucumber out of a sealed bag in the rear of the upper shelf.

"Take it," she said.

"Thank you very much, lady." He took the cucumber from her hand. "Lady drink coffee?" asked Hassan from the stove, stirring his coffeepot and smiling at her from the side.

Confused, fighting to control the muscles of her face, she said, "No thanks."

"Is good coffee," Salah, who spoke only seldom, tried to persuade her.

"Thanks, I don't drink coffee in the afternoon."

"Afternoon, morning—is good coffee." He wouldn't let up. She, already feeling the teeth of the trap closing on her, said, almost shouting: "No!" She saw Hassan open the china cabinet and take out three plates.

A moment before she abandoned her house and her baby, fleeing to the bedroom and locking the door behind her, breaking out in silent, suppressed, helpless weeping, into which dread was already creeping, she told Hassan in a soft, commanding voice: "I'll thank you not to make any noise—my baby is asleep." A few minutes afterwards, when she left her room, her eyes already dry and her voice tranquil, though her heart pounded within her, she said: "Maybe you could cook your soup up there. I'll give you a small camping stove. It's inconvenient for me here." Salah threw a malevolent glance at her over his steaming bowl of soup. And Hassan said politely, "If you please, lady, thank you very much."

For five days she heard them arriving, but by the time she had fed Udi and put him to sleep in his cot, her workers were no longer on the roof. Angrily she calculated that in the past two days they hadn't raised more than a single row of blocks above the stone rim on top of the window. Suspicion stole into her heart that they had taken on another job and, so it wouldn't slip through their fingers before they finished in her house, they had taken it and bound themselves to another boss. That was the way they did things, as the bank teller who knew about her project had taken the trouble to warn her. But in the afternoon, shaken at hearing the familiar noise of the pickup truck and, in her head composing a few harsh sentences to reproach them with, she saw the truck was laden with iron rods, thin and thick. The three of them got out of the cab and set about unloading the truck and the iron rods from hand to hand up to the roof. Calm now, from her window, she watched them at their work. She decided to rest until Udi awoke from his afternoon nap.

For a while she heard them walking around the roof dragging loads, their voices reaching her through the closed blinds of her room. Later, there was a lot of stubborn knocking, which she first took to be part of a dream, and then she heard them at the door. When she opened it the three of them were standing close to each other, with Hassan half a foot-step in front. He said, "Hello, lady, how are you?"

Inwardly bridling at the familiarity he permitted himself in asking that polite question for the first time, and keeping her face frozen, she ignored his question and asked: "Yes?" guessing they would ask permission to heat up their meal.

"Lady, we need money."

Her sister had warned her about that in their last conversation: you mustn't pay them before they've done the work as agreed. She tensed. Her voice rasped more than she intended: "Did you finish putting the iron in place for pouring the concrete?"

"We put band around roof."

"You did the band, but I'm asking about the iron. Did you get the iron ready for pouring the concrete?"

"That's tomorrow, lady."

"You'll get your money tomorrow."

"We need some. Maybe you'll give us lady . . ."

"Tomorrow," she said firmly. "Anyway I don't have so much now. I have to go to the bank."

"Really, lady," Hassan said, looking straight in her eyes and pounding his chest with his fist. "Lady believe. We coming tomorrow, money or no money."

"No money," she said, knowing how Yoel would smile when she told him about this occasion. Hassan turned to his friends, and they put their heads together and whispered. From where she was she saw the back of his neck, his dusty hair, looking gray under the woolen hat with the tattered edges, frayed yarn twisting down. His mates' brows darkened; they put their heads close to each other, taking counsel. One of them pulled a creased wallet from his pocket and seemed to be counting the bank notes in it. He had a worried expression. Within her she was already prepared to withdraw her position and say: "Look, if it's something pressing, I'm prepared to give you what I have in my purse now. . . ." He suddenly turned to her and asked, "Can wash hands in water?" He surprised her so much with the question that, like the morning when he had stood before her with a cooking pot in his hands, she said: "Certainly, certainly," pushing the door open wide, while her only wish was to slam the door in their faces.

They entered hesitantly. Now she saw that Salah was holding a large army knapsack, the kind that Yoel used to extricate from the storeroom when his unit was called for maneuvers. Hassan led the way to the bathroom, looking at her as though asking permission, and the three men made their way in and locked the door: for a long while she heard the sound of running water and the men's boisterous voices. She, walking to and fro in the living room, looked out at the large garden, across from which no other house was visible, and was gripped by sudden fear, thinking of what might be in that big knapsack. Perhaps they were assembling weapons there, spreading the steel parts out on the carpet, as Yoel had done once, kneeling on the floor and joining the shining parts one to another. Maybe they would come out in a little while with their weapons drawn and threaten her and her son? Perhaps they would take them as hostages in their pickup truck? And what about Udi? She had already run out of his special flour, and she wouldn't be able to feed him when they kept them there in their broken-down shacks in Gaza, among the muddy paths. They had shown those shacks on an American television documentary. Maybe, the thought flashed through her like lightning, she should snatch Udi out of his cot and flee with him, lay him in the back seat of her car and drive immediately to the police station on the main street.

Hassan came out first, and she was startled at his appearance. For a second she imagined a stranger had come out. For the first time she saw him without the woolen cap pulled down over his forehead. His hair, surprisingly light, freshly combed and damp, was brushed to the side, well-combed, and pulled over his temples. He wore a dark, well-pressed jacket over a white shirt and tie. His black dress shoes were highly polished.

He told her: "My friends come out minute, lady."

"Aren't you going home?"

"Have wedding from our aunt in Tulkarem. We today in Tulkarem."

At that moment the baby let out a screech more piercing than any she'd heard since the morning he had burst out of her in the maternity ward: high and prolonged, followed by a sudden silence. She herself let out a scream and rushed to the room, pushing his rolling highchair out of the way as she ran. Udi was prostate on the floor, lying on his stomach, his face on the carpet spread at the foot of his crib, with a toy between his fingers. She bent down and picked him up, carrying him in her arms, and he looked at her with cloudy eyes. She hugged him close to her body and started murmuring things without knowing what she was saying, her heart pounding wildly, making her fingers tremble. After a long while he burst out crying, resting his head on her shoulder in sobs.

"Is okay, lady," Hassan said from the doorway, and she looked around in panic, not realizing he had followed her.

"What?" she asked fearfully.

"Is okay he like so, lady," he traced his finger along his cheek and made a crying expression. "Is nothing. He good that way."

"What's good?" she asked as the baby trembled in her arms.

Hassan approached her and gently lifted Udi from her arms. "Lady get water," he said softly. "He need drink."

In the kitchen, her hands still trembling, she stood still for a long time, trying to remember where the sugar bowl was. She heard Hassan talking softly to the baby in Arabic, like a man who loves to talk to his child, in a caressing voice, the words running together in a pleasant flow, containing a high beauty, like the words of a poem in an ancient language that you don't understand, but that well up inside you. Udi, lying tranquilly on his chest, reached out towards Hassan's dark face, and

Hassan put his head down toward the little fingers and kissed them. She, stunned by the sight, stood where she was and looked at them, as the tremor inspired by fear gradually died down, and another, new kind of trembling, arose within her, seeing something which, even as it happens, you already long for from a distance, knowing that when it passes, nothing like it will happen again, and, as though dividing themselves, her thoughts turned to Yoel, whose eyes examined his son from a certain distance. He was careful not to wrinkle his clothes or have them smell of wet diapers.

Hassan looked up at her and said, "Hassan have like this at home in Gaza."

"You have a baby?" She was astonished. "You're married?"

"Also like this. Four years," he said proudly, placing his hand parallel to the floor to measure the height of his son.

"You okay," Hassan said in his soft voice, turning his face to the baby. "You big—you doctor like daddy, yes?"

With the bottle of tea in her hand, she was shaken as though by a distant alarm. Troubled by the suspicion that he knew more than he should, she said, "You can read Hebrew?" and he laughed. "I read one word, another word. I see Doctor on door in English."

"You can read English?" There was some mockery in her voice, like an adult talking to a child about grown-up things.

"I can," he answered in English, smiling, for the first time, with another smile, hidden, without the forced humility she was familiar with.

"Where from," she asked, also in English.

"From the University."

"Which one?"

"The American University of Beirut." She recognized his good accent from having heard it on television when Arabic-speaking intellectuals were interviewed. She hadn't been able to shake off her Israeli accent in the two years she had lived in Texas, while Yoel finished his degree.

"Really?" She returned to Hebrew.

"Really lady. I in Beirut two years. Maybe I be doctor that way, of babies."

"Why didn't you complete your studies?"

"Hard. Can't talk." He looked down at his hands, whose nails were free of lime. "Life like that."

Shortly after he left, joining his comrades who were waiting for him and watching him from the door, also scrubbed. She thought: they're nameless and ageless for me, in their faded black sweaters and their dirty elbows and stocking caps. They had a single face and uncouth words came from their mouths. Suddenly they were different: in white collars and jackets, their cheeks shaven, with a wife and baby and a child of four at home.

Even before she heard the bell ring she knew he had returned.

"My jacket, lady," he said and went to take his jacket, folded carefully on the back of the chair. And, at the door, with his back to her, he turned around with a carefully planned motion that made itself out to be spontaneous. "If lady want I stay now."

"Where?" she asked in astonishment.

"With lady," he answered seriously. "Mister of lady no here. Maybe need something. . . ." And she, stunned at the very words and frightened that he knew of her husband's absence, wondered if he meant what she thought she had heard. She said, "But you're going to a wedding, aren't you?"

"Going to wedding. But if lady want—I can be here. . . ."

After she had locked the door, still staggered at his suggestion, she suddenly noticed: Yoel's smell had come from the delicate odor of the fragrance on the shelf of the right-hand cabinet next to the mirror. They had used her husband's toiletries, dried themselves on her towels. She carefully put Udi down in the cot and hurried to the bathroom.

With convulsive movements, like a madwoman, she gathered up the towels and threw them all, averting her head with a bilious feeling, into the washing machine, throwing the new soap into the garbage pail. She began polishing the taps and sink and scouring with disinfectant the floor that their bare feet had trod on.

But toward evening a tense quiet descended on her, something new. At night, before falling asleep, she remembered how Hassan had held Udi close to his chest and spoken to him in Arabic that sounded like a song; his long fingers, clean for the first time of spots of paint; the English he had spoken, sounding like human language for the first time instead of the broken phrases he knew in Hebrew. Only she preferred to set aside his offer to stay with her and not consider it. She thought back over things, seeing that she had been hard on them. They had gone to a wedding in Tulkarem. Maybe they had asked for money to buy a present for the newlyweds, and she had behaved unfeelingly with them. The unease that gripped her was assuaged when she promised herself that early the next morning she would take Udi in his carriage and go out to the main street and, in the elegant store that had recently opened, she would buy clothes for his two children. Then she thought: it would not be right to offer him a gift, as a declaration of a special relationship, and not to honor his cousins. Generously she decided she would buy something for them as well. Maybe cologne like the kind Yoel kept on his shelf. If the weather was stormy, she'd take Udi in the car. An hour later, she suddenly interrupted herself as she read: if it rained hard, she'd leave Udi at the babysitter's.

She waited for them until noon, their gifts in pretty wrapping paper, tied with curling ribbon, lying on the cabinet next to the front door, and the white envelope with their money next to the packages.

⇜ ⇝

At noon she began to worry: maybe they had drunk too much and had an accident. What if the police came? She panicked. Maybe it wasn't legal for her to employ them. If they were badly injured and couldn't continue the job, the construction would be delayed and maybe not completed by the time Yoel returned. In the afternoon, tired and angry at her helplessness and concern about the future, she decided to go to the building where David was working. Maybe some members of the same family were working for him, and they too had been invited to the wedding in Tulkarem, and she could find something out from them. For a long time she waited for David, pushing the carriage back and forth on the battered pavement in front of the building site. When he came he told her that the wedding hadn't been in Tulkarem at all, but in a village near the Lebanese border. They would be coming as usual the next day, he reassured her, seeing her worried face. Afterwards he scratched the nape of his neck and asked: "So it's okay, the job they're doing?"

"I hope so," she said.

"What are they doing now?"

"They're setting up the iron rods to pour the concrete."

"Are they doing it right?"

"I don't know. I trust them."

⇜ ⇝

The next day, anger making her fingertips tremble, so troubled her breathing was affected, she waited for them on the roof in the morning after leaving Udi with the babysitter and arranging to do so again during the coming days. Hassan got out of the cab and smiled brightly at her. With his filthy woolen cap and his shoes down at the heel he was once again what he had been.

"Something happen, lady?" His voice betrayed his surprise at finding her on the roof at that early hour.

"A great deal has happened," she shouted to him, leaning over the wall at the edge of the roof.

"What's the matter, lady?" he asked, climbing the ladder on his way up to her.

"First of all, you lied to me."

"Lied?" The shadow of his smile was erased.

"The wedding was in Tulkarem?" She flung out the words, her hand on her hips, like a mother arguing with a child caught out in a lie.

"No lady. Wedding not in Tulkarem."

"That's what you told me."

"I said: my aunt from Tulkarem. The wedding not. There in village near Kibuss."

He turned to face his comrades, as though asking, and Ahmad said, "Kibuss Ga'aton."

"Ga'aton," Hassan repeated the name of the kibbutz, looking at her again.

"But you didn't say you wouldn't come to work yesterday."

"We think sleep in Tulkarem and come work yesterday. No possible."

"That's one thing," she ignored the explanation. "Another thing, David was here yesterday and he said you didn't do anything well. You didn't raise the concrete band two centimeters the way we said. And you put in number eight iron rods instead of number twelve, and you made one wall with fifteen centimeter blocks instead of twenty centimeters . . . ."

"That wall has window, lady. Must be little."

"You need a number three block near the sliding window," she exploded at his effort to fool her. "But the wall is an outer wall. You were supposed to use twenty centimeter blocks . . ." she added, scolding him, watching the color ebb from his face, and how his comrades froze behind his back.

"We do everything good. Lady want—David come here. We talk."

"I don't want you to talk!" she screamed. "I want you to work. You've been working for a month. What you've done could have been done in a week. You just drink coffee, slip away, and work somewhere else."

"Somewhere else?" he asked in amazement.

"On Monday. Where were you?"

He wrinkled his forehead in thought. "Monday we bring iron."

"Fine," she said, raising her chin and walking forward with vigor and sitting on the edge of the wall. "I want to see how much you get done today."

For seven hours she sat on the wall, without moving, not going down to turn off the water heater she had lit in the morning, suppressing the hunger that awoke within her, the need for a cup of coffee at the hour when her body was used to one, and, in the afternoon, fighting the pain in her back, which cried out for something to lean on, watching as they worked angrily, talking little, boiling water in an empty can on the camping stove she'd lent them, sitting down to eat with their legs crossed, close to each other, whispering to each other. All those hours she watched them as though riveted to the spot, only occasionally looking away from them, allowing her eyes to wander to the tops of the cypress trees and the purple mountains in the distance, the view of which, at a peaceful hour, she would enjoy. Later, when she recalled that morning, she would tremble as though the event were not irrevocably in the past: how had the courage to treat them that way been born within her? They could easily have come and pushed her, and she would have fallen and broken her neck. By the time anyone found her among the iron rods in the backyard, she would no longer be alive.

Occasionally Ahmad cast a glance at her, like a fearful child checking to see whether the ghost he had seen was still hovering in the area. But Hassan didn't look at her once. Seeing him, his clamped lips, and the line drawn behind his jaw, above his clenched teeth, she knew she had deeply wounded him, but she felt no remorse for doing so. Only the sweet consolation of someone who deals justly with himself, a feeling that rose and fell within her great anger.

They raised the iron rods over the edge of the masonry walls and laid them crisscross at regular intervals, tying them with thin wire. Afterwards they crowded steel struts into the room to support the wooden forms under the network. When they finished, they consulted among themselves for a moment and headed for the ladder, parting from her with a slight nod.

"Wait," she called to them. "You've earned your money." She followed them down the ladder and went into the house. When she came out she put the envelope in Hassan's hand. Only after they had left without a word did she remember she hadn't asked them to sign a receipt for the money or given them the wrapped parcels from the cupboard.

The next day, after leaving Udi with the babysitter despite a reddish rash on his skin showing he hadn't been changed in time, she was already waiting for them on the roof as though spoiling for a fight.

Today, she thought, stunned at the idea, they'll pour the concrete for the roof. The network of iron rods was prepared and the steel struts were in place. The wooden forms were raised, the buckets of gravel and sand were covered under plastic sheets, and the sacks of cement were arranged next to them. Today they would pour the roof and the weather was fine. The transparent clouds didn't herald rain.

When she heard the sound of the pickup truck she leaped to the edge of the roof, and even before she actually saw them she noticed his absence. Three men sat in the cab, and he wasn't one of them. Salah and Ahmad got out of the left door, wearing gray woolen hats. Then a man with a shaven head got out of the truck, looking like a fugitive she had seen in an Italian movie, who had made his way to a widow's home in a village and laid siege to it. In one look she took in his black eyes, like the maw of a coal mine. His eyebrows meeting over the bridge of his nose. A strange feeling overcame her, like when all her girlfriends had been asked to dance, and she was left alone sitting by the wall, looking at the legs moving in the dark.

"Where's Hassan?" she asked Ahmad.

"Hassan no come. This one come, Muhammad."

Observing from her corner on the wall, trying to repress the desolate feeling that grew stronger within her, she watched them put on rubber boots and mix the concrete with shovels, adding sand and gravel and pouring water, stirring it to produce a thick gray mixture in the square they had enclosed with wooden beams. Then Muhammad climbed up to the edge of the roof. Ahmad handed him bucket after bucket, brimming with the gray concrete and he swung and emptied them in big arcs over the network of iron rods, while Salah quickly filled in the space between the two wooden planks below, to stop the concrete from dribbling out.

Sitting erect on the edge of the roof, her knee swinging, her arms crossed, she felt her anger give way to disappointment at Hassan's absence. Suddenly it became clear to her that he had come between her and them, serving as a kind of protective barrier for them. Here she stood exposed to the three of them: Salah stole furtive glances at her, as though already hatching a foul plot in his mind; Ahmad smiled right at her, baring his yellow teeth like the fangs of a beast; and the new worker, standing high on the upper concrete band, his body tense, his hands on his hips, stared at her openly. From where she sat his figure looked mighty, and his shaven head resembled a crooked egg against the background of the sky above him.

She sat where she was for hours, no longer strong with the anger that had gripped her the previous morning, making her decide to sit and see with her own eyes how well they would work under supervision, but now out of fear to get up and raise her legs over the edge of the roof in front of them. They worked without stopping, diligently, bringing up the contents of the big pool of concrete and spreading it on the network of rods. From time to time they would consult each other, exchange shouts in Arabic, sing a line or two, laughing out loud into their hands. And she, sensing they were laughing at her, was angry, insulted, and fearful. She watched them cook their meal, kneeling next to each other on the torn mat, tearing with their teeth at loaves of bread they held in their hands.

"What now?" She turned to Ahmad, keeping her voice steady.

"Now must dry."

"If it rains?"

"Now two hours—good. Not two hours—no good."

"The roof is twenty centimeters?"

"Yes, yes," he said, and she thought since that morning she hadn't heard them say "lady." She turned, pointed at the floor they had left spotted with cement. "Wash that down before it dries," she ordered, pretending she still had strength.

"No dry. We put water."

She stepped to the edge of the protruding ladder and grasped the wooden rung and, as though incidentally, turned to them, "What's the matter with Hassan?"

"Hassan no come."

"I see that."

"This one Muhammad come."

"Will Hassan come tomorrow?"

"Tomorrow, tomorrow, tomorrow—Hassan no come."

"Did something happen to him?"

"He not here."

She carefully raised her legs, and when she had descended, even before her feet touched the ground, she heard their deep, guttural laugh, and she blushed. That's how men laughed at women when they spoke ill of them.

The next day, waiting at the window, she knew why her legs had taken her there, why she had arisen early to prepare the kitchen, why she had checked how much coffee was left in the bag he had brought with him from home.

Salah and Ahmad came alone. She, knowing in her heart she

wouldn't see Hassan again, was glad the shaven-headed Muhammad wasn't with them. Swallowing her pride she went out and stood before them

"Is Hassan sick?" she asked.

"No sick."

"He won't come to work?"

"He work someone."

"Why isn't he working here? Three will finish faster."

Salah, perhaps seeing through her deceptive sentences, smiled somewhere in the depths of his eyes, the mockery of someone careful not to be tripped up.

"He no want come to lady."

"He doesn't want to get his money?"

"No want," said Salah, and she imagined she heard an echo of triumph in his voice.

"He doesn't want to get his money?"

"No want money, no want lady," he said. She no longer had anything to say after that sentence, but she spoke in her normal voice: "Very well, then finish by yourselves. You can make coffee in the kitchen if you want. There's still some of the coffee you brought."

Salah and Ahmad kept coming for a few more days after the concrete on the roof had dried, removing the steel struts that held up the forms. They put in the door and bars over the window and broke through the upper room into the breakfast nook. She didn't ask about Hassan again, but they sometimes volunteered that they had met him. She, stirred by the sound of his name, gave in and made the final payment before they finished the work. Perhaps they would run into Hassan and tell him of her generosity. But they never came back. They left the walls unplastered and forgot their tools behind the wall. Shaken with fury, again pushing her baby carriage, she roamed among the construction sites and hired workers to finish the plastering: they tarred the roof, and installed the electric wiring.

⟋ ⟋

By the time Yoel returned she had a new hairstyle. They stood on the stairs leading to the bright, pleasant room on the roof, with three barrels in the corners from which palm trees sent up sharp bayonets all about, their fronds growing like a conjuring trick. He stood in amazement before the new structure and then burst out laughing. "Well, I'll be. . . . You leave a woman for two months, come back—and the world's

changed!" On the roof, his arm around her shoulder in a gesture of respect, he wandered from one corner of the roof to another, inspecting
the landscape, and sliding his hand along the walls: "I didn't want to
do it, I admit, but it's really nice. Was it very dirty?"

"Not so terrible."

"You found the workers?"

Stroking the rough wall unawares she said, "They were relatively decent, workers from the territories."

"What, Arabs?" he asked, looked at her reproachfully, getting serious.

"Arabs. You can't find anyone else. But every day a Jewish foreman
came to keep an eye on them, the one working in the building at Herzl
Street."

"They behaved all right? They didn't make trouble?"

She took a quick, deep breath, with a whistling sound, and—re-
straining the whirlpool of emotions stirring within her, looking away,
clearly seeing Muhammad standing on the edge of the upper roof, staring at her with hatred, and the flash in their eyes when she got up and
stood in this very place and accused them—seeing Hassan's fists clench
and the crease along the line of his jaw when he clasped his teeth shut,
hearing the rumble of the men's laughter when she raised her legs to
climb down the ladder—she said, "They were fairly decent. Once Udi
fell down and I was really alarmed. One of them picked him up so gently and calmed him down, you wouldn't believe it. He spoke to him
softly and kissed his fingers. Then it turned out he had studied medicine
for two years. He wanted to be a pediatrician but for some reason he
didn't finish his degree. He has a baby Udi's age and another boy of
four. . . ." Suddenly she noticed the softness flowing into her voice, be-
traying herself to herself, and she added loudly, more stridently than she
intended: "But once they made some trouble about the money and tried
to trick me by putting in iron rods that were too thin. Arabs, you
know. . . ."

Translated from the Hebrew by Jeffrey M. Green.

THE STORE

David Ehrlich

When Micha Rothman and his group founded our village eighty-two years ago, not a single road in Palestine had been paved yet, and there were hardly any settlements at all to the north and east of ours. Once every day or two a horseback rider or carriage would pass along the road, and everyone would gather around to hear the news and gossip from Jaffa and from the other villages.

Peace and quiet, that was our character throughout the years. Quiet, and hard work, and lending a hand when it was required, but also carefully guarding one another's privacy, each of us minding our own business.

We take pride in that.

With all due modesty it should be noted that our village thrived and prospered beyond the expectations of its founders. There was no farm in the village that did not supply the Tnuva company with fine milk, excellent eggs, or lusciously sweet fruit. There was no home that did not raise three or four children, most of whom returned here immediately after their army service without descending into drugs or dangerous treks through jungles. Even during the worst of the economic recession of the eighties we were far from financial ruin. No one went into debt, no one asked for help.

Even when they built the new highway, which passed literally meters from the Barkay's back fence, we weren't much affected. Villages less solidly rooted than our own went through difficult transitions when the wave of modernization washed through their streets. But in our case, either because of our lack of interest in the world, or because of the world's lack of interest in us, the atmosphere of the good old days lingered, and each of us held our own against the evil winds that blew. Even when the trucks barreled past, hauling their loads back and forth, perpetually delivering newspapers that had more colors than news, even then we could hear, beyond the roar, the rustle of the wings of birds who still remembered that, once, there were swamps here.

And then Lucy Galili died. Lucy, Elchanan's widow, was stronger than steel, with roots that were deeply and firmly planted, and the spark in her eyes seemed to have leapt from one generation to another, radiating wisdom and experience since the days of Adam.

The only thing was, they had no children.

Immediately after the funeral the great dispute over their house began. Some of us wanted to put in a library, a few suggested a small museum, and others thought that we should build a synagogue on the property.

But before the dispute could really heat up, to everyone's amazement a relative suddenly appeared. Needless to say, this person had never set foot in the village during the long lifetime of the Galilis. Moreover, there were some who remembered Lucy explicitly stating that she had no family, anywhere. But unfortunately this man, who was wearing what was perhaps the first suit that had ever appeared among us, proved that he was indeed a nephew of a cousin of Lucy's who had been killed in the Holocaust. And before we could grow accustomed to the idea and put a stop to the rest of the process, the man entered into a selling frenzy.

It should be understood that none of us had any experience with such matters. We did not know whether we should be taking legal action to try to stop the man, and if so, how to do it, and we also were unsure about the ethical justification for such a step, since, after all, the house did not belong to us.

Now, of course, we regret our inaction.

We regarded with astonishment the cast of characters that walked around and into poor Lucy's house, types we could scarcely believe existed in this country of ours, and wondered what interest they could possibly have in our village. The potential buyers appeared in succession as if in some horror movie, each with his own vision: one wanted to set up a stud farm, the second a restaurant, and the third intended to bring in beehives. What they shared was a basic unsuitability for our village, and also a complete lack of interest in the primary question of whether the inhabitants of the village wanted them or not.

Everything happened very quickly. In the course of two weeks, Elchanan Galili's house had been sold to a couple from Netanya. Rumor had it that the price reached a half million dollars, a purely imaginary sum for most of us. Until that point it had not occurred to any of us that our plots of land had any particular financial value, the whole question of price having been simply irrelevant.

From Uri Samit's nearby porch we watched them unload furniture from a truck, and then take a stroll around the orchard, and a few days later paint the house a vulgar shade of cream. Every once in a while they waved hello at us. We responded unenthusiastically. At that point we were not yet aware of how careful we had to be with this apparently naive couple.

After a few weeks they suddenly noticed that they had neighbors. Every day they knocked on someone else's door, introduced themselves, and wanted to have a conversation, it wasn't clear about what. To the best of our knowledge no one responded positively to these belated attempts at neighborliness. It was clear that they wanted something, and whatever that something was, no good could possibly come of it.

That may be why the matter of the store came as such a complete surprise.

One day Ilan, Yossi Amir's younger son, went running through the village calling, "A store, a store," his voice breaking as if someone were trying to murder him. It turned out that, overnight, they had put up a billboard the size of a movie screen by the side of the highway to draw attention and direct traffic to the old Galili house, in which they were selling junk they had acquired the devil knows where.

By the end of the week more people had wandered around our village than had come through since its founding. In one fell swoop we had been transformed from some completely anonymous place to a point of interest on the Israeli map, a well-known attraction throughout the region and a necessary stop from anywhere to anywhere. It was impossible to work in the field for more than an hour running without some dubious face popping up before your eyes to ask where the restrooms were, or how much you were selling your house for, or which way was Eilat.

That couple seemed to have a sense for what would sell. We

couldn't understand why sane people would stop on their way home from the Sea of Galilee to buy such worthless junk. We snuck in there and were amazed at the illogical assortment of things they were selling: a faded umbrella for twenty shekels, a broken toaster, an old radio with a green lightbulb, old records. Everything was in complete disarray, a mishmash of things that people had thrown out. In the middle of this mess they had draped cloths from the East, peacock feathers, broken seashells, and who knows what else. At the far end of the store sat the man from Netanya, solemnly ringing up purchases on his cash register, the bell of which echoed from one end of the village to the other, while the woman roamed importantly among the bargains, tossing around lies about the history of each piece of trash. It was especially nauseating to find Lucy Galili's blue dress in a heap of clothing, and Elchanan's broken pitchfork, and a whole host of other objects that bore so many memories for us, each of which was worth more than the gang that was putting them up for sale.

The main problem that faced us now was the inevitable corruption that awaited our younger generation. For eighty-two years we had been, without being aware of it, a place of peace and quiet, values, and beauty. And now, suddenly, the ground had erupted beneath our feet and all the filth of the country was breaking into our streets, strolling about our yards without anyone stopping it, threatening to pour its evil stench over everything.

As if in mourning we gathered to take counsel. Few of us had any ideas. After all, we were practical people, people who worked and toiled, honest and loyal as the day is long. How could we navigate the twisted ways that dominated the landscape over the horizon?

It was decided that we should have a talk with them.

Clearly, no one was eager to take the mission upon himself. Heads bowed, the delegation of three who had been chosen by lot went out to meet the couple from Netanya. It is not difficult to imagine the conversation between them, three older farmers whose strength was in their hands, not their mouths, and the slippery pair who had invaded our lives. "You can live here, that would be fine," someone said, "but you have no right to turn our village into the whole country's whorehouse." The man and woman, for their part, tried to defend themselves with clever talk and with the absurd proposition that they make a symbolic contribution to the village by erecting a monument to its war dead. The conversation became no more fruitful after continuing for some five minutes. Our people were not swayed by the lady of the house's invitation to have a cup of coffee, and certainly not to sit down, and they left more or less as they had come.

Two days passed and nothing happened. It is hard to believe that those people did not sense the ground burning beneath their feet. The village, like a living, breathing creature, was preparing to vomit them forth, and even if no one expressed it in words, the matter hung in the air as threatening and tangible as a loaded gun.

With no particular ardor and with even less skill we took the necessary steps. Katz's wife called them up to tell them that they would have to go. Then a note written in unambiguous terms was placed on their doorstep. It was clear that if that did not work, nothing would, and that with every passing day our situation was becoming more dangerous. Nevertheless, we held off for another whole day.

That night, terrible winds blew. As if in response to a call, we all assembled on Uri Samit's porch and gazed sorrowfully into the night. There, in the heart of the darkness, stood the small house, surrounded by an orchard and field and meadow, with a dovecote on the right and an abandoned dog kennel on the left, except that because the low clouds covered the moon, it all looked like one solid dark mass, whistling in the wind like a hoarse flute. None of us said a word. There was no plan. With smoldering eyes we all faced in the same direction, as if everything was perfectly obvious. What remains uncertain is which of us went first, if, in fact, anyone did. But everyone was there, walking into the darkness in a single row, tense and ready. In one motion we all lit matches, in one motion we tossed them into the thorns, and together we stood and watched the fire break out and roll from the field toward the house. From all four directions the house caught fire and was utterly consumed.

Of course, none of us intended to harm the people inside the house. No one knows why they didn't manage to wake up and escape. Did the fire spread too quickly, or were they under the influence of sleeping pills or drugs or some such thing? Undoubtedly the heaps of junk they kept in their store helped fuel the flames: the cloth went up in smoke as if it had been designed to ignite, and apparently the proprietors were simply trapped in the flaming inferno.

By the time the firemen arrived there was nothing for them to do but compliment us on our rapid mobilization in extinguishing the blaze. We thanked them for thanking us and waited for the ambulance to arrive and take the bodies away. Among us passed the thought, probably unexpressed, that we should report what had occurred, but of course we refrained from doing so.

The people collected evidence for the next two or three days and rapidly came to the conclusion that the fire had probably been set by Arabs, one of many such incidents of arson that had been spreading through the country.

We were surprised to learn that the couple from Netanya had no heirs. We were compelled to bury them and say a few nice words ourselves. We waited for a while, convinced that something was about to happen, but nothing did. We took down the sign above the store, rescued what trees we could in the orchard, and finally assembled again to discuss the future of the plot.

Again a few people suggested putting in a library, others, a small museum, and there were those who brought up again the idea of the synagogue. But because of a general unwillingness to get entangled in investments the plot still sits there, abandoned.

Translated from the Hebrew by Naomi Seidman.

A MATTER OF IDENTITY

Shulamith Hareven

The two women came at the end of the day. Winding stairs brought them to the lawyer's office, on the top floor of an old Jerusalem building. In the next room was a newspaper cutting agency, and then came the conveniences from which the smell of Lysol spread far and wide. They both puffed their way up till they got there.

"Here it is," said the older woman with a triumphant flourish. She had a flattish, distinctively Slavic face that was somewhere between innocence and a kind of pugnacity. She was one of those women whose body is not important because her actual presence means more than her shape. There she was, puffing and panting, raising her voice, waving her arms, always doing something, plucking a chicken, or cutting material with a sure hand, or dangling a baby. Always doing.

The dim light on the stairs went out. The woman groped for the phosphorescent button, but nobody had bothered to fix one on the upper floor. Or maybe it had peeled off or was out of order. Her hand collected whitewash and tiny bits of plaster. She wiped it once and again on her skirt with the motions of a peasant woman, and said to the younger woman, in Russian:

"Well, how about it, are we to enter in the dark? Go down, darling, go down and give us a little light."

"I wouldn't bother," said the other in a voice that carried constant dissatisfaction and complaint. And at that moment the door of the lawyer's office opened and a client emerged.

The older woman's face lit up. She placed her hand on the lintel of the door to make sure it did not close and leave her in the dark again.

Behind a counter sat a lean, long-toothed woman clerk with her bag open in front of her, making up her face in a compact mirror, getting ready to leave.

"We to the lawyer come," the woman explained in a clumsy Hebrew. She seemed to have grown a little smaller in the presence of the clerk, who shrugged her shoulders—her mouth was pursed in a kind of open triangle, ready for the lipstick—as she pointed toward the inner room. The two entered, and the older woman introduced herself and her daughter.

✒ ✑

In the neon light the lawyer examined the daughter's face. She was like the mother, yet unlike her. The pugnacity in her face was less innocent, more aggressive. She was weaker than her mother, not so good. She was wearing a ready-made rose-colored blouse and a snake-green skirt. Over her shoulder hung a chain with a plastic bag at the end. She ought to be wearing plastic sandals with gold or silver straps, but here came a surprise: she was wearing good leather shoes. Must have received them from the lady for whom she works, thought the lawyer, and she doesn't know how to look after them.

He wasn't particularly happy at their arrival. He was tired after a long day, and that evening he had to join his weekly group. It was his practice to meet several friends in a private seminar for expert discussions on Jewish law, and he did not want to be late, even though they had had mighty little to say about law in recent years and had exchanged jokes and scandal instead. They had all grown older.

"I heard that Mister Lawyer Russian speaking," said the woman hesitantly, in Hebrew of a sort.

"I speak it."

"Thank the Lord, my dear," she promptly went on in Russian. "It's hard for me to explain it all in Hebrew. Here's this daughter of mine, she was born to me in Russia. Me, Mister Lawyer, I'm a Russian soul from Krementchug Province, and during the war my fiancé, Stepan, just got lost on us and left me in the family way. Afterward I got to know a Jewish man there, a refugee, Perlmutter they called him, and together we traveled around so much, so much, we got as far as Turkestan, and there my daughter was born to me. And after that my new fiancé, namely Perlmutter, he wanted to go to Palestine, to Israel that is, and we went with him. We didn't have an easy life here, oh no. We lived in a convent, and Perlmutter ran away. Yes, ran away, that's what he did. I always say, why did he bring us with him if he wanted to run away? But that's what he did. You find such people in the world. And so my daughter grew up like that, and now she's a big girl."

"If you want me to look for this Perlmutter—" said the lawyer impatiently.

"No, no, what do I want Perlmutter for? I never got married to him and I haven't anything in common with him. Let him go his way and we'll go ours. That's the way things are. Only there's one thing: my daughter wants to go to Canada. And I said, good, you want to go, to find yourself a new life—go in peace. Only when we went to the consulate, they told us it isn't clear who she is, what her identity is officially, that means whether she's Perlmutter's or Stepan's or whose. I explained, I explained, and they didn't understand. And they didn't want to give her a visa. They just didn't want. That's why we are here, Mister Lawyer. That's to say, you understand the law, and you'll find us the identity of my daughter so the consul will permit her to go to Canada, and we'll wish you good health."

"That can be checked out in the population register," said the lawyer. "You have the right to go there yourself. Why waste your money?"

The woman flapped her arms in alarm.

"What do I understand of all that Population, Mister! You go, you check for us in that Population, and we'll pay you your fee, and depart in peace."

The lawyer rang for his clerk, but she had already vanished. Her time was up. So he sat down at a neighboring table with a typewriter, and with two fingers tapped out a power of attorney. The glass that covered the little cabinet of law books rang sharply to every letter he struck, and the girl stared at the glass with childish curiosity. She put her finger on the quivering glass and the ringing stopped. The phenomenon interested her. Again and again she tried to block the vibrating glass with her finger, and she felt sorry when the typing was over, staring at her finger for a long time.

Her mother signed in a slow, Cyrillic script, wherever he pointed.

She gave her address: an old convent in the north of the city. There she was doing everything, she said, cleaning up and buying greens for the convent; and there she had a little room to this day.

The lawyer fixed an appointment with them, rose, and began to lock up. The woman wanted to go on talking to him on the way, since she rarely had an opportunity to speak Russian outside her convent; but he didn't like talking to clients after finishing their business. He waited a few moments till their footsteps could no longer be heard, then he put out the light and went down himself.

Near the stairway was a grocery shop, a focus of light and life in the murky Jerusalem evening. He entered and bought rolls and the daily cheese ration for his cat. In its kitten days it had caterwauled a great deal, and he had named it Katzenbach, meaning: the Bach of all the cats. But since then it had fattened up and was quiet.

Out in the street, on the way to his car, the lawyer wondered why the woman should be so ready to have her daughter go off to Canada. Most mothers try to keep their daughters at home. And all the more since this mother was all alone.

⌁ ⌁

"The news isn't very good," said the lawyer gravely to the woman, who came alone this time without explaining her daughter's absence. "I inspected the population register. To begin with, your daughter's a minor."

"Well yes, of course," said the woman. "During the war she was born, of course she is a minor. Sixteen years old. But she's a clever girl, and a worker too. She'll manage nicely in Canada. Yes."

"And second, she's registered as Perlmutter's daughter."

"My dear, and how would you have me register her? Wartime it was, and where could a woman go all alone with a bastard baby? Perlmutter was living with me then, we ate together, we slept together, we came to Palestine together with him, to Israel that is. And how should I register her if not by his name?"

"Well, nobody's blaming you," said the lawyer. "But because of that registration your daughter can't go to Canada without the permission of her father, or the one who is registered as her father. And that means Perlmutter."

The woman was shocked.

"How is that? How can it be like that, Mister Lawyer? That isn't justice. Did he bring her up? He didn't bring her up, he ran away. But

I didn't run away anywhere, I didn't abandon her, poor bastard, I brought her up, and now he has the power to decide whether she is to go to Canada or not? And where can I go searching for Perlmutter now, tell me? These fifteen years I haven't found him. Maybe he's abroad."

"Now look," said the lawyer, "your daughter is registered as the daughter of a Jewish father, that of Perlmutter, whether it's correct or not. Which means she is half Jewish, and as a minor she can't leave the country unless her Jewish father agrees. That's the law."

"What Jewish father, Lord God in heaven?" wondered the woman. "But she's Stepan's, not Perlmutter's, and Stepan wasn't a Jew, only my boy in Krementchug Province, no, he never was a Jew, *he* wasn't." She leaned toward him and said once again, very clearly, as though talking to a deaf man: "She is from Stepan, not from Perlmutter."

"I believe you," said the lawyer drily, "but that's the law."

"Yes, it's the law," the woman suddenly agreed. "What's to be done, my dear, maybe we should look for Perlmutter. Don't worry, Lawyer darling," she said to the lawyer, "you can go to sleep quietly, I'll find him. I'll find him and I'll get permission from him."

"And if he doesn't give it?"

"Well, God will aid us," said the woman. Though she had accepted the situation, she still looked astonished.

"Only that this law should be like that, well, well! Who would expect such a thing! The law isn't fair, really it isn't fair."

The lawyer looked at her with some annoyance. For some reason he found it hard to picture the girl whom he had seen in his office as being half Jewish; but it seemed to him that the woman could not know for certain whose daughter she was. Maybe there was something Jewish about her after all, maybe she was the fortuitous daughter and granddaughter of some Perlmutters or other, the granddaughter of woodsmen or innkeepers. Maybe she was of Khazar stock. Who could know? There are so many Perlmutters in the world. Maybe she had received from him those evasive eyes, that floury pallor. Once upon a time people had known their ancestry and the families to which they belonged. A match and marriage had involved several families. Nowadays everything was at sixes and sevens. And here was this girl with her frizzled hair, her makeup, and her plastic, who didn't even know who she was and who her father had been. That wasn't how things ought to be, he thought. A man has to know what his fathers did before he was there.

The lawyer himself had neither wife nor child. He was a tall, thin, willowy man with ivory skin and carefully tended nails, about seventy years old, exceedingly clean, wearing gold-rimmed pince-nez, which surprisingly were just coming back into fashion. Since his branch of the family was coming to an end with him, he was very much concerned with his own pedigree for the sake of his sister's children, who did not in the least care who they were. He considered that it was his function in life to make matters clear to those who were not interested, to help people to see the light and the law, to fight against the chaos that continuously tries to steal back cunningly into people's wills and unchecked desires.

᠅

Be all that as it may, Perlmutter had to be found.

᠅

The woman brought Perlmutter's address in less than a week. If he had run away, he certainly had not run very far. All this time he had been living in a Tel Aviv suburb, in one of the housing projects built by impatient people with little money to spare, on flat land, where the roofs were flat and had sun-heaters on top of them. She had obtained his address from acquaintances. Only three days she looked and had already found him. So the lawyer sat down and wrote him a letter carefully explaining the whole issue. He enjoyed writing such letters, in which each detail is clarified, as though the order of writing and the exposition inevitably led to the next act.

᠅

Nothing happened for a fortnight, and then the postman brought a large commercial envelope containing a letter, written in Hebrew, to be sure, but in Latin characters.

Adoni, said the letter, *ani lo maskim.* Sir, I do not agree.

Perlmutter had plenty to say for himself. He wrote that he suffered a great deal with his liver and had married a widow with a little shop and was not making a living, and he was an unlucky fellow, and all these years he had been longing for his daughter and now she had been found at last, was he likely to let her go abroad? On the contrary, he himself would go to court and demand that she should be his daughter in all respects, just like everybody else's daughters. Let her come to visit him and he would go to the cinema with her. And let her visit them when the holidays came round and eat chicken soup with dumplings like everyone else. And just because of his bad fortune and because he hadn't seen her for fifteen years, did that mean he had no more rights? A father is a father.

The Latin script took the lawyer quite a time to decipher, for he wanted to be sure he understood everything correctly and made the necessary distinction between *lo* when it meant "no" and *lo* when it meant "his," and recognized all kinds of other differences that are perfectly obvious in Hebrew orthography. This manner of writing worked him up. He took a sheet of paper himself and began to write in reverse Hebrew letters, from left to right, and afterward the other way round, in mirror writing. He could still remember the days when he had reversed the direction of his writing from the left-to-right of Russian to the right-to-left of Hebrew. Indeed, he had actually engaged in mirror writing for several weeks. His parents and teacher had worked hard to make him understand the difference; and then, because he had forcibly compelled himself, he had at last become an expert. Now, after more than sixty years had passed, he saw that he could still write mirror writing, and rapidly at that; and the shape of the letters actually seemed more familiar to him than the standard Hebrew script.

Then he felt alarmed at the hidden strength of things that are back-to-front. He tore up the sheet as though he had been poking his nose into matters that did not concern him.

❦ ❦

"Good, you go to Perlmutter," the woman agreed, "only I won't go. You go, Mister Lawyer, and the girl can go with you, and my husband as well." "Your husband?" "Good God, of course my husband! What did you think, I would stay alone all these years after Perlmutter ran away?"

"And who's your husband?"

"You'll get to know him in the car. He's a good fellow, a Pole, in Anders's Army he was, and he was wounded as well; and deserted what's more, poor fellow, and he hid himself away. And he was starving. He's suffered a great deal in his life. A gardener he is, he helps the municipal gardeners many years already. He's strong—oho, how strong! Other gardeners just scratch a bit on top and go and plant at once, they haven't any strength or patience. But nothing like that for him. He digs, he doesn't leave a root or weed. That's how it is, a good man is our Piotr, a handsome fellow, not one of those who goes around promising and promising and promising and then runs away."

"When did you marry him?"

"Not so long ago, Mister Lawyer. Four or five years maybe."

(So that was the picture: a dark convent and a Pravoslav wedding with a golden crown held over the head of the bridegroom and a golden crown held over the head of the bride, and a ribbon joining their hands together, and nuns bringing an embroidered tablecloth as a gift, with a living chicken, which Piotr would slaughter tomorrow or the day after, and grape jam made in the convent. And the fragrance of wrinkled apples. And incense.)

"In other words, your marriage to Perlmutter was annulled and you've married again?"

"Now Mister Lawyer, look here. I never married Perlmutter, it just came about during the war, we were yearning and longing so much in Turkestan, it was so sad there in Turkestan, people would sooner eat together and sleep together than everyone go separately like a dog. They had houses there, such little ones, like cabins, with walls of earth and thatched roofs. And mud between the houses, and war, war all the time. The front wasn't near us, of course, but someone on his own could starve plenty. Easier by two it was. Sometimes one of us found a little goat milk, sometimes the other worked for a farmer and brought back a few potatoes. We lived. We had a little joy at heart, that's true, but we never spoke about it, only in the evenings. When times are hard it's better by two. I never thought then I'd have such trouble with that Perlmutter, by my life I didn't."

❧ ❧

He closed his eyes and could see. Both of them wrapped up in shawls and old faded fringed kerchiefs on account of the cold. Their ears were covered over, there was newspaper inside their boots as they moved bent-backed through the mud in the sad little Turkmeni town, with a rough-edged little tin holder for food, or maybe half a loaf, under the arm.

She was a wind-blown, largish Slav peasant woman, blue-and-milky and yellow as a harvest day, with the scent of milk still in her breasts even when she was shriveled with war, a strong girl and not bad, not at all bad but with a voice like so many Russian women, strong and shrill, and a harsh pronunciation. As for him, he was a refugee Jewish youngster, eyes close together, bent-backed, always wearing a cap, with a funny way of walking, part goat, part human being, not liking to shave, half his strength in his tears. Something within him was permanently closed to her, and that was exactly what attracted her, piercing her soul and forcing her to love him. She was gravid with both of them together, him and the daughter, and never found it hard. Day after day a train would pass near the village without stopping—for why should it stop at such a godforsaken little place?—and in the train were soldiers going home and coaches full of wounded, and the chairman of the local council speaking up for the Party and the Leadership and from time to time passing out something like an official gazette. And the children slanty-eyed, wearing embroidered head-covers like bright playing-balls sliced in half, they talk Russian at school, but they talk Turkmeni with grand-mother. And on the First of May, in spite of the war, they manage to lead a sort of procession into the sad brown village square, with flags of deep red with yellow lettering, big flags those are, covering the muddy walls. And tea. Lots of tea.

In snowy weather the woman and her Jew Perlmutter lie under all their pillows and coats, their bodies fitting together like two spoons in a drawer; and even if rivers and plans were weaving together in his head, and even if he was repeating witch-words to himself, like Amu Darya and Amazon and Rio Grande, he would be pressing closer and closer against her, like an abandoned cub nuzzling against its twin.

A goat bleating through the snow. And the odor of feathers. And the smell of cold. And the train. And sleep.

⤞ ⤝

The lawyer sighed.

"All right, we'll fix a date for next week, we'll write and tell Mr. Perlmutter we are coming. And you—don't you want to come? Are you sure?"

"I'm sure, of course I'm sure. What do I have to look for with him? God give him everything good, but he's one thing, I'm another. And my Piotr doesn't want me to go either. You, says he, you stay at home, we'll fix it all up between us men. Only I'll take the daughter, says he, if Mis-ter Lawyer says that's right. We believe in Mister Lawyer like our own father."

What am I to do, thought the lawyer. Am I to fetch this big fellow Piotr to that man with his liver in that Koppel Quarter, or wherever it is he lives, and who knows whether he isn't going to beat him up? And because of me. Between men, that is.

"Listen, your Piotr isn't going to use his hands?"

The woman was shocked:

"God forbid, Mister Lawyer, what are you thinking, my dear? Why, he's a holy angel. Put someone like him on a place that hurts and all the pain will vanish. He has planting hands, green fingers. He wouldn't hit anybody, not even a fly my Piotr wouldn't hit. And yet he's strong—oho! You wouldn't believe it. If you'd see him working out in the open, he lifts half a garden patch with a single blow, even though he isn't young. Women come to watch him when he's working in the municipal gardens, like to a show they come. Such a lovely back he has. So strong."

And that is why she wants her daughter away in Canada, thought the lawyer. Even if she herself doesn't know it. The same urge that led her to take to her heart the thin Jew who had found himself with her in the Turkmeni village was now causing her to decide wisely: one woman in the house and no more. Let the one who isn't married go away.

🖈 🖈

By chance the lawyer happened to be in the municipality that day and asked questions. An acquaintance told him that from time to time they did actually take on a gardener named Piotr, a queer fellow. Only he had not deserted from Anders's Army, but had been discharged because he was a hopeless case of mental retardation.

🖈 🖈

In the evening the daughter stood waiting for the lawyer down below beside the grocery shop. She had clearly been there a long time. As soon as she saw him she came up and began walking at his side, as though accompanying him. She spoke Hebrew.

"Why were you waiting down there instead of coming up?"

"What should I come up for?"

"But suppose I hadn't gone to the office today?"

She shrugged her shoulders.

"I want to go to Canada."

"Why do you think you'll find things better there than here?"

"Look, there's nobody who'd ever marry me here."

He was taken aback.

"Why?"

"Who would marry me?" she snapped bitterly. "A Jew? A Christian? A Russian? An Arab? One of your people? I leave a bitter taste with the boys."

He looked at her and tried to make a picture for himself. Here was this girl with the shrunken breasts, bitter; yet if only someone wanted her, if some joy were to touch her, something in her would be capable of soaring aloft. Then there would be meaning even to the physical bitterness and the horrible clothes from the market stall, and the essential thing would remain: a strong young girl in colorful clothing.

Meanwhile she tripped along the pavement, her expensive neglected shoes dragging because of a worn heel.

"I don't know who I am or what."

"Your mother says—"

"My mother says all kinds of things. She says my father was a Russian soldier."

"Why don't you believe her? I think she's telling the truth. Many things like that happen during a war. Nobody is to blame. He went off to the front. Maybe he was killed. If he hadn't disappeared, you'd be living in a village near Krementchug now, with your mother and your father."

"I'm a double orphan," said she.

"Meaning—Perlmutter?"

"He as well. He was there, and he went away."

"What difference does Perlmutter make to you? He was just a boyfriend of your mother's during the war, when times were hard. Your father was killed in the war against the Germans. You are not the only one."

She didn't even listen to him.

"All right, why didn't she marry him?"

"Stepan? or Perlmutter?"

"What do I care which? Who'll want me now? They are sure to say— that one, she's just like her mother."

He wanted to tell her she was wrong, that in our society . . . and gave up.

"That's why I want to go to Canada. There they don't know all this business, war and all the rest of it. There there are no tricks. There I can even get to know an intelligent fellow. Look at my mother, went and married the town idiot. She didn't have any choice either."

He could understand that desire for an established world so well. He also loved a protected life that moved gently according to plan, with institutions already established, containing something divine, orderly, purposeful. For a moment he thought that maybe he would adopt her as his daughter and give her an identity. But then he saw her ugly face, the iron tooth in her mouth, her childish, menacing insistence on belonging;

and he knew that he would never be able to go through with it. She is a case for a sociologist, he said to himself, for a welfare worker, but not for me. Perhaps he would talk about her to his group.

"Maybe I could work in your office?" she said all of a sudden, not believing her own words.

"Doing what? ... Typing—"

"I can learn," she suggested.

"But how? My clerk has been with me five years—six—"

"Maybe you'll need someone sometime. She may become ill. Anything can happen."

"No, no."

Promptly and without hesitation she descended a whole hope.

"Then maybe you need a housecleaner?"

"My housecleaner has been with me these twenty-five years."

She persisted with the forceful innocence of a sixteen-year-old:

"Maybe she'll die."

"No, no."

Now he sensed that this was a weed in his garden, menacing all that grew there. He stood still.

"Don't worry," he told her. "You can go home. I promise to do everything possible to get you to Canada."

She looked at him with a kind of contempt, as though this dolt did not understand what she was talking about all the time.

"So I should go away?"

"You go along and don't worry, young lady." He closed his world to her with the utmost courtesy, clearly sensing human failure in all this and therefore doubly courteous.

The child was not fooled. She raised her shoulders with a sharp, contemptuous, and despairing motion and went away.

❧ ❦

They took an interurban taxi service. As usual the lawyer had booked himself a place beside the driver. He did not always feel well when traveling and hated to be crowded among others. He himself no longer drove outside town. The speeds required seemed to demand too much of him.

Piotr and the girl sat behind speaking Hebrew, for they both spoke very poor Russian. Yet while a foreign accent could not be noticed with her, the Polish background sounded clearly as he spoke; and they were short on vocabulary. They would round things off with a gesture or a guess.

A man sitting next to them who looked like an old teacher was polite to them with enthusiastic Zionism: they were new immigrants, doubtless, who had to have the road described to them. Piotr and the girl, who had been perfectly familiar with the road for at least fifteen years, remained politely silent and did not correct him. As for the lawyer, he felt depressed and trapped. It seemed to him as though something in the logical structure of the universe had gone awry ever since those two women had come to his office late that evening. The world had become a thoroughgoing mix-up. No one was like his ancestors. Anything might happen.

When they got out in Tel Aviv, the elderly teacher hoped they would find their own place in Israel and earnestly implored them not to be alarmed at the difficulties. All of us, he said, once found it very hard to be here. We lived in tents, we built roads. And you'll do well if you go to an *ulpan* and learn Hebrew. Things will be all right. What counts is that you are at home. Nobody is going to threaten you here.

Piotr, a sentimental man, found his eyes filling with tears. Quite right, he said to the teacher, quite right, sir, this is a good country, there's nothing to fear from anybody. And as for the Arabs, God will be our aid.

❧ ❧

They took a taxi and made their way to what the lawyer had already grown accustomed to calling the Koppel Quarter in his own mind. It had been built in a hurry and was already pretty much of a slum, with peeling stairwells, balconies sticking out of the houses like drawers from a plundered cupboard, all kinds of things hanging down from them. The whole quarter was not so much an exterior as the great overturned interior of a flophouse. There was a Bulgarian sign above a cobbler's shop. A dreadful barbershop with a stench of artificial violets. Television antennas. Sand between the houses.

Years before, someone had planted white and pink vincas in front, but nobody had ever bothered to water them and they had shriveled up. Now all that grew in front were chewing gum wrappers, ice-cream sticks, dirty absorbent cotton, and pages of exercise books. In the evenings, there would be watermelon and sour milk containers, thought the lawyer to himself, and the daily journey crowded in the bus all the way to the heart of Tel Aviv and back, to sit in an undershirt and listen to the radio. Summer would be hard in this quarter, harder than the summers of Jerusalemites. A noisy quarter. Any number of radio sets blaring. And people crowded far too close, the warmth of one reaching the warmth of the next, voice touching voice, one man's smell in the other's nose. The walls were an illusion, or maybe a grudging concession to the concept of civilization.

❧ ❦

If the lawyer expected the girl to show any special feeling at Perlmutter's house, he was wrong. Her face did not change but grew even harder, with its somewhat malicious obstinacy and unresolved dissatisfaction. She was outside it all and above it all. Her hair shone with a sticky spray from the hairdresser's and looked like a sort of mouse nest rolled up on the back of her head. She wore a dress of flimsy material, the kind that is sold at bargain prices on market stalls at the end of the season. Had there been the slightest trace of ease and freedom in her appearance, it could even have suited her. But that eternal sulkiness of hers, that shackled and closed quality of stupid women, caused the light dress to seem like a piece of armor. She did not seem to move her arms at all, as though they were tied to the body, and only her shoulders jumped up and down in a wild and nervous motion depending on her mood. She looked like a woman who had never enjoyed a really good day all her life long. The lawyer had to remind himself that she was sixteen years old. To Piotr she spoke in her constantly plaintive voice, but without any tension.

As for Piotr, he was just as he had been described: big, clumsy, careful, with a big Adam's apple, dragging his bad leg and wearing a striped shirt buttoned up to the top without a tie, a jacket over it. He did not wear the collar over the jacket, a gentile habit. He walked beside her as though he were calming her and being conciliatory.

They mounted the steps. Perlmutter opened the door. He was smaller than the lawyer expected, little and creased, with his skin yellow as though it had been damaged by some chemical. There was something slightly rotten in his breath. He seemed to be older than the woman who had been with him in Turkestan, older by no few years. The image of the young, sharp, hungry Jewish boy with the cap no longer suited him, and was replaced by a picture of a Jew who must already have been about forty at the time, with sparse hair and quite a different, more materialistic, bitterness. Maybe he had had a few coins and bits of gold, and some dollars sewn into the lining of his coat, and that was why she had come to him, he thought. What do I know? Perlmutter gave the impression of a petty rogue. He lacked that aesthetic, on-show intensity that you sometimes find in big-league rogues and swindlers who are pleased with what they do.

⤚ ⤙

Perlmutter opened his arms to embrace his daughter. She allowed him to hug her for a moment, but when he wanted to kiss her, she pushed him away, her fists clenched.

"Are we coming in or not?" she asked in a vinegary voice. She had definitely made up her mind not to be excited.

"Welcome, welcome, blessings for keeping us alive and sustaining us and bringing us to this day," sobbed Perlmutter. "Rosa! Rosa! My daughter has come! What a day, what a grand day! Fifteen years, Lord Almighty."

Even his tears appeared yellowish.

Rosa, Perlmutter's wife, looked at them all with piercing button-eyes and without a sound offered refreshments: broken squares of chocolate from a large slab, presented in a glass dish. The lawyer looked around. There were two rooms, a balcony, and a tiny kitchen. In the corner stood a big old radio with a glass cat upon it. Four or five bits of electrical apparatus were joined to a single socket, their wires dangling. A Sick Fund bottle stood on the table. An ashtray shaped like a swan, another like a pink hand. And Perlmutter wiping away his tears.

"Look, just look," he urged them, dashing around and fetching heaps of old photos. "This is my former wife at Ula village in Turkestan. And this is me, and here we are together at the First of May celebration. This is the statue of Stalin here. And this is our daughter, the baby. Just look how I kept the photo next to my heart for fifteen years. I remember just like today how she was born. We fetched her mother to the hospital in a cart, and on the way, just imagine, an axle broke, and two soldiers came to help us get there in time, and she was already beginning to give birth on the way, so sure as I am alive. In a hurry she was."

"One moment," said the lawyer. "You said your former wife. Were you married?"

"What do you mean were we married? Of course we were married, what else? I don't say we went to the rabbi, not that, but we had a civil wedding, in Soviet Russia, before the official registrar of marriage—we were registered in the books of the council all fit and proper. And afterward we went to the Cultural Center with some friends, and we had something to drink, and we ate herring. There wasn't much to eat in those days, but we found some good herring. Who says we weren't married? Of course we got married."

"Then Madam Rosa is—"

"She is my wife at the Rabbinate. After we came here and this woman ran away from me to the convent and they wouldn't even let me see her and the child, I asked myself what I should do. It's impossible without a wife. I asked a lawyer, and he told me that such civil marriages don't count and I could marry a wife at the Rabbinate. I went to a matchmaker, I told him I'm ill and can't work much, but as a man—that's okay. So he found me Rosa, who has a shop. We went through with it and here I am."

Rosa, whose natural hair looked like an ancient wig, had brewed strong tea, which she presented in glasses with plastic holders. She never said a word.

"Girlie," Perlmutter turned to the daughter, "tell your father how you are. What are you doing? What are you learning in school? Do you have a boyfriend?"

She drily described her studies at the Mission School, her work as a waitress in the German Colony, and how she wanted to go to Canada.

"What Canada, Lord God Almighty? Canada all of a sudden? God preserve you, girlie, why are you dashing off alone to a foreign country? Why, this is your country, I'm your father."

"Oh, you aren't my father," said the daughter impatiently. "This is all a show. You have to put on a show, the lawyer said, so it's put on."

Perlmutter burst into tears, real tears, with sobbing and shaking shoulders.

"Well, well, you are exaggerating," said Piotr to the girl as he produced a handkerchief to wipe his hands. He had never been so embarrassed in all his life. "You don't have to cry, Mr. Perlmutter, God is merciful."

"I must ask you to behave better," said the lawyer.

The girl shrugged her shoulders.

"Okay, so I'm prepared to behave, but he shouldn't say he's my father."

"How do you know?" the lawyer asked severely.

"Just look, I'm not even like him."

They all looked at the two of them. Indeed, it was hard to find any resemblance, even with an effort. But then she was Stepan's, the lawyer remembered, not Perlmutter's. Perlmutter had only given her his name

when she was about to be born in Turkestan. And meanwhile Perlmutter finished weeping.

"That's the way it is, that witch hid her from me for fifteen years,
she poisoned her soul, so what do you want her to say now? But that
won't help you, do you hear, I'm your father before God and man, you
were born to me in summer during the month of August at Ula village
in Turkestan, in the hospital, and what's more the axle of the cart broke
on the way, so what does your mother have to say to that? Eh?"

⤍ ⤌

The lawyer tried to intervene. He was accustomed to patching things
up between people quarreling in his office. Now he began to deliver his
solemn and wordy address, appealing to their decency, their human self-
respect, their belief in the goodness within them. Even if they did not
understand, they would listen for a few moments, as though feeling that
in spite of everything there is some higher order in the universe; and they
would calm down. This time he delivered his speech in the Koppel Quarter, even though his words were interrupted every moment by a carpet-
beater overhead or a mother shrieking at a naughty boy down below.
This kind of thing was easier in the office. The lawyer drank his tea and
longed for Jerusalem.

After his speech they stopped being rude to one another, although
they did not come to terms. Perlmutter sat over the heap of photos like
a miser over coins. It was hard to understand how he could have taken
so many photos in that village during the middle of the war. Had it really been possible to obtain film freely? Or maybe this was one of the
questionable businesses he had gone in for there; so it would seem. Photo
was flung on photo, and in them all was the smiling young woman, or
he, or both of them together, or the baby, or the woman with her daughter, or he with the daughter, or all three of them together. There was
even a photo of the daughter lying on her belly, naked on a tiger skin,
all fit and proper. A family album in every respect.

"Then come to visit your father," said Perlmutter. "Spend a week or
a fortnight. I'll take you to the pictures in Tel Aviv. You'll eat with us
on Sabbath. You'll see how well Rosa cooks. You'll see. Your mother
won't recognize you. You'll get cheeks like an apple."

"I'm going to Canada," the girl burst out as though she were throwing a stone at him and began to go down the steps. The lawyer and Piotr came down behind her.

Perlmutter shouted:

"No Canada! No Canada! Not as long as I'm alive!"

⤞ ⤝

When they came down they found it hard to get a taxi. What driver would be crazy enough to go to the Koppel Quarter? Their shoes filled with sand. The girl cried, and Piotr patted her on the back as though she had swallowed a fish bone: that's enough now, that's enough.

Gulping and choking, she finally climbed together with them into a bus that pulled up into the sand and hid her face in a handkerchief. The men were silent. They could clearly feel that this was a very young girl indeed, after all. At the central station the lawyer got out and bought her a box of sweets. She opened it at once, eagerly, and began to suck.

"I'm going to kill Perlmutter," she said after the tears.

⤞ ⤝

"It's not true," said the woman. "As heaven is my witness and as I hope for salvation, I never married him at all, neither a civil marriage nor any other. I simply lived with him." And then she added something unexpected: "He was a gay fellow, this Perlmutter. I never knew any-one as gay as he was. Only he never liked to work, never."

The lawyer stared at her, at a loss what to do.

"How do you explain his story that you were married?"

She held out her hands on either side.

"I don't know, as heaven's my witness I don't know. But he knows it isn't true, so why should he lie just so? Just to harm people?"

"Maybe you'll meet him and find why he's making all these claims?"

"Piotr won't let me."

He did not know whom to believe. There was a measure of truth in both of them. He knew he would not succeed in finding the real truth. All of a sudden he had an idea:

"Listen. Maybe there's a way out of all this mess. The girl's a minor and there is a problem about her paternity. You are married to Piotr now, a Church marriage I understand. Suppose Piotr adopts the girl?"

"Adopts?" She did not grasp it.

"He can adopt her legally as his daughter, and then as her adoptive father he can give her permission to go to Canada."

A pair of starry tears appeared in the woman's eyes. She rose and embraced the lawyer's head, and then, as befits a peasant woman, she wanted to clasp him round the knees; but he would not permit it.

"May God give you everything good, sir, I always knew that your cleverness would save us all, may Jesus give you length of days, may the Holy Mother give you good fortune and everything good."

But at the door she turned round, worried:

"And Perlmutter won't object?"

"I don't think he can object. His paternity has not been sufficiently proved, and besides he has abandoned you and the girl for the last fifteen years. The judge isn't such a bad fellow."

⤝ ⤝

Her abundant joy affected him as well. He was as chirpy as a sparrow when he went home. That evening he found himself full of energy, removed Katzenbach from his knees and drew up the application for adoption.

⤝ ⤝

The judge said he wanted to see Perlmutter all the same.

⤝ ⤝

When Perlmutter entered the judge's chambers, the lawyer did not recognize him at first. The wispy sideburns on his cheeks had grown and seemed longer. He was dressed in a white, new shirt, and there was something fresh and reddish, almost blossomlike, in his yellowish color. His whole appearance had changed. He now seemed like a cheerful Hasid. The three of them sat down together: the judge in his armchair in front of the high-piled desk, the lawyer and Perlmutter facing him. The judge and the lawyer had many papers. Perlmutter did not have a single sheet of paper in his hands. Easy and smiling he sat, looking first at one and then at the other.

"Well then, Mr. Perlmutter," said the judge. "You claim that the girl is your daughter?"

Perlmutter produced a sheet of paper from his pocket.

"Your Honor, I found the birth certificate of the hospital in Turkestan. You can see by this document that the mother was registered with my family name and the daughter was registered in my name as my daughter. We were married at the village council office in front of the registrar of marriages, in a civil ceremony. And the daughter is mine, there's no doubt of it."

"How did you manage to get the woman into the hospital in the middle of the war?" asked the lawyer as though cross-examining a witness. "I thought all the hospitals were full of soldiers."

"I had my connections," said Perlmutter obstinately. "And apart from that, Mister Lawyer, you may be an important man, I couldn't say, but even if you are the most important man there is, you can't argue with my documents. Here you are, take a look, all the documents are here."

"The registration is not a proof of paternity in itself," said the lawyer to the judge.

"I understand," answered the judge and turned to Perlmutter. "Look what complications you've caused us, Mr. Perlmutter. You know that according to Jewish law the child follows the mother, and you went and married yourself a non-Jewess, and you've complicated the whole issue as a result."

"A non-Jewess?" Perlmutter started with a loud, victorious voice. "What non-Jewess? Your honor, why, she's a non-Jewess just as I'm a non-Jew. She's a Jewish girl, a full daughter of Israel. And what if she does have blue eyes, so what? Is it written anywhere that a Jewish girl mustn't have blue eyes? Against the law is it?"

⊰ ⊱

The lawyer felt as though the familiar judge's chambers had somehow left the bounds of reality. A concentrated white autumnal light making its way through a gap in the clouds was the only thing that was tangible; and it seemed to him that the scanty light was covering everything, those seated there, the furniture, the piles of paper. Sheets of light drowning everything within, while the people slowly faded away, weakening like a candle flame with the coming of dawn, their strength growing steadily less, a little more and nobody would be aware of them, just a little more and people could pass through them the way a man passes through smoke.

Bemused as he was, he thought: whatever Perlmutter points to and says is Jewish—it's as though he said, "It's mine." As though he had expropriated it. The divine hand of Perlmutter. What can I do against that?

⊰ ⊱

The judge stood up and shifted the heavy curtain to darken the room. The lawyer calmed down a bit. People and objects returned to their normal shapes.

"You realize the significance," said the judge to the lawyer in a low voice. "If the woman really is Jewish as this gentleman claims, then the girl's Jewish as well and I have no authority to issue an adoption order to the mother's husband who is a non-Jew."

"I understand, Your Honor, but I am not convinced of the truth of his statements. It all has to be clarified, it's necessary—"

Perlmutter gazed first at one and then at the other, enjoying himself tremendously. Here was a bomb he had exploded in the judge's chambers! Ever since he left Soviet Russia and the gentiles who could always be twisted round his little finger, ever since his dealings had begun with the Jewish Agency, and the Income Tax, and the Electricity Corporation, he had never succeeded in fixing a man or an institution like this. He seemed to become twenty years younger.

"How do you know she's Jewish?" the lawyer asked.

"What do you mean how do I know? She said so herself. Have you ever seen anybody lying and saying he's a Jew? A Jew may lie and say he's a gentile, that we've seen, but the other way round? Who'd be crazy enough to lie like that in the middle of the war?"

"What do you suggest, sir?" the judge leaned over to the lawyer again.

"We'll clear it up," said he. "We'll hunt for documents one way or the other. This is an absolute surprise for us." He almost added: an act of God.

"Try and ascertain the facts," said the judge, and they left the chambers.

In the corridor the lawyer said; "Listen, Perlmutter, if the woman is really a Jewess, then it's very doubtful whether your present marriage to Madam Rosa can be valid. Why should we complicate matters? Because then they'll charge you with bigamy. That may cost you plenty."

"Well, and what do I care if my marriage to Rosa isn't valid. So it isn't."

The lawyer suddenly realized that Perlmutter had met the woman in secret, in spite of Piotr's prohibition. He looked at him questioningly, but Perlmutter's rascally face gave nothing away except a cunning, opaque, secretive triumph.

✍ ✍

Then let us assume he has seen her, and let us assume that something of the old attraction is still left, and let us assume that the earth opened up its mouth and there appeared a new gateway of possibilities, a style of life, a transformation they had not thought of in advance, neither he nor she. And why not, after all? Fifteen years apart, yet he is perfectly familiar with that large white body, and she knows all his habits. Their embrace on the very occasion of meeting caused the bodies to continue on their own before either of them could decide whether or no. And Piotr and the girl suddenly lost their importance. And now he wasn't going to give her up. There's a new situation for you. A few moments of all but forgotten pleasure, and the girl wouldn't go to Canada.

≫ ≪

Perlmutter leaned over for the lawyer's ear and whispered in Yiddish: "That Rosa, she's an old maid."
And pranced jauntily toward the buses.

≫ ≪

The lawyer was one of those people possessed by an old dream that only a woman resembling him could find favor in his eyes Since he was tall, ivorylike, and black-eyed, he went looking for someone tall, ivory-like, and black-eyed who would seem to be his, one of his family. In his youth he had searched for his female twin, for his female counterpart, and when he did not find her, he gave up the search. The other, the non-family, fruitful strangeness, did not accord with his capacity. He was not inquisitive, so he remained alone. And hence it was hard for him to understand this whole incident of Perlmutter and the woman. Well then, was she a Jewess or not? Had she met him or not?

≫ ≪

He went to the convent. It was a large building with a wall round it in the north of the city. A side entrance between a stone wall and a thick hedge led to a little stone building, a kind of gatehouse, where the woman's room was. In the courtyard grew a geranium and hollyhocks. A Jerusalem jasmine, strong and sharp in the rocky dryness, spread its scent afar. Bells were pealing in the convent, whether for prayers or a meal he did not know. The woman and Piotr were both at home. He was eating while she sat beside him, her eyes red with tears. There was no doubt of it. She had been up to mischief with Perlmutter, and Piotr did not know.
She wiped a chair and seated the guest.
"Do you want your daughter to go to Canada?" he asked her sternly.
"I do," said she.
"Then why do you . . . like this . . ."
She wiped her eyes again and again. It was hard to understand how even Piotr could not realize that this was a sinful, suffering woman. Her hand beat her breast every few moments in a brief automatic movement. Her eyes were red, her hair disheveled.

"Perlmutter won't give up now," said the lawyer without going into details, so that Piotr should suppose he was referring to the daughter.

But Piotr sat, large and smiling, drinking tea in his big khaki working trousers and his striped shirt that was buttoned right up to the neck. Before him lay a chunk of bread, a cucumber, and a radish, all of which he cut up carefully into tiny, equal-sized pieces. All that was going on in the room was as far from him as noonday noises in the airfield of some other country.

"I know, I know, that's my punishment."

"Well, we'll see what can be done," said the lawyer in annoyance. His eyes fell on the narrow iron bed in the corner under the ikon. It was covered with many pillows in the old style. One red pillow had no cover on it. There was an obscenity about it, as though it ought to be hidden. Here Perlmutter had been, he thought, with his ailing liver and his rotten breath. Here all this flesh had moved under a terrifying, genuine, heady urge, concerned with nothing but itself. A man could live his whole life long without knowing that forceful drive even once. There was no appeal. *Vénus à sa proie attachée.* Perlmutter.

"Do something for us, my dear," murmured the woman, after her fashion. "And the Holy Mother will appeal in your favor, the Holy Virgin will entreat for you."

This time she chose only the mother of Jesus as intercessor, as though she could not count on the saints, who are men, to understand her properly.

Piotr rose to accompany him to the gateway. He wiped his hands clean of the cucumber with slow, comprehensive motions, which were absolutely identical with those of the woman. Then he produced a pruning knife from his capacious pocket and cut the lawyer a fine branch of jasmine.

"The scent is good and healthy," he said with a smile. "Jasmine makes you forget trouble."

His words seemed to indicate some glimmer of knowledge, as though something had made its way through the dense cover of his intelligence— but no more than a glimmer. As he stood between the iron gates of the convent, his head humbly bent and his eyes cast down, Piotr was a handsome man.

✎ ✎

The lawyer found it hard to fall asleep. It was toward morning when he did so, and he dreamt that a heavy bomber of World War vintage was about to fly, but the runway was a street full of people. When he asked somebody how this could be permitted, the fellow answered that everybody already knew how to be careful with that plane, and no special runway was necessary. He woke up startled and alarmed, feeling as though he had been almost run over.

☙ ❧

The lawyer's contacts with the world were usually well balanced. Sometimes he would witness an outburst on the part of clients, or wishes and desires of witnesses; but these could always be checked, either with the aid of that calculated and eloquent speech, or by threats of the law, or by the full authority of court and state. It was rare for him in all his legal experience to face such crazy, humiliating vitality. He felt as though any step he took in this case promptly became something else, as though people had burst into his home and turned it into a fair or a circus. Perlmutter was not the only gay dog, he thought in annoyance, they were all gay, the whole jovial gang—except the girl, the only unfortunate individual in the whole affair, more unfortunate than any person with a sense of responsibility could bear. He very much wanted to transfer the whole case to his assistant, a much younger man who might be amused by the whole business and less concerned as to what was true or not. But it was too late. He knew he would have to finish what he had begun.

Henceforward, however, he decided, he would deal with papers and not with people. His mistake was that he had been involved too much with the people concerned. Now he ordered his secretary not to make any more appointments with any of that gang for the present. Let her tell them that he was busy.

And meanwhile he sat down and drew up an application to the Ecclesiastical Institutions in Moscow, requesting them to ascertain for him whether this woman was a Jewess or not. Never in his life had he had so strong a feeling of doing right as when he drafted formal sentences, sealed the envelope containing the photographs of documents with red wax, selected himself another large thick envelope on which he personally wrote the address with old-fashioned Cyrillic curlicues, and sent the clerk to the post office to register the whole thing. He placed the registration slip in his pocketbook to begin with, then changed his mind and put it in the safe. Now nothing would go wrong, he decided, nothing would go off the track or surprise him or bring him face to face with unforeseen facts again.

☙ ❧

That envelope of his would reach Moscow, he thought, it would be lowered in the postal sack at Vnukovo Airfield, where by now it must certainly be very cold indeed and postal clerks and porters would be wearing fur hats; and afterwards the envelope would reach a minor priest, some secretary doubtless sitting in a cold office of an old church amid the scent of incense and the flickering of ikons—no, no, there was no reason for the business office to have the dim gold gleam of ikons, I am exaggerating, he thought, what must certainly be there is a picture of the heads of state; and after that the young priest in the black hat with his earlocks and curls sprouting out all round would present the material to a patriarch, an old man dressed more ornately and with a curling beard—he has it curled once a week at the neighboring barbershop—and a big cross on his broad chest and a reddish bulbous nose and any number of gold rings on his fingers. The Pravoslav Church loves gold even more than the Catholic. Doubtless this was a memory of its Byzantine origin, all the gloom and gold and hidden treasures and manuscripts and endless intrigue—and amid all this and above all this, a ceremonial that is the most splendid in the world, tasting of the kingdom on earth. The patriarch would take a pen in his hand—who knows, maybe he has a ballpoint pen by now—and would write to various regions and districts. Yet why should he write after all? The Church offices must certainly have telephones too; after all, Saint Mikola and Saint Onuphrius and all the other faded, gilded thick-beards had not prohibited the telephone. And then local priests would go searching in church registers and would find a baptismal certificate; and the elders among them would remember. And in the evening the village priest would tell an old man or woman surviving from those times that a letter had come all of a sudden from Israel, from the Holy Land, asking for documents about the daughter of Zakhar and Yevdokia, may they rest in peace. And children would want the stamps from Israel, but the priest would not give them away, being a collector himself.

🐟🐟

All that, thought the lawyer, provided that Perlmutter was lying.

🐟🐟

The Russian Church functioned swiftly. Before very long the postman brought a huge packet by registered mail, with ugly Russian stamps, showing satellites in space and the face of Tereshkova, and handsome red seals.

There was a client with the lawyer at the time. He excused himself, went into the next room, and eagerly opened the packet.

The Moscow Church wished peace upon earth to the lawyer and, God aiding, informed him with accompanying documents that the said woman was a Christian daughter of Christians for three generations back at least, her mothers and fathers had been pure and perfect gentiles even in the days of the deceased tsar, and whoever declared otherwise was uttering falsehood, and may God bless all men of truth and peace, amen.

✣ ✣

This time Perlmutter brought Rosa to court as well but told her to take a seat in the corridor and wait for him. She sat submissive and opaque, her button eyes not missing a single detail. In front of her passed people quarreling about contracts and wrangling about property, arguing and divorcing one another and complaining, most of them noisy, some of them confused. Rosa sat with her legs apart and waited for Perlmutter.

✣ ✣

The judge said severely:

"Mr. Perlmutter, why did you tell us that she was a Jewess?"

Defeated, Perlmutter hung his head:

"That's what she told me, Your Honor, and what should I do? I believed her. You can't check the papers of everybody who tells you something."

The lawyer swiftly set out to clinch his victory.

"Well then, Your Honor, the woman is a non-Jewess and the stepfather is a non-Jew. There can be nothing to prevent the issue of a legal order of adoption in order that the personal status of the girl be finally settled."

"I agree to the adoption," said the judge at length. "Mr. Perlmutter, if you have nothing more to add, you may go."

"I am a sick man," said Perlmutter. "All this excitement—"

"It's better for you this way, Mr. Perlmutter." The lawyer could not refrain from taking revenge. "Your wife is waiting for you outside. She'll look after you, take you home."

"I'm not to blame here," said Perlmutter. His face was yellow. "Believe me, I'm not to blame. I always believe what people tell me. Otherwise it's impossible to live in the world."

He went out dragging his legs. Even before he closed the door, his impatient call in Yiddish to the wife who supported him could be heard: "Rosa! Rosa! Come here."

Go on, go on, get back to your Koppel Quarter, my friend, thought the lawyer, back to the sour milk and undershirts, back to the old maid, that old button-eyed, buttoned-up saintly reprobate of yours with the legs apart whom nobody has ever seen without earrings and a round brooch. Get along with you and get out of our lives.

≈≈

From this point everything was plain sailing. The woman, the girl, and Piotr were summoned to chambers. The order of adoption was issued, signed, and sealed. Piotr, large, mulish, and radiant, pressed the lawyer's hand for a long time and wanted to shake hands with the judge as well. But the latter was the sort of man who does not enjoy physical contact. Piotr did not even notice it and pressed the corner of the writing table instead. The daughter clung to her mother, and both of them blessed the lawyer in several languages and linguistic fragments, until he edged them out of the chambers with nudges and noises, the way a driver of oxen gets a herd of cattle out of the way. There was no sign of Perlmutter or Rosa. They must have gone back home, thought the lawyer, and better that way, far better—you mustn't allow different kinds to get mixed up together, one religion with another or one type of person with other types. All that leads to confusion, to chaos, and that's one of the things that destroys the world.

In the office he called his assistant and told him the whole story; and then, well pleased with himself, he invited the young fellow to a home-fare restaurant on the second floor. Things were back to normal.

≈≈

In the afternoon fists began banging on the door of the lawyer's office. It burst open even before the clerk got there. In came a huge bouquet of red roses, uniform and coarse, fresh from a flower shop, with the requisite asparagus and the cellophane and the tinsel ribbons. Behind the bouquet appeared a gigantic box of chocolates, the kind the clerk had only seen in plate-glass windows, and which she was sure could only be props. These and other bundles were borne by four people: Piotr, the woman, the daughter, and Perlmutter. They all smelt strongly of liquor, a scent of festival that seemed slightly askew. In her hand the daughter held a large ugly crystal goblet, heavily gilded at the sides and on top and containing a heavy gold spoon of Pravoslav craft. Perlmutter had one bottle of cognac in his hand and another, almost empty, sticking jauntily out of his pocket. It was impossible even to imagine where they had left Rosa. Tipsy as they were, it would have been pointless to ask.

They burst into the room of the lawyer, who was just removing some securities from the safe. Startled, he closed it and found them round and about him. They sat him down, thrust everything into his bosom, and began singing:

"May you live a hundred years, a hundred years!"

"Here, darling, here, brother mine, drink up," begged the woman, planting the cognac in front of him.

"In crystal and gold!" piped up the girl to Piotr. "Daddy, fetch it!"

They placed the ugly goblet in front of him and poured him out his measure, so that he couldn't help but drink it. Each of them in turn took a swig at the bottle, which didn't seem to be the first either.

"But ladies and gentlemen, this is a public place, ladies and gentlemen, I thank you, but I can't work like this—"

"May he live a hundred years!"

"Cheers for our lawyer!"

"Long live the State of Israel! A glass for the Church!"

"You all think I don't know the prayers of the Jews?" The woman's face was bright and shining. "And how I know! Shema Isroil, Adoynoy Eloyheinu!" In the Yiddish pronunciation.

"Amen. Amen!"

✒ ✒

The clerk stood in the doorway. Piotr offered her his arm in knightly and gentlemanly fashion, to lead her to the table.

"Come, sister," he boomed in Russian. "Come and drink with us, we are rejoicing today."

The bouquet of roses fell. Perlmutter tried to pick it up and lost his balance. He sat on the carpet next to the roses, rolling with laughter. The girl held out her hand to him:

"Stand up, Daddy, that's not nice."

So both of them were daddy. With a sinking heart the lawyer suddenly noticed the girl's thumb, short and hammerlike, was absolutely identical with the thumb of Perlmutter. The same thumb. Truth had fled away, never to return. His eyes grew dark.

"Our lawyer is a sweetie!" yelled Perlmutter in Hebrew from the carpet.

The woman made the sign of the cross over him.

"May your Messiah come soon, and then all the world will be brothers."

"O General, lead us to the sea," sang Piotr in his thick voice in Polish. His voice was too heavy to bear, he dropped a tone and added some false notes from time to time. "Lead us to the ocean v-a-a-s-t!"

"Our lawyer is a sweetie!" yelled Perlmutter again, and this time stood up waving his hands.

"The State of Israel is a sweetie!" said the daughter. She took off her tight shoes and held them in her hand.

"After you, General, we follow and go to the sea so blu-u-u-e!"

"Drink up, my dear, drink up," said the woman wiping away her tears. "You're among brothers and sisters, don't be afraid."

Under duress the lawyer drank again. His head was really whirling by now.

"Shall I call the police?" asked the clerk, grinning broadly and displaying pink gums.

"No, no need, these ladies and gentlemen will calm down by themselves—they'll calm down themselves—just a little water—"

A plaster cast of Dr. Weizmann standing on the lawyer's table fell and shattered.

"May God forgive you, brothers," shrieked the woman. "You came to thank Mister Lawyer and you cause him damage? A lovely white Lenin he had, and they smashed it, they smashed it, the sinners!"

"We'll buy him a statue," said Piotr. "We'll buy him ten statues."

"Our lawyer's a sweetie!"

"To Canada, to Canada! Long live Canada!"

≈ ≈

The lawyer was in a state of intoxicated clarity. He felt that he was being carried away as in those distant days when, a vengeful raging kicking child, he had been swept helplessly aloft in the arms of a tall and laughing mother. He had lost his sense of balance. Strangely enough that was both a shame and yet calming. The thin, hard voices of the women, like the voices of angels, the smell of cognac, the clinking of glasses, the flashing of the transparent cellophane, and that otherwhere scent of the roses, all mingled together into a kind of warm sweet blind shameful rising wave that could not be withstood. He admitted—he could see— that something or somebody knew better than he did; but he did not know who, or what there was to know. He was surrounded by smiles, affection, kindheartedness, as though a great big world of handsome and omnipotent adults was once again accepting a naughty boy, and everything had been forgiven him most lovingly, yet what his transgression had been—*that* he could not remember no matter how he tried. He submitted to growing small. The sweet choking shame made him give way completely, drinking, raising his shortsighted, well-meaning eyes to them and responding to their smiles. He knew they had forgiven him but did not know what he had done. He admitted everything. The world beyond his own world was more spacious and sweeter than he had known. Anything could be expected there, including himself and his many reckonings. Nothing was as it should be, and everything was excused. They gave him some more. He drank with pious, concentrated intensity. His eyes clouded with tears of thanksgiving.

At length he rose with shaky knees.

"Good people, I thank you from my heart, I thank you, but go along now, go along, it's getting late—"

All four of them kissed him, two kisses from each, right cheek, left cheek, leaving a strong scent of cognac and rejoicing. It seemed that they could not leave him. Again and again they came back from the door, to thank him afresh, to shake his hands. Perlmutter kissed him all over again.

"We're interfering, enough already, enough, let's go!" said Archangel Piotr.

They departed, their jubilations rising up from the stairwell. The news-cuttings agent from the neighboring room peered in through the doorway and said, cantankerously:

"Mazal tov, I didn't know it was your birthday."

The clerk burst into a fit of laughter.

In the room remained fragments of the bust, the bouquet on the carpet, and the crystal goblet with the spoon. The lawyer felt certain he had never seen such an ugly object in his life.

"Do you want this glass?" he asked the clerk. "If so, take it along."

"But it's expensive," she said with covetous eyes.

He waved his hands:

"Go on, take it. I don't want it. And get the roses out of here as well. This isn't an actress's dressing room."

At length they cleaned up, closed and locked everything. The lawyer had a headache. He even forgot to buy cheese for Katzenbach. The engine would not ignite properly. With a thunderous headache and a sense of universal pardon and forgiveness he arrived home, opened the gigantic box of chocolates, and found that they had gone moldy with age: all were white and turned to powder at a touch. And who would buy such a box, it must have stood in the shop window for twenty years. He collected the lot and flung it into the dustbin. As he bent forward, his insides seemed to heave with all the unaccustomed drinking. Excitement of this kind wasn't for him, he told himself as he rolled up in bed without a shower or supper. Tomorrow was a new day, tomorrow would be different.

⪜ ⪜

He was almost asleep when his belly suddenly began shaking with laughter. He rubbed the sleepiness out of his eyes, sat up in bed, and found himself laughing aloud. It was only part intoxication. The laughter increased and spread like rain after a long drought, more and more. The startled Katzenbach leapt from the foot of the bed and fled into the kitchen.

"But it would be interesting to know," he said loudly to the darkness, "how they managed to get rid of Rosa."

And laughing, laughing endless torrents of laughter, he suddenly yawned spaciously, a liberating yawn, and fell asleep like a stone.

Translated from the Hebrew by J. M. Lask.

BIOGRAPHIES

AUTHORS

André Aciman was born in Alexandria and raised in Egypt, Italy, and France. Educated at Harvard, he currently teaches French literature at Princeton University. He is the recipient of a 1995 Whiting Writers' Award. He lives in Manhattan with his wife and three children.

Marjorie Agosín is Associate Professor of Latin American literature at Wellesley College. She is a well-known Chilean poet and literary critic and has written extensively on contemporary Chilean literature and culture. In addition to *A Cross and A Star: Memoirs of a Jewish Girl in Chile*, Agosín's works appear in *Happiness: Stories; The Mothers of Plaza de Mayo; Chilean Women and the Pinochet Democracy;* and *Women of Smoke: Latin-American Women in Literature and Life.*

Currently living in Calgary, Canada, **David Albahari** was born in 1948 in the Serbian village of Péc. He is the author of six collections of short stories and five novels in Serbian. *Opis smrti* won the Ivo Andrić Award in 1982 for the best collection of short stories published in the former

Yugoslavia. The founder of *Pismo*, a magazine of world literature, he is an accomplished translator of Anglo-American literature.

Max Apple received a Ph.D. from the University of Michigan and teaches at Rice University in Texas. He received the Jesse Jones Award from the Texas University of Letters and a Hadassah Magazine–Ribalow Award for *Free Agents*. Apple has edited and written many books and articles. His recent memoir, *Roomates,* was made into a major film.

Shmuel Avraham (pseudonym) was born in Ethiopia in 1945 outside of Gondar City. Before his imprisonment during the 1978 purge of intellectuals, he was an educator and government official in Addis Ababa. He lives in Israel where he works as a university professor. His retelling of his tale was aided by Arlene Kushner, an expert on Ethiopian Jewry. While his harrowing story is true, his name has been changed to protect his family.

Gil Ben Aych, who teaches philosophy at a lycée near Paris, has published four novels including *Le Livre d'Etoile* (Paris: Seuil, 1986). The excerpts printed here are from *The Chant of Being,* translated from the French by Alan Astro.

Stanislaw Benski (1922–1988), who served with distinction in the Polish Army during the war, began his writing career in 1960. As the director of a nursing home in Warsaw for the last twenty-five years of his life, Benski watched the scant number of surviving Polish Jews dwindle before his eyes. He began to write stories to preserve their memory.

Maxim Biller was born in 1960 in Prague and emigrated with his family to Hamburg in 1970. He studied German literature and journalism in Munich, where he now lives. He contributes regularly to *Tempo*, a monthly magazine. He is one of the younger members of the postmodern generation of German Jewish writers.

Matt Cohen was born in Kingston, Ontario, Canada. *Living on Water: Stories* was a finalist for the Trillium Award in 1988, the same year that he was selected as one of Canada's outstanding young writers. The Dutch translation of his novel *The Spanish Doctor* was chosen as one of the 1986 ten best books of the year in Holland. In 1992 he was a cowinner of the City of Toronto Book Award. A prolific writer and founding member of the Writers' Union of Canada, Cohen served as Chairman in 1985–1986, and was awarded Life Membership in 1996 in recognition of his services to Canadian writers.

David Ehrlich, born in 1959 in Israel, has worked as a journalist for *Ha'aretz* and *Davar,* taught at Emory University and Dartmouth College, and is now the owner and manager of the bookstore-cafe Tmol Shilshom in Jerusalem. He divides his time between Jerusalem and Berkeley.

Although born in the United States, **Ruth Fainlight** has lived in England for most of her life. She has published her second book of short stories, *Dr. Clock's Last Case* (Virago) and fourteen books of poetry, the most recent being *This Time of Year* (Sinclair-Stevenson). Fainlight has received the Cholmondley Award in recognition of her life's work. *Sugar-Paper Blue* will soon appear in a bilingual edition of poems in France.

Born in Argentina, **Nora Glickman** is a professor of Spanish at Queens College, City University of New York. She is the author of *Uno de sus Juanes* and *Mujeres, memorias, malogros,* two collections of short stories. Her play *Suburban News,* which won the Jerome Foundation Drama Award in 1993, was produced in New York in 1994.

Allegra Goodman was born in Brooklyn in 1967. Her collection *Total Immersion* written when she was 21, is set in Hawaii, where she was raised. She is the recipient of a Whiting Foundation Writers' Award and a Mellon Fellowship in the Humanities. Many of the stories from her current work *The Family Markowitz* first appeared in the *New Yorker* and *Commentary.* A graduate of Harvard, Goodman is currently completing her Ph.D. in English from Stanford University and living in Cambridge, Massachusetts, with her husband and two young sons.

Nadine Gordimer was born and educated in South Africa. She is the author of more than twenty volumes of novels and short stories, and a 1991 Nobel Prize winner. Her works, primarily about the inhumane effects of apartheid, have been published in the United States and the United Kingdom. She has lectured at many American universities, including Harvard, Northwestern, and Columbia, receiving honorary doctorates and literary prizes in Belgium, France, Italy, and the United States. Among her best known works are *July's People, The Conservationist,* and *Burger's Daughter*. Gordimer is also known for her recent non-fiction, including *The Essential Gesture: Writing Politics and Place*.

Shulamith Hareven is the author of fifteen books. *The Desert Trilogy*, recently published by Mercury House, includes *The Miracle Hater*, *Prophet*, and *After Childhood*. Hareven, who lives in Jerusalem, was the first woman member of the Academy of the Hebrew Language. She often writes about the nature of identity: sexual, personal, and national. Her book of essays, *Vocabulary of Peace*, redirects the language and perspective often used to describe Middle Eastern culture and politics. Hareven's work has been translated into fourteen languages.

In 1954, **Naim Kattan** immigrated to Canada from his native Iraq. He has written for radio and TV and is the author of numerous plays and stories. Although he is fluent in his native tongue, Arabic, and in English, he writes only in French. For two decades he was the director of the writing and publication section of the Canada Council. Since 1992, he has been an Associate Professor at the Université du Québec à Montréal. Kattan's collection *La Reprise* deals with North African Jewish immigrants in Canada, as does *La Fortune du Passager*. His work has had a strong influence on Canadian immigrant literature.

Ivan Klíma was born in 1931 in Prague where he still lives. As a child, he was incarcerated with his family in Terezín. Later, he became the editor of a Czech literary weekly, which was banned after the communist takeover. Visiting Professor at the University of Michigan in 1969, he returned home in 1970 to find that he could not publish in the State-run presses. The author of novels, plays, and collections of short stories such as *Love and Garbage, Judge on Trial*, and *Waiting for the Dark, Waiting for the Light*, his work has been translated into many languages.

Persis Knobbe, who writes in Kentfield, California, is working on a collection tentatively titled *The Morris Stories*. Her fiction has appeared in Plume/Penguin's *Nice Jewish Girls* and in *American Fiction III*.

George (György) Konrád, the distinguished Hungarian novelist, was born in 1933. His widely acclaimed first novel, *The Case Worker*, was published in English in 1974, followed by *The City Builder* (1977); *Antipolitics* (1984); *A Feast in the Garden* (1992); and *The Melancholy of Rebirth* (1995). Although he was charged with "subversive agitation" by the Communist regime and prevented from publishing for many years, he has remained in his native country.

Primo Levi (1919–1987) was born in Turin, Italy. A chemist by profession, he is known for his autobiographical account of survival in the concentration camps. First published in 1965 in English, *The Reawakening* was recently re-released. A sequel to his classic memoir *Survival in Auschwitz,* the pieces in the former collection deal with Levi's liberation and eventful journey home to Italy by way of the Soviet Union, Hungary, and Romania. His novel *If Not Now, When?* received two Italian literary prizes.

Born in Russia in 1942, **Serge Liberman** came to Australia in 1951 where he now works as a medical practitioner. He is the author of *A Universe of Clowns* and *The Life That I Have Led.* He is also currently Literary Editor of three Australian Jewish publications and on the Editorial Committee of the *Australian Jewish Historical Society Journal.* Liberman has received the Alan Marshall Award and recently compiled and edited *A Bibliography of Australian Judaica.*

Savyon Liebrecht was born in Munich, Germany, in 1948, the child of Holocaust survivors. As an infant she immigrated to Israel with her family. A writer of short stories and television plays, she has published a volume of her stories in Germany through Persona Verla, a German publisher. She has also published three collections, among them, *It's All Greek to Me, He Said to Her.* She is one of a the new wave of women prose writers writing in a strong female voice in Israel.

Norman Manea was born in Bukovina, Romania in 1936. A concentration camp survivor, he worked as an engineer until 1974 when he devoted himself to writing full-time. He left Romania in 1986 and now teaches at Bard College in New York. The recipient of Guggenheim and MacArthur Foundation Fellowships and the National Jewish Book Award, Manea is also the author of *On Clowns, The Dictator and the Artist: Essays; Compulsory Happiness,* and *The Black Envelope.*

Isabelle Maynard, who was born in China, currently lives in northern California. She was a social worker in the San Francisco Bay area for many years. She is currently an actor, painter, and an oral historian. In 1987, her play *The Ace* was produced by Talespinners in San Francisco.

Her stories have appeared in such publications as *Sideshow: An Anthology of Contemporary Fiction; The Tribe of Dina: A Jewish Women's Anthology; Fierce with Reality: An Anthology of Literature on Aging;* and *China Dreams,* which includes her story "Braverman, DP."

Angelina Muñiz-Huberman was born in France of Spanish parents; she has lived most of her life in Mexico City. Her novels include *Morada interior* (1972), *Tierra adentro* (1977), and *La guerra del unicornio* (1983). She writes regularly for the Mexican periodicals *Vuelta* and *Uno mas uno.* Muñiz-Huberman is a professor of Spanish and Comparative Literature at the National Autonomous University of Mexico.

Cynthia Ozick is one of the most innovative writers of our time. She has received the American Academy of Arts Award for Literature, two O'Henry Short Story Awards, and most recently, the Mildred and Harold Strauss Living Arts Award. "Puttermesser: Her Work History, Her Ancestry, Her Afterlife," is a selection from *Levitation: Five Fictions.* A continuation of the Puttermesser theme has been recently published in *The Puttermesser Papers.* She is known for such fiction as the *The Pagan Rabbi, Bloodshed,* and *The Shawl.* Her recent scholarly essays have become part of the canon of Jewish critical works.

Born in Guatemala, **Victor Perera** is the author of *Unfinished Contest: The Guatemalan Tragedy; The Last Lords of Palenque* (with Robert D. Bruce), and *The Cross and the Pear Tree: A Sephardi Journey.* His memoir *Rites: A Guatemalan Boyhood* won the Present Tense/Joel Cavior Award in Biography. He has been awarded the NEA Creative Writing Fellowship (1980) and the Lila Wallace–Reader's Digest Fund Writing Award (1992–1994). Perera is currently a lecturer at the University of California at Berkeley's Graduate School of Journalism.

Veronica Ross was born in Hanover, Germany after World War II and grew up in Montreal. She is the author of nine books, including *Order of the Universe; Fisherwoman; Goodbye, Summer,* and *Hannah B.* Associate Editor of *The Antigonish Review* and a teacher of creative writing, Ross has been awarded several Canadian literary prizes. *Homecoming* has been rereleased by HarperCollins in its new Canadian Classic line. She currently lives in Ontario.

Nina Sadur, born in 1950, grew up in Siberia. She began to gain recognition as a writer with the collapse of the former Soviet Union. Her prose creates a tragic but radiant world derived from the Russian folktale. Sadur's published works include a short novel, *The South,* two cycles of short stories: *Witch's Tears* and *Special People,* and the plays, *The Swallow, The Mongrel,* and *Pannochka.* She was nominated for the Booker Prize in 1993. Sadur lives in Moscow with her mother and daughter.

Steven Schwartz, born in 1950, is currently teaching in Fort Collins, Colorado. He has published two collections of stories, *To Leningrad in Winter* and *Lives of the Fathers,* and a novel, *Therapy.* He has won the prestigious Nelson Algren short fiction award, the annual O'Henry Award, and has published in the *Antioch Review* and *Ploughshares.* His novel *Shred of God* will be published in 1998 by William Morrow.

Moacyr Scliar, who lives in Pôrto Alegre, the capital of Rio Grande do Sul, Brazil, has been called the most important Jewish writer in Latin America today. He divides his time between medicine and writing. His nine works translated from the Portuguese into English blend Latin American fabulism and Jewish humor. His books have won numerous literary prizes, including the Brasilia Prize and the *de las Americas* award.

Born in 1947 in Tennessee, **Steve Stern** has been dubbed a Jewish Huck Finn. He has written two collections of short stories, *Isaac and the Undertaker's Daughter* and *Lazar Malkin Enters Heaven,* which won the Edward Lewis Wallant Book Award. He has also written two novels, *The Moon and Ruben Shein* and *Harry Kaplan's Underground.* His book of three novellas, *A Plague of Dreamers* was a *New York Times* Notable Book of the Year. Stern has also published two children's books, *Mickey and the Golem* and *Hershel and the Beast.* He is currently Associate Professor at Skidmore College.

In *Akud,* which won the Bernstein Prize in Israel, **Albert Swissa** not only depicts the reality of the immigrant from Morocco in Israel, but also evokes the vanished world of Moroccan Jewish society. His work, which often links the two countries, has appeared in *The Literary Review,* Fairleigh Dickinson University. Swissa currently lives in France and is working in the theatre.

Born in Romania, **Elie Wiesel** survived the concentration camps as a teenager and, after several years in France, came to the United States. He is the author of more than thirty books, including his recently published memoir, *All Rivers Run to the Sea*. His published works include *Night, A Beggar in Jerusalem* (winner of the Prix Medicis), *The Forgotten,* and *From the Kindom of Memory*. He has been awarded the Presidential Medal of Freedom, the United States Congressional Gold Medal, the French Legion of Honor, and in 1986, the Nobel Peace Prize. He is the Andrew W. Mellon Professor at Boston University. Most of his books have been written in French and translated into English by his wife, Marion.

A. B. Yehoshua is the author of *The Continuing Silence of a Poet: Collected Short Stories, The Lover, Late Divorce, Five Seasons,* and *Mr. Mani,* which received the Israel Prize, the National Jewish Book Award, and the Jewish Quarterly Prize. Yehoshua was born in Jerusalem and lives in Haifa, where he teaches literature at Haifa University. His diverse writings concern the metaphysical and political questions that have arisen out of Zionsim. His work has been translated into fourteen languages. While he is best known for his short stories, his latest novel, *Open Heart,* published in 1996, has brought Yehoshua a reputation as one of the world's finest novelists.

TRANSLATORS

Walter Arndt is the Polish translator of "Missing Pieces" by Stanislaw Benski, from the short story collection of the same title.

The editor of *Yale French Studies: Discourses of Jewish Identity in Twentieth-Century France,* **Alan Astro** is Associate Professor of French at Trinity University in San Antonio, Texas, and the French translator of Gil Ben Aych's *Le Chant des êtres, The Chant of Being*. Professor Astro is also author of *Understanding Samuel Beckett* (University of South Carolina Press, 1990).

John Benson is the Spanish translator of Nora Glickman's "The Last Emigrant," which first appeared in *Tropical Synagogues*.

After teaching Russian literature at the University of Limerick, Ireland, **Andrew Bromfield** moved to Moscow, where he has been working as a translator for several years. In 1991–1992, he joined Natasha Perova to edit the first two issues of the journal, *Glas: New Russian Writing*. He is the Russian translator of "Irons and Diamonds" by Nina Sadur.

Ellen Elias-Bursać, the translator of David Albahari's "Jerusalem" from *Words Are Something Else,* is a literary and South Slavic scholar. She has translated widely from Croatian and Serbian, including such works as *Holograms of Fear* by Slavenka Drakulić. She currently teaches Serbian and Croatian at Harvard University.

Sheila Fischman is the French translator of Naim Kattan's *Farewell, Babylon.*

Jeffery Green, who has lived in Israel since 1973, is the Hebrew translator of "A Room on the Roof" by Savyon Liebrecht, from the collection *Ribcage: Israeli Women's Fiction.* He has also translated the novels of Aharon Appelfeld and other Israeli writers. With Trudi Birger, Green is coauthor of *A Daughter's Gift of Love,* a Holocaust memoir (The Jewish Publication Society). He has published a novel, *Half A Baker.*

Hillel Halkin, a leading translator of classical and contemporary Hebrew prose and poetry into English for over thirty years, made *aliyah* with his family in 1970. A well-known literary critic, he has written for the *Jerusalem Report,* and is currently writing for the *Forward.* Halkin is the translator of *Five Seasons* from the Hebrew by A. B. Yehoshua.

Anselm Hollo, Romanian translator of Norman Manea's "The Instructor" from *October, Eight O'Clock,* is a poet and an Associate Professor in the M.F.A. Writing and Poetics Program of The Naropa Institute in Boulder, Colorado. His most recent book of poems is *Corvus* (Coffee House Press). Hollo's translation of Finnish poet Pentti Saarikoski's *Trilogy* will be published by Sun & Moon. Born in Helsinki, Finland, Hollo has lived in the United States for more than thirty years.

Celeste Kostopulos-Cooperman is the Spanish translator of Marjorie Agosín's "Osorno" from *A Cross and A Star: Memoirs of a Jewish Girl in Chile.*

J. M. Lask is the Hebrew translator of Shulamith Hareven's "A Matter of Identity" from *Twilight and Other Stories.*

Margaret A. Neves is the Portuguese translator of Moacyr Scliar's "A Small Farm in the Interior, Quatro Irmãos District, Rio Grande Do Sul," taken from his novel *The Centaur in the Garden.*

Ewald Osers is the Czech translator of *First Loves* by Ivan Klíma, in which "Miriam" appears.

Naomi Seidman, translator of David Ehrlich's "The Store," which appeared in *Israel: A Traveler's Literary Companion,* teaches Hebrew literature at the Center for Jewish Studies in Berkeley, California. Her translation of *Conversations with Dvora: An Experimental Biography of the First Modern Hebrew Women Writer* is forthcoming from the University of California Press, as is her new work *A Marriage Made in Heaven: The Sexual Politics of Hebrew and Yiddish.*

James Andrew Tucker, a translator for *The Hungarian Quarterly* and a Visiting Professor at New York University and Colorado College in such subjects as Greek Mythology, Greek and Latin, and Readings in Italian: Calvino, is the Hungarian translator of George Konrád's "Expectations."

Marsha Weinstein, an American living in Israel, is the Hebrew translator of Albert Swissa's *Akud.* She has also translated many of the stories that appear in *Keys to the Garden: New Israeli Writing,* (City Lights Books, 1996) as well as essays from Shulamith Hareven's work.

Professor of German and Acting College Dean at Wesleyan University in Connecticut and the German translator of Maxim Biller's "Finkelstein's Fingers," **Krishna Winston** has translated many works of German fiction and non-fiction. She is the translator of *Jewish Voices, German Words,* in which Biller's work appears.

Stuart Woolf is the Italian translator of "Southwards" from *The Reawakening* by Primo Levi.

Lois Parkinson Zamora, the Spanish translator of "In the Name of His Name" from *Enclosed Garden* by Angelina Muñiz-Huberman, is a professor of Comparative Literature at the University of Houston. She has written critical studies on contemporary United States and Latin American fiction, including writing the *Apocalypse: Historical Vision in*

Contemporary U.S. and *Latin American Fiction* (Cambridge University Press).

EDITORS

Marsha Lee Berkman's prize-winning fiction has appeared in many literary journals, quarterlies, and anthologies, including *Quarterly West, Other Voices, Lilith, Sonora Review, Western Humanities Review, Sifrut Literary Review, Shaking Eve's Tree: Short Stories of Jewish Women; Writing Our Way Home: Contemporary Stories by American Jewish Writers (The Schocken Book of Contemporary Jewish Fiction);* and *Mothers: Short Stories of Contemporary Motherhood.* She has given lectures and courses on American Jewish literature, Jewish women's literature, and Holocaust literature. Marsha Lee Berkman is the recipient of the Eternal Light Award from the University of Judaism, Los Angeles, for outstanding service to the Jewish community. She lives in the San Francisco Bay Area.

Among her diverse work, **Elaine Marcus Starkman** has published four chapbooks of poetry. Her memoir, *Learning to Sit in the Silence: A Journal of Caretaking* was published by Papier-Mache Press in 1993. With Leah Schweitzer, she is the coeditor of *Without A Single Answer: Poems of Contemporary Israel.* Her prose is found in *Vital Signs: Contemporary Fiction About Medicine; The Woman Who Lost Her Names: Selected Writings by American Jewish Women, Hadassah,* and *Studies in American-Jewish Literature.* Her two years in Israel where she lived and taught after the Six Day War have had a profound effect on her life. A resident of San Francisco's East Bay, Elaine met Marsha Lee when their stories were published in JPS's *Shaking Eve's Tree.*

PERMISSIONS

Aciman, André: "The Last Seder" appeared in *Out of Egypt: A Memoir.* Copyright © 1995 by André Aciman. Reprinted by permission of Farrar, Straus & Giroux, Inc., 1994 in the U.S. and by The Harvill Press in the U.K., 1996.

Agosín, Marjorie: Excerpt from *A Cross and A Star: Memoirs of a Jewish Girl in Chile.* Copyright © 1994 by University of New Mexico Press.

SELECTED BIBLIOGRAPHY

The following bibliography provides the reader with sources for further readings and research on modern Jewish writing. Section one includes new and classical critical works. Section two, divided geographically, lists the works included in this publication, followed by partial listings of each author's writings. Section three refers to relevant publications similar in scope to those included in this volume. Section four includes other anthologies, fiction and non-fiction, with reference to the Holocaust, Jewish tales, women's work, and recent Yiddish translations.

1. CRITICAL WORKS

Alter, Robert. *After the Tradition: Essays on Modern Jewish Writing.* New York: Dutton, 1969.

———. *Modern Hebrew Literature.* West Orange, New Jersey: Behrman House, 1975.

Baumgarten, Murray. *City Scriptures: Modern Jewish Writers.* Cambridge, Mass.: Harvard University Press, 1982.

Bloom, Harold. *Modern Jewish Literature.* New York: Chelsea House, 1990.

Blum, Jakub, and Vera Rich, eds. *The Image of the Jew in Soviet Literature.* New York: Ktav, 1985.

Cheuse, Alan, and Nicholas Delbanco, eds. *Talking Horse: Bernard Malamud on Life and Art.* New York: Columbia University Press, 1996.

Cheyette, Bryan. *Constructions of the 'Jew' in English Literature and Society.* Cambridge: Cambridge University Press, 1993.

Cooper, Alan. *Philip Roth and the Jews.* Albany: State University of New York Press, 1996.

Di Antonio, Robert, and Nora Glickman, eds. *Tradition and Innovation: Reflections on Latin-American Jewish Writing.* New York: Carol Group, 1987.

Fiedler, Leslie. *Fiedler on the Roof: Essays of Literature and Jewish Identity.* Boston: David R. Godine, 1991.

Gilman, Sander L. *Smart Jews.* Lincoln: University of Nebraska Press, 1996.

Harap, Louis. *Dramatic Encounters: The Jewish Presence in Twentieth Century American Drama, Poetry, and Humor and the Black-Jewish Literary Relationship.* Westport, Conn.: Greenwood, 1987.

Hareven, Shulamith. *The Vocabulary of Peace: Culture and Politics in the Middle East.* San Francisco: Mercury House, 1995.

Ozick, Cynthia. *Art and Ardor: Essays.* New York: Alfred A. Knopf, 1983.

———. *Metaphor and Memory: Essays.* New York: Random House, 1991.

———. *Fame and Folly: Essays.* New York: Alfred A. Knopf, 1996.

Rosen, Norma. *Accidents of Influence: Writing as A Woman and A Jew in America.* Albany: State University of New York Press, 1992.

Sokoloff, Naomi B. *Imagining the Child in Modern Jewish Fiction.* Baltimore: Johns Hopkins, 1992.

Wirth-Nesher, Hana, ed. *What Is Jewish Literature?* Philadelphia: The Jewish Publication Society, 1994.

Wisse, Ruth. *The Schlemiel as Modern Hero.* Chicago: University of Chicago Press, 1971.

2. WORKS BY AUTHORS INCLUDED IN THIS ANTHOLOGY

Each entry begins with work reprinted in these pages, followed by the author's publications in chronological order.

North America

United States

Apple, Max. "The American Bakery." In *Free Agents*. New York: HarperCollins, 1984.

———. *Roommates: My Grandfather's Story*. New York: Warner Books, 1994.

Goodman, Allegra. "The Four Questions." In *The Family Markowitz*. New York: Farrar, Straus & Giroux, Inc., 1996.

———. *Total Immersion: Stories*. New York: Harper & Row, 1989.

Knobbe, Persis. "Here I Am." Published for the first time in this anthology.

———. "The Nose-Fixer." In *Nice Jewish Girls: Growing Up in America,* edited by Marlene Adler Marks. New York: Plume Penguin, 1996.

Ozick, Cynthia. "Puttermesser: Her Work History, Her Ancestry, Her Afterlife." In *Levitation: Five Fictions*. New York: Alfred A. Knopf, 1982.

———. *The Messiah of Stockholm*. New York: Alfred A. Knopf, 1987.

———. *The Shawl*. New York: Random House, 1990.

———. *A Cynthia Ozick Reader*. Bloomington: University of Indiana Press, 1996.

———. *The Puttermesser Papers*. New York: Alfred A. Knopf, 1997.

Schwartz, Steven. "Madagascar." In *Lives of the Fathers*. Champaign: University of Illinois Press, 1991.

———. *To Leningrad in Winter*. Columbia: University of Missouri Press, 1985.

———. *Shred of God*. New York: William Morrow, 1998.

Stern, Steve. "Bruno's Metamorphosis." In *Isaac and the Undertaker's Daughter*. Providence, Rhode Island: *Lost Roads*, #22, 1983.

———. *Lazar Malkin Enters Heaven*. Syracuse: Syracuse University Press, 1995.

———. *A Plague of Dreamers: Three Novellas*. Syracuse: Syracuse University Press, 1997.

Wiesel, Elie. "Kaddish in Cambodia." From *The Kingdom of Memory: Reminiscences*. New York: Simon & Schuster, 1996.

For Elie Wiesel see also Romania.

Canada

Cohen, Matt. "Racial Memories." In *Living on Water*. Ontario: Penguin Books Canada, 1988.

———. *Emotional Arithmetic.* New York: St. Martin's Press, 1995.

———. *Last Seen.* Toronto: Random House of Canada, 1996.

Ross, Veronica. "The Ugly Jewess." In *Prairie Fire* 17, no. 3 (Autumn 1996): 176–180.

———. *Hannah B.* Stratford, Ontario: The Mercury Press, 1991.

Central and South America

Mexico

Muñiz-Huberman, Angelina. "In the Name of His Name." In *Enclosed Garden.* Trans. by Lois Parkinson Zamora. Originally published *Huerto cerrado, huerto sellado.* Pittsburgh: Latin American Literary Review Press, 1988.

———. *Dulcinea encantada.* Mexico: Joaquin Mortiz, 1992.

Guatemala

Perera, Victor. "Mar Abramowitz." In *Rites: A Guatemalan Boyhood.* San Francisco: Mercury House, 1994.

———. *The Cross and The Pear Tree: A Sephardic Journey.* San Francisco: Mercury House, 1994.

Chile

Agosín, Marjorie. "Osorno." In *A Cross and A Star: Memoirs of a Jewish Girl in Chile.* Trans. by Celeste Kostopolous-Cooperman. Albuquerque: University of New Mexico Press, 1994.

———. *Surviving Beyond Fear: Women, Children, and Human Rights in Latin America.* Fredonia, New York: White Pine Press, 1992.

———. *Happiness: Stories.* Trans. by Elizabeth Horan. Fredonia: White Pine Press, 1993.

———. *Starry Night.* Trans. by Mary G. Burg. Fredonia: White Pine Press, 1996.

Argentina

Glickman, Nora. "The Last Emigrant." Trans. by John Benson. In *Tropical Synagogues: Short Stories by Jewish–Latin American Writers.* New York: Holmes & Meier, 1996.

———. *Uno de sus Juanas.* Buenos Aires: Ediciones de la Flor, 1983.

———. *Mujeres, memorias, malogros.* Buenos Aires: Mila, 1991.

Brazil

Scliar, Moacyr. "A Small Farm in the Interior, Quatro Irmãos District, Rio Grande do Sul, September 24, 1935–September 23, 1947." In

The Centaur in the Garden. Trans. by Margaret A. Neves. New York: Ballantine, 1984.

———. *The Carnival of the Animals.* Trans. by Eloah F. Giacomelli. New York: Ballantine, 1986.

———. *The Volunteers.* Trans. by E. F. Giaomelli. New York: Ballantine, 1988.

———. *Max and the Cats: A Novel.* Trans. by E. F. Giacomelli. New York: Ballantine, 1989.

Western Europe

England
Fainlight, Ruth. *Dr. Clock's Last Case: And Other Stories.* United Kingdom: Virago Press, 1995.

———. *Fifteen to Infinity.* Pittsburgh: Carnegie Mellon University Press, 1986.

France
Ben Aych, Gil. Excerpts from *The Chant of Being.* Trans. by Alan Astro. *Yale French Studies* 85 (1994): 17–24. First published as *Le chant des êtres.* Paris: Éditions Gallimard, 1988.

———. *Le Livre d'Etoile.* Paris: Seuil, 1986.

Germany
Biller, Maxim. "Finkelstein's Fingers." Trans. by Krishna Winston. In *Jewish Voices, German Words: Growing Up in Postwar Germany and Austria.* North Haven, Conn.: Catbird Press, 1977.

———. "See Auschwitz and Die." Trans. by Krishna Winston. *In Jewish Voices, German Words: Growing Up in Postwar Germany and Austria.* North Haven, Conn.: Catbird Press, 1977.

Italy
Levi, Primo. "Southwards." In *The Reawakening.* Trans. by Stuart Woolf. New York: Random House,1993.

———. *Survival in Auschwitz.* Trans. by Stuart Woolf. New York: Simon & Schuster, 1984.

———. *Moments of Reprieve.* Trans. by Ruth Feldman. New York: Viking Penguin, 1995.

———. *The Periodic Table,* Trans. by Raymond Rosenthal. New York: Schocken, 1995.

Central and Eastern Europe

Czech Republic

Klíma, Ivan. "Miriam." In *My First Loves*. Trans. by Ewald Osers. New York: HarperCollins, 1985.

———. "A Childhood in Terezín." Trans. by Paul Wilson. In *Granta* 44 (Summer 1993): 189–208.

———. *Judge on Trial*. Trans. by A. G. Brain. New York: Random House, 1994.

———. *The Spirit of Prague and Other Essays*. Trans. by Paul Wilson. New York: *Granta Books*, 1995.

Hungary

Konrád, George. "Expectations." Trans. by J.A. Tucker, *Commentary*, (June 1996). Volume 101, #6 pp 46–47.

———. *The Case Worker*. Trans. by Paul Aston. New York: Harcourt Brace Jovanovich, 1974.

———. *A Feast in the Garden*. Trans. by Imre Goldstein. New York: Harcourt Brace Jovanovich, 1992.

———. *The Melancholy of Rebirth: Essays from Post Communist Central Europe*. Trans. by M. H. Helm. New York: Harcourt Brace Jovanovich, 1995.

Poland

Benski, Stanislaw. "Missing Pieces." Trans. by Walter Arndt. In *Missing Pieces*. New York: Harcourt Brace Jovanovich, 1990.

———. *The Survivors: Three Left* (excerpts from the novel). Warsaw, 1986.

Romania

Manea, Norman. "The Instructor." In *October, Eight O'Clock*. Trans. by Anselm Hollo. New York: Grove/Atlantic, 1996.

———. *On Clowns: The Dictator and the Artists: Essays*. New York: Grove/Atlantic, 1993.

———. *The Black Envelope*. Trans. by Patrick Camiller. New York: Farrar, Straus & Giroux, Inc., 1995.

Wiesel, Elie. *The Night Trilogy: Night, Dawn, The Accident*. New York: Farrar, Straus & Giroux, Inc., 1987.

———. *The Town Beyond the Wall*. New York: Schocken, 1988.

———. *The Gates of the Forest*. New York: Schocken, 1989.

———. *All Rivers Run to the Sea: Memoirs*. New York: Alfred A. Knopf, 1995.

Yugoslavia (currently known as the Federal Republiic of Yugoslavia)

Albahari, David, "Jerusalem." From *Words Are Something Else*. Trans. by Ellen Elias-Bursać. Evanston: Northwestern University Press, 1996.

———. *Tsing*. Evanston: Northwestern University Press, 1997.

Other Diasporas

Australia

Liberman, Serge. "Two Years in Exile." In *On Firmer Shores*. Brisbane, Australia: Globe Press, 1981.

———. *A Universe of Clowns*. Brisbane: Phoenix Publications, 1983.

———. *The Life That I Have Lived*. Melbourne: Fine-Lit, 1986.

———, ed. *A Bibliography of Australian Judaica*. Sydney: University of Sydney Library, 1991.

China

Maynard, Isabelle. "Braverman, DP." In *China Dreams: Growing Up Jewish in Tientsin*. Iowa City: University of Iowa Press, 1996.

———. "The House on Fell Street." In *Fierce with Reality: An Anthology on Aging*. St. Cloud, Minn.: North Star Press, 1995.

Egypt

Aciman, André. "The Last Seder." In *Out of Egypt: A Memoir*. New York: Farrar, Straus & Giroux, Inc., 1994.

Ethiopia

Avraham, Shmuel, with Arlene Kushner. "Escape Westward." In *Treacherous Journey: My Escape from Ethiopia*. New York: Shapolsky Publishing, 1986.

Iraq

Kattan, Naim. Chapter Six from *Farewell, Babylon*. Trans. by Sheila Fischman. Tapliner, 1980.

———. *La fortune du passager (roman)*. Montreal: HMH, 1989.

———. *Le repose et l'oubli*. Montreal: Éditions Hurtubise HMH, 1987.

South Africa

Gordimer, Nadine. "My Father Leaves Home." In *Jump and Other Stories*. New York: Farrar, Straus & Giroux, Inc., 1991.

———. *July's People*. New York: Viking Peguin, 1982.

———. *Something Out There*. New York: Viking Penguin, 1986.

———. *The Essential Gesture: Writing, Politics and Places.* New York: Viking Penguin, 1989.

———. *None to Accompany Me.* New York: Farrar, Straus & Giroux, Inc., 1994.

Israel

Ehrlich, David. "The Store." Trans. by Naomi Seidman. In I*srael: A Traveler's Literacy Companion.* Ed. by Michael Gluzman and Naomi Siedman. San Francisco: Whereabouts Press, 1996.

———. *Be-miluim.* Tel Aviv: Yediot Aharonot. Forthcoming.

Hareven, Shulamith. "A Matter of Identity." In *Twilight and Other Stories.* Trans. by J. M. Lask. San Francisco: Mercury House, 1992.

———. *City of Many Days.* Trans. by Hillel Halkin and the author. San Francisco: Mercury House, 1991.

———. *Thirst: The Desert Trilogy.* Trans. by Hillel Halkin. San Francisco: Mercury House, 1996.

Liebrecht, Savyon. "A Room on the Roof." Trans. by Jeffrey M. Green. First appeared in *Ariel Magazine: The Israel Review of Arts and Letters.* In *Ribcage: Israeli Women's Fiction: A Hadassah Anthology.* New York: Hadassah, 1994.

———. *It's All Greek to Me, He Said to Her.* Jerusalem: Keter, 1992.

Swissa, Albert. Excerpt from *Akud.* Trans. by Marsha Weinstein. In *The Melton Journal* (Autumn 1992): 15.

———. "The Encounter." Trans. by Marsha Weinstein. In *Keys to the Garden: New Israeli Fiction.* Ed. by Ammiel Alcaly. San Francisco: City Lights Books, 1996.

Yehoshua, A. B. Chapter Eleven from *Five Seasons.* Trans. by Hillel Halkin. New York: Doubleday, 1989.

———. *Mr. Mani.* Trans. by Hillel Halkin. New York: Doubleday, 1992.

———. *Open Heart.* Trans. by Dalya Bilu. New York: Doubleday, 1996.

3. OTHER RELEVANT WRITINGS

Argentina

Gardiol, Rita, editor and translator. *The Silver Candelabra and Other Stories: A Century of Jewish Argentine Literature.* Pittsburgh: Latin American Literacy Review Press, 1997.

Canada

Krakofsky, Shel. *Listening for Somersaults*. London, Ontario: Parchment Press, 1993.

Richler, Mordecai. *Solomon Gursky Was Here*. New York: Alfred A. Knopf, 1990.

China

Krasno, Rena. *Strangers Always: A Jewish Family in Wartime Shanghai*. Berkeley: Pacific View Press, 1992.

Costa Rica

Rovinski, Samuel. "The Grey Phantom." In *Clamor of Innocence: Central American Short Stories*. Edited by B. Paschke and D. Volpendestra. San Francisco: City Lights, 1988.

Cuba

Behar, Ruth. "Mi Puente/My Bridge: Revisiting A Jewish Childhood in Cuba." In *Bridges*. Vol. 4, issue #1 pp. 63–70.

Czech Republic

Lustig, Arnost. *Street of Lost Brothers*. Evanston: Northwestern University Press, 1990.

Egypt

Alhadeff, Gini. *The Sun at Midday: Tales of a Mediterranean Family*. New York: Pantheon, 1996.

Ethiopia

Shelemay, Kay Kaufman. *A Song of Longing: An Ethiopian Journey*. Champaign: University of Illinois Press, 1991.

Westheimer, Ruth, and Steven Kaplan. *Surviving Salvation: The Ethiopian Jewish Family in Transition*. New York: New York University Press, 1993.

Finland

Katz, Daniel. "The House in Silesia." In *Books from Finland*. Trans. by Herbert Lomas. Helsinki: WSOY, 1989.

France

Friedlander, Saul. *When Memory Comes*. New York: Farrar, Straus & Giroux, Inc., 1979.

Halter, Marek. *Children of Abraham*. New York: Little Brown and Co., 1990.

Meyers, Odette. *Doors to Madame Marie*. Seattle: University of Washington Press, 1997.

Germany

Sichrovsky, Peter. *Strangers in Their Own Land: Jews in Germany and Austria Today*. Trans. by Jean Steinberg. New York: Basic Books, 1986.

Weil, Grete. *The Bride Price*. Translated by John Barrett. Lincoln, Mass.: David R. Godine, 1991.

Greece

Fromer, Rebecca Camhi. *The Holocaust Odyssey of Daniel Bennahmias, Sonderkommando*. Tuscaloosa: University of Alabama Press, 1993.

India

Daniel, Ruby, with Barbara Johnson. *Ruby of Cochin: An Indian Jewish Woman Remembers*. Philadelphia: The Jewish Publication Society, 1995.

Iran

Barkhordar-Nahai, Gina B. *Cry of the Peacock*. New York: Crown Publishers, 1991.

Israel

Amichai, Yehuda. *Yehuda Amichai: A Life of Poetry; 1948–1994*. Trans. by Benjamin & Barbara Harshav. New York: HarperCollins, 1994.

Grossman, David. *The Book of Intimate Grammar*. New York: Riverhead Books, 1991.

Katzir, Yehudit. *Closing the Sea*. Trans. by Barbara Harshav. New York: Harcourt Brace Jovanovich, 1992.

Oz, Amos. *Under This Blazing Light*. Trans. by Nicholas De Lange. New York: Cambridge University Press, 1995.

Italy

Sava, Umberto. *Stories and Recollections by Umberto Sava*. Trans. by Estelle Gilson. Bronx: Sheep Meadow Press, 1993.

Lithuania

Jacobson, Howard. *Roots, Schmoots: Journey among Jews*. New York: Overlook Press, 1995.

Morocco

Canetti, Elias. *The Voices of Marrakesh*. New York: Farrar, Straus & Giroux, Inc., 1984.

Netherlands

Hillesum, Etty. *An Interrupted Life: The Diaries, 1941–1943; and Letters from Westerbork*. Trans. by Arnold J. Pomerans. New York: Henry Holt, 1996.

Poland

Bukiet, Melvin Jules. *Stories of an Imaginary Childhood*. Evanston: Northwestern University Press, 1992.

Fink, Ida. *A Scrap of Time and Other Stories*. Trans. by F. Prose and M. Levine. Evanston: Northwestern University Press, 1995.

Hoffman, Eva. *Lost in Translation: A Life in a New Language*. New York: Viking Penguin, 1990.

———. *Exit into History: A Journal through the New Eastern Europe.* New York: Viking Penguin, 1991.

———. *Shtetl: The Life and Death of a Small Town and the World of Polish Jews.* Boston: Houghton Mifflin, 1997.

Romania

Lentin, Ronit. *Night Train to Mother.* Pittsburgh: Cleis Press, 1988.

Russia

Brodsky, Joseph. *Less Than One: Selected Essays.* New York: Farrar, Straus & Giroux, Inc., 1987.

Emiot, Israel. *The Birobidzhan Affair.* Trans. by Max Rosenfeld. Philadelphia: The Jewish Publication Society, 1981.

Spain

Alexy, Trudi. *The Mezuzah in the Madonna's Foot: Marranos and Other Secrets.* New York: Simon & Schuster, 1993.

Sats, Mario. *Tres Cueñtos Espanoles.* Barcelona: Sirmio, 1988.

South Africa

Freed, Lynn. *The Bungalow.* New York: Simon & Schuster, 1991.

Zwi, Rose. *Safe Houses.* North Melbourne, Australia: Spiniflex Press, 1993.

Sri Lanka

Ranasinghe, Anne. *Desire and other stories.* Colombo: English Writers Cooperative, 1994.

Tunisia

Memmi, Albert. *Pillars of Salt.* Trans. by Edouard Roditi. Boston: Beacon Press, 1992.

Turkey

Roditi, Edouard. *The Delights of Turkey: Twenty Tales*. New York: New Directions, 1977.

United Kingdom

Feinstein, Elaine. *The Border*. New York: M. Boyars, 1990.
Kehoe, Louise. *In This Dark House*. New York: Schocken, 1995.
Louvish, Simon. *The Silencer: Another Levantine Tale*. New York: Interlink, 1993.

United States

Bellow, Saul. *Herzog*. New York: Viking Penguin, 1989.
———. *Mr. Sammler's Planet*. New York: Viking Penguin, 1996.
Goldman, Ari. *The Search for God at Harvard*. New York: Ballantine, 1992.
Kamenetz, Rodger. *The Jew in the Lotus: A Poet's Rediscovery of Jewish Identity in Buddhist India*. San Francisco: HarperCollins, 1994.
Kazin, Alfred. *A Walker in the City*. New York: Harvest Books, 1969. Reprint 1995 by Harcourt Brace.
Lester, Julius. *Lovesong: Becoming A Jew*. New York: Arcade, 1995.
Malamud, Bernard. The Complete Stories. New York: Farrar, Straus & Giroux, Inc., 1997.
Roth, Philip. *American Pastoral*. Boston: Houghton Mifflin, 1997.
———. *A Philip Roth Reader*. New York: Farrar, Straus & Giroux, Inc., 1980.
———. *Zuckerman Bound: Trilogy and Epilogue*. New York: Farrar, Straus & Giroux, Inc., 1985.
Singer, Isaac Bashevis. *Shadows on the Hudson*. Trans. by Joseph Sherman. New York: Farrar, Straus & Giroux, Inc., 1998.

Venezuela

Segal, Alicia. *Cláper*. Trans. by Jean E. Friedman. Caracas: Planeta Venezolana, 1991.

Yugoslavia (currently known as the Federal Republic of Yugoslavia)

Kis, Danilo. *Encyclopedia of the Dead.* Trans. by Michael H. Helm. New York: Farrar, Straus & Giroux, Inc., 1989.

4. OTHER ANTHOLOGIES

Argentina

Landis, Joseph C., ed. "Modern Jewish Studies: Argentine Jewish Writing." In *Yiddish* 8. Flushing: CUNY Queens College, 1992.

Austria

Lappin Elena, ed. *Jewish Voices, German Words: Growing Up Jewish in Postwar Germany and Austria.* Trans. by Krishna Winston. North Haven, Conn.: Catbird, 1994.

Canada

Oberman, Sheldon, and Elaine Newton, eds. *Mirror of a People: Canadian Jewish Experience in Poetry and Prose.* Winnipeg: Jewish Educational Publication of Canada, 1988.
Sinclair, Gerri, and Morris Wolfe, eds. *The Spice Box: An Anthology of Jewish Canadian Writing.* Toronto: Lester & Orpen Dennys, 1981.

France

Astro, Alan, ed. *Yale French Studies: Discourses of Jewish Identity in Twentieth-Century France* 85 (1994): 17–24.

Israel

Abrahamson, Glenda, ed. *The Oxford Book of Hebrew Short Stories.* London: Oxford University Press, 1996.

Alcalay, Ammiel, ed. *Keys to the Garden: New Israeli Writing*. San Francisco: City Lights Books, 1996.

Kurdistan

Sadar, Yona, ed. *The Folk Literature of the Kurdistani Jews*. New Haven, Conn.: Yale University Press, 1982.

Latin America

Goldemberg, Isaac. *The Fragmented Life of Jacobo Lerner*. New York: Persea Books, 1976.

Stavans, Ilan, ed. *Tropical Synagogues: Short Stories by Jewish-Latin American Writers*. New York: Holmes & Meier, 1994.

United States

Kaplan, Judy, and Linn Shapiro, eds. *Growing Up Red*. Champaign: University of Illinois Press, Forthcoming.

Solotaroff, Ted, and Nessa Rapoport, eds. *Writing Our Way Home: Contemporary Stories by American Jewish Writers (The Schocken Book of Contemporary Jewish Fiction)* New York: Schocken Books, 1992.

Holocaust

Amery, Jean. *At the Mind's Limits: Contemplations by a Survivor on Auschwitz and its Realities*. Bloomington: Indiana University Press, 1980.

De Pres, Terence. *The Survivor: An Anatomy of Life in the Death Camps*. New York: Oxford University Press, 1976.

Langer, Lawrence. *Art from the Ashes: A Holocaust Anthology*. New York: Oxford University Press, 1995.

Tales

Schwartz, Howard, ed. *Imperial Messages: One Hundred Modern Parables*. New York: Jason Aaronson, 1990.

————, ed. *Gates to the New City: A Treasury of Modern Yiddish Tales.* New York: Overlook Press, 1971.

Women's Work

Antler, Joyce, ed. *America and I: Short Stories by American Jewish Women Writers.* Boston: Beacon Press, 1990.

Bruck Edith. "Lettera alla Madra." Trans. by Brenda Webster. In *13th Moon: A Feminist Literary Magazine,* 11, nos. 1 and 2 (1993) pp. 161–168.

Diament, Carol, and Lily Rattok, eds. *Ribcage: Israeli Women's Fiction.* New York: Hadassah, 1994.

Domb, Risa. *New Women's Writing from Israel.* London & Portland, Oregon: Valentine Mitchell, 1997.

Kalechofsky, Roberta, ed. *The Global Anthology of Jewish Women Writers.* Marblehead, Mass.: Micah Press, 1990.

Kaye/Kantrowitz, Melanie. *My Jewish Face and Other Stories.* San Francisco: Aunt Lute's Books, 1990.

Klepfisz, Irena. *Dreams of An Insomniac: Jewish Feminist Essays, Speeches and Diatribes.* Portland, Oreg.: Eighth Mountain Press, 1990.

Marks, Marlene Adler, ed. *Nice Jewish Girls: Growing Up in America.* New York: Penguin Books USA, 1996.

Moskowitz, Faye, ed. *Her Face in the Mirror: Jewish Women on Mothers and Daughters.* Boston: Beacon Press, 1994.

Niederman, Sharon, ed. *Shaking Eve's Tree: Short Stories of Jewish Women.* Philadelphia: The Jewish Publication Society, 1990.

Yiddish Translations

Forman, Frieda, Ethel Raicus, Sarah S. Swartz, and Margie Wolfe, eds. and trans. *Found Treasures: Stories by Yiddish Women Writers.* Toronto: Second Story Press, 1994.

Katz, David. *Oksforder Yiddish: A Yearbook of Yiddish Studies II.* Newark: Gordon & Breach, 1987.